All This is So

John Roe was born and brought up in rural Lincolnshire in the United Kingdom. He later read History at St John's College, Cambridge, and acquired a degree in English from London University. After graduating he taught and travelled in Europe and Africa and wherever there were mountains. At twenty-eight John married Ella Burley and began a more organised life altogether, as well as two children, Christopher and Madeleine. John taught in Rhodesia for several years and then came to teach in Australia. He loves to read, travel, grow flowers, coach soccer, and keep the company of his grandsons.

ALL THIS IS SO

JOHN F. ROE

Wakefield
Press

Wakefield Press
1 The Parade West
Kent Town
South Australia 5067
www.wakefieldpress.com.au

First published 2002

Cover artwork by Drew Harrison
Cover designed by Dean Lahn, Lahn Stafford Design
Text designed and typeset by Clinton Ellicott, Wakefield Press
Printed and bound by Hyde Park Press

National Library of Australia
Cataloguing-in-publication entry
Roe, John, 1935– .
All this is so.

ISBN 1 86254 579 0.

I. Title.

A823.3

Publication of this book was assisted by the Commonwealth Government through the Australia Council, its arts funding and advisory body.

"It's a poor sort of memory that only works backwards," the Queen remarked.

Alice Through the Looking-Glass

Prologue

The pigs could not recall November but it had always been a bad month. The second week brought Martinmas and although it often brought the mild weather of St Martin's summer few of the pigs survived to enjoy it. Most farm animals died placidly but not so the pigs. The fury and outrage in their protesting screams came equally from those face to face with the butchers and from those others further away, who, sensing the blood and smelling death, cried out in scraping metallic shrieks that told both of their own dread yet, strangely, carried through the air their clumsy, unformed, unpractised sympathy to those of their brothers and sisters whose turn had come.

Though not wild pigs they had not been domesticated into complacent bags of fat; in the forests that seemed to have no boundary, save perhaps the seas, the pigs had lived full fierce lives. Sometimes wolves, and even on occasion bears, had encountered them, but the pigs believed wherever they happened to be in the forest was their own territory, and whatever the predator the boars rushed forward on their stumpy legs driving bodies like wedges, each hair a bristling shiny wire, wet mouths agape and bullet eyes red. No sidestepping, no manoeuvre, they drove in like torpedoes. Left in peace the pigs foraged for food, ploughing up the leaf mould and top-soil with rubbery noses, sneezing triumphantly at unearthed tubers, crackling acorns in their long narrow jaws, uprooting festoons of ferns with a flourish. At night they slept, humped on their sides, snoring or muttering in dreams, and best of all when the sun warmed a clearing they lay basking blissfully, like wheatsacks fallen from a dray.

Pig-herds watched over them, often small boys who lived alongside them. Each generation of the boys, entering without realising it into the pigs' community, passed on the pigs' mythology in old tales of how wolves had been outwitted and savage dogs sent whimpering away. For their courage and intelligence alike the boys admired them, but above all were captivated by their boisterousness as the pigs busied themselves through days seemingly always too short.

The pigs were not always merry companions, and sometimes eyed the world malevolently and dreamed darkly, dreams best forgotten of the sick man who had stumbled and not been able to escape from underneath their sharp stamping hooves, the old woman charged off her feet in the feeding-pen, and the baby left at the furrow's end they had chomped up. The older men knew the pigs' moods and the boys soon learned that they could be herded and driven only on sufferance, and only because their herders were close kin to them, so close that to the pigs' minds they were the unpigs, perhaps pigs themselves in some far off time, like themselves in everything except being magically able to kill those they loved, and love those they killed, which no other creature understood.

He had remembered it all once. In Westermain in November night came early, and the days themselves seemed unlit when the cloud blanket lay featurelessly thick. The boy walked four miles to the hall, setting out as dusk fell and knowing that he would walk back through a cold, lonely night. In the summer months he might have passed the pigs, but not after Martinmas. He knew some of the pig-boys and had shared a desk at school with little Pete Gibson who had two fingers missing on one hand. "Pigs have got sharp teeth, Harry," little Pete had told him.

It was different in the hall, warm enough to sweat, particularly in the anonymous comfortable company of a packed crowd. He would either choose one of the seats in the very back row or else sit on the wooden floor close enough to touch the stage. Once in his place he could relax, close his eyes and know he was there by the smell that hinted, as wine does, at many things: stored apples, old crushed velvet, soap-scrubbed hands, and faintly the tang of powder and paint. The boy would choose the front when he wanted to be near to the jugglers, the acrobats and magicians, and most of all the glittering blue-painted eyes and the imperious aura of the actresses. In the great faraway city of Limber every girl and woman would shimmer like them, he knew.

That night, though, he chose to sit at the back, because this time he was concerned far more with the words. He didn't know what they would be but he felt they would be for him alone. His fellow playgoers, he knew, were more fond of plays that told of the One God and the many gods, though also enjoying fables and comic misadventures, where the masquers, dancers and clowns held sway. All that evening, and later at home in his bed, he shivered at the words, trying out those he could remember and thinking of the worn old king, of the passion of the earl's restless son, of the power hidden in the ambivalent young prince. It was hard to know where his own sympathies lay for the earl's son spoke as the boy would like to have spoken:

An if we live we live to tread on kings,
If die, brave death when princes die with us.

When the earl's son, at bay, cried out, like defiance itself, "Doomsday is near, die all, die merrily," the boy knew the words' power instinctively; he had understood the play though his own world was calm and untroubled by earls. In fact he was not really sure what earls were, though they behaved rather like magnates and the boy had heard of them. He knew the prince would and should win, and he quite liked the prince too. And then looming among the characters was the huge fat man who jested as he jeered at honour. Everyone else in the audience cheered and laughed when the fat man appeared but the boy bit his nails. The fat man guffawed at the recruits in his charge saying they had lately come from swine-keeping, from eating draff and husks. Before long they were dead and the boy thought of little Pete Gibson.

He knew nothing yet of the blood that ran in his own veins, but he knew he liked the play and that it was realer than his real life. Perhaps there would be another play like it.

It was June but by next June the month would have become almost as mistily uncertain for them as for the pigs who now were rumbustiously content. The pigs butted a gap in the fence and munched the cabbages and broke down the pea-sticks and galloped to and fro on the small patch of lawn, while the small boys shrieked warnings and imprecations at them and had to pull up some more of the pea-sticks to beat them, urgent lest the door should open and the witch-girl emerge to trap anyone found in her garden. Soon enough she appeared, limping along on her crutches, and they fled away through the gap, though the girl seemed disinclined to display any of her powers. Nevertheless the young man who followed her into the garden appeared to be an appropriate friend for her for he laughed and some of the pigs came to him and pushed him with their wet noses and were repentant, or so the boys told the older pig-herds later. The witch-girl had laughed too and over the fence had offered the boys drinks, but they shrank away, being too wily and cautious to believe it was the apple-juice it looked so much like. They would have taken the drink from the young man whom they knew to be only an innocent visitor who had clearly been entrapped by the girl's arts and deserved better. He had bright hair cut so short it bristled and he seemed to them to have all the qualities of a master of pigs.

It was intriguing when the pigs wandered this way for the boys could speculate about the witch-girl's house, and keep watch over its visitors. The young man was far from the only caller; there was also a succession of the Twisted Folk. When no one could hear the pig-boys called them 'Twisters', though the boys' parents had recently become inclined to scold on hearing the name: "More people are twisted than you think. They have big hearts and braver than most."

Though the young man came usually to call on the witch-girl most other visitors came to see an older lady. This was an insoluble riddle for the pig-boys, for the girl called her mother, a dubious relationship, for the kindly lady with greying hair (which she liked to dye black) had delivered several of them in difficult births. She could also help the sick, she played the organ in the village church, and when snow fell on the nearby hills she took a toboggan out under the stars and sledged laughing in the darkness. Children of all ages liked to join in with her, though nervously if the witch-girl came too and fell off in the snow and giggled, though that was clearly how she would behave if she were disguising her nature.

Both women went often to the village graveyard and there would trim the graves' edges, two in particular, and plant flowers: lupins, irises, Michaelmas daisies, anything that would divide and multiply. On these occasions neither spoke much and what they said made uncertain sense. Once the older lady had heard someone remark that it would be nice for something to happen exciting enough to talk about for a year, and had replied sharply that it had happened, and not so long ago, and the more exciting the more graves to put flowers round. The villagers spoke politely to her but yesterday's rain was fresher in their minds. She was different from them and that was enough. Once the Merganser Companions had come loping through the trees and their captain-general, Silky Wilkins, had stopped to sit in her garden, which was a satisfactory topic for conversation for a while. It was said he had spoken to the witch-girl's mother through a long afternoon, and then knelt down for her to stroke his forehead. But then who could believe the pig-boys?

The house was built on the river's south side. Behind it were low hills which channelled the river, and a village straggled up the hillside. Because the house had been built near the hilltop it was exposed to fierce cold winds that swept in across the leaden sea which the river entered five miles or so to the east. Every other house huddled beneath the wind but not this house; it had been built high, three storeys of grey stone each with a row of small, square windows, beneath a high-pitched slate roof. Among the nearby squat houses with mossed pantiled roofs, even the occasional thick thatch, it was straight-backed, angular and uncompromising.

The man who owned the house was old but he felt older. He spent most of his days in his own room, and there he tried to think about the past, which was like thinking about a country he had never visited. The present made his past seem so long ago that it was as if it had hardly existed. His room had several shelves of books, among them many tall black ledgers with purple spines, one for each year, which could verify that something had once happened. Each contained the voyages of the fishing-boats in that particular year, with their catches and sales, the names of captains and crews, and the occasional black-bordered entry: 'Ingomar Jonsson, lost overboard, 27 May'. 'Euan of High Dyke, crushed chest, 5 October'. Two lost that year was sad but not exceptional. And the noting of help and recompense to the families, the records of weather and of the lack or profusion of fish, the encounters with other boats, the times of tides, and all the mystery of the sea.

Some of the ledgers, those in his wife's handwriting, he could hardly bear to open again. Always a poor scholar himself he had been delighted when she had taken over the ledgers, though she kept them differently from anyone else, being inclined to insert drawings or stick in a feather from a seabird, or a flower brought back by their eldest son that he had found growing on the cold shores where the ice-bears lived. The old man thought her not very business-like but the trade prospered and the little fleet began to acquire new trawlers, though his eldest son, Andread, had snarled at the Matrix's ban on big ships: "This is a fishing-smack, not a ship. Still, we can always catch sticklebacks in it."

Then after three sons came a daughter and his wife gave her own life to save the baby, or so the midwife told him. For two years after that he had sailed on Andread's every voyage, every time further north, every time the hold more dangerously deep-loaded with fish and the rigging hung heavier with ice, until the giant rolling waves, sixty feet high and miles long, had the last word. "Why my son?" said the old man, who having persuaded Andread to sail in December knew the answer. "Why not me?" but he could find no answer to the second question.

The ledgers had stopped and never been restarted, though he suspected his second son kept his own records, as well he might for the fisher-folk said they would sail round the world if he was their captain, even far to the south where the stars themselves are strange. The old man said his first son was the greater sailor; as for the third son he might make a good farmer. About his daughter he tried not to think for she lit up the big cold grey house and sometimes seeing her at the far end of a long corridor he took her for Laura. Then he tried not to say, "Hello, Ladybird," because that had been his name for his wife when they had first met, she sleek in her grown-up red dress with its big black spots.

There were times when the old man wondered about his mind. Everyone had told him his sons were coming home again and his daughter had filled the house with flowers and painted a sign saying 'Welcome home' to hang over the garden gate, but only the youngest one had come. Certainly he had not come alone and for a few days the house was alive again with people but his daughter had not seemed glad. A simple man, who had apparently come to stay for a long time, irritated him by moving into his second son's bedroom. He perplexed the old man most, even more than the disturbing woman who rarely left the simple man's side. Once he asked the woman if she knew when his second son was coming back.

"No," she said.

The memory had teeth and claws. Perversely it did not loosen its grip, despite their being a people who shunned the memory of their past.

The stars were shining so faintly that the light as it penetrated under the bridge was only visible as a sort of skin that separated water from air. Beneath each of the spans the stubby boats and punts lay tied against the stonework of the piers. Neither the boats nor the men and women in them were visible save as the darkest of shadows, and the workers rarely stayed more than the three hours after midnight, frowning at each other when a tap or scrape hinted at their presence, though an occasional bat flickering through the arches or an inquisitive otter surfacing at the end of its bubble-chain were all that observed them. The river was deep at the centre but its current slow-moving, retarded by the reed-banks and swamp-lands of its fringes. It was an old river, inscrutable, its waters unlikely to reach the saltiness of the sea.

They had first screwed rings into the stonework to hold fast their boats, then in the darkest nights gone about their plans. Even with black clothes and blackened faces they did not come when the moon was up. The bridge was rarely used after sunset, though a few times feet pattered across above the boatmen's heads. There were often noises as of men and animals somewhere not far off, and sometimes fires glimmered, dogs barked and cattle lowed.

Once enough of the stone facing had been removed to make an opening wide enough to crawl into the boatmen tunnelled inwards, excavating quickly, dragging out the lumps of rubble that were the filling of the big smooth piers, gently lowering the broken boulders to slide silently down into the dark deep waters. When they had hollowed out a chamber sufficient for three or four of them to crouch in, they brought boxes and stacked them neatly in the space, filling any gaps with loose rocks and soil, and mortared back into place the facing-stones. They repeated the process for each of the piers, and all this with a sort of mischievous self-reproach, for although they used the bridge infrequently it was shapely and they admired shapeliness above almost every quality. Mischief was in their blood; they were not a mighty people, so their protests against their various neighbours tended to be pinpricks and minor vexations. Their plan for the bridge, however, was not small, and their hopes ran high. Times were changing. The bridge had been there forever, as far as anyone knew, though it was so slightly used that a cartload of hay crossing it while two small boys fished from it made it seem busy. Yet the weeks that had just passed had been very different: war and many deaths had come to the bridge and the tramping of feet across it had gone on all through the daylight hours. The new people from the south were sweeping across the land, and how could the Matrix stop them? In their homes in the woodlands the men and women who had laid the plan for the bridge trembled at their own presumption, hoping the plan might not also turn out to be part of their long misfortune. In this their memories were refreshed and recreated by such incessant reminders that there could be no soft forgetfulness.

But some were doubtful. They thought the signs harder to read than most found them. One of the women, in daytime her eyes were shielded by dark lenses, put the doubts clearly: "The Matrix is not finished. We saw Billy Scarlett the Once-Dead still alive and many more. Let us hope our King is right. What we are doing is something, but still only the work of a hidden people."

It did not make her popular but they knew it was true.

It was a cramped room with a musty smell of earth and tree-roots and another pungent, salty smell he didn't like to think about. Someone was breathing heavily in a corner, difficult sobbing breaths, but it was hard to see, though a wavering suggestion of light was percolating into the room. A few moments ago the room had been a frightful shambles of a place where men blindly struck blows into the dark before it could grow steel teeth. The darkness had torn open his stomach and broken his nose but he was still alive.

From outside he heard an unfamiliar voice saying: "Go home. In the morning it will all be different." The voice was cold; he had heard voices like it before but not recently. Over the last year or so his days had been so good and this morning it had been good again to wake and stretch and plan the day over breakfast – a carnival day with masks for fun. His own mask was smashed now, but he pulled another one away from a dead face and put it on, still sitting down. Eventually he got to his feet, his hands pushing the pain back inside his shirt, and walked slowly to the door. He wanted to crouch over and cradle the pain but forced himself to stand upright and step outside. Though the air was smoky the lanterns' light made brighter patches and he saw enough to know his enemies had won.

Someone spoke to him as if he was expected but no one else seemed immediately concerned so he took a cautious step backward into the trees, then another, then sideways behind a fallen trunk covered in ivy and now a screen of criss-crossing alders and hazels hid him so he took another step and another. He knew he wanted help and he wanted to be out of this wood and its dense tangles, so unlike the columned trunks in grassy glades that the foresters tended. It was chiefly a hazel wood, the branches that were regularly cut back for wattle-hurdles and eel-traps regrowing rapidly from the stumps and enmeshed with blackthorn and sycamores, while nettles, ivy, brambles, foxgloves and wild yellow irises crowded towards the light. After some moments he could go no further so he lay and waited. Though certainly he could not outrun the man with the cold voice, at least where he was he would be hard to find. It hurt very much to breathe.

Before long they came, looking and calling. At first they called out, "Hereward, where are you? Hereward?" but the words meant nothing to him. Soon enough the words and tone alike changed and he heard his own name and knew they came for his death. It seemed there were no gainful reasons for them to do this. He had seen dangerous times but he recalled no long or deep resentment. How could he, it was all so distant now? There had been the games with the Twisted Folk but surely that was unimportant. It was all so unfair.

After a while the noises of people pushing through the undergrowth faded away leaving only the sounds of the wood talking to itself, branches chafing, an owl calling, and once a cough and snuffle near by that he guessed to be a badger. Soon he would have to move but, hearing Hay church bell chime midnight, he decided to wait an hour. Anyway, lying still didn't hurt his chest so much.

Between twelve and one the noise started again. At first it was slight and not close but gradually it drew nearer until it became a voice that called his name, crying out "Where are you?" over and over, a woman's voice, high and eerie in the darkness. He was sure he did not recognise it. It never occurred to him to answer, no more than he would have answered the dead voices from his past, and he fully expected the voice would go away. But it went on, cajoling and admonishing him, even crooning makeshift rhymes.

Come now, come now, don't be hard to find,
Think about me, think about me – let me touch your mind.

The Matrix had had failures and successes. When it had succeeded, more often than not it was because it was still attuned to its original bargain, contracted so long ago no one knew who its signatories were, though perhaps it had been intended that all people and all living things should be represented. As with all mighty intentions there were, sheltered under its umbrella, lesser failures and minor successes, but few could argue that the Matrix had cherished the trees. Certainly there were inhospitable places where the trees grew ill, such as the Glassy Country, or places they had not colonised, such as the empty windy grasslands around the Fence and the gibber-plains of the Mesa. Yet elsewhere were rich compensations spread: the far deep forests, oak, ash and hornbeam, the greenwoods where the pigs rooted for beechmast and acorns, the friendly spinneys and coppices of birch and alder spring-carpeted in bluebells and primroses, hedge-rows of shady elms and shapely chestnuts where children learned of falling branches and shaky tree-houses, weald, holt and brake, a name for every tree and every disposition from the magic grove to the garden orchard to the holly tree in the churchyard red with berries just when it should be.

He was at ease in the woods, and why not for he knew them as he knew the vapour that came misty from his mouth on frosty mornings, part of his own warmth borrowed from and shared with the cold air. So borrowed from the woods were the tottery cabins he and his young friends had built and slept in to awaken with their hair and eyelashes wet with dew and daylight already making bars of light through the hazel-pole walls. Other friends, the pig-boys, sometimes joined them for breakfast, scrambling eggs in a black pan to dump on bread-slices. Even his own room at home had oak-leaves carved on the bed-head.

Now he was alone in the wood with his fire nearly out but he was content. The night was clear and the road he had just left and was to walk again in the morning was close by. Tomorrow held much promise and interest. As for tonight the wood was his friend, nor did the Green Man of the pig-boys' stories concern him. Though by custom the law reached only as far into the forests as the eye could penetrate, the boy felt no fear. He would be careful as he had promised his mother, so he did not sleep near his fire.

He slept the light sleep of animals, so light that he could tell without waking when a stir of wind cooled his face. Feet stumbling and trampling through the ferns brought him awake and he slid gently out of his blanket long before the noise came close. There was the sound of a fall.

"Stand up, you little rat! This is bad country for the likes of you." The voice and the words had a coarseness the boy found offensive. There was a crackle and a flare of light and he knew someone had kicked his fire into life. "Get some wood for it then." Now the boy liked the voice even less. He put his feet down softly, like leaves falling, and came slowly towards the fire. He wanted to be looking from the shadows into the light, as the wolf looks.

There were two figures in the firelight, a tall one standing, a small one kneeling to put sticks on the fire. Suddenly the standing figure laughed and made a jerking movement of the arm and the other staggered, overbalanced and fell, twisting to avoid the embers. Then the boy saw the rope; it had risen from the ground as it was dragged taut and it had been tied round the small man's waist. His face was unmistakably clear. Not the guffawing man but the other, the boy had seen him only a few days before, smiling and showing his neighbours on an inn-bench party-tricks with dice. He was a twister, obviously, but the boy had liked him at once.

At the edge of the circle of firelight he was still unseen, so silent he had to give a cough to announce himself. The tall man was round in a moment and a long knife was in his hand. The boy slid neatly into a shadow, his hand reaching back over his shoulder and from his pack, where he kept it strapped, the bayonet hissed as it came out.

"No one should be tied up like a mad dog," he said.

"It's a twister. Are you blind?"

"What about Dole River?"

"That was a lot of lies. Now get out of here, whoever you are. Your mother's missing you."

The man could not see the boy clearly, so in the dim light he might have missed the eyes. But then he should have caught enough in the voice to know that here was a young raptor, who would never forego or forget these fierce sweet moments.

It was a memory one day but not the next, and then more of a mirage of a memory, simmering and shimmering separate from anything of substance. Since it was all he possessed of his early life he was very familiar with it, perhaps too much so for it had acquired a patina of wear, here an extra skin of tiny emphases, there its own skin worn thin by probing. Imprisoned inside the memory's glass bubble the scenes were fierce and vivid, but nowhere connected with what he knew or could imagine of either his past or present self.

It was hot in the bubble, the sun a burning presence too glaring to look towards in a sky that was an unflawed blue glaze. The metal in his hand was so hot he had to change hands to hold it, though it was unclear to him what it was, other than that it was a weapon, maybe a rifle, though he thought not, maybe a blade of some sort. Below him and to every horizon, for he was high above the ground, stretched a parched and rocky landscape resembling no place he had ever seen except in this memory. In small stone-walled fields rocks protruded hotly through a soil which itself lay in hard clods, as if baked on the day the plough turned them over. He knew without knowing how he knew that the patches of glossy dark green trees with golden fruit neatly hanging on them, as if placed there as decorations, were orange orchards.

The wooden floor of the third storey of the rolling tower creaked and shuddered. The men packed round him swayed, those near the planked sides reaching out to keep their balance. He knew them all, had known them a long time, though their names were strange, names such as Ivo, Gilles, Heppo, Lothar, Agmundr, Reynald. Through cracks in the boarded-up sides of the tower the top of the city wall was visible, creamy stones roughly plastered into place but with black marks of ash and burns, where the wooden barricade that the defenders had erected to raise the height of the wall was now burning and disintegrating. Outside there was a crash as a wooden gangway was flung out and onto the wall-top, and the first man was across in four or five bounding strides, ducking his head and plunging into the flames. Now the memory had almost unwound itself, for he, Ivo, Agmundr and the rest followed in a rush, the wooden bridge tilting and bouncing terrifyingly above the chasm of hot bright air. Then his feet were on solid stone and he caught a glimpse of the city below, domes and spires and palaces, shining white and ivory and pearl-grey, the city dreamed far back in their own stumpy churches and muddy fields.

The arrow went into his throat, neatly finding the notch in the breastbone. Thinking he was glad he had taken communion that morning before the assault, he fell. For a second, face down, there was the gingery smell and taste of dust. Then nothing.

Examining his body, inspecting his own face in the mirror, he supposed himself to be in his thirties. Apart from that one recollection, nothing else remained of those lost years. Anyway, it was not likely to be a true memory since there was no sign whatever of any scar or mark at the base of his throat.

I

"That Petergint, or Pergint, whatever he's called, suits Demetrius well, Martin."

"Why's that, Red?"

"Lots of reasons. Neither of them seems to know what he's doing for a start, they both talk too much, and neither of them's very amusing. It's all right for you, larking about as a troll."

"Thank you, Red. That's kind of you!"

"I wouldn't choose it. I'd rather live with cheese and garlic in a windmill, far. Demetrius should stick to my play, Martin, even if you haven't much to say in it."

"You're right. 'Come, neighbour, the boy shall lead our horses down the hill.' It isn't much, and even then I've never been sure how to say it. Could you actually put a horse on a lead? I thought they were big powerful creatures that liked to run about."

"I think they were, but friendly as well."

It was pleasant to be strolling along in the afternoon sun, the breeze just rippling the barley fields, and Green Lane beneath your feet. Of course there were many green lanes, but this one was always smooth, straight and level, and both of them were walking home. There was danger, there always was, but less so, thought Martin, when you had Red Buckle for company. In any case they had seen no one since leaving Bran village, where Demetrius's troupe were to perform that night. About six in the evening they would walk back together and act their parts. Martin enjoyed watching Red in the role of the wild young magnate. It suited him well, so much so that sometimes Red would threaten to win the final sword fight instead of losing it. Occasionally they would speculate as to why Demetrius arranged for this play to be performed so much more frequently than any other in their repertoire. For three months now the company had swung through the villages round Ingastowe, never bothering if the audience was two farmers and a cow, or if the stage was the cobbles of an inn yard, though in a week's time they were to be in Hay village to perform in the banquet room of the Misses Shepherds' grand house.

Red Buckle and Martin alike were puzzled by Demetrius. The big man paid generously and Martin in particular was glad of the payments, but he would stick so closely to the same play. Occasionally the Petergint Story was acted, 'as a special treat for the Twisted Folk,' Demetrius would say. Then Martin liked him less, and Red would suggest sharply that Demetrius stick to playing fat bullies. The company also had a number of shorter plays and interludes, including one Demetrius had written himself, called 'Lamorak and the Beanstalk'. If things didn't work out, he told them, then they would do it all again next year. When asked what he hoped would work out, he laughed and said that it was personal.

Then a girl stepped out on to the lane, a small figure appearing a hundred yards or so ahead of them. She was clear to see for there the lane ran along a sort of raised causeway over some marshy ground. She was holding a bunch of flowers. Martin hesitated and Red Buckle, who feared nothing and no one, understood the hesitation and paused too. As if the path ahead were a stage, two men climbed up out of the bushes of the embankment and one took the girl's arm. The men seemed to be speaking to her. At first she pulled away but then clawed and struck out so fiercely that she broke free and ran along the path towards Red and Martin. They saw one of the men chase her, while the other stood laughing, and as the pursuer caught her she screamed and turned to scratch and kick. Horrified they watched her flung down and his boot slam into her back and then her head.

Though experience and advice alike suggested to Martin and Red that they stay safely clear of the Daylight People's affairs, they ran forward. But the action had not finished. Out of the elderberry bushes on the opposite side came another man. Moving swiftly and silently, he sprang on the girl's attacker, dragging him down the bank into the shadowy undergrowth. Now the second of the men who had accosted her reached the girl, arriving at just the same moment as the two part-time actors, so that they stood on opposite sides of the body. The man's eyes flickered over Martin: "Get out of here, you dirty little twister!" He pulled a handgun from his belt. His gaze turned to Red Buckle. "You too, if you know what's good for you."

Martin shivered when Red said, as if in mild conversation, "Do you want to kick her as well?" He could now see that the man facing them was a Matrix soldier, a frightening contingency. For some moments now the branches of the bushes at the bottom of the slope had stopped waving, and the choking noises had stopped. Only one man was scrambling up the bank. Martin recognised him as a millworker from Hobson's water-mill in Hay.

The newcomer was breathing hard. He wiped blood away from deep gouges on his face and pushed past Martin who shivered at all the pent-up fury there. The Matrix soldier lifted his gun. "All of you walk away," he said. "Go somewhere else. I've warned you."

Then the millworker was coming forward, screaming as he came. Red Buckle knew it as the fighter's scream that chills and slows the target. The shot came fractionally late, just after the fierce collision that sent the soldier staggering and the gun flying sideways. Red stepped forward but now the soldier was more intent on escape. Within seconds the big man from Hay village was back on his feet and in pursuit.

Martin took off his jacket and spread it over the girl, but Red picked it up and handed it back. "Let's go, Martin. She'll live, I think."

"What about the other soldier, down there in the bushes? Do you think he's dead?"

"I don't know. I do know if they find you here you certainly will be."

"And you, Red?"

"Yes, probably me too."

II

"We were coming down Station Hill," said George Littler, "down from the Barr plantation and we'd heard the clock strike five." The dialect was thick but because everyone else spoke it there was no misunderstanding. Zjelko noticed how eyes swivelled upwards to where, above the dark beams, the worn old mechanism of the great clock gave order to their lives.

One man in particular strained his ears for the muffled clack as the pallets slipped into and out of the crown wheel's teeth. The clockwright spread the clock on the drawing-board of his mind, his thoughts easing the worn cogs round a revolution, stroking bars that were pitifully frail. More mutton-fat, he thought, tallow, oil, then add wormwood so the mice and rats aren't tempted to pilfer the grease from the old clock's innards.

"Down in the old Station yard we saw these two. Later we found Adelie. How is she now?"

"Someone'll be over by and by," said a tall bent man with a black bar of moustache, and the people in the room swayed their attention to him and back to Littler with the patience of unlettered people who know that words made quickly are like bread made quickly, the inconsistencies not kneaded out. Also they knew that foresters like Littler, who talk to seed and sapling and squirrel, are naturally slow of speech.

"We'd heard a shot. This fellow," Littler's voice was tinged with condescension, "must have shot at Orr . . ." He paused. "With a gun," he added drily, and his hearers smiled; no self-respecting forester would even possess a gun. "Missed. Orr was probably a few yards away, so he wouldn't be likely to hit him." The villagers looked at Zjelko standing impassively, arms folded, his straight back leaning gently against the lime-washed wall of the big room.

"Well, we heard the pigboys shouting and when we got there," Littler went on, "Orr was on top of him, shaking him like you see Ragnar shake a rat, so me and Alwyn thought we'd better do something. We got 'em apart, and then some of the lasses hoeing the ridges in the Station field came over, and we all came down here together to the village." And the bits in between everyone knew, embroidered by forty-fold recounting. Orr had gone to the house of Hobson, the millhouse whose flour-smelling attic had become his home. The rest had walked down to the headman's dwelling, which was in fact for them the nearest house in the village, standing the other side of a lane that ran along by the potato field. There Zjelko had been ushered into a dark, over-furnished room and a few moments later the headman had come in and they had sat opposite one another in big cushioned chairs. Quietly the old man had explained that this incident called for a full village meeting, which he was having assembled that night, and that Zjelko ought to stay and speak at it. Until then Littler would sit with them lest Zjelko take exception to the way the headman was conducting affairs.

Zjelko had given Littler one short, overbearing stare which said plainer than words that he was only staying because he wanted to. In fact, he liked neither the look of Littler, who was a looming figure even in a chair, nor the presence of Ragnar, who was a fully-grown gray wolf. It was well-known that only the foresters from the deep fastnesses had wolves as companions. Maybe this Littler was a bit more than a cloddish stump-digger. There had been no more talk, for Zjelko found it hard to follow the village folk's speech, and they had sat waiting through the long twilight until he fell into a doze, disturbed only by the big cockchafer beetles that occasionally tumbled down the chimney and rattled in the pile of pine-cones that filled the wide raised hearth.

Now as the big soldier leaned against the wall of the room listening to the woodman's deep gutturals his mind turned in the treadmill of his predicament: soon he must speak, yet what could he say? To speak directly would be to invite retribution; nor was he certain that his version of the truth was not, in any case, some higher fabrication. It certainly sounded feeble enough to him. Yet where was there a plausible pretext for assaulting a child? If only, he thought, she hadn't broken away long enough to scream, and if she hadn't been so strong. She couldn't be older than thirteen, it wasn't natural.

These were outlandish folk who regarded life differently from others who met death less frequently; they knew the ferret's teeth in the rabbit's neck, the cow dead in labour. He had heard once of a sow that had eaten a baby, and how they had hanged it. That was a different village, but the same province, and the girl wasn't that much more than a baby after all. A girl-child and alone, and he from a far province. In every way it would outrage them. The lanterns cast none too good a light, and he found it difficult to gauge the expressions. The women looked at him much longer than the men, and desperately he groped for some chart to help him pick his way out of this peril. An accident? He could hear the iron laughter that time-worn evasion would provoke.

"Well, Art?" The high female voice snapped Zjelko alert, and the dark roomful of faces focused on the new speaker.

"Yes, Anna?" said the headman.

"What are we waiting for?"

"Well," said the old man, "first we must hear the stranger's story."

"Yes, Art, that's a good idea. I mean when we've heard him tell us what he did to Adelie will we have to wait then?"

"Oh, no, he'll have to go trotting back to the fort then," said another voice.

The headman sought the most soothing tone he knew: "Anna, and everyone, my friends, and you, Matrix soldier, all of us know that the free meeting of a village decides matters of justice in our community, over all except the monk-people, and our decisions rule vagrants and visitors . . ."

"I am neither," interrupted Zjelko loudly and leaned back deliberately. He might be at bay, but it could be far worse. He thought it most unlikely that the girl could recover, at least for several days, and no village in all Westermain would let a twister testify or even appear in its court. That just left the madman.

"He lies, he is one at least," a voice called deeply from where the listeners packed thickest, and mutters of approval came like the pebbles churning in a wave's backwash as it ebbs off a shingle beach.

"But is he?" said the headman quickly. "The comings and goings of the Matrix soldiers, and remember this is not a militiaman, are beyond our law. Most of you have seen them escort the caravans to and from the markets, and if they trample in our crops, or billet themselves without fair payment, do we arraign them in our meetings? No, they ask us how we have been wronged, and they set the matter aright, both the recompense and the punishment."

"Why did you call this meeting then, Artis?" said Littler, one of the few men in the room who used the headman's full name.

"Because," replied the other, "this is much more than trampling crops. Also it seemed too much to touch us all not to call you together, and because I and all of us wish to know how it came about. Nor yet do I believe many of the grains have fallen through the hourglass in this matter."

"So, let us hear the soldier speak."

Zjelko pushed himself upright. The talk of whose jurisdiction this affair fell under was a loophole. It was tempting to demand that he be returned to the fort, but awkward and embarrassing for his commander, and a postponement of an inquiry that he was not looking forward to. Perhaps it would come to demanding his release, though scrutinising the women's faces he suspected this avenue of escape might be more apparent than real. Something in his native stubbornness and that apartness which is part of the mystery of all uniforms urged Zjelko to see the matter through. He felt no compunction for what he intended to do. He liked to do things in his own fashion, and for others to give way to his strength and experience.

He had been infuriated by almost every event of the day. Being told to kidnap a girl was, he thought, pointless, and then she had resisted so ferociously, spitting and snarling. It had been a pleasure to see Vanya knock her head on the stones, the only redeeming feature of the day. Though the girl had seemed quite alone a man had appeared silently to drag Vanya down the bank into the dense thickets. Then the twisters had come strolling along as if they owned the path. Inwardly he cursed them and he cursed missing his shot and even cursed the herd of dun-coloured pigs that had scattered squealing into the trees as he ran among them, and the pig-boys who had shrieked incoherently at him. He wished he could have had a few moments alone with the pig-boys and given them real reason to shriek, but there had been no opportunity. With no shots left he had not wished to end up like Vanya; the guns they were given were next to useless, he thought, but he knew it was more the way Orr had rushed at him, unhesitatingly and screaming as he came. Just as well that lumbering great lout of a forester had appeared.

Zjelko could see Orr staring into a yellow flame, and the flickering light on every plane of his face marked him an outsider, a man not related to these burly villagers, their blue eyes wide, blond hair matting their forearms, their women only a little smaller and no less stolid. They were a people, thought Zjelko, not unlike their big, creamy-yellow buttercup-munching cows, but the strange man with the empty face who had pursued him, the man called Orr, where did he belong in this pattern? The soldier felt not a flutter of remorse at what he was about to do. Even if he had he would have stifled it. Vanya did not deserve to be choked and left in the brambles.

"Friends," he began, "when have you ever known us to be murderers? When did a Matrix soldier hurt anyone save outlaws and twisted people and those who serve the magnates? Your headman has told you what you already know, that we live under the law. We recognise offence where we commit it; we are quick to recompense when we transgress."

Zjelko was not sure he had all the local words right, nor for that matter that the ways of the Matrix soldiery were so extremely scrupulous, but the effect was encouraging; the whole room, even Orr, was waiting on what was to come. "This afternoon the two of us found a girl near a big barley field. She was unconscious where the lane runs on top of a high bank . . ." He paused for the anticipated questions that came together from a dozen mouths.

"Two . . .?"

"Who were the . . .?"

"Who else was there?"

"Apart from me? My comrade, of course. We found the girl lying on the path. Two twisters were running away. I felt sure that would not have been kept from you." He paused to let the barbs sink in, wondering how much Orr had spoken of the killing. "I set out to chase them. My comrade stayed behind to care for the girl but he was dead when I returned. Sooner than stay there to be ambushed by a gang of twisters I made my way along the causeway towards this village, which I could see behind the trees. A man followed, caught me up and we struggled." The murmurs were rising, but Zjelko lifted his voice over them: "He is sitting there now. He is the one you call Orr."

'Now I have set my foot into this river I must cross it,' thought Zjelko, his mind racing in the uproar. The dark room was full of sound and movement: above the people's heads pigeons shuffled on the wall-top where roof and rafters met, and a bat skittered down to the door and away along the long lobby to the starlight. Only by the side of the miller was stillness, although Hobson, a small man but powerfully built, was on his feet, banging his fist on a table-top and shouting his support and approval for Orr. By his side Orr sat silently on the stool he had occupied throughout the meeting. His gaze was fixed upon Zjelko, and as their eyes locked together the soldier saw that the ruminative film had gone and the stare was alarmingly intent. Once Zjelko had looked down from a river's edge and seen a crocodile's hooded eyes peer speculatively up at him. The same sense of coldness, of his body hair prickling, ran over him.

"Orr's no twister and he never harmed a living thing!" Hobson bellowed. "Why do you think little Adelie went out walking with him? Why did her mother like them to be together? Because he's gentle, gentle as can be, and there's not a one of you as can deny it!"

"That's right!" shouted another voice. "Tell 'em, Hobby!"

"It's right enough," called another. Shadows danced darkly over the walls and the ring of people tightened as passion drew individuals towards the centre to press their point. Those pushing forward met the backs and shoulders of those who wished to hold their places.

"Either he or the twisters killed my friend!" shouted Zjelko. "Has he said nothing about his afternoon's work at all? Go on! Somebody ask him."

"Why is this the first time we've heard of this killing?" shouted Hobson in return, and the miller's stocky figure pushed closer to Zjelko's big form.

"Because the headman kept me in his house and allowed no speech or discussion before this meeting."

"Words, excuses," snarled the miller. "You could have told Art easily enough, and anyway if Orr killed your murdering friend there's many here will want to thank him for it."

Zjelko laughed and stared down at the miller. "Tell me who he murdered since he's the only one dead."

"Now, hold hard," the headman said. "Whatever has come into our lives this day will not be driven out by shouting. Yelling at one another won't separate grain from chaff."

"No, nor do we want your old proverbs, Art," snapped Hobson.

Zjelko's eyes followed each speaker and his nerves were taut with concentration on the currents in the room, as a man on a high wire must know the merest flexure of the airs over the abyss. From his position near the door he was the first to see it open. The woman who came through was small and slight, unlike most women of Hay village, and in the shadows her black coat made the others slow to notice her, though the headman saw her come.

"Welcome to the meeting. The child will be well?" said Artis doubtfully, feeling in his heart that whatever had come into their lives that day was not to be so easily driven out.

"She will live . . ." said the woman, though her terse words carried little comfort. Silence hung round and spread from her, and the meeting waited for the great massy burden to be split into pieces, each piece a word, so that all might share, and perhaps by sharing lift it better.

". . . if you can call it living." And the people took the words as you lift a sack of grain, trying it gently because shortly it will have to be heavy on your shoulders.

"She will be sick then, Nell?" asked a voice at last.

"No, neither sick nor well, nor quick nor dead. She is both crippled and out of her mind."

The faces looked round at one another. Their community was a strong one in many ways, they could care for a member who was crippled, but the maiming of a mind, especially a mind keen and brilliant as this little one's had been, that seemed to sap the spirit of all. Passion had run slack, as water in an eddy retains its weight but loses its direction. Conversation swirled gentle with sympathy. Zjelko relaxed, his breath coming more easily. Remarks he had overheard in

Artis's house had made him almost sure the girl would not be capable of speech, but it was reassuring to be certain, for she may well have recognised him again; she had been so strong and fierce, biting and scratching, screaming only once.

The images and perplexities took but seconds. Throughout the room private conversation became noisy debate with a high female voice calling out: "Will this take all night? The poor soul wasn't hurt in an accident, or have you forgotten?"

"Aye, what has Orr to say?" said another, adding, "He hasn't said aught yet."

"Ask him if he's killed anyone today," said Zjelko.

"Did you, Orr?" said the headman into the mystified silence.

Orr's head came swivelling round and he looked at the headman with a long stare that seemed to be focusing on the wall behind him. "Yes," said Orr at length, removing the incident from others in his head and observing it, before putting it back next to the sound of rooks cawing their late afternoon way home to high elms.

"Then why did you not speak of it?" the headman asked. The room was quieter now than it had been all night.

"I don't know. Does it matter?" said Orr.

"Deaths matter," said the clockwright, speaking for the first time. "Or do you disagree?"

"Some matter," said Orr, and now Zjelko felt the tide turning his way with the answer. He thought it rang true, though he would never have said the same in the circumstances, and Orr's tone was so neutral, as if he had lost interest. His words and demeanour were reminders that here was an outsider, a stranger.

"Speak straight, Orr, lad," said the miller grimly.

"If it isn't too much trouble," said another voice.

There was a muttered chorus of approval for this, the level of sound rising steadily, and then came shouting:

"Why are we wasting time?"

"We know he's a killer, he says so himself!"

"It wasn't a life for a life either!"

"You can't trust him!"

"Maybe he did it!"

Zjelko was waiting for this: "Of course he did! And he killed an innocent man for getting in his way. He wanted no witnesses. He would have killed me too, if the forester hadn't come along. Now ask him what he and the twisters meant to do to the girl if they'd had the time!"

Hardly were the words spoken when a savage cry chilled the blood of the hardiest. A lantern was smashed sideways, a table toppled, and shadows and bodies collided and spun as Orr, teeth bared, came driving through the group around him and all of his weight thudded into Zjelko's chest. The back of the big soldier's head struck the white wall a flat echoing smack and he fell forward. As he did so Orr hauled him further away from the wall by the front of his tunic, side-stepping to let the bulky body tumble past. Before Zjelko had fallen Orr had clubbed him across the head, two or three blows that sent him sprawling dazed among table legs and dust and booted feet. Another swinging blow cannoned into an anonymous shoulder and the sheer press of twelve or fifteen bodies bore Orr back and away; strong hands pinned him against the wall where, seconds before, Zjelko had leaned. The latter in his turn had been hauled up, and from a table-top seat stared dazed, dishevelled and furious, at his assailant. Flames ran over the oil that had splashed from the broken lamp and feet kicked them out. Orr suddenly, unexpectedly, cried out again, animal-like, and the men who held him shook him silent. The room, darker now, throbbed towards a decision.

"This Orr-stranger is not one of us." The clockwright seemed to speak for many. "He appeared from who knows where, his thoughts are strange. Myself, I believe that, in a moment when he knew not what he did, he attacked Adelie. We saw, we heard, his fury a moment ago; we know also that he has killed once already today. For that, too, unless we do something, we will all suffer. I do not think it altogether his fault. I do not believe that he knows what is right, or what is truth. He sees the world through a broken glass, as Unmen do."

Listening, Zjelko thought that Orr was ill in his head. The man seemed not to care what was happening, as if the present had no presence and he was only watching it happen to others. He wondered if Orr could possibly be an Unman, or perhaps one of the Old Ones, but he had only heard of the Unmen, who anyway never seemed to leave the sinister shelter of their city of Regret, and the Old Ones, while certainly they were ill in the head, were physically indistinguishable from everyone else. Whatever the truth, Orr didn't fit in this village. "I do not think," said Artis in a tired old man's voice, "that we shall uncover any more of the truth by debate. This is a free meeting and can judge Orr, who is now a village man. As for the soldier, he chose to be here and must accept the consequences. First let us decide whether Orr struck down the girl so that she will never walk straight again. Vote as your hearts and minds tell you."

"They can only tell you one thing. Orr had nothing to do with hurting my daughter. I am her mother and I can assure you of that."

Nell's voice rang out. "I know him well and he would not do anything like that."

"Newcomers sticking together," said Carver Jacques. "Knocking little children around and seducing their mothers. Give me five minutes alone with him." There was a shout of approval from parts of the room, and Nell's retorts were drowned.

The business of voting was customary, though not for years had so ugly and foreboding an event called for the little beads which each person there placed in a box to record a vote. Men and women edged forward to the dais where the headman sat; he watched the black and white beads filling the box. The verdict would be clear and he felt a surge of relief mixed with remorse. Not all voted, it was not compulsory, and the majority was not much in excess of the hundred and fifteen beads, representing half of the village's grown folk, which were needed to be decisive.

"One hundred and twenty-nine say guilty," said the old man quietly, when the counting had been done. "For the killing, as Orr has admitted his responsibility, we do not need the beads. As headman I find Orr doubly guilty. For the death of a soldier, to be delivered to the fort in the morning; for the attack on a girl-child and the destruction of her mind, sending her half-witted to walk in a light that is half-dark, I sentence him to walk in the half-dark . . ."

III

The soil was good: black, crumbly, moist like treacle cake. Tsiganok liked the feel, the coolness of it. Because he was old he worked gently, and there was a relishing in all he did, in the raising of forkfuls of earth, turning them over and seeing the darker soil lifted from beneath the surface, shaking earth from weeds' roots and flicking them deftly to one side, occasionally, with slow ceremony, depositing an earthworm into the open for his companions, blackbird and robin. The soft brownish female blackbird stepped trustingly between his boots, her eye a bright bead, clawed feet sinking into the soil's tilth; the robin came in sharp-eyed ravenous rushes, or retreated precipitately into a bundle of old pea-sticks, his breast like a stray patch of red flannel caught in the twigs.

Tsiganok's plot lay on a hill-scarp and, although he worked facing the slope, often and again he would break off to gaze out into the air below him. Under a grey February sky through which broke slanting columns of sunlight his gaze could move for twenty-five miles across the low wooded valleys which ended half-way to the horizon, where the long blue horizontals of the fenlands began. He loved it all.

It had not always been so. He had come here a young man, lean and arrogant, bred in the islands which, lying south of the Matrix capital, seemed to provide so much of its drive. In those days this land had been merely a draught for him to drain. Now he knew he had poured his own draught back into the cask, and though there were regrets, they were few, and those the three o'clock regrets that all men have when dawn seems a long way off. Now part of him was the old stone wall that formed the upper boundary of his piece of land; it rose from coils of brambles and patches of nettles at its base, half-covered in dusty ivy but with fifteen feet of creamy limestone topped with battlements, and on the far side the guard-walk, and beyond, the bailey, the barracks, the bugles, the boots crunching on gravel.

Daylight wanes quickly in February and the north-east wind soon chills the body, blowing down from the wastes of the grey sea forty miles away. Tsiganok polished his fork with a stone, and pushed open the wicket-gate into the lane. A man was standing there; as Tsiganok turned left to his lodgings the stranger fell into step with him.

"Cold," he said.

Tsiganok shrugged. "You young men shouldn't feel it," he replied amiably. Their breath was visible now, the vapour white in the dusk. The stranger swung his arms across his chest and flexed his shoulders.

"Here," he said to Tsiganok, and held out a leather bottle. The old man pulled out the stopper and sniffed. Its scent was raw, like wet barley with a touch of fern and brown water, its taste was like fire and he felt warmth spread down his chest and fill his belly.

"Moonshine liquor. Thank you. A good drink." He handed the bottle back with a grin.

"Are you a soldier?" said the other.

"Once," grunted the old man.

"Ever go back to the fort?"

"Not really." There was a silence. They walked companionably, hands in pockets, Tsiganok's fork beneath one arm. Smoke was rising from the chimneys in the valley to join a layer of mist from the river flats. Here and there windows were lighting up; the town was drawing in upon itself. An inn sign hung silhouetted above them as he halted. "I live here, comrade," he said. "Thanks for the company and the drink."

"Good night," said the stranger. "Oh, by the way, did you ever come across a soldier called Zjelko?"

"Yes, I know him," replied Tsiganok with a quick glance. "He comes in here for a drink most evenings. Are you a friend of his?"

"Well, I only met him once," replied the stranger, "though I'd like to see him again. Good night."

The old man watched him go quietly away between the houses.

George Littler blew at wood chips in the hearth. Dusk had come into the wooden cabin, closing in around the circle of light from the oil lamp. Littler squatted on a rough stool, hunched inside his jacket and fur hood. He sighed and looked at the two beds. The top one held only bare boards and a folded grey blanket. The blue pack and the swansdown sleeping-bag had gone, and his companion had gone with them. The long, slow talks, the easy silences were over, and Littler wondered if ever he would see his strange acquaintance again. Share a wilderness cabin with a man for two seasons, hunt by him, tramp alongside him, eat with him, sleep near him, and you have to begin to know him. Orr had first come to the cabin when September was turning the ferns saffron, two months after the day Littler had dragged him off Zjelko in the way-station yard. He had spent the autumn and winter in the forest until February brought the celandines out in the hedge-bottoms, the rooks began patching the high tracery of the elm-tops with heaps of twigs, and he departed.

The forester recalled Orr's appearance in the woods, the months just fading the memory round the edges as always happened with the Daylight People. Inside George Littler's head the events of each day lay in sequence and would fade in sequence. A kettle standing on two bricks in the corner of the room caught his attention and thus led the facts of his day, and all days, moving his meeting with Orr one step further away, pushing it back down a queue of incidents and impressions.

That autumn Littler had been building a shelter for the pheasants. It was a rough square of four branches tied horizontally between some tree-trunks then roofed with smaller branches and bracken. Littler put corn for the birds under it in winter so the grains did not get covered in snow. He was a forester and thus Orr had not taken him unaware. George had watched him coming between the trees, the blue pack a strange colour, different among the woodland's yellows and buffs, ochres and oranges. Orr had approached and leaned on a tree-trunk, hitching his pack half on to the thatched shelter, taking the ache from his shoulders.

"They didn't hold you long," said Littler, thickening a thinnish patch with a handful of ferns.

"Long enough," said Orr and his fingers moved automatically around the eye-socket, smoothing the eyebrow ridge and resettling the black patch where it had chafed one side of his nose. "How did you vote that night?"

"White bead," said Littler.

The forester had hated the trial. Like all the villagers he had been vaguely aware of Orr's arrival two years or so ago, drifting in from nowhere, inquiring for work at the mill, staying on in the quiet place. Most had not disliked him, though some, such as the three Jacques brothers, had been irked by his not seeking their noisy company. Despite Orr's reticence, his workmates had liked his unobtrusive presence, and the other stranger, the woman Nell, who had arrived not long afterwards, had seemed close to him and had been happy to see Orr watching over her daughter. It was quite common for him to be spoken of as an Unman, as was Adelie's mother, since both were newcomers to the village.

"I believe you," said Orr, and the ghost of a smile twisted the corners of his mouth. "I wouldn't have stopped here if I hadn't thought that."

"Where are you going now?"

"Anywhere," said Orr. "Into the forest. Not back to the village."

"Have you no home, no family?"

"I don't know," said the man with the empty eye-socket. With the exception of the flash of something happening in an unknown siege that may simply have been recounted to him, though it felt more immediate than that, no figures drifted across his memory's empty screen. "I suppose I may have, somewhere," he added with a shrug.

Littler threw a handful of golden wheat under the shelter and nipped one or two grains in his front teeth, sharing the satisfaction of the pheasants in their floury solidity. "Stay here a while," he said. "You're already in the forest." He hoisted the corn-sack on his shoulder, hefted his axe, and as he did so Orr reached down and picked up the woodman's hammer and bag for him. The two men nodded simultaneously and walked into the shadows under the oaks and beeches.

That evening, as Littler had cooked supper for them, Orr took the axe round the back of the cabin and split logs. They were mostly pine logs from the plantations the villagers used for firewood, planted as seedlings by Littler and other foresters and cropped in a twenty-five year rotation. With the night dark outside the lean-to that sheltered the log-pile, occasional hail-showers rattling on the split-pine shingles, Orr was enjoying himself.

He stood on a soft carpet of sawdust and chippings bringing the axe down in long swinging arcs that sliced the pine into clean, scented billets. The wood split crisply. Whenever a heavy knot deflected the blur of his downward stroke Orr simply reversed the log and chopped into it from the opposite end. He wished it were so easy to by-pass his own affairs. Perhaps the incidents leading to the loss of his eye had galvanised his short-term memory, since he recalled with ease, though uneasily, all that had happened the day he had met Zjelko and most of the events of the subsequent months. Now, too, he was finding it possible to establish a focal point in his days. Where before he had not discriminated between the cloud shapes and his coming to the village, now he was beginning to acquire the habit of establishing landmarks in his mind's scenery. Though he did not know it this made him unlike almost anyone else in Hay or for miles around.

But where he was from, who he was, why he laughed and why he cried, were hidden from Orr, and there seemed no way to understand by going back to his birth and childhood, for the log could not be cut from that end. Twice Orr's axe missed a log and he knew that his single eye had misjudged the distance. On both occasions he thought of his ordeal after the Hay village meeting and the blow that followed ripped venomously into the wood, flinging it clattering against the sides of the shelter.

Orr took an armful of chopped wood into the cabin and stacked it near the fire. Together he and Littler ate soup thick with onions, then damper bread and smoked bacon slices. Later he unpacked his bag and climbed to the top bunk. Long before the firelight stopped flickering among the rafters he was asleep. In the lower bunk Littler lay, not ill-content. Neither was a man who made demands upon another, and that suited each of them well.

November ended in dark days and cold rain that made Orr's eye-socket ache. It had not hurt him for weeks and he thought with gratitude of the small, gentle man in the abbey infirmary, and of the smell of the herbs packed upon his eye and the talks on pain and suffering which Orr, with his brief memories and outraged, amputated nerves, had for a time argued were one and the same.

Littler and Orr rarely spoke together at any length. However there came a day when, high on a rocky spur with snow-showers blowing horizontally into their faces and the white blizzard-mist filling the valleys below them, even Littler called a halt to work. With Orr following, he led the way down towards shelter and found a hawthorn coppice, its trees black, gnarled, rock-tough in their long struggle against the wind's attrition. The two of them ducked into the lee of a dense clump, relieved to feel their exposed faces at once less raw and smarting. Littler pulled dead leaves and twigs into a heap and lit it, cutting the match in half with his knife, lengthways, and sliding the carefully saved half-match back into its box. The flames hesitated, discouraged by the damp, then crackled and sent up a wavering plume of white smoke. The coppice was strewn with fallen leaves and soon the men were ungloved and warming their hands over the small hot fire.

"Two hours, Orr," said Littler, "then it'll slacken and we can make for the cabin. Have a rest."

Both men were oddly comfortable. After a time, encouraged by their closeness and slow easy talk, Orr asked the woodman: "George, who do you think attacked Adelie that day?"

Littler stared downwards into the fire's red centre. Hitherto their talk had been of trees, birds and snow. "The Matrix soldiers. Must have been," he said finally.

"You're right. But why?"

"Who knows? Why do men attack women? Why does the pike attack the dace?"

"But they aren't the same," protested Orr. "If you mean men who desire women in fear, they are different from fish eating fish to stay alive."

"Different in one way, Orr, but in other fashions, just the same. Men and fish, they decide on things when there's no other road they'd sooner follow. Their bodies and the time make the action." The forester's speech was slow as he felt his way through the unfamiliar wood of words and ideas. "You see, Orr, I found out a piece of news later, weeks after that day. One of the Twisted People told me. That soldier had been in the village before. I wonder what brought him. He believed no one saw him, but few except the foresters ever bother with the twisted ones. Or talk to them."

There was no gap in the grey cupola of falling sleet around the coppice; Orr cast about, frustrated, for some feasibility to which Littler's information might lead. "So why did Zjelko and the other man come back to the village?"

"Who knows?" said Littler.

"They must have been looking for something or someone."

"It's possible."

"Do you think Adelie interrupted some plan? Just surprised them on the causeway? While I was dozing, of course."

The bitterness in the words made the forester lift his gaze from the fire. "Don't be so hard on yourself," he said. "You're a good man and Hay is a good place."

"I found that out, all right!" Orr's voice was flat and cold, and he slowly lifted the patch off his eye-socket. The remaining eye fixed itself on Littler in a peremptory stare, so that the forester, who had never been intimidated in his life, needed all his stubbornness to return the look.

"Go easy, Orr," he said, and a second or two later the patch was back, and the introverted look returned as Orr shrugged himself into the bow of the tree-trunk. "One man knows. Try asking him."

"I think I might," said Orr, though so softly Littler was uncertain whether he had spoken or whether the wind had rattled the leafless thorn twigs

December came and the winter solstice: one of man's most ancient festivals, time to propitiate a sun which seemed to pause, too lethargic to climb the southern sky. Littler gave Orr a pair of fur gloves he had made. Orr, touched by the gift, decided to call at the abbey. The snow-crust was firm and glittering beneath his feet and the whole land frozen like crystal in a silence so complete that even thoughts might echo.

The abbot was hunched at his table as Orr was led into the narrow second-storey room with its six high arched windows down each of the two long sides. One view was towards the wooded valleys from which he had just come, the other revealed a huddle of buildings clustered around a church-tower, whose old clock's lost minutes the clockwright would soon have to recapture, as he did each solstice, winter and summer, whenever there was a noon sun to make a shadow fall on the sun-dial. Across the white pine table were blood-red sun-splashes, the burgundy stain of noonday winter sunlight diffused through red window-glass and wine-glass. "It'll soon be Christmas Day," said Orr.

"So it will, my dear fellow," said Abbot Huw of the Cappacian Order.

"Here's a present for you." Orr bent to his sack on the floor. From it he pulled two pheasants and an ermine fur and laid them on the table. The intricate bronze dapples of the pheasants' plumage, and especially the cavalier colours of the neck and tail feathers gave an air of barbaric splendour. The abbot smiled. Since November the abbey had served up dried and flavoured meats. "The fur is a present for the almoner," said Orr.

"Ah, the almoner, yes," said the abbot, and rang the small bell on his table. The monk who answered relayed a summons downstairs and within two minutes a small, dapper monk appeared. "Greetings, Father," he said shrilly to the old man. "Greetings, Orr. I hope you are not here as a patient!"

"Brother Kay," said the abbot, "Orr has brought you a gift." Kay's eyes went to the ermine and he smiled in delight. "He probably believed it a suitable gift. My dear Orr, even rabbit fur is considered ostentatious among serious almoners, many of them prefer good coarse hessian against the skin."

"Orr, would you believe," said the abbot, "that our almoner could vex the harmless brothers last night at supper by asking them whether it was possible for an all-powerful supreme God to create his Son on earth and make him his equal, and still remain supreme? Brother Kay, take Orr away with you, and for your sins meditate upon vanity and contumacy. Oh, by the way you may sew the ermine on your collar. Wear it with humility."

The two left the room, down spiralling stone stairs into the great undercroft. Orr lifted his hood into place and averted his face for here were men from the village, craftsmen, lay-brothers and the sick, who had occasion to visit the abbey. Together, unnoticed, Orr and Kay slipped into Kay's small dispensary. "Well done, Orr, Huw loves pheasant, though no doubt he'll give them to the novices and make us all feel gross," he said, closing the door. "And thank you for my fur." He ran his finger along its black and white hairs. "How is your eye?"

"Which one?" said Orr.

"H'mm, much livelier than when you came here for sanctuary."

Last July. They both remembered it well enough. Here in his dispensary Kay had been mulling blackcurrant wine for an asthmatic brother and had filled the room with steam to ease his breathing. Then there had been the disquieting pad of running feet, the sound of urgent voices, and the abbot had come through Kay's doorway with his prior and a sweating figure whose fingers could not contain the blood pooled in his eye-socket, for it dribbled down his cheek and neck and seeped under his soaking shirt. There followed days of sick agony and the slow recovery, during which Kay had always been ready to talk with his patient, despite the frustration of answers which were a mixture of cynicism and obliquity, a frustration thoroughly compounded by the abbot, who replied, when Kay asked why the villagers had taken out Orr's eye, "To stop themselves seeing, simpleton."

Imprisoned by the villagers in the church vestry that summer night Orr had spent an hour made savage by pulsing, throbbing cymbals of pain rocking his whole skull and a great hate-filled loathing for the clumsy injustice that fate had visited upon him. So intense was his elemental protest that, without knowing why, several times that night men looked suddenly behind them at the church tower above the trees.

There were two doors to the vestry, one leading into the chancel, the other out into the churchyard, and each was guarded from the outside. Orr heard the guards change on the second and third hours after midnight. And then, while he had sat head in hands pondering ruses such as feigned unconsciousness, a scratch had come at the churchyard door, and, when he failed to move, a gentle tap. He had listened at the door, ear pressed to the crack between its solid halves. Even then chance had been his salvation. Turning away he had gripped the iron ring of the handle to steady himself, balancing awkwardly on the narrow threshold. The latch had lifted and to his amazement the door swung in towards him. He stepped out. At the base of the wall the unconscious sentry lay, breathing heavily. On cat-feet Orr melted past him into the shadows of the big holly-trees that lined the path from the vestry to the road.

Thanking whomever had intervened on his behalf, he had considered searching for Zjelko, but only briefly, realising he had no notion of where to begin. Moreover he was desperate to find relief for the lacerated flesh of his eye-socket, and the pain had put him in mind of the abbey. A mile or so out of the village, it lay among wet fields, alongside the beck, squat substantial buildings, home for a community of some forty monks and a number of waifs who looked to them for shelter. Orr had stolen through the village's dark empty streets and, once away from the houses, had run slowly through the dew-wet grasses of a green lane, once startling a dog-fox as it walked across his path. Only when he heard behind him far-off shouts and the barking of dogs had he increased his speed, soon to come jogging into the abbey's cobbled courtyard, where sleepy monks peered mildly at him.

When Orr had thrown off his fever, for the wound had gone septic, he remained many days in the sanatorium, not the larger infirmary but a small chamber with three beds, recuperating, talking with Kay, watching the swallows gathering for their long southward flight. The monks had been good to him, teaching him unexpected skills: preparing skins, tanning, dyeing and sewing. He had made himself a pack and a sleeping-bag, stuffing it with downy swan-feathers. Ready to leave, he had left like the swallows.

"I feel much better now," said Orr. "I shall always be indebted to you."

"You were much more interesting than cowherds with toothache," said Kay. "Remember to keep clear of Matrix soldiers."

"Have they been here since?"

"No. They came to the village though. The elders knew you had sought sanctuary, but no one ever let it out. I suppose they thought you'd been punished enough."

"Punished?" said Orr. "Is that what they called it?"

"Now don't be frosty," said the almoner. "Do you want to play chess?" At Orr's smiling nod he fetched the apple-wood board and the pieces and placed them on a low table. "Orr," he said, "if I ask you nicely would you give me one grain of corn for the first square on the board, two for the second, four for the third, then eight and so on. I want our pigeons to be plumper."

"No, because I don't own all the grains on earth. You've asked me that before."

"And you remembered it. What's happening to you?" They moved the pieces to and fro.

"I remember quite a lot now," said Orr. "One day I shall remember everything."

"Then you'll be a good candidate for abbot. Though presently you don't remember enough to stop playing that bishop move."

"It's a good variation," said the abbot from the dispensary hatch, taking the board in at a glance. "It throws the centre wide open later on."

"I know," said Orr. "I like it, even if the attack takes a long time," and he tapped a bishop.

"Are you adjusting that piece?" asked Kay.

"Just for now," replied Orr.

"It's an important ecclesiastical piece," said the almoner. "That's why it moves obliquely."

"I think I would prefer 'mysteriously' to 'obliquely'," said the abbot.

"Slantingly?" enquired Kay.

"No, no, 'mysteriously' will do, if you please, almoner."

On they played through the short winter afternoon, engrossed in the ancient game. Orr had learned it with such speed that Kay, who rarely found an opponent to match him, was having to exert all his skill. He wondered if chess was part of whatever Orr was remembering more easily now. He pushed forward his pawns to disrupt Orr's pattern, though feeling that such a strategy was too predictable. Indeed, his efforts soon ran out of steam and Orr dislodged the almoner's hold on the central squares.

Deepening dusk stopped their contest. Orr suspected his renewed presence in the abbey might have been noted by villagers and, reluctant to ask for sanctuary again, was eager to pass under the eaves of the forest. He peered out of the dispensary hatch across the wet cobbles of the undercroft, through its arches to the cold landscape. The trees and hedges were flatly black as if drawn in charcoal on its glazed expanse.

"Time to get back to George," he said. "You don't feel like resigning I suppose?"

"I've thought about it." He stepped swiftly over to Orr's side in the doorway, perky and sleek as the bulfinches he fed on the window-sill.

"What made you stay?"

"Someone gave me a Christmas present."

"What's that got to to with resigning?"

"Everything," said Kay. "It's often tempting to resign, Orr. I know that well. For instance, in my work patients sometimes get delusions about the grandeur of physicians but no real man of medicine shares them. Do you think I enjoy wives asking me if there's any way to stop their husbands dying? I want to say, 'Don't delude yourself, sister, I can't stop myself dying. You'll be asking me next to stop night coming.' Then I get a gift or some good luck, so I say that it might as well be me that tells them, and I come back here the next day instead of resigning and keeping bees. No, we'll carry on with the game later." Somewhere nearby a crow squawked derisively. "Did you know, strange friend, that once there were physicians who could give life and hold back death? Perhaps they still exist, men trained by their cities and societies and supplied with medicines from wherever in the world they wished? Few sicknesses or afflictions could stand before them. They were conquistadors, while we pick herbs in the hedge-bottoms. The prior runs our community for us, does it well. The masons who built this room built it well, the spiders make good cobwebs in the corners, but for all I know my patients would get better without my help. How do you think a spider would feel if he wasn't sure whether it was his web that was catching the flies?"

"Who knows?" said Orr. "But where have they gone, those conquistadors?"

"The abbot once told me that they may possibly have taken refuge in the heartlands of the Matrix, or maybe even beyond that, but really he suspects they were overwhelmed by the numbers of the sick. Yes, you needn't say it. He's an infuriating old man, I agree. But he's sharp enough. He always says that knowing how little he knows qualifies him to be abbot. Why don't you talk to St Huw the Enigmatic?"

"Why has he never said much to me?"

"He's a humble man," said Kay, "and probably he thinks he has nothing to say that you would want to hear."

They fell silent, standing in reflection. Orr fidgeted with his coat, contemplating the long trudge back to the forester's cabin. Darkness was collecting where the trees stood thickly. "Kay," he said, "you never really thought of resigning, did you?"

"No," replied the little monk. "No. Why do that when one can still hope for a draw?"

"Don't even say it as a joke then," said Orr, turning and smiling. Big in the doorway, he seemed to be holding back the snow and the dusk. Kay patted his arm, and they shook hands, the almoner's small fingers engulfed by Orr's thick gloves.

"When did a man with an ermine fur collar not manage a draw at least?" said Kay.

Orr struck out through the shadows. As he strode away from the abbey's shelter into the wind he turned and shouted, "Thanks for everything!"

There was no reply except, as Orr reached the first sheltering trees, faint and far behind him he heard a crow. He sniffed abruptly, then smiled. Crows were entitled to an opinion too, he thought, so long as they didn't always want the last word.

IV

The shrinking of the glaciers marked the beginning of the Holocene Age more than ten thousand years ago, and as the ice retreated great lakes of melt-water formed on the westward side of the chalk ridge. Shifting and confined, the water gnawed and chafed at the chalk, flowed down fault lines, dissolved the soft rock and gouged out a channel through which it rushed eastwards to the great new sea which was drowning the mammoths' grazing-grounds.

The millennia went by and men coming along the north–south causeway of the chalk ridge crossed the traffic of river-folk travelling east and west along the river. On the bluff above the river was the highest spot that the winds keened round in a thousand miles and more. The winds had blown over fens and oceans, over great alluvial plains and frozen muskeg. Indeed, modest though the height of the chalk-ridge was, a line drawn due east would have had to reach distant ranges even beyond the Matrix influence to find any spot as elevated.

The crossroads became a camp, the camp a settlement, the settlement a village. An empire crowned the ridge with a fort to guard its communications, though a yet more ancient palisaded mound had preceded the fort when the musk-oxen had roamed the valley. The barbarians sacked the fort and halfway down the ridge built their wattle huts clear of its stone shadow. As the years tamed them they fell prey to a warrior nation, who rebuilt the fort and crystallised their fierce new faith in a mighty cathedral. The small town grew and sprawled down from the ridge into the flat-lands, swelling to a city thousands strong. A sulphurous pall blackened the cathedral for three hundred years as the first age of machines came to the city. A million strong in teeming towers the city bellowed at perihelion.

Orr had lodged for a night at a hospice which the monks maintained on the opposite side of the river-valley from the great cathedral on its ridge. Kay had directed him there. The next day he walked into Ingastowe, the city, though few gave it its name, for where was there another city? Entering from the south-east Orr passed cavernous hulks of buildings gutted long since of metal. Even those in best repair had lost their roofs and where once had been windows were ragged holes in the masonry. Others had served as quarries for stone and their timbers had been burnt as fuel. Rubble, plaster and the mould of decayed plants lay where once there had been smooth floors. Here mosses throve, liverworts, periwinkles and thistles; often there were great clumps of dusty stinging-nettles, coarse fleshy-leaved docks and everywhere, always, unassuming grass, lifting the foundations.

Orr observed it all with detached interest. It was beyond his reach. Only the effects of the past half-year illuminated his thoughts. The account was paid where Adelie was concerned, but the matter of the eye was yet to be settled. So, single-mindedly, shark-like in purpose, he came up the long wide road towards the fort, which he saw above him on the ridge-top. Here and there as he began to climb he registered houses that were less dilapidated, some inhabited, and a slight traffic of people and animals was beginning to move. The higher he climbed the narrower grew the streets, twisting up the hillside, full of unexpected lane-ends and gates.

Eventually he emerged into a wide area of trodden earth and cobblestones that lay before the west door of a cathedral. From Hay village the cathedral was visible on the horizon but as he stood before it the building staggered him. Its mighty size and complexity dwarfed such other buildings as he knew and he was struck with wonder. Across the other side of the empty expanse stood a fort; its stone matched the stone of the cathedral. From the keep flew a blue and gold flag. A dribble of people came and went through a small door in one gate-tower though the big gates were closed. Orr turned his back on the cathedral, noting it as an enigma that he might one day ask Abbot Huw to unravel.

The wind knifed along the length of the cathedral walls, eddying and swirling at the west front, making those people facing it hunch their shoulders and lower their heads. Orr, conscious of the need to conceal the patched eye-socket which marked him so clearly, welcomed the excuse to pull his hood close to his cheeks and over his forehead. He had not shaved for several days and his face looked darker and more lined, as if he had retreated behind a barrier. On his eyeless left side he seemed totally unapproachable, his face like a house-front, its window shuttered.

He drifted slowly towards the high wooden gate to the fort. There were a few soldiers, some strolling away across the cobblestones and down the steep lanes of Ingastowe. Another group with packs and bedrolls seemed to be returning from some errand.

The gate-tower door pulled him smoothly towards it. He had no plan except to move in the direction that beckoned him. What would happen would happen after he met Zjelko again, but did not yet concern him. He had little or no conception of long-term consequences, though his mind chafed at this without his understanding it.

He peered through the stone tunnel that lay behind the postern and saw a green close-mown turf bailey surrounding a tall grey keep. The view covered only a few degrees but he thought that barracks, armouries and kitchens must lie somewhere to either side of his range of vision, probably tucked beneath the walls and inside the five towers which buttressed the fort into a rough pentagon. Orr moved back into the recess of a doorway and waited.

The hours went by and the pattern remained the same. Orr felt the cold seeping into him, but he remained in the vicinity of the gate, chiefly sheltered inside his doorway but occasionally walking for a few minutes at random, though he was reluctant to move out of sight of the gate. He was disappointed not to have seen the man he hungered to meet again, but he was absorbed in the routine around the entrance to the fort. There was plenty to interest him for although his mind was becoming more selective in its observations he retained much of the impressionability of his days as the miller's labourer. So while he studied the faces of the people, particularly the soldiers who came and went past him, and noted weapons and pondered activities, he also scrutinised the stray dogs that wandered across the wide yard, and the dandelions growing between the cobblestones. But no soldier looked like Zjelko, big and blunt-faced with an indolent arrogance.

Orr wondered about the Matrix, its peoples, its domain and what aspirations drove it where this land was concerned. George Littler had said the land was part of the Matrix but also the Outland of Westermain. He supposed the fort might guard a frontier, though he had no notion where this frontier might lie, or indeed whether it was the sea-coast itself, which he had heard was forty miles away. No one in the village had spoken of any power that might disturb the hold of the Matrix. Wondering about it passed the time.

Several times a bugle called from inside the walls, and at about midday there was a sudden, jaunty and raucous trumpet-call which drew attention to one of the side streets from which marched out into the wide space between cathedral and fort a flamboyant figure, dressed all in bright yellow and blowing on a tarnished old trumpet. Behind him emerged another, towering nine feet tall, followed by a man with coal-black skin who, as he walked, kept six glass balls aloft in a whirling shower. Several handcarts followed, carrying a clutter of bags and boxes on top of an assortment of crates. The axles screeched and the solid wooden wheels rattled on the cobbles. Alongside and behind the carts there ran a swarm of urchins, as eager as the seagulls that follow the ploughshare, and just as ready to sample whatever should be revealed.

Orr smiled a rare smile as the nine-foot man began a grotesque sword-fight with the man in yellow velvet, who was attempting to reach his tall adversary with great leaps into the air. Behind them their companions were pulling the carts together and laying planks across their tops to form a rough scaffolded dais. The giant was trapped and slain and lay briefly revealed as a man on long stilts, before disappearing with the others behind the carts. Already other players of the troupe had begun to weave their spells over the audience of village-folk in to visit the market, as well as children, tinkers, housewives and old people braving the cold, all of them transfixed by the tale of the three men who set out to kill the ogre Death itself.

Though Orr knew this tale, he was unwilling to look away from the spectacle before him. He forgot the makeshift dais, the threadbare finery and even the cold wind. The actors fetched it all vividly to life. As the plot unfolded, the irony of the fatal trap that lay in wait for the would-be slayers of Death gripped all that watched. So when the voice spoke to one side of Orr it caught him unawares.

"Good to see some players back again. What have you in store for us tonight?"

Orr started to spin round, for he recognised the voice, but before he could do much more found himself looking at heavy, yellow shoulders and a feathered hat. The actor was addressing a farmer's wife. "The climax of our tale is near, madame," he continued. "See how they drink the poisoned wine." Then looking back the man in yellow picked up the soldier's enquiry as deftly as his juggler might have brought a wayward ball back into orbit. "In store for tonight, sir, we have for you the high-fantastical tale of Petergint, of his great hopes and small deeds."

"Ah, trolls and the button-moulder," said Zjelko.

"Aye, the button-moulder. Are you never afraid that he isn't waiting to mould you into buttons?"

Zjelko chuckled. "The trick, friend, is to know him when you see him."

"It is, it is," said the player-chief.

The playlet was now at an end and shortly after, with a word of farewell to the soldier, the leader of the troupe scrambled on to the stage to advertise their play, which was to be performed, he announced, with the gracious permission of the garrison commander, in the donjon of the fort. There the ground floor would be roomy and warm enough for all those people who, he felt sure, would be unable to resist this dramatic banquet so carefully prepared for them, in which he would in person naturally portray the hero, a role which few actors nowadays cared to attempt lest audiences compare their well-meaning but ingenuous efforts with the now definitive performance which that evening they would be privileged ... but here he was cut off by a good-natured uproar during which he disappeared grinning into the fort's little gate.

During the rhetoric of the man in yellow Orr had held himself in check only with the utmost difficulty, and he had sidled through the crowd to a position from which he could see Zjelko without being seen. The laughter and the disappearance of the chief actor signalled the break-up of the gathering, so he had only a brief opportunity to watch Zjelko, who was now walking back into the fort. But it was enough. He was close now. Relieved that the soldier was still stationed at the fort, it was a relief too that he looked the same: bleak, imperturbable, self-centred. You would expect him to look no other way, reflected Orr. Yet, he thought, it will not be easy to reach him in the fort, and less easy to reach him uninterrupted, except, of course, that he must come out.

What would bring him out Orr could only guess at, but the best chance seemed to be that Zjelko would look for somewhere to relax. So he left his doorway and spent the afternoon looking into the taverns that lay behind poky doors in the twining streets below fort and cathedral. He was delicate in his questions, as wary of arousing suspicion as a fox that comes to the henhouse by three or four patient circles. Twice he sat and drank a mug of beer, and once he ate some bread and cheese, and always he kept his empty eye to the wall or in the dimness. Fortunately, the sky showed few blue patches, the little rooms were poorly lit, and the brief February daylight was drawing to its close.

Orr learned nothing. He had spoken of soldiers, musing on their ways, supposing aloud that they were good customers, but though there had been responses none had been helpful. He moved along, walking the narrow paved streets, staying close to the hilltop. He felt mildly irked by his failure, as he had done sometimes at the chessboard when he had set traps for Kay so subtle that the almoner had not even seen the bait. But he was pleased to be so near: even, he thought, looking across a vegetable garden that sloped up to the castle's wall, within calling distance.

An old man came through the garden gate into the lane, close to where Orr stood. He was polishing his fork with a stone, and as he strolled down the lane Orr fell into step with him. The old man looked cold, his eyes were watering, and impulsively Orr pulled out a leather bottle Littler had given him. The old man took it, drank and coughed. "A soldier's drink," he said, and Orr, hearing it, felt as he had when his involuntary push had opened the vestry door. So they walked the lane together until the old man halted at an inn door. Orr had missed it in that afternoon's hunt for information. He said simply, "Did you ever come across a soldier called Zjelko?" The old man knew of him, he said, and most evenings he drank in that very inn. Orr would have been surprised if he hadn't said as much. He looked up at the inn-sign. It said, in green letters on white, 'The Wait-a-bit Inn'. "Good night," he said.

Tsiganok watched him go, his mind pondering how best to use what now he knew. The one-eyed man had arrived, at last, and was asking for Zjelko, just as his son-in-law had predicted might happen. He shivered and took a last look down the lane but no one was there. The wind had dropped, and a mist was rising from the flooded river meadows.

V

Ceil had followed the camps for most of her life. As tiny Ceil, daughter of Tsiganok, she had played in the gravel of parade grounds from the polar cap to the hot deserts. A soft beauty made her look fully-grown at fifteen. Innocent in her new-found power she fluttered like a butterfly fresh from the pupa. In the village where Tsiganok that year was quartered there were few to notice her but the clumsy local boys; then Zjelko arrived with a reputation for valour and tall tales of distant lands on his lips, to sweep her away.

The years had gone by and the bloom had long gone from the marriage, as it had from Ceil's hopes and skin. Still only in her early thirties her face was hardening into that bright mask which women use who shrink from reconciliation with age or loneliness. Two daughters dead in the womb had embittered the mask. Zjelko's fierce sexuality had become a coarseness that repelled her, his toughness a carapace for nothing, and she knew it. He knew she knew, so there had been other women. Her life ahead she saw like a long road with tall poplars, those straight and shadeless trees, on either hand, and she walking alone between the trees, until one day she would fall and not be able to get up, and what would it all have been for?

Who knows what she thought when the talk of the one-eyed man came into her life, for she was not certain herself? Often in the previous autumn Zjelko and Tsiganok had sat long over empty glasses, and she, shut out of their muttered conversation and only slightly interested at first, had heard Orr's name as you might hear rumours of a distant storm. Ceil wondered what had happened, but Zjelko was silent on the matter. For once his attitude perplexed her. He was wary of the strange man's coming, though as the autumn and winter went by, seemed to regard his appearing as more and more unlikely. Yet he was uncertain of his ground, and always wished to know should there be any news.

January stretched into February and the cheerless, raw, dyke-brimming days followed one another, until a day came when her father, whom she treated with an impatient tolerance, entered the inn swelling with a bullfrog's self-importance. The three of them rented the topmost storey of the rambling old Wait-a-bit Inn where, below, Ceil helped to serve the customers when trade was brisk. In the low, panelled parlour people were eating and drinking who normally would have dispersed homewards. Today they were waiting for the players' evening performance in the fort. Ceil was not popular among the regular customers to whose half-hearted attempts at joviality she never responded. A few came from the garrison, the rest were townfolk, mainly red-faced middle-aged craftsmen or noisy apprentices. She had grown accustomed to them; they were as anonymous as the roadside poplar trees.

But today felt different, for in had come her father and there was no disguising the purpose in his stride. Though Tsiganok was now growing old planting lettuces and picking beans, more than once he had stood stark-faced to watch the wild people's war-front, sparkling with steel, roll towards him, his comrades and John Cortez, his favourite marshal. Now he could snuff action. His wrinkled walnut face smiled as he came towards Ceil.

"He's here," he whispered, and looked over his shoulder.

"Who?" said Ceil. She bit back the sharp responses for she liked her father thus. It was like finding an old picture of him between the leaves of a book.

"The man they call Orr," said Tsiganok. "We walked together down the lane from my garden. He gave me a drink."

"Where is he now?" said Ceil.

"He went away. He'll be back though. He asked if I knew Zjelko."

"Did you tell him who you are?" asked Ceil.

"No. I told him Zjelko sometimes drank here. He'll be back."

Ceil felt nervous as if the future was tugging at her sleeve, stirring itself. The restless players were in the town, and now came Orr, the Old One, as once she had overheard her father eerily call him.

"Did you see him clearly?" she asked.

"Of course I did," said the old man.

"What was he like?"

"Quite big," said Tsiganok, "light on his feet, only one eye, sort of . . ." He hesitated, seeing again the detached expression, but unable to name it. "Sort of different, he seemed to be."

Two travellers came to the hatch for food, and Ceil cut them thick slices of pork from the joint on the counter. She hacked off hunks of bread and gave them a plate of butter. Tsiganok looked at her quick, capable hands, and the long black hair, and for a moment felt again a gleam of the wild glamour fathers dream for their little girls. One day, he had told her long ago, we'll climb the stile and walk down the field and come to the old stone barn, and inside we'll find a white unicorn with a long silver horn and eyes like stars. "What then?" she had said, and he had told her, "We'll take him home and you can ride him down the road." She had smiled at the thought, her wide eyes blue as the shadows on the unicorn's white coat.

"What are you going to do about this man?"

"Me? Nothing," said Tsiganok. "He's too much for me to handle. Zjelko's on guard duty tonight. See if you can persuade the stranger to stay late. And perhaps if he drinks a few too many he may say more than he intends."

Ceil sniffed and turned away. She did not often work in the evenings, and she found her father's suggestion distasteful. "I'll be upstairs," she said. "Tell me if he comes. Though what it matters to me I can't imagine."

The old man went out into the night. He turned to the right where tall houses pressed close together. Twisting up alleyways and through a passage that ran beneath a terrace of dwellings before long he was in the open space between fort and cathedral. The thin sound of singing voices came from within where vespers was being celebrated but he turned his back on the music and walked to the fortress-gate. A sentinel appeared from an alcove where he had been keeping warm by a fire. The two knew each other and the guard readily sent a message that Zjelko was wanted at the gate. When Zjelko arrived Tsiganok saw to his surprise that his son-in-law was wearing the blue greatcoat that the Matrix troops wore on campaign. He still used his own for gardening.

"Well, old man," said Zjelko. "Be quick, we're moving out in an hour. Trouble near the estuary, though we're not sure what it is."

"How long will you be?"

"Hard to say. Three days perhaps. We're taking twenty men, though nearly all militia boys, and plenty of firearms, for what use they both are. Even so it shouldn't be longer. But what do you want?"

"The man Orr is here," replied Tsiganok. "He spoke to me in the lane near the Wait-a-bit. He asked about you."

"What did you tell him?"

"I told him you sometimes went there for a drink. Nothing else."

Tsiganok looked round the guard-room. Its worn stone floor, wooden benches pushed back against the walls, smoke-blackened beams and narrow barred windows had been part of his life. Zjelko scraped his hand back and forth across his chin, and the old man heard the stubble rasp. Finally the soldier shrugged his shoulders and said, "Let the poor sod be. If he's still here when we get back, well, we'll see what we'll see."

Feet clattered and mantles swirled in the passageway, and the room filled with men, tightening buckles and adjusting packs, their urgency ending the conversation. Tsiganok turned away. Outside it was still and misty, quite windless. Somehow he felt cheated of action. He walked slowly home and pushed open the door of the inn, wondering whether to go upstairs to his room, but then going into the long bar. Ceil's dark hair, half-way down her back, caught his eye, and as his glance lifted past her shoulder to see if she had company he felt the cold stare that was checking each newcomer who entered the room, and knew that it was Orr.

Ceil, too, had known who it was the moment he entered. She had been talking idly to the innkeeper's wife. Orr had come over to them. "Something warm to drink, please," he said.

"Hot wine all right, and honey? You sit down over there," said big Magda, and Ceil watched him sit quietly near the fire-place, behind the scarred table on which the old men played long games of dominoes.

When Magda reappeared with the drink Ceil intercepted her. "I'll take it for you," she said, and the older woman was glad to let her. Ceil placed the drink in front of Orr, the honey-and-cinnamon-fragrant steam tickling her nose. She hesitated by the table a long five seconds, not knowing why she stood there. Suddenly she murmured, "They are expecting to see you."

The face was unruffled, and now with the hood pushed back she saw the black shadow of the eye-patch, and the single grey eye observing her. "Sit down, if you like," he said quietly. The voice, like the face, had the neutrality of a stone, and Ceil felt herself piqued by his lack of reaction, and irked with herself that after so many bruises her vanity should still try to reassert itself. "Who is expecting to see me?" he asked, when she had seated herself.

"Zjelko."

"Ah, well," said Orr. "See with both his eyes, I expect. And use both his hands. Hard hands, though maybe only for children."

"I know," she said softly. Men were often afraid of her husband, but not this one. He had the look, she thought, knowing what she meant by this but having no better word for it.

"And how could you know?"

"I know because I was a child when I married him."

"So," said Orr, and looked carefully at her, "the past is your business, but the little girl – certainly he was not married to her."

"I don't know what you mean." Her voice was shaking; she was reluctant to hear of this girl-child. Orr sighed and unlaced his fingers from around the cup upon which he had been warming them. For the first time Ceil felt his attention on her, and she watched as he almost smiled.

"Well, why should you know what I mean?" Orr spoke gently

and she smiled at him shakily, and then saw his gaze lift to the opening door. Turning her head she saw Tsiganok standing squat in the doorway squinting at them. Ceil turned back to the table, but Orr lifted a hand towards him. The old man nodded back reluctantly before turning and disappearing into the night. "He soon went."

"Up to the fort to tell Zjelko, I expect," Ceil murmured.

"How do you know?"

"He's my father."

"You're Zjelko's wife. You can tell him. Why should the old man bother?"

"Because those two are friends," she replied, then thought, bewildered, 'Where does that leave me?'

Orr lifted his cup and drank; the fermented sweetness was smooth in his throat. "I should like to see the travelling actors perform their play," he said. "If you were differently connected I would have asked you to join me, I'm sure you would be good company."

Ceil's thoughts whirled but she could not help responding, unpractised though she was in the game. "I'm afraid not, though in different circumstances it would have been nice," she said.

"Chance meetings often are," said Orr. This light exchange surprised him, used as he was to men talking gravely. Like chess, the banter echoed something lost deep in his memory, but what it was he could not tell. They went to the door together and out into the night. Orr lifted his head. The clouds had gone and the stars were frosting the sky.

"Do your people have names for the star-families?"

"Yes," she replied.

"What is that one?" He pointed upwards.

"Orion. The hunter."

"And that?" asked Orr, indicating the next constellation.

"The one close to Orion? That's the Castles in the Air." She was grateful the dark prevented Orr looking at her. She wondered if there could be such a constellation somewhere. It seemed unlikely.

Ceil had been right about her father. Tsiganok had hurried back to the fort. He was nervous of the man's inexorable look. Because in some ways he was obtuse and believed that Ceil's marriage had not altogether been ill-made, and because he and his son-in-law were men of similar mould, and who thinks ill of himself, or perhaps just because his daughter's dreams had been always hidden from him, whichever it was, Tsiganok believed his daughter's welfare was threatened.

He was lucky. In the short term, that is. The captain on watch was Alrik Alriksen, who had questioned Zjelko on his return from the village, and the next day had led a patrol that had searched the area. At the time Orr lay in the abbey's sanatorium, but the soldiers had been distracted by false trails that some of the villagers had suggested. More than seventy people had put white beads in the voting box, and while not hostile to the soldiers they did not feel any compulsion to aid them.

Alriksen heard of Orr's appearance in the town with that pleased anticipation that an angler feels when a big fish darts from between stones among which he had not expected it to lurk and hangs quivering in the current. If outlaws refused to stay in the forest then they should expect no mercy. Together he and Tsiganok stood in the draughty guard-room.

"Thank you for your assistance," said Alriksen.

"It was only my duty," replied the old man, though conscious that involving others in family vendettas was less than satisfactory. He wished that Zjelko had told him more about the incident in the village.

"Show us where he is," ordered Alriksen, and the six soldiers who had been summoned from the keep came closer. "Identify him and then keep back. Not that I expect any real trouble. Right, off we go."

They missed Orr in the darkness. It was easily done for there was a tangle of alleys and lanes between the fort and the Wait-a-bit Inn and people were making their way up most of them, pressing along as the rising tide floods into the creeks of the saltings. Orr went into the fort with the crowd. He knew what he was there for, though unprepared with any plan other than his determination to come upon Zjelko unawares. So he crossed the green bailey, marking the walls where their darkness blocked out the stars, noting the long wooden quarters of the militia, the armoury and the forge. Tsiganok, according to Ceil, had come here to speak to Zjelko so he had to be somewhere in this stone pile. Orr merged himself into a family group that was entering the keep, climbed its half-dozen worn steps, followed them towards the sound of laughter and voices and music, and found himself in a huge room that covered almost all of the ground-floor.

At the far end was the same wooden stage the players had used earlier in the day, and upon it the black man was taking hen's eggs from his mouth and ears. Beneath his mesmeric stare an uneasiness was creeping into the audience's laughter and applause. There was nothing of the mountebank about him, more the relaxed dignity of an artist amusing himself tuning his instrument. Orr found it hard to look away, but he needed a niche to watch from and he chose a place at the very back close to the entrance; now anyone coming in would be looking away from him. The room was filling and Orr scanned the faces flushed in the flares of the cressets. Vitality pulsed, the men in the ruddy light looked bigger, the women brighter, the children bolder. The drum on the stage was throbbing like the beat of a heart.

It stopped suddenly and the old woman Osa was on stage listening to Peter's wild tale of the great buck that he found: "Hidden by a clump of alders, He was scraping in the snow-crust, After lichen."

The images came clear as bells on a frosty morning. As the player-chief moved the audience swayed with his gestures.

Tsiganok and the patrol reached the inn. Two men stood at each of the front, side and back doors while Tsiganok went inside. The old men were shuffling the dominoes in the chimney corner where Orr had been. Nor was he anywhere there, it was clear. 'Would our marshal have been here?' thought the old veteran. 'Would John Cortez have been waiting like a chicken in a coop?' The thought surprised him and he tried to wish it back into the void where thoughts wait to be made.

"What happened to the one-eyed man?" he said to fat Magda, who had apparently not stirred since he was last there.

"He must have gone out," said Magda. "Isn't he there?" She had seen soldiers' helmets go past the steamed windows at the end of the room, and she saw blue greatcoats. She felt no wish to be part of any ambush. "Is this some sort of trap?"

"He's a murderer. Of course it's a trap."

She sniffed noisily. "Well, he's not in it."

Tsiganok had already turned away. Soldiers looked at him stonily as he went out. "He's gone," he told them.

There were footsteps on wooden stairs and the rattle of a lifting latch. Ceil appeared at the foot of the narrow stairs. She was holding a candle; the draught fluttered its flame sideways.

"Where's the man with the eye-patch?" said Tsiganok.

"He's gone. He said he was going down into the lower part of the town, near the river. He has lodgings there."

"Talked to him a long time, did you?" a soldier asked.

"No," said Ceil. "I took him his drink, asked if he lived in these parts, and that was all." 'Or nearly,' she thought, 'but what is the rest to you, or to anyone but me?'

"Look," said Alriksen, who frightened her. "We're going to scout around a bit longer. If you do chance to see him again get a message up to the fort. All right?"

"Yes, we will," said Tsiganok. Ceil said nothing. In the sky mighty Orion was brightest of the star-families.

The story of Peter was weaving its spell. The vast magical world with its small human hopes and fears held the crowded room rapt. Orr was loath to move from where he sat, back pressed to the wall with a black-shawled, sharp-featured old lady on one side and a narrow aisle to the door on the other. But he had scrutinised the faces of the few soldiers in the room and it was now time to look elsewhere for his target, so he slid from his place and, unobtrusive as a cloud-shadow, drifted outside.

The passage to the inner bailey was empty, and soon he stood under the stars again. A silhouetted helmet above the battlements drew him across the grass to one of the towers. Once there, he mounted the spiral stone stairs like a cat, feeling his way by running his fingers up the cold groove cut as a handgrip in the wall. As he stepped lightly out of the tower and on to the limestone blocks of the sentry-walk he saw far beneath him the scattered lights of the town, a dusty glimmer of far-away candle and hearth-light behind narrow windows. To one side of him lay an unguarded drop of twenty feet or so to the gravel walk beneath the wall's inner perimeter. Orr edged nearer to the parapet's solidity.

Ahead of him Orr heard two sentries' voices distinctly in the cold stillness and knew at once that both were strangers to him. As they parted to continue their separate patrols one turned back towards him and he retreated into the dark shaft of the tower. It was almost his undoing, for from beneath him he heard a foot scrape on a step. With one soldier approaching the tower along the wall and someone mounting from below Orr sought urgently for some line of retreat. The only possibility lay behind him – an embrasure and within it a lancet window, unglassed. He squeezed through, hoping the outer sill would extend sideways. Although the stone sill was no more than the width of the opening, there projected out to left and right two gargoyles, long-necked stone grotesques that many thought were sculptures of the Twisted Folk. Reaching high and digging his fingers into crevices Orr placed his foot on a gargoyle's neck and stepped out to stand in a black airiness. Pressed tight to the wall his cheek felt its cool roughness. From far below his feet he caught the creaking whisper of tree-tops. A man stepped just past him, out onto the walkway and spoke to the nearer guard. Orr made out some sort of warning, and the sentry replying dourly, "I've seen naught but owls and heard naught but dogs."

Both soldiers began to move away towards the second watchman, to Orr's huge relief, for the trembling in his legs was increasing with the strain of his position. He had just placed his left foot back on to the sill when, with the gentlest of foot-falls, a deeper blackness emerged from the stair-well and slid past, the shock freezing Orr in the arch like a stone statue in its wall-niche. Dark as it was he recognised the player-chief. Orr's heart was pounding and his nerves felt unbearably taut. The actor had now gone far enough along the guard-walk for Orr to slip from his perch and move swiftly down the stairs. Whatever drama was to be played out up there above his head he left to others and went on, intrigued but undeflected.

In the militia quarters there were small groups of soldiers at whom Orr peered through the windows; but always their faces, build or gait revealed them not to be the man he sought. Briefly he contemplated leaving the fort and resuming his surveillance of the gateway in the morning's daylight, but then there was even less likelihood that he could come upon Zjelko alone. Feeling that his best chance was still while the play was disrupting the garrison's routine he went back before long into the keep. The actors were well into the play, and Orr saw the chief of the players, the man whom last he had seen soft-footed on the stairs, was now Peter seeking the hand of the troll-king's daughter amid the mob of the king's troll-subjects. The torch-flames fluttered and the trolls swirled so violently around Peter that it was hard to distinguish the actors behind the masks.

"Dash him to shards on the rock-walls, children!" said the troll-king, and the lesser trolls pursued Peter round the stage, hooting like owls, baying like wolves, whining and hissing like cats. Orr recognised their king as the black juggler, but the crouching, dancing figures behind chilling masks were nothing like the jesting band who had pushed the cart up the cathedral hill that morning. The mock hunt was at its most frenzied and the whole suffocating atmosphere was beginning to discharge in screams from some of the children in the audience, swelling the stage-rabble's cacophony. Amid the conventional goblin-masks were lizard skins too real to have been painted on, displaced eyes that stared alertly, parchment faces that sweated real sweat. A whisper had started nearest to the stage: "Twisted ones, the Twisted Folk." Orr caught the murmur as it rippled backwards; the air like tightened fabric, vibrating, waiting for the weakest thread to snap. Orr, rapt in what was happening, felt vaguely the pressure of eyes upon him. Turning towards the aisle beside him he looked full into the face of Alrik Alriksen.

Alriksen had never seen Orr before and was not certain he faced him now, but the man he had stumbled upon fitted the description Tsiganok had provided. Then Alriksen made the error, rather than calling for assistance, of grasping Orr's shoulder, intending to propel him outside. At the same time he beckoned to the nearest soldiers in the room. Events then began to accelerate, for Orr, who loathed being manhandled, shrugged his shoulder free and when Alriksen's hand went to the long dagger at his side he smashed his forearm into the officer's face and sprang clear into the aisle. Alriksen's yell of pain and the shouts of the approaching soldiers as they pushed people aside to reach the affray made heads turn among the audience, and as someone bellowed, "Watch the doors!" even the actors faltered and looked around.

There were only five or six soldiers scattered through the room, but they moved quickly, either to guard the doors or come to Alriksen's aid. Orr was intent on not being cornered, and fortunately for him the crush of people, the semi-darkness, the milling excitement and the fact that only Alriksen had seen him clearly, helped him and hindered the pursuit. He found himself reluctantly having to push his way away from the doors and towards the stage, where the crowd was thickest and concealment easier. Above the din he heard the player-chief shout: "There he goes! Stop him!" and saw him pointing to the far side of the room. The other actors cried their advice, and even the eeriest of the troll-children pointed and shrieked, "Look, look!" at nothing at all.

Glancing up Orr caught Petergint's eye and the actor unmistakably gestured for him to reach the stage. "Up here," he called urgently as Orr pushed nearer. With a run and a jump Orr sprang on to the stage. "Now down the trapdoor," the actor whispered, pushing him ahead as the two dropped into the claustrophobic shoulder-high space beneath the stage that served both as robing-room and to allow spectacular entries and exits. It was fusty and hot, lit by an oil-lamp and strewn with costumes and stage-properties. "Put this on, quickly," said the actor, shoving a fur coat and tall hat into Orr's hands. "Then get among the crowd and make for the doors. We'll divert them."

The diversion had already begun, for two of the quickest-witted actors had dashed down into the cluttered space, fashioned makeshift patches for each left eye and disappeared again. Their leader himself now emerged, both with his own eye-patch and with others which he began persuading baffled members of the audience to wear. Orr, glancing out quickly from the stage, saw a chaotic scene which he was certain would in moments become a very different one of anger and violence, when the soldiers realised the nature of the actors' buffoonery.

He mingled as inconspicuously as possible and edged towards the nearest exit, where three men, shoulder to shoulder, barred the way. Orr saw the dull gleam of gun-metal keeping back the packed and jostling press in front of the soldiers and tugged his hat-brim low over his forehead. Not far away an actor with an eye-patch had been hauled to where Alriksen was now on his feet; the officer took one look at the face and tore off the patch. He gestured behind him and his men pushed the actor into a corner where several of the troupe, their masquerade over, were penned.

After a brief respite Orr felt the trap closing again. Then he saw faces beginning to turn to the stage, drawn to a dance and gleam of flickering light. There on the front of the stage the juggler was spinning two shining silvery globes, one on each forefinger. Now faster, now slower, they spun, and cries of delight came from the children as the juggler made them jump above his head and change places. "Home," he said. The balls swayed and made smooth patterns. Orr felt he was falling down a funnel of fog. "Home," said the voice again, soft and deep, and the word spread through the room, stilling the noise. Now the fog was warmth and soft, deep darkness, as gentle as June dusk under the white chestnuts. "Careful with the little ones," said the juggler, and there was a sigh from the gathering. Alriksen stepped backwards to make a space for two small boys to get past him. The balls spun slowly, and wobbled. With the soldiers who had barred their passage leading them, the people flowed gently out into the night.

Militiaman Tonald was eighteen, though perhaps his age made no difference, and the arrival at the gates of the steadily moving audience from the play had been an impossible dilemma. "What was I supposed to do?" he went on. "I told them to halt but no one seemed to hear. I said I would fire but there were so many children at the front. I could have fired into the air but I don't think they would have heard. Anyway, some of our men were walking with them. It was hopeless. I'm sorry."

"Dismissed," said the commander, who had been eighteen once. He looked round the ring of his regular soldiers: two plodders, one cynic and two capable professionals. Two more, both good, out in the field with patrols. Not so bad for a backwater with Limber allocating us only nine men, eight now without Vanya, he reflected. Lucky it was Alriksen at the play, at least we salvaged something out of that debacle.

"Well, Alrik," he said. "Explanations?"

Alriksen had been considering the matter for hours, his feeling that he had, on the previous night, touched the hem of a strange cloak. "Well, sir," he began, feeling his way, "this Orr, as you know, has already killed one of us, and we have already searched for him in and around that village. There are suggestions that he – ," he hesitated, " – that he is an Unman."

"Round here if you come from the next village you're an Unman."

"No, well, it's just what I heard. Zjelko's father-in-law told me yesterday after he saw him in the town that he may be pursuing some grievance against Zjelko. He literally slipped from my hands yesterday, and he is clearly lucky or resourceful."

"We are not getting far," said the commander. "Correct me if I am wrong, but we have a recognised and outlawed murderer, no one denies that, as well as an assaulter of young girls – or so the Hay villagers decided – amusing himself at a play in this fort. First, why? Second, why, when he is almost captured, does a troupe of actors rally round him? Why, please?"

"Sir," put in another voice. "These actors are no ordinary troupe. Backwoods companies sing songs about marrows. They don't employ powerful mesmerists."

"A mesmerist perhaps capable of wide hypnosis. We must certainly not trifle with him. Is he a Twisted One?"

"Not possible to say," replied Alriksen. "He got away."

"How long were you in a trance?"

"I don't think I was. Rather I was thinking about what he said, about 'home' and 'being careful with the children'."

"Same thing. But you did stop some of these actors getting away?"

"Four, sir,"

"Out of ten or twelve. And this grievance against Zjelko? Does that require this man to come and see a play?"

"We need more information, sir," put in Alriksen. "Otherwise we can't make anything of this business."

"Where do we get this information?"

"We have prisoners."

"Who when questioned had nothing to say, I understood."

"Sir, they were not questioned very hard."

In the silence Alriksen, like a man who sees fault-lines appearing in the ice on which he stands, realised he had gone further from the shore than was wise. Eyes looked at him from around the table.

"I believe you wrote a much-admired paper," said the commander, and his voice creaked like the fracturing of ice. "It was about . . . refresh my mind, please."

"The psychology of officer-garrisons, sir."

"Ah, yes. But not the psychology of hard questioning?" Alriksen dropped his gaze. "Torture," went on the short, unsmiling man, "is for the magnates' women. I hope you never meet them. Nevertheless, we are dealing with the death of one of my command and the killer entertaining himself in our midst, and I like that no more than you do. Should these players turn out to have abetted the man Orr, as they certainly seem to have done, we shall be fair and we shall give one of them a quick death, perhaps one of the Twisted Ones. Meanwhile this is what you will do, so listen carefully . . ."

The night had been raw, even for the beavers in their lodges and the owls in their feather cloaks. Dampness was cold in rotting grass clumps and under last year's leaves. The three of them were in a man-made cavern. It burrowed beneath the plinths and foundations of what had been great buildings, but were now broken ground, barrows and hollows where the common land began at the edge of the town. Martin had found it for them in the night, telling them in his unexpectedly quiet and gentle voice that he had heard there were thousands of such subterranean caves wherever one of the great towns had once been. "I think they must have been kin to the burrowing moles," he said. "Or perhaps they were a weak people who would have liked to come out of the earth-shadows and walk abroad in the open meadows but the stronger races would not let them. If that was so I pity them."

With the wariness of fugitives they had gone deep into their tunnel before lighting the fire around which they sat huddled, dozing, heads on knees. Dawn had come imperceptibly, its faint chill light creeping into their refuge. "You haven't told me who you are," said Orr.

"Orlando and Martin, at your service," said the juggler, looking back at him across their small fire.

"Yes. You told me your names. But who are you all?"

Orlando shook his head. "To tell you what would interest you about us I should have to tell you about yourself and that is too long a story to be told now."

"And what sort of story is it?" asked Martin. "Demetrius never told me. We like stories. Good stories. We don't want to hear the story of the mushroom sower." He grimaced at them, his swarthy alert face crinkling.

"It might even go back to that," sighed Orlando. "Most things do."

"Then I couldn't bear to hear it. I don't know how you can bear to tell it, though you two are the sons of gods, while I'm only one of the bastards. Or maybe a son of the sower," concluded Martin sadly.

The two dishevelled, tired and hunted sons of gods looked awkwardly at one another. "Well, I hope," said Orlando, "that this story we're in now does not turn out to be such a sad tale as that one." Beyond the ragged entrance of the tunnel the outline of trees was emerging, charcoal on grey, and they heard the bellowing of bullocks on the move.

"I'd better go," said Orr. He wondered vaguely where his two companions might intend to go. They ought to move soon for a more conspicuous couple would be difficult to find. They would not merely be noticed but gaped at in astonishment. One ebony-skinned, tall, powerful, stately, and to call the other human might be misleading, it seemed to Orr. With his neck and wide shoulders cramped not much above his navel there looked to be no space for the torso to hold heart and lungs. Though his legs were slim and straight he stood less than five feet tall and his arms reached close to the ground. Their flight from the fort had left the pair dressed in theatrical costumes thought appropriate for a troll-king and his subject. From across the dying embers the two were looking at their fellow-fugitive, one like a figure from myth, the other from a fever-dream. Orr had recognised Martin at once from their brief meeting beside the unconscious girl Adelie. A girl whom he had been trusted to watch over, he reminded himself constantly.

"No, no, let them chase after us," Orlando mused. "We avoid them by staying still."

"Gnomic," said Martin. "And I ought to know." He laughed, and Orlando, who already knew it, and Orr, who hadn't been sure, felt his humanity.

"This gnome and I have to find our friends. Some I know escaped from the fort, though I fear not all. So we should stay in hiding close to them, even if the town is like a trodden anthill for days to come. You are becoming notorious, Orr, also easily recognisable in that smart fur coat."

"Unlike us," said Martin

"Perhaps none of us will blend into easy anonymity with the people of these environs . . ."

"Spare us, Orlando," said Martin. "Pity us simple folk."

"Beware, Orr, of devious people, for they alone profess to be simple folk." Orlando smiled.

"If I weren't simple I would be home in bed," muttered the small man, though the others caught the suspicion of a smile on his face.

"We need food and water, and we need a plan of action," went on Orlando. "Above all we must plan to find Demetrius."

"The leader of your troupe?"

"Yes. It is he who, properly, should answer your questions since it is he who has tried so hard to meet you. You may learn from him whom we all are and why we hoped to find you in this province. Or at least someone like you." Orr fell silent. The last half-year had allowed him to accumulate many experiences but one made all the others hazy: whenever he wished to glance to his left he was made aware of the amputation of his vision. In the monastery and in the forest his revenge had been fermenting, and he meant, if he could, to exact it. Yet when Orlando had spoken he felt, for the first time, that another future was opening before him, one leading away from his intended direction. He said slowly: "I have my own plans which are unconnected with Demetrius. Perhaps our paths may cross again, but further on in the wood, I think."

"Some of our troupe may now be dead," said Martin. "There were others of my folk among us, and such vermin as we are do not live over-long. If they are dead they died to let you get away. Think of them sometimes. They will be company on this path of yours."

"I have thought of them," Orr replied curtly, stung by the remark. "Yet Orlando says it is too long a story to tell. I'm grateful, of course, but it seems to me I did not ask your aid. Was it not freely given? Am I your debtor?"

"Certainly not, Orr," said Orlando. "You may be right in what you say. But today, as you walk, the sun will warm you and the grass will be soft under your feet. Listen to the birdsong and watch the hazel putting out its catkins. They do not hold you their debtor, but are you quite sure you are not indebted to them?"

"Of course he's sure," said Martin. "In a minute he's going to say he didn't ask to be born."

"That's not fair, Martin," Orlando responded. "Look, Orr, if you'd like to stay, we'd like you to spend some time with us. Give us a chance. And yourself."

"Myself?" Orr frowned. "A man is his memories, they are his real shape and self. I've just got two years' memories, so I don't know much, though I do know why I'm called Orr. Would you like to hear?" Martin nodded. "Everyone in Hay village, most of them anyway, thinks I'm dull-witted or slow. When I first got there they asked me my name and I said I wasn't sure, but it was something like Wood or Ford. That was the best I could do, but they started calling me Orr. It wouldn't be such a bad name in itself, except to them it was 'Aww' or 'Err', just another way of saying 'stupid'. Would you like your name to be 'Stupid'? Of course, the monks don't say Orr that way, or

Adelie, or her mother, Nell, or Hobson or George Littler but there are plenty who do. Convenient too. Easy to blame the local simpleton when a nice girl gets attacked. Easy to hold him down and gouge out his eye. A lot easier than blaming the Matrix soldiers when you have to serve alongside them in the militia. But someone's going to pay, don't worry. That's how it is, Martin, and I hope you like my story."

Outside the tunnel mouth a tawny sun had risen and tattered rags of clouds were silhouetted against the oranges and resigned reds of the eastern sky. "Goodbye, then, Orr, or Wood. But if your steps bring you back this way remember this spot. If we are not here ourselves we will leave a message under this flat stone." The juggler slid his fingers under the stone's edge and lifted one side. Woodlice rolled themselves into brittle balls and a polished black beetle ran away from the light.

"Goodbye," said Orr. "And I am truly grateful for your help."

He moved quickly, climbing to the brow of the high hill on the far side of the common lands and there retrieving his pack and sleeping-bag from the hospice. Then there was no urgency for him to move far until night came so he wandered into the woods that lay on the slopes and crest of the hill. They were leafless overhead, being all deciduous trees, chiefly beech and birch. Winds noisily tossed and bent their topmost branches that formed high vaulted arches above him. He walked through the aisles of trees, enjoying the sheltered feeling they provided; down at his level the dead leaves barely fluttered as the cool airs wandered between the slim trunks.

He met a forester cutting mistletoe, chopping away the parasite where its light-coloured wood had sent clamp-like jaws gnawing into the darker branches of its host-tree. The patches of mistletoe looked like swarms of bees hanging clustered from the branches. The plant had long narrow fleshy leaves and was full of green berries. "They seem to do no harm for years but the tree won't thrive once one has got a grip," said the man, glad of someone's company.

They walked and talked together through the afternoon. The forester knew George Littler. He was more genial than Littler, or perhaps just lonely and pleased to have a visitor. He spoke fondly of the foresters' gild, and, vehemently and at length, of those earlier, now distant, years when the great woodlands had almost disappeared. He told of the whole company and hierarchy of trees: the sovereignty of oaks, the fickleness of elms, the age of yews, the perfume of pines and the magic of rowan-trees. "But you see," he concluded sadly, "the old people cut down their trees. They wanted the land to grow food. Cut them down and where will your children get timber and warmth? And trees give us air, the air we breathe. Did you know that? How long can you live without food? Maybe two or three months. Without drink? A few days. Without air? A minute. They're wonderful trees are, wonderful." He patted a silver birch, feeling its roughness where the once pale and papery bark had split as the gnarled trunk had grown out of it. Higher up its trunk was smoothly white; though spring was coming only last year's leaves sprinkled the tree with yellows and buffs and faded greens. On the ends of the young chocolate-coloured twigs were slim purple and green buds.

The gesture made Orr think of George Littler and how at night in the cabin George had sometimes tried to speak of his passion: the mysterious bounty of trees, of how, like a rich hinterland, they stretch away from the settled areas, of how they offer everyone a partnership of breath-taking generosity, of how their hidden depths feed and nurture that desire to live close to strange and ancient lives. Some of this he had told Orr, though perhaps it was not altogether for telling; words can only be constricting when your deepest consolations are cramped into them.

As blackbirds were pouring out the evensong they save for spring daylight's last cool hour Orr departed, slipping alongside hedgerows and by apple-orchards. In the dusk he came up the long forlorn street of decayed buildings he had first walked along only the previous morning. The first placard he barely noticed, the second he did not bother to read, but a third soon after made him curious, and he stopped to read it. In a red border, large black letters said 'Outlawed', and beneath was a list of five names. With that odd, small shock you feel on seeing your name somewhere unexpectedly inscribed he recognised his own name. Another name, 'Demetrius', was also familiar.

Orr had only seen one such notice in his time in the village but knew what it meant. Outlaws, and he was one, forfeited the protection of the law; usually they departed into the forests, sometimes to be tracked down there by those who refused to forego the blood-feud, the vindicators. He wondered if Demetrius might even have been executed that day, since he had probably been captured at the fort, though his crime, so-called, was rather complicity than anything. The placard hung there, as the commander had intended, eye-catching in its black and red colouring. Orr went on. Like the salmon which goes upstream confident of its passage even as it launches itself in coiled leaps at the impassable new dam wall that has transformed the old valley, he began to climb. From where he stood the ridge-side rose to where the cathedral loomed over all, and as he climbed the hill steepened, so that his strides shortened and he leaned into the slope. Yet he pressed upwards. The wish was the action. What else was there to do? Night was settling like silt in the narrow lanes as he threaded his way numbly onwards, not bothering to take cover when anyone passed. Some familiar line of the eaves and twist of the small street he was in drew his attention and he realised that the Wait-a-bit Inn lay a few doors further on. Its door must have been opened and shut for he could hear the sound of singing cut off almost as it began.

Zjelko may be with his wife, thought Orr. I will go to their room and settle this once and for all. Almost at ease he went on towards the inn. Ceil knew who it was even as the handle on the inside of the door turned downwards. The fluid shape of the future must be responding to the pressure and intensity of my wishes, she thought, just as the priests said happened when you prayed. She was sitting in a chair by the window when the door opened; she guessed his errand from the silent way he stood no further in than the doorway.

"Are you alone?" he said. She nodded. "Your husband?"

"He went out on a mission early last night. He has not yet returned."

"So," he said, "he was not in the fort last night after all. When do you expect him?"

"I don't know." She was made nervous by his directness.

"Where was he going?"

"If I tell you," said Ceil, "will you say why you seek him so urgently?"

"Why not? It is no secret."

"He went north-east. Up towards the estuary."

"I see." He looked carefully at her, wondering if this direction was too quickly given to be true.

"And why do you seek him?" she asked. She saw him growing tense again, drenched in purpose.

"For myself, I seek an eye for an eye. For my friend, to ask him if there is any reason why he should not be treated as he treated her. In court he bore false witness against me, and you can see the result. The crime I suffered for, he committed."

"And what about this friend he has ill-treated?"

"She is young, a girl. They said her mind was deranged and her back and legs paralysed by what I did to her, but he did it, him and his friend."

Ceil leaned back and closed her eyes. The muffled sounds of the inn came more clearly up through the floorboards.

"Whoever we are," she said flatly, "our fate is defeat. All of us. Many a time I have told him that somewhere someone will find him and will treat him as he has treated others. He is an arrogant man, a bully who holds other lives cheap and his own dear. I do not ask you to forgive him, because I have too much I do not forgive him for myself. In any case if it were not you collecting the blood-debt it might be someone else to whom he owes less. Just a girl, was she? I might have guessed. I will show you the road. It is not easy to find in the dark." This time, as they stepped outside together, the stars were blanketed by cloud. She began to lead the way downhill but Orr stopped her.

"That way is south."

"It will take us a round-about way," she answered, "but it avoids the fort. You should not go near it."

"There is something I wish to see there," said Orr, "or rather not to see. I do not need to go close."

"Have you seen the outlawry notices?"

"Yes," he said. Not much later, like hares from a hedgerow, they were peering out from a lane across the empty, cobbled space where first he had seen the wandering players. Above the battlements rose a small observation tower, and from its side a beam suspended a form that twisted and swayed in the wind. A sack had been drawn over the head. Too small for Demetrius, Orr thought.

A man and a woman walking together is an ordinary enough sight and no one spoke to the couple as they made their way round to the north-east quarter. The woods here pressed much closer to the town for there were no grazing lands on this side. A misty rain was beginning to fall and occasionally larger drops slipped from the branches overhead and fell on them. Looking along the paved road to where it disappeared in the darkness and murk, both caught the faintest of far-away sounds ahead of them, a distant murmur coming across the miles through the windless night.

Ceil came close to Orr, so close that he felt her tremble. Along the road a dark shape was coming towards them. It lurched and staggered as if a huge bat had been maimed and dragged itself fluttering along the ground. Behind his shoulder Ceil whispered, "It's an Unman," but knowing only the name Orr gave no heed to her fear. Sobbing breaths were clearly audible, though now the figure was lower to the ground and moving slowly. Swathed in a dark cloak and crawling on hands and knees was a man. He must have seen Orr's boots for he looked up, the whites of his eyes clear in the drabbled face.

"How far is it . . .?" he whispered, and then began a long bubbling cough. Orr took hold of him beneath the armpits and lifted him backward into a sitting position, feeling his coughing jerking the body forward as he did so. As he put one arm across the man's back to steady him he felt with a shock two arrow shafts embedded there.

"Let me lift you on to the grass," said Orr, but the man shook his head with a feeble vehemence, and pointed back up the road.

"Tell the fort," he gasped. "Trapped . . . help us . . . back there." He made as if to crawl on, but was so weak that without Orr's support he would have fallen face down. The rain was matting his hair and streaking the mud on his forehead.

"What can we do?" Ceil's voice caught Orr by surprise.

"For him? Fetch help and quick." They heard again the faint noises from where they guessed the wounded man had come.

"What about his message?" asked Ceil.

"For help from the fort? I've no time for delivering messages."

"He's just a young militiaman, some boy from round here. You can tell. I shall get help for him."

"Very well," said Orr. "Let us put him here under these trees." He gestured up the road. "I'm sorry to leave you but I must go on. My friend cries all the time, and I miss my eye. I don't think it was right for anyone to to take away my eye."

"I understand," she said.

VI

The farmhouse lay alongside the road, four miles north of Ingastowe. The Matrix soldier and the remnants of his militiamen had come a long way that day to reach it, twenty miles of marching, turning, fighting and marching again through hour after hour that had strained their discipline and resources of will to the limit. They had raised a hornets' nest on the estuary, a wild place at the best of times; there muddy creeks sluiced into the drab olive-grey water of the miles-wide river that chewed at its banks with fretful waves that broke in muddy foam. The first patrol had taken the girl clumsily and been trapped before getting far. Zjelko's relieving force had extricated them, but the river-people, refusing to be daunted, had harried the Matrix troops back down the road towards the fort. More and more men joined the pursuers, swarming out of villages and woodlands along the road. This girl's father was no unknown ploughman or woodcutter but a deeply respected patriarch, a sea captain with a strong following. Now both old and sick he had entrusted the command of the pursuit to his second son who, pressing furiously in chase, had finally cornered the remaining twelve in the barns of the farmhouse. There would have been thirteen had the young Janitza not been dispatched in the hope of bringing back help from the fort, now tantalisingly near.

"Here they come!" shouted Zjelko. Through the darkness and across the yard in front of the barn came the rush, like a black wave beating on a stone jetty. Zjelko wondered desperately what new ploy the river-folk would come up with this time. His fellow officer had gone down at midday in one of the savage little melees which they seemed to have been fighting all day long. Since then he had held his men together single-handedly, feeling for his enemy's tactics, out-guessing them when he could, stoically taking losses when he guessed wrongly, and always fighting in the pitiless, wily way that was his nature. The short axes smashed into the doors of the barn and its timbers splintered and cracked in a dozen places. Zjelko had with-drawn his men from the windows and blocked them up with wood; although they would have allowed his men to fire into the attackers he had too few to dare to expose them.

They had stacked heavy sacks full of grain waist-high on one another ten feet in from the door. The axes crashed, filling the barn with noise, and from outside came a roaring of formless shouts and yells. Zjelko waited. The assault on the door could be a feint; if so where was the killing thrust aimed? Or had the yellow-haired man with the boy's face who seemed to lead every attack been too subtle for him? Perhaps the door was to be the main breach after all. Still he waited where he was, in the loft of the barn with five of his men, the smell of dust and mouldering hay, of hemp and leather, pungent in his nostrils. Below his other six crouched behind the breastwork of sacks. If all of us were down there and we had the ammunition for a volley we could really hurt them, he thought, and caught the faces turning to him anticipating the order to leave the loft. Agonisingly he hesitated until over by the gable-end there came the rattle of falling lime and tiles and a bird's nest fell like a dry sponge at his feet. As if at a signal the shouts below increased and above them tiles were prised and torn from the roof, the slats were kicked in, and one form, then another, dropped through the opening into the loft, one's legs swinging through as the first fell. Zjelko fired as the first attacker landed on hands and knees, the shot jolting him against the wall, leaving the second man to his sword or bayonet-men. Reloading would have taken too long so, springing onto a barrel-top, he hoisted himself through the hole and on to the roof-ridge, deflected an axe-cut with his rifle-barrel, and kicked at a ladder. It moved easily, scraping and sliding away across the wet tiles and from below him he heard shouting and a crash as it fell. He was gladdened by the cordite smell, the din, the forge sound of the axes; here he was insulated from that daily life in which the teasing dependencies of gentleness and affection hung twisted on his bull's shoulders, irking him.

Before the arrows could search him out he ducked back into the loft. His defence was holding; he had lost one man in the scuffle below, but the attackers had lost more and another two in the loft. There was neither noise nor movement outside now so he took the opportunity to look at his prisoner. They had tied her wrist to a harness-ring on the wall and told her to lie down on the straw. He lit a stump of candle that showed her face wild and stained. Her eyes rolled as he came nearer to her. Images of another girl and a man with an empty face pursuing him along a high bank disturbed him. The whole pointless business of kidnapping children mystified him. Nothing happened for years and then orders to send two more off to Limber. One day, he thought, it will get me killed. He reached out to pat her shoulder but she flinched away, awakening in him a different set of painful memories.

Almost gratefully his mind returned to the youth with yellow hair, and the nature of his next attack. The feint, another feint, then the point? Or was one of the feints not a bluff? Guess right and you get another guess, he thought ruefully. Yet it must be nearly nine o'clock. If Janitza made it back he will be getting a hot drink from the kitchens, while the commander puts another relieving force together. Better make it a good one, there must be over a hundred of them out there by now and it's only our having the girl that's holding them back from burning this barn down with us inside it. This abduction business is madness. Nothing could be better designed to make trouble for us, Zjelko thought.

An hour went by. The rain eased and the moon crept from one bank of cloud into another. In the farm house, in the out-buildings, among the trees around the farm, the river-folk and their allies moved quietly to and fro. Zjelko told his men to loophole the walls, and he stared through the slits they made, peering in every direction. Once a flight of arrows came through the shattered doors, plunking suddenly into the wheat-sacks or rapping into the far wall, but no one was hurt. The smell of smoke briefly worried the besieged men but they saw that it came from many small fires that the besiegers had lit for cooking or simply to keep warm around. The fires encircled them, the small glows patching the night. Zjelko's men rummaged through their packs and shook their water-bottles.

Towards midnight came more firing, this time both arrows and gunfire. Zjelko, who knew that few guns save Matrix weapons had been seen in this province for several lifetimes, guessed that the firearms had been taken from his dead comrades. Again the attack was ineffective. Still, there was movement all around the farm though not close enough to the barn to be threatening or even to offer targets. Zjelko counted the ammunition – twenty-five rounds between eleven men. He wondered if a few random shots towards the fires might induce their foes to think they had plenty to spare, but he decided against it. Whoever decreed our fighting should be chiefly hand to hand ought to be here now, he thought. Some of his men dozed but others maintained a close watch, the inactivity sharpening their instincts for the ruse they felt sure the river-folk were hatching.

In the depths of the night an object was thrown into the barn. It clinked across the floor and lay shining innocently in a shaft of moonlight. Opening the locket they saw Janitza's face, and knew there would be no relieving force.

The long dark hours went by torturously slowly for men woken and woken again to stand watches. Occasionally they would hear voices, once wild laughter that set them looking uneasily at one another, and now and again came the desultory arrows.

Cockerels' long brazen calls brought Zjelko to his senses with a start and he looked up to have a mug of warm milk put into his hands by a grinning militiaman Yalkin. Over in a corner another of his men was still milking a cow, the white jet spurting into a helmet. Two more helmets lay at his feet in the straw, brimming with milk that steamed in the cold air, its fragrance as soothing as its sweetness in the mouth, its warmth in the belly.

"Some cows came through the yard," said Yalkin. "So I just persuaded one in." He laughed. Zjelko stretched and went to a loophole, smiling; it was good to still be alive, with the sun coming up and fresh milk to drink. The farm lay very still in the clear light. He felt sure there had been bodies outside the barn, but they were gone, though he saw the broken ladder he had pushed off the roof. Not far away cows were lowing insistently, their udders full, and he heard birds singing and ducks calling from a brown pond, but none of the noises his ears strained to detect. No one was there.

Zjelko waited with cold restraint. He hid all his men for an hour, forbidding the slightest conversation or movement, trying to reverse their enemies' ruse of enticing them into the open. But no one came to investigate the barn except an old tortoiseshell cat. Finally they moved out. Zjelko led the way, sticking to open fields wherever possible. He wanted to be quite sure his hostage could be seen with the rifleman walking close behind her. On the skyline the cathedral appeared and the march quickened towards it, a spring in the steps and a lift in the voices. Zjelko chose a little-used track in from the town's northern outskirts, suspicious until he could actually stand in his own barrack-room, but they met only small children and dogs. The girl was flagging and her face was ashen. He kept up the pace, wary of narrow streets, but soon emerging close to the cathedral. As they walked across the wide cobbled space that separated it from the fort he followed his men's upward glances to the dangling figure above the battlements. Speculating morbidly as to its identity they walked thankfully up the gate-tunnel past the two men in greatcoats warming themselves at the guard-room fire.

"Hey, we're back," said Zjelko, as he brought up the rear with the girl. The guards turned quickly, one stepping between him and the girl. He was young with long flaxen hair.

"Jackyboy!" the girl cried.

Zjelko hardly heard, and was still staring hard when he was shoved into the guard-room where there was another man, this time lying on a bench, looking too tired ever to stand up again.

"You!" he said.

"That's right," said Orr.

VII

Jackyboy never stayed idle long enough to wonder what drove him. He swam like a fish and fished like an otter, playing in the sluices and along the gravel-banks of the mighty estuary. He knew the far, oozing depths out in the middle of the river, where often when the fog came down he listened for church-bells or cows to guide him to the shore. He sailed in coracles, canoes and skiffs, bobbing like a cork in the tide-rips where the currents gnawed at the mud-flats of Skua Point, the hooked spit which for miles separated the silt-grey river from the salt-grey sea. Quick of hand and sharp of eye he chafed at anything that would not bend to his will, tackling it with a tenacity and grace which won the adulation of the young and the admiration of the elderly. His father had regularly taken his squabbling brood out with the fisher-fleets, and Jacky at ten years old had balanced on the pitching deck of a fishing-smack and gutted the great tarnished-silver codfish until his fingers bled, hauled in the trawls until his hands were cut to the bone, and stared at the big bergs dipping past until his eyes stung.

The Matrix strictly regulated the size of ships, which rankled with Jackyboy's father as it had with his father before him. The cockleshell boats found long sea-voyages hazardous, but as the sweet-fleshed fish spawned and swarmed in the ice latitudes, the mariners either netted the less productive coastal waters in comparative safety or took the widow's way up to the fish-rich northern seas. A big green roller like a hundred-ton cat's-paw plucked Jacky's brother off the stern-rail one wet night, and the bereaved family's loss festered into sullen resentment at the Matrix's regime and regulations. It seemed that the Matrix pressed down on maritime folk, on footloose or ambitious people and on traders, harder than on simple tillers and sowers and herdsmen, and the slow bitterness of the Dorn family smouldered on, as heat can lie unsuspected in a haystack.

Then that morning Astolat, Jacky's young sister, a girl as quick and precocious as April lightning, was snatched from the family orchard by a Matrix militia patrol. The mariners and river-dwellers had pressed after Jacky as unhesitatingly as they would have followed his boat in through the fog-banks. They pinned the patrol in a wood and when Zjelko's relieving force extracted them Jacky led his band of friends and allies in one stinging attack after another in the long pursuit southwards towards the fort. The firearms kept driving them back but they followed his yellow hair like a talisman.

In the farmhouse kitchen he was walking restlessly round the room, nagging at the problem: to overwhelm the trapped Zjelko in a way that left his sister unhurt. His mood and movements grew more frenzied together, as he kicked at chairs, licked his lips, picked at his knife-hilt, clicked his fingers. All day long they had been feinting, avoiding the head-on charge into gun-fire, but this patience for subtleties was now as thin as cat-ice. The fish-captains, farmers and forest-folk looked in his face, saw authority, and waited for him to outline a plan. Walking into the kitchen, into their conference, came a man with one eye.

"Who's the captain here?" he said. The glances answered his question without a response.

"Who wants him?" said Jacky Dorn.

"Are all the soldiers dead yet?"

"Not yet," said the youth. "And who are you?" For it seemed odd to him that he should be standing answering questions.

"Orr. At least that's what men call me."

"Well, since you seem not sure who you are, try to say what you want," said Jacky tartly. "Can you manage that?"

"I am here to collect my blood-debt," said the newcomer quietly. "Unless you have collected it for me."

"From one of the bluecoats? Then we all run along the same track," said Jacky, pushing back his hair from a face like a blade. "My friends and I are collecting for our brothers and neighbours. You may find them littering the road from here back to the estuary, but these other Matrix people have my sister in there," and he pointed through the window to the shadowy bulk of barns and outhouses, "and if she is hurt I mean to swim home in blood."

"How old is she?"

"Eleven."

"Mine was thirteen," said Orr, and now the others' stares were intent on him.

"Why does the Matrix do this?" asked someone.

"We shall ask the dead," someone else answered.

Standing unseen beneath a walnut-tree's wide canopy Orr watched across the farmyard. He saw the besiegers surge against the door of the barn, hewing at it with axes while others at the rear swarmed silently up a long farm ladder and prised tiles from the brown barn-roof. "Hard for us," said a man alongside Orr, "hard to catch them unawares." Even with the words a shot cracked out from the loft; there was the smithy sound of steel on steel, and shots from inside the door staggered two of the axe-men. Orr saw two men grappling at the top of the ladder before the defender kicked it away. He knew him at once and nodded to himself. Zjelko's debts weren't proving easy to collect. But now it would be different. He went back into the farmhouse.

Jacky was not long in coming back, with three of his comrades. He was shaken and bruised for he had fallen twenty feet from the rickety ladder when Zjelko had dislodged it. Blood was coming out from under his finger-nails where they had clawed at the old tiles as he slid down the roof, and his voice was choked with fury. "Next time, we'll get them," he grated. "Next time!" In his pale face his eyes rolled blue and white.

Orr felt the suggestion of an idea struggling to the surface of his mind. 'Move by standing still.' He remembered the words though not the speaker. "Don't try to get in the barn," he said, and saw the uncomprehending faces lift towards him. "Let them come out." He knew they were listening impatiently, giving him a few seconds to show himself more than a night-time nobody, claiming to have the same grievance as theirs. Then the idea swam up, and he saw its outline as you see a fish's in a net by the water swirling round it.

"Where would they go if they could leave the barn?" he said.

"The fort," one of the men said curtly. "Where else?"

"Then tempt them out."

"They may choose to wait here for reinforcements," said another.

"If anyone knows they're here," said Orr.

"A messenger got out. Got past us," snapped Jacky. "So we haven't much time to waste on conversations."

"The messenger never got back." And now Orr saw the fish's silver back. "Not with two arrows in him. I passed him on the road. In the morning if no one is here they will come out. Carefully, but they'll come. Then we – "

"We?" said Thorsten, the sluice-keeper's son. "Did we invite you?"

"Who asks leave who comes for the blood-debt?"

"Astolat – " and Jacky's voice made the syllables sound like a broken window banging in an empty room " – my sister, expects me. So what's this plan? Just be quick." His face was white and feral.

"We should be waiting for them," went on Orr, "in the only place," and he could see the fish flapping on the sand, "they so little expect to see us that their swords will be sheathed and their guns on their shoulders, and that place is – "

"Inside the fort," said Jacky. "Where else?" He started to laugh. It was so merry a laugh that his companions, gaping at the dripping shape of their future, began to laugh with him, and even Orr was drawn to smile. He recalled a village song that only came out when the fire was dying and the glasses were empty: 'The road that goes over the wide world's end, Is lonely walking without a friend.' There would be worse friends to walk with on that highway, he thought, than this wild, quick youth.

They needed little time to develop the plan. Jackyboy's Uncle Isak would stay at the farm with twenty men, to see that the besieged defenders remained in their refuge through the night. Just before dawn Isak and his men were to slip away to the north leaving an avenue of escape temptingly available. Most of the remaining rivermen would drift silently towards Ingastowe to rendezvous in the woods close to where the road entered the town's north-east corner. A few others would backtrack up the road to where the earlier skirmishes had taken place and spend the depths of the night hunting out the Matrix casualties and stripping off the blue uniforms, which they would then carry southwards to the meeting-place.

Orr went with the main party. His months in the forest had taught him much: where no one would have thought to turn aside he saw a broken hawthorn that lay with its roots in a pool of water and stepped off the road into the trees. The Matrix messenger was propped against a tree-stump staring past Jacky and his followers, several of whom crossed themselves rapidly. "Take his locket," said Orr, "and let someone go back and throw it into the barn. Then they'll know they have to take a chance."

Jacky lifted the chain over the cold face and passed it back. "We'll need the uniform too," he said. Orr nodded. Fatigue was slowing his thoughts and he felt chilled and heavy. "Let's wait here," Jacky suggested. "We need sleep." The order was passed back, the men pushing in among the dripping trees and on sodden leaves and bracken searching for a little softness. A few spoke in whispers but most were silent. Like hunting-dogs they turned over once or twice, sniffed, coughed, and fell asleep inside their cloaks.

The searchers had brought three uniforms to the rendezvous; the messenger's was already there. An hour later four men were clattering and clumping noisily up the alley that doubled along the north side of the cathedral, twisting through a maze of lily-ponds, sun-dials and mossed buttresses, masonry some of which hadn't seen the sun for well over a thousand years. It was a grey half-light and there was smoke in the air from cooking-fires. From far below in the valley cockerels called, and small birds were beginning to cry thinly. Dampness filmed their faces and beaded their helmets. Their eyelashes blinked cold dew onto their cheeks.

They marched out into the wide space between cathedral and fort and across the grey-wet cobblestones. 'Still only one body on the beam,' thought Orr. Dim stone kings lined a parapet over the cathedral's west doors, and above them mullions and stone tracery reached up to the sky. Ahead bulged the fort, a stone cliff in their path.

Jacky had seen fiordsides taller than the cathedral and icebergs bigger than the fort but they had been part of the landscape's enormous unconcern. These buildings were surely the artefacts of the Matrix and his mind momentarily floundered, limed in his own presumption.

His nerves pushed him forward alongside Orr. "Wait," he said, very quietly. Orr looked round and saw the rifle muzzle. "Just in case. Let Thorsten go first. You stay behind me."

Orr reached over and patted Jacky's shoulder with a gesture that was only for the watcher on the wall. "No," he said. "I've waited longer than you for this." Orr turned and walked on. The others could hear him whistling. "Good to be here," he called over his shoulder, his voice loud in the enclosed silence, and a helmeted head reappeared and looked down at them from the wall. Jackyboy lifted a hand upwards in a casual wave and the figure returned his salute. Now they were directly beneath the dancer on the beam and from inside the barbican came the sound of footsteps. Jacky's arm came out of his pack's shoulder-strap, but he shrugged it back when he saw Orr shake his head. In a few seconds they were inside the arched entrance. A soldier standing there had seen them approach, familiar in the uniforms, but only when they were almost upon him did he feel a sudden doubt at the strange faces under the curved helmet-rims. It was too late then. They caught him as he slid unconscious down the wall. The second guard had his back to them as he collected firewood from the log-box. He turned into the guns and steel blades and the young staring faces.

"How many look-outs on the walls?"

"Two."

"Thorsten, up on the wall with me," said Orr. "You two have got to keep this gate open." He saw Jacky hesitate and added, "You've got the hard job."

The stone steps that wound up to the sentry-walk were inside a tower further along the wall. Now it was light enough to pick detail from what had been only silhouettes and they flitted cautiously along the base of the wall. There was neither sound nor stir as they mounted the stairs. The sentries were standing together looking out towards the cathedral, and Orr and Thorsten in the tower tensed as one sentry pointed out across the void.

Then quickly but without hurry they walked towards the soldiers. Over by the cathedral there was a slight stirring, and both sensed a sudden change in the sentries. As soon as one dropped a hand to his belt Orr catapulted into his stride, thankful that again the uniforms had brought them so close. Chest-on he cannoned into the first sentry, pinning his arms to his side so that they somersaulted stunningly on to the footworn limestone. A startled shout from the second soldier meant that Thorsten was fractionally late. The shout became a scream and Orr, wrestling to hold his man down, wondered who had gone over the edge of the sentry-walk. There was the patter of swift feet, a rifle butt came past his head, and the man beneath him went limp. Lights were flaring now in several places, and there was a rising of voices somewhere below them. Still on his knees Orr saw Thorsten beckoning from the battlements.

In answer the men from the Big Grey River swarmed out from the shadows of doorways, of wall-ends, of buttress-shoulders, of tombstones. They raced across the cobbled space and Orr, getting to his feet, saw beneath him their fastest runners burst into the fort, as waves flood through a gap in the sea-wall, so eager that they seemed to swirl in the funnel of the gate.

The river-folk were made vengeful by their losses of the day before and galled by the unbroken resistance of Zjelko's trapped force. From the start it was hopeless for the young militiamen of the garrison, most caught in their barracks and without firearms. There had been dead brothers and cousins on the way down from the estuary, but according to custom the river-people's grievance was only with Astolat's abductors; they were ready enough to be merciful with the youngsters in the fort, and although there were a few sharp clashes none lasted long.

Orr, Jacky and his two followers had shed the blue coats and tunics lest their own friends mistake them, and even then they looked not unlike many of the recently awoken garrison, some of whom had fought bare to the waist. Jacky's blond head was their passport as they made their way to the tall tower of the keep. If resistance was to be drawn out it would be there; if it went on much longer Zjelko's men would certainly not walk into a fort that was a clangour of metal and roar of voices.

Inside the keep passages and stairs twined away in a stone anthill. Orr and Jacky, with the young man's closest followers, hesitated and peered about in the gloom, then dashed towards a stairway that led towards the sound of voices above. At the top, just before it widened into a landing, where there was room for but one man at a time, they met Alriksen. Thorsten, the sluice-keeper's son, came backwards down the steps, his eyes glazing as he fell. Orr watched Jacky go next up the stair, which spiralled always to the right to hamper the climbing right-handed swordsman. Who would tell Thorsten's father and mother? Jacky presumably, thought Orr, but what words would he choose to say there would be no grandchildren and no dozing over a fishing-line with the floodgates left to younger, firmer hands?

Someone whispered in his ear and he swung around to an empty darkness. His skin prickled and he felt his face tighten and teeth bare. He took two steps back into the passage and the voice whispered again, brokenly, as if apes wept inside his head. To one side he glimpsed tunnel-like steps that descended to an iron door, the frame outlined by a faint light seeping through. Orr pushed at the door and found the handle, but it was impossible to move; looking closely he could see bolts going across from door to jamb. He heard the heavy scrape of the iron latch inside then footsteps coming to the door. A low voice called, "Who is it?"

'Not that question again,' he thought, but he answered, "Orr," which seemed as good an answer as any.

"Are you alone?" said the voice within.

"Yes, I'm alone."

As at a password the bolts shot back and the door opened before him. He paused in the threshold. The voices in his head had subsided to the crackle of sunstruck grasshoppers. The room, suffocatingly low, was huge, extending below much of the area of the keep; its rugged ceiling, black with moisture, was supported by massive rough-hewn vaults that formed a series of alcoves around a flagstoned central space. Most were full of barrels, but a few were barred across the front, and two of these cells were occupied. The prisoners were at the front of the cages, hands gripping the bars, and Orr recognised immediately the blunt features of the player-chief. With him stood another of the troupe, wearing the chequered coat of the actors. In the next cell Orr saw, with that jump of the heart with which you recognise the human form misshapen, two of those he had heard called 'sons of the sower'. One grasped the bars with dully scaled pangolin hands, the other peered over a thyroid growth that bulged from his neck like some coarse fruit. Their eyes fixed on him. Orr felt the wordless noise in his head stutter with hope and fall quiet, and at once he knew its source. A lantern hanging from a bracket gave a shadowy illumination.

The man who had unbolted the door stepped back a few paces. "How right it should be you," he said. "I think I know you, though you won't know me. I am the commander of this garrison, and guardian of the north-east quarter of the province of Westermain. Did my notice bring you here?"

"Was that it hanging from the tower?"

"Ah, who are you to talk so? You killed a man. I hanged one of the twisted creatures." Distantly shouts came from the stairway, though outside the keep the noise had died away. "Defeated, it seems," said the soldier. "A pity it should end like this. I would have preferred to choose my own company to die in, but it was all too sudden. How could the sentries have missed that many?"

"What do you mean to do?" asked Orr.

"Easy. Take this lamp and ignite this fuse." He lifted the lantern from its bracket. "We keep our gunpowder down here." He gestured towards the barrels. "Antiquated, of course, but Limber is too careful to issue us with proper ammunition, for reasons that I won't bother to explain. We make our own. By now many of your men will be in the keep. I hope they enjoy their victory. Briefly enjoy, that is."

Orr came across the threshold and into the room. Although he crouched his head occasionally brushed the damp stone of the roof. He pulled the Matrix sword from its sheath; holding it he felt clumsy and uneasy. The Matrix captain did likewise, transferring the lantern to his left hand. Orr moved to his left, favouring his only eye as always, hoping to entice the commander away from the fuse. The man followed and Orr now found himself with his back to the bars of the cells that held the actors.

"Be careful," said Demetrius behind him. "This is bad, Hereward, but Regret was worse."

Orr nodded though the remarks meant little more than that he was being mistaken for someone else. He shuffled sideways, closing on the fuse. As he glanced down at it, for so far his eye had been on the sword-point that flickered in front of him, the soldier kicked the door shut and, reaching backwards, slid the bolts into their sockets. Orr came up on guard with too little time. The first thrust was at his stomach; it jarred his wrist as he parried late and awkwardly, and, stepping back hurriedly from the second thrust he thumped into the bars, which left him no room for movement. The blade came under his block and drove into his chest. He felt that momentary disbelief, thinking that the actions of the last few seconds could still be reversed, but his left hand came up to curl around real pain.

"Well, now." The commander ran his finger down the flat of the blade and wiped the blood on to his breeches. "No strangling from behind, no sleepy sentries. Just the two of us. How do you like it?"

Into Orr's mind came a picture of Adelie's thin face and old blue frock, he smelled lilac, and heard the throb of bees in a lime tree. With his arm jammed under his rib-cage to lift it, for it hurt less that way, he stood flat-footed in the louring room while they traded blows until the steel spat inch-long yellow sparks, glittering like flakes of hot metal. The watchers in their cages fought with him, pressing onto the bars as he attacked, wincing as he defended. No one spoke, lest voicing hopes should blight them. The commander's every skill was lashed by the rage of Orr who fought as a blacksmith might fight in a smithy, crowding and clubbing his opponent. But he was fighting a professional soldier who weathered the storming rushes grimly, waiting his moment. It had to come for Orr's parries consisted largely of throwing himself to one side. Then the swords locked and slid together until the hilts touched, and Orr did not know the riposte that would prevent his opponent's weapon rolling free first. Even then he almost twisted enough to evade the thrust, but it went clear through the upper muscles of his right arm. His hand jumped and jerked like a dying chicken's claw, opening and closing in empty reflexes, and the sword rattled down on the flag-stones. Both men's breaths came sobbingly loud. Orr dripped sweat and his veins pounded in his fury.

"You fight well," said the commander, panting. "Go on. While you've got the chance. Take the two men with you, if that's what you want." Orr swayed, the room seemed dimmer, and his head buzzed. Orr glanced at Demetrius, then pointed to the other cell. It hurt too much to talk; anyway he was past words now. The bees would be carrying orange balls of pollen to the hive. "No, Orr. Not the twisters. They stay."

So Orr took his left hand off the hole in his chest, and dropped to his knees, groping for the sword. The commander shook his head, and watched him stagger to his feet. Dying head down was a steer's death. The room was now so dark the shadows weren't there. They both looked at the lantern. The flame was shrinking, smothered, down into the wick. Orr was on his feet, though the pain in his chest had to be lifted too, and there was a liquid, coppery taste in his mouth. But, in hope that the darkness would help him, knowing there was one more blow to take, he stumbled forward, because at last the commander had his back to the cages, took the blow, and in a brutal, stumbling embrace both lurched against the bars. 'Come on, Demetrius,' Orr prayed. 'Here's your chance.'

*

Exactly as Orr and the three river-folk had come walking up to the gate of the fort just before daybreak, so came Zjelko and his men with the girl two hours later. Where the first group had been tense the second was relaxed, where the first was nerving itself for an exploit the second was congratulating itself on surviving one.

"Here they come!" whispered one of Jackyboy's people standing half-way along the tunnel, masquerading as a guard. Orr lay on a mattress against the wall. His wounds had been bandaged and the bleeding stopped. Once he had seen an eel, thicker than a man's arm, impaled on on a sharp stake: the workmates of Hobson the miller, with whom he had lived in the earliest days he could recall, had fished it out from the brick-lined pool called 'the deep' in which the water-wheel churned. The eel had tried to writhe and twist away from the pain that transfixed it. He too found himself twisting his chest to ease the throbbing yet, like the eel, finding the movement brought no release. His arm was numb from two wounds and he had lost much blood, but he had demanded to wait in the guardroom, and after what had happened no one wished to deny him.

Jacky waited with him, quivering like a spring. He peered out just once, impatient to see his sister. Feet tramped past the door. Zjelko came up the tunnel last in line. He stuck his head in the guardroom and called out, "Hey, we're back." At least someone might ask what had happened. Ahead in the tunnel was a scuffle as the river-folk disarmed his surprised men. Orr heard Jacky say, "Remember me? Last time we met was on the roof of a barn. Come in. Somebody here wants to meet you."

Someone else pushed Zjelko further into the room. He looked down. "You!"

"That's right," said the one-eyed man.

The room was filling now, with big smiling men who patted the girl and congratulated her brother. There was an air of boyish delight: the river-folk could not have been more gleeful had they been mannikins who had tripped a giant to send him sprawling in the dust.

"What about the prisoners, nephew?" said Uncle Isak.

Jacky laughed. "Lads from the villages, like us. Send them home." He was euphoric, basking in his sister's adoration. Zjelko was bustled away, looking dazed by the somersault of events. When about noon Orr had felt able to rise he promptly set out for Zjelko's cell, but after three steps fell in a dead faint on the floor. His reputation was high and there was no shortage of volunteers to carry him the three miles to the Cappacian monastery. He had mentioned earlier his intention to seek the healing aid of a monk called Kay there. He was put on a litter and, with a small escort, carried down the hill, through the deserted fringe of the town, across the common-lands where new-born lambs scattered in front of them, and up on to the rolling forested ridges which led south-eastwards to the monastery. The clouds had thickened and, as they changed litter-bearers at the foot of the escarpment before the ridges, light snow began to fall, hesitating downwards and melting as it settled. The landscape was quiet. On the road the disturbed crows rose, flew ahead and paced about again. Demetrius, taking his turn at carrying, felt vaguely irritated by them. If they were sensible they would fly away over the woods instead of inconveniencing themselves.

He looked at Orr who was still unconscious. It had been a long journey to find him. He hoped it would turn out to be, well, satisfactory. An old bell tolled three in a fold between two spurs of the ridge. The litter-bearers kept to the ridge rather than wind down into the village, walking across the headlands and alongside ragged hedges where the birds'-nests clung blackly exposed. Orr swam up to the brink of consciousness. His face was the waxen colour of the sky. Among the spiky branches of the thorn hedges were occasional red berries that the birds had overlooked. As their colour caught Demetrius's eye he glanced sharply at Orr. If red bubbles began to froth out of his mouth they might just as well leave him under the hedge with last year's leaves. But though the one-eyed face seemed to shrink a little during the journey and the lines from nose to jaw deepened to trenches, the red phlegm never came.

A short steep lane led down to the flat, wet meadowlands that surrounded the abbey. The buildings were quiet, shabby in their mixture of stone, brickwork and timber, patched around the chapel that had once been enough for the half-dozen, long-dead pioneer brothers who had brought back the promise and excitement of God. Kay came out to meet them. "I should have known. Bring him inside."

They did so and Orr, hovering between the slow world of the half-awake and the quavering, deliquescent mindscape of dreams, felt the jolting end and the featherbed's softness accept him. On the pillow his face smiled faintly, but the watching men could not have guessed that he had gone with a friend to pick daisies.

VIII

The world of the Matrix moved very slowly. Partly this was by force of necessity, for communication at the periphery of their zone of influence was usually as slow as a man running, occasionally as fast as a heliograph winking from parapet to hill-cairn. The horses had gone. There was nothing faster. There might have been, but it was the will of the Matrix that it should not be so, and the years had so confused this will with the natural order that now they were one and the same. Like a vast glacier the Matrix responded with no convulsion but with inexorable slow pressure. Jacky's uprising was as if a man had held a flaming blowtorch against a wall of ice; a cavity melted in the ice, for a time, but the torch couldn't blaze for ever and before long back would come the inching ice, slowly healing over the wound.

However there was no account anywhere of the Matrix failing to respond eventually. But in this remote maritime province neither was there any record of revolt. The northern seas were little travelled, and when the far-off marshals led their troops to battle they headed deep into the great arid land wastes or down through the passes of the purple-white mountains that formed, respectively, the long southern and south-eastern frontiers of the Matrix. Beyond these frontiers dwelled turbulent people; sometimes for years, even many years, the Matrix heard little of them, only to find them suddenly pillaging the Outlands and borders as mindlessly as soldier ants.

Internal uprisings anywhere were rare indeed, and no one had heard of a successful one. Dissent was muffled by the Matrix's subtle and essentially gentle philosophy of the origins and application of power. The emergence of a Jacky Dorn was not unique, but the circumstances, which time makes always different, on this occasion had conjoined favourably for him. For a start, an organised garrison, though a small one, had been outwitted and overwhelmed; then it had taken place in February, a month when both fields and forests were lying fallow, so Jacky's force did not melt away. Indeed it swelled, in a buoyant, boyish way, with bubbling recruits, glory-seekers, sightseers and playful ploughboys, all of them dazzled by their cousins' exploit, and only too happy to share in making the tale ever taller. There might have been a worse time for the militia of Unity to be asked to move against the new occupiers of Ingastowe fort. But perhaps not.

*

Orr could sit up in bed now. His wounds were sore and whenever he so much as turned his head he felt across his chest the punctured muscle-sheath throb. But he was alive and he bit into the brown bread and in his mouth was its grainy rough flavour, the milky-salt softness of butter, the sweet ooze of honey. The afternoon's light was enough still to show him his companions, Uncle Isak and Demetrius, big men looking bigger as men in heavy coats or cloaks do in bedrooms, sitting with Abbot Huw and Brother Kay. Only an unpredictable future could follow this day's events.

"Demetrius gives good advice," said Isak. "Though I will say my nephew is a quick pupil and doesn't need telling twice."

"He needs to be quick," muttered Demetrius. "Next time the professionals will come."

"Tell me again," Orr interrupted. "When did you first know they were coming?"

"When they were two days march away. That comes of having foresters with us. I think they must get the trees to pass messages along," Demetrius laughed. "I'm sure most Matrix officers regard you outland people as barbarians or just wild innocents, because they train the militia always to fight the same way, a nice simple formation which they expect you will buzz round like wasps jittering round a jam-pot. Make a stand on a bare hillside or a plateau or inside a fortress, anywhere that's not messy and tangled and there's no need to manoeuvre. Keep it simple and march an extra hundred miles rather than get in a muddled skirmish in a wood."

"That's right. When we chased them south from our river," recalled Isak, "even then they stayed on the open ridges. This time when the Unity militia got near to Ingastowe we were behind them in the woods. Luckily their commander didn't sidestep or withdraw."

"What did he do?" asked Orr.

"He thought all of us were there in the woods, so he decided to rush the fort. Like ordering a hammer to rush an anvil." Isak, who had been in the fort, smiled coldly.

"Towns are no place for troops," Demetrius added. "Particularly towns with high buildings and narrow streets. Tactics don't exist when you can't see further than the width of the street."

The four men, so unalike, gazed reflectively at one another across Orr's brown blankets. All knew how it had gone. Two had been there and the flow of wounded men into the abbey had said enough for the monks to have pieced it together hours earlier. The Unity militia, sucked into chopping scuffles in the blind alleys and sunken lanes beneath the walls of fort and cathedral, the javelins and harpoons pouring down from high windows, harassed into ever smaller groups in gardens and backyards, or trapped in streets full of burning straw, had as little wish to fight on as their opponents had. "What's our quarrel?" Jacky had said often enough. "We're all from Westermain, aren't we?"

"May I ask, sir," asked the abbot, "how you are so well-versed in military lore?"

"Just picked it up here and there, Father, like most of us."

"In your travels as a troubadour?" asked Kay. Demetrius said nothing, his beefy face expressionless.

"Are you familiar with the heartland of the Matrix, or did you pick up this knowledge in the provinces?" the abbot said gently.

"Like I said, just here and there. A bit of time in the militia."

"By the way," said Orr. "Your friend the juggler said I had something to learn from you." In the silence Orr had a brief image of a flat stone, of fingers raising its edge. He was not sure now that he wanted to look underneath. The room was uneasy, for three of the men openly liked Orr.

Demetrius heavy-shouldered, blue-jowled, with the skin creased and weathered red over the wide calm face, was more reserved with his sentiments. His flamboyance on stage was curiously at odds with his present self-contained demeanour. "Well," he said, "you may want to keep it private." He shrugged his shoulders and looked emptily at the far wall. "I think I probably would in your place." His words were like stones dropped into a dry well. They fell rattling on the pebbles at the bottom and there was no relief in them. Even their echoes were brittle.

"Will it matter if others hear it?" said Orr, beginning to grow impatient.

"It might, that is hard to say. Others may find you different."

"Then keep it to yourself," said Orr. "You were about to tell me part of my past, I think. But there is much else on my mind. In a month, or a year perhaps, I may want to hear your news sufficiently to ask you again." He leaned back, resting his head on the bare wall behind the bed and dropped his right eyelid. He looked tired and uninterested and it came as a surprise to the others when without moving, or opening his single eye, he spoke again: "Why do you seek me out in this quiet corner? What can you desire of me? Whatever you have to say, I think you need to tell me more than I need to hear."

Demetrius laughed, a big chuckling laugh to ease the sting in Orr's words. "Of course I do," he said. "I do need to tell you. It would be hard to deny it. As for your not wanting to hear, well, believe me, I sympathise with you. I don't much like hearing from my own past."

"I suppose you know a lot," said Orr, and a grating edge had come into his voice. "Maybe that's what they call wisdom. Perhaps you and your friends think I'm an ungrateful man. But let me tell you this. My friend's life has been broken to pieces and one of the men who did it lied to save his skin and that cost me my eye. They scraped it out with the point of a knife. My friend was just a child and if someone doesn't try to balance out the scales then what are friends for? Until I've dealt with him you ought to stop spinning words round me."

Huw, Kay and Isak sat quite still. Demetrius got to his feet, settling his big coat around his shoulders and feeling for the buttons without looking away from Orr. He reached behind him and pulled open the door. "I came a thousand miles to find you, and I hoped you would recognise me or at least trust me. But if you won't even listen then we won't bother with that. But I'll tell you one thing. Your name isn't Orr. Kay tells me that was some of the villagers' paltry idea of a joke. It's Hereward, and a name to be proud of. I'll tell you the rest whenever you ask, and how I let you down in the past. But we didn't let you down at the play, did we? I knew you'd come to one of the plays sooner or later. I saw you watching us. I even followed you up on the wall of the fort because I wanted to see you again. Hereward told me he never missed a play if he could help it."

"You're starting to tell me my past again. That means you've already started to use me. Let's go our separate ways."

Demetrius turned and walked away. He didn't slam the door behind him. In fact he pushed it further open with his foot so that it rattled against the wall and swung in the cold wind. The abbot reached out gently and closed it.

"A strange man, is he not, Father?" said Kay conversationally.

"Not really, Kay. All of us have pasts we have in part dismissed."

"I meant our friend Demetrius."

"Oh, him. A troubled man, I would say. Just possibly a strange one too," replied Huw. "My sympathies are all with Orr-Hereward in this matter."

Orr's ruffled temper was smoothed thus, as the abbot had intended, of course, and after a while conversation wandered pleasantly, as Isak told them of calmer days when all that mattered was the moods and tides of his river, and Huw looked back even further to the years he had passed in the mendicant branch of the order, a young man walking the roads which led to faithless communities.

Night came on and they parted, each to lie in bed, each letting his mind toy with the images he had acquired that day. Huw, Kay and Isak slid reflectively down into sleep, but Orr lay awake for hours. Usually he would at this time try vainly to look into the abyss of his past, a vertiginous, comfortless blackness that gave no sign of whatever he might have seen or known, but now it was different. Hereward – it was so friendly, as easy to wear as a pair of old shoes. He had vestigially responded to Wood as a name, but this was different. It had a shining to it. It was a name that deserved to be kept bright.

IX

March went. April came and went. Ceil came to the monastery one morning through hawthorn starred with may, the field-hollows full of rabbits, lords-and-ladies aflower in the hedge-bottoms and faraway cuckoos calling in the blue distance. Hereward saw her coming from far off. He carried three Matrix scars but he was able to do light work now his muscles had knit together and his strength gathered. The prior had employed him that day in the pigeon-loft. The pigeon-cote itself was part of the monastery's tallest building, being a short tower perched on one end of a big barn. On all four sides of it were many small entry-holes for the birds, and through them you could see for miles in any direction. Ceil's yellow dress was easy to see, and he watched her approach. As she came into the yard beneath him he lost sight of her, feeling curiously regretful. He went on with his work, absentmindedly daubing the walls of the loft with their spring coat of limewash. The voice from below in the barn took him by surprise.

"Hullo, anyone up there?"

He opened the trapdoor in the floor and looked down. "Yes, I am."

"You must be better," she called up. "Are you working?"

"Yes, I am."

"Beguiling conversation!" shouted Kay, who was ferreting about in a corner of the barn scraping cobwebs off the wall. "Go on up and have a look at the pigeon-cote," he suggested, and Ceil climbed up the steep wooden steps with their treads worn so thin in the middle that they bowed under her weight.

Sunlight and wind were filling the cote with a bright flutter, and as her head came through the trapdoor her black hair blew back from her face and Hereward saw the bruise, a purple shadow darkening her temple. "You got back safely that night then," he said.

"Yes. What happened to the young man?"

"I'm afraid he . . ."

"Don't tell me." She turned away and stared stiffly out of one of the holes, and Hereward picked up a brush full of whitewash and slapped it onto the flaky plaster. He felt, miserably, that he had given her another bruise and was thankful for the flight of pigeons that came swooping towards the loft and on to the landing-board, feathers fluttering and claws rattling in through their holes.

He took a handful of wheat from a bag and walked across to her. "They'll want something to eat," he said. "They like this." He tipped the grain into her hand. "I don't even know your name."

"It's Ceil."

"Mine's Hereward."

"Really? I thought it was Orr."

"It was, not long ago. But Orr was more of a nickname than anything."

"I like Hereward much better," Ceil assured him.

A pigeon had perched on his wrist and he stroked its feathers softly, admiring the sleek greyness with the white ruffles on each pinion's end. The pigeon cocked its head and stared onyx-eyed at Ceil.

"Your eyes are a lovely colour," she told the bird.

"So are yours," said Hereward, saying it as she had spoken to the pigeon, because it was so, and to say thank you to the providence that had left him an eye to see blueness. To his dismay she gave a half-sob. Without thought he took her hands in his, feeling their warmth, and a layer of his cold purpose thawed a little.

"Hereward, listen. I should have told you this at once. I came to tell you Zjelko has got away from the fort." A film came down over Hereward's face and he pointed wordlessly at the bruise. "He came to the inn in the night and asked where he could find you. I told him I didn't know and he called me a liar."

"I suppose he'll think of coming to Hay," Hereward muttered, and now she felt hardly present to him at all. "That's good. It's time to settle this thing once and for all. When will it be?"

"He may come tonight, I think. He cannot stay long in this area and he must know that someone will tell you he has escaped." Suddenly, unexpectedly, he smiled at her. She had never seen him smile before. "What is it?" she said nervously

"Look, there's a rainbow." He pointed over the treetops and she realised with a shock that she was the well from which he drank delight. When he reached down and touched the bruise she turned her face away hoping he could not see the tears welling in her eyes. Before he could say more she shook her head.

"It doesn't matter," she said, in the hopeless shorthand of syllables. Hereward's instinct told him this was another castaway like himself, clinging momently to the same spar, and that all this was hopeless, so he wiped away the tears and smiled at her again and wished time would be still.

It was, almost. Zjelko lay in hiding in the hazel saplings of that same embankment where he had watched Adelie kicked unconscious. He stared unblinking at the village, beyond which lay the abbey. The hazels did not move, nor did the rainbow dissolve. Kay in the barn was still, his hand reaching upwards, full of cobwebs, contemplating their strange healing properties. Jacky sat motionless in a tower looking at a list but seeing the sea. From a narrow hole in the ground misshapen Martin peered up at the rainbow's perfect arch.

Then Hay church clock began to tick again. Zjelko sucked at his water-bottle, Jacky yawned, and Hereward and Ceil started down the ladder as Kay's hand scraped more webs off the wall. He saw them look at each other and was glad.

"What would you like to do?" Hereward asked her.

"Whatever you'd like to do."

"You've been listening to the pigeons too long," said Kay as they passed him.

The golden afternoon passed by. Later, in the twilight they ate supper with Kay. Ceil had been teasing Hereward affectionately about his long tangled hair, and after a while he slipped out of the room. On his return, his hair trimmed, he looked younger, different. He was carrying a Matrix battle-helmet. When her face blanched and hands clenched round her cup, Kay said very gently, "Are you all right?"

She drew in a deep breath, like a swimmer about to dive, and Kay glanced at her perplexed. "It's not as bad as all that. In fact, it's probably an improvement," he smiled.

Hereward sat beside her and as he took her hand in his, he felt it tremble. "Are you all right?" he repeated the question.

"Yes, it's nothing." Whatever had stalked into the room had to remain nothing, she thought. In a corner of her mind she mourned the small coquetries with Hereward and the brief afternoon when the fields of buttercups they crossed had dusted their shoes with gold, and the wild roses had tugged at them as if loath to let them leave the pastoral they walked in like figures entwined in a tapestry. Happier, she thought, those born in the interstices of history. How could she ever have hoped to reconcile the gentle constituencies of love with this marked man? His was a face born of a distant past, there being fewer born like him now, and others felt around him a hem of apprehension and precognition. Partly it was this that had swayed the verdict in Hay village court towards guilty.

She knew he was the man she had always been waiting for, and with equal certainty that it was not going to last, in fact had probably already lasted as long as it would. He had pulled the old cloak's hood over his helmet and she knew he was leaving.

"Is this going to solve anything?" said Kay slowly. He felt he had left it too late. "Talk to the abbot about stolen children. He did mention it once. He gives good advice."

"No, too late for that. Goodbye, Ceil. Thank you for everything. I enjoyed the walk this afternoon."

Outside it was a soft, warm evening, a smooth velvet darkness into which he blended. He had made his plan. There were four ways to reach the abbey. One was from the north, but from this direction Zjelko must come openly along the village's main street and on down the highway from village to abbey. Hereward discounted this at once. Then there was the grassy track through the meadows along which he had run to find sanctuary with his bloody eye-fluids running down his cheek. This was a lonely path, the one Hereward would have chosen himself, but he doubted Zjelko knew of its existence. The third, the water-meadows and cow-paddocks behind the abbey might just be passable, though they were always marshy, with deep muddy dikes. On the high, drier side of the village was the ridgeway track along which he had been carried in a litter. It came down from the ridge into a lane shaded by ash-trees, and enclosed in tall hedges of crab-apple and quickthorn. This would surely be Zjelko's choice.

Hereward walked for two hundred paces up the lane, crossed a stile into a field of kale, lay down in the wet grass of the headland and then silently wormed his way backwards on his stomach and lay concealed under the thick, crinkly leaves, settling himself to watch the lane through the less leafy growth at thc bottom of the hedge. An hour went by. Once an old lady passed slowly along the lane, and once the coughing snuffles of a sow badger and her cubs drew his attention, but otherwise he sensed only the rustling of the kale leaves and the raw green smell of them and the tiny white moths that inhabit the black tunnels beneath the leaves. The evening dew was beginning to dampen his clothes, but he made no move as another hour went by. A wafer of moon had appeared, and the shadow of a barn owl came floating along the grass near him. It saw the paleness of his hands, but glided on, deterred by the bulk of his back. Before dawn the squeaking traffic of mice and voles would know of the owl.

Alerted by the bird he became aware of a faint pattering or throbbing, not unlike his own heart-beat; as he pressed an ear down he could sense it in the earth. There was another sound too, a rattling not far off in the rows of plants, and he guessed he was not alone in the field. He was just about to rise from his hiding-place when, only a few paces away, a darker patch detached itself from the night and moved in front of him. The white owl had been as soundless as a snowflake, but this time there was the swish of boots on grass and the creak of leather. As the figure reached the stile moonlight shone briefly on a rifle-barrel and the hedge's shadows fell away, revealing the square-shouldered cut of the Matrix tunic. Hereward was on his feet. He pressed close in to an ash-tree and gave Zjelko time to move further down the lane, then climbed the stile to bring himself on the same side of the hedge. As he had hoped, the tall lighted windows of the abbey's chapterhouse neatly silhouetted the Matrix soldier.

Then he heard rapid footsteps, and saw another, smaller, figure running fast up the lane in his direction, not bothering with concealment. Her hair fluttered out and he knew it was Ceil. He quickened his pace and then heard her frightened scream, as the soldier suddenly stepped out of the shadows where he had paused to watch her approach. She tried to pull away as he took her arm. Hereward thought of Adelie lying on the causeway but now he was running forward on his toes, moving the grass but silently, as wind-ripples do. Perhaps Ceil had revealed his presence for the rifle swung towards him, but now he was only a few paces away. He heard the rifle's whip-crack, but before the flat echoes had slammed across the valley he drove the man backwards to the stony ground. He had waited a long time for this moment. He gripped hard round the soldier's neck and held him face down. This Zjelko was not easily subdued. He lashed backwards with his boot heel, numbing all of Hereward's leg from the knee down and then bent forwards suddenly trying to drag him clear over his head. Yet it was none of those manoeuvres that loosened Hereward's hold. Almost a year ago he had broken Vanya without thought, instinctively and quickly. Now the one-eyed man was slowed by a sudden image of himself garotted from behind and as, momentarily, he relaxed his hold, the soldier tore himself groggily free, gasping for breath on his hands and knees.

He never saw the rifle butt that Herward brought down on the back of his head. "That was for a friend of mine," said Hereward, and dropped the gun on the prostrate figure. As he did so he was aware of Ceil pulling at him, and looked up. Her face looked terrified, worse than it had on encountering Janitza, the harmless wounded cadet. A row of pale, blurred faces, grim beneath the Matrix helmets, was closing in. One was a short, tubby man, but though Hereward saw the emerald star emblems flicker on his epaulettes, he neither knew them as the insignia of a full marshal, nor would he have cared if he had known. He saw only Zjelko standing by the stocky man's side.

"Stop him. He's an outlaw, sir! He's killed one of our men before!" shouted Zjelko.

"Hold him," said the marshal.

Hereward's world wobbled. He looked at the unconscious figure at his feet. Were there no stilling consequences?

"Don't anyone move, please." The rifle had appeared in Ceil's hands and there was an unfamiliar rasp to her voice. "I won't miss." Her eyes were steady on the marshal, but she spoke over her shoulder. "Go back in the forest. Don't let them hang you, my love."

X

There were only ever three marshals of the Matrix. The unmapped ice-cap to the north was an unconsidered waste, the domain of the blizzard and ice-bears. Tortured plains of sastrugi at the centre and buckling ice-floes at its rim made it as hostile as some far-off frozen planet. So there was no marshal for the northern lands. However, to west, south and east were marcher provinces, which all in different fashions had to be directed.

Peace was a rarity for the Matrix. Why this was so no one really understood. The thinkers of the Matrix had proposed various answers: the demands of people upon resources was one, another the cruel supposition that peace-loving societies merely acquiesced in their own demises and thus thriving societies were ipso facto belligerent ones; a third was that civilisation is by its nature a destabilising activity, that complex unities and communities attract the competition of primitive cultures, even as other plants and grasses will always try to colonise rose-beds – or again, and this was roughly the view of the order of Huw and Kay, that war is simply mankind's imperfections writ in large characters, as clear a fingerprint as was the rose when God put his hand down.

The marshal of the west was always known as Wulf. He had died four years ago, eight years before that, and an unbelievable twenty before that, so his lives had been long ones. Of course, that was how the western marshals were. Guarding and guiding mainly maritime provinces called for craft, for the patience to make concessions to buy time to erode those concessions, for knowing when to do nothing. But when Wulf's troops did move he marched with them, when one of his men had no food he did not eat. Soldiering was a profession for only a few in the Matrix or its provinces, so it was left to local militias with a handful of experienced instructors. The tactics were simple: a line of infantrymen with their short stabbing swords swung underhand, and a few hand-guns. Behind their lines or within their squares they kept the riflemen, usually pushing them forward only to use their long bayonets. Point-blank was the only effective range for their firearms, and point-blank meant, more often than not, that the enemy's charge crashed into the stubborn, sweating, cursing infantry, the journeymen of the army who, for more years than any man knew, had been the stretched muscle and sinew that guyed upright the bones of order.

In recorded history no Matrix marshal had ever fought anywhere except in the centre of the front rank. That was a marshal's doom and privilege. He set his battle in order, simply, so that, as far as possible, not much could go wrong in his absence, and crossed himself. The Matrix people would fight where they must, and, though their ancestors had once reached out to the stars themselves, their weapons were unreliable guns and swords that broke. This way, the people fought, not their weapons, and they understood war's wrath.

No one knew who had been the first Wulf, and the name had had many legatees, though by no means as many as the names of the southern and eastern marshals. Cortez held the southern frontier; he was the most charismatic of the marshals and the most often consumed. Although by custom the man assumed the mantle, submerging himself in the office, very occasionally a leader became celebrated in person, and none more so than that Cortez under whom Tsiganok had served, John Paul, whom death had seemed reluctant to take.

The present Wulf stood on the moss of a green pathway on a warm, still May night, smelled cabbages and a crew-yard and lily of the valley, and looked into the black eye of a rifle barrel, knowing that this was where it all ended, because she couldn't miss and he knew she was going to pull the trigger. It was his business to know. But he had heard of an outlaw helping to lead the rebels, and if he could be seized now the insurgency might well be nearly over. His captains would see to the rest.

"You'd better be sure it's him," said Wulf to Zjelko, in the thick accent that was almost the only part of his old self he allowed himself to indulge.

"Marshal, I'm certain."

"We'd better take him then," the marshal told his escort, and almost casually reached for his hand-gun, and saw her pull the trigger, or rather, because it was too dark for that, saw it in all her movements, and his shot sent Ceil tumbling backwards. He was so engrossed in registering the final night-scents of his life that he took some seconds to grasp the meaning of the empty click.

At his side Zjelko gasped and jumped forward, kneeling to feel for a pulse. His sudden movement momentarily distracted the patrol, and they were a second's thought and ten paces behind Hereward. He was running with the speed of animals, who know speed is life and there is no point in anything but now. His pursuers, running swiftly in his steps, kept him in sight only briefly, for he swarmed up a wall, his hands scraping cushions of moss off its rounded top, and dropped into a cluttered back-garden, full of chicken-coops and leafy runner-beans just starting to twine up tall sticks.

The noise drew the pursuit and he darted up a garden path, past the side of a cottage, and out on an earthen track. Without breaking stride he was across it, vaulted a wooden gate and landed in the trampled plash cows leave at the gates of their meadows. It was one of the tiny fields common in the area, and Hereward turned sharply along the hedge into the corner of the field where gorse and birch offered dense shelter. In seconds he was into the furze, and belly-down on the powdery soil rabbits had thrown out of their warren. He looked back, for the first time feeling his throat hot and parched.

Hereward took a deep breath, held it and then breathed silently out through his nose. There was movement on the road but he was fairly sure that the soldiers weren't aware of his hiding-place. He was right. They spent no more than a few minutes scrambling through the dark labyrinth of hedges and banks. Their voices came clear through the night and then the sound of footsteps withdrawing.

There was not a complete silence. When the footsteps faded Hereward could sense a dull noise he had noticed earlier, a vibrating in the earth, as if a giant were drumming on the ground with huge fingers. As he lay pressed to the earth he saw grains of loam shaking down from the edges of the rabbit burrows. Then the cause of the vibration became clearly recognisable as many feet running, jogging rhythmically, and then the road he had dashed across a few moments earlier was full of movement, of stirring, a subdued jingle of metal and the sharply drawn breaths of many men. Like a black tide under the familiar steel helmets came the first of the Matrix companies, their skirmishers in front and then the main body running steadily six or eight abreast between the hedges. The weight and purpose of their movement told Hereward as clearly as words that this was neither patrol, cohort, nor even single regiment. He remembered the crackling feet in the kale-plants and knew that the Matrix had from somewhere silently conjured up an army. They must be pouring towards Ingastowe along at least three parallel tracks as well as running like hunting-dogs over the crops and meadows. He guessed that the burly stranger he had first encountered and grappled had been one of the scouts reconnoitring ahead of the main body. "They'll send the professionals," Demetrius had said.

Hereward, for the first time in his brief, patchy memory, felt puny. Only minutes ago he had felt bewildered by events, now he sensed the events were not so much random as responding to wills more potent than his own. He preferred the first case. Yet the thoughts were fleeting, for his stubbornness hadn't learned to be easily deflected. So he got up on his feet and, twisting through the gorse bushes, patiently unsnagging his cloak from the brambles, came out on the far side of the thicket. There he turned his back on the road and the pounding feet, and ran in the hedge-shadows towards the abbey. The ground was swampy, and though he tried to step on the tussocks of coarse grass his feet were soon soaked. The abbey itself lay among wetlands, and after stumbling across three fields he saw the tower of the pigeon-cote ahead. When he could hear above him the pigeons crooning and whirring their wings he realised how silent it was now the Matrix force had run into the night, as if they had passed in a dream.

He went between the barn and dairy, through the unlit, vaulted undercroft, and into the small doorway of the almoner's domain. Kay was there, bending over a bench, grinding up paste in a mortar, then looking up and smiling.

"Did you see them?"

"Yes, I saw them," said the little man. "Ceil came out to tell you they were coming. Did you have time to finish your own business?"

"No."

"Did Ceil find you?"

"Yes."

The almoner looked suddenly ill. It was Hereward who spoke: "Where did they all come from?"

"Out of thin air. I don't think anyone dreamed there were so many Matrix troops within a hundred miles, and the river-folk in Ingastowe certainly won't be expecting them. It will be a tough nut for Jacky to crack, particularly if he is surprised by their coming."

Hereward's head lifted as he gave his grey stare. "You know the roads."

"I can't go," said Kay.

"Why not?"

"The abbot wouldn't let me interfere."

"Why?"

"I've told you before," said Kay, "to ask him yourself."

"Go without telling him then."

"He trusts me," said Kay simply. "And I trust him to know what's best."

"You helped me when I was hurt and hunted."

"That was different. To succour the distraught is part of our mission."

"All right," Hereward said, "I'll go myself. But you'd better know Ceil is dead. Someone shot her. I want to bury her first. Then I'll go."

He went out into the night. It was so quiet now he could hear the pigeons' claws click on their perches. He turned into the mossy lane where in that unforgettable second he had seen Ceil fall into a shapeless bundle, and had raced away aghast. The track was quite empty. He knew exactly where she had fallen, for to his right was the wall he had scaled and the garden he had run through earlier that night. He retraced his footsteps. Had she been wounded and carried away? His eye still held the image of the shuddering impact and he relinquished that possibility. He might find her body but she would be gone.

The grasses at the verge of the track were trampled wherever he looked, almost up to the stiff quickthorns, proof of the passing of many feet. The tall-stemmed chicory, hawkweed and spikenard, that had waited winter-long for the warmth of May were broken-stemmed and bruised. Dark though it was it seemed impossible he could not find the body. The Matrix troops had surely been moving too fast to have disposed of her. Under the hedges were drifts of nettles and he foraged among them, his hands swelling with the white blisters of their acid. There were only rotting branches and molehills.

Now he was investigating spots he had examined earlier. An hour went by, as doggedly Hereward pursued his search, now moving further along the lane in the direction of the village. When the Hay church clock tolled four strokes it sounded clear and close in the silence. The eastern horizon was awash with a pallid light. The lane steepened, meeting a ridge, and soon it would lead out on to open sheep-pastures, where he knew there could be no point in persevering.

He was standing irresolute when for the second time in moments the long silence was broken. From ahead came a hollow knocking, like a woodpecker but louder. He walked towards the noise but it stopped abruptly. A thick screen of black yew-trees lay before him. He skirted swiftly round it, his foot met a stone slab and he stepped over a clay pot full of marigolds. Inscribed in stone he made out dimly 'Emma Hobson, Beloved Wife', and realised where he was. Hobson kept those flowers always fresh, and he had accompanied his friend here on two or three occasions. Wreaths of morning mist were draping the headstones and at first the place seemed deserted. Then a figure on the far side emerged as if climbing on to a stage. Hereward had no trouble recognising the bull-neck and wide shoulders.

Sweat patching his shirt, Zjelko scrambled out of the hole. The hole looked to be waist-deep in the red-brown clay. Close to it were Zjelko's weapons and a rough wooden cross. The soldier picked up a bundle wrapped in a blue greatcoat and lowered it out of sight. Hereward walked quietly to the grave's edge and stood on the weapons. He even had time to look down and see the corner of a black coffin that the digging must have exposed before Zjelko had noticed his presence.

"Is she inside the coat?" said Hereward.

"What's it to you?"

"You can't hit her any more now." Zjelko made no reply to this but shrugged his shoulders. "Your special skill, hitting girls, isn't it?" He glared across the heap of earth, knowing he was being goaded. "Nice having both eyes too."

"What makes you think we wanted to hurt that girl? Why should we? We had no choice. You ever been in an army? You're taught to obey orders. And who gave you the right to even talk about my wife, when we had fifteen years and two children together. You didn't know her. All you did was let a marshal use her for shooting-practice, then run away!"

Hereward frowned at the rush of words. Two large earthworms were wriggling frenziedly on the freshly turned soil. "Obeying orders, were you?" he asked after a long pause. "Your commander's?"

"I suppose so."

"He told you to kick a thirteen-year-old girl almost to death? I doubt it."

"We were told to bring her to the fort. She started screaming. I didn't want her hurt. It was Vanya who kicked her anyway. And he didn't kill her, remember that. You were the only killer that day."

"One life for one life. Everyone knows that's the law. The girl is not dead, but it's not life when her friends pull her round the village on a chair with wheels, and she knows neither her mother nor enough to lift her own food to her mouth. And it's one eye for one eye. You owe me. Your wife died trying to help me, so she bought you one hour. That's not quite the law, but fair. Though if you would like to settle things now . . .?"

"We'll meet again, Orr, don't worry." Zjelko threw the spade in the grave. "Maybe you won't be so cocky next time." He walked away through the mossy tombstones, gallingly leaving his weapons under Hereward's feet, and spat on the last stone.

When he had gone Hereward filled the hole and then looked at the words carved into the cross. 'Ceil Zjelko', he read, then two symbols that meant nothing to him. He picked up the cross and the short sword and sat down in the daisies and dandelion tufts. The sword-point was awkward to work with but he soon splintered away the second word; he contemplated hacking off the symbols but left them and scratched into the wood the outline of a bird. He meant it to be a pigeon but it turned into just a bird. Laboriously he cut the word 'Love' and then the letter 'H'. It took a long time but now there was nothing else that he wanted to do more, so he didn't hurry. The sun came up, linnets whistled in the hedges, curlews dodged and piped in the fields around the graveyard, and larks sang irresistibly in the sky above as he worked at the wood.

When he had finished he pushed the cross into place, and set off towards the road to Ingastowe. His eye-socket ached and he found no satisfaction in what had happened.

XI

Jacky came awake that morning almost regretfully for the cares of command chafed him, and in his heart he knew that his people should not be here looking idly out from the fort's walls at the wide cloudscapes. One consolation was the arrival of Astolat who had come visiting from the estuary to see her brother. Clutched under her cloak she carried with her a miniature fishing-boat, made from the creamy-grey narwhal horn. She had bought the bone from a northern sea-gypsy and her father had carved it. News had travelled along the chalk-wolds from Ingastowe to the Big Grey River that Jackyboy was fretting at a table in a tower. He put her gift on his window-sill.

In truth many of his friends had already gone, and in their stead had come ne'er-do-wells and vagrants. He had been irked by his uncle telling him that he was acting like a magnate. Jacky had tried to say that all he wanted was the chance to build a big ship, which was true in itself but Isak only responded that there must be less dangerous ways to do so. What had begun as a fit of fury and swelled to a famous exploit was now declining into a sour occupancy. Jacky thought sometimes of Orr-Hereward. His uncle had told him of Hereward's sharp words with Demetrius, and Jacky was sorry that the latter had departed. He wanted to go to see Hereward but he hoped the one-eyed man would come first to see him. However, he thought, he might take Astolat on a visit to the abbey where Hereward the inscrutable lay convalescing.

Thus was he speculating when the news came that the wide sweeping common-lands south of the town, usually shared by the sheep and bullocks, were swarming with Matrix troops. He strode away to see for himself, leaving behind him the aggressive roar of a disturbed hive as his men buzzed with the news. Among the tumble-down walls of the ruins that fringed the town were numerous observation-points. It's true enough, he thought, staring out across the dewy expanse. On the lower lands of the green common bullocks paddled deep in marsh-buttercups, then the slopes rose to the closely bitten sheep-runs. Above, crowning the ridge, were the Matrix regiments. The sun was behind them and their uniforms looked black, but catching the early sunlight the battle-flags danced cornflower-blue and gold. He recalled Demetrius's words: 'They will fight in the open – on a plateau or ridge-top if they can.' Fleetingly he considered retreating into a siege, not picking up the gauntlet, but that was no way for him. He was a northerner and his blood whispered only defiance. In the marrow of his bones was the melancholy of long dark winters and green-yellow summers that you snatched at before the darkness came again. If this is the darkness, well, it has always been coming, he thought, and he went and stood out in the open. He was Jackyboy, born John Dorn, twenty years old, and this was no day for hiding behind walls.

Wulf, western marshal of the Matrix, born Rocco Barbella, looked through his telescope at the town. They wouldn't be long in coming – there was a youth there now, looking up, shading his eyes, conspicuous with his long yellow hair. Wulf thought of the olive groves and how his parents still shook the olives on to sheets laid under the trees. This land grew no olives, here they cooked in cow-fat. Here even the light was diffused with green, and the grass's roots would grow quickly into his arteries, for this was the place from his nightmares. Only another John Cortez could stand unscathed for long in the front rank, not simple Rocco Barbella, third son of an olive-farmer.

He didn't wonder what had brought him here, for he never questioned the high ideals the free servants of the Matrix cherished. His instructors had taught him much and he had tried to teach it in his turn. The Matrix is stretched very thin, but then it always has been, though now more than in the past unnerved by the shadowy Unmen: if it is to be overthrown that will be because the time is ripe. Neither Rocco nor the men who fought alongside him would ever consider abdication, he knew.

The marshal looked round at his infantry and smiled. For many of them it had been a hundred-mile sea-voyage, then forty miles up-river cramped under the hatches in barges and scows, then running with their packs on for hours through the dark fields and woods. What had he done to deserve men like these? Most were sitting or even lying down, talking, and Rocco heard some of them near him start up the 'Sandman' song, the militia's favourite. It came plaintive and slow-beating:

Twice last night,
Once the night before,
I heard the Sandman
Knocking on my door . . .

It chilled Rocco, as did their other song, 'Too-tall Poppies'. Both had melancholy refrains, and he wondered why they never sang the one he liked best, the rollicking 'Hey, Hey, Joe Hammer', but they hadn't done for years. Once there was the sea peacock blue through the pine-trees, and walnuts and red wine, strong-scented in the mouth, and in the evening down to the inn and a game of cards with some school-friends; now it's murdering women in lanes.

"It won't be long now, sir," said a voice behind him.

Turning he saw one of his captains. "Not long at all, Lucien." Even without his glass he could see the nearer streets of the town glinting with steel and dense with hurrying figures, the roads disgorging them on to the grasslands below.

Twice last night,
Again just after dawn,
I heard the Sandman
Blowing on his horn.

Behind him the line was waiting, his own place vacant like a missing front tooth. Wulf was trembling. How many times did the tide have to come up the beach before it washed the last sandcastles away? After a while he went to stand in his place, observing without surprise the shouting, many-coloured column that was forming a quarter of a mile away to his front, exactly opposite his position.

Around him the militia were mildly curious. "Wulf looks pale," said one. "Anything here to be worried about?" They were, as always, a mixed bunch – masons, musicians, metal-workers, miners, mountain-men, mill-hands – and dealing with warlords and magnates was much the same as cleaning house. You did it when it needed doing. Also they had four companies of the Merganser Companions, two on each flank. The Companions' marksmen would soon pick out the rebel leader, and, with their leader eliminated, the led would be more likely to play football together than be enemies. This little magnate would soon know all about the Sandman.

Once or twice, when the May breeze veered south so that it blew towards him, Hereward thought it carried the faint, confused sounds of an affray far-off. He felt irritable; he had long rehearsed his encounter with Zjelko, and he was unsure exactly how he had been diverted. The tender shoot of his feelings for Ceil had clouded the issues, along with Zjelko's claim to be doing someone else's work. Had the same instruction applied to Jacky's sister, Astolat? What did the children possess that made their abduction desirable? A just revenge required clarity; here were muddied waters and unexpected eddies.

Withdrawn in his thoughts he did not at first draw the correct conclusions from the two men who ran panting towards him, and, seeing him, stopped and scrambled through the hedge and away across a field. Further on a group squatting under some bushes withdrew hastily deeper into the cover of the thicket. There was a corridor of trees ahead and beyond it, over the shoulder of the ridge, the wide expanse of the common-lands. He was hastening along this avenue when its far end was blocked with figures, an unkempt crowd, some running, others trying to support comrades who hobbled jerkily or had to be supported. Again as they saw him men began scattering off the road but this time, he saw uneasily, several stayed to block his path. They had tight, shocked faces that shone with sweat. Blood clotted their clothes and forearms.

"What news?" asked Hereward, halting, and saw disbelief in the row of confronting faces. They exuded the hot-eyed menace of ill-treated dogs. Some of those who were slipping away halted and turned back. Hereward stared warily, as they began to edge round him in a crescent, but by the time they had nerved themselves for the onset there was no surprise left.

Thankful for the sword, which he had recently used to whittle wood, Hereward retreated coolly before a flurry of crowded, clumsy stabs and thrusts. Concentrated on the dangers closest he was sent staggering as a rock clattered against his helmet. The shouting voices in front of him became more vicious, but with them came another distant yell. Hereward saw brown and green jackets behind his attackers, and suddenly there was space around as the Companions' skirmishers jogged past, waving and grinning, shouting "All right?" at him.

Hereward reached up and felt the dent in his helmet. As he did so he remembered which helmet he was wearing and slipped it off and held it under his arm. Should he be an ally of the Matrix or not? The result of the battle could not be in doubt. The Matrix light troops were dispersing the stragglers and beaten remnants.

He walked along under the trees until he emerged on the brow of the wide green pastures sloping down to the town, pausing once to drop the helmet into a bush. Along the contour he was standing on was the aftermath of the struggle. It was not yet eleven in the morning but, as Hereward walked towards the wretched jetsam lying there as if abandoned on the hillside by some long ebbing, he could see the way it must have gone. Nowhere had the Matrix line broken. Only in its centre, where the wild column had charged up into it, were blue uniforms lying. Standing above them, still as boulders in the grass, were the bitter-faced picquets watching over their dead. Their eyes swivelled with Hereward as he walked quietly by but only when he stopped and looked back at a face he thought he knew was there a sound or movement. The greased click of a rifle bolt and a lifted muzzle directed him away so he went towards the shabby piles, like picked-over clothes at some wilted market, that formed the high-water mark of the river-folk's assault. Among and beneath the heaps there was movement, slow, reptilian. The wounded were many. A few men and women were picking their way through the cheerless scene, or kneeling pitifully to shed tears for someone. Whether this was how all adventures ended Hereward could only wonder.

Just ahead of him was a grave. It seemed a day for graves, though there was only as yet one here. Though Hereward did not know it the soil had closed over Rocco Barbella, his men's last tribute. Later they would build a cairn. He had been fat and his hair was going thin, he was fond of card-games and drinking red wine out of the bottle, but when they came up the slope, like wolves after a caribou, crashing through the swordsmen and into the bayonets, he had been there to meet them, to drink his own blood and to die like a marshal.

Hereward had come to a standstill now, as if he had realised the truth of the equation which states the higher the endeavour the greater the waste. Almost under his feet a head lolled sideways and the yellow hair fell off the discoloured face. He knew it at once under the bruises and the mud, indeed had been expecting to see the face somewhere in these piles. He slipped a hand inside the shirt and felt the heart beating. With so much blood it was hard to see Jacky's wounds clearly. There were cuts and stains in his shirt and a wound in the thigh, but the worst seemed in the throat, and the flies buzzed thickly there.

Hereward staggered as he got Jacky up cradled in his arms, and plodded down the hill. There would be water somewhere, he thought, water, bandages, shelter, maybe food. He was sweating, Jacky being heavier than he looked, and he tried to stick to the narrow paths the sheep had made where he was less likely to stumble. Reaching the monastery was out of the question, he thought.

Towards the bottom of the slope it suddenly occurred to him that down there, not far from the road leading to Hay, was the entrance to the tunnels in which he had hidden on the night after the play. Gritting his teeth he crossed the road and into the broken ground where stumps of brickwork poked forlornly through the grass. Before long he had found it, a twisting, narrow passage into a long masonry cavern in which the echoes and draughts told of further tunnels beyond. There in the dim light he saw the flat stone. On it was a casual charcoal scrawl, but he knew it at once for an 'H'.

XII

The water was holding its lisping conversation, a silver-green gurgle of syllables, even familiar phrases, repeated, though not quite in the same order, as in idle talk. Over the moss-smoothed stones, between grassy banks, the beck's soft inconseqential murmur went on, soothed by the ribbons of water-weed.

Martin had heard the murmuring on the day he was born, his mother praying as she laboured to be delivered of him that he should not be too provocative a parody of humanity. He had fished for the beck's minnows and rainbow sticklebacks as a tiny child, and had fallen into its coldness as unperturbed as the water-rats which dive in from the banks in their matted brown fur. Now he lay in one of his favourite places, his nose just above the water and his head poking out of a burrow which emerged in the stream's bank. With a big root of an ash-tree as its lintel the burrow was visible only from water-level, though occasional otters and dragonflies observed it. Martin could reach idly downwards and break off sprigs of watercress to chew on, and behind him hear the soft voices of his family. Soon it would be dark enough for them to come out in the twilight, and to find the green lanes that would let them run all through the night if they wanted and not be tired.

One lane in particular he favoured: it ran eastwards, over the long embankment, then turned off along the edge of a barley field, over a stile and into a field next to Shawpits Wood. The turf there was always smooth, full of dips and hummocks. The villagers called it Hollowhills Field, but, just as bees fly first to white clover, the Twisted Folk favoured one special hillock, towards which a buried cromlech drew them like a lodestone. Further on, the lane passed a disused church, sited where once other village people had felt the place answered when they spoke, and further still, the lane reached the horizon, where the mighty cathedral lifted like a stone beacon. Martin often ran hirpling along it, a four mile run, stopping at the subterranean maze on the edge of Ingastowe to check messages left for Hereward. Then he would run back along the grass on paths only his folk could see, and into his tunnel fresher than when he started. On his expeditions he rarely saw anyone, though hares and pheasants, fallow deer and frogs, let him pass through their world as if he went invisible. Sometimes he would lie high in the oak-tree that grew over the barrow-tomb, and once a grey wolf had halted and looked up at him with glowing topaz eyes. A big forester had followed, walking beneath the boughs, and had smiled and waved the comforting old sign of the crossed fingers that Martin liked. Martin dropped an acorn at his feet and the man put it into his pocket.

Now as Martin lay in the tunnel he felt his feet being tugged, and knew without asking that it was his younger sister wanting to go out or maybe just to come and eat watercress with him. So he wriggled under the root and, putting his arms elbow-deep in the water, pulled himself out into a frog-like crouch. Squatting there, his stunted trunk bringing his head lower than his knees, he knew he was one of the shapes that made the Daylight Folk so uneasy. His sister reached out her small hand and he put a bunch of watercress into it, and gave a warning whisper. Someone was approaching; he could feel footsteps, a plodding, heavy sort of walk. Martin stayed perfectly still, though to see him whoever was approaching would have to turn off the track, walk down the water's edge and then part the screening osier-beds. He heard a voice, so apparently there was more than one person. Then the uneven steps resumed until they reached the small bridge ten yards upstream. Martin saw two men silhouetted against the western sun, one leaning heavily on the other.

"This should be the place," said one, looking at an object in his hand. Martin quivered with excitement. He knew it was a map. After all he had drawn it, had indeed drawn several, each clearer than the one before, burning the lines into birch bark with a red-hot nail. He began moving up the stream to the bridge, habit making him stay concealed. He knew that voice, but who was the other one with long yellow hair? As he crouched where the water slid smooth and glassy the men were almost above his head.

A tired voice said, "What do we do now?" and Martin looked up as a bruised face glanced down over the bridge's wooden handrail. "God in heaven!" The man took a shaky backward step.

"Not God. Just me." The little man grinned. "Sorry to disappoint you." Hereward was smiling as Martin scrambled on to the bridge and met Jacky's fascinated stare.

"John Dorn, meet Martin, actor, wit and very brief acquaintance."

"Very brief friend, if you please," said Martin. "Oh, yes, we won't forget what you did in the fort." He gave a jerky bow to Hereward, and reached out and took Jacky's hand. "I think you'd better lie down. Come on," he continued with a wave. "I don't know how you're standing, anyway. It isn't often that you Daylight People get invited into the home of a twisted family, is it? Actually this is the first time I've heard of, at least in this part of the land."

The soft evening was drawing on. There was a field of turnips on one side of the track, on the other an unkempt pasture, ragged with gorse and bramble. The beck wound away under a tall ash then between leaning willows and the roots of young willow-herb, purple loosestrife and tall clumps of rushes. Down the arcade of the willows the gnats were dancing their drugged aerial pavane.

"Lead the way," said Hereward. He hoped it would not be far to Martin's home, though the nearest woodland looked half a mile away. Could he carry Jacky that distance?

The little man skipped across the bridge and, leaning over the bank, pointed downwards. "Use the front door."

Jacky and Hereward looked over and down. The bank was shored up with a wall of old flaking bricks, and halfway down it was the circular hole of what looked like the mouth of a piped conduit.

"It's ever so humble, but then we're ever such humble folk," said Martin. As he spoke a stifled giggle came from the green depths of the clubrushes and sedges behind them. "Come on," he added, hopping down the wall, to drop neatly on to a flat stone that rose just above the water.

"Can you do it?" asked Hereward, and Jacky nodded and reached his legs down to the stepping-stone.

"Steady," Martin advised as Jacky swayed on the stone. "Now you've got to crawl. Hereward, you come down and help when I'm in the opening." He slipped into the pipe as smoothly as a startled snake can disappear into a fissure.

It was dry, even dusty and went straight ahead for about twenty feet. From where it then turned came a faint wavering light. Gripping snags in the pipe to worm himself along on his stomach, Martin turned the corner, hearing Jacky behind him. The conduit went further on, but the light was coming up through a circular hole in its floor, and he lowered himself into a low candle-lit chamber. Jacky followed.

At once Martin was supporting him. "I didn't realise how bad your hurt was." There was no disguising the wetness on the shirt-cloth with which Hereward had bandaged the wounds in neck and cheek, nor the red stain where a marksman's ball had slammed into his thigh. "Here, lie down." He pointed to a low couch against the wall and Jacky thankfully collapsed onto it. Hereward had now entered through the shaft, and there was a hint of other presences in the chamber, candlelight gleaming on an eye and briefly silvering the paleness of a thin face. The whole room was screened with woven hangings. Where they joined there were rustlings as someone else peeped in. As their eyes adjusted Hereward and Jacky began to discern a busy tapestry crammed with figures. As the curtains moved the frieze took on a demure life.

Martin stepped through the hangings, then reappeared with a flurry; behind him, more hesitantly, came a grey-haired woman who, though a foot taller, seemed to be sheltering behind the strange little man. "My mother," he said. "Mother, this is Hereward the one-eyed, as I'm sure you realise, and this is a friend of his. And now, you two, what about something to eat and drink?" He and his mother deposited earthenware vessels on the woven reeds that carpeted the floor, and poured liquid into a glazed mug that he put into Jacky's hands. It was warm and a heady fragrance came off it of berries and poppies and leaves. The steam alone was relaxing and Jacky drank deeply.

The woman lifted his legs on to the couch and covered them with a blanket. "Eat later," she said. "Sleep now." From the pillow the young man from the river smiled up jauntily and she shook her head sadly. Martin guessed that she was wondering what purpose of fate had put herself and her children into such a stamp that she had to wait all her life for one of the Daylight People to smile at her. Behind her two more female faces appeared and looked down at Jacky though in his drowsiness and the dim light he did not notice them. Soon he was asleep.

Hours later Hereward awoke with a start. Momentarily there was nothing in his mind except the sensation of the feather mattress yielding beneath him and the blankets keeping him warm. Tiny, bright dust-specks thronged floating in a narrow shaft of sunlight but the room was otherwise dark. He shook his head as if to shake open a hatch and let his memories out. They began sidling into his consciousness. There in the lane was Ceil, dead. How short a time ago he had walked with her through a golden afternoon. He heard again the spade knocking the cross into the soil as the sun rose, saw the Matrix picquets stare at him over the dead. He wondered why it was that his actions spread, first as ripples, then as waves swamping people he never knew.

"Hereward," said a voice from the darkness.

"Jacky Dorn. Go back to sleep."

"I've been thinking about Zjelko. He got out of those cells under the keep, and I and my men were to blame. He owes you an eye, doesn't he?"

"Well, it's a longish story."

"I've got the time."

"You should get more sleep, Jacky."

"I can't sleep, and it would be interesting."

"All right. Since I've never told it all to anyone here it is: it will pass the time until the little man comes back." He began at the beginning and told how his desire for justice had driven him for almost a year, and how when the face-to-face moment had come his will had been diluted through a membrane of modifications. "Was Zjelko merely obeying another man's orders? Doing another's dirty work? As he said, Ceil was his wife and I hardly knew her. And she died to let me get away from the Matrix troops, out of a trap I'd put myself into. And I ran away. I was afraid." The voice grew lower, until the words were more like thoughts.

Jacky considered the questions. Eventually he said slowly: "You did what you had to do, as far as I can tell. You gave Zjelko one chance. Maybe she bought him one. The woman was woeful luck. I'm really sorry about that. I can't answer your questions except to tell you what my father told me. He said that when I was born I inherited two rights only, to be alive and to be a man, and the time to be angry is when others try to take them away. That's why you got angry about that girl, and why I got angry about Astolat. If you do nothing when someone hurts your sister or your friend, then you're less of a man. If you're too weak to be angry and act they've taken your manhood away earlier. It all comes down to that in the end."

"Does it? Oh, does it?" The voice came out of the gloom. "If only things were so simple." The speaker must have been listening concealed by the arras, or from within one of the tiny cells or chambers that led off the main room. She emerged clapping her hands in belittling applause. As she came through the sun-shaft the two men saw she moved with the litheness of the young, though her face was clouded by curtains of rust-red hair. "You, Tyr-Hereward, wouldn't agree with those idiot's remarks, I know, but you – " she turned the fullness of her derision on the flushing Jacky, " – what do you or your father know of rights? Your self-esteem gets dented and you feel angry. That's all. But what about the thousands of times when you've been the one crushing out the aspirations of others trying to be men and women? What does that make you?"

"I don't know what you mean." Jacky sounded bewildered and hurt. "Whose aspirations have I ever crushed?"

"Mine for one," she said. "Look around you. It's not uncomfortable, I suppose. But it's an animal's den, isn't it? An underground rat-hole for twisted rats, isn't it? Why don't you feel angry about that? Aren't we fit to walk in the daylight? We've had that right taken away by you and people like you. If it hadn't been for Tyr-Hereward my sister and I would have opened your wounds while you slept." Her husky voice became a venomous whisper: "Was there a cripple in your village, or someone dumb, or a hunchback? Was there?"

There had been, a hunchback boy, just the same age as Jacky, and he began to sweat as he thought of the jeering, the pursuits, the stones that had driven poor Oxback Willis away into the trees.The girl saw Jacky wince, although he didn't know he had rounded his shoulders. "Oh, the hunchback boy," she hissed. "Did you do anything to stop the others?"

"Go away, Kit, go away at once." Martin had suddenly appeared, and the authority in his voice was new to Hereward. "These are our guests and friends."

"Yes, I'm deformed too," she snarled, and leaning close pushed her narrow forearm down into Jacky's face. "Feel that, and be angry about it."

Martin's long spidery arm seized her shoulder before she could move further. "You disgrace us all. Apologise." He shook his sister sharply.

"Never." She slapped Martin's arm away and scowled.

Martin turned towards the others: "Hereward, forgive us. This is poor hospitality."

Before Hereward could speak she was contrite. "Oh, Hereward, my tonguc runs away with me. For you I say I am sorry. Just you." She pushed back her hair and he saw the pale intense face. "May you walk in the daylight," she said clearly to Jacky, and then as she passed Hereward: "No one can stop us now." Her voice was so low only Hereward could hear it and he felt the sudden pressure of her fingers on his sleeve as she passed, as if she were assuring herself that he was there in the flesh.

"My apologies," said Martin. "Lie back." He pushed Jacky gently backwards. "She eats herself up as flames do. How she's lasted this long I can't tell. But today's our special day, you see. It's probably the first time your people ever slept in one of our homes, at least in this valley, and that is a shock to her, and to me too. And there's something else you have to know before you're too harsh on us. It happened a few years ago now."

Martin hesitated, thinking back. It had been one of those days best left to corrode in the deeps of the memory, for the grapnels of words hauling it out scraped it to a painful brightness: Easter Sunday and the church bells ringing, the smell of charred meat and smoke from the fields as the cattle were burnt in piles, their carcases awash with disease, the land too dry all that winter and spring, the top-soil starting to blow like dust, the thick rain-clouds always rolling on past.

"The villagers were frantic. There was drought and the cattle-plague. Who knows where that came from? It was tempting to blame someone. We came out in the fields, to listen to the bells, as we often did. My father hurt himself climbing over a fence, and he must have tried to hide in a cowshed. I wasn't there so I'm not sure, but I think his leg was broken. They found him among the cows. There were still a few healthy ones." He told the story vaguely so it didn't hurt too much. Anyway the listeners wouldn't want to know how the family had searched and then in the moonlight seen the body, recognising the little bat hands, just wide enough for the nails to go through. "It turned out like this." He fetched a candle, lit it, and showed them one of the scenes sewn in the wall-tapestry. Jacky and Hereward gazed grimly at the figure stretched on the barn door. The detail was intricate, exact, achingly close. "Kitfox and Fleur sewed it." The sisters had been too young to remember, but he and his mother had taken the cadaver down and later his sisters had turned the family threnody into thread. Their father's long hair had been full of burs and goosegrass clung in the furry hands. They had even got that in their embroidery.

Suddenly and certainly Hereward took the candle and blew it out. He put an arm around Martin's bowed shoulders and clumsily patted the averted face, feeling it wet with tears.

At a chink in the curtains Fleur tugged at her mother and older sister. "Look!" she whispered. "You see. Tyr-Hereward understands."

"Of course," said Kit.

Martin lifted his head and smiled waterily at both men. "I'm all right now. I try not to think too much of the long-ago. It will fade."

"Why," asked Hereward, seeking an opportunity to change the subject, "do you call me Tyr-Hereward?"

Martin lit the candle again, and beckoned him to a corner of the room. The glow illuminated the trees, flowers and animals that climbed out of the frieze and into a story and curled back. Often it wasn't easy to distinguish between men and animals. The little man laid a forefinger on a figure. "There, that is Tyr." The figure had been sewn tall and straight with a bird on the shoulder, but what drew Hereward's gaze was the left eye-socket covered in a patch. "There he is again." The finger pointed out another scene. "And again."

"Did Kit sew those too?" Jacky almost sat up, curiosity offsetting his weakness.

"Those?" Martin laughed. "They were done by my grandmother's mother, maybe her mother too, and they were probably copying them. That is One-eyed Tyr who loved the Twilight Folk, all children and animals. One day he will lead us out under the sun and teach us not to be afraid. But there was a price. The Daylight People asked for an eye. Look on his shoulder. What is it?"

They looked at the scene and back at him blankly. "A bird," Hereward suggested.

Jacky, who had owned one once, called from his bed: "A hawk. I used to have one." The two sisters and their mother had slipped back into the room; stories drew all their people like moths to a lantern.

"What is it, Mother?" Martin didn't even look round.

"Tyr's white falcon, my son," she said softly.

"We knew it was you." Kit sounded triumphant. "We heard how you were angry about Adelie. Tyr in the story was very angry when little ones were hurt. Look at your bird. You keep his hood on and then he won't fly at mice and small birds. All the great stories are true stories."

Martin moved the candle and pointed to another scene.

"Now only the white falcon remains," Martin's mother replied. "Tyr was lost. He is supposed to come and help us, and he does, but then he disappears. All the great stories are sad stories."

"But that is all it is, a story," said Hereward. He could feel their minds weighing him.

"Yes. But they are real feelings inside the story: hopes that we cling to and fears that should not be let into the world. There was never an impossible story that was worth telling."

They stood in silence. All of them were in one way or another aware that their own lives were falling into tales. A name from among them might last, but to be the unsung foundations on which the heroes towered was a more likely outcome, those anonymous figures who were sometimes frail – 'And all that year the people were afraid' – sometimes enduring – 'We are the people, we have no truck with kings'. One tale's ending was another's beginning.

XIII

The Twisted Folk had come from miles around. They had run through the soft late afternoon to the Hollowhills Field, singly or in groups, from lonely hilltop spinney, from riverbank rush-bed, from abandoned croft. One big family had come from Lichgate Farm, where herons looked out of the crumbling window frames of mouldering upper storeys; no one else would live there because the damp, old apple-orchard was that eeriest of places, a graveyard from the bad times with the soil covering sadnesses beyond bearing.

The news of Hereward's presence drew them to the field to talk, to see him, and to drink together the thickening scents of evening with its promise of change. Infants dabbled at the pond's edge, young ones flirted together, leaving their initials in the smooth grey bark of the chestnuts, the older men and women greeted relations, exchanged news and smiled warily at Hereward. He too felt the field's attraction. Sloping, dimpled, odd-shaped, it had occasional oak and one or two lime trees that cast dark pools of inviting shade on the short turf. Beneath one was a green pond palely freckled with the tree's papery seeds; crested newts walked underwater on a sunken log.

He looked up at the cathedral on the horizon and wondered about the strange gathering. He kept inside him his reckoning with Zjelko, knowing that thinking upon it blew it, as if it were a slow-burning coal, into a red incandescence. It would be less simple than it might have been once, he thought, because these favours kept mounting up, and he felt now he owed something to Martin, and perhaps to this odd gallery that had gathered in the field, as difficult to see as brown moths are against tree bark.

Another favour revealed itself during the evening when a tall red-haired man came strolling into the field, joking with everyone he met. Hereward was surprised that one of the Daylight People should be accepted so openly, but more so when he discovered that Red Buckle considered himself one of the Twisted Folk. Then Buckle remarked casually that he was pleased Hereward had escaped from the locked church and that it had been a pleasure to hit the guard on the head. "Especially when it was Lew Jacques!" he said and laughed. When Hereward began to stammer his thanks Buckle shrugged and said that he and Martin had seen what had happened to the girl and it was the least he could have done. "Where's your sister this afternoon?" Buckle asked Kit. He was tartly informed that Fleur was playing nurses, that she was boiling up soup for an unwanted guest and that she was a silly girl, but he only laughed again.

A boy and girl from Hay came hand in hand through the field carrying a basket of mushrooms. They saw Hereward and stepped past him uncertainly, but he leaned against one of the oaks, wondering how a field that moments before had been full of life could look so empty, though Red Buckle waved cheerfully at the pair and made no attempt to avoid being seen.

"We've had a life-time of practice," said Kitfox in his ear. "Even the rabbits aren't as cautious as we are. They don't have to be. Courting couples won't bother them."

The village girl looked back twice as if she caught the flicker of a movement where none should be, but after that there were no disturbances until Martin beckoned. "Time for supper."

A group of figures headed off with Hereward tall among them. Only one man, swarthy, unkempt, battered as an uprooted tree stump, his skin the colour of earth, came above Hereward's shoulder. They made their way along a sunken lane, the hedges on either side meeting above their heads, the wild roses splashing the dusk with white rosettes. The church rang out the hour distantly and further away still it was echoed by the abbey's chime. The track sank deeper through banks of ferns and the group led Hereward into the green depths, crouched ever lower until the loamy smell told him they were underground.

"The badgers hollowed it out first," said one, "but we've used it for generations. It's always been my home." He gestured round a cavernous room walled and vaulted with mud bricks. From high in one corner came what sounded like the placid night-time buzzing of bees. "No good for honey, but they keep strangers away. I expect they lived here before us." Hereward saw a wicker bulge in the wall near the ceiling, and the man caught his glance. "Their nest opens outwards, of course, or we wouldn't be sitting here."

"Hornets," said Martin, and teeth glittered in grins round the circle, for all had suffered stings from the tetchy insects. "No daytime visitors."

"Why did we come here?" Hereward asked.

Eyes turned towards him thoughtfully. The question had been blunt, but the Twisted Folk were not displeased. It was a sign of a difference they expected. Tyr in the story was not content to do nothing.

Martin explained from his squat, grasshopper's crouch: "We are the family heads of all our people from the cathedral to the ferry. Beyond those places are other families, and more beyond them, and we keep in touch with some families that are further away than anyone can run in three days." He paused, looked around, caught the nods, and plunged into the tale. "A year and a half ago the Tyr-whisper came: that Tyr was somewhere near if only we could find him before he went away again. Twice in my life the Tyr-whisper has reached us, but the first time it was far, far away, and we could do nothing. This time the sign was here, close, and I was one of those asked to search, I and one from each of the other four families. There is only one way we can mix easily with the Daylight People. By custom we work with the travelling troupes." He paused for a moment. Always the same, the years going by like dandelion seeds on the wind and the hybrid and aberrant looked always to the world of entertainers. Several of those present had worked at one time in the troupes, drawn by a chance to see the Daylight world from within.

"I joined the company of Demetrius and we looked in and around Ingastowe for almost half a year. That is, Demetrius looked for Hereward, we for Tyr. Several times I thought I saw the sign, but was always mistaken. Then we turned back almost within sight of home, playing in the stone fortress. It seemed we had missed Tyr, missed our chance perhaps for generations, and then . . . They say you counted all people equal that morning in the fort prison, whatever their family."

It hadn't really been that, thought Hereward. It had been the red wetness of blood in his palm when he lifted it off the pain in his chest, and the sweat mingling with the blood. It had been sheer asperity that boils over rather than be coerced.

"What you did that morning," went on Martin, "and the mark of the eye, they were almost enough. Then there was Jacky, the white falcon, who hunts with you. It had to be you. Then you went away after our first meeting." Hereward recalled it well: the stricken face of the little troll in the cavern with his lordly black companion. "One cannot force Tyr, one can only find him and the rest is fate. For the first time we, the Twisted Folk of this part of Westermain, think we may have found him. Now we will follow and wait."

"How can I be the one you've been waiting for? I'm a man, not a legend, not someone out of a dream." Hereward shook his head in exasperation. "I don't understand any of this. It would be misleading you if I tried to put on this mantle. Anyway it wouldn't fit."

"If you don't try it on how can you know?" someone asked gently.

"For the same reason that you know who you are. I am not this Tyr. Surely I would know if I were."

"No," said Martin. "That may not be so, for you may still become Tyr. Can any man tell what he is to be in ten years time? Also you told me once how you could recall nothing of your past. May you not have been Tyr then and forgotten it?"

In Hereward's mind there was the village mill-house, the grindstones, the mealy smell and the white dust, and he was glad of them, but he accepted that his forgotten past was trapped in an impenetrable black monolith, as lost as if it had never been. He rubbed his forehead and pushed back his hair. "I can't pretend to be someone I'm not. You wouldn't want that, anyway."

Hereward hated this. The evening in the field had been pleasant; he liked their shy company and the ill-made bodies were becoming more familiar. Next to him the lumbering hulk of a man heaved a deep sigh, but nobody spoke. The hornets rustled in their skep. "I'd better go," he said wearily. He would have been grateful for advice. Unthinkingly his hand went to his eye; one part of the future, at least, awaited him

Kitfox's voice came from outside the entrance: "Have you men finished your debate?" Hereward saw Martin pull down the corners of his mouth and roll his frog-eyes.

"Yes. Come in, please," called Jesse, the tall grey man, and in came the families, soft-flowing as the dog-rose scents, whispering against the walls, leaning together holding hands, children on mothers' laps. Jesse's family brought out cheeses and honey and rye bread, which no one would touch until the oldest there had chosen a morsel, and Hereward had been pressed into taking some. He felt rather than saw their presence around him, as their dark, warm, sweet interdependence pervades the bees clustered in their hive. Their thoughts folded him round, soothing and child-like in their trust. He almost dozed, pondering the riddle of Tyr; irked by it, yet not feeling committed to any action. He wondered how this figure, if he ever came, could possibly bring the sunlit lives these deformed people were hoping for.

And before long story-telling began around him. Sometimes it was almost news, like the story of the battle on the High Common and the dead marshal who lay up there, sometimes gossip like the story of the girl who left blackberries and walnuts where one of the young foresters would find them, and Jesse's oldest daughter blushed and shrank among her friends as it was told. Yet gradually the stories winnowed away down to the ones sealed into unalterable words: the gentle fable of the swallows in winter; the tale the players loved to tell of indomitable Fat Jack Laughter who never forgot the green fields; and the terrible shiny legend of Baldwin.

". . . and when Baldwin held the gift in his hand the ice-diamonds that the Queen had sent him to seize from the stars had all melted away and gone. 'Go and try again,' said the Queen, kissing him, and then Baldwin reached out and touched her face, and the melting water ran down her cheeks in salty drops and she was icy cold. 'Take care,' said Baldwin. 'This time I brought tears, what may I not bring next time?'"

There was an uneasy silence for everyone knew the second and third journeys of Baldwin well enough; they touched too nearly on their own crookednesses and blemishes. Martin and Jesse and the stump-like man and the brothers from Lichgate Farm could feel thoughts not their own creaking and shaping themselves in their heads – the odyssey of Baldwin, and his return with the spores, when he held out his charred wrists and the hands had gone. Most would have preferred the saga to stop before reaching this point, even though the story was imprinted on the dancing atoms of their thoughts.

"It's a long way," said one of the brothers from the lonely farm. "Further than a heron could fly in a month."

"Where?" Hereward was still not at ease having his thoughts read.

"Only the Matrix can tell you about the children."

"You shouldn't go on your own," added Martin.

"I'm not even sure what it's called," Hereward muttered to himself.

"The city of Limber," said a voice.

"All roads lead to Limber," said another.

"And none to Regret."

Pause, slightly, because the litany requires it, then all together, softly, even the little ones: "You find your own way there."

This time the silence seemed palpable. The next words took a lot of saying. They came at last, thick and stuttering, from the big gnarled man, his tongue clicking in his roofless mouth: "Is Tyr g-going?"

There was a wail from one of the walls where the women sat, "Ai-aiee, stay, Tyr!" and others echoed it, "Stay, Tyr, stay!"

Hereward glanced at the entrance and back at the gathering. He tried to catch Martin's eye but the little man looked away. A baby had crawled between Hereward's feet and he tried carefully to extricate his foot. Eventually he picked the baby up and saw hope hesitating on the faces around. The mother made a roo-cooing like a dove. The prospect of the city of Limber was wavering when another voice went through the room like an icy draught.

"Leave him alone," said Kitfox. "Let him be. You are selfish, all of you. This is Tyr. If he wishes to go to Limber then that is best. He is not just our Tyr. He belongs to all the children of Baldwin, to those who live on the further side of Limber just as much as to us. He must soften the wrath that the heart of the Matrix bears for us. And where is their heart? In their great city, of course."

She stamped her foot and flung back her hair, and her words rang in the room. Except for what the black glove concealed she was, along with her younger sister, the fairest of the fair, yet ever, thought Martin, unwavering in her was her cardinal passion, the deliverance of the Twisted Folk. He was inordinately proud of her. "Kit – " he began, sensing there was more.

"Hush." She wanted no elder brother's admonishments. "Excuse me, Tyr-Hereward," she continued decorously, and scowled at her brother's sudden smile. "You are right to go to the city of Limber, I am sure of that, but as Jesse says, it is far, far away. It must be easy to find, I suppose, as all roads lead there, but that is not to say the roads are easy to travel. Have I not heard also that you are outlawed where the Matrix is concerned? You must not attempt this alone. None of us has been out of this land and certainly never over the sea where Limber lies. So, as everyone is equally inexperienced and as I was the first to suggest it, I shall accompany you." The last few words were said quickly and with a defiant lift of the chin as if to keep her head above the surface of the babble that rose round her.

Eventually it was grey Jesse who stilled them. "We all admire your spirit. But you should ask Tyr-Hereward first, I think."

"You want me to come, Tyr, don't you?" she said, staring at him with such intensity that he was unable at once to say 'No'.

He was interrupted in his search for mollifying words by her brother. "You cannot go. I must forbid you. It would be a hard journey for anyone and a thousand times more so for one of our women."

"Do not bully me," she said. "I shall go if Tyr wants me."

"I forbid it," Martin repeated quietly. "As you would do in my place." Turning round he went on: "Hereward, our friend, we wish that you should do whatever is your will, but ask if one of us may go with you. Admittedly we are a small people, perhaps only good for acting, but it is time we spoke out of our own mouths. Will you choose one companion from us?"

Hereward had been thinking quickly for he sensed that where Kitfox went, with her startling grace and turbulent temper, crises would follow, and yet was vexed that he could only disappoint these trusting, haunted people who had mistaken him for this long-awaited Tyr. His first instinct was to refuse, but then he pointed wordlessly at Martin. He couldn't bring himself to look at Kit but he heard her gasp and the door clatter open as she plunged into the night.

XIV

The grey wolf sat at the back of the chantry and listened to the singing. It was not the only creature there. Ants laboured across the tiled floor and butterflies opened their wings languorously on the gratings of the windows. The singing voices floated through from the main choir-stalls. George Littler scratched the wolf's head, tickling its ears, rubbing its neck under the coarse ruff of hair. He had said his prayers as best he knew. He had prayed for his trees, feeling them soothed by the rain, sensing their capillaries lifting the amber sap, encouraging the filaments of root hairs to dissolve their way into the limestone's minerals – yet gently, for the limestone too was good and in some other time the tiny sea-creatures' surrendered lives had made the stone. What else would foresters pray for?

The chantry was full of flowers, with carved leaves and twigs curling out of the wooden crucifix. It was one of Littler's favourite places. Like all of the monastery it lay just right, aligned on the beck, sheltering beneath the shallow ridge. It focused his prayers, concentrated them. It reached backward into time – his wooden bench was smooth with use – and forward too, prayer by its nature looks forward.

Littler knew that, by ancient custom, candle compline was said in this small room just after night-fall, lit only by its altar lights, so that anyone might attend, Twisted or not. Some years ago there had been objections but Abbot Huw's predecessor had met at the door the jeering crowd pushing it open and said he was holding a service for those who cared to worship, so whoever wished to make a mockery of the service should step forward. Abbot Daniel was built like a bear, and on cold nights, as that one was, the heavy old Matrix greatcoat that he wore over his surplice hung on him like a pelt. No voice was raised against him in the stillness. The occasion had become a story, the villagers' favoured way of recalling past events.

Ragnar snuffled and clicked his claws on the stone, for someone else was coming in. There were two. They knelt at the front, right on the altar steps. A child and his mother, thought Littler. Both looked round at the door and the woman beckoned. Another figure joined them, and Littler felt a prick of surprise. After the months Hereward had spent at his cabin he would recognise him anywhere. He hadn't seen him since February but had heard rumours of his doings; his presence like low cloud did not disperse easily. He looked the same still, walking carefully as if restraining himself, his pale face swivelling steadily to bring his good eye round. Ragnar whined quietly and began to wriggle forward on his belly. There were only five rows of seats so by the time Hereward had knelt next to the woman the wolf had reached him. Littler, too, came forward quietly and knelt on the animal's other side, smiling as he heard Hereward's mock-stern voice: "Ragnar, put your tongue in."

For a time there was only the sound of the silvery voices:

We see your print in seed and rain,
You, Lord, the end we'll never know;
You are the light, the dark, the pain,
You are the way we have to go.

And side by side, laborious, slow,
There come the trees, the grass, the stone;
How could we leave them, Lord, you know
You are no way to walk alone.

George Littler had been waiting for that verse. "There come the trees, the grass, the stone," he sang quietly to himself. It was his favourite hymn. Looking sideways he saw to his surprise that it was no child beyond the woman; the sallow, seamed face and round frog-eyes had seen as many years as himself, he thought. This was a bold spirit, to be out like this at midday, though this chantry was the likeliest place in the village to find one of his people.

The air was still and drowsy, and before long even the hymns died away. Littler could only wonder what had brought this odd trio to the Chapel. The small man and the woman knelt silently, foreheads pressed on the cool wood of the altar-rail, holding their hopes in their minds, shaping and refining them, giving them intensity, as one does in prayer. Finally their prayers were disposed and presented and, for Martin and Kit, quite unchanged. They had been offered up before, and were like golden coins in a poor man's purse, much-inspected and satisfactory. Hereward's prayer was torpid in him, like a bubble suspended in tar; he felt it inappropriate, sulphurous in this cool sanctuary, yet not completely out of place for revenge is much entwined with justice and often with an ardent love.

A quick glow of pleasure warmed Hereward, for he liked Littler. The forester was so quiet, yet reassuring, his shoulders wide inside the old leather jacket, the smile gentle on the tanned face, the big hands on the altar-rail stained and grained with woodland colours. The four walked outside in a group and stood on the edge of the stone culvert along which the monks had here neatly channelled the beck.

"Well, Orr."

Hereward smiled, knowing the other's slow conversation. "Well, George, it didn't turn out quite as I hoped. Though I found out my real name. Hereward – I quite like it."

"I did hear something of your goings-on."

"Oh," said Hereward dubiously.

"I heard about dressing up as soldiers." Littler puffed out his cheeks. "My word, clever! And I took you for a boar-pig in the bracken, all snarl and sharp tushes."

They both laughed softly, and Littler, catching the sardonic upward smile at his elbow, asked, "Who's your friend?"

Martin sniffed noisily. "Good day, George Greenwood." He grinned as the forester looked hard at him, and held out an acorn on the palm of his hand.

Littler took it and chuckled. "Which family are you? Lichgate Farm? Bracken Hill? Shawpits? Or maybe Sheepwash Bend?"

Martin nodded at the last name. He was mildly surprised at how many of the families Littler knew. He felt a poke in his ribs from Kit. Her face was averted, her fox-red hair bundled under a drab shawl. Her disapproval was almost tangible. Hereward, seeing her gesture, assured her that George was a good friend, but she was silent and scowled at the ground. "Have you anywhere to stay?" asked the forester. "The bunk's still there."

"Tyr is staying with us." Kit sounded so firm that Littler raised his eyebrows and whistled so that Ragnar the wolf got up and looked about. "We're going to Limber," she added abruptly. The statement plunged awkwardly into their midst, rather as an elm tree will, on the calmest day, dangerously discard a high branch. Her determination was no less clear then Hereward's.

"You are going home," said Martin firmly, though he looked hopefully round for support.

"Limber? Is this an Orr-Hereward plan?"

"I suppose so. And not Orr any more, thanks."

"You'll need all your prayers. What chance do you give yourself of getting there?"

"Hard to say."

"All this," Littler's gesture encompassed the past, "is still on account of what happened that day?" When Hereward nodded he sighed. "You know I've always felt bad about that day. If I hadn't interfered you would still have your eye. I should have kept out of your affairs."

"No. You did what you had to do."

"Maybe. That doesn't make it any different. Doing what you think best at the time is all right at that moment . . ." Littler struggled with the intractability of words. "But you're responsible for afterwards too. Like with trees," – relieved to be on familiar ground – "sometimes it's best to cut one down, but then you don't just forget it. You plant another. It's a matter of balance."

"Was that why you looked after me last winter?"

"Partly, I suppose, but that wasn't much. You might reach Limber, though having your acorn-friend here makes it hard, and if you take her . . ." He was unsure about the girl and her kinships, but there was a feral look there, the features palely sharp-drawn, hollowed under the cheek-bones. Then she stared, disturbingly, full at him. She pulled back the shawl to see him better, pinning it under her black glove, flaunting at him the too-narrow shape inside its dark fabric. "Well," he went on, knowing now, "with her you'll have to fight your way through every village you pass once they see that glove, and – "

"I only am going of my people." Martin interrupted, his voice very clear. He seemed taller.

"Hmm, you might manage, come to that. But, Hereward, somewhere you'll need help, and who better than one of the tree-guild? I'll always have friends along the way."

There was quiet, save for the beck sliding and gurgling among mosses and the skylarks singing like angels overhead. Instinct urged Hereward to travel alone, but deep in his mind lay the long shadow of Limber. "If you really want to come," he said, "then I'm glad." Now there were two strands of friendship entangled round his future. At first he would stride along, and they would be light as cobwebs. He gave it no real thought, calcined by his purpose: finding the way to Limber would not be hard, as land-roads and sea-lanes alike led there, its imagined domed and towered skyline already silhouetted on the horizon.

The late morning was so warm and complaisant that any plan seemed good. So they would walk to the hidden home beneath the stream-bank of Sheepwash Bend, say their farewells, and set out along the road to the coast. Unfortunately they passed Lew Jacques who gestured crudely at Kit and shouted after them that any twisters found near Hay would get hurt. Hereward started to turn back but George held his arm. "Don't waste your time with him," he said. Kit smiled to herself: passion was always easier to glimpse than thought, and she liked the smokiness in Hereward's mind. It encouraged her hopes of the wrath of Tyr rising and the changes it might bring.

*

Next morning saw them on the road. It was a cool grey day, good for walking. By midday they had left Ingastowe behind them, the cathedral quietly sinking in the horizon's haze. Now they were on the plateau to the north, whereas Hay village had looked up at the cathedral from its valley to the south-east. Hereward found its different silhouette had whispered words to him that he could not quite catch.

They passed the place where Hereward and Ceil had met Janitza crawling towards them, and later the farm where Zjelko and his small force had been besieged. Hereward was more at ease now that they were moving and he told the others the story of that night.

The road was straight and lay along the edge of a plateau. Tracks led off down the escarpment to where settlements crouched on the spring-line. The limestone springs gave water clearer and cooler than rain, George Littler told them. The road was generally empty, but once they passed a small trading caravan coming inland from the sea. "Traders, Hereward," said Martin. "They don't seem to mind us Twisted Folk." He told the other more of the traders: they were inveterate news-carriers; they had no guild because gold or barter was for everyone. "Same as actors," he added.

Later in the afternoon they began to overhaul another caravan. It consisted of a dozen oxen, panniered, their backs draped in bright blankets, their carts rattling and swaying. From beneath the dusty hooded canopies babies looked out, and behind ran thin dogs that yelped as Ragnar-wolf loped in from the roadside bushes through which he had been prowling. "Wolves will walk alongside us," said Littler, "but they'll follow at no one's heels."

The traders' looked askance at the wolf but their faces stayed expressionless. Their jackets had curled sheep's wool collars, the backs patterned with coloured beads and dyed designs. They reminded Hereward of Jacky; they had his restlessness, some of his agility. They were less bluff, not so tied to the soil as most of the people he recalled encountering. He wondered about Jacky lying in Martin's dark chamber like a broken-winged hawk. Their parting had not been easy, and Martin in particular felt anxious. He had watched the young man's gaze go to Kit as if he had come through the desert and she was cool clear water, though for her part continual biting gibes were all she had offered him.

The traders did not welcome questions about themselves, but were always happy to talk about business. George Littler inquired about their wares, this being mannerly. Merchandise could provide conversation for weeks on end. Malt, hides, wax, wool and rope – usual enough going north, they said. The other way, salt – this was called the Old Salt Road, wasn't it? – brought south from the coastal salt-pans ahead of them. Then there was fish and, if you were lucky, sea-things, silk from far away, or ivory, or amber. And the Matrix asking for toll-money, whenever honest people tried to set up their stalls at a market. Times were hard. Perhaps times had always been hard though, or were they just getting old? The tanned faces smiled slightly at their new company. Who ever saw an old trader? they said. Old men didn't walk twenty miles every day in sun, rain and snow.

As evening approached the caravan halted where pine-trees straggled on a sandy heath and turned off the road. "Do you use the same stopping-places?" Littler inquired.

"Depending on the season, yes," said one. "Good weather now, so we sleep out, and sand's comfortable to sleep on. Pine-wood burns well too."

"Plenty of rabbits," added another.

Supper that night was rabbit, caught by the traders and shared with the three travellers. George put mushrooms and wild celery into the pot, while Martin, during the afternoon, had picked a big bunch of watercress. The traders ended supper by boiling a can of water into which they dropped black flakes or leaves from a small wooden chest which was then locked and put away carefully in a cart.

"Tea," said George. "When did I last see that?"

"Would you like some?" asked Gildas, who from the others' slight deference appeared to act as spokesman. He poured the liquid into their mugs. The scent and flavour stirred distant thoughts in Hereward's mind. Somewhere once he had lifted a delicate flowered cup, while round him gentle voices had . . . Then he was back in the ring of firelight, holding a thick mug, one of a circle of figures with beyond them the shadowy outline of tethered animals.

"Only traders seem to drink this now," said Gildas. "It's a sort of custom. I couldn't guess how old our tea-box is."

Relaxed by the mild drug it was easy to talk. "Have you ever been over the seas?" asked Hereward. Somewhere ahead of him, he knew, were the grey waves.

Gildas smiled reflectively. "Yes. Three or four times. Always to the same place."

"High Altai." Another voice.

"That's where we get the tea," added another.

"You can buy or sell anything there." It was as if the mere mention of High Altai started all the traders talking. After all, they told the three travellers, where else would a trader want to go but the great free port lying where two oceans mingled, its southern hinterland the strange lands beyond The Great Dessication, across which the camel trains brought to High Altai exotic goods to sell. Far out at the fringe of the Matrix's suzerainty, at the tip of a rugged peninsula, they said, it was difficult to reach except by sea and it was a law unto itself, a huge half-fair, half-warehouse, a by-word for the unaccountable and outlandish.

"Does it lie on the way to Limber?" Hereward queried.

"It does indeed," replied Gildas. "By sea there is no other way except past Altai. Though I doubt if it's the safest."

There was a rueful laugh. The seas east of High Altai were notorious for predators, they explained. Honest men sailed there in strong convoys. "All the same," the traders agreed, "once you get your stuff ashore there it's safe and likely to fetch a fair price."

"Could we find a ship sailing there?" Hereward asked.

"Maybe." Gildas sounded very doubtful. "Only maybe. Remember it's a long way from here, and the Matrix doesn't like us traders much and it likes big ships less. You couldn't sail there in a coaster; we wait for a whisper of one of the sea-gipsies' carracks. One came a week ago, I hear, so there may not be another for months."

"Sea-cargoes are for young men," said someone. "We've got families. Salt's a good steady living."

"You're welcome to come with us up to the salt-pans," Gildas remarked. "After that you might try Old Man Dorn. If you can get him to speak."

The three travellers exchanged quick glances.

"Would he be the father of Jacky Dorn?" asked Hereward.

"The one who died in battle? Yes. And we saw his sister not long ago. The old man's supposed to be about as tough and stubborn as flint, but let's see how he takes this news."

"Was she all right?"

"More or less," said Gildas. "Except she was with a Matrix patrol and they certainly weren't going anywhere near the estuary."

"No, they wouldn't be." Hereward's voice was calm, though several faces glanced up suddenly as if distant lightning had flickered. "One more victory for the big people, one more defeat for small people."

"Sometimes they forget small people have long memories," George Littler said softly.

"And good friends," added Martin.

Gildas lifted his mug of tea. "Here's to little people!" His voice echoed away among the moths and shadows.

Hereward felt a nudge at his elbow and Martin whispered: "We ought to send this news to Jacky, I think."

"Yes, we must. Perhaps our friends here can pass a message on to traders going back towards Ingastowe."

Gildas nodded agreement but Martin shook his head. "I'll send the message. I must pay for myself on this journey." He rose and disappeared among the clumps of broom. Quietly the traders watched him go.

"That piece of news won't take long," murmured one of them. The others nodded.

"Not so many of the Twisted Folk nowadays," said someone. "These sandy lands were full of them once. Easy to burrow into, I suppose, and no one ever wants to plough here."

"What is the story of the Twisted Folk?" asked Hereward. It was a question which had lain long in his mind. He thought suddenly of Kitfox and Jesse and of how they believed he was in some way their emissary, Tyr the One-eyed.

"Probably I know no more than you," replied Gildas. "All I can say is that they haven't always been with us, or so it seems, for some say they came later, though always persecuted and in hiding. Sometimes – like your friend – they resemble us in many ways, sometimes they are more like misbegotten monsters. Those they keep hidden, of course, though I believe there aren't so many born like that as there were once."

"You can find big gatherings of them sometimes," one of the traders added. "Hundreds and thousands of Twisted Folk live around the Glassy Plains; a bad place that, not many trees grow there." George grew sombre at the thought.

"They're different in themselves too. Magical people some of them," went on Gildas. "Thought-readers and diviners, shamans, we don't usually have much to do with them though."

"Glass," said someone across the fire, "they like objects made of glass: lanterns, lamps and little sharp tools, knives, scissors, needles. And specially clocks and watches."

"Birds," said another voice, "song-birds, hawking birds. They like to trade for them."

"They're firm believers too," went on Gildas. "When the Old People burnt God it says in the story that the Twisted Folk tried to put out the flames with their hands. Remember Baldwin?"

Hereward did remember hearing of Baldwin, the story still glowing in his mind: Baldwin, his hands charred when he brought back the bright key that unlocked the stars.

"What do they trade with?" asked Littler.

"It depends where they live," answered Gildas. "We sometimes get this." He reached behind him to unbuckle a pack and passed across a stone, frozen florets of lilac in white.

"Chalcedony," said Martin. "Lovely. Where did you get it?" No one had seen him emerge from the bushes but he was there.

"Miles away and years ago," said Gildas. "Swapped it for my wife."

There was a stir and rueful laughter where the women sat. "Poor Gildas," said one of them.

"No life for a woman, travelling the roads. I expect she's found a nice fat butcher or baker by now."

That night Hereward lay awake looking upward at the pines shrugging themselves in the wind; the rosiny air was full of their soft colloquy.

"Jacky will know in the morning," came Martin's voice. "It took a while to find one of the green lanes, but then I only had to wait. I said that Tyr wished to send news! So that will make it travel faster."

"I wish you'd forget this Tyr business."

"How can I?"

"Well," muttered Hereward, "what if we meet Tyr himself on the way? He won't be pleased that I'm pretending to be him."

"Let me worry about that."

There was the sound of faint laughter. "It's not funny."

"No," said Martin. "I know. Sleep well." Hereward rolled on to his side so that he could see the little man. Chasing dreams, he thought, almost everyone's hand against him, looks like half a frog, and still he's laughing. What am I worrying about?

"Goodnight, Martin. My thanks for sending the message."

XV

George Littler and Hereward took turns staring through the iron grille. By standing on the fixed wooden lockers that lined the room they could just see out. Outside, the sunlight was dazzling, the burning white light of a hot country's sun.

They heard the bellowing roar of a huge crowd. The noise was nothing new to them. Before today it had been intimidating and fascinating, like hearing from a safe distance a huge beast of prey roar in its hunting; now it pounded them with the weight of a cataract. On other days the noise would have come over the city to the wall; then every man there would turn and look across the fringed palm-trees and the fig-trees in courtyards and the pink and purple bougainvilleas that scrambled over white garden-walls, looking, eyes shaded, to where in the city's centre loomed the sand-coloured ziggurat they called the Drome. When the Drome spoke workers on the wall and foremen alike paused to listen. It had many voices, impatience, rapacity, implacability, rancour, even admiration – but none were gentle or laughter-loving.

You walked out of the Drome a free man or they put your body in a pit somewhere. So it was said on the wall, anyway. Through the bars George and Hereward had watched the sailor from the Big Grey River walk slowly away from them along a roofless passage towards the raked sand of the arena, until the brick quoins hid him from view. As he had left, the door of the room had been thumped back into place. The roar swelled again, battering round them, and they guessed that the crowd had seen the big seaman emerge from the tunnel into sunlight. The din slackened for a few moments, enough for them to hear drums throbbing, and now, thought Hereward, Rigger must be looking at the black square of the tunnel on the opposite side of the arena and wondering and praying hard. Every packed tier would be watching. Then the roar exploded, though loaded with a sort of droning ululation that the Drome spectators used to show their disapproval. In the room they saw the guard, ignoring them, standing with his back pressed to the bolted door, arms out at either side as if to barricade it with his body.

George, his face shocked white, was shaking his head as if a clawed and frantic creature were trapped inside his skull. Glistening sweat ran out of his hair, making his skin a mask. Hereward felt something so cold crawl into his mind that he gripped the forester's bare arm to remind himself of the warmth of flesh; he kept his eye on the barred grating because whatever it was would suck all the light out of the world if he didn't. But he pressed the intrusion down in his head and put honey-bees and daisies and Ceil's blue gaze around it.

So this is how it is, he thought, even in here safe behind that door it hurts like they said it would. What is it like for Rigger, out on the sand, looking in its face? Outside even the drums had faltered, though the noise was starting to build up again, now shriller, underpinning screams, hysteria inflating itself. All right for them to scream, high up on the marble terraces with cool drinks and shady awnings, what about us with it only a few steps beyond that door? But anger was feeding into him, and he felt the emptiness quail, the thing that, like a lump of misery, sat dumbly in his mind. He snarled at the impatience that had brought him into this room that smelled of death, and the fury sent him striding to the door, where the guard moved aside appalled, never having known anyone force his way out though many outside had tried to get back in. Hereward dragged out the heavy wooden bolt, shoved it in his belt, and opened the door.

Outside it was hot, stiflingly hot, and the clamour was frightening, an inchoate dementia. Hereward ran along the passage towards the noise. The reptilian coldness in his head was swelling, but he put his hand round Ceil's slim fingers in his mind and never wavered in his stride. Suddenly he was in the great, walled, sand-floored pit held in an inverted cone that men meant when they spoke of the Drome. Above him the smooth walls stretched, then the watching tiers of people, their heads like the sand-grains that make the sloping sides of the ant-lion's trap – and to Hereward as meaningless and distant as is the sand to the ant when it turns to face the ant-lion's jaws coming out of the floor. With the sun overhead there were no shadows, and the colours were glaring greys and harsh yellows.

The moment before his emergence into the arena the crowd-noise had climbed again; now it was a howl and he feared the worst. Then he saw what grimly he had expected: the man from the cold estuary was lying face down in the sand. Often men ran for the walls in scrabbling circles, like the poor ants and beetles, but Rigger must have stood and waited, and now he was lying in the hot sand at the feet of the hulking figure.

Most of the watchers had seen Hereward by now, and a new note infused the noise, bringing the figure's stare round searching for him. His head felt invaded, violated, as if another existence were in there with him, relegating him into a passive corner. He fought the hallucination back, and now he knew that the creature in front of him was an Unman. Night after night when work ended they had talked of the beast but seeing it was different. It was an enormous, lurching humanoid with pale lashless eyes in a face that twisted and worked, its tangled hair like left-over straw. The sand and dust swirled up around its feet so that it seemed to bring a restless dry wind.

Hereward shook his head to clear it of the howling images jetting out from the Unman, not discrete but a broadcast of its own condition.

Briefly and contemptuously it acknowledged Hereward as 'you', and when he came closer threw at him a mesh of its stinking, necrotic hopelessness to halt him in his stride. But Hereward called up his rune and her laughter was still proof against the thing. Then the Unman turned and bent over the sailor, reaching down to throttle him, knowing that in order to go back through the bolted doors and sleep, eat, drink and lie in its feculence, it must fight to the death. Somewhere in its fog of images a chance osmosis gave Hereward a hint of a name and he called out in a voice which carried across the arena to its furthest tier: "Lokietok! Turn around, Lokietok!"

Blue. Dancing, limpid, glittering blueness dripped off the bows in ropes of bubbles and lay beneath them in glassy swells inside which fish hung suspended as if in cobalt. Cloudless above them stretched a blue canopy. The very air they breathed was blue, and the light so clear that George Littler felt he could see for a hundred miles and more. He seemed too near to the sun, exposed in this empty warmth where all the horizons were looking at him. His woodcraft was nothing here, yet he thought that for all its perilous openness, its watery convexes restless beneath the keel, it was beautiful, this southern ocean.

It had come upon them suddenly, the blues they moved through and the violet depths over which they floated, far different from the grey cloud-cover under which they had embarked from a weed-hung jetty in chill thin rain. As Gildas had suggested they had sought the aid of Jacky's father. Rheumatic and bitter he now rarely left his house save for melancholy visits to Thorsten the sluicekeeper. The old man listened head-down to their story, lifting his gaze coldly only when his children were mentioned. Three days later they had seen him standing in the rain at the jetty's end, staring after them as they departed. As they rounded Skua Point the tide was gurgling up the deep, black creeks that fissured the mile-wide foreshore, then galloping across the flat mud and sand faster than a man can run. A lone fisherman, pulling an occasional grey flounder out of the turbid water had watched them go.

*

Rigger tried to remember what he was doing face down in this sand that grated dustily between his teeth. All he could think of at first was the voyage, that sea-journey that the mariners had thought of as a holiday. His head ached and his hand came up to feel a bruise swelling. Then understanding began to return, for the big feet, the legs like columns that stood within inches of his eyes, belonged to the Unman, the terror that he had been pitched against in single combat. More, he thought, a death-sentence than any sort of combat. How do you fight an Unman? It simply knew too much, and, worse, its mind mirrored you the pits into which it was condemned to stare: knowing no one would weep when it died; merely existing, isolated from time before or time after. An ineffable loneliness had poisoned everything for it.

Then the nightmares focused elsewhere. Rigger looked up dizzily and retched as the swirling dementia touched him again, for the Unman had noticed him move. Then he realised why this respite had come, for he saw Hereward poised in front of the huge creature, and with that look which so often set him apart. There was a charged and quivering intensity about him – the forces of the Unman were indeed besetting him, but he had neither run nor been frozen immobile. As the sailor watched, Hereward edged in closer. As he did so Lokietok swayed, like an enormous snake poised erect on its coils, watching for an opening to strike.

The crowd was quieter now, fascinated by what was happening and sensing that the Drome's operations had miscarried. There were two factions in the crowd, though only one was at all vocal. These were the warrior-people of El Daro. They called themselves simply the Daroi, the Men. They had overrun High Altai several months earlier, ending its centuries-old history as the emporium for two continents. The remnants of the merchant population sometimes went to the Drome but only in hope to see their overlords die. Naturally they had to watch quietly.

If only we had known, thought the crew of the *Swan* and their passengers, as they had thought again and again over the last half-year. But they had only known what Gildas the trader had said, that the quickest way to Limber lay past High Altai, and no one had conceived of the coming and the conquests of the Men.

The *Swan* was the pick of the Dorn ships, most of the sailors were veterans of a score of fishing seasons out in the deeps, and Dorn's sister's son, Lars Gustafsson, was the captain. When they were well out to sea he had handed a leather bag to Hereward. It was heavy with silver and ivory counters, both good Matrix currency. For the crew this had been one feast day after another, with no trawls to be dragged achingly over the sides, no ice to be chipped off the rigging, only this hot sun dazzling them as they sailed through the unknown to where voyagers said High Altai would lift over the eastern horizon if you went south till the butter melted and then three days due east. And eventually they had seen it, the chalk-grey peak of High Altai like an upright tusk, the thousand-foot-high sides smoothed and plastered to run the rainwater into its cool hidden reservoirs, and behind the peak the peninsula stretching, its lion-brown ranges of hills rising to the edge of the Mesa far beyond. As they had drawn nearer they had made out white cubes of buildings that rose up the peak's sides.

Hereward had noticed the captain's eyes narrow as he first stared at the city, then lifted a stumpy black telescope and focused it carefully. "Turn her, Rigger. Due north," he had said quietly, nodding his confirmation as the helmsman glanced across.

"Why are we turning away?" George Littler had asked.

"Just a feeling," said Gustafsson. "Lots of galleys in the harbour. Don't like galleys. Never have."

Poor Lars Gustafsson was never far from his crew's thoughts. It had never been right for him from that moment on. The manacles, the long hot hours labouring in the stone-quarries or on the massive sandstone wall they were laying across the isthmus that separated the peninsula of Altai from the empty mesa country beyond, the lumpy barley-bread and the cold porridge, the mosquito-ridden nights, how they had loathed their servitude. But none loathed it more than Gustafsson, pining for his grey seas dimpling under the nearing rain-squalls and the bluebells blowing in the birch wood behind his house. As soon as he could he had put down his name to fight in the Drome, though all of his crew begged him to have patience and await some other chance of escape. His crew asked him to think of his wife and child but Lars replied that he could think of nothing else. Hereward said nothing, though his face was bitter, and Martin, whose eyes rarely left him, had seen how he had stared with his eye on the Drome as it had bayed on that afternoon the captain of the *Swan* went into the arena.

Now here they were on the same desperate recourse. The only compensation was that 'the Men' with their rigid honour-code would never question the victor's right to freedom once he had hazarded his life in the arena. And what ill fortune had sent out Lokietok, the caged Unman, which alone was never released save into the arena, and then tempted back into its compound with meat to await the next crowd to flock to the unforgettable orgiastic afternoons. As you walked out on the sand you never knew who or what might emerge from the far door. The use of weapons was also an arena convention. These could be agreed on, or decided by chance if there was no mutual consent, though Lokietok fought always bare-handed, his keepers being unable to communicate over any matter of choice.

Now Hereward had forced his way in out of turn, spreading confusion among the warders of the Drome, none of whom would risk going out and closing with Lokietok. The Daroi were fascinated that the newcomer was still on his feet. This was a warrior after their own primordial hearts, and the roar rose again as Hereward feinted in and out searching for one chance. He tried not to think consciously lest Lokietok be able to seize upon thoughts as well as unleash them, and he prayed that from somewhere in his unrecollected past some suddenly remembered skill might come to help him.

Yet the oppressiveness of Lokietok seemed now not quite so unrelentingly murderous. Instead of the totality of the Unman, the unalloyed and contemptuous otherness that a man might feel for an embedded leech as he burns it out of his skin, there were different tendrils that reached out inquisitively to finger Hereward's thoughts. It was Lokietok's first hesitation. In a moment of indecision the Unman's arms dropped, briefly but long enough. Months dragging blocks in a stone-quarry had hardened Hereward and he felt the first impact of the wooden bar jar into his shoulders as it knocked the Unman staggering, and his second and third blows sent it to its knees. As he lifted the bar again Rigger watched the creature look up dazedly and its lips groping for words; he saw Hereward unaccountably step backwards.

High above the scuffled sand and the gasping figures the chieftain of the Daroi watched from his cool pavilion. He found it surprising that the creature had been overcome, and irked at the loss of so rare a show, but, like a child who keeps a poison-snake in a box, his vexation was not unmixed with relief at its end. For it was the end. The Unman who had been for months a ravening terror had succumbed limply when confronted by some shabby stone-breaker. "It was a coward at heart," said the Man, and looked round at his retinue. They nodded confirmation and he gestured to the far side of the arena.

Within moments a group of men in leather tunics and aprons carrying axes and spades ran across to where Hereward and Rigger were standing, their minds wonderfully at ease. With Lokietok unconscious their thoughts now had a sunlit immensity to dance across.

One of the aproned men gesturing towards Lokietok, spoke in the clicking talk of the Men. "What did he say, Rigger?" Hereward asked airily.

"I think he said to finish it off."

The Drome workers nodded vigorously. One of them said in the Matrix tongue, "We bury the Unman."

"It isn't dead," said Hereward.

"No. You finish it. You won." They looked down at Lokietok. The Unman seemed oddly vulnerable, lying on its side as if asleep. Then its hands uncurled and the fingers flexed. A gibbering began behind Rigger's forehead. Something shapeless was whimpering and shaking, craving the sunlight and warmth towards which it was labouring. In his head a polyp was swimming up from deep, deep water, straining to reach the air and the wavering light. "Hurry," said the spokesman for the labourers. "It wakes."

"Are you asking me to kill the Unman?"

"Yes. Or we will." One pulled out a short sheep-slaughterer's knife. They looked unconcerned, blunt-faced and mechanical, as the workmen in abbatoirs look.

"Wait," said Hereward quietly.

"We can't. It's got to be done." Another put his hand in Lokietok's tangled, dusty hair and tugged his head back.

"Leave Lokietok alone." Hereward's voice was a whisper this time. The grave-diggers looked at him indifferently. Very little surprised them. Two of them closed in to separate him from the Unman, two others doing the same with Rigger.

"You've been good so far," said the one who did the talking. "Don't be bad now."

Despite their stolid demeanour they were nervous, Hereward guessed, for Lokietok even semi-conscious must be infiltrating their minds as well as his. What happened next unnerved them completely. George Littler had never been little even as a very young boy and from nowhere he dropped a massive hand on the shoulder of the man holding the knife.

"Don't, son," he rumbled. He was smiling, a big bear of a figure. With wonder George had watched Hereward go out to confront the Unman, knowing his own feet would refuse to move any closer than the passage into the arena. He had forced himself to accompany Hereward to the Drome as a sort of second. A gentle man, he had hated even entering the place. He was reluctant to put ferrets into a rabbit-warren, even when the rabbits chewed the bark off his tender saplings, and he tried hard to avoid stepping on beetles, but now he turned his heavy hand edgeways and chopped it down into his other hand, like a blunt axe, rehearsing the blow he would use down and across the Unman's neck, even foreseeing listening to the vertebrae crack.

"It isn't worth it," he said benignly and flapped his arms vaguely as if to drive off a flock of importunate turkeys. "Can I borrow that?" he added, and plucked a hatchet from its unresisting owner's fingers. The workmen withdrew to a safer distance. "That's right," he called after them. "No point in us hurting one another, is there? We're all just simple sailors and labourers here."

"Well, George," said Rigger. "I suppose you came at the right time. Though I doubt if anyone knows what will happen now. Hereward's gone mad, of course, but that was always likely."

They were both looking at Hereward who, to their amazement, had slid an arm under Lokietok's head and was lifting the Unman into a sitting position. "You know what that thing is, Hereward, don't you?" Rigger said grimly. "It's what our old village priest used to call a cacodemon. It's not only a demon, it's a sickness. I know because before you stunned it it was . . ." Rigger sought for words, ". . . it was like pus and darkness in my mind. Didn't it feel the same to you?"

"Yes, Rigger, it did. And it was all the things you say. But just as I hit it, you see it was too late for me to stop, it, or he or whatever its name is, dropped its arms and spoke, not only said something but thought it too . . ."

"Said what?" asked George into the silent pause.

"It said, 'Let's be friends.'"

Rigger and George stared quietly at the creature until they were startled by a trample of footsteps as one of the Daroi combatants approached, his dark face decorated into a death's head mask. His cloak swung crimson and his words were caustic and impatient, though his glance strayed warily to the Unman who had relapsed into unconsciousness. "You have not kept to the order of the Drome," he said. "Two have fought against the creature, not one. You," he looked at George, "should not be here either, hod-carrier. Go back and wait. The other two must come with me. El Daro will decide what you have deserved. The monster is to die. Its time is finished. It was not a true warrior and served only as a cheap excitement."

Hereward muttered, "It wanted to be friends," almost too quietly to be heard.

"Who are you, anyway, painted man?" Rigger said, longing for violence that did not involve Lokietok. "You try facing the Unman when it wakes. If you're really a man, that is."

"I am Moskander Daro, first of the blood. That is enough for lime-mixers to know." He paused as the three men before him glanced suddenly each at the other. "Ah, you recognise my name."

Rigger came a step closer. "Yes. I have heard it before. You won't know mine. Nor Lars Gustafsson's either, I suppose?"

"I do not wish to talk. The crowd is impatient. So is my father."

"You haven't answered my question." Rigger had to shout now over the noise. He picked up a spade and swung it to and fro playfully. "So I'll answer it for you. You killed Lars in this arena. All he wanted was the chance to go home. What did you want?"

Moskander unslung his assegai. "Step aside."

"I think you should run." Rigger smiled as he spoke, a toothless, uneven grin. In the early days the guards had beaten him unconscious with pick-handles when he had refused their orders, breaking his teeth and jaw but not his free spirit. "Fight or run. Lokietok is waking. Our friend. Five to one you run."

Behind the death's-head there must be some doubt or why paint it on? The mere thought of having befriended the monster was macabre, and even as Rigger smiled at such a claim the Unman sat up and stared around. At once it disordered the worlds of Rigger and George with its comfortless perspective of futility racing towards dissolution. Like thin roots its thoughts wound into Hereward, gnawing at the block in his memory, the more lavish for their loneliness The Daroi warrior shrank from Lokietok and ran blindly without hope.

The watching thousands were uneasy. Never before had they felt the presence of the Unman for so long, and many pressed towards the gates. The chieftain of the Daroi stared at the swirling movement round the exits, and spat yellow phlegm at his feet. "Who will rid us of that plague-spot?" he said. His closest followers looked at him and he saw lips pull back from teeth as dogs sense fear. There would be no second chance, he knew, and scowled behind his black beard. Unbelievably the men in the arena were walking away.

"Let's get out quickly. There'll be real trouble soon," George said. The four started to run. Rigger found himself running alongside Lokietok, matching the Unman's long shambling strides. It was gabbling over its shoulder to Hereward, words illuminated with sinister images like a monk's manuscript of the subconscious.

Close Warm Blackness

Then feet raced down the tunnel to the bolted door.

Plasm Tissue Bone

Rigger crashed his axe into the wood.

Apart Fracture Disjoint

And again. The door split.

Dust Necrosis Nothing

Lokietok's hands drove into the gap and splintered it apart.

Nothing Dust No-breath

They flung themselves through the broken hole and into the room.

Walls Choking Corners

The corridor beyond was empty and their running feet raced among their own echoes.

Outside Emptiness Stars

Another door. Hereward tugged and it opened to white sun and a white road.

Warm Hereward Heart-beat

On through walking people who scattered like blown leaves.

Others Eyes Chaff

Blue sky. Running past lime-washed buildings and camels that shied from them. With every speeding footfall, the Unman scattered its singularity, washed crimson and misted vermilion to hold the dark away. Rigger, who had often sailed to the ice-fields, felt he was running among the northern lights. No words were spoken. The three men knew where they were heading, and at first Lokietok followed close, a runaway boulder bounding down a hillside. Better to keep ahead of the insolent lonely brute, thought Rigger and George, but Hereward let the giant run close to him.

"Why should he not go free?" said El Daro of the Men. He gnawed at the dried meat. The cook could have softened and flavoured it, but it reminded him that he was desert-bred. It would last for hours yet and then he could eat the sultanas. "He is like one of the Daroi. Better. Did any of you face the Caged One alone? And the others did not run. I like these sea-people." He thought that this would gall his eldest son. Had not thousands seen him run from the Drome?

"So we are no longer a proud people. We sit and talk," said the eldest son, "and these few hold our quarries against us, and laugh. To let them go ..." The chieftains who led the lesser clans waited quietly. Sooner or later the younger man would challenge his father; this might be the time. "They have some magic over the creature. I do not believe that otherwise they, or anyone alive, could stay near it."

"Strong wills." El Daro shrugged. "That's their magic. Offer them a place in my clan. We could use men such as they are."

All round him his dark-faced followers listened unsmilingly. Perhaps El Daro was jesting, but perhaps he wasn't. And if he wasn't his words had the faint putrescent light of decay, and they watched for that phosphoretic glow.

The Men had come a long way, a hemisphere of miles across wide steppes, through jungle basins, lonely across the savannah. Sometimes they hived off a clan or two of their people who fell in love with the skies they found themselves under, but always the main body stared at the beckoning horizon. Beyond it was a life different from planting and picking crops and going home to bed. For they feared that if they stopped this is all they would have left to do.

At some time in their past they must have heard a first rumour of the Matrix. As the Daroi moved towards the north, a generation had passed and another and still the emptiness had lain ahead of them, though one day the fabled place would lie in their path like a silver bar along the horizon.

The Men reached High Altai, led to it by its trade routes. Its wealth delayed them, its novelties fascinated them. They played with it like a glittering toy. When the merchant princes of Altai warned them that if they went further north and inland across the mesas they would be in the lands of the Matrix they had laughed. How can anyone own the land, they said, or the rocks under the earth. Does the Matrix own the air too? And the clouds?

"I do not care about the quarries. Perhaps we were wrong to build walls round this place and wait in it. However I hope it is not true that they laugh at us. That is something different." It had been a long time since anyone laughed at El Daro. Now his voice had the sound his men understood. Moskander Daro who had been about to speak suddenly changed his mind. "Give them a choice. The three who came to the Drome are free to go. They deserve it. The rest stay and work as before. As for the monster, they must kill it, probably when it sleeps."

"If what we have heard is true, it is their ally," said one of the Daroi chieftains. "They may refuse the offer. What would you do in their place?"

El Daro stared hard at the speaker. He knew and liked him so he let himself be placated a little. "That would depend on the value they put on their lives. Myself, I would spit on such an offer." The chieftains, none of whom could conceive of abandoning his clan, nodded agreement. Woe to whomever stood to block their dream-path, free and calling them on. Surely the sea-people felt the same – or why come to fight in the Drome?

The quarries were empty. Limestone was dug out of huge opencast pits, but there were mines too, long deep tunnels that followed wriggling lodes, the roofs forever dripping, homes for glowworms and bats, and in their pools blind fish. Led by one of the quarrymen – he had been a goldsmith before High Altai was overrun – the crewmen of the *Swan* and their companions from the stone-gangs, about two hundred of them all told, had slithered along the tunnels. Xavier the goldsmith, Martin, and George Littler were at the front, the squat man able to see far in the dark and the width of George's shoulders a gauge to measure whether everyone could squeeze through the gaps. Far behind to the rear came Hereward with Lokietok. The Unman, sensing the main company ahead, was satisfied with the distance, and Hereward wished to keep the swirling gibbering muted. In a dark cramping tunnel Lokietok's brand of vertigo could create a wild disaster.

The tunnel was lower now. Hereward walked bent forward and behind him Lokietok shuffled like a gigantic crab. Perhaps in thought too there was something of a crab, there being none of the connections and sequences of logic, only an endless flickering and ricocheting.

Stone Rock Clay

The images pressed their smothering weight downwards.

Shale Roots Worms

Lokietok's phototropic yearning was churning upward to the surface.

Sand Thyme Goats

Far above there would be goats gnawing the thin grass.

"How long have you been in High Altai?" Hereward did not like where the Unman's images were tending. He spoke the words, having discovered that the giant would respond to words with words, though slowly in a thick voice and always implying impatience.

"Before the Men," replied Lokietok.

"Long before?"

"Long?"

"Can't you remember?"

"Not clear. Like tomorrow." Lokietok resorted to an image of himself poised on a tightrope over an endless invisible abyss that he had always been crossing.

"What's your first memory?" Hereward expected the same dark fog and was startled by a multitude of overlapping glimpses: herring gulls following a ploughman, an aching tooth, climbing in the comfortable branches of a chestnut tree, a fire with potatoes blackening in its ashes, the muscularity of flesh clamped between clutching fingers.

Hereward felt cold. His own first memories of the early days in Hay village, the scattered recollections of working as a mill-hand, were similar in their randomness. It had taken the shock and impact of what had happened to Adelie and Ceil to provide perspective. If nothing was worth remembering more than anything else, he thought, then where was the meaning of it all?

Far ahead of them faint lights illumined the hole the tunnel made in the darkness. They had been descending gradually for more than an hour but now they were climbing, and several times stones came rattling back towards them. Hereward felt spent. The afternoon was not half over and he should have been fresh but the Unman's presence was fatiguing. Despite the uneasy attraction that it seemed to feel for him it exuded an unthinking remote danger as lightning does.

Then there came an ominous clatter of falling rocks, a scream and voices shouting. Dust billowed back down the tunnel fogging the dim light. Hurrying on, Hereward saw Carlin, the *Swan*'s first mate, lying half-trapped under a scree of rocks. From the middle of the column Rigger had come back to the rock-fall and with his axe he levered a wooden prop out of the boulder-pile. Now splintered, it had once supported a treacherous arch of stone. Men looked at him as the roof creaked and the eyes were white in dusty faces. From far away through the honeycombed rock came a long yammering barking. "Hunting-dogs," said someone grimly. Even the men pulling rocks off Carlin's legs paused.

Throughout their masters' long-drawn odyssey the dogs of the Daroi had always followed them. Men and hounds had grown so close as to be strangely alike. Touchy, careless and savage, they regarded all other peoples and most other animals as irreconcilable rivals. The Daroi had never stayed still long enough to create a past for themselves and the dogs even more embodied that truculent insubstantiality: what dog can boast of the history of dogs more than that they ran and bit?

The scent in the tunnels was thick and easy to follow and they swept along it like a mustard-coloured bore funnelled between steep banks. Those at the rear snapped and howled impatiently and this was the noise that chilled the escapers.

Rigger slammed his axe into the butt-end of the pine-log prop. It bit and locked and he dragged it out and drove it down into the notch. The prop split and between the two lengths of wood they tied ragged cloaks and shirts. The mate's leg they bound with belts between two spear-shafts. It was done quickly with a few quiet words, but just as they finished there came, first into their thoughts then into the lantern light, the huge shuffling Unman. Most of the men who had stayed near the rockfall withdrew along the tunnel, leaving Hereward, Rigger and two of the sailors along with the crippled man grimacing at the pain in his leg. Lokietok regurgitated into their minds white splintered ends of bone grating among skewered nerves.

"Dogs," said the Unman tersely. The short meaningless lives of dogs, cramped in their narrow skulls, driven by shocking necessity and the appetites of hunger and procreation, Lokietok knew and broadcast all their dim agony.

Meat   Musk   Muscle

Hereward, bending to help pick up the makeshift litter, felt his arm pulled and saw the Unman gesture at him to move. The roof creaked again, a crack opened and a stream of dust came sliding out. Lokietok dragged again at Hereward, who snapped, "Wait, can't you!" but the giant shouldered him onwards, trampling indifferently across the injured seaman who cried out in outrage.

"Run, friend," said the clumsy voice. Clearer and nearer came the howl of the hunting-dogs. Passions beat in the dimness like the wings of frenzied bats. Rigger stared at the Unman in rigid fury and the two sailors gazed wide-eyed from a bend in the tunnel to which they had retreated. Almost engulfed by the bulk of the Unman Hereward was being pushed away from the approach of the dogs. A clumsy craving and imploring was the only glimmer in Lokietok's cheerless mind; that and a fragile conjecturing of a companion to hold off the final loneliness. The pagans in their pyres and pyramids love company.

Part of this penetrated to Hereward but he let his questions wait and, dodging past Lokietok, dashed back to Carlin. Now the pursuit was so close he could hear the sound of voices. There seemed some hesitation and he wondered briefly if the presence of the Unman could also deter dogs. He had not long to wait for an answer.

Moskander Daro knew deep down that this chance had to be taken. He tightened his grip on the leash as the heavy beast on the end of it growled in the back of its throat. He had given up trying to tame it, but proud to possess an animal that, by its ferocity, had cowed the fiercest of his clan's dogs, spurning the pack to run always by itself. It was a chieftain's escort. Now, muzzle close to the damp floor, it ran intently along the tapestry of scents that stretched so temptingly ahead. One of the smells was a warm glowing ribbon among a grey festoon and, drawn by it, it lunged against the rope. When Moskander Daro dragged back it turned and slashed at his hand. Suddenly, unrestrained, a wolf drove like a grey wedge snapping between the yellow flanks of the rearmost dogs.

Hereward knew the howls came from threateningly close. Within seconds there was the scuffling of clawed feet along the passage and the first hound came out of the darkness. Turning, he just had time to register the redness in its mouth and the glitter in its eyes as it sprang shoulder-high at him. He tripped on the rocky floor and fell, with the dog holding on to his arm, working its jaws to bite through his thick jacket. Its hot breath steamed and smelled like raw meat.

The tunnel clanged with cries and the rabid barking and snarling of hounds. Hereward drove his hands deep into the thick ruff of fur covering the yellow beast's neck, striving to link his hands round its windpipe. Its teeth slashed at his wrists and he saw the flesh tatter.

Above and around him was a swaying, gasping struggle, a bedlam of noise and flailing bodies. Dogs dripped from Lokietok who, standing astride of Hereward, was blocking the tunnel. They hung growling from the giant's thick arms and leapt at chest and shoulders. One that had burst past lay yelping, its back broken, where Rigger's axe had chopped it down in midspring. Hereward felt hands drag him backwards as a *Swan* sailor hauled him out of the snapping tearing pyramid round Lokietok.

The noise was a constant shrill din, a murderous uproar. These were yellow hunting-dogs, and they smelled the blood of their own pack-mates and tasted blood in the bites they inflicted. Lokietok raged and spat, hurling one down to find two more springing for the throat, clothes almost torn away so now the dogs found an easier target. For everyone else, part of the confusion was distinguishing real animals from the shadowy creatures of Lokietok's mind.

Teeth Fur Aorta

A big grey beast broke past the pack slashing at the yellow dogs as it came, going for the throat of the dog that was flinging itself at Hereward. Bones crunched like dry twigs underfoot. Hereward recognised Ragnar, the wolf-friend of George Littler.

Rigger lifted the axe again as more dogs closed in and it jarred into the low roof as he did so, jamming deep into a crack. He twisted and wrenched to free it and saw the crack widen and branch into other cracks. Dust blossomed and fogged the air. He wrenched again, coughing, and a single great block, like the keystone of an arch, crashed thunderously to the floor. "Lokietok," he shouted, "get back, you son of a bitch, the roof's going!" Dragging dogs, the Unman spun, awkwardly and heavily. Rigger had released the axe and was holding the edges of the gap made by the dislodged rock. The stone slabs swayed and shook above him, and he straightened his back under the terrible heaviness. Now the Daroi, left behind by their dogs, were close, slowing in their pursuit only as they felt the aura of Lokietok waiting for them. Only as Lokietok turned away up the tunnel did Moskander Daro press forward with his men. There, towering in the dimness, he saw Rigger and their eyes met.

"Get clear, Hereward!" Rigger yelled. How long he could have held up the intolerable tons above him would never be known for another rush of dogs knocked him off balance, his arms convulsed and in a welter of rubble and dust the roof collapsed.

The price had been paid. George had dragged Carlin up the tunnel as Hereward tore himself loose from a dog's grip and sprang backwards. A falling rock had struck Lokietok, but the Unman crawled to safety. Only three dogs had survived on the fugitives' side of the rockfall, but not for long as most of the *Swan*'s crew, and others too, had by now come back along the tunnel, drawn by the uproar.

George, Hereward and others turned and went back towards the fallen rocks. Lokietok's disapproval showed itself, clogging their thoughts and feet alike as if they ran in dreams. All of them seemed to feel powdered rock gagging in their throats and great slabs waiting for them. They bent and heaved at the nearest boulders. Every man knew the task was futile but none would turn away. If only Lokietok had not hindered them, George thought, and from somewhere along the tunnel came to him the paranoid merry-go-round from which the Unman seemed never to dismount.

Dark *Deep* *Lonely*
Vault *Fetor* *Vault*
Lonely *Deep* *Dark*

XVI

A few sand-coloured houses crouched on a hot gravelly plain waiting to be forgotten altogether. Once two roads had crossed here, but now travellers were few indeed. The place lay a long day's journey inland from the bay where the sea-gypsies had put them ashore. Over the Empty Levels lay Limber, the gypsies said, somewhere over there, pointing inland. The road has to lead there. Somewhere out there beyond the Levels, Martin told them, is where Demetrius lives, in a place called Venask, on the southern slopes of the Sawtooth Ranges. When the other two asked how he knew, he laughed and reminded them: "Still alive, you know." He had told his friends before there were no stupid Twisted Folk – only the smart ones were still alive.

The place they now found themselves in had an inn, more a hut than a real building. The owner had looked dubiously at them when they asked for a room before suggesting that though he had none they might sleep in the barn. "Not much of a place, is it?" said George Littler. Sometimes he thought about the forest and the young beech leaves like pale green chiffon, but it was all faraway and growing less distinct. He wondered if he would ever see it again.

"It's waiting for something that's already happened," said Martin. The last year had changed him very little. The Daroi, who had never seen anyone like him, had not disliked him, and his skills with stone had been profitable for them all. Hereward had changed more: the others were uneasy with his tolerance of Lokietok, for whom they felt no affinity whatever.

"I was glad to hear of Jacky Dorn," said George, hoping to rouse Hereward's interest, but the one-eyed man only nodded. A message had come through trader friends of Gildas: Jacky had sailed for Limber with several of his father's ships and the message was that he would wait somewhere on the Seven Hundred Steps of Limber. Gildas had sent them two bags, one of ivory, another of amber, and his apologies for not knowing High Altai was now a place to avoid. In one bag was a present for Martin, who grinned when he saw it, saying that it might come in handy one day.

"I'd nearly forgotten Jacky Dorn," said Hereward. "I wonder if he's got the patience to wait more than a week for us." It was uncomfortable in the barn, with its floor of trodden sand, but they were long used to sleeping on harder, colder floors.

George tried another topic: "The ship will be well on its way home now. With Carlin and Gilbert and the others." The ship had come ghosting in to the inlet in the milky light of daybreak, her sails and the sea and the beach all the colour of dull pearls, and the dew saturating the marram-grass on the dunes where they waited. The lonely rendezvous had been arranged by the merchants of High Altai.

After Rigger's death Hereward had brought his party of seamen and Altaic dissidents on through the tunnels and into the catacombs under the great rock. Here was a refuge neither Daroi nor dogs could penetrate. Many levels down, guarded by layers of pitfalls and oubliettes, flooded shafts and blind alleys, the jacquerie that was the remains of a free merchant-people waited, trying to forget the old days of chaffer and auction. They had not found it difficult to smuggle out the survivors from the *Swan*'s crew along the coast, nor to get news to the sea-gypsies who, having suffered themselves from the Daroi confiscating goods and ships, had slid in from where they had lain concealed just over the horizon.

"Rigger didn't make it, though," said Hereward. "Or Lars." Or others too, their names slipping now.

"The best go first," said Martin from under his blanket. "Ratfish live for ever."

George chuckled. "Lokietok should be all right then."

They heard Hereward turn over and sigh. "Lokietok's not so . . ." He began and stopped. "Just different." The others made no reply, being too tired to debate degrees of difference, and were soon asleep.

A steep escarpment further inland overlooked the paltry buildings and, crouched halfway up it, Lokietok watched with pale eyes the last few lights dissolve. The road came up the ridge, a good place to wait. The dawn would bring Hereward.

Wind *Alone* *Echo*
Quartz *Starsleep* *Dark*

Through the cold night the mesa mice ran past the Unman's feet and the spiders netted the tops of the stunted salt-bush scrub with silken mesh, the stranger in their world half-sleeping like some huge wary ape. His mind still simmered sluggishly, an asphalt pit disgorging an acrid vapour of obscure images. Waking, Lokietok waited, occasionally reaching out lazily to crush one of the small orange spiders.

Spider-flesh *Powder* *Apart*
Dust *Falling* *Frailty*

The sun came over the horizon already stark and hot and the landscape spread itself flat and wide below the scarp. Lokietok's sharp hearing caught from the east the clink of metal, the rattling of chains and buckles, and then there came, black against the sun's disk, rocking and swaying towards the buildings below, a string of camels. On several were men riding, though most were pack-beasts. Silently around them walked other men, twenty or so. Lokietok didn't count. The spiders in their webs hadn't been counted either. A lizard was sunning itself on the stones. The Unman reached for a rock.

In the barn Martin, Hereward and George sat comfortably on bales of hay. Eggs had been easy to find and they had bread in their packs. They licked the egg-yolk from their lips. Martin started singing to himself:

All I had to give was love
But Billy gave her honeycomb . . .

"Ever been in love, Martin?" asked George.

"Lots of times. It didn't cost anything, and the girls never knew. Even if I'd had some honeycomb I don't suppose . . ."

He broke off and George followed his gaze out through a slit in the barn wall. Swaying into the one dusty street of the settlement came the first of the camels, its head high, upper lip curled superciliously back. A man rode high on its double saddle between the neck and hump. It was draped in threadbare blankets and leather bags crammed full of gear hung from its sides. The man ignored the barn. On his knees lay a rifle and bandoliers crossed on his chest. Before the camel had passed with a squeak of leather and jingle of harness, another was in sight and then another and another, softly padding along on their wide, sponge-like feet.

Martin peered from the barn door to watch them pass and reported that men and camels had stopped at the inn. All three watched men bring water from the inn's well and splash it into stone troughs. When they had been unloaded the camels pushed forward side by side to suck thirstily, not moving for a quarter of an hour. Finally they were hobbled and the men disappeared inside the building.

The three walked down the road towards the camels. Hereward ran his hand across one's warm, woolly hide as it towered above him. "Now if we had two or three of these," he said reflectively.

"Would they sell?"

"We'll go in and see, George."

The main room of the inn was long and cool, stretching right across the front of the building. Behind a counter stood the owner, who glanced up in surprise as Hereward came through the beaded curtain that served as a door. Most of the camel men were drinking and talking at a long table that filled the centre of the room. Two were playing backgammon, another was standing with his hands on the counter.

"Three glasses of wine. Red, please." Hereward had acquired a taste for High Altai's cheap wine while working in the quarries. It was helpful in forgetting what was painful to remember. The innkeeper looked at him and back at the other man at the counter. Hereward with his blind eye on that side was only slightly aware of anyone else there. As he pushed a coin across the counter, a hand fell on his arm.

"Wait your turn," said a voice. "One-eye." The man picked the coin up, looked at it, and placed it in front of Hereward. A few half-interested glances came their way. "Same as before."

Hereward looked at the speaker, seeing a short, heavily built man, his face deeply tanned but with startling light-blue eyes. There was something familiar about the faded old coat with its metal buttons. "Thirty days food for twenty of us. Don't keep us waiting."

"It's no good, Hasso. We haven't that much. Not till after the next harvest." The innkeeper sounded desperate, and when he caught sight of Martin's frog-face staring up from counter-level he closed his eyes. His demeanour suggested someone who had almost ceased caring.

"Three glasses of wine." Hereward didn't like to hear what seemed like extortion, but after the Drome and Lokietok not much seemed substantial.

"And one for Hasso," said Martin. Hereward might be stiff-necked but twenty to three looked no good odds. Four, if George whistled for Ragnar. The glasses were filled and Hasso clinked his on Martin's.

"What's the world coming to?" he said obscurely, adding mildly to the innkeeper, "Round up that food by midday." He inspected the strangers. "What are you three doing here?" he said.

"Well," it was George who replied. "We were hoping to buy animals, maybe oxen, for the journey across the Levels." He gestured north-eastwards.

"No good. The land's a desert. It eats beasts like that. You want camels, like us."

"Would you sell us any of them?"

"Maybe," said the other, and Martin, listening, caught the faintest inflection in his voice. It reminded him of Jesse, the grey man, who when he went fishing and felt a tug on his line would say 'maybe' just like that if anyone asked if he had a bite.

"How much would you want for one?"

"Hundred silver, two hundred ivory."

Hereward, leaning with his back to the counter, not liking the smiles in the room, frowned and interrupted. "Fifty silver. And we choose the animal."

Now there was laughter. Even the backgammon and card players looked up. "Two hundred for that," grinned Hasso. "Silver."

"Done," said Martin. "Provided it's double or nothing. We'll play you for the camel. One game of backgammon."

"So, four hundred for us if we win, assuming you've got it, and a camel for you if we lose. I suppose you'll want the gear thrown in as well." Hasso gave a toothy smile that didn't change his eyes at all. What chance was there of this ragged trio having more than drinking-money? "Where's the money?"

"We've got it," said Hereward. Martin knew well that Hereward had never looked in Gildas's bag.

"All right, one game then. Should be interesting. Henrik, you play for us."

George Littler wondered about Martin. He respected his sharp mind, and although he had not heard of his having any liking for backgammon he assumed the little man must be confident in himself. "You play him, George." The forester opened his mouth to protest, but heard Martin whisper, "Still alive, George," grimaced inwardly and walked over to the table. He picked up the dice-box and shook it but it gave no rattle. There was a moment of confusion as the men round the table looked under plates and behind cups, even on the floor, but the dice remained obstinately missing.

"Innkeeper, have you any dice?" Martin enquired. The man hesitated as if pondering the question.

"Well, perhaps if I went – "

"What about those?" said someone. Two dice were sitting on a shelf in front of some bottles. The innkeeper shrugged and deposited them on the counter. Martin passed them to George who dropped one in his box and flipped it over on the wooden board. Henrik did the same and each lifted his hand simultaneously, Henrik showing a three and George a one, the black spot sharply incised in the cloudy-green jade. Henrik covered the fifth point in his inner table. George rolled a two-one and ruefully moved his stones off his own one-point.

Hereward stood watching. He hadn't counted Gildas's gift but by weight alone there couldn't possibly be enough silver and ivory. It would be an interesting game. He noted the firearms, where they lay, how near each was. A rifle lay just to his right. He stretched casually and took off his jacket, throwing it on to his shoulder. Perhaps in a few minutes he could drop it carelessly on top of the gun.

Henrik threw eleven and ran one of his back stones. George threw a six-two and stared grimly at the numbers. It was early in the game, but as there was only one game the luck had no time to even itself out. He moved his stone on the three point another eight steps forward. Hasso and his men were pressed close, their support for their comrade almost tangible, and they shouted when Henrik picked off the blot with a double-one, and again a bellow of noise when George's double-six left his stone still sitting forlornly on the bar.

"Never mind," said Martin, who was kneeling on the bench to lift himself high enough to see the board. "Better to have your luck at the end than the beginning." But though George threw some better throws Henrik's position grew stronger; he played carefully and gave no chances. Before long he began to bear off his men, George still having six stones outside his inner table.

Hasso leaned forward and picked up the doubling cube as Henrik removed his first two stones. He placed the 'two' face up and looked at George, who glanced across at Hereward but there was no comfort there. Indeed Hereward was not even looking at the board; his grey eye was fixed on Hasso's face and he had edged closer to him. George stood up and gestured towards an empty corner of the room but, though Martin wriggled through and followed his friend, Hereward only shook his head.

"You decide," he said.

Around the table they were slapping Henrik on the back, all being good enough players to know a won position and anyway sympathising with Henrik, who was not to be envied taking Hasso's risks for him.

"How much have we got?" asked George.

Martin shrugged. "Maybe enough if we quit now."

"What would you do?"

George looked down at the thin features under the tousled black hair. He recalled the little man lying down in the rubble hacked off the quarry face they were working, so tired he would have to be carried back to the huts by Rigger, who thought it a privilege. Lying in the stone-dust or in Rigger's arms he would sometimes sing:

It's been the loveliest day, Louise,
Could you ever imagine one better?

In his turn Martin looked up at the patient face and its half-exasperated smile. He thought back to days when he had watched unseen as George had planted trees near Martin's home: how fondly George had looked at the seedlings as the big brown hands unwrapped them from damp rags – oak, beech, elm, trees for the centuries ahead, and his favoured chestnut-trees, to be planted along green lanes which they would shade with broad leaves and illuminate with white and pink candelabra, waiting for autumn and small children to gather and fondle the shining chestnuts.

"You can have my share," said Martin, smiling.

"And Hereward's?"

"His too. He doesn't care. Surely you know that by now."

"I don't think we've much chance."

"Backgammon's a game where you need a bit of luck. Let's throw a few doubles."

"Right," said George.

They made their way back to the table. George picked up the cube and put it in front of himself. He shook the dice and flipped them out. One fell on three, the other rolled and spun on its corner, hesitated with the one uppermost, but still had enough motion to turn again. "Double three. That's better, Martin."

Henrik threw a six-one, and with no stone on his one-point could only bear off one more. George threw again and the room fell silent as the dice rolled on the table. There were two fives. George cleared his outer board and took two off the five-point. His stones were evenly spread, while Henrik had five still on the six-point but another five snugly off the board and it was his turn.

Six-four: he looked ruefully at his empty four-point, took one off and moved another down.

George picked up the jade dice and fondled them. They were beautifully made, semi-transparent. Holding one up to the light he could just see, as if through green water, the six shadowy spots on the far side from the one dot that was facing him. He threw again. Five-one. The one had toppled slowly, displaying the five for long enough to make his heart jump. "Nearly," he said, looking down at Martin, surprised to see his face dripping with sweat and his fingers clenched whitely to the table's edge. The little man's eyes did not leave the dice even as they disappeared in Henrik's scarred hand. With their two following throws each player cleared four more, though Henrik with no stones on the five, four and one-points had a face like grey slate. Five-one, and he took one of his sixes off. He was still three ahead and time was running out for George Littler. The forester glanced over his shoulder at Hereward and saw that his friend was smiling faintly. He threw again and put two more stones in their niche. Henrik's four-two only allowed him one off, but so did George's three-one.

Now George had four stones left, one of them on the six-point. Henrik with three, and his turn with the dice, removed two more. With one left, and with a look of wary satisfaction, he pushed the little green dice over to the forester.

"Double six coming up," said Hereward. The laughter elsewhere sounded strained.

"Let's hope so," muttered George. Martin pulled over a jug of water and filled a glass. A premonition stirred in George's head and twitched in his hand. He shivered and one of the camel men rose suddenly and peered from a window at an empty, dusty street. The red and white discs seemed meaningless, and he shook his head, noticing Henrik do the same.

"Last throw," said Martin. "Water for luck." He held the dice over the glass. "Anyone object if I drop them in here?" His question was met by silence. Somewhere Lokietok was slouching towards them.

"If no one objects, then." There was a splash. The dice sank slowly, wobbling. Several of the people in the room were not even looking, but those who were saw the first six appear, then the other, even as they settled. They were still like that on the bottom.

"Well, well, would you believe it?" Hereward broke the silence. "And nobody objected either."

Hasso spat on the floor. "Only because something just walked over my grave." Several of his men nodded at the comment. He glared at Martin. "You little son of a whore, what sort of a throw was that?"

"You owe us two camels, then, since you doubled," said Hereward, "and the gear." His hand was under the jacket. Hasso saw it there, but now his face showed nothing and he gave a nod.

"Where are you going?" he asked.

"Inland," George replied quietly. "I hope the gear includes water-containers. This looks a dry country."

Hasso sniffed and gestured his men towards the door. "Let's get them the stuff. Two camels and their gear lost to a twister. All fair and square." He gestured at Ragnar, lying alongside a bucket of water on the verandah. "Next time we'll play the wolf."

"Well, it's been a nice meeting," said Hereward, and George and Martin looked at one another in resignation.

Hasso, who had lived on his wits for a long time, had learned to be wary of intensity of purpose; it often went along with the unpredictability of illogic and he could do without it. He marked Martin down as a trifle to be dealt with later and noted Littler's solid presence, but Hereward irked him. The one-eyed man meant trouble, and Hasso surprised himself by thinking briefly of how in the gloom beneath the green pads and pristine blooms of the lily pond unimaginable spined conflicts churn the mud.

Nevertheless, though he felt himself cheated and challenged, he smiled inwardly. He had never seen jade dice before but he had heard of them. Also he had noticed who had picked them up.

XVII

It was their fourth day out on the tableland and late in the afternoon. They had tramped all day, steadily consuming the miles across the flat landscape, navigating by their shadows, walking on them at midday when they pointed north and gradually as they lengthened letting them veer away to their right. The two camels slid along tirelessly, roped in single file. Sometimes Martin would scramble into the saddle and ride. It was easy to daydream in the saddle, pleasant to be alone after the cramped life in the quarries, detached by the surprising height of the camels and lulled by the comfortable rhythm of the ride.

Their dreams were as random as clouds, though Martin returned most often to be refreshed by the myth of Tyr, and how Hereward had come back from the Drome. 'Tyr would have come back,' he told himself. George thought inevitably of the trees, pondering how he would forest this land: slowly, he thought, bushes first to shelter one another, then shrubs with lance-like leaves hanging vertically, not catching the sun, thin feathery leaves, mimosas maybe. Not you beech trees, he denied them affectionately, you stay in the cool mists. Hereward gnawed at his inaccessible past, or toyed with available thoughts, wondering, for instance, if all girls and women lived with the fear of predators, recalling how the fear had visited Adelie. Thinking this, his mind convulsed and pulse inflamed to impulse so that he grew impatient with the slow horizon receding ahead.

For several hours on this fourth day the three had been travelling across a featureless expanse of gibber stones, between them and the skies that encircled them being neither a tree nor any growing thing more than a few inches high. The mesa's flatness gave the illusion of walking in a great shallow saucer, in which moving towards the rim never took them further from the centre. The view never varying they gazed usually at their feet or the ground just ahead, observing the endless permutations of pebbles of every shade from a rusty orange to a creamy white. Occasionally the stunted desert plants were decorated with flowers, small pink and white rosettes as crisp as if modelled there. Among the sand and gravel, hardly to be distinguished, were tiny skulls and scattered femurs, the cenotaph of marmots, mice and skinks.

The camels baulked at passing a patch of saltbush – at last something to chew on – so it was decided to halt. The big beasts, divested of the gear and water containers and hobbled, ambled off, the bells round their necks tinkling as they bent for mouthfuls of the spiky bushes. Hereward took a shovel to scrape a shallow trench in the sand in which he could spread his blankets, while Martin, his mouth parched, went to the water-tanks.

Far behind them Lokietok walked along their track with huge strides, catching up at sunset, there to eat, drink and, best of all, be close to Hereward. Then would come sleep and the next dawn the Unman would wait for them to move off before following, keeping below the empty horizon, sometimes chuckling when anguishes and appetites were for a time not uppermost in the inflamed brain.

Orchid *Entwinement* *Mistletoe*
Link *Loop* *League*

Martin, having quenched his thirst, had broached their second water-tank and was baling water out of it and into the first near-empty one. They had noticed how awkward it had been for Kar-Loom, the big lead-camel, to carry the tanks, which were hung either side of her, when the heavier one continually unbalanced her load. His sudden cry brought the other two to their feet. George had no recollection of hearing Martin cry out in all their acquaintance, either in shock or pain.

"What is it?" he called.

The little man beckoned them over, dipped a saucepan full of water and passed it over. "Taste it." Hereward took a mouthful and spat it out in disgust, handing the pan to George who licked some water off his finger.

"Sea-water. Brine."

"Yes, George. Our friend Hasso," said Hereward.

"Now look what I've done." Martin was ashen under his tangles of black hair. "I've ruined the rest of our good water too. I ladled brine into it. I'm so sorry. I knew you would be better off without me."

"No, we wouldn't," George cut him off. "It's not your fault. How could you know?"

"It is my fault," insisted the little man. "It was the dice and the game. We took their camels and their water because I tricked them. I used my gift to cheat them, and I've always known better than that. My family would be ashamed."

"Don't feel sorry for them." Hereward dismissed the matter. "They were a rabble. By now they'll have left that place to starve. They don't feel sorry for you."

"That isn't the point. I have my gift. It comes with this body, and it helps those like us feel more equal, but it's not to be misused. If it is, then you are right not to want me in your world. Not so much you two, you understand, but people in general."

"Oh dear, and there was I thinking I was good at backgammon."

George feigned shaking his head regretfully and saw a flicker of laughter in Martin's eyes.

"Dice fall as they fall. It's not the first game won on double-six. Anyone knows that throw was perfectly possible by chance. Forget it." Hereward's words were so like him, thought Martin, always the future and the past pulling the present in half.

The sun was dipping below the earth's rim, leaving behind its canopy of deep pinks and apricots that merged upwards into violet convexes. They used the salty water to boil rice, but ignored the salted meat and fish. Their small amount of fruit they saved. Later it might save them. A wash of inconsolability and vain expectations overflowed into their thoughts and they knew Lokietok was near. Martin felt it least, as a blighting presence coming close, but George could not bear the arid, brutish perspective, which belittled all he held dear. He took his plate away to eat near the camels.

Rice *Grass* *Chaff*
Belly *Flesh* *Juice*

Lokietok's disapproval of the offered food was obvious, and Hereward, with a sigh, set out to explain the predicament. It proved easier than he had expected after Lokietok took a gulp of the salt-water. The outburst shook them all, and from inside the Unman's brain came flickering glimpses of a torturous waterless expanse, where winds that now never blew had gnawed caries into stumps of rock bedded in shale and ash, a place that rolled through a dry, starless void. Hereward knew it for what it was and shuddered, for around him the desert was incredibly beautiful – it stirred and vibrated, ringing in the dartings of the little thornbills and the dancings of the lightning overhead.

A big hand pawed Hereward's shoulder, the gesture awkward in that no smile or softening of the features accompanied it. Lokietok spoke in a creaking, unpractised voice – "Wait!" – before running off into the night, once looking back and rewarding Hereward's wave with a gurgling shout. Less than a minute had passed since the Unman's arrival, but this speed of decision they now accepted as usual. It never seemed to pause for reflection.

"Where is the demon going?" Martin wondered aloud.

"Southwards." Hereward stared into the darkness.

"Back to the village? Eighty miles? A hundred?"

"Who knows?"

George rejoined them around the fire and they talked on quietly, sitting with blankets about their shoulders. They made their plan, each contributing not so much ideas as character. So George gave them an outline: walk and ride by night, find shade and be still by day; then Martin drew the detail: insights of the earth-children, little tricks of distilling to catch dew and condense vapour on cold metal, of sucking stones and blades of grass. Hereward's determination to push on gave the picture a rippling wash of urgency.

They slept early to wake at midnight and were soon on their way, navigating through the darkness by the stars. The land was cooler now, more attractive; like a woman behind a veil it whispered to them without words. Ragnar appreciated this return of his ancestral ways and ranged happily invisible alongside them. Feeling more inclined to talk than in the hot daytime they questioned Martin on his gift of moving small objects. When asked if it was easy to do he laughed and reminded them of the backgammon game. He told them such gifts were family traits, and elusive ones also, often missing a generation or two. His talent was not accounted much among his people, who prized more practical skills such as bone-setting or animal-calling.

"We nearly lost, even with my own dice."

George Littler laughed. "So they were yours."

Martin reached in his pocket and held out his open palm; the two jade dice sat there pale in the moonlight. "A present from Gildas the trader," he said. "Very thoughtful of him." He told them most of the throws had been unaffected. "Maybe there were one or two doubles, maybe Henrik didn't get many at the end. Maybe it was all luck."

"That's what I told you, even if the double six at the end looked watery," remarked Hereward.

"Well, dice move more slowly in liquid, gives you a bit of time."

"Does it help having jade dice?" George asked.

"Just a little. I wouldn't like to try with iron. But it's a strange fact, and any dice thrower will tell you this, if you really want a number it starts to appear a little more often than it should."

Hereward smiled. "So Henrik didn't want to win quite as much as we did?"

"Ordinary people don't as a rule."

"And aren't we ordinary?"

"No, Hereward, you are certainly not. George and I are indeed ordinary persons, but behaving in an extraordinarily stupid way. We could be back in Hay watching the trees grow."

Hereward laughed and the other two were glad. It was better without Lokietok. Perhaps somewhere in the expanse behind them the Unman might disappear for ever, though all three of them sensed that they would meet Lokietok again. George and Martin pushed the thought away: it was like the brine gurgling in the barrels, an unpalatable prospect.

They strode on, the miles unrolling beneath their feet, the camels swaying along with the squeaky sounds of leather, and occasional coughs or snuffles. Ahead the land was clothed in shades of grey and the sky a dark, crisp black, with the stars scattered across it in what they never felt as random sparks. The galaxy's axis banding the sky was too emblematic a highway for that.

"Beautiful, the stars, aren't they?" George said softly.

"What would the night be without stars?" murmured Martin. "We're lucky to have them. I think they're like dreams. They disturb us at times but who'd want sleep without dreams? It wouldn't be anything at all, would it?"

"One day we shall have to find out about the stars . . ." Hereward hesitated.

"Why?" prompted Martin.

"Not us, perhaps, but men and women in time to come. I don't know how but I'm sure we have to try."

"When we find out might there be nothing left, like sleep without dreams?" Martin asked.

Hereward laughed. "I doubt it. What's the biggest number you know? There'll always be another bigger one. But we're born to try."

"Does 'we' mean all of us?" George gestured around. "Ragnar? The owls? The spiders?"

"I expect so," said Hereward. "If it didn't you wouldn't be interested, would you?"

They laughed together and first George and then the others began to sing:

So side by side, laborious, slow,
There come the trees, the grass, the stone;
How could we leave them, Lord, you know
You are no way to walk alone.

"We'll not leave you, Ragnar," said the forester, as the wolf ran near them.

The end we seek we cannot know,
Whose framework is the questing clay,
But we'll not leave the search when, Lord,
You hung the stars to light the way.

That night they went on for many miles. On the way they sang and laughed for now there was no way but forward, and though they sensed their fellowship was surrounded with sadnesses each of them was determined not to be the one to let melancholy through into their charmed circle.

Early in the morning the sun beat down on them. Flinching from its thirsty rays, they scooped trenches in the sand between the wiry saltbushes and laid blankets over them as shelters. All day long they stayed still in the shade, dozing like lizards with their eyes half open. Now they did not talk and their breathing was shallow, for they begrudged every wisp of vapour that their bodies exhaled, and when sweat ran down their faces they lay still, not touching the moisture, for it cooled as it dried off. Flies settled on them, or sat in dozing congregations on their blankets, and ants ran across their legs in tickling files. Not until the sun touched the horizon did they move, shaking sand from their clothes and pushing swollen tongues between their teeth to feel crusted lips.

"Time to go," Hereward said. He wanted to ration his words, lest from his open mouth the great dusty mesa should suck his juices to leave a rattling husk.

Each in his different way was determined not to add to his companions' load even by a word, and the little man, particularly, felt sure that some time that night or the next, unless they were delivered from their ordeal, he would simply fall down and not be able to get up. As the night wore on he began to labour to keep up with the two big men who were striding forward as if in a trance. Once, somewhere out in the darkness to one side, there was a scuttering of frantic movement, a high squeal and a snap, and they guessed that Ragnar had killed and was quenching his thirst with blood. The thought of the salty hot liquid made Martin retch. All his life he had lived close to the sound of water, its coolness always refreshing him, and its wavery quicksilver an element to love. Needing to change his thoughts he was forcing himself to consider the whereabouts of Lokietok when, for the first time in hours, Hereward spoke: "What are you thinking of, Martin?"

"Not much, Hereward."

"No regrets?"

"None," said Martin bravely. He had so many regrets that they seemed to beat like wings round his head: his lost friends, his strange little delved-out house, the children he had never had, the kisses he had never given or received, the green, green fields, and somewhere inside he gave a silent sob. "None at all. What about you, Hereward?"

"If the worst comes, and we're not finished yet, believe me, then I'll regret that you and George followed me here, but" – he ignored

George's dismissive snort – "if this is the end I'm sure I couldn't have chosen better company. We all have to die once, but look. There are the stars overhead and this wide strange empty land around us, and here we are walking upright across it, and our minds are clear and our strength still in us. So sometime we all stop walking, tomorrow or the next day or the next. And what did we miss? Some slow wasting sickness? The feebleness of the senile? The misery when we couldn't stand the pain? Here we'll die, if we do, looking at the sky and listening to the wind."

They were silent. It had been a long time since Hereward had spoken so candidly.

"How long then, Hereward?"

"Maybe tomorrow, maybe the next day, if you think like that."

Miles further on the night ended. They staggered towards an anonymous piece of ground that looked sandy enough to scratch holes in. As they knelt hobbling the camels George felt a cold draught almost whisk his hat away. It came from a hole among the stones. From a far-off past he thought he recalled a frustrated forester who had tried to plant trees in porous limestone plains telling him of blowholes such as this. Somewhere beneath there would be caverns. The three of them widened the hole to show a drop of eight feet or so into a smooth tunnel up which air was whistling. Down into the darkness they went, the tunnel fetching back thoughts of High Altai.

"It's too narrow to go on," said Martin.

"I don't like it anyway," muttered George. "It's shelter from the sun, but too cramped for me. Let's sit here where we can see the light."

Ragnar came and looked down at them but departed. The wolf was noticeably less active now and George wondered if it could still catch one of the nimble desert rats – should any still be about now that the sun had burnt away their velvety darkness. Half the day dragged by when Hereward, realising that the light coming down the blowhole was far less strident, twisted himself to his feet and climbed out to look at the sky. Flat grey clouds were masking the sun and he called to the others that it was time to move.

Three hours later Martin's legs wobbled and collapsed. They waited for his eyes to open then lifted him on to one of the camels. "Due north to Venask," he said. "Then north-east for Limber." Later, as the sun sat briefly on the horizon like an amber dome, he fell off unconscious and they tied him across the saddle.

These were pack-camels that plodded sedately at the end of a line threaded through a peg grown into their nostrils. When led they kept up unconcernedly with the walker's pace, but ridden the pace slowed to an amble and none of the three knew if it was even possible to make them trot, let alone gallop, or how to control them if they did. Yet ahead to the north, and for the first time, the horizon did not lie in an unchanging flat line. The jagged edges of what might be distant mountaintops had just become visible.

Hereward, calculating distances, hoped the mountains were less than a day's journey away. If not they might as well be the crater-walls of the moon's calderas. In his imagination the peaks were snow-tipped; where drifts melted damp lichens grew and lower was the first thin turf with moisture trickling among fern-roots. But that way lay madness and he strode on mechanically. Thirst was shrivelling him, but his stride didn't waver. The clouds thickened above him so that in order to tell his way he had to wait to glimpse the stars in one of the great cloud-canyons.

Some time far into the night Hereward found himself walking alone, except for the small body draped across the camel he was leading, and so turned in his tracks to find George Littler. Though he shouted no one answered and he almost despaired, for he could not remember at all where he had walked nor when George had first disappeared. He hated turning back to the south but there was no choice, and eventually it was the howling of the wolf that led him to the body. The camel that George had been leading was gone, so he urged his own beast to its knees and dragged the big man on to the back saddle from which the water-tanks had once hung, then tied a strap round his waist to hold him on. A glance at Martin showed Hereward that he had not recovered consciousness.

Going to the animal's head he took its lead-rope, paid it out for about five paces and knotted it round his wrist. Overhead the tumbling cumulus clouds rolled past, shimmering cloud-lightning illuminating their fringes. There was no thunder though the night was unexpectedly warm. Hereward turned to the north, shakily but inevitably settling on it as the compass needle does and falling into his steady accustomed pace. This, he sensed, was the last halt he would make and this time he intended to walk off the rim of the earth – for once he stopped and lay down there would be no going on.

As he strode along Hereward felt strangely both light-headed and light-hearted for, though thirst tormented him, he was in his heart's imagination utterly calm, having reached that rare condition where there are no choices left at all and thus no perplexity of spirit. The hours went by with the clouds and he contemplated dying and laughed aloud, unaware of the unconquerable will that was driving his feet. In the depths of the night the ghostly company came: Jacky first, laughing with him, throwing his yellow hair back, and Kay, the almoner, who shook his head at him in affectionate exasperation; then in the lightning's glow he saw Zjelko waiting like a thick pillar in his path but when he reached him there was only an old thorn tree. Abbot Huw and Gildas watched him pass and the juggler's glass balls dissolved into the stars of Casseopia ahead. Once someone scrambled on all fours alongside him and wept, and whoever it was pressed into his hand a cold nose like a wolf's.

There were real cicadas round his feet that buzzed and leapt as he passed and the mesa was a less silent place than it had been on earlier nights. The dawn refused to come. He fell and the camel strode on past him unknowing, its rope dragged him across the stones before the pain in its nostril brought it to a standstill. He lay there for a while until Rigger came from behind the rocks and lifted him to his feet, so that Hereward felt ashamed to have fallen and went on for a long time unaccompanied by any imaginings. The ground was rising steadily so that his steps grew shorter and he noticed with surprise how quickly daylight was coming. There were some trees now and the ranges had grown closer. The dawn light showed him how still and pale were his two companions, their only movement a slow nodding roll of their heads against the camel's woolly flank as it plodded and swayed behind him. He would not stop, though now he felt so tired that he needed to push each knee straight to complete every step.

Ragnar appeared and walked nearby for a while and then Hereward seemed to be walking alongside a low ragged wall. On the far side there would be water but he knew it for the wall that marks the boundary the living cross to become the dead, so he resolved to keep back from it. Try as he would the wall twisted and turned to lie always in his path to the north. Eventually as the sun glinted to his right he tugged the unwilling camel and began to climb over the wall, his shadow coming with him, his blistered hands and feet aching as the rough stones scraped them. Stones rolled backwards and he slid with them, but the raptor's genes pulled him upwards to the wall-top, as jerky as a wired puppet, and when he fell sprawling down the other side the same elemental galvanism twitched until he stumbled to his feet.

North was Venask, then think about Limber. So one step north, another step, then one more. And more, an hour of them. And then more. And more. There was the sound of singing in his ears, and he would have sung himself had his mouth not been so dry that he could no longer move his tongue or separate his lips from his teeth. And more. With the singing growing sweeter.

XVIII

The Seven Hundred Steps was a staircase and a fair, a peepshow and a university, a market and a ghetto, but above all it was a rendezvous. There was a step or a landing, an alcove or an embrasure, for everything from the first tryst of sweethearts to the last tristesse of suicides. The steps themselves even felt different, granite or marble or slate, and the passing of numberless foootsteps had put a worn curve on the lower ones, though up near the crest of the hill-face few people climbed past the six hundredth step and there the slabs were level and glossy underfoot. Along its lower reaches it was shaded by trees and sometimes lines of washing hung across the stairs; often its parapets wound among tiled roofs and its landings made small plazas among the terraced sandstone houses that, like pale honeycomb, had been attached to the hillside's every niche. The little-frequented high steps were a dizzying ladder beneath which you saw, almost between your feet, a great expanse of roofs, ridges, towers, treetops and chimney-pots that ended to north and south in the smoky olive-green of the distant countryside. Turning and looking back, or eastwards, one gazed out to the dancing lavender and silver stripes of the sea that rose to the cool opalescence of the horizon. High or low the steps had names, and up here was the single Duelling Step and higher there the Nightmare Pavement, a flight of twenty narrow steps that had no wall or rail but sidled up a rocky buttress with on either hand great gulfs of air through which storks and ravens slowly beat.

It was said that, on the Steps, you could buy anything, or meet anyone. A man and a woman were sitting down at the Hundredth Step where it widened into a promenade among fountains that pattered under the green shade of plane trees. They were listening to a singer, one of the balladmakers who brought news from afar. He was singing a song of the Daroi and their pillaging of High Altai. Though the merchants of High Altai with their single-minded pursuit of profit had never endeared themselves to anyone, nevertheless the Matrix people felt some qualms at their fall, as adventitious as the fall of apples dislodged from a tree by a small boy's kite. The way the Daroi had paused nervously in High Altai, even building defensive walls, was a tribute to the reputation of the old Matrix, but the confrontation never came and now, disturbingly, the Daroi outriders were pushing north again, still unopposed.

Though the song told some of this it was to provide a background for the adventure of the man who had fought and tamed the monster:

So if you too get tired of stepping aside
In the road when the canker walks by,
Let's drink to a fighter who wouldn't give in,
To the man with the patch on one eye.

The singer concluded with a flourish of chords on his instrument. He held out his hat at arm's length and spun round looking at his audience, before clapping it unrewarded on his head with a laugh. It was as if he knew it to be no more than a gesture. Indeed there were a few disapproving murmurs and a number of people walked away. So it was to the minstrel's surprise that the young man and his woman companion rose and came over to him, the man speaking in one of the northern outlander accents: "We'll drink to the man with a patch on his eye. Come and have one with us."

"Why not?" said the singer. He liked the straight gaze and had noticed the way the outlander's words had been pitched loud enough for everyone nearby to hear. Something in the casual sprawl as the man leaned against a wall had marked him even before he had got up. The long yellow hair that framed his face and the old brown hat crammed on the back of his head reminded the singer of the dangerously insolent look of a hooded hawk.

"Come away, it's Mad Jack and his woman," a fruit-seller with a basket of grapes and oranges said to her daughter, and the name was repeated like an echo.

"Oh, Mad Jack, is it?" remarked the singer. "They say you're worth a verse or two yourself."

"Did you hear that, Kit?" laughed the yellow-haired man, looking down into the woman's eyes.

"Yes, Jackyboy. And I've heard what happens to tall flowers."

He grinned and gestured to the singer. "Come on. We'll find a quiet spot."

The trio walked along the terrace that led off the Hundredth Step until they reached a stall that sold bubbling soda drinks. An old man gave their table a wipe with a cloth and put tall frothing glasses in front of them, pushing away the offered payment. "Free for you, Jack. And your friends."

"My, my," said the woman. "Free fizzy drinks for the new king. Mad Jacky the First."

"Here's to him," said the old man.

"Here's to the man with the patch on his eye," said Jacky Dorn. They sipped at the drinks and he held the question in his head as a little boy holds in his hand a snowball so nicely rounded nothing will stop him from throwing it. "Why should he be in High Altai?" he mutttered, partly to himself. "It can't be him."

"Of course it is. His name is Tyr." Kit was impatient. "Martin will be with him. And the forester."

"That I don't know. It's only a song I learned from another ballad-maker. I am sorry there is no more."

"No more?" said Kit. "Why, that will be only the beginning."

It had been so long for Jacky, waiting for his wounds to heal, getting back his strength, and then the long voyage, the ship sailing unnoticed past High Altai. Weeks later from the ships they had seen the gilded domes of Limber catch the morning sun. Jacky had said his farewells and gone ashore, and every one of the crew was sad to see him go. Though the sea had taken his brother Andread years earlier and the Matrix had seized his sister, and loss had undone Old Man Dorn, it was Jackyboy who had always been beloved of the fisherfolk, the more so for they felt he would, comet-like, blaze only briefly for them.

The woman, the crew called her Lilith, they were not sorry to see leave, for she spoke rarely, and then cynically, and her tawny hair always clouded her face. The sailors saw Jacky's face as he looked at her and feared lest she drain away his powers. On the voyage she had heard them talk of Jacky and she knew that he had fought and killed in the fury of battle, but reading his thoughts it was clear that he regarded this as lightly as the fall of hail, for what other course had been open to him than to fight the power that had taken his sister? Somehow to inflame in him some unwise passion would be different and as he was the only person not of her own people whom she knew at all well she had made him the very paradigm of her people's oppressors, not easily done when he had laughed and whistled tunes and asked if he could teach her to fish, but maintained by thinking of the family tapestry, her father's last agony brocaded on it.

Together Jacky and Kit had tried to learn the ways of Limber, hunting through its labyrinth for news of Hereward and Astolat, sifting the words of singers and talkers, traders and artisans, even children. Ten fruitless days had passed since their landfall and they had learned nothing of Hereward or of Astolat. Then Kit had insisted on their following the hoary advice of the first line of a Limber nursery rhyme – 'The First Ten Paces is the Place to Watch Faces' – and wait on the Strangers' Stairs that were the first ten of the Seven Hundred Steps.

Before Jacky and Kit reached Limber neither had seen a city. Ingastowe had been a city once, before the Broken Years, and to both of them it seemed big, though the Matrix captains posted to its fort had called it a mossy market town. Limber was different. A hundred Ingastowes and more would have fitted into it. Jacky and Kit had heard vague tales of children brought to Limber but as yet nothing more, and the sheer size and activity of the city was still bewildering to them. Jacky had an indistinct memory of Hereward saying that he enjoyed hearing stories and watching plays so also kept a watch on the steps around the Hundredth Stair. There were to be found mimics, musicians and masquers, both master-actors and mountebanks, as well as tellers of stories, news and gossip, among whom the day passed quickly.

When Jacky and Kit had first come to frequent this part of the steps they soon noticed that it was regarded by a gang of older youths and trouble-makers as their territory, where traders could be harassed, the entertainers forced to pay a sort of intermittent tribute, and even passers-by intimidated and abused. "Where are the boys in blue and gold, when we need them?" a stall-holder said to Jacky, but nowhere was there any sign of the fighting militia that Jacky had seen on Ingastowe Common.

Nestor the Fat hadn't always been fat but pickings had been too easy of late, both in flesh and goods. Several times he had seen Kitfox on the steps, and his inquisitive mind had noted how her hand was kept either hidden under her cloak or carefully gloved. Seeing her walking alone one evening he had followed her through the twilight and watched her, excitement stirring hotly in him. Daintily, as fat men often can, he had climbed up the spiral staircase on to the first balcony of the tall grey house she had entered. In one room a candle flickered into life so it had been easy to note his target. Sweating, he tried the door-handle very softly, felt it open before him and smiled as he settled his lucky brown hat on his head.

The room was bare and simple, a bed, a chair with a sheepskin on it, a table, and one deep narrow window with a plaster saint standing on the sill. Kit had let the bougainvilleas trail in through the window, though their gaudy purple bracts were no substitute for the cool soft mint, watercress, forget-me-not and willow-leaf verandahs of her own hidden, faraway home. Her senses were far too sharp not to hear the creak of shoes outside her door or to miss seeing the door-handle move. She knew that Jacky was not in his room across the corridor, for she had left him deep in talk down at the foot of the Steps, her departing remark about talking less and doing more giving him that baited look she was coming to know well. Once or twice she had almost regretted her barbed tongue but no one, she had reminded herself, should be as reckless, as open, as fortunate, as John Dorn. Still having not understood that northern melancholy upon which his buoyancy floated she regarded him as a true representative of the overbearing Daylight People. It had been easy to persuade him to bring her to Limber, easy to bend him to her will, when one gentle word rewarded him for days. And, of course, no ploy was a fraction so successful as to let her gaze stray to another man, even allowing herself once to meet the stare of Nestor as he sat among his cronies.

Nestor came soft-footed into the room and closed the door quietly behind him. Kit shivered. All her life she had lived on the edge of danger, but always there had been friends around her to make it less lonely. Among the Twisted Folk in her backwoods province perils tended to come as unpredictably as lightning does. She knew at once that this fat man, carefully latching the door, was a quite different danger, and for all her self-reliance she was afraid.

He must have sensed her fear. "Now don't scream or shout," he said in a calm voice. "We don't need to be rough." He came closer, his bulk barring the way to the door. "Where's your friend?"

"Down at the harbour," Kit said. The harbour was on the far side of the city and Jacky had been there a number of times, but as far as she knew he was nowhere near the harbour now. If the fat man had time he might be slow. "And now get out before I scream for help, gutter-rat."

"Well, well," chuckled Nestor – he was so close that she could smell his breath – "and what about this?" His big hand shot out, gripped her left wrist and pulled it towards the candle. He tugged at the black glove and, without fingers to clench, it slid off easily. "Gutter-rat is it? And what does that make you?"

No one for years had seen what Kit's glove concealed but now they were both looking down at the narrow paw, covered in reddish-grey fur that grew sparser as the paw widened into her wrist and forearm.

"Still going to shout for help?" The voice was thickly satisfied and she knew that now he was confident of his power to humiliate and hurt. When he had entered the room he might still have been shaken off but not now. "I thought when you kept that hand hidden on the Steps you might be ashamed of it. I've a good nose for you slippery people. Let's see if any other part of you is deformed."

Letting go of her wrist he dragged downwards at the top of her dress, and as he did so Kit struck at him in a frenzy, the claws extending from their pad to slash red lines across his face and tear open one corner of his mouth.

She screamed then, for the only time, for Nestor, instead of releasing his hold, pushed her backwards and when she fell back on the bed held her down and grinned with his lacerated features. "You'll be sorry for that." He licked at the gash in his mouth and hit her across the face so that she, who had never been struck in her life, was horrified by the weight of the blow. She shut her eyes as the second blow came down.

No one had come to help Nestor's earlier victims but he had been playing with the laws of chance a long time. The infinite mounting number of tiny events from a pause to brush away a mosquito to hastening his pace past the Drug Steps, everything combined to bring Jacky, with his silent, swaying fisherman's walk, to the stair-well just as the scream came down it. The scream might have come from any of a number of rooms but not the cracks of the two slapping blows and he opened the door and flowed in as coldly as a draught. He had bought a new gutting knife for himself with one straight edge and one serrated, and he came behind Nestor and placed the knife-point behind his ear.

"Stay very still." The words had the chilling hiss of a snake, and Kit felt Nestor go still. "Are you hurt, Kit?"

"A little," she said.

"Take his fancy dagger out of his belt." Jacky's tone was unfamiliar to her.

"What are you going to do?" Nestor blustered. "Try thinking how many friends I've got."

"Oh, dear," said the icy voice, and the knife-point's pressure increased.

"Just give me a chance." Nestor had heard people begging him for a chance and was surprised how alike his voice and theirs sounded.

"How many chances did you mean to give my woman?"

Kit began to say something and bit her lip. This was not the boyish young man trying to do favours for her on the ship or bringing her violets on the stairs. She guessed it must be the other Dorn, the one she had only heard of, whose exploits at Ingastowe were now easier to understand. And it took a full marshal to stop him, she thought.

"We won't be long, Kit." Jacky picked up the brown hat and put it on his own head. "You, whatever your name is, you won't be needing this."

She washed herself but did little else after the two men left, thinking all the time: 'I suppose I've done it. He'll murder him in some dark corner and then he'll not be the same Jackyboy ever again.'

But she found no satisfaction in the thought. Her feelings had become so ravelled but she had known that one thread of them was her half-wish to drag Jacky into the penumbra of self-loathing that was so familiar among her people, to cloud the bright mirror of his confidence and candour. This fat man would know all about it, she thought, would have seen her as someone to introduce to the company of the soiled.

In the wet darkness no one noticed Jacky and the fat man. They were walking close together and the knife-point was pressing into Nestor's back. One of the sea-squalls not uncommon in the gulf waters was sweeping across the city, the first drops of rain bouncing on the Steps and the wind churning the palm fronds. The terrace that here was slate, tough and grey, was starting to glisten with the water. When they reached the Steps they began to climb. When Nestor attempted to speak there was only a silence at his side and a sharper pressure in his back. As they climbed other people became fewer, though Jacky had a sense that for at least a hundred steps someone was not far behind. Sometimes when he glanced back a shadow would halt and merge with a wall or tree. The night was opening up around them, spacious and black, though the lights of Limber vibrated mistily below. They were high now, among the academies, the wide forums where there was learning of all kinds to be found, with shops that sold books and maps, paper and pens. Astolat would like this part of the Steps, thought Jacky. Though busy in the day, now the terraces were deserted. Rain was falling steadily, the breeze sweeping it across the city so that sometimes the view disappeared and clouds were creeping down those Steps still above them.

Nestor slipped, stumbled and tried again: "Where are we going?"

"It's where you're going," said Jacky in his cold voice. He was unsure of how to deal with Nestor. Steeped as he was in the Matrix code of a just revenge, he was aware that recompense for an attempted rape was not death. No doubt Nestor knew it too, at least in theory.

The footsteps behind had not gone away, though in the rain it was impossible for Jacky to make out who else was climbing. Before long they were past the Six Hundredth Step and Nestor was gasping for breath. An unexpected flicker of lightning showed Jacky that whoever it was following them was much closer now, and he stopped to see if the figure would also stop. Nestor took the chance, as Jacky turned to look back, to collide heavily with him and, as Jacky staggered, the fat man was away, running hard for the higher Steps.

Nestor was climbing fast, but then paused and looked back. Jacky, closing fast, wondered if he had turned to fight, and then saw the reason for the hesitation. Ahead lay the series of uneven sloping steps that was known as the Nightmare Pavement, rain bouncing off them like steam, water cascading both down and off the sides. They were for the young, the daredevil and the nerveless in the daylight; now in the dark they were all that their ominous name promised. They may have been two paces wide, but with sheer space on either side they seemed to dwindle upwards into a black tightrope as Jacky looked up. He had never had reason to climb this high before, but he came upwards fast.

Still Nestor hesitated. Then the fat man took another ten or twelve steps on, now holding out his arms as the wind tugged and battered at him and the abyss gaped on either side. His costly leather boots slipped on the wet stone and, sick with vertigo, he crouched down in a huddle. The exposed steps ahead were uninviting for Jacky but he had walked too many icy, sea-swept decks to be afraid. He climbed on, pulling the brown hat down, raindrops falling from its brim like a veil.

Seeing him come Nestor crawled a few more steps upwards, ape-like on all fours. Ahead the Steps narrowed and, as the gap between the men diminished, Nestor took one despairing glance at the giddy prospect beneath him, turned sullenly, and with a rat's desperation launched himself feet foremost, sliding downwards on the slippery stones meaning to thump into Jacky, kick out and sweep him over the edge. Jacky, who more than once had jumped rolling barrels that were careering across a pitching deck, sprang clear over Nestor, one foot just brushing his chest. Though he slipped on landing, Jacky steadied at once and watched Nestor. The fat man was still sliding, scrabbling futilely at the stone; then he slithered over the edge and clung there, legs swinging beneath him, feet struggling for footholds but finding none. Jacky stepped carefully round the fat man, avoiding a hand that snatched at his ankle, and walked down to a less precarious perch, ignoring the threats and promises and raving. Nestor had a fair chance of regaining safety if he could swing himself up. A better chance, Jacky thought, than Kit had had. He was satisfied that the would-be predator was as terrified now as his victim had been earlier that evening – and by the laws of the Matrix and the Outlands alike that was just.

A few steps further down he saw a man climbing upward, and guessed him to be the shadowy follower who had been trailing them for some time. As they passed the man spoke in a whisper: "Have you finished?" Jacky nodded. "I'm glad," the man said. "He can tell me what my son's last words were. That's fair, isn't it?"

"That's up to you," said Jacky. He went on, looking back once when he heard the scream but it was too dark to see anything. The evening was one that he hoped would fade as so many others had and would do. He thought of the Matrix marshal: fat, and shorter than the street bully, the marshal had stood like a bulldog, his feet dug into the grass of the common-lands south of Ingastowe. That had been different.

He had descended almost to the Five Hundredth Step when he found himself passing again between the big buildings of the academies. Glancing casually into the window of one of the many bookshops he saw a book of animal pictures. 'Astolat would like that,' he thought to himself.

Hundreds of miles south-west of Limber the host of El Daro was making camp on the first night of their northward migration. Beyond the curve of the globe to the north-west, where the daylight lasted longer, the monks were singing vespers, and Martin's mother and younger sister had walked to the Hollowhills field to ask, as always, for news of Martin and Kitfox. Lokietok ran like a tireless engine across the gibber plains of the Mesa. Demetrius got out his black trousers and pressed them for the morning service. Hereward in the darkness was hauling George Littler up on to a camel's saddle. Through the world, asleep or waking, the lives of its people moved in a mesh that none could comprehend.

XIX

Dominic Santos was late for church. He was annoyed with himself for he did not like to be late now that Demetrius had come back to Venask. The heart of the village almost stopped when Demetrius was away with the Sawtooth Mountain militia or on one of his acting expeditions. Now Nana would open the shutters and not spend her time upstairs with her white cats. And Dmitri would make the feast-days go properly as he had when he was young.

Of course he didn't look young any more. He was thicker round the waist, heavy in the chest and shoulders, but Dominic thought of long-gone feast-days – this surprised him for his past rarely intruded on his present – and of the slim Dmitri running at the front in the races across the meadow. Now no one bothered with Venask's feast-day and they had started to quarry in Midsummer Meadow. Always six rows back in the nave, on the right-hand side, that's where Dmitri would sit, where Nana sat when she didn't play the violin. When things stayed the same it was better, easier to recall.

Already the day was growing hot as Dominic tiptoed into the church's coolness and sat quietly at the back to avoid the disapproval of the old ladies with their grey eyes and lavender-scented dresses. Through the glass the sun was refracted, lilac and green, and between the windows saints looked mildly down from their niches. Side by side above the altar hung the first Christ on the cross and the young Christ in the flames. Dominic shivered, touched by gladness. Father Anselm was reading to the congregation.

"Thorns also and thistles shall it bring forth," he read and paused. "We know the land, it can be often hard as well as sometimes kind. Our fields are not short of thorns and thistles, are they?" The congregation stirred and smiled. "But when man is not there how the thorns and thistles sigh for him. Without him to name them and be scratched by them they are merely plants. But man makes each plant separate, alive and apart from other plants with his love. Hills would not be there to climb if there were no mankind, nor rivers to cross, they would be just rock and water. To observe all creation, my friends, not only as it is, but as it has been and may be at once, is a price we pay and a privilege denied to all other kinds." The priest looked round and knew from the faces that watched him that they understood his words. "Be glad then that there are thorns and thistles, for imagine if there were only pliable sap and cellulose that always conformed to our whims. To what hopes and dreams could we ever aspire?"

Dominic listened and pondered the words at the same time. They made sense to him though they filled him, as Father Anselm's words often did, with a sense of gravity that it was he, Dominic Santos, who had helped to love the world into existence. Of course it was no new idea; their priests would often speak of this fearsome trust to be both earth's maker and its caretaker. That trust always had been part of his faith. The history of the Matrix peoples, as Dominic understood it, was the story of how these feelings had been installed in their minds, had instilled themselves into their deliberations.

A hymn began. Dominic guessed it had been chosen for Dmitri, and the church was so full of voices that it rang like the air inside a drum. The singing escaped through the door and wandered around the churchyard and down the sandy lane.

The end we seek we cannot know,
Whose framework is the searching clay;
But we'll not leave our quest when, Lord,
You hung the stars to light the way.

Sitting near the doorway Dominic was the first to notice as a figure swayed and blocked the light. As it lurched into the back of his pew, the hollow crash sounded louder coming between the verses. The man stumbled sideways past Dominic, who saw people stare in astonishment at the face darkened with black stubble, the lips caked yellow, the cheeks sunken, the skin grey. Hands and face alike were a confusion of scratches and abrasions, and an eye-patch hanging loose on a cord had been dragged off an empty socket in which the skin was slackly gathered like a tortoise's. But the man held himself upright and went on down the aisle. When the musicians shakily played the tune and a few voices bravely tried to sing then the mouth opened and the harsh croaking voice joined in:

We see your print in seed and rain,
You, Lord, the end we'll never know . . .

The children in the front rows gazed wonderingly as the figure came slowly among them. When his thighs struck the altar-rail it shivered and creaked, and the man stepped back and then forward again as if blind. The flutes and violins making the music faltered as the man lifted his foot and placed it over the rail, and the old ladies, who had seen one another grow tired, sighed at his tiredness as they watched him try to pull his weight over.

"You are the light, the dark, the pain, You are the way we have to go," sang the voices as Demetrius, running, reached Hereward with Dominic only one pace behind.

The church felt colder now, though the morning sun outside had already dried the sun off the grasses and brought the blue lizards out. The congregation felt themselves hemmed in, not by the shabby figure standing astride the altar rail but by the world or some part of it he had left outside. The children, unmoving as small carvings, sensed only that outside their church was a strangeness, but the older people felt a dilating menace that drained the meaning from their service.

Demetrius' hand lifted gently to restore the patch to the eye-socket and Dominic heard him say, "Do you know me, Hereward?"

"I know you." The voice was thick.

"Let us help you." Dominic put a hand under Hereward's arm. The pressure mounting in the church was distilling into images, meaningless as calibrations on an unknown scale, existing but not informing:

Doorhole	*Ganglia*	*Hessian*
Striding	*Lungs*	*Vinegar*
Giving	*Gift-sack*	*Wetness*

Yet these were cerebrations instinctive with rage and loathing, not inert as calibrations are.

"What's outside?" Demetrius spat the words, but Hereward lifted his arms from their supporting shoulders and staggered down the nave towards the door, pausing briefly at the gleam of water in the font then dipping his head to drink.

As Demetrius filled a ewer with water Dominic followed Hereward into the sunlit porch. Looking over the one-eyed man's shoulder, he gasped at the Unman's size, as it stared at them over the churchyard wall like a huge clumsy scarecrow, the ball of the head a bulging turnip. He was only too happy to stay in the porch, the familiar canticles behind him, and allow Hereward to walk over to the wall and distract the Unman. Both were looking towards a wood known to Dominic as Tiptree Wood; then Dominic saw the creature reach a long arm over the wall and pass a sack across to Hereward before shambling away. The images littered behind it faded.

Then Demetrius with the water and the first of the congregation appeared from the church, until everyone including Father Anselm came flocking under the tamarisk trees. The children running ahead saw the camel first, then the wolf, that lay flat with its nose between its paws. Then they saw, propped against a pile of stones, the two bodies.

"It's Martin!" Demetrius stared down. "Little Martin from the players."

Dominic took the jug, tilting it so that water flowed into the big man's mouth. Shivering and wondering at the misshapen body he did the same for Martin. What did it mean, these strangers coming into his village? Twisted Folk, men with a wolf, a monster, and a one-eyed man who knew the seigneur? He glanced again at Hereward, who was holding a sack that had swung from his hand since the Unman had passed it over the wall to him.

"Come along," said Demetrius. "They certainly can't walk so we must carry them. Two for the wolf-man, whoever he is, and be gentle while that wolf's watching. I'll carry the little troll." He picked up Martin as easily as lifting a leaf and grinned at Dominic. "Unless you'd like to carry him, Dom."

"No, no, Dmitri." The pig-keeper's mouth dropped open and he stepped back hastily.

"If you knew him, you'd know it was a privilege. Caroline, lead the camel and someone bring the sack."

Full of conversation and wonder at what their Sunday had brought, the procession moved off, back past the churchyard, turn right at the windmill, over the foot-bridge, where for a while the camel baulked at the narrow planks, and up the dusty street to the big stone house with its closed white shutters, which had always belonged to Demetrius's family.

Nana was in the open doorway. "I thought all this was over," she said tartly. "Bring them into the kitchen. Good morning, Father, perhaps you could disperse your flock now. Hurry up, Dominic!"

Dominic grinned. "Yes, Nana, madame," he said happily. The kitchen was still the same, still the smell of wax polish, plum jam and gingerbread. "Give madame the sack, Dan," he said to the boy who had carried it and was staring around open-mouthed.

"Too many years since little boys played in here." Nana ushered out the boy along with everyone else except Demetrius, Dominic and the three travellers, two still in comas and Hereward too exhausted to move. She opened the sack and looked into it. She did not cry out at what she saw but shook it out on to the table. The arm rolled once and lay still, tattooed with blue designs and the word 'Venask'. "One of the little boys once, I think," she said softly, her eyes on Dominic whose gaze had moved from what lay on the table to the three strangers.

"And to think I was glad to see them." He spoke almost to himself. "You understand, Dmitri, that not much happens here. Why, it's a big day for me when a sow has its litter. When we were young this was the happiest place in the world. I know I've never been anywhere else but I still think it was."

"I know, Dominic," Demetrius said gently. "I think it was too."

"Swimming in the mere, that was fun, and when the weeds caught me you and my brother Hasso dived down and pulled me clear. What about the bullfight when Hasso used Nana's table-cloth for a cloak? I can still show you where it gored me. Well, today, just for a few minutes it was like being young again. Can you understand that?"

"Of course, Dominic dear," said Nana. "Being young is an adventure. How many times have you heard of the adventures of Baldwin, told to little children even, but would we want Baldwin to come towards our children with those smoking stumps of hands? And Hasso, he has been walking on the sword's edge too long not to fall off. Do not weep. Let Dmitri deal with it."

"It is Unmen's work," said Demetrius gently. "And can you not see that these three would gladly change places with you." Though maybe not Hereward, he thought. "They will tell me the story soon."

"Very well, Dmitri," said Dominic, and Demetrius noticed how grey were the hairs below his cap, "but I shall take my brother's arm with me. It may have been an Unman's gift, but I know not how it was his to bestow. Goodbye, Nana."

"God bless you, Dominic," said the old lady.

XX

It was raining still in Limber as Jacky came out of the grey house where he and Kit had taken rooms. For once he was not sorry to have left Kit. She was in a black mood, scowling and shaking at the same time at the thought of Nestor's hands on her. Jacky would only say of the fat man that he had suffered an accident, and Kit pressed so hard for details that they parted with impatient and hurtful words. It was rare for him to go long without thinking of her, hoping for some sign of affection.

She, in her turn, fretted at the thought of him, often reading his mind, impatient at his candour and generosity, gnawing at his beliefs for a weakness. Finding him brave, kind and forthright, but openly captivated by her, she was woman enough to want to keep him so. In Hereward's mind she had sensed something like a deep black pool, from which might emerge more than just his past. Jacky, she knew, was only in Limber for his sister, but Hereward was of the ancient family of Tyr, and thus was drawn without knowing it to the sky, the law, and weapons.

Jacky had been left in charge of the whole house by its owner, who was quick to obtain such a janitor in exchange for two rooms' rent, and had made acquaintances among the occupants, feeling much sympathy for some and little for others. With the old dusty couple or the shy country girl Jacky was gentle, but at the man who looked at him from a door that writhed with poppy fumes or at the woman with her face pock-painted and fashions that imitated the Twisted Folk he stared hood-lidded until they turned away to make remarks that set their companions laughing. There was about him an innocence that challenged or disconcerted many of the people he met in the city.

As he walked along the terrace to where the Steps reappeared in their ascent he mused upon those who dwelled in Limber. Where does its heart beat, he wondered, where is its strength? His progress was delayed, for the news of Nestor's end had soon spread. There were people who smiled at him as he passed, some waved, and an old lady brought him a tiny basket of pansies and put them in his hand. At the eating-house where Nestor's underlings usually gathered he saw only two of them, and he took off the brown hat and held it out tauntingly to them. When neither reacted he clamped it firmly on his head and walked on.

The first three or four Steps above this terrace were known as the Drug Steps and here Jacky picked his way among the blank-faced figures. The wasted faces and marionette movements shook him with impotent grief. Better be Andread, frozen in the green sea, than these marooned creatures, he thought.

Higher on the Steps another flight began that, though empty the previous night, was now lined with people, two or three to a step, keeping to the left for others to climb or descend. Jacky knew about these Steps, though he rarely went above the actors' area. They were called, obscurely, the April Steps, and were thronged with the workless that gathered there to sell their labour. Here were makers of shoes, candles, hats, paper, or glass, those who could write, calculate, keep records, run estates. In front of some were symbols – a piece of wrought iron, an open book – or samples of their work, rain-wet gloves, cups and furs. Others stood there with nothing, the older ones looking tired even though it was early morning, the young, particularly the girls, still ready enough to glance hopefully from under dripping hats at any likely passer-by. Most of the unskilled hoped for employment as servants, perhaps valets or maids, one of the occupations which subject you to another's will, and Jacky shivered at the thought of such constraints, hands not his clamping an invisible yoke on his shoulders. Better have milk pails swinging from the yoke's ends, or even pull with the bullocks at the plough, he thought grimly, remembering an old smallholder, Henry Fowler, who had taught him the art of ploughing and had many times pulled to help the beasts. "You walk along behind and break up the soil for me," Fowler would tell the little fair-haired boy whose bare feet crumbled only the smallest of clods. He was called Old Henry by the time he was thirty, because that sort of work ages men faster than years do. Henry, with his feet set in the furrows, grumbling about trampled seeds and 'fair treatment', to put him down on the Steps would be like exhibiting an old puzzled badger at a fair, lost and blinking.

Jacky was glad when these Steps were behind him and he climbed on through the rain. The rain was a gauze curtain past windows and noisy in pools, here and there making small waterfalls from one step to another. For three days and nights he had been coming up to the Five Hundredth Step and the academies that lay just above it. Today, he hoped, would be different.

Jacky wiped the rain off his face as he halted in an archway. Beyond it lay a cloister and then an impression of tall grey buildings, of many windows and stone colonnades. He reached inside his cloak and gave his knife a loosening tug, then walked in past a lodge without disturbing the porter. The previous night he had seen a child disappear through the door at the end of the cloister, so he headed for it, his mocassins soft on the flagstones. Pushing the door he saw it open on to a stair, so he climbed upwards. At the first landing a long corridor stretched away ahead of him, doors opening off on either side. In the musty silence of cool stonework there was a whisper of rustling, scratching, squeaking sounds from behind the nearest door. He tried the handle, found it opened, and looked in. The room was empty of people but, intrigued by the scuttling noises, he inspected what he took to be a large glass box, taller than he was and divided into many levels, like a model of a great building. Running along its foot-high passages, scrambling up ramps or slipping down chutes, alone or in groups, fighting, mating, eating, asleep or even dead in corners, was a horde of rats. Inside their box the squealing must be deafening, he thought, watching in fascination. With rats, in general, he felt no qualms, liking the harmless water rats, and admiring house-rats' courage even while conducting a desultory war on them, but this mass was different. Near the trough of food scraps on the lowest level the rats were all energy and aggression, their speed of movement almost too quick for the eye to follow; yet on the higher levels they were apathetic, often with their fur matted, some with bites showing red against the grey. The darting lower level rats looked out and saw Jacky, rearing up on their hind legs against the glass wall to watch.

Walking round the box he found on the far side, this time attached to the wall about waist-high, another, much smaller, box-like world. It had been filled with earth shaped into a lacy filigree of tunnels along which ants trotted in purposeful columns. All here was order and intention, and Jacky, despite his urgency, was tempted to stay and observe.

His inspection of the room was almost complete when he noticed a third community, less obvious by being set into the wall, and also behind glass. It was a water-world, forested by undulating fronds of aquatic plants, inhabited by a population of fish, molluscs and larvae. Looking through the green-tinged water he could see clouds beyond, and realised that the far side of this world was the outer wall. Water-beetles skated on the surface and bees were alighting to drink. He saw the grill that allowed them to enter and meshed this world firmly into a wider pattern. With some reluctance he left the room, his mind taking the information to ruminate over.

In the distance he seemed to hear music, very faint and intermittent, as if distant doors were briefly opened to release it and then closed to cut off the sound. In the music was a sweet complexity that brought back tales of sea-nymphs, the choirs that the fishermen anchored at night off strange coasts said they heard singing among the trees that fringed the beach. It comforted him to think that if such sounds and his sister were together she would be safe. He would reach the music soon, it was dancing up the corridor towards him.

Jacky smiled to himself. Frequently in Limber he had been handed strange fruits – pomegranate, guava, papaya, nectarine, granadilla, cashew apple – their soft perfumed tastes as exotic as their names to a young man from the cold estuary where only green apples grew easily. Holding each fruit he would wonder what new flavour was waiting, as if the tree had grown it especially for him. This place was like that. It signalled to a dormant sense in him that he could not even name. He licked his lips in excitement and was inclined to open more doors had not the music then swelled and tinkled towards him. A man in a long cloak was approaching from the direction of the sound, but he merely nodded and smiled at the young man and walked straight past

Jacky pushed on and opened the last door to find himself in a very large room, a cavernous hall of a place, and soon realised he was in an upper gallery. On a stage far below him were many people with musical instruments. He went forward to the balcony to observe them more closely. Almost at once and without surprise he saw Astolat. She was in the front row with a violin tucked under her chin, her eyes fixed on the conductor of the music. As he watched the musicians ceased to play and he heard a scattering of applause from below. Craning over he saw a number of people on long benches who were presumably an audience. Postponing the imponderables, such as why his sister had been carried off to play a musical instrument with which, he felt sure, she had no previous acquaintance, he looked round for a way to descend, eventually spotting some stairs.

Without thought he loosened the blade in its sheath, a reflex such as a hawk might perform, unsheathing its talons as it hovers above the netting of an aviary, staring with its yellow eyes at the fluttering finches, fascinated by a caged commonwealth of birds.

At the lowest stair he pulled aside a velvet curtain. The orchestra was dispersing from the stage and he noticed all ages there as the members found seats for themselves. No one looked at him as he stood there, the curtain in his hand, gazing into the hall, scanning the benches. Then quite simply, as if it were a moment no different from the previous one or the next, the meeting he had so determinedly sought arrived. She was sitting with several other children, talking and balancing her violin case on her knees, so he walked quietly across, sat behind her unnoticed, and, leaning forward so that his chin touched her shoulder, spoke softly: "Astolat."

"Oh, Jacky!" she exclaimed. "Jacky! I said you'd be here before long." Turning she addressed her friends, "Look everybody! My brother's here. Watch out, I'm going to sit with him." She scrambled, giggling, over her bench and sat close to him, holding one of his hands in hers and pressing it. "You never sent me a letter and I often wrote to you. Father wrote and said you'd sailed. He only wrote once though and what he said made me cry."

"Well, he misses you so much. Everyone does. But there's no need to worry. We'll go home now and go on with our lives." He gestured at the room: "Later you can tell me about all this."

"Are we going home now? This moment?"

"If you like."

"Can we just stay and listen to this?" She pointed to the stage, where a man was now seated at a piano with a woman standing by it holding a violin. The lilting, rippling piano notes began, sustaining the violin's sound, its clear high melody seeming to balance on the accompaniment. It built patterns of exquisite order, symmetrical as snowflakes, yet developing ever towards some envisaged design, never static but ephemeral as its composer's own mind, its notes shimmering now as they had when he first transcribed sounds that themselves fluttered as flames do in a dance that is their own passing.

Listening, Jacky moved from a slight and impatient interest through attention to absorption, sitting perfectly still as he tried to cope with this enchanted encounter. His mind raced to compensate for a lifetime's unawareness of this shapely sweetness. He tried to grasp ideas which, like wind-tossed leaves, would not stay still long enough to be examined. When the music ceased he was left with only one thought, as if a single leaf had been picked up and pressed crisply between the pages of a book: that full, intense and ardent as his life had been, the ice on the fishing-boats and the blood on the grass, there had all the time been an unimagined universe elsewhere.

There was applause, echoing in the big room, and Jacky clapped his hands together until his sister had to pull at his arm. "Ssh, Jacky," she smiled, "I didn't know you liked it so much."

"Astolat, we have to talk alone."

"This way," she said and led him back the way he had entered, up the stairs and through the long dim corridor.

"What is this place?"

"This? We call it Rats' Alley."

Jacky frowned at his sister's words and muttered something to himself. Halting briefly he knocked on the door of the rats' room as they passed.

"Why did you do that?" demanded Astolat.

"So they wouldn't think I had forgotten them."

"Hmm," she murmured, glancing up at her brother through her long lashes, making no comment as they went along the cloister, from which rain was dripping like a bead curtain, until she had steered him to a stone seat from which they could look out through the arches on to a damp green square of lawn. "I only got one letter," she said again. "From father. He didn't write again."

"Have you missed us?"

"Yes, terribly." A tear slid down her face. "I cried all the time at first."

"Well, it's over now, and you can tell me what you have been doing all these months. And why is this place so quiet? I thought it might be – "

"Like that farm when you and Uncle Isak and the men came for me?"

"Well, perhaps."

"You haven't brought them all with you this time, have you?"

"No. I brought just one friend."

"Where is he?" she inquired.

"Not far away. It's a lady."

"Oh." Astolat pondered this news for a moment. "Jacky, you aren't married, are you?" When he laughed she patted his hand. "You laughed! The first time. Before, you always used to laugh. Where did you get that hat? It doesn't suit you."

"Same old Astolat, always asking questions. Let's forget Limber for a while. Are you ready to go home? Now?"

"Yes. I've only my clothes and books and some pictures I painted, and I'd like to keep the violin if I can. Can I say goodbye to my friends?"

"Of course you can." His mood was changing and his nerves growing tense. It was all too easy. Which leaf did he have to lift aside to see the brown twine of the snare. When would he hear the thin click of the wire trap? Or had it already happened? Not for him but for her?

Astolat ran off in a flutter of curls and dark green dress, leaving him sitting and trying his test of imagining what in these circumstances some of the people he knew would do. Neither his father nor his older brother would have lasted this long alive, he thought, and he could easily guess at his father's contempt for 'fighting against feathers' as he would have described Jacky's progress in Limber thus far. Kit with her preternatural talent would have done better, covering her tracks with confusions, but he could not hope to imitate her.

Hereward was different, he caused events and people to react around him. Thinking of this, Jacky thought of the loop of wire, and of putting his head in it, not jerking and choking like a terrified rabbit but giving it a little tug so that whoever put it there would come and see. So he went back to the first room in Rats' Alley, opened the door, walked to the big glass compartment and drove his heel into the side, leaving a jagged hole and reminding himself vividly of winter mornings and breaking the ice in the cattle's drinking-trough.

"Good luck, rats. I don't think you deserve this place," he said.

XXI

The big honey-coloured house had belonged to Nana and her family for more generations than they knew. As a thousand hands wear glossy the handrail of a balustrade so the house wore the imprint of those who had gone. Underneath the window of Hereward's bedroom a sundial was built into the wall, put there as a sign of hope, Nana told him later, in the bad times when the clouds had covered the sun as if for ever. When he asked how long ago that was and what it meant she smiled and said that perhaps the long winter was just a story.

For the rest of the day and all night the travellers had lain without waking between cool white sheets, and when Hereward did wake the others had gone from the coma of exhaustion into a gentle sleep. He washed in a white bowl that stood ready on a table in his room and walked down a long corridor with arched doors on either side, so wide it accommodated wooden chests and tall carved cupboards and was still spacious. Finding a stairway he descended into a hall floored with cool creamy marble, then followed voices to where Nana was organising breakfast. A girl was setting trays with grapefruit, brown bread and butter, bowls of cherries and glasses of milk.

"Hereward, already up!" Nana exclaimed. "Come and eat. Elena can take trays up for the others." He thanked her with his slow smile and sat down. "My nephew Demetrius is in the garden somewhere. Talk while you eat, if you feel like it, but nothing serious until everyone is here."

So she told him that lilies were her favourite flowers, that she had not visited Limber since she was twenty, that it had rained in the night, and that no one wrote letters to her any more. Her white cats with blue eyes came up on the arms of the chairs and she tickled their ears. When he had finished breakfast she took him into the garden and, holding his arm, walked along the sandy paths bordered by box hedges that formed a knot garden bright with roses and delphiniums, gentian and nasturtium, saxifrage and peony, all clustered and mingling with one another. "Too old to bother with it," she said smilingly. "Though it's looking better since Dmitri stayed at home more. I'd forgotten how good he is at gardening." Hereward had a sudden recollection of Demetrius's big choking hands reaching out through the bars of a cell, dark under Ingastowe fort, but he put the thought aside. They walked across a lawn that wound under pear trees still flecked with late white blossom. "This was where I first met my husband," she said. There was a wooden seat under the trees. "He was sitting just here, looking as tired as you looked yesterday, but he stood up when he saw me and asked if he might rest in this garden."

"Then he was as lucky as we are."

"Very gallant, Hereward," said the old lady jauntily. "I hope he thought he was lucky. Everyone seemed to think he was a lonely man, and in a way he was, because of what the Unmen did to him at Regret, but he was never lonely here if I could help it. It didn't last long, our marriage." They sat on the seat and looked down the lawn to where a peacock was spreading its freckled fantail, rustling the medallions of enamelled green and glossy violet towards the peahens in their modest speckly plumage. "Oh, I knew he was my man straight away." Her voice was soft. "He didn't need to dazzle me like that vain fellow." The peacock poised its crested head and sunlight slid along its neck feathers. "When a woman meets her man it's like going over a ridge and seeing a new country spread out below. All that new prospect, that once unguessed at world, is hers to have. At least that's how it seemed to me. This is eighteen years ago and I was well into my thirties then, and I don't remember much clearly unless I write it down, but I won't forget him."

Looking up at the old house among its attendant trees Hereward wondered why she was talking to him, a stranger, as if she was taking up a familiar topic. A green wooden door in the garden wall clicked open and Demetrius came through towards them. He looked relaxed and jolly, Hereward thought, very different from the tired master-actor he had last seen in Huw's monastery. On that occasion Demetrius, like Nana a few moments earlier, had spoken as if somehow their lives and his intersected. "Well," Demetrius said with a smile. "The eye of the whirlwind. Sitting here with blossom on your shoulders, while the rest of us get swirled around and our hats blown off. An Unman lurking in Tiptree Wood, looking out through the branches, Hasso Santos's arm in a bag, to say nothing of Martin Wash-the-sheep asleep upstairs. You used to stir things up in the past, so I suppose we shouldn't be surprised."

"You should be more hospitable, Dmitri," said Nana. "And enough of the past."

Hereward frowned at another of those suggestions that his past was possibly less inaccessible than he had supposed. Postponing the matter, he said to Demetrius, "What do you know about Lokietok the Unman, who has followed us since the affair at High Altai?"

"What affair? Tell us what you have been doing since we last met."

So Hereward in his own spare fashion told of how he had met Zjelko again and set out for Limber to find the people who had given the instruction that had resulted in the misery inflicted on Adelie and probably, for that matter, many other children. "I've thought about it a lot. I killed that day and I am an outlaw for that, though I did lose an eye. One death was enough, or too much as the law runs, but what Zjelko said made sense. Someone somewhere gave the order. That order must have come from Limber, all the others do. So that is where I go. My friends have their own reasons for the journey."

"I know why Martin is here. You are the Twisted Folk's Tyr. The one who buys their freedom from what they call the Daylight People. The other man I don't know, but friends are always good to have."

"I certainly am not Tyr, whoever he may be," said Hereward sharply. "But you know much about the Matrix and its ways. Am I wrong in going to Limber to find this man who said my friend's happiness should end when she was only thirteen years old?"

"What if there isn't one man or one woman but many, perhaps thousands? In a way you are asking me to explain a whole society."

"No, I'm not. I'm asking a question. You don't have to answer, since I shall go anyway. But I do know that someone, somewhere, decided. It may have been a leader or a representative of many, but he was in that position because he wanted to be. I may be simple, but I know that. If he didn't want to be there deciding the fates of others then he wouldn't be. If he didn't like that decision much, but he still decided to make it, then it was because he wasn't prepared to forego the satisfaction of making other decisions. Either way he is responsible. Someone has to pay."

"I'm not sure of the reasoning. Certainly Zjelko owes you an eye, I can see that, though the Hay villagers might be just as responsible too. But Adelie isn't dead, so no one owes that life. And if she were I'm not sure it would be owed to you personally."

"All debts will be paid. That will be that."

"I doubt it," shrugged Demetrius. "The debtor too will have friends."

"Friends? People like that have no friends. Small folk have friends, that's why I'm here, but who could be friends with someone who causes girls to be kicked until their minds have to escape out of their heads?" Hereward rose as if the words themselves had lifted him from the seat, then stared down from the scratched face with the grey eye so oddly flecked with yellow.

"Now, Hereward," said Nana, "you are very tiring. You are in too much of a hurry. Though that doesn't surprise me."

"I'm sorry, and I'm grateful for your kindness to us."

"It is nothing. Now you should go and wake your friends, and the cats and I will walk in the garden. It is entertaining having adventurers in the house again, speaking of the wide world. Sewing seams and pruning fruit trees can pall after a while."

As she spoke George emerged from the house and came across the lawn, his gaze flickering from turf to shrub to herb, naming the trees as he came: plane, ash, sycamore, elm and the mimosa which flowered only once every twenty years within the prospect of Ingastowe Cathedral.

"What a lovely garden. But where does the water come from?" He lifted his eyebrows sedately at the others' gentle laughter.

"What a question!" Demetrius exclaimed. "No wish to know where he is or how he got here! If Hereward hadn't told me I would have picked you for a forester already. So you like the garden?"

"I do. All things are good that I see. Though these old brick walls will catch the afternoon sun and apricots would ripen there, perhaps with melons to shade the trees' roots, maybe strawberries too . . ."

"Are you missing your woods?" asked the old lady.

"Very much. This is the first time since we left Hay that I've been in a garden, and we haven't even seen a real forest. That great blue sea and then the plains of the Mesa like a dead sea-bed, not even a bush, not one that you would call a proper bush. But thank you."

She smiled and her fingers played with the brooch that pinned her shawl together. It was shaped like a double star, two emerald stars. "Come along, cats." She walked away and the cats ran after her.

"Hereward, I have to thank you, too," George said. "You got us through the desert. My thanks. I don't know what else to say."

"Nothing," said Hereward quietly. "I'm sure there are many forests in the world, greenwoods and leafy places. When we find ourselves in them you must lead us. Meanwhile if Demetrius and Nana permit we can rest and recover our strength in this fair house."

Demetrius shook George's hand and they were strolling towards the house when the garden gate rattled open, a voice shouted, "Hey there, Demetrius!" and Martin appeared, his face shiny and wet hair dripping on his shoulders. "I think your maid-girl got nervous when she saw me, so I went for a bath in the weir. Lots of old friends, otters and herons and mayflies, and some new ones too. You've got swimming tortoises!" He laughed and fished a baby turtle from his pocket. "I enjoyed it till Lokietok came down to drink."

"Any signs of the Folk?"

"A few, George, though not very recent. So, Dmitri, this is your home. I guessed when I saw the peacocks and the white cats that you used to tell me about. I know how we got here; I listened to the village children talking. Baldwin's first cousin, with ten camels and five Unmen brought us, I hear." He glanced at Hereward. "Maybe with a bit of help from you, old friend."

"Only five Unmen? Give them time!" laughed Demetrius. "And my guess is it was you who navigated the way here."

"Oh, maybe," said Martin. "In Westermain you would never stop talking about your place in the ranges on the Mesa's edge, so I tried to remember that. But I'm sure you can guess who wanted to come the quickest way to Limber."

So they walked in the garden and George and Martin were happier that day than for many months. The stone tomb of High Altai and the dusty sarcophagus of the Mesa had almost gathered them in, but both places lay safely behind them and the trust and patience of their fellowship had grown firmer every day, each of the three appreciating what lay in their comrades. Particularly was this so with Hereward who, cut off from his past, had been deprived of the memories of others' affection and regard. So it was that Adelie, and briefly Ceil, had become to him as singular and unforgettable as Eve in the garden. All day the bees boomed softly in the trees and thronged on the lavender hedges, the butterflies floated on warm air-currents, and the pink hibiscuses swelled their daily garlands of flowers that would fall in the night to lie on the sandy paths like balls of crumpled tissue paper. Hereward, sitting in a wicker chair in the shade, watched Demetrius come and go, saw him water the carnations, rasp his palm across the warm stone of the birdbath's rim, tie a vine branch back to its arch, sleepwalking the day away. Sometimes he would whistle a tune or sing to himself, just a few words and then let the songs slip back to sleep.

Under the willows where the kingcups grow,
Lived a fish and a frog and dee-dah-doh . . .

The words seemed to talk of things that made no sense in themselves:

When mud was dry and dust was wet,
Godolphin's donkey went back to Regret . . .

Hereward guessed they were Demetrius's keepsakes.

George had gone off with the old man who looked after Nana's beehives and was happily making frames for the bees to extend into honeycomb. Martin stayed with Nana in her sitting-room as she rocked back and forth in her chair and asked him questions about his family and his home. He answered politely and carefully and after a while she desisted. Then he amused her with stories of acting in Demetrius's troupe.

Darkness comes quickly in the lands where the sun is strong, and Nana had decreed that they should all dine together in the late evening when the air was cooler. There were tall clocks with brass faces that chimed the hours, their mellow sounds mingling in the corridors, and at nine o'clock Hereward came down the stairs, his reflection dark in the ivory-framed mirrors, his fingers brushing lightly over the lapis lazuli boxes that shone on the marquetry of table tops, his feet echoing on waxed wooden floors or silent on white fur rugs. Sitting in its village that perched on the edge of the great empty plains, the house was like a creamy convoluted shell on an expanse of beach. The table glowed in the candlelight, the silver and glass sparkling.

Nana was waiting on a window-seat, where at the casement, drawn to the candle flames, big moths whirred and the flying ants beat their wings until they fell and lay in heaps like wispy shavings. The white cats stood on their hind legs and patted at the moths. Martin came in and gazed wide-eyed at the room, thinking of bone forks and food wrapped in leaves, of milk in earthenware bowls, the cream yellow on top. But he reminded himself that in some way he stood here for all his people and restrained his wonder. Nana's hands encrusted with jewelled rings, as had been fashionable when she was young, spoke to him of the Daylight People's confidence. It was conveyed less by the gems than the certainty with which they were displayed, as if she had never known a doubt. He, George and Hereward wore shirts or tunics, grey or fawn, borrowed from Demetrius's wardrobe, though Demetrius himself wore nothing but black. The food was unfamiliar, sharp and appetising, tiny spiced fish and olives, a smoked ham in which Martin could taste oak leaves, with artichokes and tarragon. Demetrius filled the glasses with the village's red wine.

George and Martin had the natural courtesy of people who eat little and like to prolong their meals by eating slowly, and Hereward had his own unruffled manner. Nana thought them all very proper and tried to encourage an exchange of anecdotes, but the tone grew gradually more serious.

"Do you ever hear from Orlando?" asked Martin.

"No," replied Demetrius sombrely. "Though I did catch a rumour that he had crossed the Fence, the eastern frontier that is, and disappeared there somewhere, probably in Unman country. That is all I know. A pity, he would have made a good rector of the Matrix."

"A rector?" said Hereward. At his side the little man's eyes narrowed as he felt Hereward's attention focus. "Is a rector of the Matrix a leader of the Matrix peoples? One who makes big decisions?"

"Yes." Nana made her voice gentle for she sensed the new tension. Demetrius leaned over with the wine carafe but Hereward put his hand over his glass.

"So did they give Zjelko his instructions?" He was choosing his words carefully as one strings beads on a bracelet. "Are they the end of my search?"

Demetrius shook his head. "To bring the children to Limber was a long ago decision. Always in earlier times the children came of their free choice, the responsibility of their parents, to be taught at the academies so that there should be a treasure-house of learning and philosophy, so that knowledge and wisdom should not be lost. Only the sharpest minds were offered the chance. Was Adelie like that?"

"Once. Not any more. No free choice there."

"It was not like that in the old days." Nana's voice was sharp. "I do not like to hear the old Matrix criticised. There were men in those days. They did not war on children. I know. My brother and my husband went with Lamorak to Regret, though that was before John Paul and I were married. I have never seen my brother since. I know as much about the twilight of the Matrix as most." She paused and they sensed that, invisible to them but very clear to Nana, the dead had come into the room, young and at ease, resting their arms on the backs of the chairs. "Perhaps you would drag the Matrix down," she went on, "but whatever takes its place will not be those brave sweet innocents I knew as a girl, and my grandmother and her grandmother before her knew as girls."

"They still let bad things be," said Hereward.

"Yes, Hereward, and maybe they do, but it was the free folk of the Matrix who struggled hardest to drive out the badness. But think of the story of Baldwin for a little while. I am sure you know it well enough."

"Baldwin the Gamecock," said Martin, "and his three journeys. Which do you want?"

"The second," said Nana softly, "was always too hard. The magic draught from the well at the end of the world. No, that will turn out to be the bitterest of all his quests. I was thinking of your own story, Martin dear."

"'And when at last Baldwin found the key he picked it up to bring it back to the queen, though it had been told him that he would never pick up anything again. It dazzled him so that, though he carried it, he could not look at it, and as he bore it in his right hand towards the Queen it burnt his hand away, then he bore it in his left hand, but the key burnt that one too, and it fell on the ground and there it lay, burning up the animals and the insects and the flowers, its heat turning rivers into steam until one day it slid into the deep sea. But its discharge had poisoned the seeds and eggs and wombs of many things, not least the Twisted Folk, and all the horses died . . .'"

"Enough," said Nana. "It is too painful, except for one small victory. Most old stories tell the hopes and fears of many generations intertwined, but it was the Matrix people who made some restitution for they forebade the Queen ever to ask again for the key and eventually, untouched, it lost some of its power and the sea hid it. Long ago was the Blessed Time when all the world was a garden, or so they say." She smiled at George. "And I suppose all the men and women were gardeners. But that did not last for ever, and, though we do not know enough history to comprehend the decay of the Blessed Time, there seems to have been a time when man grew obsessed with machines, which themselves grew so powerful that no one could imagine stopping their operation and they took away responsibility. Baldwin's quests were at that time and, brave and determined though he was, there followed an age so fraught with misery that no one had the time or inclination to record the tribulations they had brought upon the garden, what we now call the Broken Years. But civilisation grows as naturally as plants and though much of the world lies beyond our knowledge now, at least here, under our familiar stars, the Matrix attempted its own form of regeneration, and tried to make the world happy again." She sighed deeply and pushed back her hair.

"It is hard to explain because the roots lie so far back," said Demetrius. "But my uncle, Nana's husband, was a marshal of the Matrix – those are his insignia she is wearing." Nana's hand lifted to the green stars and briefly polished them. "As Southern Marshal he should have died quickly but he was different, the survivor that random events select. You understand that when the Matrix fights no marshal fights elsewhere than the centre of the front rank. If the cause is sufficient to ask men to die for it then what leader would ask for any other place? And no man is ever made to fight. If free people do not wish to fight then so be it; it would be a paradox to enslave men to fight for freedom, though we have met enemies who believed otherwise. The greater the power and the responsibility then the greater the peril, that is the Matrix's first principle, though no man need wear the stars."

"Do the marshals decide the wars the Matrix enters?" Hereward enquired.

"Only those small affairs in the Outland provinces that are a matter of keeping the peace – as at Ingastowe not long ago. But to fight beyond the frontiers is decided by the rectors, who are the ministers, or leaders if you like, of the Matrix."

"So what is their peril?"

"You can guess surely. If a rector at the table in St Xavier's votes for war, then there is only one logical step that follows." He looked around at all but Nana, who knew anyway. Martin, who had several glasses in front of him, arranged them in a line then pushed another one into the centre. "Quite right, Martin. Front rank. Responsibility is reciprocity, that's the commitment a rector makes."

"What if the rectors decide on war and the regiments are not willing to go?" asked George.

Demetrius laughed. "Then there is no war. They clearly do not represent their people. I do not suppose it to be an ideal system, but its roots lie in the Broken Years, and perhaps earlier, when peoples fought one another and within a year or less were allies, even friends. What had happened was that the men and women making up those people, by abdicating their responsibility, had made themselves unfree. When they woke from their war they found that only their leaders had wished war to come. The Matrix taught its leaders to play chess with knights that could cut them in pieces. The game was still played but only after much thought."

"All this I can understand," said Hereward, "and it is no doubt as you say. But war is not all – nor even very much – of the life of the Matrix. To me it seems well-organised, holding distant provinces together but without force in most cases. Am I right?"

"Yes, though in all societies there will be areas where consent is less than complete, or, to reverse the condition, where desire for change is lukewarm. Maybe the world of ants is equally acceptable to all ants, but humans could not remain human under those conditions. The Matrix's day will be done when enough of the people living under its laws find them too alien or too arduous. Certainly it is weaker than it was."

Martin spoke into the subsequent silence: "My folk find its law very arduous indeed."

"I am sure you do," Demetrius agreed. "You are the most vexatious and grievous of the Matrix's concerns."

"Of course we are. We are the blemishes, the degenerations, the blighted of the human stock. The pig farmer kills the runts before they breed, I can understand that, or at least doesn't mind if they die. But you know that we are immortal souls, and that is the grievousness."

"That is true, Martin," said Nana. "And I am sad to say that as far as I know you are the only one of your folk who has ever entered my house. Please tell me of your people, if you wish to do so."

For the next hour Martin told his people's story or answered his listeners' questions. He told of the guilt, the impotence, even the warped pride, with which they reconciled themselves with their history, of how born always to obloquy, at times to persecution, they knew their unpardonable transgression well enough. The others round the table heard of how the Twisted Folk bred crookedly and, unable to find for themselves a true shape, they had always regarded the human figure as their own lost pattern, longing after it yet ashamed of their yearning. On a few occasions, to Martin's knowledge, Twisted Folk had slipped across the barrier. Born with shapely bodies they had left their kindred to live in and marry into a Daylight community. Some of their folk, Kit was one, said the little man, saw them as renegades, but more often those they left behind felt ambivalent, partly abandoned and their own predicament more bitter, partly pleased as prisoners are who learn of a fellow-captive's escape. After all it was a birthright reclaimed, and they were a branch of the tree of man and the great trunk nourishes straight and crooked branches alike, however far down in the forest's green deeps it may seem to lie. When he had finished his audience understood how unshakably the Twisted Folk believed that they along with all men had their ancient story and their unfathomable ancestry in common.

When Martin had finished there was a long silence, as if everyone had suffered some loss. Eventually Nana spoke again: "That you should grieve is not surprising. Our forefathers made mistakes, I am sure, as they set out to give humanity back a world commensurate with our instinct for wonder, to make the world young again. I can't get out of my mind this thought of their lonely crusade that was to make them the prey of the cynical, the mercenary and the greedy. I think of them on their long slow crusade, with always hanging on their flanks the camp-followers quick to set up their booths at every nightfall to dispense irony and ridicule, to question their sincerity, to traduce the weak and sap the will of the uncertain, the pedlars who sold decline as reality. But envious always of the dreamers' courage. The dream you can see still, for in part at least it came true. You, George Littler, are one of its instruments. They dreamed you and they dreamed the forests you tend. Now I am getting upset again, so you can tell us about your work in the forests."

The travellers looked at the old lady and wondered at the vigour in her words. The dream seemed far bigger than their own, encompassing the forests, justice, the fate of the Twisted Folk and much more, twining them into a vision for which they were means not ends.

"Well," George said reflectively. "A forester is a sort of caretaker, if you know what I mean . . ."

In Limber it was raining and the Steps were very slippery.

XXII

Jacky, sitting at his favourite table, looking out over the counterpane of tiled roofs and leafy treetops, wrestled with his decisions. Astolat was happily eating gingersnaps, getting cream round her mouth and licking it off delicately with the pointed tip of her tongue. She was not displeased to hear that her education at the academy was to continue for a time, though Jacky had not consented to this with any enthusiasm. When Kit had refused to return to their homeland with him, saying that her own decision was to wait for Hereward and help him change the minds of the lords of Limber, he felt he could not leave her to face alone dangers such as Nestor, or worse. He hoped not to have to wait long for Hereward. Also he held in his head a new piece of knowledge. He could not yet think how to exploit it, but he was sure it was important

It had begun when he had released the rats from their glass world. He had expected some reaction, which was why he was clear-headed and ready when quiet footsteps came up the stairs of his lodging-house and a firm knock sounded from the door. When he had freed the rats he had stopped at the porter's lodge and told the man on duty that, if anyone wished to know where the rats had gone, the person to ask was John Dorn, brother of Astolat Dorn, at the Hundredth Step. This, he had thought, would be enough to summon someone to his house. He had told Kit of his actions and, taking her advice, the three of them had waited in an empty ground floor room and watched for visitors. About twilight they had come, two men and a woman, all wearing long cloaks with, embroidered on the front, the device of the open book, which Jacky recalled seeing carved in stone on buildings just above the Five Hundredth Step where the academies were.

"Here they are," whispered Kit. "No weapons and a woman. Do you think you can manage?"

"I doubt it. I'm just a poor fisherman." Jacky had learned that the more Kit was concerned the sharper her tongue, and now rose less often to the bait. "Can you pick up anything?" He never doubted her ability to intercept thoughts, though dubious when she said that he or anyone could do it, if only they would look at the thinker.

"It's too dark," she replied. "But they are uneasy, though the woman less so. Please don't try the simpleton fisherman pose."

"That's Sister Francesca," chirped Astolat. "She's nice."

"Wait here," said Jacky. "Watch the street, Kit. There may be others."

"Very good, Jacky. Now you're thinking like a twister."

Halfway up the stairs he saw brown cloaks clustered at his door. Seeing no point in subterfuge and confident that Kit would have warned him of any hostile intent he invited the visitors inside and lit candles. They watched him carefully as he moved about. He watched too, seeing sharp intelligent faces but not, he thought, dangerous ones. "Well, what do you people want with me?"

The woman spoke: "We came to see that Astolat is well."

"Very well. I am taking her home."

"Does she want to go?"

"Of course," he said sharply. "You would if you were dragged out of your home at her age."

"Well, yes, I was." Jacky, surprised, looked hard at the woman, who went on: "Naturally I was miserable for some time, perhaps longer than Astolat has been. Then I discovered a world beyond the mud huts of my village and a life as a household drudge. In the Limber academies all that matters is to let minds grow and expand. Some minds have great potential. Astolat's is one such."

"My folk do not live in mud huts. Our home is as fair as any I see in this city. We have no truck with opium. We are no man's servants either. We have lived on the Big Grey River as long as men have sailed boats. Do not confuse your childhood prospects with my sister's."

"Well," said one of the men, "why not ask her if she is glad to leave us?"

"I have asked. She wishes to go home."

"Do you not wish her to go more than she wishes it?" Jacky shrugged his shoulders but did not answer. After a brief silence the man went on: "Why not visit and see what the children do?"

"You wouldn't want me there. I would let the rats free again."

"Not if you understood why they were there in the first place."

"I understood enough." He could wait to have the glass prison explained. Confident that he could take his sister away safely, he asked unimportant questions and eventually the group departed, Jacky having agreed to do nothing precipitate, and to visit the academy again. He watched them disappear towards the noise and lights of the Steps, then joined Kit and Astolat in his room. His sister was tired and soon asleep and when she was breathing deeply he related to Kit what had been said.

"Did you believe them, Jacky?"

"Yes, I think so. They didn't say much but I wanted to let them think I was fairly easy-going."

Kit gave a shriek of delight, flicking back her long red hair, a rare smile illuminating her usually caustic expression. "Easy-going!" More giggles followed at the thought. "Did they ask about your hat? They must know about Nestor, everyone else on the Steps does. Were you sharpening your knife during the conversation? No, don't smile yet, Mad Jacky, because the two men aren't quite men."

"What do you mean by that?"

"Well, men, but not as you are a man nor even as Martin or I are human, if you count us as such."

"Don't talk like that," Jacky protested.

"These two are different, anyway. I felt their minds as they came and left. They have a layer that hides their deepest thoughts, a condition I have never met before, and what is hidden is mean and grudging. It is not easy to explain."

"Try. I am one of the free people. What I meet in Limber disturbs me every day but it does not frighten me. If these secretive men who came into my room knew that I had you to teach me they would do well to be afraid."

"Maybe, maybe, my Jacky. Let me try again. You know that feeling that something lives in us, travelling in our bloodstreams, lodging in our heads? Think of sunlight's glitter on water, it can't exist without the water. It must be invisible sunlight and only when it dances on the ripples does it have a body. Whatever dances inside me – I don't know what its source is – is in you too, easy to see because with you it's merry and irrepressible. But they didn't show it. At least the two men didn't. They were just . . ." She hesitated, searching for words.

"Like animals?"

"No," said a voice from the bed, and they turned in surprise, thinking Astolat asleep. "No. Not like the badgers and rabbits and thrushes."

"Do you know them well?" asked Jacky. Perplexed and proud, it came to him how his father had always said she was 'the deep one'. She was so small still, he thought, like a doll.

"They teach us in the academy. They are clever. One helps us to learn about the rats and ants and the other creatures that live in that room. We learned a lot about them, but it was what he didn't say that made me think." Her small face was set and the way she lifted her chin and her straight stare reminded Kit of Jacky. But she thought that the little one was subtler and one day someone might be sorry for having brought her to this place. "When I heard that the rats had run away I knew who had let them go. In lessons I used to watch the rats and listen to the talk about the strong and weak, and the access to food and so on, but there were two facts no one mentioned. First, the rats hadn't put any other creatures into a cage, and, second, they knew about the outside. I could see them looking and I tried to send thoughts to them. I don't suppose it worked. Can you do that, Kit?"

"No. Though I have a friend who can sometimes do it."

"Well, when I heard you talking about the light that lives in us and is part of the outside, you know, like sunshine on water, I felt sure that all the creatures are a bit like that. They all share it. Maybe not so much as people, but what about the ox and the ass? They rejoiced, didn't they, and I expect it was because the babe was born for them too, and for the rats. Probably for the plants too, in a way. What I mean is Sister Francesca knows this but the other two don't, or they behave as if they don't. I'm sorry if that's not clear, but . . ."

"It's clear enough," said Jacky and Kit nodded agreement. "So tell us more about these teachers."

"Not all the children find them strange, and I didn't at first, but they won't let the sunshine thing show in their lives. I think it's in them but it can't shine out because they deny it's there. They watch the rats and tell us that mankind is as voracious, as vicious, as they are, and only when we realise this can we do something about it. But whatever lives in us isn't interested in food, and doesn't need to shelter, does it, Kit?"

"Of course not." Kit was playing with her black glove, tugging it gently as if to take it off.

"Can you guess, Kit, how I think of what's inside me?"

"A diamond?"

"Oh, nearly. You are clever. A star, a very small star, that joins me to all the other stars as far as there are stars. Bright and part of a great pattern, my star is. Sister Francesca says I took all of time to make."

"You did," said her brother. "And you are a special girl, but you must go to sleep."

And amid much protestation that she was not even slightly tired and that she was old enough to look after herself Astolat dozed off, as the rain stirred in the leaves outside the window. Kit and Jacky talked on for an hour of the shields in the minds of Astolat's teachers, wondering how to use the strange fact they had stumbled upon. Kit resolved to watch closely and, if she could, detect more of these empty people, as she called them, in the streets of Limber.

"I think there must be some connection," she said, "between these people's minds and bringing Astolat and other children here."

"Why is that?"

"Because everything connects."

"Go to bed, Kit-philosopher," he laughed.

XXIII

Meat *Flesh* *Tissue*
Redness *Wetness* *Fibre*
Teeth *Salt* *Sinew*
Fur *Skin* *Vein*
Drink *Swallow* *Throat*

The belly's cravings were converted into pictures by Lokietok's brain, a row of images that let him know hunger in another way than pain. The familiar gallery led nowhere, save into contemplating itself, a sequence that Lokietok would have preferred to evade, had it not been for the dim remembered pleasure of meat. The rubbery parasols of mushrooms, the brittle scraps of insects, the thinness of leaves, were swallowed so that the gnawing hunger stopped. When there was nothing else Lokietok ate mud. But finding meat, that was different, worth rehearsing.

An animal was trotting along the edge of the wood, teasing the Unman's hunger.

Wind *Scent* *Stillness*
Hands *Throat* *Fur*

There was no name for the animal. It could be eaten and that was all. There were no names for any animals or birds. The animal was close now. It came over inquisitively to the shape that lay unmoving in the leaves. Curious, but confident in its own strength, it circled the prostrate figure casually and poked it with its nose.

Hands *Throat* *Tight*
Hair *Teeth* *Claws*
Hot *Mane* *Tight*
Pain *Chest* *Arms*
Teeth *Tight* *Close*
Fingers *Grip* *Softness*

The animal fought ferociously, growling and snarling, slashing its claws down Lokietok's chest and arms, struggling to sink its white fangs into flesh. But with the huge hands deep in the ruff of wiry fur they rolled in the crackling twigs of the wood's floor, brown leaves clinging to the bloody gouges in Lokietok's shoulders and chest. Though the animal's teeth slashed out again and again towards face and neck, the Unman drove both arms out straight to keep the creature away and finally the pressure of the grip closed its windpipe and stopped its breath. It went limp but the Unman's fingers remained clamped until several minutes had passed.

The kill had not been easy, no rabbit or tame farm animal, but here was food for days and though tired and sore Lokietok was mindlessly content, ready to eat and doze. Almost any man would have been in a state of high nervous fatigue, but, the struggle over, for the Unman there was a brief lassitude and almost a sense of ease. Lokietok's world was a bed so terrifyingly narrow that there was no space to turn over for any other consideration than to exist at whatever expense. So now a sharp-edged stone was found and a leg severed from the body and the remains hoisted up to hang in the crook of a tree, grey fur dripping and draggled with blood.

Birds *Meat* *Beaks*
Crows *Craws* *Leaves*

Plucking up an armful of ferns and twigs Lokietok climbed up again and covered the body so that from below it looked like the ragged and ill-made nest of some large bird. That done, it was time to sit against a log, moss-grown and damply cool, sucking and chewing on the leg. Until encountering Hereward, eating had been done in a daze untroubled by thought. Now, as the sun came dappled through the ash and oak screen and teeth scraped away at the bone beneath the chewy redness, there was time to consider Hereward, fetch him into focus, repeat his movements, give him his name, none of it necessary but curiously pleasant:

Man *Hereward* *One eye*
Unman *Man* *Noman*

There was enjoyment in this struggle to cope with subtleties. Lokietok vaguely conceived of the world as being a million competitors, but Hereward was different, and clearly neither Lokietok-like nor hostile. Nor was he a part of the world that was simply there: the branches, the cloudshapes, the reflections on water.

Unman *Uncloud* *UnLokietok*

And as this got nearer to what he probably wasn't but no nearer what he was:

Sunlight *Marrowbones* *Nopain*

Lokietok found this a soothing category, at least nearer to being a satisfactory impression of the perplexing one-eyed man, and ambled out from under the trees and across a field of short grass. The Venask children had used it for their games before the news and menace of Lokietok had blown like a spiteful wind among the houses, and families counted their children, even their animals, every hour. Beyond the field chattered a stream that ran through the village, under an arched bridge that the main street crossed and into a pool that invited you to fish for the trout in it. Twenty miles on, the stream would dwindle away among stagnant reedbeds and cracking mudflats that were the northern margin of the Mesa, but its water was always sweet to drink and Lokietok splashed down into it, careless as a drinking bull, and gulped from the shining surface.

So close that he could almost reach out and touch the big shoulder, Martin lay still and deep between the clumps of redhot poker flowers that were themselves contained by the hanging green ribbons of willow branches. Though many of the plants were different in this land the red and yellow spikes were familiar, as were the arums, sedge and marsh marigolds that were tickling his face, and he was almost as comfortable here as on the banks of the dear friendly beck that washed past the tunnelled entrances of his own family home.

Fascinated, Martin watched Lokietok lap at the water. He found the lumbering giant unbelievably loud and careless, sloshing clumsily through a marshy patch, leaving deep water-filled footprints in the mud when a few paces further on was smooth stone. Martin winced as the big feet trampled out through the blossoms. He could hear the jaws scraping at a long piece of reddish bone from which hung some grey hairy skin. Occasionally the Unman spat out a piece of gristle. At first Martin thought it was part of a sheep, but the fields were empty of farm animals, and the hide too furry from what he could see.

He followed, keeping out of sight. It was getting warm now and grasshoppers fizzed like mechanical toys as they rocketed out of the disturbed grasses, but Lokietok paid no heed. Before long Martin found himself entering a wood and ahead saw Lokietok sitting against a boulder, chewing contentedly. The nearest tree was big and shady, a sweet chestnut of which Martin had seen few in Westermain. With its smooth, regularly branching limbs it was temptingly easy to climb. The little man reached for the lowest branch, his strong arms lifting his slight body with silent ease. As he climbed his attention was all on the big figure below him, and, at first ignoring the occasional drops of moisture that fell on him, he was surprised to see a red blotch on his forearm. Looking up he saw a misshapen bundle jammed in a fork of the tree, draped in ferns and grasses but clearly a body of some sort, from which the droplets of blood had fallen. A tremor of angry disgust went through him and, quieter than any squirrel, he climbed up to the fork and pulled the greenery away from the head. It was easy to recognise – a notched ear, a flash of white hair down the muzzle. Martin knew he was looking at the remains of Ragnar, the wolf that had been George's companion for as long as he remembered, that had rediscovered the forester at High Altai, had accompanied them across the Mesa, and was now carrion meat in a tree. It can't stay here, thought Martin, who had grown to like the wolf for its dignity and loyalty. Tugging the body out from between the branches he found it too heavy to hold without losing his balance and had to release it, noisily bumping off branches and snapping twigs as it fell and landed with a sack-like thump inches away from Lokietok's head.

Alert, the Unman stared upward and Martin knew he had been seen. Then they came, the ego pulses that Lokietok flung out, and because they came from not quite man and not really beast they were comfortless and savage. Guessing that he was receiving the faintest echo of the howling in Lokietok's head, Martin consoled himself. The impact was fierce enough but he knew from their encounters on the Mesa that his own inheritance and deviations reduced the pressure others felt.

Meat *Belly* *Tongue*
Thief *Enemy* *Dwarf*

In the mesh of assertions some were simpler to grasp than others, though each flowed into all, and Martin knew at once that the intent was to kill if he stayed anywhere near the carcass. But George was his particular friend, he had liked the wolf, and he had seen danger before so, instead of signalling retreat by withdrawing through the branches, he leaned down and spoke slowly and clearly: "Go away. No one wants you with us."

Lokietok made no answer other than to snarl and, coming to the foot of the tree, reached for the lowest limb and began to climb. Martin looked down at the unkempt hair, stiff with dust and with bits of bark and dry grass tangled in it. Seeing the big muscles flex and tighten over the shoulders a coldness ran through him, more wholesome than the fears that Lokietok usually induced but frightening, and he searched upwards for branches that would take him where Lokietok's weight, three and more times his own, could not follow. He swarmed nimbly up, the tree being one of the most convenient the wood could offer for climbers; with regular strong branches there were frequent hand and footholds. Below him he saw Lokietok climbing slowly, sometimes hesitating before trying a branch but following steadily.

Now the giant reached out and snatched at his foot, and Martin scuttled out along a long thin branch, one that projected out at a shallow angle. He was now so high and exposed that above him was only blue sky. He could see out over Venask's small rockwalled fields, the grass thinner and browner than in his own homeland, a stone-built farm or two, cloaked in the green-black of pines and cypress, then the village, its houses clustered together. Nana's big house was clearly visible, a tendril of smoke above one of its chimneys. Perched where he was he felt almost outside the tree, and noticed butterflies rising and dipping just above the topmost leaves.

Lokietok had climbed high too, his weight making the slender boughs tremble. Martin retreated until he had nowhere else to go. His branch was bending perilously. The Unman had stopped climbing, hearing protesting creaks under foot, but reached up and tugged at the branch that held Martin, trying to dislodge him or to snap it off. Neither attempt was successful though the branch swung precariously as if a storm whipped and bent it. Martin held on grimly, and, when Lokietok ceased shaking his refuge and slid back to rest in a crook between two bigger boughs, found himself sweating.

Though nervous and afraid he was not terrified; the villagers of Hay had certainly reduced him to terror at times, so he knew the difference between that and fear. Lokietok had now climbed well down the tree and was wedged in a fork of the main trunk, remaining still for long periods. Only when Martin changed position or came lower did the Unman move and then only until Martin had returned to his original perch. Sometimes Lokietok gave a disapproving growl, and whenever both were still Martin felt far more strongly the brutish images invading his mind. There was not, he thought, the paralysing effect that George in particular experienced, and he wondered what in his own unique twistedness immunised him against it.

Though Lokietok seemed unable quite to reach up and seize or dislodge him, the creature's presence was so physical. It was like being in a room confronting a large and dangerous animal, as opposed to being in the same room in total darkness, not knowing what was there and waiting nervously for the first touch of hair or scale or skin. Living among the Daylight People was like the latter situation, with the further unpredictability that on some days they would be as gentle as George Littler.

An hour passed. Martin was wondering how long he could stay where he was, but then Lokietok climbed down and went to the wolf's corpse. This was dragged to the foot of the tree and another piece of meat severed. As the meat was torn clear of the skin blood bubbled from the corner of Lokietok's mouth. Martin watched in revulsion. What relation could the monster be to the merry, cruel, gentle, terrifying Daylight People? Unconscious or asleep it resembled Hereward or George far more than he did but, awake, seemed from another world. George had loved Ragnar as he loved the shapes and lives of the trees, the primroses and mosses beneath them and the moon entangled in their branches. Martin knew this and felt the same feelings himself, but the Unman seemed not to care for anything else that dwelled on earth.

He scrambled far enough down to flick a twig on to Lokietok, and called down, "Who are you?" which provoked a snarl, and then images that coupled Martin with Ragnar as a broken bundle of joints to be dismembered and devoured. The giant reached up for the lowest branch but Martin merely climbed further away and when the creature went back to eating he returned to hang not far above, a sequence that repeated itself twice more until Lokietok appeared to grow accustomed to the relative nearness of the little man. The huge figure stood under the tree chewing and looking up. After a while Martin tried another and much simpler question: "Are you staying by this tree?" He had watched Hereward talk to Lokietok, a slow process full of frowns and gestures with words kept brief and responses articulated in pictures. So while the first question had produced only paranoia, the second gave back images of waiting, first in light, then in dark. The thick voice, the tongue labouring in the mouth, said, "Tree, day, night." The words were superfluous, for Martin registered pictures of the tree with a figure trapped in it in a deepening darkness. As you might flick through a book's pages receiving half-glimpsed impressions until one's thumb holds down the required place, so it was with Lokietok. Apart from the relevant response there were other fleeting scenes, often ones of food, hunting, gathering or killing to sustain the belly, and then, undefined but inescapable, attenuated as the wood fibres of the pages, its brutal loneliness.

Martin considered asking about this loneliness but wishing to simplify the question said, "Have you a friend?" Instantly the response came, a sunburst of colour, reminding Martin of the sun shining behind Hay church's stained-glass windows, the figures aureoled in golden green, the sky an unreal violet.

Stoneplain Hereward Friend

Along with the response was a craving that Martin found hard to grasp. It disturbed him that the nearest emotion he could find was his own folk's desire to find Tyr, the one who would make life better. But, since Hereward seemed to have enough to carry, he said coldly, "Hereward no friend." He tried to accompany this with an image of Hereward wrenching his hand out of Lokietok's grasp. Lokietok faltered for the first time, or at least looked round and brushed a hand across the face as if to disperse mist. "Kill. Wake. Eat. Sleep. Those are all you know. No friends."

"Friend!" shouted Lokietok in a sobbing howl.

"No. None. Never. No friend." Martin repeated the image,

strengthening and clarifying it, and eventually Lokietok flinched. "You killed Hereward's friend," he added, and kept the image steady in his own mind. Now the figure below was no longer upright but slipping into a crouch, arms folded round its head, grinding it down on to the knees. As Martin stared in sad wonder the Unman fell sideways, lying on the grass. He had seen fits before but never shared the mental misery. Now Lokietok was drowning in some churning vortex, sucked under by the 'kill-eat' dark waters and the thin bright rope no longer there to cling to, a rope called 'friend'.

Martin was appalled. Even now he felt that Lokietok could not have really grasped what friendship meant; perhaps it had been a dimly felt idea, yearned after but imperfectly realised.

The danger having passed, Martin climbed down and even touched Lokietok's shoulder but there was no reaction. Later in the day he returned to the wood bringing Hereward and George, though not Demetrius who for two days was away from Venask. Lokietok, hard to see in the dirty grey smock, crouched in the shade, so still that the flies walked undisturbed on the eyelids and between the lips. George did not speak at all but took the remains of Ragnar and buried them deep. After a time he and Martin returned to Nana's house, but Hereward sat through the dewy night beside the unmoving shape. Several times he wiped dry the pale face, not knowing whether the wetness was dew, sweat or tears. Once he lifted the big hand and held it briefly, noticing for the first time that Lokietok wore a ring. It looked as incongruous as a necklace on a bear. The ring was a silver band; it had an onyx stone, on which a symbol, perhaps a figure four, had been inscribed.

At dawn Lokietok stood and stretched, then walked placidly away across the fields. Hereward walked alongside, giving an occasional steering tug on the arm. A child may pull a bull along by the brass ring through its nose, and nothing in the landscape or the grasses awakens in the bull any memory of its ancient self. So it was with Lokietok. Hereward eventually left the mute giant at a herdsman's disused hut.

Back at Nana's house he asked her whether she had ever heard of such a reaction. She told him she had: "When one finally despairs, the monks call it wanhope." It did not seem right to Hereward. Recalling the fiercesome spectacle in the arena and the furious fight with the Daroi hunting-dogs this eerie senescence unsettled him.

In the three days that followed no one but Hereward went to see Lokietok. Hereward found no way to converse but the two would sit silently. Once, while he was looking at the coppery disc of the moon just above the horizon and wondering idly about the legend of the footsteps on the moon, he turned and saw recognition stir across Lokietok's face as if broken glass should stir to fuse itself again into some shape. "What is it, my friend?" he asked, but the fragments had fallen apart again and the big unkempt head returned to its aimless rolling and nodding.

XXIV

The fire crackled cheerfully and though it was a warm evening the bushes and low trees that ringed the hollow in which they had camped seemed to lean inwards to it. Demetrius threw the chopped cabbage on to the metal platter to join the strips of mutton already sizzling there. He added rice and onions, stirring them all together. It pleased him to cook using an old shield as a pan, a trick he had learned from his uncle John Paul. "Who wants a bright shield?" the marshal used to say. "The fewer people that see one the better."

Later they ate hungrily, for the day had been a long one. From the ridge above the camp it was still possible to see far back the foothills on the edge of the Mesa that hid the village of Venask and Nana's comfortable old house. Hereward thought back to the previous night. They had all dined together and the dark table had again glittered with silver and glass. Then, just before climbing the long stairs to his bedroom, Nana had taken him aside.

"I heard you went to sit with the creature in the cowmen's hut. That is what my husband would have done, you know. This is not the first time you have met the Unmen. Tomorrow Demetrius will show you my brother's little book. It may help your memory."

"Thank you, madame. I fear nothing so far has done. Thirty-odd years and nothing but a sort of dream." He found himself telling her of the shining city and the flames, Ivo and Guillebrand and the others swarming over the parapet of its wall, and then the arrow.

She shook her head. "Were they the walls of Regret? Perhaps not. My brother wrote that it was a different city. But often it is merciful to forget or not to know the truth. Think of the flies in the spider's web, the mouse in the snake's jaws – one wishes for them a mindlessness where fear and dread cannot come. Nevertheless read the book and listen to what my nephew has to say. He longs to tell you. I will say goodbye now as you will go too early for me."

The next morning they walked down the long lawn and out through the green gate in the wall, striding away into the misty dawn. But from the first ridge beyond Tiptree Wood they looked back to see Nana had opened her shutters. Lokietok prowled a half-mile or so behind them as they walked. Demetrius, who was accompanying them for a day's march, often stared back. "I haven't set eyes on the Unman yet, and I don't want to. Tonight, Hereward, I'll tell you why." George approved, being also happy that Lokietok kept out of sight.

After supper Demetrius joined Hereward, while the two others talked drowsily on the other side of the fire. He was carrying a small book, its edges ragged and the stiffness long gone from its black cover. "Nana said you might like to read this," he said, holding it out tentatively. Hereward took it.

Tucked inside the front cover was a piece of folded paper. Lifting it out he read:

This book belonged to my brother Constantine. It was given to me by my husband, John Paul, for six years Marshal of the Southern Matrix and one of the longest-serving marshals. For five of those years we were married, though I saw him all too little. Only two men went further on Lamorak's first expedition. At that time he met my brother. He told me that Constantine spoke often of Venask and our old house. John Paul brought this book back here from Regret.

The paper was signed 'Nancy Villiers'. The fly-leaf had a faded inscription at the top: 'With love to ... on his first ... summer ... father, mother and ...' Then followed the words of a psalm and Hereward, flicking rapidly through a few pages, found a psalm on each right-hand page with the left side left empty, thus interleaved throughout the book. On some of the blank leaves were tiny drawings, sketch maps and arrows that indicated phrases on the opposite page, as well as a series of brief irregular entries. It seemed some sort of journal or commonplace book. Hereward recalled Hobson the miller keeping such a book with pressed flowers mounted where here there were psalms.

'This the first day of May we set out. We are ... but having Lamorak to lead us. Beneath him all are equal ... calls me Con ... my friend John Paul ...'

Opposite this some words were underlined: 'Thou shalt break them with a rod of iron'. Hereward read on, as the pages turned growing engrossed in the story that was emerging from the patchy sentences with the faded words that were forever lost.

'Today is the eighth day beyond the Fence ... is empty ... in great grasslands ... Lamorak walks ... before we stop, nor change places with any man. The moon is not up. We reach Regret when ...'

Lamorak's expedition was strong, Hereward discovered. The book told more; they were the chosen, selected by Lamorak himself and ranging from warriors who were household names in Limber to untried boys. As they travelled they became warier and stained their clothes the colours of bark and leaves, all metals dulled and spoke in whispers.

'... fire in a hole in the ground. We grow closer ... men turning back. John Paul and I read this book every night ...'

'Hide me under the shadow of thy wings.'

The notes revealed something of Lamorak's intention, that the Unmen be trapped and destroyed in their city or settlement, for none knew what it was or looked like. 'They are not men,' Constantine had written, 'but self-created ... after the ... Years. So they hate us ... and scheme ever to make themselves masters.'

The words on the facing page had been ringed heavily as if he had sought assurance: '... the Lord shall swallow them up in his wrath and the fire shall devour them.' Hereward pondered what he had read. He had heard vaguely of Lamorak, but only that he had led some exploit of which no one really knew, or was willing to divulge, anything significant. He read on.

'More have left tonight, some secretly, others after ... John Paul and I are both anxious. Those of us left try to stay in the trees. The land itself does not like our presence ... I wonder if we are ...'

And arrowed: 'My strength is dried up like a potsherd.'

'Five days march from Regret ... This land is so empty. We talk only of home and ... small things.'

'Thy rod and thy staff they comfort me.'

'... we could not though there was one only and our hearts turned to water. Only when Lamorak came up and ... a solitary? He says the others will be less but hate us more ...'

Hereward wondered if the expedition had met someone like Lokietok. What did Demetrius call him? An ur-Unman? Did Lamorak really hope to get anyone home from Regret? He thumbed through the next pages quickly, the written entries being very short, until a paragraph caught his attention.

'Today I am writing by daylight. We are close to Regret. It is built of wood and thatch ... luck surely cannot last. I think we have been seen, though we are so few ...' There were some crossed out lines that might have been a poem, then the words, 'I do not expect to come back, so this may be my last entry. Constantine Villiers.' And underlined in the psalm: 'Into thine hand I commit my spirit.'

Surprisingly then the handwriting changed, though as with the previous writer most of the words were missing or illegible: '... I cannot tell but only two ... hundreds only two ... I could go no further ... farewell to Lamorak and Constantine my friend to ask their forgiveness in my weakness. A reconnaissance that Lamorak ... Next time ...' Several blank pages followed before the new writer spoke again. 'It is time to go. I have found nothing and am lost in these grasslands. The city of Regret is not where we first thought ... the Mesa country and is called Venask ... if they judge me faint of heart it will be true.' Here the writer had not only marked lines but had copied them across in capital letters: 'For it was not an enemy that reproached me; then I could have borne it ... but it was thou, a man mine equal, my guide and my acquaintance.'

"Demetrius, who is this writing now?"

"John Paul, later a marshal of the Matrix, and my uncle by marriage."

"So there was no assault on Regret?"

"No."

"And John Paul brought this book back to Venask?"

"Yes. He stayed near Regret for months searching for my father, but he was never found."

"And Lamorak himself?"

"They say he came back, took years to recover and then went to Regret a second time. He said that he had a secret key that he had found the first time and with it he and others could seize part of the power of the Unmen, perhaps all of it. There were only twelve on the second expedition, and eleven of them were Old Ones, because in the words of Lamorak only they could break the heart of Regret. I was the twelfth, the only one from the Daylight People. He couldn't leave me out, you see. Constantine Villiers was my father."

"So you went to Regret too."

"Seven years after my father disappeared. That was where I met you."

Hereward turned over the later unmarked pages of the psalter, sighed and said, "Did you?"

"Look, let me tell you about it. I tried to tell you in the monastery at Hay. It matters to me, you'll see why."

"All right, we owe you something for your hospitality at Venask."

"See if you think you owe me anything after you hear what I have to say. This is eight years ago and fifteen now since my father and John Paul went with Lamorak. Regret is six hundred miles north-east of Limber so it took us a month to reach the Fence and cross the grasslands. Gradually we began to know one another. We all got on well together, though everyone was very different. You were the only one from Westermain. I'd never met anyone from there. Lamorak called you Hereward, but to the others you were often Harry. I don't know which was right. Regret didn't frighten you or the others but it filled me with fear. In the last week I was sick every night thinking about it. Then we saw the city. I do not understand why my father wrote that it was wood and thatch. Perhaps it was then. Now it is white marble, reflecting the sun, built on islands in a blue lake that reaches almost to the horizon. I remember there were long causeways leading out to it. Then Lamorak told us that the weakness of the Unmen lay in their minds and that we must enter the milieu of their thoughts to overcome them. A woman had shown him how this was done and he would show us."

Demetrius's story grew more detailed as he related how the Old Ones were instructed in the method of entering the Unmen's mind, for, he told Hereward, their mind was a shared one. When they were warned that to do so they must fall into a coma from which there was a chance of never waking back into themselves, the Old Ones laughed.

"You didn't laugh, then?"

"No, Hereward. The woman knew I was afraid. She told me to go home. I was weak and ashamed. That night I left them. With the woman. They were in a coma, lying in the grasses. They were a different breed, you and the rest of them. I just quietly slipped away. Even the Unmen's trees and grasses told me to save myself, or save my soul. I've been ashamed ever since. That's why I didn't want even to see the Unman that follows you around. I should have gone into Regret with them, not run away.

"Afterwards I served with the Matrix militia, pretended to be brave. Trying to become another John Cortez, you see, for five years. It fooled some people, though not Nana and certainly not myself. Then I thought I would try to find you if you were still alive. With the others I had nowhere to start, except one had the speech of the Archipelago and another said he was a Lettlander, little things like that. But you once said you lived within sight of Ingastowe Cathedral and that helped me. Also you sometimes spoke words I knew, like: 'An if we live we live to tread on kings, if die, brave death when princes die with us.' So I brought that play and a few more to Ingastowe and there you were. You, and not you, and everything faded into nothing since you had lost your memory. You looked very different, much older, but it had to be you. Ingastowe Cathedral had pulled you back. But you wanted nothing from me. I understood that. So I never got to say sorry. What if my father had had someone to help him? One more man to help, in the place you and the others went into, it might well have made all the difference."

The evening light had nearly gone now, though there was enough to outline the branches black and grey above them and show the trees like slender stone columns. "Maybe," said Hereward. "It was a long time ago. Let me think about it."

"In the morning," said Demetrius, "I shall go back to Venask. I hope you find what you are looking for in Limber."

They went back to the fire, and Martin laughed when Hereward asked drily, "Did you enjoy working with Demetrius?"

"He enjoyed it. He didn't have to play trolls and calibans and idiot-tinkers. He was the hero."

"A hero who ran away. You got to be the King of the Glassy Country."

"Thank you, Dmitri. I didn't have to join your troupe to be one of the Twisted Folk."

"I gave you a crown."

"A paper one. I liked it best as the man in the moon's dog. I got a real collar. Do you remember coming to watch us, Hereward?"

Hereward nodded. The past was starting to rearrange itself more satisfactorily in his head, instead of its events running like ants in a line. Now he was stringing chosen beads on to a cord.

"I think I'll go for a walk," Hereward said. "If he wishes, Demetrius can tell you what he has just told me. I was dozing, Demetrius, when Adelie was hurt, so one day I'll have to explain that to her. Everyone would like to change part of his life. Don't fret." He walked away to find Lokietok, who kept some distance from Demetrius, the latter having told the others that he never wished to set eyes on an Unman.

The massive figure climbed to its feet, shook and yawned. Images fluttered but only of the night, the trees and the moon, refracted as through thick glass. The two strolled on, leaving the quiet voices behind. The air was warm, caressing and densely scented, spicy barks and leaves and pine-needles fusing together, woodsmoke somewhere hinting its presence.

How much stranger than the blend of scents, Hereward thought, was the mixture of personalities of which he was part. Do we blend, like the woodland's scent, and become more than ourselves? Into his mind came the notion of his parents and the parents of George, Martin and Demetrius. As he had met only Martin's mother it was not a clear picture, but he imagined them as being not unlike their sons. Behind them were their parents and beyond more pairs so that the line stretched back into a twilit past, back through the Broken Years, far back, long lines of people diverging like the ribs of a spread fan towards a fringe of indistinct squat ape-like forms bent as if they had emerged from caves. Then his mind's eye returned along the fan's ribs back towards the four of them. The figures were relaying down their lines, one to another, an aura of light until his and his friends' parents passed the glow to their sons and daughters. Not long after the light had left their hands, to illuminate their children, the parents' shapes went dark. He left a faint glimmer lingering round Martin's mother whom he knew to be alive. The whole analogue surprised him, jumping into his mind fully-fledged as it had. Behind him Lokietok grimaced uneasily as if waking from a disturbed sleep. Hereward wondered briefly about the Unman's ancestry, but Lokietok had ceased to communicate even the old terror.

So many men and women had lived to make him, lived to make everyone alive, an almost endless succession that had passed on not only his body and mind but whatever simultaneously led, drove and illuminated them both. He felt a deep sense of awe at the thought of bearing the commission of so many. Though it was paradoxical that he should be acting out a purpose without knowing what it was, that remained a paradox only if one accepted its terms. The light knew the purpose, he was sure. It hadn't come from the beginning of time for nothing.

In any case he did have a purpose for the present, to head on towards Limber. After that he might go back and work at the mill in Hay – though as he was still an outlaw that could be difficult. It nagged at his mind that he had killed Adelie's attacker though she was not dead. It was an imbalance that disturbed him. Maybe it would be corrected. Maybe, he thought, if it coincided with the shimmering light's purpose.

A little owl called 'hoo-hoo' ahead of them and he saw its stubby silhouette. Cicadas hopped underfoot and twigs crackled as Lokietok trampled carelessly among the bushes. A day's journey behind them Dominic Santos's body had just fallen on to broken twigs among chirruping cicadas. The Daroi warriors were eating pork and wondering why anyone could be so stubborn as to fight for pigs.

XXV

Jacky could read and had been able to do so since he was a tiny boy, but had read very little. At least, he had read often enough but there had been only a small number of books in his father's house, apart of course from the many fishing records and ships' logs which his family had preserved and perused over many generations. Jacky had read the records many times and knew most of the books by heart. Astolat, who read avidly and fretted for new material, would laugh at her brother and his handful of much-loved stories. Like all his friends and acquaintances, he could recite the history of his own family and of the estuary, but these were songs and poetry, legends and anecdotes, that could make you hold your breath or tremble or laugh: 'The men who killed death' or 'The mushroom sower' or 'The night great-grandfather Ulf saw the ghost' and hundreds more. Neither Jacky nor anyone else had ever seen these stories written down. He did own a sort of bestiary, which Astolat herself liked to read, telling of the various creatures that lived on or by a river. To his surprise he was holding another copy of it at that very moment in mid-morning as he sat in one of the academy libraries, with Astolat peering over his shoulder.

He had found a picture of an otter, one of his favourites. She smiled, reaching across to run her finger-nail under a sentence: 'They are family animals.' "Like us, the Dorns," she said gravely. He had accompanied her to the academy for the last three days, though Kit was yet to appear there, preferring to wait on the Steps for Hereward.

Disturbing rumours were beginning to circulate of the northward movement of the Daroi. A few of the wanderers on the Steps had seen them, and the number of refugees was increasing. "When the storm comes where do the leaves go?" Kit said. "We shall see more of these displaced people before long."

Jacky was amazed by Astolat. On many occasions, particularly when the fishing-boats had reached the northern islands, he had watched the seabirds, white as snowflakes against the wet cliff-faces, rolling, looping, sideslipping, playing with the air, an exhilarating capricious element to dive into and wrestle with, plumage fluttering over singing sinews. Yet into the tangled, frothing breakers was no place for Jacky's boat, and best left to the fulmars and petrels. Astolat in her new world was just as at ease as the birds in theirs, and Jacky as ready to watch in admiration.

The first principle of the academies seemed to be that there should be no teaching as he understood it, or at least no instruction, its pupils simply being asked questions, some starting 'How?' or 'What?' but most beginning 'Why?' The children's mentors then listened to their responses as they sat on a bench in a cloister or had them delivered at the counter of a shop or across a table in one of the squares off the Steps. The previous day Sister Francesca, sitting with Astolat at violin practice, had leaned across, plucked one of the instrument's strings and said, "Why?" Now Astolat was trying out her ideas on her brother, skipping unselfconsciously through a maze of possibilities.

"Come on, Jacky. Why does this string go 'ping'? And don't say because it does!"

He grinned at having his answer predicted. "It goes 'ping' because of the way it's made."

"Good. It must go 'ping' because it's made of gut and it's thin and flexible, not brittle. Now if you took it off the violin and put it in your pocket what noise would it make? A mouse sitting on the violin and one in your pocket, not mine – " she giggled " – would make the same noise, wouldn't they?"

"More or less," Jacky agreed.

"So what does the string in your pocket need?"

"It needs to be taut and it needs to be touched."

"That must be right. Is the mouse the same?"

"How do you make a mouse taut?" He turned his head away so that she could not see him smile.

"Not the mouse, silly, whatever it is that goes 'squeak'. Does it make it taut and then touch it with something down here?" She pointed down her throat.

Jacky pulled the string tight between his hands and it thrummed gently in vibration. "Like that, maybe?"

She ran a finger up and down the string making it squeak. "Or like that?"

"Wait a bit," he said, the game intriguing him. "It's wet in a mouse's mouth." Astolat giggled again. "If we hold the string tight, like this, under water, and then pluck it, will it go 'ping'?"

They went up to what the children called Rats' Alley. The big glass booth had been repaired and the rats inside it were all near the food trough. "They've got some more, Astolat."

"No, Jacky. These ones didn't run away. Look, they've got tags round their legs. That's how to recognise them. Anyway there's food in there. Where would you rather be, well fed in a cage or starving out of it? Don't answer, it's not a fair question. It's what Sister Francesca calls 'imaginary limitations'."

Who can tell where a butterfly will alight when it flickers

crookedly through the garden? Astolat, like butterflies in this, was also like them in rarely staying still. There were so many nectaries to sip. She pushed her hands into the water-creatures' tank, the violin string between them. "Ping it," she told her brother. When he plucked the string it made a noise, lower but clear enough. "So what's between the string and our ears makes a difference. But does it change the sound or make it harder to hear? I'll go in the corridor and ping it and you close the door and listen."

So it went on all morning as Astolat investigated her world, tinkling with laughter as she bounced her views and surmises off her brother. About midday they found themselves out on one of the terraces leading off the Steps, a terrace with pools above which dragonflies hummed. Jacky fetched his sister pastries soaked in honey. The dragonflies were absorbing her attention and her mouth was full of food; the rare break in the barrage of questions allowed Jacky to change the subject. He hoped she would treat his question as she did all the others, another air current tilting the birds' wings. "Astolat," he said slowly, "are you happy?"

"Too hard, Jacky, it depends on . . ."

"I know, on what happiness is. Just let's pretend we know what it is."

"Then, I think sometimes I am, and sometimes I'm not."

"If we were back at the river would you be happier than you are here?"

"Yes, I expect so. I know you would be happier, back with the otters and water rats. So why aren't we going? And don't say because we're not." Jacky gave a long sigh, and was silent, so she answered her own question: "You want Kit to come home too, and she's not ready."

"Not yet, Astolat. One day, maybe."

"Jacky?"

"Yes."

"Do you think we were meant to be happy?"

He shrugged, staring at her in affection. Over her shoulder he could see Kit walking towards them. She was dressed all in black, the long sleeves of the black dress half hiding the black glove. She rarely wore any other colour, and apart from the soft black shoes she had acquired on the Cobblers' Steps her clothes had all been woven on the looms of her people somewhere near Hay or Ingastowe: black flowers and ferns on her dress and behind them a black sun against a black sky. Chin up and eyes narrowed she walked with quick light steps like the fox in her name, and just as wary and poised. Even sitting she sat on the edge of her chair and Astolat, who could not sit without lolling back or pretending her seat was a rocking-chair, said enviously, "Oh, Kit, you always look so cool."

"Hmm." Kit was fond of Astolat whom she found entertaining and easy company, a rest from the ambivalent emotions aroused by her brother.

"Kit, do you think we were meant to be happy?"

Jacky flinched, expecting the answer to be Kit at her most vinegary, and he was thankful for her mildness: "I think we were meant to try to be happy."

"How do you try?" Astolat went on.

"Well, for a start, by changing whatever makes you unhappy."

"Is being happy the same as not being unhappy?"

"I don't think so. It's probably different for everyone but I suppose being happy is when you can be a man or woman or bird or tree as fully as possible and being unhappy is when someone or some circumstance stops you. There's maybe some area in between where nothing is stopping you being yourself except your own . . ." Deep in thought Kit patted the table top with her gloved paw, and saw Astolat's eyes widen at its strange narrowness.

"Laziness?" the girl asked, looking away.

"No, not really."

"Inertia? That's what stops lots of objects moving."

Kit smiled. "That's nearer, but not quite. Some people just don't think they can be what they dream of, and end up saying 'if only' all their lives. Did you notice my glove? I always wear it because I have no hand, or not one like yours anyway. People like me are called twisters, as I'm sure you know. What else do you know about us?"

Across the table Astolat's blue eyes were wide and her small hands had clenched into fists. She was busy with her thoughts, riffling through them, catching here a word or phrase, there a picture: mothers in Ferris's Landing looking up, dreading to ask the midwife, or little Adrian, so happy as an infant then aging a year for every week until his parents shook like quaking grass. Astolat's father had taken Adrian up on the ness and 'they' came and took him for one of theirs; then Oxback Willis, and the picture in Jacky's book of the faun playing panpipes. "I know you are different."

"What happens when there's sickness in the village or in the flocks, or a child's lost, or a pig goes missing, or the church steeple gets blown down?"

"I'm not sure," Astolat faltered.

"Ask your brother."

They both looked at Jacky but he stared away to the deep blue of the bay where the masts were thick as reeds. "You tell her," he said tersely.

"All right. Though I think she knows. What happens is that someone in the village or on one of the farms, it doesn't matter where, gets a crowd together and they go out hunting. It's exactly like killing badgers, you need some dogs, some spades and probably some sticks and rope, perhaps matches. Then when they've chivvied some of us out of our holes or cellars or wherever we've tried to make a home then the fun starts, particularly with the girls or women like me, those that are not too twisted or too old. That bit isn't like badger-hunting, of course, but the end result's not much different. Some places are better than others. Hay valley is one of the better ones, apart from my father being killed there."

"I'm sorry, Kit." Astolat wished Jacky would speak.

"I know."

"Is there any way to make it stop?"

"The only way I can think of is to bring the Matrix on to our side. They have always left us alone as long as we stay in the dark, hidden away. There is a legend that one day we will find someone to help us. My brother may have found him. We call him Tyr, or Tyr-Hereward. Like the old weapon-god with one hand he has one eye. I am waiting for him to come here with my brother. You see some of us got tired of saying 'if only'."

Astolat had listened with interest. She rolled her eyes, sucked her lips in and made a series of grimaces designed to help her think, then took another pastry and munched it: "Can you do something for the Matrix so valuable they will want to reward your folk for ever?"

"I can't think of what, can you?"

"Should we tell them about our teachers? You know, the two who came with Sister Francesca."

"Maybe," said Kit. The idea had merit, she thought, but not really enough weight.

"Jacky," said Astolat finishing off her pastry. "Look at them!" The dragonflies were very near the table, the sun turning their wings to the thinnest golden shavings as they hovered. She made the violin string resonate and watched the insects carefully. Did every insect vibrate its wings at the same speed? What about other stringed instruments, cellos, pianos even? No dragonfly would obligingly sit on a violin, but a piano? "I could try a bee in a piano, Jacky. Then if it buzzed like one of the notes . . ."

"Maybe a bumblebee would be better," Kit suggested.

"Jacky, can I have this last cake? Sonics is fun, isn't it, Kit?"

Through a mouthful of cake, Astolat added, "I'm still thinking about what you said. You know, about getting the blame for the church steeple."

Her brother shook his head. He envied Kit's ability to cope with an Astolat conversation. "That bee in a piano . . .?" he said.

XXVI

Movement was life for the Daroi and they had not found the Levels or the Mesa difficult. Their vast cattle herds had provided them with milk and blood, and halfway across it had rained heavily, so heavily that water lay in wide muddy sheets through which they waded. Had the rain not come they would still have reached the green mountain ranges on the other side but not so many of their cattle would have survived. This would not have caused them any great concern. "It is the way," they would have said and shrugged. "Yesterday ten cows walked with us, today we have five. So? I am still I. We are still we, the Daroi. Now we will walk faster."

But most of the herds lived, so they came on more slowly. Some of their people stayed behind in High Altai, not many but often as they roamed they would leave colonies behind, small principalities that would before long sink into the original peoples of that place. Even with greater numbers there was never really the lust for dominion; the way was all and the settlers' hearts were with the wayfarers by now unimaginable miles along, rapidly folding the tents in the morning, in the evening looking lovingly at the horizon. The front of the migration was now through the southernmost Outlands and filtering into Ambria, one of those lands that had been part of the Matrix as long as there had been such a sovereignty.

The Daroi, for whom war happened between one step and the next, expected to do battle at any time, not least in that for a full generation and more they had heard of the power and wrath of the Matrix, as warning and expectation, as simple as 'in the south it will be hot'. Yet in all their migration never yet had they seen the blue and gold banners or looked at the blue line of the Matrix's fighting-men waiting on the ridge or at the river. The very first of the Daroi to do so was to be the clan of Zander Bey, which somewhere near the centre of the twenty-mile-wide advance had camped that night in a small village of stone houses clustered around a squat slit-windowed church.

The Daroi took what they wanted, which was almost always food, but when thwarted became murderously ill-tempered. They had a proverb, 'Whoever owns the chicken, no one owns the eggs', and owning very little themselves were impatient with unfortunates such as Dominic Santos. Dominic's body lay in the bushes on the edge of his garden, but though almost hidden it had not escaped the notice of the man who came walking in from the north. Miles back he had smelled the smoke of hundreds of fires, but not until he looked down at the friend of his boyhood had he begun to think what he intended to do.

The fiercest of the fighting-men of Zander Bey, every one of whom aspired to lead his clan one day, just as twenty others like Zander Bey waited only for El Daro to hesitate, sat along the sides of the long table in the big house. Tireless and strong, black moustache thick under a hooked nose, their leader was as formidable as he looked. The maid-girls, who had not fled the house only because Nana remained, brought in bowls of soup, hesitantly, like timid ghosts, listening to the Daroi's strange sing-song version of the Matix speech that most had learned in High Altai. Nana had barely spoken a word. Her world had collapsed around her but she did not acknowledge it. She stood silent and gazed out into her garden, the green stars glowing on her dress.

"Why are we so unwelcome?" asked Zander Bey over his shoulder. "Is it that we are strangers? In our tents the stranger takes the first drink and the choicest bite. You are not poor, this house has many fine rooms, more than you can use, you have food enough." He gestured at the full bowls. "Will you go hungry tomorrow?"

"You are not guests," said Nancy Villiers.

"You are not hospitable. Should we sit in ditches while your velvet chairs stand empty? Are we less than your cats?"

"You do as you do because you are many and I am an old woman. If my husband were alive there would be no unbidden people in this house."

"It would have been good to meet him," said one of the young warriors. "We have met no real men yet."

"Only pig-keepers pretending to be men," said another.

Just outside the door Demetrius stiffened as he caught the last remark. He had been uncertain of what to do, but now he walked softly away down the corridor and mounted the long stairs. He went to his own room, entered it and opened another door into a small boxroom. From a tall wardrobe he took the faded blue tunic with the gold epaulettes, put it on and placed the hanger back on the rail. Opening drawers full of linen scented by small bags of lavender he lifted the sheets and shirts and from beneath them removed his weapons. He made a brief round of the room, glancing at pictures, opening another drawer to look at the handwriting on old letters, fingering a sea-shell, stroking the backs of his books so that they sat level with the edges of the shelves, and then took a last look out of his window, noting sadly that the big pear tree no longer filled his view but lay mutilated on the lawn, its smaller branches having been carried off for kindling. Going back down the stairs he searched his mind for a line from his days as a player but found only someone else's: '. . . a man can die but once. We owe God a death.' Whose line had it been? One of the Twisted Folk actors, he thought, one of Martin's cousins. Demetrius was oddly pleased to have said his farewells in such a way, quiet and composed. To die suddenly, he thought, means no time to say goodbye properly. Now he was ready.

Along the corridor he met one of the maids in tears, carrying a tray loaded with plates and food. "Oh, Dmitri," she whispered, "they are drinking too much in there. I am afraid for madame."

"Who killed Dominic?"

"The first one on the left as you go in," she said.

"Pigeon pie," he murmured, and picked up a slice from the tray. "Lovely pastry. Wasted on them. Now you go home. Take the others. Don't talk about it, go on!" The laughter round the dining table was so loud that he stood a moment unnoticed in the doorway by all but Nana, counting the heads, even taking another bite at his piece of pie. Then he came forward in three fast strides and the gun's hammer was back under his thumb and the muzzle against Zander Bey's temple.

"Before the feast best count who comes for the broken crumbs," his aunt said into the silence.

Zander Bey pulled his lips back in a snarl that showed his teeth filed to points. It was the mark of a close-quarters fighter of the most dangerous sort. "Who are you?" he said, lifting one finger to his men to keep them in their seats, and Demetrius saw him tucking his feet beneath him ready to drive upwards.

"I live here. This is our house, mine and my aunt's. She does not wish to fill a murderer's cup." He pointed at the man on Zander Bey's left, who stared back with a short laugh that had nothing in it but defiance. Others were almost imperceptibly edging their chairs back from the table.

"Stay still," said Zander Bey. So this is one of them, he was thinking, watching the big freckled hand that was only inches from his eyes, one of them at last. We had to meet them in the end, the lords of the horizon, always somewhere north of our future until today. "If we leave your house," he asked mildly, "do you expect us to run away?"

"No. I expect you to come back to find me, ten, twenty at a time, with your dogs to help you. Remember to bring men as well."

Again the Daroi shivered and stirred round the table, straining like their dogs for action, but never looking away from the gun. Surely they don't think they can reach me before their chieftain is dead, thought Demetrius, and hoped they wanted him kept alive. Candlelight showed the whites of their eyes as they stared at him. "Up," he said, lifting Zander Bey by his long black hair and walked backwards out of the dining-room and down the corridor that led to the front door, pulling the Daroi after him with one hand but never letting the gun barrel relax its cold pressure. The rest followed as closely as they dared, as he knew they would. The grandfather clock chimed deep and mellow, then began its nine strokes and elsewhere in the house, echoing in its high rooms, the silvery bells of smaller clocks. The corridor widened into a hallway and just to the side of the big front door was a small room that was used for coats and umbrellas, walking-sticks and hats. Demetrius, who had already selected it, backed into its entrance and held Zander Bey in the threshold. "Open the front door and walk out," he called to the group crowding along the corridor after them

"Do you want us to go?" asked the first man as he passed within arm's length of the Daroi chieftain.

"Yes, fool!" snapped Zander Bey.

The others followed and as the last one stepped outside Demetrius pushed the chieftain towards the door, and spoke in his ear. "Now let me hear you say 'Please let me live', and loud so those outside can hear."

"Why should I?"

"Because those were the last words of my friend Dominic, or something like it."

"If I do not say it, we will come back and kill you," said the Daroi. "But no one else. We will spare the old woman and her house."

"Say it loud. Very loud," said another voice, an old thin voice but peremptory and commanding. "Do you think to frighten me, the widow of a marshal of the Matrix?"

Zander Bey wanted desperately to live and to repay this moment a thousand times over, and though he could not bring himself to speak loudly he still had the gun barrel against his head and so he muttered the words. "Louder," said Demetrius. "Dominic didn't whisper, did he?" The Daroi was full of a deadly rage that was fast eroding his instinct to survive, his humiliation bubbling and hissing in his head, like acid falling on lime, seething in ochre foam and exuding a choking gas. He took two paces down the stone steps that led straight on to the village street, and then came the gunshot ringing in his ears and he was still alive, but could not endure what had happened, so he let his legs slide past him, pivoting on his hands, gripping a stone step, and when his scrabbling feet hit a lower step launched himself back towards the doorway. Demetrius's knee snapped upwards, taking Zander Bey so heavily in the face that he was lifted in a somersault through the air to collapse like a puppet at the foot of the steps. The

Matrix handguns were inaccurate and limited to one cartridge but Demetrius had always intended his only shot for Dominic's killer and not for Zander Bey. At such close range he had not missed.

For a few seconds no one moved and Demetrius, looking down the six white steps and over the low wall capped with pink and crimson geraniums, drank it all in: the long sandy street, now filling with faces and noise, men shouting and feet running, the smells, pines, dust, smoke, the scents of a warm evening, familiar as the palm of his own hand, the splash of white roses in a nearby garden, the yellow of a lighted window in the first shadows of dusk. Then he stepped back inside the door and bolted it all in one fluid movement. Behind him he saw his aunt standing at the bottom of the curved stairway at the far end of the long hall. "Into the cellar, Nana, quick." She turned and made for the kitchens.

Next to the big kitchen-stove there was a brown door. Demetrius and Dominic as boys had been fascinated by it. In winter you could hear water lapping behind it when the well in the cellar floor overflowed, and floating boxes and jars would nudge the inside of the door, their gentle tapping like water-beasts to the small boys' imaginations. Demetrius followed his aunt down the corridor, the crashing at the front door behind him filling the house with splintering noise. He was about to swing into the kitchen when there came a pounding rush of feet and a roaring of voices, and he saw a dozen of the Daroi, their curved sabres gleaming in front of them, each shoving the other to be first to reach him. They had clearly entered the house by the garden door while their comrades had been held up at the main entrance. He sprang backwards and into a small anteroom, which offered at least temporary protection. He bolted this door too and jammed a chair under the handle. Outside there was a babble of voices, which increased as the main door was unbolted and many more poured into the house. Demetrius jumped back as the window set high in the wall was shattered by a stone, but the window's smallness and the shape of the room would, he thought, protect him. The noise outside stopped after a while and there was a knock on the door.

"Can you hear me, Matrix lord?" He recognised the voice of Zander Bey.

"I am no lord," he called back.

"This house is a great house. What else are you?"

"A man of this village and a free servant of the Matrix."

"So. We are the Daroi, also men, and we offer you, man, a choice."

"Say it then. Is it between bad and worse?"

"You must decide that. If you stay in the room we shall burn the house, and you in it. There is much wood in the house, yet it will not be quick, I think."

"And the choice?"

"To let you out. You bring a weapon, but no guns, and then you walk along the street. Whoever wishes to bar your way shall do so. To the death."

"How many wish to do that?" asked Demetrius. Clearly the Daroi did not believe in the Matrix's law of a just and exact revenge.

"The brother of the man you shot, his father, his dog. I, Zander Bey, for my honour. Then I do not know. Why, do you wish to say, 'Please let me live'?" Outside the door there was a clash of voices, then silence and Zander Bey again. "Many wish to be next, but say you will not last long enough, so as to that we must wait. Do you wish for time to think?"

"No. Tell them to be ready," called Demetrius. "Be ready yourself." He smiled to himself. It was the end of his journey, there was no doubt of that, but often lately he had found himself trying to relive his younger days, taking walks he had first walked long ago, looking for familiar trees, for the holes in the streambed where the fish that had once been used to hide from the boy he had once been. Now these newcomers would change all that, so that before and after their coming would be like before and after the bad years that cut us off from the Blessed Time for ever.

Then, waiting in the street, was the fear he had met on the grasslands near Regret. He didn't wish to think about it though it was drawing him out for this final encounter. So he opened the door and stepped out into the hallway. The Daroi drew back to clear a path to the door and down the steps, and then closed in behind.

The twilight had almost faded, but the street sparkled with torches and light spilling into it from the open doors and windows of the houses that lined it. He looked along the far side, seeing a farmhouse, a barber's shop, a butcher's, three or four dwelling-houses that were all tangled together so that he had never been quite sure which family would answer any particular door, then the bridge over the stream, and a bend to the left. The near side was roughly the same, though the long wall of Nana's garden stretched for some way before the next house on that side. The third house on the right had espaliered apricots that grew on its front wall. Demetrius could not see them but he knew they were there. In all his life he had rarely seen more than twenty people in the street at any one time, but now there were two long banks of faces and a buzz of many voices. From the middle of the road he could see many of the folk of the village, some half-hidden behind the Daroi, others at upstairs windows or perched on walls, even little children peering past the folds of the black or chequered cloaks the Daroi wore. He knew why they were there, his own people. He had been their ornament and pride, the chosen one who went with Lamorak to Regret, who had led the Sawtooth Mountains militia, for whom the world had unfolded so that he had seen its lily petals, while they had seen only the clasped green calyx, working and living about this spot for all of their enclosed lives. So this was the time of the paying of debts, to die as befits one whom the world had favoured. Let them take this moment home to the cottages, whisper it in bed, embroider it in the telling so that the children do not cast themselves as victims too easily. Polish tonight into an amulet.

But Demetrius was thinking of another time altogether, that he could recall because he thought of it every day: nearly nine years ago and the Old Ones laughing.

He took off the blue tunic, folded it and handed it to a woman standing near the gate of the big house. She was one of Nana's oldest acquaintances and he knew her well. "Look after this for me, Mary, please."

He had been little birds-nesting Dmitri to her once, with a brown corduroy jerkin that was too small and boots that were too big. "I will, Dmitri," she said.

He pulled out the Matrix sword. It was short and broad, a sword meant for crowded melees but he knew it well, and he knew that not many fights last more than seconds before the fighters close. He kept the long hunting stiletto in its sheath under his shirt. Ahead of him he saw a man step into the middle of the road and there was a long-drawn sound from the crowd, like a sigh of satisfaction. As Demetrius walked forward the noise swelled and swirled around him. The Daroi warrior waited and then came in fast, wiry in build and light on his feet, and Demetrius parried three rapid sabre cuts. Though he felt the sabre jar his arm its weight was not enough to jolt him back, and he smiled grimly to himself. When he had the warrior with his back to the crowd he drove in and left him no room to move except forward on to the Matrix blade. It had only lasted seconds. "Some company for Dominic," said a voice in the crowd.

Shrill through the uproar he could hear other friendly voices calling his name. Oddly it pleased him a great deal and he walked on watchfully. Behind him a figure bent over the body on the road, then straightened up. Demetrius stood still and the man came closer. He was older, probably the father to whom Zander Bey had deferred his own challenge, a different fighter, grey-haired, stripped to the waist, with grey on his chest, and bigger than most of the Daroi. Over his shoulder he held poised a short lance or assegai, with two or three more strapped on his back. Demetrius wondered how good he was with them. He knew how good he was himself, certainly not Baldwin or Lamorak or one of the shining names, but he was experienced and calm, and his teachers had considered him an apt pupil. He watched the throwing arm carefully, instinctively pushing his chin behind his right shoulder.

The man had stopped. Three paces to his right two of the yellow hounds snarled and barked ferociously, rearing up on their hind legs as they strove to reach Demetrius, almost dragging off balance the men holding their leashes. Their twisting shapes caused Demetrius to flick one quick glance in their direction and he knew it was a mistake even as he did it. The arm came forward like a striking snake and, flinching to his left, he felt a hot punch in his side. The grey-haired man was reaching his arm back for a second throw but Demetrius was much too close. The instant pounce and thrust flung the lanceman among the legs of the crowd, though the Daroi yelled as they saw Demetrius tug once and again at the spear shaft projecting from just above his hip.

From her gateway Sylvie Patillo, the first girl he had ever kissed, was weeping for fifteen-year-old Dmitri, their eyes meeting as he twisted like a gaffed fish. "Behind you, Dmitri!" he heard her scream. He tore out the spear, appalled by the pain that came with it, just as the dog was on him. The yellow hounds of the Daroi had only one master in all their lives; brutish and aggressive, they loved once only. When the lance-man went down his dog came at Demetrius like a beast from a fever-dream. As it sprang chest-high at him he flung up his hands, but the impact sent him crashing backwards on to the hard sand and the beast, yammering and growling, bit at his arms as he held them across his throat and face. It had torn wounds in both arms before he had time even to think and its panting, flesh-smelling breath was hot in his face, spattering him with saliva and blood. Driving his left arm up into its jaws he felt the fangs scrape on bone as his right hand frantically searched under his shirt and found the knife-hilt. He was semi-conscious with pain and revulsion at the half-mad creature pressing him down, mauling him, but the long, thin blade slashed in and out like the sting of a giant scorpion until the growling became a shrill howling and then there was silence.

Demetrius rolled the animal off him and lay looking up at an indigo sky in which one big star shone off to the west. Over his own sobbing breaths he could hear someone crying and the buzz of many voices. Then, moving one limb at a time, angularly and clumsily like a damaged beetle, he got to his feet and wiped his face with his right hand. He didn't want to look at his left hand.

The centre of the road seemed empty now. What were the conditions of the gauntlet he was running? If there really were any. To the end of the street? Venask was not large, the street narrowed into a dirt track only five minutes walk away, so perhaps to the end of the road. The road had no end that he knew of, unless it was the gates of Limber. I suppose it was the road they meant, he thought, not that it matters much.

Then he saw, silhouetted fitfully, Zander Bey standing on the bridge over the tumbling stream. Demetrius knew the noisy water became a smooth flow through the twin culverts before swirling in the deep pool beneath the terrace of the tavern. The Daroi chieftain was alone on the bridge, his back resting on the parapet. He came forward barring Demetrius's slow approach, knife-point upwards, filed teeth bared.

"I am Zander Bey Daro. Remember me, Matrix lord?"

"Should I?" Demetrius had lost his sword, perhaps in the dust beside the dog, but he still had the stiletto. He thought back to his militia instructors, Alain and Bernard, their long ago voices clear in his head and he wondered if they were old men somewhere along the street. It was possible.

Zander Bey came in fast and out again as swift as a swallow in full flight sips at a pond. Demetrius struck late and saw the smile on the thin dark face; he felt weak and he knew the lance wound was bleeding. The Daroi came in again, feinted high and struck low, poised on tiptoe, all hesitations gone; in again, another feint, no opening this time, but even twisting away was tiring. In again and again. Demetrius was sweating heavily, the sweat salty as he licked his lips. His left arm was not responding properly and the Daroi, having seen it, was circling to come in on his left every time. Silently he repeated the oldest axiom of all: however good he is, even the best, if you hold on long enough you'll get one chance. This one is good, he thought, but he's prolonging it, showing off. Demetrius flexed the muscles in his left arm and felt their response twitch, then let his arm fall slack again. Zander Bey came forward high on the balls of his feet, smooth dancing steps that never let one foot ahead of another, and Demetrius swivelled at the centre of the circle and imperceptibly let his heels down and his feet begin to drag. The dancing figure that was almost round behind his vulnerable side darted in for the slash upward at the heart. Demetrius forced himself to keep his left arm hanging limp and tried to avoid the blade by swaying back but it went in just below his collar-bone, scraped on it and tore through. 'Too fast,' he thought, 'and I'm too old. One chance, please.' Though there were waves of noise sweeping round him, voices crying out and shouting, here at the vortex they were not sounds he could distinguish. He let the movements resettle into the circling pattern, knowing there would be another clash within a few seconds.

'Don't think about it,' said Alain's voice in his head. 'Defend. You'll know it when it comes.' Then Zander Bey was on him again and there was the chance, plain as the gleaming star in the west. The Daroi chieftain was just too close in to Demetrius's vulnerable left side and he shouted at his left arm and its torn muscles responded behind a screen of pain and the arm clamped round his adversary, locking the Daroi to him chest to chest. Zander Bey's arm went back to strike and Demetrius had to drop the stiletto to catch the knife-hand by the wrist. He saw the filed teeth bare as the lips drew back and felt the mouth search for his throat. Filled with disgust, Demetrius threw all his weight forward and in a shambling brutal embrace the two staggered five or six paces and fell into the stream's swirling knee-deep current.

Demetrius had fallen into this stream a dozen times and more as a boy and knew every minnow and eddy. The faces that pressed and bobbed on the parapet and the figures that thronged the bank saw the white water welter and break over Demetrius's back. Seconds and then minutes went by and his back was like a new brown boulder in the water, but in the dusk no one saw that Zander Bey was pinned, drowning, to the stones of the stream-bed, until Demetrius turned for the bank and a new log rolled away with the current. Once the water swept his fumbling feet from under him, but he crawled to the steep bank and many hands hauled him out.

Looking up Demetrius met the gaze of Father Anselm. Somewhere mistily in the old priest's head was a christening day: Constantine Villiers and his wife bringing the babe to the font – and now this battered triton, streaming with water, his wet hair flattened as the babe's had been.

"Well, Father?"

"What is it, my son?"

"Did I do well?"

"Yes," said Father Anselm. No other answer seemed right at the time. The priest put Demetrius's arm over his shoulder and stumbled as he felt his weight but together they staggered across the bridge to the village shop that sold items as various as candles, liquorice, needles and combs. The Daroi had gathered curiously around, so close it seemed the weight of their breathing pressed on the pair. There was a bell at the door that customers tinkled to fetch the old lady Beatrice from the back parlour in happier days.

"Far enough," said Demetrius. "Now tie my wrist to the bell bracket." His voice was faint, and the street was rising and falling beneath his feet, as if a giant were casually flicking bights along it as children do with ropes and whips. Now the rise of the bridge and the road in front of the shop were jammed with faces and the voices were like a million bees. What had been the clan of Zander Bey buzzed as it instated a new leader. Whoever he was would come forward soon and as the claimants eyed one another Father Anselm, using the cord of his cassock, tied Demetrius's arm fast to the bell overhead.

"Pray for me, Father."

"Any special prayer?"

The pain in Demetrius's side was throbbing in time with his pulse and he could not think easily. "Perhaps to forgive my pride. I ran away when I went with Lamorak. Nobody in Venask knew that, except Aunt Nana. But I didn't run today. Is it a sin to be proud?"

"Not much of one," said Father Anselm.

For some time nothing happened save for the occasional clink of the bell as Demetrius swayed. Then at the far end of the street came the noise of many feet and voices, one voice used to command raised above the others. Demetrius lifted his head and saw the colours, the blue and gold bright in the sun, and the sun-browned faces, heard the crash of their feet, and the sound of their voices. They were singing 'One more tequila', the song he had sung with them in the militia. He heard them laughing and laughed himself. The Matrix had put forth its strength again and he was glad, though he was unsure why the sun was so bright.

El Daro pushed through the crowd, his brothers either side of him and paused at what he saw. The warriors of his own clan tramping behind him also pushed through and stopped. When he said loudly, "Where is Zander Bey?" he was told that the eels were eating him. "Give me a lance," he ordered, and went across the bridge. There in the darkness lit by wavering flames, was a scarecrow, eyes closed, hanging from a shop doorway. His arm went forward and back three times, and then once more. At each thrust Demetrius lurched away and the bell tolled thinly. El Daro turned and strode down the street. He felt uneasy, the air tasted dusty and hot, and silence followed him.

As Father Anselm lay in bed, unable to sleep, he thought how somewhere pride and love get mixed up. Maybe Demetrius had been too proud to run twice, but the priest also knew how much he had loved Venask and its folk. Maybe Christ had been too proud to run.

Sylvie Patillo cried herself to sleep but was woken at three in the morning by the crackling roar of a huge fire and the screams from inside the burning building as those of the Daroi who had slept in the big house struggled to escape from the locked and smoke-filled rooms into the corridors, where Aunt Nana walked rattling her big key-ring while her cats ran and flinched from the flames.

XXVII

For a week Hereward, Martin, George and Lokietok progressed steadily north-eastwards. The land through which they passed consisted for the most part of undulating wooded ridges, with small streams running in the valleys between. They saw few villages but guessed from the worn tracks and the footbridges that more were hidden in the folds of the hills.

On the eighth day, to George's delight, they met a forester, who came silently into the firelight as they were settling down for the night, speaking quietly with George for an hour or so. When George was asked about their low-voiced conversation he replied that it had been chiefly of trees but that the forester had told him that not many days march to the north the woods thickened into the fringe of one of the fastnesses. The visitor had sympathised with George over the killing of Ragnar, and had stared grimly at Lokietok, who, half hidden in the undergrowth, sat looking over Hereward's shoulder, the Unman's usual nightly station.

Two days further on they met a woman washing clothes in a stream. George knew her at once as a forester's wife. "See how she leaves no trail," he said, "though she probably goes to that stream every day. We don't move even dead leaves without cause." She soon guessed his craft and they walked back with her to the house, a long, low, wooden building in a clearing, with a verandah on which rocking-chairs stood in the sun. Close by a child's swing hung from a walnut tree. Her husband, Karl-Pieter, joined them and, though as undemonstrative as most foresters, insisted that they stay at his home.

Their arrival was fortuitous, for that evening George began to sweat and tremble, alternately burning hot and shudderingly cold. "Too many mosquitoes," said Karl-Pieter. "He has swampwater fever or ague or whatever you people call it."

"How bad is it?" asked Hereward.

"It varies. For me and my family, nothing much. The body gets used to it. For him, not good, unless we have help and medicine."

"Can we get help?" Martin enquired anxiously.

"Yes." Karl-Pieter smiled. "Since it's you, Martin, your long-lost cousins will help. I will go and ask them. You should come with me, though not the Unman. That is a creature that has no place here."

Leaving George in the care of the forester's wife they set out into the warm summer twilight, Karl-Pieter and Martin deep in talk. Hereward walked behind with the forester's two small boys for company, smiling his reluctant smile as they kept up a steady conversation.

"That's our paddling pool."

"It has fish in it."

"And kingfishers."

"Do you like birds?"

"We have a ship that father made for us."

"Have you been on a ship?" As Hereward felt that some answer was expected he nodded and smiled. "What was it called?"

"The *Swan*," he said, to approving smiles from the boys at such a proper name. This parade of clear pools and gleaming kingfishers, and comfortable green turf was the world he had enjoyed briefly in Hay village, lifting sacks of grain, and watching spring unroll buttercups across the mill's meadow so that the women of Hay knew to bring out their carpets and beat the dust from them, as if they were the swallows that also know their own meetings and departures.

Now they were walking along a disused cart-track, a green lane where the grass grew even, except for two deep ruts that wheels had worn. After a mile Karl-Pieter put up a hand to stop them. "This is as likely a place as any," he said softly. "Now children, behave properly."

The two little boys promptly disappeared through a gap in banks of brambles where, Hereward noticed, the wheel ruts also turned off. As the men walked quietly after the boys Hereward and Martin saw the track become stony and then end in a steep-sided hollow that had been bitten out of the valley-side facing them. "A lime-pit," said Karl-Pieter, and the others nodded, recalling similar ones near Hay. "Good stuff, this, for sandy soil and heaths. Look!" He pointed ahead. The pit was being gradually reclaimed by the plants: there were clumps of thistles, snow-in-summer, red valerian, scabious and scented herbs that Martin did not recognise.

Ahead of them were the two boys, one sitting on either end of a long crumbling slab of limestone, and between them, his clothes as grey as the rock, making him at first hard to see, was a short, broad man whose hair, entangled in leaves and flowers, hung down to his waist. As they drew near he smiled, black eyes glinting above a black beard, and lifted a hand as they reached him, the backs of the hand and fingers furred with coarse hair.

Karl-Pieter patted the open palm. "How's the King?"

"Oh, him," grinned the man. "I suppose he's all right. How's Elsa?"

"Very well."

"Good. She's well, the boys don't seem to be dying" – and he reached out and tickled one of them so that the other, protesting, came close to be tickled also – "and you three look well, so this must be a social call."

"Only partly. We have sickness in the house. A stranger from over the seas, but a friend of my companions here. He has the swamp fever."

The man turned to Martin. "Well, little man. Is he a good friend of yours? One of us perhaps?"

"A very good friend and a good man."

"But not one of us. Never mind. We'll come this evening." Quick-footed he ran through the bushes and scrambled to the skyline of the hollow. Hereward, looking around thought he saw a face among the bushes, but when he stared closely saw only the leaves swaying and catching the light.

Karl-Pieter saw his gaze and chuckled. "Not bad for one eye. How many did you see?"

"Maybe one."

"That means there'll be five at least. In your country are there Twisted Folk living near you?"

"Certainly," said Hereward. "Martin here and his family, and about six other families not too far away. Though in all the long ways we have been since leaving home we have seen no more. Perhaps there are fewer than I thought."

"That will be because you have been in lonely places where few men and women have ever lived. The old cities are desolate now, but those are the places for the Twisted Folk. A hundred miles north-west of here are twenty or so of these old cities, and no one at all lives there except Martin's people. Those living here," he gestured round at the meadows and coppices, "are their outliers, for this is the edge of their ruined land. Their King will protect them from the Matrix, they say."

Dusk deepened into warm night as, later, they sat round Karl-Pieter's table. Outside one of the windows, silhouetted against the moon, was the black arm and shoulder of Lokietok. The Unman stood motionless near the house side, sombre and unquestioning as some lonely megalith. When the knock came at the door Martin ran to answer it, for George had fallen into delirium, his pillow and sheets wet with his sweat. It was the bushy-haired man and behind him others, tall men with long grey cloaks disguising their strangeness, if indeed it was a visible distortion, but not hiding the moonlight glinting off metal. "Come in," said Karl-Pieter. "You know me well enough not to need your escort."

"Of course," said the man. "When did a forester break his word? But we doubt the giant that stands by your wall. So my brothers will watch outside if you do not mind." He came inside and as the group moved towards the bedroom he shook his head. "Now, you wouldn't need me to assist you in planting seedlings, would you?" He closed the bedroom door and they sat down to wait.

Leaves rustled outside and owls called. Once came heavy footsteps as Lokietok trudged off into the trees, but it was otherwise dark and still. The boys had gone to bed and Martin was talking quietly with Karl-Pieter. Hereward sat idly letting his gaze wander round the room. This was not a cabin or woodman's hut such as George lived in. The walls were wood-panelled and there was a stone fireplace. In unexpected places lurked carved wooden shapes, a snake coiling up a table leg, tortoises emerging from the window sill, fawns' heads supporting shelves, and on one arm of his chair Hereward saw a tree carved and on the other the skyline of a city. He was running his fingers along the tiny prominences of towers, roofs, and crenellations, when looking up he caught Karl-Pieter's eye

"Your carving?" he asked.

"Yes. The tree for my work, the city for what I used to do. Most foresters had fathers to learn their craft from, but I've been one for just ten years."

"What was your work before then?"

"A lay-brother in the teaching guild." He paused. "In Limber itself, among other places."

"Why did you leave?" asked Martin, intrigued by a forester who had come late to the profession.

"What was there to stay for? The Matrix is dead, though it doesn't know it. At least that's my opinion. We know what it stood for, and its people were proud to be part of it, as long as its dream was still part of its future. Now the dream has been dreamed what vision does it have?"

"Is that why it would not fight at High Altai?" asked Hereward.

"Where do you find enough fighting-men when they have been ridiculed for so long, told they are barbarians, their honour denied? It is a miracle the militia can still hold down the magnates. But each year it gets harder. The long insistence on forebearance has gone on too long now, I believe. Our young men have been converted to thinking that there is a virtue in yielding, perhaps as recompense for some ancient guilt, or perhaps it's just easier that way. Everything that their hearts bid them believe they have been taught to doubt."

"Does your leaving the Matrix not weaken them further? Some may have listened to you," said Martin.

"Perhaps that is true in a small way. But what of my children? Here they breathe free air, not decay. The deer do not press opiates on them. The work I do will one day be seen as the most important of all the labours of the Matrix, to harvest the trees and care for them as carefully as men have always cared for their other harvests. This land we are in was once a semi-desert, arid, harsh, like the Levels further south. We, that is the trees and the people, made it good land again. Repeat that a hundred times, then a thousand, and that is no unworthy achievement."

A door opened and the man who had been tending George appeared. "Sit down with us, Ulmo," said Karl-Pieter. "Is it the ague?"

"Yes. He is ill now, but the elixir will help. Tomorrow he will be cooler but very weak. He should rest now, a week at least, and then move slowly for a while. This fever is a strange one; it will return once a year or thereabouts, but as a shadow of itself, not dangerous but there will be sweating and shaking and troubled sleep. Though we don't need that for troubled sleep, do we, Martin?"

"Surely it is safer here on the edge of the Glassy Country?" Martin wondered.

"It is. Give me a razor and I am all right until the next shave is due. You are too easily marked as one of us. Also I have protectors."

"Martin has protectors." Hereward's words were spoken with no emphasis, but it was one of his rebuffs for anyone who cast him too readily into a part. George Littler had once amused Martin by saying that he thought of Martin as one of the long-stemmed mushrooms suddenly lifting perky heads from the leaf mould, but saw Hereward as a thistle. Thistles made no attempt to hide their frosty colours and arrogant purple tufts, hacked down they did not die. They were not plants to which a gardener could make concessions.

"Very good," said Ulmo. "You protect him then. It sounds from your response to be necessary. Here we need no help from the Daylight People. In the Glassy Country there is us and our King."

"Are we in the Glassy Country?" asked Martin. "I've never been sure whether it was an old tale."

"No tale, Martin. You are not quite in it, but very close. It stretches far to the north and west. It pays no homage to the Matrix, or anyone else. Better not to war against our King, or to tax him or to go within his boundaries. Most people know this. Those who don't know learn."

"There is a saying in the Matrix," interrupted Karl-Pieter, "that it is not difficult to win a battle in the Glassy Country, but impossible to win a war."

"What is he called, this King?" asked Hereward.

"He's called the King," said Ulmo, "as far as I know. He has no other name. I've never met him or even glimpsed him from afar. He lives in one of the ruined cities at the centre of the Glassy Country, and I would rather not go there."

"Why is that?"

"Because it is customary not to, Martin. On the boundaries of the Country we are like these Daylight People, so alike it is easy to pass for them. But the nearer the centre the more it seems that the human mold was altogether broken and the die lost. I cannot imagine the form of the King who never strays from the centre."

"Could this King's name be Tyr?" asked Hereward, and Martin nodded approval.

"No," replied Ulmo. "He has no name, as I said. He may not even be a man or woman. You cannot understand what the interior is like. Nor must you go there, ever. I know nothing of this Tyr, except the Tyr in the stories."

The talk rippled away along other channels, until Ulmo rose to go. "Take this," he said. "It is a remedy that will not fail. Give it to George once a day until it is used up. The colour of his skin may change slightly but that is not a bad sign. Farewell and God go with you." They stood on the verandah to watch him go. Shadows detached themselves from the trees and went with him. Some time after they had lost sight of the visitors laughter came floating back.

"The Folk are different here," Martin remarked enviously. "Not like – not like fugitives."

"Why should they be?" said Karl-Pieter. "Yes, I know what happens in other parts of the Matrix and perhaps beyond, and I understand the phobia that underlies the persecution. When you have children you understand better. It is worst just before the child is born, and you are nervous through the first year until you are assured that all is well. Even back in the Blessed Time, it is said, children of that sort destroyed a family as often as not. But these Twisted Folk have their own homeland and that makes a difference."

"Yes," agreed Martin, "and they carry weapons and laugh aloud in the open. It must be good to have a King."

Hereward stared out into the darkness as they spoke and his mind juggled with the design and pattern, so infinitely complex, of the world through which he moved. Though his own quest remained unchanged the further his journey progressed the more he became aware of a profusion of other travellers. Some moved fast, some slowly, some drifted, some moved unswervingly and intently, and those nearest to Hereward by their very presence deflected his course or impeded him in his progress as a crowd of runners does in a race. He sighed and stood motionless as Lokietok came out from the trees, gripping the verandah rail to gaze into Hereward's face. "Where are you going, Lokietok?" he wondered aloud. "And where have you been? Was it dreadful?"

The Unman's face creased, the mouth opening and closing slowly like a snail's wet mouth. The others had gone inside as soon as Lokietok appeared so no one saw Hereward reach forward to hold one of the massive hands. Hereward, whose lost memories must have held joy and trepidation enough, had found in his life's new morning in Hay both a vivid happiness and a terrible anger, and both still shook him as they might shake a child, so he recognised at once the glow of the Unman's delight. Inside the house heads jerked upwards, as people glance quickly at windows when the lightning flashes outside. But there were no clouds at all, nor any sign of lightning.

That night Lokietok slept warm in the ferns, and George's breathing grew calmer. In the morning the big man was weak but coherent, and in turns they all talked to him, the boys fascinated by him and gradually over several visits making the transition from standing in the doorway in the morning to sitting on his bed at night, until their mother had to drive them away. By the time a week had passed they were his warmest admirers, and when Hereward and Martin returned each night from accompanying Karl-Pieter on his work, assisting when asked, which they did gladly in some recompense for his hospitality, they saw how steadily their friend's health was improving.

Their days in the woods were full of interest. The forester showed them the trees that had been felled over the previous months. "Beech, in November, they need to be really hard, no sap in them, other trees in winter, sometimes oak in spring. The carters are starting to move them now, that's why they've been sawn and trimmed, the trunk for the carpenters and wagon-makers and builders, the branches for firewood for the village and the twigs for bakers and potters and so on, to heat kilns." He was modest, saying that he was inexperienced but was trying to learn fast, that the local craftsmen had taught him more than he had ever dreamed there was to know of the lore of the forest, how beautiful trees may grow too quickly, how trees grow differently in hedgerow, wood or park, how elm planks in seasoning will develop transverse ripples while oak and ash will bend in a lengthwise shallow curve, and a store of knowledge that when it was instinct would make him a true forester. "That I will never be," he added, "but my sons will, I hope."

Now George was out of bed and eating breakfast with the others. Big bowls of thick oatmeal porridge were on the table and Martin was decorating the top of his porridge with honey, making golden coils and flourishes, concluding with an 'M' in the centre.

Hereward, carrying a bowl that steamed whitely in the cold air, had departed to find Lokietok. A trail of footmarks led away from the hollow in the ferns where the Unman slept. They were freshly made, the dew trodden off the grass and brushed off leaves so that the track shone emerald against the untouched mistiness. As Hereward, unsure whether it was worth following, was standing doubtful, there came surging around him the rage of Lokietok, buffeting his senses as a great wave will tumble the surprised swimmer in its uncaring depths.

Cage *Bars* *Grill*
Spear *Pain* *Gaff*
Dark *Chain* *Sand*

Then nothing. The trees were back, so were the blackbirds scraping among dead leaves and the smell of woodsmoke. It all faded away, the pikes jabbing and prodding the Unman backwards until behind the grating of the cell it waited on the wet straw in the darkness for the next bloody spectacle. Running, Hereward saw Lokietok ahead on one of the cart-tracks that led through the woods. A hundred yards or so further on where the track wound out of sight men were standing watching. The patterns painted on their long wooden shields and on their faces were familiar enough. Choking and coughing in the dust of the High Altai quarries, he had seen those patterns high above him on the lip of the stone-pit where the guards watched indifferently over the men toiling below. In the Drome, in the streets, in the tunnels below the port he had seen them. The Daroi must be moving quickly now, he thought, moving fast to make use of what was left of the summer, perhaps feeling the pressure of the hordes behind them. Had they recognised Lokietok? It was not difficult. The Daroi, Hereward knew, were not a particularly forgiving people, so he tugged the Unman's arm and together they ran back to the forester's house.

"What will you do?" asked Karl-Pieter on hearing the news. The three travellers had been friends long enough now for each to know the others' thoughts, and they nodded when Hereward said that they had no intention of drawing unwelcome attention to a family which had shown them so much hospitality. "Do not be anxious for us," Karl-Pieter assured them. "I have cabins deep in the forest where no wandering folk will come. My family will go to one of them today. For the villagers here it will be harder, of course, though the Glassy Country is not so far away."

"I doubt the Daroi will fear the Glassy Country," said Hereward.

"So much the worse for them," Karl-Pieter's wife said tartly.

"Though it does seem there will be new lords in this land from what you say. Our old lords have forgotten how to fight it seems."

"The Daroi may move as swallows do," said Martin encouragingly.

"Swallows also stop, Martin. These people, from what you have told us of them, have come through hard, barren lands. To stop here would be natural. This would be a good place to call their own – though I can hardly believe it is all happening. But if you must go on, then Limber is to the north-east, and the only road takes you through woods and farms until the Hogsback Ridge. There you will look down on the River Dole, and see a long stone bridge, with a tower at the far end. Maybe it is guarded, as beyond the river one is in the home provinces of the Matrix. And travel slowly for George's sake."

They strapped on their packs and with reluctant farewells, for they had grown to like the forester and his family, the three set off along the grassy track. When the track took them up a rise and clear of the trees they saw that ahead lay a land rolling like waves to the blue northern horizon. Behind them, dwarfed by the distance, Lokietok lumbered tirelessly along the trail, and that evening far back to the south, smudging the sky like an approaching rainstorm, was the smoke of a thousand campfires.

XXVIII

Although Kit's home was on the bank of a stream she had never learned to swim. Indeed only in winter and early spring would the stream itself rise more than knee-deep – it was utterly different from the Big Grey River in which Jackyboy had swum ever since he could remember. Jacky's river was tidal for miles upstream from its estuary and its waters were deep and treacherous, always fogged with silt and the deep riverbed for those who swam down towards it was not easy to discover, except that the water became thicker like liquid dust. Jackyboy and his friends would feel the soft sucking of the mud as it began to envelop their ankles and calves and then they would kick fiercely up to the surface. Kit had seen him dive from the jetties that waded on stilts into the harbour of Limber and heard him say how clear and warm this water was. "Not like the grey old river," he would say. She had seen the estuary when they sailed from it and thought it bleak, colourless and cold, but knew Jacky was pining for its hazy dove-grey and wet pearl hues. "Dirty old river," she would say, so that he grew vexed with her.

"I don't call your beck dirty."

"That's because it isn't," she would retort.

He would shrug and concede the verbal skirmish to her and slip into a nostalgia she couldn't disturb, thus without knowing it winning a sort of victory. The rank river-meadows that flooded every spring, the leaden sea with its line of white that moaned beyond the sandhills, the turnstones and sanderlings that ran in and out of the retreating tide, the gulls speckling the sky over the cliffs, the bell-buoys that rang hollowly through the fog, all were his and he had been theirs, and watching him she knew exactly where he had retired to, as if wood should fall to contemplating its own grain.

Astolat persuaded him to enter a swimming race, part of the sea-festival. It was known as the jetty race, and from the jetty furthest north along the Limber shoreline to the most southerly one was a long hard swim. Jacky, as always, was keen to impress Kit and soon leaving most of the swimmers behind found himself engaged in a contest against a tubby man of about forty whom he recognised as the harbourmaster himself. To someone used to the great river that flowed past his home this warm sea, its waves like the steady breathing of a sleepy leviathan, sapped none of his strength, being so salty and buoyant that Jacky lengthened his usual stroke along the water rather than churn through it. He reached the jetty first by ten seconds and hung in the water with one hand on the bottom of the ladder to wait for the harbourmaster to reach him. "Well swum," he said, holding out his other hand.

"Too old," laughed the other. "Where did you learn to swim?"

"A long way away."

"I thought so. All those bubbles and foam. Like an egg-whisk!"

Jacky smiled. "Swim quick to keep warm in my country." Hoisting themselves up the ladder they walked along the jetty letting the sun dry them. A convoy of ships was entering the harbour from the south and they stopped to observe them.

"How do they stay afloat?" wondered the harbourmaster.

"What are they?"

"Refugees. Not the first, but they're coming thicker now. They think Limber is some sort of haven, I suppose. It's this Daroi migration."

Their conversation was interrupted by Astolat, who arrived breathless having run down the jetty to make sure that her brother realised she at least had known without doubt he could swim faster than anyone. Walking back she held his hand and looked down through the cracks in the boarding to where the blue water was occasionally clouded by silver-grey shoals of tiny fish moving together, their bodies always aligned similarly, even in sudden changes a thousand heads swinging at once. Astolat stored up this image but seeing Kit approach left the how and why until later.

"He won, Kit!" she announced. "I knew he would."

"Well done, King Jacky. Don't forget your crown." Kit spun the old brown hat through the air for him to catch and cram on the back of his head.

The four of them were off the jetty now and walking along a wide stone wharf against which a fleet of ships were moored: stained much-used fishing-boats, little skiffs, sleek caravels, short dumpy hoys. Jacky gestured at a big schooner. "We'll build ships like that before long. Our trawlers are all right for fishing trips but they won't show us the whole wide ocean. Something tells me the Matrix regulations won't be so well kept in my country soon."

The harbourmaster said he was unsure of this, but thought it quite possible. They walked further, flanked now by the gently bobbing ships on one side and on the other by a long terrace of stone warehouses. Out in the bay the refugee ships were edging closer. Some were sailing, others appeared to be drifting, but on each the deck was dense with people and every possible space ramshackle with animals, poultry, chests, mattresses, boxes, bags, the timeless flotsam of displaced and homeless people. A tall white tower marked the centre of the wharf, rising like a campanile above the warehouses and stores. Its windows had balconies and three storeys up a man was leaning on the balustrade and looking out across the harbour. "This is my home," said the harbourmaster. "Come in, if you like. Have a glass of wine." Jacky, who had always liked looking down from high airy places, nodded with a smile and they followed the man up a succession of stairs to a spacious square room from which, through archways set in each wall, you could see far in every direction. To the west rose the buildings of Limber, the Six Hundred Steps climbing sinuously through them and then above the last rooftops as if the highest peak wore a stone sash. The group went to the opposite arch and lined the balustrade. "My younger brother, Michael Novak," said the harbourmaster. "I'm Conrad Novak." They clasped in turn the hands held out to them. Below them was the harbour, a long deep inlet protected on its seaward side by a low rocky arm of land which dwindled to a point ten miles south of them, the point ending with the exclamation mark of a grey lighthouse.

Michael Novak was a slight man with grey curly hair and dark eyes, quick and neat in his movements. He flicked three glances along the visitors as they spoke, and then one more back at Kit, as you might glance at a hand of cards to decide whether to play or to shrug and wait for the next deal. "Those are not the accents of these parts," he said. "Somewhere way off to the west, beyond the sea. Am I right?"

"Yes," said Jacky. "Westermain, I think you call it."

"What do you call it?" asked Michael Novak.

"It is a big land, big enough for many places and people. I come from the Big Grey River. Kit is from the Ingastowe valley. I expect they mean nothing to you."

"Not at all. I know exactly where they are. Ingastowe would be about fifty miles from the river, though still your nearest town. Kit probably lives very close to it. The Matrix lost a garrison there, a small one, in a local uprising, then a relieving force and even a marshal."

"How do you know that?" Kit was totally alert now, her mind reaching out to Novak's thoughts in the way you might feel for a doorknob in a pitch-dark room, carefully, no need for bruises, it has to be there. She did not wish Jacky to be at a disadvantage.

"I am a rector of the Matrix, it is my business to know. Also the marshal was Rocco Barbella, a friend of mine."

"I can't say I'm sorry for him," said Jacky. "Nor for anyone who helped to bring my sister here. And I thought rectors fought in the front rank. I don't recall seeing you there."

Astolat could feel the coldness spreading from her brother. So could Conrad Novak: "This is my house. I would be obliged if you did not quarrel here."

"You are right," said Kit. "Jacky, don't be so hasty. Why should this man have anything to do with Ingastowe or Astolat?"

"No, he is correct to be concerned." The younger Novak was clearly not intimidated. "He deserves an answer. It is no secret. Brothers have come before, fathers, uncles, whole families, with the same problem. Poor people may arrive on their own but we have known a small army come."

"I am on my own. Nor are we poor. If my sister does not return there will be others. That I promise you."

"These family feuds have happened before, as I said. And I agree not all the Children in the Academies are as happy there as I was."

Astolat, who had missed nothing of the exchanges so far, piped up, "Were you at the Academy?" in so shrill a voice that Novak had to smile.

"Certainly. Though when I was a boy I lived close by so it was easier for me. You will have noticed that many of the Children are from Limber and a smaller number from faraway provinces."

"But why was I brought here?" Astolat had all the directness of her age.

"That's not easy to answer properly. The academies are old and no one can know anything but a fraction of the past. Maybe they were there before the Broken Years, who knows. But that was a terrifying time, when even the sun, they say, lost its strength, and the Unmen and Twisted Folk came among us. We can guess that what went before was a mighty civilisation – when a giant falls the corruption of his flesh does not happen overnight. But when the flesh has dissolved the bones remain and we have to erect them again because if we don't then we can never stand on the giant's shoulders. We don't want that particular giant back to repeat his fall so we clothe his bones with different flesh, our own. That flesh is us, that is the peoples of the Matrix, or at least our hopes, faith, imagination, beliefs and ideals. The bones are the earth's own laws, the behaviour of its atoms and the knowledge of them, what we sometimes call the many gods. Hopes are everybody's, they need no provision. Knowledge is different, it is always there but not always accessible, as if the giant's bones were lost and had to be found and then grasped, lifted up, arranged. That is what the Children do, or are taught to do. They are the future, as they should be." Michael Novak turned away and looked out to sea. The explanation seemed to have tired him. Or bored him, thought Kit.

His brother broke the silence: "Jacky, you mentioned the size of your fishing-boats. Why did the Matrix make such a regulation, do you think?"

"To keep us weak. With big schooners we could sail far away, find new fishing-grounds, open new trading routes, discover new lands beyond the Matrix's grasp. Sovereignty. And we would be safer in big ships. Andread my brother is dead in the green sea, but the wave that took him overboard would not have come halfway up the side of a big ship."

"Men have made big ships before. I am a harbourmaster and I know. The sea-gypsies have their big carracks today, and the Matrix has some fair-sized ships. But if you wanted to build a carrack how many trees would you need to cut down? Let me tell you. More than a thousand. That's right, believe me. Fully grown oaks in your land, teak in hotter places. Think of your nearest oak tree. Lovers like its shade, little ones like its branches to climb, old people like looking at it and listening to the wind in its leaves, even the pigs like its acorns. Now chop it down and see what a gap it leaves, then cut another, and another, and now your village isn't the same, is it? It won't be for the next century even if you replant at once. That's just three trees and you need many hundreds more yet and you still can't build your big ship, not until the wood is seasoned. The trees themselves are only part of the reason for that regulation, so you see it wasn't lightly decreed."

"I understand that," said Astolat. "It is interesting. What are some of the other reasons?"

"There are many," Conrad Novak responded. "Let us say that after twenty years everyone has a big ship like yours. So you, or someone else, decide to build a very big ship. But it isn't possible. Built too long, wooden ships bend and distort. So you build with iron or steel."

"Iron?" Jacky laughed. "Is there that much iron in the world?"

"Certainly there is. There may be iron ore near your village. It will need hundreds of men to mine it, tear it out of great pits and shafts in the earth, hundreds of others to melt it in furnaces heated by coals that hundreds more have dragged from other mines, while yet other hundreds hammer the iron into metal plates and sheets. Your village will see the cinder and slag piles rise like hills round it, and your own saliva will be black with the dust. But now you have a big iron ship and you will be proud and satisfied, and you can travel far in it. As for the children and old people they can stay behind and look at the dust and the tree-stumps. Still want a big ship?"

"Is that 'imaginary limitations'?" asked Astolat.

"Very good," laughed Conrad as Michael Novak returned with a tray bearing glasses of white wine. "Perhaps! Perhaps we could just extend the possibilities to having your brother's ship and your own unruined homeland as well. But I haven't finished with the iron ship. You see, it's a machine, an apparatus that applies power to perform its task. In a way, I know, fishing-boats are machines too, but they need you as much as you need them and more. Not so your iron ship. Eventually it will not need you at all, only other machines to direct its course, load and unload it and so on. When it doesn't need you, Jacky, you can stay at home and enjoy the view too."

"Are the Children taught this?" Kit inquired. She was less interested in the answer than watching Michael Novak.

"About machines? Yes, though it is more important to have knowledge of the how and why of the elements, the cells, and all the powers and logic of the world. Once the Children design machines they lock themselves into a path we have been down before. That may be not altogether undesirable but it is better their minds exercise their knowledge and stay flexible."

"It takes time to find things anew," said Astolat. "Shouldn't we be taught why the rats live as they do in their box and why clouds make rain?"

"No. That way knowledge becomes a sacred mystery, a ritual." He talked on as the afternoon became evening, explaining how hierophants guard abracadabra, weighting the syllables with virtues when the ague it is supposed to affect has long become dissociated from it. In the twilight the far-off lighthouse beams occasionally lit the refugee boats, yawing and pitching, even in the low swell, as a broken-winged moth hobbles across dust and gravel. Conrad told them how the Matrix had always struggled to preserve a precarious equilibrium, guarding its dominions frugally, a small victory here, a small defeat there, reluctant to develop weaponry which would set it far ahead of its enemies lest it disturb the precious balance. So the regiments treasured their few guns with worn-out rifling as if they were the last in the world. Everywhere was the same balance: wood was used as it grew but it had become customary for the foresters to maintain the tree-cover, and for the people to accept this restriction as naturally as the workings of osmosis, for, as a fluid percolates through its membranes into a thirsty cell, so were the trees released, but if the woodlands grew sparser a sort of nervous pressure caused its replenishment.

It was Astolat who voiced another hovering question: "Conrad," – she gestured to the road below their balcony where the refugee stream had thinned but not disappeared as the city absorbed the shabby procession – "these are dangerous times for the Matrix, are they not?" Both Novaks nodded in agreement. "Then why have you, a rector and a harbourmaster, spent your evening talking to strangers in this way?"

"Well, first of all I know a little about your brother. And since he insists on playing with that knife let me say I wish him no harm and understand his desire to take his sister home. I also know who used to own that hat."

"Jacky, who used to . . .?"

"Ssh, Astolat," said her brother.

"Also you all seem to sympathise with what I say about the Matrix, or part of it, and perhaps because natural fighting-men are not so common as they were. Why else would Nestor have lived so long on the Steps?"

"Who is . . .?"

"Astolat!"

"Jacky, Sister Francesca says I must ask questions if I don't understand."

"In a while, then," said Kit soothingly.

"I have seen your fighting-men," said Jacky. "They didn't run."

"Too few," sighed Conrad Novak. His brother had relapsed into a permanent silence, it seemed. "I think we have become too subtle, too self-conscious. Always we have sought consent, always the diminution of power. That is another legacy of the Broken Years. Now our people have grown to expect that other forces and dominions will seek our consent, and that to be powerless is good in itself."

"Is that why so many wish to be servants of others?" asked Jacky, thinking of the crowds on the April Steps seeking such occupations.

"Probably. What do you think of being the servants of the Daroi? If our people wish for peace then Michael and the other rectors are obliged to pursue that wish."

"That sounds like the peace the cliffs made with the sea," said Jacky. "To agree to dissolve into sandgrains so the waves won't batter them. It will be more placid on the long flat beach, but who will remember there were once cliffs?"

Conrad Novak sighed: "So you would fight. Tell us what for."

Jacky did not hesitate: "Easy. To stop anyone hurting whatever I hold dear."

"And that is?"

"You know, the river, Christmas Day, lying in bed listening to the wild geese."

"And messing about in boats," added Astolat.

"Yes, that too, and people, all sorts of people, like my father, and Astolat and . . . Kit," Jacky finished with a rush that made Astolat giggle and Kit look at him carefully.

"Yes," said Conrad. "That's what makes you and your people so hard to shake off, like young bulldogs. What is important to you are simple matters, lots of them but clear. For us, we have one big vision – the Matrix dream, I suppose you'd call it – but it's so big it's hard to imagine it ever disappearing, whether we defend it or not. It's like freedom, you can only ever imagine it extinguished when it's gone. Who can conceive of the sun dying? I can't, but I can imagine a candle going out. Anyway, who wants to fight for the Opium Steps or fight to have a chance to be someone's valet?"

"But," said Jacky, "you fought at Ingastowe, which is a city for us but would be lost in a corner of Limber. So why not fight these Daroi tribes who will crumble your city as well as your dreams?"

"There has to be an end some time," Michael Novak put in. "Perhaps we got tired of always being in the front line. That happens too, you know. We've held the line ever since the Broken Years and now almost everyone seems to want to tear down the dream our ancestors made into truth – the Daroi because it makes their lives look cramped and their past an empty waste, Regret because it wants only its own dream to be real. And as for the Twisted Folk, they would be happy to dance on our graves." Kit nodded and clearly agreed. "Why we fought at Ingastowe isn't easy to understand, except that one of the signs of a loss of nerve is to fight small peoples only, to turn on them in the name of principle. A little battle in Westermain made us feel brave. Many of our citizens hope only for a quiet life and subject peoples are quiet. The men till the conquerors' crops or mind their cattle, the women clean their houses for them or nurse their babies, spared the unending wrestle with decisions and sacrifices that come with freedom. Doubtless there is more to it. Perhaps some feel that victims have a strange strength of their own that sustains them."

When Jacky said that none of this was plain to him the rector invited them to be his guests at a debate in St Xavier's the next day. Jacky, his sister and Kit took their leave and walked back to their lodgings, their senses sharpened by the words they had heard. Many of the faces that passed seemed secretive; passers-by who sidled close to the walls, or in crowds jostled and shouted among themselves, the words coarse and ugly. Often the clothes were shabby, not with wear but with a show of poverty, patches that were badges not mendings. Below the tawdriness simmered a restless petty violence. At the stalls in the plazas they noticed a continual pilfering of fruit and trinkets.

A youth snatched a handful of flowers from a barrow and shoved them towards a girl who flung them down with a screaming laugh, the petals and stems disintegrating under careless feet. The flower-girl called after the youth who returned only to yell abuse into her face.

"No, Jacky!" Kit exclaimed, but by the time he had reached the stall the youth had disappeared into a thronged alley. When the flower-girl looked warily at Jacky she was heartened by what she saw, for though the seaman would sometimes hood his eyes and stare icily, his face all harsh planes, in this smoky street he was so upright and assured that where he walked a space opened.

"Two red roses, please," he said, very correctly, and placed in her hand a coin that was more than enough for the roses and the stolen flowers.

"It's too much," stammered the girl.

"A present from the Big Grey River," said Jacky and, when he received a puzzled look, smiled so that she was compelled to smile in return, wondering at him as half-hearted anglers used to finding flatfish and sucking lampreys might wonder to see a shining salmon surge beneath the oily debris of a muddy harbour-mouth.

As they returned to their lodgings the air grew sultry as if thunder was close, though more as if its heaviness came from the people around them. The loud music, shrill voices and glittering eyes made Astolat stay near to Jacky, as did Kit, for in the crowd were many who pushed and shoved mindlessly. Twice they heard Jacky's name called out and, turning, saw no particular speaker, but noticed a sort of unpleasant laughter on some of the faces.

At the steps up to their rooms Kit pulled Jacky's sleeve and whispered that a man was following them. He glanced down and nodded, never doubting that what she said was true. "Go upstairs," he said. "Let me give him something to laugh at."

"I think he means no harm," she said, but she and Astolat went on ahead and Jacky stepped into the porch just inside the doorway. There was no waiting, the man walked straight past him without noticing and began to mount the stairs. From behind him Jacky said, "Hey," a quiet sound that can mean almost anything, but said like that was as chilling as the snake's hiss when feet step too near its head.

The man turned and smiled. "John Dorn?" he said.

"Yes." There was no answering smile.

"Can we sit down and speak for a few minutes?"

Jacky pointed upwards and they mounted the stairs, into the room where Kit and Astolat were standing by the window.

"My name is Kopa, of the Kopa family," the man began. "You may have heard the name."

Though it seemed not completely unfamiliar Jacky could attach no significance to it. The stranger was tall, with a prosperous look about him, the gloss that a hothouse puts on its plants. Rings, including a crested seal-ring, shone on his fingers.

"My family home is close to the Steps." Jacky glanced across at Kit, who merely lifted her eyebrows. "We have never met properly before today, though I have taken the liberty of observing you in the streets and speaking to others about you. In truth it was more often they who spoke to me and mentioned you. I heard also that Nestor has no more use for his hat. You have become a name on the Steps."

"A name to be shouted after him by troublemakers," snapped Kit.

"That's to your credit. Some may pretend to deride, but it is envy that they feel. The flower-girls and old people tell a different story, and I speak for all of them as well as I can. I am the rector for the Steps and the inner city."

"Are you?" said Jacky mildly. "Pity you didn't do more about Nestor."

Astolat gave Kit's sleeve an anxious tug, but Kit patted her shoulder. Though her hawk was ruffling his feathers, she detected no malice in Kopa.

"I'll keep it simple," said Kopa. "All rectors must provide successors to take their chairs when they resign or die. It is not easy to find men or women willing to serve in this way. What I have learned up and down the Steps, and seen for myself is enough to convince me that I am right in asking you to be my replacement as rector."

"That's ridiculous." Jacky wondered if this were some extraordinary mistake.

"Take time to consider it. Remember you are in no way bound. You may resign whenever you wish and in any case I am not retiring yet. Remember too that I do not ask lightly. Kopas have lived and died here for as long as the Matrix has existed. Those of us that have been rectors never thought our position other than an honourable one."

"How do rectors choose their replacements?" Astolat's voice was bursting with approval.

Kopa smiled at her eagerness. "It's easier than you might think. We listen for names and eventually one starts jumping up. To be honest I was probably chosen because I was my father's son, and I have been a flimsy rector at best, but I care for this city in my own way."

"If you are serious," said Jacky quietly, "I thank you for your confidence, however you came to acquire it, but we are to return to Westermain in the near future, so that is the end of it."

"When you say 'we'," Kit interrupted, "you don't speak for me. I will wait here as long as I have to, years if necessary." There was a long and uncomfortable silence, before Kopa departed with Jacky's promise to meet him the next day.

After Astolat had gone to sleep the two sat together, for hours passing only an occasional remark. A thought began to stir in Jacky's mind. When Kit fetched a hot drink he warmed his hands on it and smiled, and she was nervous, knowing only that the idea had made itself a pleasing shape.

XXIX

Waiting, good-naturedly if rather bored, for their captain-general, Andre-Leander Townsend, to return were the Companions of Kittiwake. Kittiwake Island had been given to them as their home by the Matrix in recognition of some long-ago feat of valour. It was a pledge that those who died in the southern companies would lie in its cemetery within sound of the sea and the kittiwakes and their comrades' voices. A thousand miles to the north-west of Kittiwake lay Merganser, the island of the northern Companions, some of whom had fought at Ingastowe Common.

It was not unpleasant in the fields and coppices round the Old Stone Bridge, and those Companions who did not feel like bivouacking in the thickets that lay along the Dole River could generally find room in the tower that stood at the northern end of the bridge. The Dole was brown and muddy; you could see spirals of mud swirling in the currents and eddies, and it was wide, so wide that looking across it from water-level its surface had a colourless glassy sheen like a turbid sea. It had no banks but disappeared into swampy reed-masses or floating weedbeds. Even quite far out there stood skeletal trees, long dead now, with the water half-way up their trunks, and terns, herons and egrets, sometimes a sea-eagle or two, used the bare branches as perches or nesting places.

The Companions knew about the Daroi and why their captain-general had placed them where he had. Even if they had not known, the steady stream of refugees, coming towards them over the Hogsback Ridge, six miles distant, and down the long slope to the bridge, would soon have told them. Across the centre of the bridge the Companions had constructed a wooden barricade, high and solid, signalling their intentions clearly, but the refugees they allowed through and sent further north, moving them through as cheerfully as possible. Refugees have a spiritless grief, but with both the river and these casual joking people between themselves and the Daroi they seemed to regain some hope.

Hereward, Martin and George, with Lokietok not far behind, also looked down from the ridge that evening, seeing the long coils of the river and the thickness of the vegetation, particularly on the further side. Here and there flat green islands separated its main flow. To the east it flowed into an almost impenetrable delta, a quaking water-world. They had left Karl-Pieter's house several days ago, picking their way along the ridge until they reached the road. It was not crowded though there were groups at intervals all walking in the same direction. Most of the people had carts, even in a few cases a sort of sledge, and in these or in the packs on their backs were the few possessions they sought to keep. Along with them came cows, bullocks and sheep, though from the stained bags and boxes it was not difficult to see they had often slaughtered their animals for meat on the journey. From the ridge's highest point, looking backwards to the south, you could see the road winding down the reverse side of the ridge before disappearing among the trees. Several times it emerged briefly, but in the middle distance of grey-green folds of pasture and woods the road could be traced no further.

A whitish-grey haze behind the travellers stretched from east to west almost as far as the eye could see, the smoke of the Daroi fires signalling where the Men had reached that day in their march. In some spots a tall thick column of smoke marked a bigger fire, the smoke rising straight at first, then drifting away at an angle as the breeze caught it. A faint smell of burning was in the air. Talking quietly over what they had seen Hereward, George and Martin walked on towards the bridge, though Lokietok trudged in silence along the verge, his strange milky eyes unfocused. Once, walking past a small herd of cows, he seemed to be part of them, and as they might pause to crop a mouthful of grass so the Unman occasionally tore off a handful of greenery or sour fruit to munch on.

They reached the stone bridge and walked on to it. Whereas the refugee procession had eyes only for some distant sanctuary, George and Martin wondered at the bridge's strength and solidity, and at the skill of the long-dead engineers, even leaning over the parapet to admire the strong grace of its arches. "How could they build these piers and foundations in the middle of a river?" Martin pondered aloud. Though if the Daylight People could build Ingastowe Cathedral then no marvel was beyond them, he thought.

"They made coffer-dams, a sort of watertight case, that were put right down to the river-bed," said Hereward. "Then when they reached rock they would build upwards."

"How do you know that?" asked Martin. Hereward only shook his head. It must have filtered through, he thought, from his past.

They passed through the opening in the wooden barrier. No one seemed to want to stop them and the men on the bridge casually waved them through. As the three looked around curiously, wondering who the bridge guardians were, Lokietok, towering seven feet tall, neither looking nor speculating, came to the barrier, having to duck low to get through the roofed gangway. The Companions who saw the Unman squeeze through were suddenly all alertness, and watched fascinated as Lokietok tramped past. Beneath the straw-like hair was only an empty fog in which everything had disconnected. A stone on the road was not a stone to Lokietok, for if it had been it would have been part of a bigger stone or the sum of several smaller stones, or a flint, or a cobble or a meteorite, an arrowhead, a fossil or a moonlet, the analogue of the dust and the diamond. The Unman knew a stone as the stone might be if there were it alone in an otherwise empty universe. So with all things: they were, that was all. Lokietok did not know or care if the wind moved the branches and leaves of the trees, or whether they, like fans, whipped the air and caused the wind.

In the dusk the Companions were lighting fires, letting the smoke drift over them to keep away the mosquitoes, cooking up their suppers of fish or waterfowl, with wild rice that grew plentifully on the muddy flooded grasslands. The three travellers started to make their own fire, but the Companions squatting round the nearest one were ready to include them in their ring when they found out that these were travellers from beyond the Dole who had seen the Daroi at close quarters.

More of the Companions gathered round in the darkness, strolling over in twos and threes to hear of the backgammon game or the death of Rigger. As Martin told them of the Drome they listened in fascination, glancing often at Hereward as the tale unfolded. In their turn the Companions told their own stories, which usually related who they were and why they were there. There were common links: often it was just the glamour of the Companions which had drawn youths from distant villages where only the weather changed, or men hiding their past or forgetting lost loves; some had come to buy the farm, the land with which the Matrix compensated them at five acres a year. The numbers of the Companions from either Kittiwake or Merganser never rose above two thousand, their exclusiveness being a source of pride. Being a law unto themselves they had no social barriers in the companies, and later that evening Martin, to his delight, found himself sitting next to one of the Twisted Folk, who greeted him as a long-lost brother. There were men from Westermain who spoke exactly like Jacky in his hard, clear accent, and who told Hereward that they knew of Old Man Dorn. Most were Outlanders, some from the furthest fringes of the Matrix and beyond, even two cousins who lived so far away no one quite knew where it was. The two spoke in voices like thin-drawn wire and laughed when they fought. There were even sea-gypsies born and bred on their ships, their home ports far across some unimaginable ocean. Andre-Leander Townsend himself was one such, and with much hilarity the Companions claimed that he had been expelled from the sea-gypsies for being regularly seasick. Even Unmen had reputedly enlisted from time to time, though presently there were none.

As the groups round the fires expanded they started their favourite and interminable argument as to the fighting qualities of the different provinces and regions. Most favoured their own homeland, or that of the cousins, who were considered crazy because they did not take up the offer of the farm and appeared to have enlisted in search of an enjoyable adventure.

Hereward, Martin and George were listening in amusement to the cousins telling a rambling story about the dangers of sharks, which no one else could dispute, never having encountered one, when there was a stir of movement towards the bridge. From where they sat it was no more than a raising of voices and a swaying of lights. Men rose to scan the river and its far bank, but only a few reflections undulated on the water's surface and in the still warm air even the twigs and reeds were silent. Then there came a bugle call, a short lilting string of a dozen notes. The Companions, who knew the calls as they knew their own names, referred to them as colours, or gave them offhand titles; this one was blue, or 'half-awake'. "Who's going to see what's happening?" asked one of the cousins, making no attempt whatever to move.

One of the Westermain men got up. "I'll go," he said. "Then I shan't have to listen to shark stories."

Hereward too got up. Though the stories amused him he felt restless, a sense of slightly losing impact and direction in his search for retribution, rather as a shot arrow towards the end of its flight feels the wind and airs starting to deflect it, the earth tug it. As the pair walked towards the bridge Lokietok appeared from among the trees to follow them. Already thirty others had gathered on the bridge, looking through the passage-way, or climbing up the barricade, to gaze over the top as if leaning on a wooden serving-counter. Hereward stepped through the opening and saw in front of him the reason for the bugle call. Two of the Daroi, long shields and faces alike painted and patterned in red and white, their dogs at their heels, were standing halfway across the bridge. A refugee family that had arrived at the further end of the bridge was hesitating there. One of the Daroi, glancing carelessly at whoever emerged from behind the barrier, slid his eyes past Hereward and then sharply back, frowning to himself.

In the captain-general's absence the Companions were led by his deputy who, having been alerted, now came through the wooden barrier. When told that the first of the Daroi had set foot on the bridge he had lifted his eyebrows and sighed resignedly: "Nearly time to earn the farm again."

"What do you want?" he said tersely to the painted figures standing just within the dusky lantern light.

One gestured at the wooden wall and called out, "What is that?"

"What does it look like?" said Franz Schroeder. Franz 'four farms' they sometimes called him. Hereward had heard him spoken of around the fire. He was from Lettland, proverbially the most stiff-necked of the Matrix suzerainties. It was a Lett trait to answer a question with a question.

"Why is the river passage barred?"

"What is it to you?"

"We are the Daroi."

As this did not seem to call for a response there was silence until eventually Schroeder said, "Never heard of you," and turned his back. He was about to step through the opening when one of the Daroi, responding with the same brute impulse as would one of their dogs to an aimed kick, reached back and whipped his throwing-arm forward. Hereward instinctively lunged across, slamming Schroeder into the bridge's parapet. The assegai thrummed and quivered waist-high in the wood of the barrier, but the Daroi were running, fleet as deer, back across the bridge, black shadows quickly gone. Several Companions came through the barrier with a rush and others vaulted down from their viewing place on top. Hereward, sitting up, saw light flash on their weapons, but Schroeder, from the ground, spoke before they could pursue: "No, no. What might be waiting at the end of the bridge? There's lots of time. And I'm all right, so don't fuss." Reaching a hand out to Hereward he added, "Thanks to you, and I won't forget."

As Hereward grasped the hand and pulled him up Schroeder was already examining him. Behind them the Unman growled, a warning roll of far-off thunder, but Hereward spoke reassuringly and saw the pale eyes film over and the lips open slackly. In the maze the silken thread which had for a few seconds tugged urgently was loose again.

Hereward and Lokietok went back to the fire where they had left George and Martin. Finding it was easy for there was much laughter and singing among their new acquaintances, though of an unusual sort. The two cousins, having claimed that they could sing all five parts of a part-song simultaneously, were doing their best with a children's song Hereward recalled having heard in Hay village:

As I was making buttercup chains,
My sweetheart picking daffodils and daisies . . .

This, to the amusement of the Westermain Companions, was being sung in an absurdly rustic parody of a Westermain accent. Martin wondered again at how easily the Daylight People compressed their lives into the present, singing as the future began to dam up against their provocative little barricade.

Was Hereward part of that future the little man wondered, looking at him as he rejoined the group, the black tangled hair pushed roughly back, the eye-patch on the cord, the face and neck burnt brown from when Hereward had laboured in the shadeless quarries of High Altai, and the big hands still scabbed and scarred as stone-workers' hands are. Then Martin and even the most carefree of the Companions looked up as, looming into the firelight, swam into view the bulk and strangeness of Lokietok, the straw-like hair and ponderous head, the skin pale and matt as a peeled mushroom.

About midnight Hereward dropped off to sleep in a hollow scraped in the dry soil. The night was full of sounds, the bass chorus of bull-frogs, whispering leaves and water-flags, the lapping, gurgling sounds of the river, a last crackle of sticks from the fire, a quiet voice somewhere, all part of it. Martin stayed awake longer, revolving ideas in his busy mind. He was confident in Hereward, for this was Tyr-Hereward, he knew it. The Drome, the Mesa, the muzzled terror of Lokietok, all were surely part of the experience of Tyr. How strong he would be soon. Yet Martin felt that neither he nor any of the Twisted Folk were doing enough to help, and since he thought his people, though not in general timid, had been intimidated, his mind turned to an authority that sounded in no way daunted or diffident, the King of the Glassy Country.

Daylight came and the ashes of the fires, a hundred and more of them, were blown into flames, twigs dropped on them and the Companions changed their sentinels again, being as careful as they seemed to be careless. About noon the bugle's call was a howl – two notes, high, low – ominously repeated over and again. "Red! Red!" the Companions muttered to one another in their camp-places up and down the north bank of the Dole, and waited for the runners. Before long the runners came and the companies of Urbano de Vito and Oyvindsen of Thule, each a hundred strong, filed towards the bridge, with two more companies to wait in reserve on the road that led northwards from it, while the other captains, sixteen of them in all, deployed their men in vantage points along the river, watching for boats and even swimmers. Hereward and Martin, feeling unnecessary and left behind drifted down to the bridge and found a spot where the river edge was eroded into a cliff which provided an uninterrupted view of the bridge and river; George walked away from the river and into the trees.

The watchers had not long to wait, nor did they easily forget what they saw. Across the river, still hidden by the foliage and the tall trees, drums began to beat and from what seemed far away came an eerie sound that made men glance uneasily at one another, a crackling rhythm as if a huge snake rattled a thousand brittle vertebrae together as it writhed forward in mile-long loops. Then on the far river-bank the reeds and bushes shook and took on life as the thousands of Daroi concealed among them came pressing down to the water's edge. Half-glimpsed faces, shields, and torsos came and went, a black nest of shining scorpions seething angrily among pulled-aside grasses. Then came the Daroi column, fifteen abreast, tightly packed, moving down the highway and out on to the bridge. At every fifth step the warriors stamped down their feet together with a thunderous 'Ah!'

Martin was sure that the Companions behind the barrier would feel its wooden construction shaking, and even feel the bridge, for all its massiveness, ripple beneath them. Another five steps and another crash. 'Ah!' came the roar, drowning even the howls and snarls of the Daroi hounds as they jostled to find places in the thick of the column. The warriors held their long narrow shields on one arm, the other hand carrying sabre, lance, javelin or stabbing-spear. Their hair had been stiffened and reddened with clay so that it stood out spikily from their heads. This was the Daroi battle column that had brought them across two continents. The Companions on and behind the barricade were staring almost transfixed. 'Boom, boom, boom!' spoke the gongs in the trees and the Daroi beat their weapons on the edges of their shields, making the eerie rattling noise.

Though more than a hundred yards away, Hereward could sense the charge building up. Two or three more of those five-pace advances, the pounding of feet, and then it would come. He felt Martin trembling by his side. Smallish at this distance they saw Schroeder step out through the passage and lift his hand. The front of the column paused and in the silence his voice was loud and clear.

"Go back. We have no quarrel with you." His words hung in the stillness. "Your women and children need your care. Your old people too. Why do you wish to fight men you have never seen in your lives? We are like you, ordinary men, not kings or chieftains. If your King wishes to fight then let him do so, but we hope to meet you as friends."

The packed ranks of the warriors paused momentarily and heads turned to find their spokesman. The clan chief pushed forward clear of the front rank. "Friends would not stop us crossing a bridge!" he shouted. "We fight those who are ready to fight. Open the bridge and we will be your friends."

The column seethed and pushed and scores of the yellow dogs filtered through to the front like the spume that precedes a wave up the beach.

"That we cannot do," Schroeder called out. "Yet if you go back to your camps then we can meet and talk more. How can we be friends until we have learned to talk together?"

"We do not go back!" the chieftain shouted. "We do not go back for water or fire, for desert or forest. We do not go back for men. We are the Daroi. No man owns this river. Any man may drink from it, or fish in it, or cross it if he wishes."

"So be it," replied Schroeder. "Though I think that you and your King wish to cross more than the men who must force the crossing. So now I speak to them and not to you. Daroi men, we on this side are men like you. You go your way, let us go ours, surely the world is room enough for that."

But the Daroi leader had no inclination to debate with Schroeder. The road on the far side was far too tempting. Turning he gestured to the column as it pulsed behind him, and Hereward saw them imitate the leader's five steps and heard the thumping of the stamped feet. Schroeder had gone back now. Then, as if the starting-gun of a great race had been fired, the mass was released with a roaring shout that sent waterfowl panicking into the air for a mile up and downstream of the bridge.

Only a single span separated the Daroi from the barrier, perhaps forty paces, and they had covered half of this before the Companions responded. Somewhere Franz Schroeder had dropped his hand in a signal. The gunfire crackled like flames running through long dry grass, and the bows and crossbows many of the Companions favoured twanged and snapped unheard above the din. Every one of those watching along both banks of the river saw the column stagger, its leading ranks going down and those following stumbling and pitching forward. A second volley shook the head of the column. The riflemen were firing through apertures and loopholes, then walking back to reload, their second rank stepping forward to take their place. One of their bowmen came toppling backwards from the top of the barricade. Martin shuddered at the sight of the carnage on the bridge.

The Daroi swarmed forward across the dead, they ran along the parapets and sprang at the top of the barricade like apes. Sheer pressure drove them to the face of the wooden wall and their spearmen forced the Companions' riflemen back from the loopholes, thrusting their lances through or seizing the rifle barrels and striving to drag them away.

"Kittiwake! Kittiwake!" yelled the Companions, their cries like the sound of seabirds over a storm. On top of the wall metal flashed in the sunlight, but the gunfire was ceasing. A Daroi warrior was over the top and jumping down, then another and another. The wall-top was like the crumbling lip of a dam through which water spurts as the stones and earth disintegrate under the pressure. The watchers saw the Companions suddenly retreating, running back along the bridge, some even diving into the river. Through the broken doorway and over the top the flood poured. As the company from the bridge ran back the company of Oyvindsen of Thule was revealed standing in line and the carefully prepared volley came like a metal hailstorm, sweeping whole sections of the bridge clear. There was a pause as the Daroi took cover among the bodies or on the further side of the barrier. Around the dead the dogs ran frenziedly and the baying set Hereward's hair prickling as he remembered the tunnels beneath High Altai. Where the bridge reached the northern bank its downstream parapet joined the base of a brick tower, four storeys high. It was garrisoned and, although it did not bar the road, Hereward thought it looked a daunting prospect for anyone to pass beneath its walls. Oyvindsen's men had filtered into the trees and bushes on the opposite side of the road, which then stretched emptily up the valley side to the north. The Daroi looked at the road and must have known it was a killing-place and their front ranks hesitated.

It was time for Schroeder again, and he came out on the road. "Everyone's glad of an excuse to listen," said Martin. Only the dogs yammered on.

"Go back!" Schroeder shouted. "Go back and talk among yourselves. We war only on kings. There is no man of you I would not have for a friend, except the one who drives you on to our weapons. This is a wide world," – he gestured round him to the horizons – "and we wish only to stand on a small part of it. Why does your King wish to be lord over us, when before this day he had never seen or known us?"

Though the Daroi clan had many of its warriors just behind the barricade others of them had gone back across the bridge. After half an hour's inactivity Hereward and Martin were joined by two of the men whose fireside they had shared the previous night. With their clothes a screen of leaves and twigs and their faces smeared with mud and sap the men were not easy to recognise, until their nasal voices revealed them as the cousins.

"What do you expect to happen?" Hereward asked.

One of the cousins said that the Daroi would not be deterred by Schroeder's words for long.

"They haven't got halfway across the bridge to go back now," added the other. "They are probably getting themselves a new chief."

"Poor fellow. We've got marksmen like Alvin Costello."

Later the cousins drifted off, chatting cheerfully, and shortly afterwards Martin left too. "I can't stand any more of this," he said as he walked away. "I'd sooner be with Lokietok."

Before long the clan must have found its new leader. Hereward could see the other clans watching on the river's far bank, or packed on the hillside, even on the ridge above the Dole valley, as the second attack was launched. It swept clear across the bridge before the Companions cut the column in half, and under their fire those in the rearward part retreated, feigned death, or sprang over the parapets. The vanguard tried to turn into the trees but the undergrowth was thick and the Companions were waiting. For the Daroi only the road led away from the dying and they scattered along it in dismay, either back towards the bridge or on into the northern distance.

Hereward walked down to the road and looked around. Those Companions who had not reoccupied their barricade were tending the wounded of both sides, giving them water, bandaging wounds and trying to cope with the Daroi dogs.

It was in Hereward's mind to press on towards Limber that evening when Martin reappeared and pointed to a Daroi warrior sitting propped against a rock, his head lolling back. "On his cloak," he said quietly. Hereward saw it at once, a double star, deep glowing green. He had last seen it, or one exactly like it, on Nana's dress back in the big house in Venask.

XXX

The Matrix, like all empires and principalities before it, was driven by the heartbeat of its past. Impulses from a thousand years ago move through people as mysteriously as blood through the veins, but nothing absorbed the Matrix more than the problem of rule and government. Somewhere in their race memory lay the wreckage of their ancestors' civilisations, when the sirens of power sang too enticingly and men and women strove for positions which allowed them the intoxication of bending others' wills to their own. In the Broken Years, however, it was well not to attempt to control or coerce any man. Were not the carriers of the virus of power far worse than the lepers, who asked for nothing but care? So eventually had come the rectors. They were not elected. No decision of the rectors was enforceable. They existed to confirm what the people had decided. As the years passed the rectors found that if they concerned themselves with the safety of the people then within that framework most other dispositions would develop by general consent. Sometimes ancient policies became philosophies, such as the attitude to the forests. When this happened there was a sense of satisfaction that law had become custom and equity fairness.

Not far from the Limber waterfront loomed the mighty church of St Xavier of the Flames, huge among the labyrinth of palaces and gardens, abbeys, smaller churches, the great Sweetwater aqueduct, theatres, basilicas, galleries and columns, all of which clustered around it. Most of the buildings were ablaze with mosaics and frescoes, their floors cool underfoot with marble, their windows an iridescence of rose-red, sea-green, coral and amethyst, everywhere an intricacy of tesselations, on walls, on ceilings, in basins where water tinkled as it curved from the mouths of stone dolphins. St Xavier's itself was a cascade of domes, each poised above its corona of windows; in its cavernous interior shafts of downward-piercing light stood like pillars of bright air. Where one of the shafts made a pool of light in the centre of the wide floor it illuminated the round table of the rectors. Seated at it they were dwarfed by the space round them. The first-ever council had wished for a position for the men and women who were ministers which would at once diminish their stature while augmenting the sense of the importance of their work. Here, tiny and exposed in the great church, was now the accustomed place.

Debate and discussion were public, and those who gathered to listen could vary from a few passing visitors or worshippers to the swarming thousands who, once in a lifetime, would surge into St Xavier's to hear for themselves the crisis their way of life was entering. Jacky, Kit and Astolat were sitting that morning with Conrad Novak close to the front, long before the ten rectors were due to appear at the table. When they did enter there were only nine. "Look, Alexis is late," said Astolat.

Kit was thinking of Hereward; she expected that, if he reached Limber, he would mete out the same brutality that Adelie had undergone to at least one of the rectors who approved of the policy of the Academies. One would be fair, but Tyr might not stop there. It would be interesting to know if the policy concerning the children had been debated in recent years, she thought, or had been merely inherited. Only once since leaving Westermain had she heard a rumour of Hereward and that was unconfirmed, but her talent had allowed her to look in his mind. What she had sensed there had been as uncomplicatedly direct as a baby's craving for its mother's milk, and as strong and stinging as sunlight is when concentrated to a point through a lens. So unless he was dead he would come, and then somebody in Limber was going to get hurt. How this might help the Twisted Folk was unclear.

Her thoughts were interrupted by the opening speech of one of the rectors. There was no leader and the opportunity to introduce and speak on a topic was circulated round the table. The city knew with the instinct that bees have for their queen's uneasiness that Michael Novak would call for war. Through the previous night fires had burned on the Steps, outside his brother's waterfront tower, in the parklands, on the crest of the ranges. On some fires straw effigies burned, stuffed inside the blue greatcoats of the militia. Novak stood up and looked round the table and then across the space surrounding the rectors to the people beyond, the nearer rows seated, then standing figures, and, in the galleries high above, faces that looked down as pale blurs.

In the front row sat each of the three marshals. Occasionally a marshal would attend to receive his instructions, but for all of them to be present was rare indeed. Jacky had heard a low jeering noise run round the nave when they had entered. The same noise began again as Novak prepared to speak, and there were patronising smiles and glances passed between some of the rectors.

"Fellow-rectors," Novak began, "and fellow-citizens. It is my duty to try to express the will of the people and that is what I now do. Only two of the last ten generations have seen war and no one at any time wilfully desires to look upon it. I do not mean the nagging conflicts that our marshals have to contain almost always beyond our borders in the empty lands and sea that surround us. I mean a great war, one that unhoods its face and asks us all to fight together, or at least show that we are prepared to fight.

"Ten years ago we began to hear whispers of the Daroi, a people as numerous as the locusts and as hungry. Then they were one sea and two deserts away. Today they are burning our villages in Ambria and all the lands north of the Pale Mountains. Very soon their vanguard will be across the Dole River and into Sylvania. Whether they mean to break the King of the Glassy Country we do not know, but it seems more likely they will head straight towards Limber itself."

"Will they, Jacky?" whispered Astolat.

He put his arm round his sister. "It won't happen."

"Their numbers are huge, for really they are several nations in one, and what we are meeting is the leading fringe. Far behind their front they are moving towards us like migrating ants, so far back that our grandchildren may still face their columns. This is a good land, fertile and bountiful, soft under green forests, watered by clear streams, and a land that we and our forefathers made so, for once much of it was a dusty wasteland. Both this, our home, and our way of life in it are, I believe, worth defending. If the Daroi come on unchecked you may be sure that everything will change, and the great expanse that the Matrix has tended so long we will need to tend no longer, for we shall have forfeited the privilege of doing so.

"I do not wish any man to be my subject, but nor do I wish to be subjected to anyone else. I would hold it shameful to be one of the generation that extinguished the dream. Thus I propose that the will of the Matrix is that we remain a free people whatever the sacrifice, and that the marshals be given armies that are capable of keeping faith with those that have made the same sacrifice in the past."

"What sacrifice have you ever made?" a voice shouted.

"Send your own children!" a woman yelled.

"Empires and commonwealths are centuries in the making," Michael Novak went on as if there had been no interruption, "but a few days in the destroying. Civilisations have died before. When the people looked down into the bay and saw the incomprehensible fleet drop anchor like wooden swans, or when the men that were not like themselves, men with no hair on their faces, began to bring the magical trading goods that they could only covet and admire and buy with their land, or when the new priesthood was proclaimed that turned their homely worship into dirty little tokens and taboos, always there must have been a moment, early or late in the encounter, when that civilisation came to believe in its own death. Once one believes in that one is dying.

"Perhaps some of us have looked at the Daroi and believed in our death. I have not. As I speak of them I see a struggle with an unknowable end, but ask yourselves why they paused so long in their advance when they took High Altai. I will tell you why. They looked at us and were troubled by their own insolence. Some of them may have seen death, but now they think they were mistaken and we are too craven to stand and face them. The Matrix has kept its faith through bad times and good for a long age. It is late, perhaps too late to save all we hold dear, but if all else falls in the wreck we shall have saved our name." He paused and there was silence, into which he spoke the traditional closing words: "I, who try to speak for you, salute you."

Sitting next to Novak was a dark-haired woman with a square lace cap weighted with pearls at its corners. She stood and said, "I believe the will of the Matrix is expressed in this proposal. I, who try to speak for you, salute you."

After the previous long speech this sudden addition to the support for Novak came as a shock to most. Conrad Novak muttered to Jacky, "I don't mean to be cynical, but it's easy to be brave from the safety of the Archipelago." The woman's brief response seemed to have left the next speaker unready and Conrad took the opportunity to explain to his group that the Archipelago lay south-east of Limber, and no one was quite sure at any one time which of the hundreds of islands was acknowledging the Matrix leadership. He added that the islanders' unruly semi-autonomy was put down by the mainlanders to the protection the seas gave them. "Only Osprey and Kiretha are big enough islands for people to live on and be out of the sound of the sea in a winter gale."

Nevertheless that was two votes for confronting the Daroi, and Jacky was looking at the third rector rising to speak when he noticed a dark object falling down the shaft of light from one of the high galleries beneath the main dome. What looked like a leather bag had been thrown arching outwards and it plunged on to the table with a heavy thud, then burst open, splattering with red liquid the clothes and faces of the rectors, some of whom recoiled in disgust or sprang to their feet to look upwards. A hooting cheer erupted from above. Before long an attendant arrived with cloths and a broom, but was dismissed by Michael Novak. "Let it stay as it is. What is more suitable? Blood is the currency of freedom."

Jacky was not the only one to notice the sideward glances and the smiling shrugs among some of the rectors, and several were dabbing away the sprinkled blood and carefully mopping dry the table-top directly in front of them.

If the last speaker had been brief the next said only a little more. It was Marcantonio Colonna, by upbringing one of the Children. He spoke for one of the immediately threatened areas, the delta of the Dole. "Same old difficulty. Trap set by words. 'War is bad.' But 'war' is a word. Stops us thinking properly. Too little correspondence to reality. Statement likely to be in part true, but the degree of truth limited by random factors. Should therefore be 'War contains bad elements'. Cells in my body conflict, bad for some but not bad for all cells or all milieu. Proposition should be 'Preserving our existence as a society is desirable'. Forget war's morality. War is a method, not good nor bad but either necessary or unnecessary on balance. Alternative method non-resistance and, I believe, consent to the extinction of our society as now constituted. The will of the people is best expressed by the proposal before us. I, who try to speak for you, salute you."

"Conrad, will five votes be enough with just nine rectors here?"

"No, my dear." The harbourmaster smiled down at Astolat's inquisitive face. "Not even all ten votes would ensure a war. But any majority would mean that the marshals would have the permission of the state to name a rallying day and prepare for the disposition of the men who would muster to it. It's as unsystematic as a system can be without simply dissolving."

"Does it work?" Jacky asked.

"It has so far. The Matrix peoples have always kept their nerve and avoided the temptation to shelter under a powerful authority. In the middle of a meadow you can be struck by lightning, but in a dungeon you can't. So who's better off in a storm?"

Astolat appeared eager to deal with this question but was finding it difficult to make herself heard. The news of the third vote had filtered outside the cathedral and from the streets came the response, a clamouring that threatened St Xavier's as if it stood assailed by a sea of noise, the shouting, shapeless at first, gradually turning into a chant of "Make peace! Make peace!" The cathedral seemed a diving bell lodged on a reef where with waves booming against it the divers inside are unable to converse for the noise. Kit's head was aching now, for the chant was being taken up by the people packed inside and she wondered what would happen if the next rector to rise did not advocate peace. Conrad Novak whispered the name to her: "Osric Sheer, from the Steppes." She stared intently at Sheer but looked away and pulled her black hood tight when she saw that he was disquieted enough to scan the gathering's front rows uneasily.

Eventually he spoke: "I'm just a simple sort of fellow, like most of us here, but I know empty slogans when I hear them and so do you." Instantly approval came in an outburst of clapping and foot-stamping, it being already likely which way this vote would be cast. "These Daroi are wanderers – they'll move on, that's what nomads do for a living. Even if they stayed, well, they're men and women, they've got families, same as us. Maybe there might be a bit of change – what's wrong with that? They seem to me to have a real community spirit – we could learn from that. Better than being on the Opium Steps, take my word for it. Colonna goes on about semantics – you see, Marcantonio, I know a few long words too, you didn't expect that – but I prefer good honest words like common sense, just the same as you folks out there. I know you can't weigh freedom with scales but if they want to share our freedom and live like us what's wrong with that? Let's have some logic here. I'm sorry I haven't a way with words like Michael has, and Marcantonio for that matter, you see I didn't get the chance to go to their smart academies. Even if I had I'd have come bottom of the oratory class, no doubt. That's all I've got to say. You all know me – you know I'd sooner be somewhere else drinking a couple of beers – and if you want peace you know I'll always do my best for you."

"Osric'll make peace!" screamed a voice above the cheers.

"Make peace! Make peace!" echoed the chanting outside.

The applause swirled round the spaces of St Xavier's, hands clapping, voices shouting down from above.

"Have you finished, Osric?" asked Michael Novak bleakly.

"Sorry. I who try to speak for you salute you." Sheer lifted both hands above his head as torn-up pieces of paper fluttered down like drifts of white butterflies.

Jacky gazed around. "Does everyone here agree with him?" he said to Kit.

"Judging by the noise. But then you can't hear the ones who are silent, can you?"

"Not everyone's here, either," said Astolat. "There are lots of others. What about them?"

"I suppose they wish it would all go away," he said, "so they can get on with their lives, and fish and farm and so on."

"I'm sure they do. Exactly what my people have been hoping for since we appeared on Earth. And," Kit went on tartly, "I wouldn't be surprised if these Daroi turn everyone else into Twilight Folk. It would serve the Matrix peoples right. For us, of course, it would be more of the same."

A woman stood up to speak. "Three–two," said Kit and when she sat down that was the count.

"How did you know that?" Jacky asked, and Astolat leaned over wide-eyed to listen, but Kit shook her head and muttered words they didn't altogether catch, about having more difficulties than usual with these rectors being all rhetoric and artifice.

Another vote was cast for offering a welcome to the Daroi. As those outside learned the voting tally the chanting became louder still. Again there was movement in the gallery and, even as the next rector began his speech, eyes were drawn upwards. Others followed and soon hundreds saw a grotesque dummy being lowered to hang swinging, suspended by a rope round its neck. It was crude, with straw-filled body and limbs sticking out like sausages, but its makers had aimed for no likeness, choosing to staple to the chest a large placard bearing the name of Michael Novak. Over his shoulder Jacky saw other placards held up on sticks by people who had pushed into the back of the listening crowd. Many were white with a black skull and all carried the same inscription: 'No war'.

Another of the rectors, a bent white-haired man who supported himself with a stick, spoke briefly and cast his vote to fight. "One for Limber Port," whispered Conrad Novak. "I think he might have voted the other way if there hadn't been so much noisy persuasion."

Frowning to herself Kit agreed. "You're right. Very strange."

A stone, flung over the heads of the nearer people, bounced on the table, skipping as if across a pond's smooth surface, and a voice shouted, "Old men always vote for war. They haven't long to live anyway."

Michael Novak was on his feet again. "If there is one more interruption of this sort the cathedral will be emptied to allow the council to continue." Another outburst of jeering greeted this remark, but calm was restored, Novak remaining standing until there was quiet.

"Can't the ordinary folk have a say?" asked Osric Sheer, earning himself the applause of much clapping as if the audience signalled that it could respond to reasonable comment.

"When they stop throwing stones," replied the woman from the Archipelago.

The next speaker made his opening point clearly enough: "Fellow rectors, in war there is no choice but to win. That is in a war where losers do not survive, as distinct from minor conflicts for limited gains of territory or a change of some small regime. So we must win."

Jacky liked the gruff voice and the face that looked seamed, down to earth and wise. To his surprise Kit from the corner of her mouth murmured, "Four–four."

"Didn't you hear?" he said quietly. "He said the Matrix must fight."

"No, Jacky, he said the Matrix must win."

"Yes. I heard him."

"Wait and see." Sometimes she wondered how Jacky made his way through the world. In a crowded street the hurrying walkers move in many directions untouching, avoiding an unlimited number of collisions, even brushes. How would a thousand hurrying blind men cope, she wondered. In the end they probably would survive but, as they could only wait and see, at what cost in bruised frustrations?

"Let us be realistic. Is this a war we can win? From what I hear of these Daroi they will not disappear. The breakwater will stop the first wave and the second, but it can't stop the tide. This is not like anything we have faced before. If we fight then we cannot be sure of winning, and even if we hold them back then it seems to me we are declaring war on behalf of our children, our grandchildren, even their children. Have we the right to do that? You might say that in the future we, or they, can make peace . . ."

"Make peace! Make peace!" repeated the chant, first from below and then from above as if a wish had been made into a ball and bounced in the shadowy nave before being thrown and caught high in the galleries and clerestories.

"You might say it, but it would not be true. What stored memories of hatred would underlie that so-called peace? We would leave our children a desert of resentment and ask them to call it peace. The peace of exhaustion, the peace of surrender, the peace that the rabbit knows while the weasel digests its mate, these are phantoms of peace. Let us offer the Daroi friendship and trust. You, the people for whom we try to speak, have the right to expect that of us. I believe that in our tongue our nearest translation for the word 'Daroi' is people. That is what they are, people, as we are, who have no reason to desire war with other men, women and children. What is more, we should be seen to be genuine in our desire for friendship, open-hearted and generous. I therefore give notice of my intention to introduce the topic, as soon as deferrals permit, of abolishing the office of marshal. Let us pursue peace without reservation and without reproach. What worthier cause do you know?"

The rectors seemed to be aligned into two groups of four with two yet to speak. One of these was Alexis Kopa, the other the rector for the Outlands who now stood up.

"I speak for the Outlands," he began, "the traditional allies of the Matrix . . ."

"Is that what we are?" Jacky muttered behind his hand to Kit.

". . . and there are more than fifty Outlander peoples; they are as varied as the Free Port of High Altai, the desert settlers of the south-east, and the different parts of Westermain. Some are lonely islands where a few crofters live frugal lives, others are crowded, with busy contentious folk, such as . . ."

"Such as Lett! Get on with it!" someone shouted and there was laughter.

"My point is that embodying so many diverse places is difficult, the more so in that there is virtue in both sides of the argument . . ."

"Not in my opinion," said Jacky to Kit.

". . . nor do I feel happy when we consider proposals in terms of rights, as several of us today have done. It does not seem to me that we necessarily have a right to stop these Daroi in their tracks." A buzz and throb of voices rose at this. "It is absurd to say they have a right to do as they wish in their migrations or invasions or whatever one calls them." The voices went from a purr to a snarl that developed a ragged edge after Michael Novak smiled. "What we need to ascertain is whether or not we have the will to survive. Fortunately for me the responsibility of my decision today is not so great as it might seem, as if we have this will then no remarks of mine will change it, and if we do not then I cannot summon it up. It does not come when one beckons. So far this civilisation we call the Matrix has always had the ability to survive against all competition. From this survival has been derived the idea of rights. I do not wish to go into the conundrum of when morality and survival conflict. It is, in any case, an issue for little children to sharpen their debating skills on, although it would be surprising if one could find a moral action which did not permit the survival of the greater number. If you doubt me then imagine yourself outside your burning home with your babies asleep inside it."

The rector halted as a man came pushing through the crowd standing in one of the aisles. There was an urgency in his passage and noisy reactions – as when a man pushes through a bamboo thicket the canes clatter and sway. Reaching the table he placed a folded paper in front of Michael Novak. From where he sat Jacky could see the elaborate purple seal and guessed from whom it came. Seals were an antiquated device, using them a harmless quirky indulgence, but it seemed to suit Alexis. Novak broke open the seal and read the paper, pushing it to the nearest rector from whence it was circulated round the table. An expectant silence fell as Novak stood up to speak: "The rector for the Seven Hundred Steps has resigned as of this morning. I think we need a short break in our meeting as his nominated successor has not yet accepted the rectorship. We shall reconvene in fifteen minutes."

The announcement produced disarray among the rectors, who rose hurriedly and moved towards the chapter-house in busily conversing groups. The cathedral was filled with an intrigued hum of speculation, as if at the interval of an absorbing play. Though the voting had yet to take place, the general impression was that four votes on either side were committed, but that two rectors, the Outland rector and Alexis, were as yet unconvinced by either argument. If, well into a chess game, one were to remove a white bishop and replace it with a white knight, the game would pause for a time as the position was inspected and the strengths of the other pieces redefined. The white knight may also turn out to be a black rook; among the rectors only Novak and Alexis before that day had set eyes on Jacky and they were far from certain.

Jacky felt Astolat squeeze his hand. He gave her a quick smile before turning to Kit. "What do I do now?" he said quietly.

"It's your decision, Jacky. I can tell you this – the truth's getting as twisted as my hand in this debate."

He spoke across Astolat to Conrad Novak: "How serious a man is Alexis?"

"He liked a quiet life," said Novak. "He would have hated this crisis. I can't predict how he intended to vote – perhaps under the pressure you get in St Xavier's he might have sided with Sheer."

"Did you know him well?" asked Jacky.

"I've visited his house. He had a strong sense of family; he showed me his portrait gallery and many of the portraits were of Kopas who had once been rectors. You got the impression he was whimsical and elegant, but he would not have resigned his responsibility as a caprice."

The rectors were reassembling round the table. Jacky caught Michael Novak's eye and rose to his feet. There was a mutter of questioning going on and then a few shouts. He thought he heard Nestor's name. He felt very young and when he looked at the circle of rectors he detected a hint of condescension, and some allusive smiles that came and went.

"From a jack to a king," murmured Kit. "Well, well, well!"

"Do you accept the position?" Michael Novak called out.

"Take it, Jacky," whispered Astolat.

"All right, I'll do my best," said the white knight.

XXXI

The double brooch was in Hereward's pocket, and now he knew most of the sad story of the events in Venask. The Daroi who had worn the brooch had been reluctant to tell what had happened until Lokietok had begun to stir on the roadside. As Hereward lost patience so did the Unman begin to shed some of its apathy. Though but a shadow of its former self, the shadow was still a slavering menace.

Blood *Sinew* *Gut*
Wetness *Fats* *Teeth*

The images had slurred across and the pale eyes had focused on the man with the brooch. It was more than enough. Shuddering, the warrior had related the last hours of Demetrius, the burning house with the screams behind the locked doors and shutters of the flame-filled bedrooms, the old lady they had found later in the cellar under the ashes and debris. "We played dice for the brooch," he said. "I do not know who first took it." Martin thought the Daroi was lucky that the Companions were all around, and were being gentle with the wounded captives. He did not wish Hereward to be alone with the man who had worn the brooch. Lokietok was agitated and went off to prowl among the trees not far away. The nearer Companions eyed them speculatively.

Hereward, George and Martin moved little for the rest of the day. The road to the north still had some fugitive Daroi on or near it, and Hereward kept taking the brooch out of his pocket. Once or twice Martin thought he saw him speak to it. In the late afternoon sun they were sitting on the banks of a small creek trying to formulate some plan. "I am tired of being chivvied and chased," said Hereward. "It is time these nomad people met someone who said 'no', apart from Demetrius, and I think these Companions are the ones to do it. They have already done it once today, and if they intend to do it again I shall offer to help. I do not like thinking about what happened in Venask."

"Do you no longer wish to go on to the great city?" Martin asked. "There is the matter of the girl."

"I have not forgotten. But we are already inside one of the Matrix's home provinces. So far we have not learned much of the way of their world, but now we shall see the Matrix fight for its life. Then we shall discover what ideas it holds most dear, because it will hold on to those the longest and sacrifice others. Also we shall meet the ministers or rectors or whatever they call their leaders, because they, it is said, fight in their front ranks. So they should be here soon. Then I will have a chance to ask them who decided to take Adelie from her mother."

"If you mean to stay and help these Companions, Hereward, then I don't think they will want me," said Martin. "But I understand you. You liked Madame Nancy Villiers and so did I. She was kind and brave and I remember what she said about the people of the Matrix and how they dreamed this world for us. Well, my people's part was to be the incubus that presses dreams out of shape, I suppose. I can't forgive that or forget it, but – "

"But," said George with a frown, "you have to wonder where the Matrix people are?"

"I don't know," said Hereward. "It is hard to understand. These Companions are brave, but they are few when one looks across the river." Their eyes lifted to the columns of smoke that stretched downstream and up as far as the eye could see. Clearly the Daroi were enjoying having plenty of cooking-fuel after their journey across the treeless mesa. The lowing of cattle made a constant undertone from where, on the far side of the Dole River, herdsmen were urging thousands of beasts into clearings or thornbush enclosures for the night.

"I think," said Martin, "we should go and see the King of the Glassy Country."

The other two looked at him and let the idea diffuse through their other thoughts.

"He is far away," said Hereward.

"Not so far. And he will want to see you."

"No, he won't," interrupted Hereward. "He's never heard of me."

"He's heard of Tyr."

"Martin! I thought that idea had been forgotten." Hereward felt remorseful when the little man looked cast down, but he was distracted by a buzz of voices and by some of the Companions running out on to the road and then calling the news back to others: "He's back."

"It's the captain-general."

"It's Andre-Leander." This last was from Lucas, one of the cousins, neither of whom seemed at all respectful of rank.

Hustle and movement ran through the Companions and it became clear that Townsend had come to speak to the men of de Vito's company, among whom the three travellers had already made some acquaintances. Before long they had assembled. It was now twilight and the wetland mosquitoes were singing round their heads as the captain-general addressed them. Hereward and his friends stood unobtrusively and listened.

"You fought at the bridge today and I'd like to ask you about that," said Townsend. "But first I have news from Limber – the runners are taking it round the other companies."

"Is the news bad?" asked de Vito.

"I'll keep it short. The rectors by now may well have voted for peace." Townsend meant to go on but there were many responses.

"Surely they're not surrendering!" said Lee, the other cousin, voicing the general opinion. When Hereward glanced at his friends in surprise, George said quietly that he supposed that meant there would be no chance to meet the rectors.

"If the vote is for peace there will be no armies to help us," Townsend continued. "Some volunteers, I suppose, if we decide to fight it out, but that's all."

"Fight it out?" asked a voice in the dusk. "What are the odds?"

"Five hundred to one, maybe more," Townsend answered.

"About two hundred to one in fighting-men," de Vito added.

"That's all right then," remarked Lucas.

"But we don't have to fight now, assuming the Matrix does offer peace. So, if we withdraw and move off into the forests, will the Daroi leave us alone? Yes, I think so, after all they seem to be heading for Limber. It's the treasure-house of the world and no one's ever sacked it. They won't bother with us." Townsend lifted his voice over the buzz of comments. "That's right. It's the heart of the Matrix, though it's nearly stopped beating. We never thought we'd see the day. Like earthquakes, floods, forest fires, plagues, you always think they'll happen somewhere else. But it sticks in my throat that the rectors may propose no resistance. Is that the wish of the Outlands? I cannot believe it is. When their turn comes, and it will, sooner or later, will Westermain sue for peace, or Lett, or Thule or any of the others?"

"We wouldn't!"

"We wouldn't!"

"Of course we wouldn't!" said the simple voices.

"I know that," said Townsend. "But what about your people at home? If we fight then they will have to face the Daroi peoples when they have been hurt. The Men will not be inclined to be merciful to beekeepers and fur traders, ploughmen and bricklayers."

A voice said, "If we don't fight they will be contemptuous of our people, they will feel no caution and put them to work the more quickly."

"Let me tell you my view," interrupted de Vito. "The Outlands have always been sheltered by the Matrix. I know we chafe at their regulations but children always chafe at their parents, and sometimes we have squabbled as children do, but no other powers have threatened us. But children must grow up, and it seems our parents are grown old without our noticing. We must start to care for ourselves and let our own folk tell us whether to fight or not. Until we know how the Council voted there is time to show these Daroi and their dogs a thing or two."

As de Vito was speaking Hereward noticed Townsend staring into the trees and followed his eyes. At first the Unman was hard to see standing among the trees back from the edge of the clearing. While undisturbed Lokietok was simply there, like a tree lopped off at head height, but then responding to Townsend's gaze came a faintly exuded menace, a warning mental growl. While no images were implanted in the minds of those around, nevertheless some taste of thought formed itself, rather as happens with those who flavour what is apprehended with optimism or pessimism. Lokietok moved out of the trees to stand within arm's length of Hereward, who could see the Companions' leader scrutinising the dishevelled clothes, and the scratched, scabbed face and hands of the Unman.

Townsend came across, nodded amiably at George and Martin and shook Hereward's hand. "Schroeder told me you knocked him out of the path of an assegai. He said that you are travelling with an Unman, even that you are friends with the creature. Is that true?"

"Yes," said Hereward. "Ever since High Altai."

"Wait a minute, I heard a rumour – no, I heard a song – about a man with a patch on his eye. Did you fight in the Drome at High Altai?" Hereward nodded. "Were you a prisoner of the Daroi?" Townsend caught the glances from Hereward's side. "All three of you were?"

"So was Lokietok."

"Stay close," said Townsend. "I've still to meet any of these Daroi people. I need to ask you about them."

Across the river the drums were beating again. The Companions did not anticipate a night attack, knowing night-fighters are rare among tribal people, but the drums were not difficult to understand. 'Tomorrow, tomorrow, tomorrow,' they were saying. "We should not fight head on again," Townsend said to de Vito. "You did well, but it will bleed us to death. Can we possibly win any confrontation with these people?"

"It doesn't look like it." De Vito's response was blunt. "Sixty years ago, maybe. The Matrix was different then, or so I have heard. Not now."

"Then let's really give them something to remember us by."

"What? I don't think we can."

"I don't see how we can either, yet," replied Townsend. "But there ought to be a way. Call a meeting in an hour. Something different, you, me, Schroeder, the Children."

"The Children?"

"Yes. There are bound to be some in the companies. Come on, how would you match up to the best Daroi warrior?"

"He'd probably beat me."

"Perhaps. It would be close," said Townsend. "Now, what about their best-educated man or woman against one of our Children?"

"I see what you mean," said de Vito.

The Children came. There were fifteen of them, most of them in their twenties. Townsend explained the reason for their assembly. The Children's eyes lit up; no one in the Companions had asked about their talents before. Their confidence was almost palpable.

"Give us the problem," they demanded. Townsend gave it to them.

"How many answers do you want?" asked the Children.

"I want an answer," he replied, "that makes the Daroi turn away, because this world, what we call the world of the Matrix, is too fragile. They will destroy it in their simplicity. I wish it to have a chance to fulfil its promise."

"They have not learned the power lesson," said one of the Children.

"They are young," said another.

And a third: "Do you wish to destroy them if they will not turn away?"

"No. Show them they should set limits to their own power," said Townsend.

"Do we teach them or let them learn?"

"Imaginary limitations!" chorussed several of the Children.

"Sister Francesca!" laughed others. She had taught most of them, in memorable classes on logic.

"Will this be a long debate?" inquired Townsend.

"As long as you want." The Children knew the answer to that question.

"Well, give me a quick answer to think about." Oyvindsen of Thule gave the answer. Most of the others frowned. Like mathematicians, given several answers they would always prefer the most elegant. Oyvindsen was being inelegant.

"But does that exist?" As Townsend spoke the firelight lit the underside of his features, so that for a moment his face looked like a skull with a candle inside, a child's turnip mask.

"Not in these times, but we could make it."

"Surely that is like those weapons from the Broken Years that need a thousand mines and factories and ten thousand engineers and mechanics working with materials we no longer possess in any quantity."

"No, captain. Poisoning the air needs some easy chemistry, that's all."

"Poisoning the air?" Hereward heard George mutter. "Surely they don't mean it."

The Children had pressed round Townsend in the centre of the clearing, but in a wider circle enclosing them was an audience of de Vito's company, along with Hereward, George and Martin, steadily swelled by men from other companies drifting across to listen.

Townsend dismissed Oyvindsen's proposal: "You know perfectly well we can't do that. That's the old problem back again. We have to fight close enough to feel the enemy's breath and tell the colour of his eyes. You know that. It was my fault anyway, asking for a quick answer."

The talk went round and round the circle for an hour, the Children floating ideas as shapely as soap-bubbles and joyfully exploding each other's creations. Frequently they walked over to the three travellers to ask for information about the Daroi. Hereward and his friends found themselves answering questions on whether the Daroi could read and write, the value they placed on their herds, their methods of recording events, their fear of death, the hierarchy of their clans, their concept of a god or gods and many more.

One of the Children introduced himself as Sammy; a short stocky young man with a fringe of fair hair, he took Hereward on one side for twenty minutes and catechized him on his time in High Altai and what he knew on how the Daroi viewed superstition, luck and magic. "You see, Hereward," he concluded, "I want to know whether they see themselves as driving the future or as it driving them."

"That isn't easy to say, Sammy. All I can tell you is that they often speak of fate. By that they seem to mean living in a sort of partnership with the wind and the horizon, their herds and the clouds. I'm sorry – that doesn't help you much."

"No, it's a great help. So the future's driving them! Good."

Sammy went back to the inner circle and asked, "Can I have a go?" which produced a round of good-natured banter, cries of "Sammy's woken up," and Townsend's ready assent.

"All the ideas have been good, but we need to do something very long-lasting. There's no point in winning a year's grace, nor even ten. Even if we could defeat them in battle, and that isn't going to happen, then it might make them pause, but not stop. What will make them stop is not wanting to come here, into the Matrix lands, that is.

There are probably lots of ways of making this happen." Seeing the Children stir, Sammy added, "Well, relatively lots. For instance we have considered the idea of making somewhere else more desirable. Desirable for them means desirable for their herds. We have heard of nomad people destroying irrigation works because they like dry grasslands and open steppes. So making the land too wet might be another way. But a better way, I think, would be to make a legend."

The Children were avidly attentive now and the whole clearing became very quiet. This was like a steeplechase; Sammy was jumping the ditches and hedges and they admired his style as they watched him run. "To make a legend we need their doom or defeat and then they should find some way of coming to terms with it, so that there is a cabbala or taboo which says that the Matrix lands are unlucky, forever proscribed."

"Sammy, I hope this is no will o' the wisp. Are you saying this needs us to defeat the Daroi first and make them a legend second?"

"No, captain," said another of the Children. "*They* have to make the legend." Sammy nodded approval, the first of the hounds having reached the hare.

"Most legends are the same," said someone in the quick speech of Westermain. "We are on the edge of one. Up there," he pointed to the west, upriver of the Dole, "lives the King of the Glassy Country. Why does the Matrix not rule those lands, not even to spread the kindly forests there?"

"It is an unlucky land," Oyvindsen suggested.

"Yes," said Sammy. "The Matrix made itself a legend. The land is bad, says the Matrix, glass, not soil, an unlucky place, with stubborn primitive people and a magical king. So leave it alone even if it isn't convenient to do so. The land lies on a straight line from Limber to Westermain as well as to Alba and other provinces. All roads lead to Limber but not straight there, those from the west have to swing right round the Glassy Country."

Other Children seemed to think they had been quiet long enough: "Is it a rule that history is the reverse side of legend?" asked Oyvindsen.

"Empirical rule, maybe."

"Argument from analogy, anyway."

"Not really."

"Yes! Implied analogy."

Townsend lifted a hand before more of the Children could pounce on Oyvindsen's suggestion. "One at a time," he said. "The captain's just taking his mind for a walk."

Hereward smiled. How exasperating the Children were and how

well their name suited them. They seemed absurdly young, even Oyvindsen, who looked near to forty.

"Since we agree there is a legend," Sammy went on, "then surely there must have been a base, an occurrence, from which it grew. If that was recorded it is now history, but only the King and his folk will have preserved it as history, and they won't mention bad luck or magic. If we found out what their ancestors did to deter the Matrix, then we might be able to repeat it and leave the Daroi to transmute it into legend."

"Wouldn't it be quicker for us to make a legend for them?" de Vito asked.

Sammy shook his head. "It would be quicker, captain, but we couldn't possibly construct it from outside the Daroi beliefs. Lucky charms, bad luck signs, nursery rhymes, words that mean nothing to outsiders – we have to leave all that to the Daroi. We need to know the truth of what the Glassy Country folk did to the Matrix."

Gradually their meeting wound down. The Children, who had enjoyed it, were reluctant to go, but they strongly approved of Sammy's analysis, and pressed Townsend for action on it. Townsend and Oyvindsen left together to walk back to the fires of the latter's company.

"Who's going to ask this King then?"

"Obvious, isn't it?" said Townsend.

"Crook and Hex?"

"Yes. And the other, the little one."

"He's not a Companion. Will he go?"

"He's been in a Daroi prison, hasn't he?"

Martin consented to go after consulting with his friends. Both urged him to be careful, Hereward adding that he hoped to be busy in Martin's absence. He did not enlarge upon this but seemed more interested in toying with the brooch. In the first light of the next dawn Martin and the only two of the Twisted Folk who were then among the Companions set off into the west. As the three of them climbed up out of the river valley, below they saw George wave to them and Lokietok emerge from the trees to peer down into Hereward's hand.

XXXII

The chapterhouse of St Xavier's was very private. It was a spacious room with one marble pier in the centre from which twenty ribs made a high vault. Plain wooden chairs with their backs to the wall made a full circle. Standing in a small group were the rectors who had called for war, and with them was Jacky Dorn, holding himself upright and looking full into the eyes of whoever spoke to him. When he felt others appraising him he had a kind of hauteur and already those looking at him felt that Alexis had made a typically unpredictable choice. 'Who is he?' thought the Lady of the Archipelago. 'Those eyes like blue holes in a mask, and I hear he dwells on the Steps. Limber doesn't breed many like him. I'm afraid he might stir things up.'

'An outlander,' said Marcantonio Colonna to himself. 'One who thinks with his blood. Already he's made his decision. At least it is easy to predict what he will do.'

Jacky was listening politely to Michael Novak, the latter simply asking him to express the will of the people of the Steps and the inner city as correctly as possible. Jacky nodded and inside his mind he stored up the words and the impressions. Probably most thought he was putting them into the pan of a balance to weigh against those that the peace party would provide for the opposite pan. Colonna however had guessed right. Jacky did listen closely and he was interested in the ideas and some time in the future he would consider which group had counselled him the better. But that was all.

There were four rectors in the group round Jacky, Novak, Colonna, the Lady, and the rector for Limber Port. A tentative silence had fallen as Novak finished when the chapterhouse door opened and Amalrik, the marshal of the southern frontier, entered. "May I join in?" he asked.

"Of course, and are your regiments ready to fight?" asked the Lady.

"Maybe. We could have fought more easily at High Altai, but we got no encouragement, if you remember."

Novak shrugged. "You know what everyone thinks of High Altai. Any proposition to fight there would have received little or no support. We had to defer then. This time I think we may win in the council. The Daroi advance gave us some more votes, two at least."

"If you go on deferring much longer," said Amalrik, "the Daroi will be holding dog shows in St Xavier's. And what about you?" He examined Jacky curiously. "There wouldn't have been many younger rectors than you, not that it matters. Made up your mind yet?"

The marshal's presence was so compelling and calm that Jacky nearly answered in spite of himself. However he held back the words and instead gave Amalrik the long cool stare that Kit called his Daylight People's look. The marshal only smiled back. "I expect these people have given you plenty of good advice," he said. "I won't repeat their ideas. I'll give you my own view, forgetting my position and the aspirations of the Matrix for the moment. This is it. Humans are born to fight. I don't mean to fight other humans particularly, but to fight whatever looks to have got us beaten. Why, some records say men's footprints are on the moon, and if they are they will be again, and if they aren't then one day they will be. It won't be me that walks there, but on the other hand there are some achievements and even one or two ideas that I don't want to see extinguished. There are people who believe that nothing justifies fighting. I know that it's all very complex and we could argue for years about it and yet it's simple enough inside my head. There is evil in our world. There's good too, they are a match for one another, they have to be. You know this, I expect, and if you don't I can soon show you some of both. You might say you don't need me for that, but you look young and strong – and, yes, I've heard of Nestor – and I think you won't be so well acquainted with evil. It searches out the small and the frail and the friendless because it savours their terror, and they are much easier to push into despair. It might disguise itself and come and tempt you, but it won't by choice assault you. After all it wasn't you Nestor wanted to be alone with, was it? My guess is he was very respectful to you.

"The people you should ask about fighters are the eighty-year-old woman being raped or the baby having a red-hot coal stuffed into its mouth, and I've come across both so I know. If they could put words together they would tell you there was nothing in the world that mattered more than that their misery should end, or even better that it had never begun. If only someone had been with them ready to fight on their behalf. Then the bully and the brute would have gone away, or put on a respectful face.

"End of lecture. No, one more suggestion. You are probably going to hear a lot, from Osric Sheer in particular, about how the cure – violence or force or resistance or just standing up, depending on who's talking – is just as bad, or that the poor offender is misunderstood or ill. You then have my approval if you push a hot coal into Osric Sheer's mouth. Speaking as a private citizen, of course."

With a flurry of brief farewells he had gone. The Lady of the Archipelago shrugged as they heard him clattering away down the cloister that led back to the nave of St Xavier's. "He makes it all sound so simple," she sighed. "Give a surgeon a knife and he wants to cure everything by cutting."

"You're arguing from analogy, just like Amalrik," said Colonna. Jacky was surprised by their responses. He had liked meeting the marshal. The rectors were, he thought to himself, not sufficiently ardent in their cause, slightly too inclined to see arguments for the other side. Whether, in this world of policy, a fierce and passionate advocacy was wise he was unsure, everything being so unfamiliar. Novak was unperturbed enough to pat Jacky on the back, and there being little left to say he was left alone to meet Sheer and his party for a while. The final decision was to be made at the table under the dome at noon, in one hour's time.

Sheer came alone to meet Jacky. He expressed no concern that Novak's group had spoken first, and explained that Alexis Kopa's resignation had come as a complete surprise to him, as had his replacement. "You look very young," he told Jacky. "Nothing wrong with that, so does Colonna. I hear your sister is one of the Children. She looks very bright if that's her sitting next to you in the cathedral. Now, the other girl – I'm not so sure she's good company for you. No offence, you know what I mean. As for Nestor – well, we won't miss him."

"Do you know what I had for breakfast?" said Jacky.

"We had to start somewhere. I'm a bird-watcher; imagine me trying to identify a bird in a thorn tree, spotting pale ruffles on its wing feathers, part of a buff chest, a glimpse of a bronze eye, though most of the time there's just a wind-flutter of leaves. It could easily be some finches, and you lean in to see, parting the branches, and then 'kek-kek-kek', it comes exploding out and this is no little bird but a peregrine falcon, yellow-clawed and slate-beaked, avian death, and you wonder how you could have been so mistaken. I mean like Nestor was mistaken."

Jacky's monosyllabic responses did not encourage conversation and before long Sheer left. Expecting to see others of Sheer's party he was surprised when Kit entered. There was a buoyancy in her step and a glow on her face. Even the black shawl had been pushed away, and though he was disturbed by the warm softness of her breath on his face as she put her arms around his neck, he held her close with one hand and stroked her dark red hair with the other. "Kit, what is it?"

"Oh, Jacky!"

"Something's happened to Astolat?"

"No, of course not. But I have to talk to you before you make up your mind. You see Sheer and some of the other rectors asked me how you would vote, and I said you probably weren't sure. And then they asked if they could do you a favour for joining them. Well, I thought I would ask if the Twisted Folk could be free, no one's hand against them, a free and equal people within the Matrix and all the provinces. I expected them to have no interest, or just suggest some petty concessions, but they just smiled and said 'Why not?' I think they mean it, though Sheer's mind is cloudy, hard to understand. But they agreed, Jacky! Just like that! Years beyond memory in burrows and bolt holes and it's all over. Two seconds, that's all it took!"

She looked up at him, but there was no response. Even his arms fell away until she found herself holding only one hand. "Jacky?" she whispered. It was a dream, surely, that dream she had when her hand had fingers on it, delicate long fingers with oval nails, and in the dream she used a knife and fork and scissors, thimbles and needles, fitting her new cream-skinned hand carelessly into or around the implements. Then she would wake to find it under her cheek, the hair coarse bristles, the pads leathery, the vestigial claw where on her other wrist her pulse beat in veins of the palest blue. She closed her eyes, and the tears began to slide out from beneath her eyelids, running down past the corner of her mouth, leaving shiny trails.

The debate had meant little to Jacky, because inside his head he had held his own conference: 'What would my father do? What would Andread, my brother have done? Would the river people be proud of me? My grandfather? His grandfather? Uncle Isak? Thorsten the sluice-keeper's son?' His blood whispered the answer along his veins and arteries. Ever since he had stood up in St Xavier's there had only been one response. Now he felt a pain in his stomach, a twisting coldness as if a snake moved blindly there, writhing in the gastric acids. He knew what he had to say: that the people on the Steps had looked to him, because what stared at them from the future was subjection, either to the Daroi or other predators who were quick to smell weakness, that the Matrix had conceived and upheld a vision, flawed as it may be, that had given men and women a chance to grow tall, and now it was crumbling there were few to come to its aid, and, most of all, that this was a hollow achievement for the Twisted Folk, a bribe that only bought others' complaisancy. "You have to earn it," he said. "It doesn't come this way. Freedom's harder to get than that. You're going to say that I've always been free so what do I understand. I just know you can't buy it cheap."

"Jacky," said Kit, "I don't care if it's dear or cheap. Are you going to fight for the Matrix? How many of your river-people did they kill? Have you forgotten Astolat? They chain up your own sister, they make you sail small ships that drown your brother. How can you make excuses for them?"

They were still standing hand in hand. She was crying as she spoke, and after a while she pulled her hand away, tugged up her shawl and tucked her black-gloved paw inside it. Her wariness was back, he thought sadly. "They say there are desert flowers that bloom for one day in a lifetime," she said. "I hope their petals last longer than mine did."

Long before the hour had passed the cathedral was again awash with noise. It battered back and forth, the waves of sound bouncing and mingling as water-waves do in a sinkhole when the sea beyond the rocks surges into it. The news had spread through the city, even to those few hitherto unaware of the voting, though the cathedral could take no more than the crowd that was already pressed inside, nor could the nearer streets, and all movement towards St Xavier's was choked by a stalled press of people. A feeling was growing that the Matrix would fight, so much so that the southern marshal was pondering whether he could find the forces to hold the line of the Dole River, and the protestations of Sheer's supporters were growing more acrid by the minute. With nothing to separate them the partisans of both sides were smouldering with a pent up anxiety that was only one more shouted insult away from mindless aggression. Petty looting was occurring on the fringes of the crowds just as random lightning flares round the main bulk of swollen storm-clouds. The main stroke was still gathering in the black-purple cloud-centre but its electric taste was already in the air.

The other rectors were seated round the table as Jacky pushed open the door that led from the cloisters to the northern chancel. Many in the galleries could see him there and the formless noise began to focus itself into a clamour of "Peace! Peace!" and then gathered the shape it wanted: "Vote peace! Vote peace!" There was another current of noise too, itself strong and forming a chant of "No surrender! No surrender!" People dragged at Jacky's clothes and screamed advice as he pushed forward, the smell and closeness, the glittering eyes and the shrillness of the voices all reminding him of once scrambling up a cliff face where seabirds squalled round him as he hauled himself up ledges where their shabby nests crackled underfoot and their white droppings splattered thick on the rock.

Suddenly up in one of the ring-galleries someone released a white chicken. Awkwardly, with a strenuous fluttering of wings, it came slanting down, pale through the light beams and grey through the shadows, bouncing off a pillar, squawking and clucking, to land in the space surrounding the table and run mindlessly underneath it and out again. "Chicken-heart!" came a voice from somewhere, then several, "Chicken-heart!" and then it was hundreds. Someone stepped in front of Jacky, but the way opened up again as he pushed the man aside. He could think only of Kit as he had left her, standing alone in the chapterhouse, her face bright with tears, his thoughts drawn as helplessly to her as the earth's dark waters are drawn by the moon. He was through the crowd now and a few steps took him to the only empty chair, though he did not bother to sit down until Colonna pulled his arm.

Michael Novak rose and lifted a hand above his head and the noise receded, silence moving out from the centre. The cathedral grew still and all inside heard the uproar outside grow fainter as the news spread that the decisive vote was imminent. "Does the new Rector for the Steps wish to speak?" Novak asked.

Colonna nudged Jacky, who looked startled and there was some faint laughter. He shook his head.

The actual vote was a strange and longstanding ritual. On the twelfth chime of the cathedral's bell that signalled noon each rector would rise simultaneously and hold outstretched in both hands a silk square, blue to assent to, and gold to deny, the proposal being decided. The bell pealed out its first stroke and the other rectors, as was the custom, rested one open hand on each square.

Astolat saw Jacky staring down at the two coloured silks in front of him. She had never seen him look worse. His face was gaunt and the blue eyes had a glaze to them. There were nerves jumping in his face.

"It's not fair!" she screamed into the silence.

XXXIII

"Who wants this piece of toast? Lokietok?" The giant made a noise not unlike a chuckle from deep in the chest. All round the fire the Companions of de Vito's company had pulled up logs and about forty were squashed together on the rough seats. In the darkness of the forest others of them surrounded further cooking fires, from which smells of woodsmoke and supper wafted in the air. Lucas, sitting next to Lokietok, said, "Put some honey on."

The Unman munched the toast, rumbling that honey was good, and Lucas remarked amiably, "Tastes better than blood, eh?" There was a mental purring from Lokietok which Hereward could sense from across the fire. By their familiarity the company of de Vito acknowledged that Lokietok, the previous evening, had passed their only test, and for the first time in the giant's recollections, such as they were, there was the feeling of being one of a fraternity.

"It's high time we were put at the back," said Alvin Costello, his black hair and milk-white skin clear in the firelight. He nursed one arm in a sling, the hand and wrist swathed in bandages. The others chorussed their agreement. The captain-general had pushed their company right to the back of a twenty-mile file. It had meant marching those twenty miles that day but he said they had earned the position. They were deep into woodlands none of them had ever entered before and now the other nineteen companies formed a reassuring screen between them and the Daroi host.

Hereward pondered what had happened over the previous week. It was only a week since they had parted from Karl-Pieter the forester, though it seemed far longer. The four of them had tramped through pleasant countryside, arriving at the Old Stone Bridge late on the fourth day. The first of the Daroi had reached the bridge that same evening. On the fifth day the Companions had fought at the bridge, and on that evening Townsend had returned and Hereward had listened to the conference of the Children. Early on the next day Martin and two of the Companions had left to enter the Glassy Country. That same morning George had come to Hereward saying that he wished to follow Martin into the forest but would return to the Companions before long. During that night de Vito's company had penetrated the Daroi encampments and on the seventh day the company with Hereward and Lokietok had marched away into the woodlands.

Behind them Townsend had left the Old Stone Bridge free for the Daroi. If they crossed and went on northwards to Limber then on their western flank would lie his tiny but undismayed force, still almost undamaged. Would the Daroi turn and swat at them? After the wildness of the previous night it was highly likely. Now the nomads would need time, probably a full day, to reorganise.

They have a lot of time, thought Andre-Leander Townsend, years of it. The Children had better know what they are doing.

"Andre-Leander knows what he's doing," said Lucas. "He's not a bad diver, either. Can you dive, Lokietok?"

"No," growled Lokietok, and gave images of water in spate, better left to water-creatures.

Weir Stickle Pike

Hereward gave the emerald brooch a polish and thought about the little psaltery in his pack. 'Rebuke the company of spearmen, the multitude of bulls.' The book had this trick of apt commentary. He hoped to find out more from it.

"Lokietok, your turn for a story," Lucas said.

The Companions chaffed at the Unman's reluctance, and before long the forbidding face turned to Hereward who, sensing the call for guidance, said soothingly, "All right. If you like. If not, another night." He was anxious that there might be a tale that would tell truly of the weary purgatory that the giant inhabited, a tale that might estrange Lokietok from any form of fellowship, and reflected ruefully that such a meeting as this would have been inconceivable before the events in the wood outside Venask.

Then, accompanied by a flow of images which embellished the thick unpractised words, came Lokietok's story. "There was first Lokietok. Father of all Lokietoks. In the sun, running, eating . . ."

Muscle-pull Sinew-tug Ligament-flex

"Doing things," suggested Lucas.

"Night comes next. Darkness. Rest. Lokietok listens to box." The audience were baffled here, particularly as Lokietok added a twangling tune.

Cogs Axle Wedge
Pinion Spring Box

Eventually one of them recalled a little box on his mother's window-sill. "A musical box, was it?"

"Music in box. Inside head is music in box. Sun comes again. Lokietok runs, eats, drinks water, shelters from rain. Night comes. Lokietok sleeps. Men come. Take off his head. Take box. Gone. Sweetness gone. Honey gone." The listeners waited, unsure if the story was complete. But there was more. "Sun comes. Lokietok runs, eats. Night comes. Lokietok rests, listens, but nothing. Lokietok asks men for music again. Men say, 'What music? We do not know of it. It has never been.' Every day Lokietok runs under the trees, in sun and shadow. Many days go by. Now the children of the father of all Lokietoks do not recall music. Music is forgotten. Perhaps it was a dream. Some say it did not happen."

The Unman's short story had been made longer by the images and pauses that inhabited it. Particularly among the older Companions it touched forgotten regrets for the days before their own music had stopped playing.

Hereward could only stare at Lokietok, astonished at how the Unman could have found such an analogue for Hereward's own yearning for memories earlier than his coming to Hay. If he knew who he once was, he wondered, surely it would be easier to find a future, just as hearing a string of notes helps to make the next one in the sequence recognisable and proper. Though, he speculated, might not the opposite be equally true, that any note of the sequence draws as much of its rightness from the reverse order, that is from the sounds that follow as well as precede it, and if the note is too easy to anticipate from the order of its predecessors then might it not lack some virtue?

"Good story, Lokietok," said Lee and Lucas together, neither of them actually thinking it was, but cheerfully making allowances.

"Good story," said Costello, thinking it was, his people behind the mountains of Far Westermain being tellers of tales of drowned kingdoms, lost treasures and forsaken children.

"How are you feeling, Alvin?" It was de Vito, stepping into the circle, making his nightly round of the evening fires.

"Lucky to be alive," said Costello.

"You, Hereward? Not all the Companions' enterprises turn out that way."

"I'm all right," said Hereward. Someone had stuck tape across his forehead above the good eye; the gash beneath the tape ached even though one of the Companions had stitched the torn eyelid neatly back into place.

"Still got the brooch?" inquired de Vito. Hereward opened his hand and firelight glowed red in green, flame on silver. De Vito addressed the ring of Companions: "Know who owned that?" and, ignoring the disrespectful mirth at Lucas's suggestion of 'Lokietok's auntie', answered his own question: "John Paul the Lonely." Even those who knew little of the marshal's exploits were silent. The name had become tinged with autumnal loss; it was a link back to the time when Lamorak was young, before the marigolds died, and before the lustre of Limber grew dim in ways that they of the generation after John Paul could not comprehend. "With him and his men the Daroi would never have seen High Altai."

"Pity they aren't here now when we need them," said a flat voice from the ring.

"They are," said de Vito, gesturing around. "We've got each other and we've got the captain-general, so we're exactly the same as John Paul's men."

Most of them knew about the brooch. The Daroi prisoner had told them part of the events in the village street of Venask and how the big house had burnt in the darkness; he said he had won the brooch in one of the gambling games that the Daroi played for the treasures they picked up and dropped like jackdaws. He had been sent away with food and drink back to his own people, in keeping with the Companions' philosophy on leaders and led. Even though the Matrix usually asked them to subdue frontier warlords there was always a leader; it might be a brigand chief knowing only contempt for the law, or an imam inspired to substitute charisma for the law, or oligarchs who wished the law to be a sword rather than a shield. This time what was crossing the river was different, an unlaw which would dissolve whatever opposed it, but it had to have a leader, so on the previous night five of the company of de Vito had volunteered to search him out.

With gaps in his company, de Vito had not hesitated to accept Hereward's offer to cross the river. He did not know the grim man with his preoccupied face but he did know it meant using one fewer of the hotheaded youngsters, and he trusted his own instinct. Going into the Drome of High Altai and then defying the Daroi was enough for de Vito. As for the question of Lokietok, he thought that what a man does with his shadow is up to him.

Hereward watched Lucas give Lokietok more toast and thought back to the river crossing and what had followed. Had it really happened only the night before? It had begun in the late afternoon when the captain-general had himself gone down to the Old Stone Bridge while de Vito, Hereward, the cousins and a young Companion called Halloran lay concealed behind the wooden barricade, peering through its loopholes. One of the high taunting bugle calls of the Companions had fetched Daroi warriors rushing on to the bridge like ants disturbed in their nest. Townsend had walked out from the barricade towards the southern bank and called: "I am a Matrix lord. I am alone. I wish to speak to your chief if he will come out of his tent."

Then he had leaned on the parapet, watching the brown water sliding by some thirty feet below. The minutes too had slid past, but quite suddenly El Daro was standing at the end of the bridge. Townsend had held up his hand, and, made his points quickly and simply to the chieftain, explaining that with a world elsewhere the destinies of the two peoples need not collide, though gradually changing the tenor of his argument as he had striven to isolate the will of El Daro from the wishes of his followers.

"You, El Daro, you alone, bring your people forward. Why cross this river, when north of it are only many deaths? I must warn you of this." Were the Daroi to make a myth then its foundations would probably be bones, just as childhood's rhymes are so often thus founded.

"The Matrix will ask for peace with us," responded El Daro. "We shall mingle together. Their leaders have said so."

"I speak for the Outlands."

The chosen Companions had passed an eyeglass from one to another, carefully memorising El Daro's face and clothing, even the stance and walk. On the southern bank a log had nosed gently in among the reeds. Dressed in a Daroi leather tunic, his hair stiffened with clay and face dark with charcoal, Alvin Costello had hung hidden behind the log. He had actually enjoyed his mile-long voyage down the river, floating along so quietly that black cormorants had alighted on his log and preened their plumage, drifting with him on the warm, brown water on which many pale leaves floated. He could just catch Townsend's voice from the bridge, saying that mice wished for peace with snakes, and would no doubt also like to mingle together, but that El Daro should take a different path.

"Do not ask," El Daro had said. "It is fate that wills it, not I."

"No, it is you." Costello could hear both men clearly now.

"I am my people," the nomad replied. "The sky above us and this river below, the wind and the way before us. I am all this and this is I. I do what I have to do."

The captain-general had watched Daroi warriors edging closer to the bridge and been alerted by El Daro's knee lifting a little. When his foot had stamped down for the charge Townsend, not being the fastest of runners, had vaulted on to the parapet and gone down into the river in a long dive, spears following him like bright shadows. The many watchers had seen him emerge, dip under again, reappear further upstream and tread water until a canoe had come slipping out from the bushes to collect him.

Heavy black clouds had built up through the rest of the day and at midnight had blotted out the moon and stars when de Vito and his group had crossed the river, again just one log, but this time with five pairs of hands holding its branches down like an outrigger. The current had moved them smoothly along and they had been careful not to let the ripples tinkle on their shoulders, even though a strong wind had been noisy in the treetops and reed-beds. In the tall bulrushes they had met Costello. He had gestured westwards and whispered the whereabouts of El Daro's camp among the hundreds of encampments marking the vanguard of the Daroi migration. He had watched the chieftain return there that afternoon. Then they had worked on darkening their skins where water had removed the grime, putting on their Daroi clothing, and trying to fan out their hair in the case of those such as Hereward and Costello who kept it long enough. The leeches which had attached themselves to their bodies they picked off quickly.

Hereward knew that El Daro slept on grass or sand, surrounded by his family, and his clan, with beyond them other clans, and alongside them as they slept a great horde of dogs that dozed, whimpered in their sleep, or stood, muzzles raised, and stared about them. Halfway between midnight and dawn, that most empty of hours, Costello and Halloran, the stealthiest of the group, had slid towards the clearing in which somewhere El Daro was sleeping. There had been lightning playing among the clouds and thunder had rolled and boomed off to the west. The Daroi clothes they had carried across the river smelled of cowdung and smoke, heavy enough, they had hoped, to fool the dogs. Ten minutes later Halloran had returned to report that Costello was hidden in a tree looking across the clearing where the clan of El Daro slept. He would have a chance if the Daroi could be persuaded to rouse themselves and light lanterns and fires, and thus reveal and expose their leader. "Let's get on with this before the rain comes," de Vito had muttered.

"So how did you manage to wake everyone up at three in the morning and get them to provide some light?"

"Easy," said Lucas. The plan had been refined earlier that day in the knowledge that the Daroi were not night-fighters and that they loved their cattle. The camping ground that El Daro's clan had chosen was, as a matter of precedence, close to the river and bridge, this being the forefront of their advance. Lesser clans were camped further away. "I quite enjoyed the next bit," Lucas went on, though regretting saying this when he saw Costello stare icily at him. "Not for long though," he added and the listeners, who knew it had been bad, were thankful to have avoided most of the frenzy and fury.

The clan adjacent to El Daro's clan, who were just as proud and possessive where their cattle were concerned, had been horrified and disbelieving to be woken by wild rumours of men with torches firing the thornbush enclosure and driving away the herd. Thinking they were dealing with cattle thieves the clan had swarmed in the wake of the beasts like enraged bees.

"Whose idea was it to stampede the cattle?"

"Just something I once read about," said de Vito. Though what happened after that had been no one's idea.

Dust *Hooves* *Drums*

Fire *Thorns* *Horns*

Perhaps Lokietok furnished the images, perhaps they were there already.

The cattle had been easy to drive, skittish and energetic as they were with two days of restful grazing. The wind had exploded the tiny bracken fires into flaring channels that had sent the herd panicking along the river's bank towards El Daro's camp-site. The bellowing, snorting tide of animals had bucked and jostled as they ran, with Hereward running on one shoulder of the wave, Lucas on the other, and Halloran, de Vito and Lee driving the rear along, torches in hand, both the cousins screaming like wild-eyed minotaurs.

The Daroi child fretted by his dreams had woken, and stood up. Drowsily his mother had murmured to him to lie down again but he had drifted across to the dogs to find his puppy. Seeing only other dogs he had been searching sleepily among the nearby bushes when the dancing flames, blown sideways by the wind, had caught his eye and he had gone towards them. Behind him the cattle had begun to run, and the wall of bulls at the front had crashed towards him, trampling the low bushes irresistibly before them, in a dream more terrifying than any of his three-year-old nightmares. Hereward, running hard on the left point of the onrush, had seen the boy, dashed across the front of the beasts, swept him up by one arm, and raced for safety. The outermost animal had flung them both into a tree trunk and they had fallen, to be sheltered by the tree long enough for Hereward to struggle to his feet. Five seconds later the pursuing Daroi had surrounded him.

*

"The cows certainly made everyone scatter," said Costello. He thought he would never, even with the Daylight People's inevitable forgetting, lose the picture of the turmoil and tumult as the herd, scattering everything before them, had rampaged into the clearing where El Daro had set up camp.

"El Daro ran just in front of me," said Lucas. "I saw him."

"You hadn't been waiting for him for hours," said Costello. "I had." Even in the firelit darkness, the chaos and the urgency, dazzled by lightning, he had not missed. "Of course I didn't miss. I gave him a better chance then he gave our brother Demetrius."

"Do you think they have any normal games?" wondered Lee. Having postponed the time with stories they were readier to talk about it now, none of them really understanding that they had to talk and talk until there was some insulation round the events to deaden the shock.

"I thought it was the finish," said Lucas, and the listeners muttered nervously among themselves. The very thought of Timmy Halloran's ordeal sent a cold shudder through them.

There had been no escape for Lucas, who had ridden the horns of the stampede deep into the encampment of El Daro's clan, or for Halloran dragged down by the dogs, while de Vito and Lee had disappeared as smoke dissolves into darkness.

The games of the clans were in no way playful, but barbaric ordeals. In the darkness, still fogged with dust from the cattle's passing, the Daroi had selected Halloran to begin. El Daro was dead and though unsure of how he had actually died they had been determined that anyone who had helped to kill him should also die. The night had throbbed with passions that only a retributive auto-da-fe would slake.

A rope had been looped round Halloran's waist so that it extended about eight paces to either side of him. A Daroi fighting-man had held each end and tried to drag Halloran into the big hotly blazing fire by dragging on the rope. Halloran's strength had allowed him to pull the rope, even to drag one of his opponents near to the fire or at least to keep himself away from it, and his speed of foot and dash did not make him an easy target, but after a minute his breath had hurt his chest and his hands had bled raw from the rope. Three times he had been dragged close enough to the fire for it to scorch him, but each time he had managed to keep his executioners off balance as they had striven to hold him still by keeping the rope taut between them. Whenever they had done so Halloran had flung his weight towards one of them unbalancing the pull, and more than once he had contrived to get the rope across the fire hoping it might burn and break, though each time the Daroi had flicked it out. After five minutes fresh men had taken the rope.

"Have you seen it before, Hereward, in High Altai?" asked one of the Companions.

"No," he said. "I've only heard about their customs, though the Drome was fairly similar." He told them what he had learned in his months in the quarries: how the Daroi seemed driven to enact bloody spectacles from time to time; how the ordeal of El Daro's clan was peculiar to them, in its appalling nature a sort of demonstration of their primacy, the other clans having fierce, even lethal, trials, without such unforgiving cruelty.

"I'll see it in nightmares for the rest of my life," said someone.

"We all will," de Vito said, and they nodded. What faded in the Daylight People's memories did not necessarily fade from their dreams. Here was the dream to come: Halloran stumbling into the fire, the sparks exploding round his feet, tripping and falling headlong to scramble and plunge in the flames, the Daroi jerking the rope tight as he rose outlined in flames and beat at his hair and clothes, drowning in a fountain of fire.

The Companions who had not been there felt sick. Those who had seen it looked different, their eyes losing focus, their arms pressed to their chests, several of them giving short, spasmodic groans. Lokietok moaned deep among them.

Someone muttered, "No prisoners now," the lips saying the words without the teeth opening. Most were looking at Alvin Costello as he retched, then dropped on hands and knees to vomit. Everyone knew that Costello's night was scorched into his mind as cattle are branded. Those who had been there had smelled the charcoaled flesh. It had filled the clearing and the smell, the drifts of smoke hanging among the tree trunks and the formless shouting had reached out into the closer encampments, drawing from other clans more and more of the Daroi, including those who were holding Hereward in a sort of uncertain restraint.

"No choice, Alvin," said Lucas.

"You did well," said his cousin.

"Sit up, Alvin," said de Vito gently. "Have a drink. You gave him a quick, clean death. If it had been me in that fire I would have been praying you were out there somewhere."

"No prisoners, Urbano," another voice advised de Vito, who

considered reminding his men of the Companions' rule, but bit his lips close, thinking the captain-general smart in putting the company well away from the bridge.

Costello's first shot had not missed El Daro. Through the shouting of men and the screaming of women, the barking dogs and the din of the cattle and thunder, few people had heard the gunshot and no one had noted from where it came so Costello had lain very still along a big branch watching the happenings below him. The events had chilled him but when he had seen Halloran being dragged ever closer to the fire and heard the unhinged yelling and brutal laughter he had made ready and known what he must do to the fiery scarecrow that had been his friend. He had liked Halloran, a very quiet man who had preferred listening to talking.

This time the Daroi had heard the shot clearly, some even seeing the muzzle-flash. Though in the shouting and manhandling of Costello's capture they had been unsure whether he was the rifleman who had shot their chieftain, it had not mattered. Among the crowd had been many from the clan that the rifles had swept off the bridge and Costello they regarded as their own special enemy. Known as the wrestlers, as El Daro's closest followers were the burners, they too had a game that was an ordeal. Hereward had not seen the burning, having been brought into the wrestlers' camp by his captors. Several had recognised him, spreading the news that here was Lokietok's challenger from the Drome. The woman whose infant he had plucked from the path of the trampling cattle, still trying to express her gratitude, had not moved from his side.

The game of the wrestler clan was simple. At a table under the trees Costello had his hand locked into that of a massive Daroi warrior, who by general consent though not much acclaim had been elected to compete in the ancient contest of arm-wrestling, and both had rested their elbows on the table. Costello, who was wiry and slim, had no chance and within seconds of the signal to start, seconds filled with a whirlwind of noise, his arm had been driven backwards and, for it was really no more playful than a crucifixion is, the cruel game had ended. Hereward had seen Costello's hand impaled on the barbs of a stubby black spike, blood oozing and pooling in the cupped palm as the hand had twitched like an inverted crab.

*

"It hurt all right," said Costello. "But it was far worse for our Saviour. I deserved it. He didn't. Nor did Timmy Halloran."

"I thought we were finished." The cousins rarely managed a serious comment, but Lucas was in earnest this time. "Just as well Hereward decided to play the spikes game."

The mismatch of Costello and his powerful opponent had been an anticlimax, having far less of the rabid effects of the fire-death, but there had been an ugly moment when the Daroi had pulled Costello's hand back out through the barbs. Hereward had almost felt the fragile bones splinter and a spasm of rage had gone through him, some of it directed at the savagery of the Daroi, for there was no way not to breathe in the meat-smell from Halloran's pyre, but more an anger with circumstances. Though he had the green brooch it had been Costello who had avenged the deaths of Demetrius and his aunt, and as hard as he pressed towards the eye of the storm the more had he been frustrated and diverted.

Hereward had stood long enough in the magic circle that had formed round him, so he had pulled out the double green star from his pocket and thrown it so that it landed on the table. Then he had tugged off his tunic and shirt and the Daroi around him had roared rapturously. Lightning had forked savagely overhead, causing a nearby tree suddenly to split and start to burn. The first swollen raindrops had begun to slop down

"It must have been my birthday, after all," said Lucas, and the others smiled, knowing the cousins had their carefree reputation to uphold. "I thought I was next for the burners. The clan was talking about the Drome and saying the burners weren't having Hereward. Well, I just watched and hoped. Hereward didn't look as big as the Daroi but he looked like a wrestler. He wasn't as ugly either. And I started to pray that Andre-Leander hadn't forgotten us."

"Nobody forgot you, Luc," said one of the gathering. "Not with all the noise, the fires and smoke. Andre-Leander knew better than to stop us. It was only the width of the river away."

Costello retched again, drily, his empty stomach spasming. Lokietok reached over from the fallen log he sat on. One hand clumsily patted Costello's heaving shoulders and the Unman made a strange crooning noise far back in the throat.

Costello looked up and grasped Lokietok's hand. "It's all right.

Thanks, Lokietok." Hereward stared, as did the watching Companions, pondering how monsters can be surprising and ogres sometimes not ogrish.

Hereward had felt the pressure driving at once on his hand and arm and, locking his muscles tight, he had let the pectorals take the strain. His arm had tilted from the vertical about an inch, but holding it there he had pumped in air through his nostrils for his teeth and lips were jammed shut. With the Daroi's face inches from his own Hereward could see sinews in the neck jumping and veins bulging. Suddenly the warrior, driving fiercely forward again, had forced Hereward's arm to tilt further under a force he could not hold steady. The noise around them had increased, rain pounding the trees, a formless yelling, a chorus of savage cheering, the volume rising as the nomad warrior, giving another surge, had gained a few more inches.

Hereward had fought back, both men's arms vibrating with the strain. He knew that evenly matched arm-wrestlers will sometimes not give way before a bone snaps, and, though it was impossible to hear, could sense his arm creaking. When he had flicked a backward glance at the eight-inch spike, its whole length darkened and moistened by Costello's blood now washing away in the rain, he had heard cheers. Angered, he had driven upwards and forwards, catching his opponent slightly relaxed and forcing the grip back to the perpendicular. The Daroi's immediate furious response gained nothing this time.

Smoke eddying through the clearing stung his eye and he could hear the crackle of burning bushes somewhere nearby. Sucking in the smoky air greedily, he had tasted salt in the rain streaming down his sweating face. Readying himself for a big effort of his own he had suddenly spotted a face he knew poised very close to him, the face of someone for whom the crowd had parted as he had pushed his way to the table's edge. Hereward had known him at once as the man he had last seen in the tunnels beneath High Altai, and before that on the sand of the Drome. Another surge came on to his arm but he had held it steady gulping in air, wondering how much strength the other had exerted. Somewhere, beyond the din and cheering around them, there might have been rifle-fire. It had been hard to be sure through the din of the watching Daroi and others further back shoving continuously to reach and glimpse what rumour spilling out told them was a desperate and balanced contest. Attitudes had wavered, taking uncertain shape as shadows do. The Daroi wrestler's aggression had made him few friends even in his own clan; the clan of the fire ordeal felt aggrieved that a neighbouring clan should hold three captives, particularly when one, Costello, had almost certainly shot El Daro.

Hereward had now held the locked arms vertical for four minutes. In his muscles was the time he had spent catching eighteen-stone wheat sacks sliding down the chute of Hobson's mill and tossing them into a pile on the dray, there was the hewing of stone and the swinging of pick and hammer in the quarries of High Altai, and there was who knew what in the years he had forgotten. The size and temper of the Daroi wrestler had meant too many favours, too many followers and not enough challengers, or none like the weight of wheat and the stubbornness of stone. His arm had bent back an inch, and then another.

"So you had met this new high chieftain before?" asked de Vito.

"Yes. Lokietok and I met him in the Drome and then in the tunnels under High Altai. I was surprised. I thought the tunnel roof might have fallen in on him when Rigger died."

Lokietok rumbled an odd mixture of words and impressions:

Locks *Bars* *Cage*
Tunnel *Dark* *Dogs*

Moskander Daro, saturated by the rain, had watched the wrestlers' deadlock for several minutes. Too impatient to await the outcome, and perhaps suspecting Hereward of stalling for time, he had flicked his reversed assegai backwards into Hereward's face. The blunt end of the shaft had rasped agonisingly across the eyelid of the one good eye. Distracted and blind Hereward had had his arm driven back and back. Yet even with the spike's tip sharp on his hand and the Daroi warrior with the advantage of pressing downwards he would not give in. In his blindness the other senses had responded more sharply and he had felt the rain whipping him, matting his hair, heard the many voices more clearly, smelt the nomad smells of dogs, leather, milk, and the coconut smell of wet dust, even sensed the wooden edge of the table flake slightly.

The voices had roared again as Hereward's arm moved upward. With thunder rumbling above he had lifted again, and kept the gain. The hefted wheat and the hoisted stone had brought his arm almost upright. Now many of the Daroi had taken his side, admiring his fortitude. They had become engrossed, even the sound of rifles and a renewed howling among the dogs failing to distract them. Hereward in his blindness had heard rifles and dogs, but above all a sudden clamour of jeering and disapproval. Moskander Daro had turned back, and lifted his assegai, spear-point forward and poised, as his father's had been poised before Demetrius.

"I saw a tree move," Lucas recalled. "I thought you were a tree, Lokietok."

Lokietok had crossed the river with the Companions whom de Vito had swum back to summon, and the Unman, who took orders from no one, had pushed ahead into the trees sensing blood and a fiery dying. Since the encounter with Martin and the fall into wanhope the monster had lost some of its broadcast terror, though it made little difference on this night when terror itself was abroad.

Moskander Daro had felt his own danger, though Lokietok's anger lacked the full, fearful anguish of the Unman that thicks the blood with cold. In the lightning's flash the Daroi around the wrestlers had seen Lokietok fling aside those in the way, sweeping the Daroi wrestler to the ground with a swinging arm, then seizing Moskander Daro to lift him high in the air. Costello and Lucas had sprung up and run to where they had glimpsed de Vito and several Companions. "We could see you slashing the dogs away," said Lucas. Then had come a long tearing scream. Lokietok carrying Hereward on one shoulder had come pounding towards the river through milling cattle, the remnants of the stampeded herd. It was very dark now the rain had extinguished the fires.

"Then we saw Lokietok carrying Hereward," added another. "You wouldn't want to be the Daroi that got in Lokietok's way."

"So now they need another high chief," said de Vito. "Two in one night." Hundreds of the Daroi and many of the Companions had heard the scream and Costello and Lucas had seen Moskander Daro lying on his back on the table, impaled on one of the long spikes.

"Not an easy way to die," said someone.

"Better than burning," said Lucas.

XXXIV

Far from his home as he was Jacky did not, as most exiles do, long to return. Perhaps he was too young. Unlike those exiles who are old the young can always expect to return provided they do not wait too long, and Jacky had no future that ever occurred to him other than to go trawling in the cold seas north of the Big Grey River. He had moments of homesickness but generally there was too much to occupy him, and when he swam in the warm rock-pools of the Limber coastline or between the jetties in the sun-soaked harbour he had occasional premonitions that these times would return to tug disturbingly at him when he hauled on the trawls or when he walked home from the quay in thin drizzling rain up paths that were beaten tracks of cold mud.

Nevertheless he could just as easily recall tenderer images, time not having blurred them so much as was common among his people: foxgloves so tall in the woods they reached up to the branches of the hazels, blackbirds' song like the clearest water, the apple orchard's whiteness dappled pink. He was never more content than in the memories of his church, its stones and mortar, its wood-carvings and sandstone font, the tiles underfoot, the clock and always the bells. His world drew much of its symmetry from its church, just as spreading ripples do from the stone dropped in the pond.

Throughout the Matrix the faith in the one God and the many gods had spread to fill the vacuum the Matrix had created by the philosophy that power over one's life should never willingly be allowed to fall into another's hands. Their people embraced the law, but that other polarity, order, they held discreetly at arm's length. Instead their own faith had made order, and things were done because they ought to be done, which was both nothing new and a fair assay of a civilisation. The response to wrongdoing in the Matrix was a sort of outlawry, usually left to the church. For the thousands of small settlements this was enough, for there was everywhere a foundation of consent in laws which were nine-tenths belief, and little sympathy was felt for the felon and none for the impenitent. Instinctively the people of many lands knew that if they relinquished the responsibility for order, primarily by abandoning their faith, there would be nothing to stop it being taken up by those who, clothed in authority, would impose as many lifetimes of tutelage as their subjects would bear.

Astolat, Jacky and Kit had quickly found a nearby church. It was a narrow grey building full of arches leading to other arches and built into the side of the Steps at about the ninetieth level. All three of them thought it rather small but there was always room inside. Its priest was old but seemed young, for Father Stanislaus was quick-witted and loved to be active. Because his flock was ever-changing and often from far away he found nothing strange in the three new members. The matter of Nestor's death vexed him for a while but Jacky said only that he had died from a fall, and had not spoken again of it.

Now Jacky was a rector, had been one for almost a week. After the peace debate no one had seen him for several days, but this Sunday he appeared for the morning service. Usually he was almost lost in a group, the flower-girls, shopkeepers, lodging-house owners, and their lodgers from the countryside, anxious girls and young men looking for work, these and more would sit near him. They were glad to have him as one of them, along with his bubbly sister and his reserved lady-love, for so the gossip on the Steps tried uncertainly to account for Kit.

Now that reserve seemed to have spread to Jacky – not only was he a rector but he had voted for peace with the Daroi. It was confusing. Peace was what everyone wanted and yet the Daroi were burning farms and villages as they came, breaking down the water-mills and aqueducts as if hundreds of years of caring and sharing were nothing. Somehow people sensed that if their land bred more men like Jacky it would have been the Daroi holding conferences on whether to seek peace. His vote may well have reflected the fears of the elderly and the careful, the timid and the weak, and no one questioned the good faith of his decision, which was plausible enough, but there was disappointment that he had not detected in them a fierce defiance, and resignation that such an attitude had been insufficiently felt and not often openly displayed. The people of the Steps were unaware of the true reason for Jacky's voting as he did, but when the news filtered in of the Companions barring the bridge over the Dole River it sent a redeeming flicker of pride through the city, and no one scolded the children playing in the streets and shrieking, "Kittiwake! Kittiwake!" in their games of chase and struggle.

The churchyard was shady, with golden cypresses like columns around its sides and stone benches against the walls. Occasionally Father Stanislaus would hold services in the open air and often there were weddings held there. The narrow tower of the church had storks nesting on the top and the grey angular birds floated high above in the thermals that spiralled up off the foothills of the range behind Limber. People stayed to talk although the mood was too anxious for the usual exchange of pleasantries. Eventually the priest reached Jacky. "Well, you are finding life difficult."

"Yes," said Jacky. "Nor do I think it will get any better."

"Why do you think that?"

He looked at Kit and he couldn't say the words. He couldn't say that he thought he was the last rector of the Steps, or of the Matrix itself, though perhaps for a few years there might be a puppet-rector with a Daroi mentor. How could he say that he sensed that Sheer and the others were not interested in peace but in some pursuit he could not grasp, and most of all he would not say that Kit's tears in the chapterhouse had mattered more than all the tears of the future because he loved her. "Oh," he said "I'm only a fisherman and I should have stayed one."

Kit, watching him, knew all the reasons that he kept silent, and Astolat, who guessed some of them, said, "You did your best. It wasn't an easy choice," and gave a sweeping glance around that when it alighted stung like scattered droplets of boiling water splashed from a kettle-spout.

"Astolat is right. People understand you tried your best," Father Stanislaus agreed.

"They understand nothing," said Kit, and she walked away, furious with herself and everyone else.

Shortly afterwards Jacky and Astolat joined her. The warm sun soothed them as they climbed to the Two Hundredth Step where Astolat was due to practise in her music group. Jacky and Kit then made their way through a maze of courts and terraces to where the mansions of the rich quarter were clustered together. Rather to their surprise they had been invited to a gathering at the home of one of the rectors. Jacky was unenthusiastic but Kit pressed him to go, not wishing to offend the man who was one who had assented readily when she had proposed the bargain that delivered Jacky's vote.

The dwellings grew more opulent as each street led to the next, white towers looking over tall garden walls, from behind which palm-trees rustled and water fell musically into fountain pools. The house itself was easy to find, a swirl of people at its gate distinguishing it from the quietness of its neighbours. Entering they found themselves on a wide sweep of lawn, the further end of which appeared to hang suspended over the uninterrupted blueness of the harbour. "I hope we know someone," said Jacky who had so far seen only strangers.

"Won't all the rectors be here?"

"I doubt very much that Novak or Colonna will," he replied.

There were no familiar faces to be seen and so they walked slowly towards the long verandah under which most of the guests seemed to be standing in the shade. Long tables stood against the wall of the house holding silver plates piled high with many foods, a profusion of colours, the pink of smoked ham, the amber of melon, the black and red of caviare. Jacky thought wryly of barley bread and salt herring, Kit of white cheese, walnuts and brown rabbit-gravy, just as Martin had gazed at the jewels on Nancy Villiers' fingers and thought of Fleur's necklace of acorns. Neither felt like eating but Kit took two glasses of wine, greenish-yellow and bright, and looked up at Jacky as they sipped.

"It's the foam on the wave, Jacky." She nodded at the opulence around them. "Enjoy it. It lasts about as long. And stop thinking about the estuary and all those harvest suppers, or whatever your family used to celebrate."

"We weren't farmers," he sighed, "but we used to have nice picnics."

"Oh, you're hopeless. Come on, at least let's see if we can find our host."

This, after a while they managed to do, finding him talking to Colonna, who had been invited after all. Their host was the rector who had argued that they should only fight if they knew they could win, a burly man with bushy, grey hair. "Ah, our new allies," he said heartily, and there was a stir and turning of faces in the long high room where they now stood. He lifted his voice: "The new rector of the Steps and his lady. A welcome increase to the average intelligence of the Council."

Laughter followed but it seemed harmless enough, and the babble of conversation broke out again, though conversing was not easy in such a noise and to Jacky it seemed to be nothing but a collection of dozens of argumentative speeches delivered to small inattentive groups who responded with indifference. Nor did he like such talk as he could hear, slickly coarse with what the speakers perhaps took for peasant vulgarity, or the clothes modishly patched and ill-fitting mimicking the dress of poor people in fabrics no one but the wealthy could hope to possess.

"What are they doing here?" he whispered to Kit.

"Being seen. Gossiping. Looking for patronage, or something to refresh their appetites. Careful, you might be it. Wait a minute, they might be it too." She nodded towards the garden, and, following her gaze, he saw a man and woman walking across the lawn. Both were tall and slender, brown-skinned with narrow faces and long black hair spread stiffly wide by oils. The man wore a leather tunic and the woman, despite the heat, a jacket that was beaded in swirling patterns and trimmed with furs. Alongside them trotted a big yellow dog with a spiked collar. They came arrogantly, staring about them, occasionally glancing at the windows and balconies that rose upwards in tiers. Jacky guessed that he was, for the first time, setting eyes on the Daroi, and the murmurs around him confirmed this. A prickle of excitement and intentness went through him.

"So," said Kit, "these are the people who put Tyr-Hereward into an arena. That would have been worth seeing."

The Daroi had almost disappeared in two separate circles of interested guests, and around Jacky and Kit another group was beginning to form, with among them a face he knew. "Enjoying yourselves?" said Osric Sheer. "I expect all this will be very new to you."

"Really?" said a woman at his elbow. "Why is that?"

"They come from Westermain," explained Sheer.

She gave a little scream. "Oh! Don't the men there each have many wives? Or are their bodies all covered in hair? I know it's one of the two, isn't it, Osric?"

When Jacky said nothing Sheer prompted him: "I think you should answer the lady, John."

"It's nothing like that," he said.

"What did you do before you were a rector?"

"In Westermain? I was a fisherman." Jacky had always been proud of his sea-skills, and although he caught fish he loved them at the same time. There was nothing laughable about the mackerel shoals surging in the grey swells with a November wind pelting the sleet-squalls across the icy deck, so he was perplexed when his answer produced shrieks of laughter.

"Do you expect lots of questions on fish in the Council?" asked someone.

"Which way will you vote in the next debate?" inquired another.

"On what topic?"

"You see, we know more than you do!" the women screamed, and Kit's face grew darker.

"It's come up before," explained Sheer. "How do families deal with babies who are, well, to put it simply, twisters? An awkward problem, isn't it?" He glanced at Kit. "Nothing personal, dear lady."

"What do you mean 'deal with'?" Jacky asked.

"We mean encouraging the families to, well, just quietly let them go to sleep."

"I won't vote for that," said Jacky. "Babies, even those born . . ." He hesitated, for the ground ahead seemed riddled with pitfalls. "You can't do that . . ."

"Yes, go on," said the voices.

"But they are immortal souls, aren't they?"

"Tell us more!" the voices shouted. He heard someone say, "A fisherman and a philosopher," making him feel even more hot and flustered, and he knew it was futile trying to reason in this pandemonium.

He was beginning to say that it wasn't right, and looking across to Kit for help when support came from an unexpected quarter. "Good, fair-hair," said the tall Daroi woman. "If they had to carry their young in the womb across the desert they would speak differently. Does your woman have babies?"

She stared down at Kit who returned the stare with a glare, and snapped, "What's that to do with you?"

"Can you not find a man?" The Daroi woman sounded quite happy to trade rebuffs. "All the better if there are few babies here. The more room for mine." She gave a glance around that took in the slopes, the harbour and the distant ranges. "There is much good land here and we shall live in peace together. Your chiefs are sensible, some of them. Tell me, is there one here?"

"Yes, madame, most are here," Sheer replied, laying an arm on Jacky's shoulder. "I am one and my friend Jack here is another. So is our host." He gestured to where the grey-haired rector was talking to the Daroi man.

"So," she said, picking out Jacky again, "you did not wish to oppose our coming. You know what is good for your city."

"Leave him alone," said Kit. Her voice had that high warning throb to it, the one with which wildcats confront one another. It sent a tremor through the group. The Daroi woman knew the tone at once for what it was, but not all of the others around them were prepared to trust their instincts.

"Who is this giving orders?" said a fat little man.

"Not much breeding," said the youth standing next to him and, encouraged by laughter, added, "In more ways than one, I see."

Jacky's fist took the youth full in the face with a noise like a stick breaking, and suddenly he was alone as space formed round him.

"You barbarian, it was only meant to be a joke!" shouted someone.

Jacky took three fast steps into the crowd and dragged the speaker into the space. "No voices in the crowd," he said. "Let me hear you tell my woman she's only half-bred, and we'll see if she enjoys the joke." Almost as he spoke he felt his arm gripped and twisted up behind his back, but this, compared to the water-torture of words, was far too easy, and he simply dipped his head forward and then jerked it up and back. Something cracked and Osric Sheer was backing away with his hands over his face.

"You stupid fish-eater," he said thickly and spat a tooth on to the grass.

"Hold your tongue, Sheer. As for that, I'm not so stupid that I don't know a traitor when I see one. You betrayed the Matrix. You know these Daroi folk won't be satisfied until everyone's a dog and they're top dog."

"You voted for peace!" screamed a voice.

"I suppose that does make me stupid," snapped Jacky. "As stupid as the sheep who wanted peace with the wolves."

"It would be better if you left," said the grey-haired rector. "You have spoilt what was supposed to be a happy occasion."

"And take your misbegotten little harlot with you," added Sheer. Kit knew what Jacky would do, or at least knew that he didn't care what he did, so it was no surprise when he stepped forward and cracked his open hand stingingly across Sheer's face. It wasn't a slap, it was more like a camel kicking. Three large men appeared in answer to the host's call for his retainers.

"Just going." The gutting knife was in Jacky's hand and he was up on his toes swaying from one foot to another, lightning looking for somewhere to discharge its white lash.

"That must be a fish knife," the Daroi woman remarked.

Kit shook her head, thinking that to inflame the lightning was really not necessary at all. "That's right," he said, "and for gelding dogs."

They went out together, everyone else staying a respectful few paces behind. The iron grill gates slammed as they left.

"At times you've got a nasty tongue, Jacky."

"I'm sorry, Kit. I must have wrecked your agreement. You know, about your folk."

"Who cares?" He looked at her in astonishment, but she just smiled. "Sheer let his guard down," she explained. "For the first time. He's one of those who mask their minds, but he forgot to stay calm this time. Perhaps it wasn't such a happy occasion. Anyway, he never meant to keep that pledge. He just wanted to play games with you. To say nothing of his playful plan for our folk's children. He's a nasty misbegotten creature. And I mean that."

For several minutes Jacky walked in silence absorbing what he had just heard: "They seem to like playing games with us, Kit."

"They enjoy it, Jacky dearest. Forget them. Let's do something we enjoy for a change. I'll take you for a picnic."

It was the first endearment she had ever used to any of the Daylight People and she nearly regretted it, but he hadn't seemed to notice so perhaps she could be forgiven, she thought.

XXXV

The group was deep into the Glassy Country now. They had become four on the first night of the journey when George Littler had joined them, catching them up with his long forester's stride. Even on the first night Martin had been tired, for the pace was gruelling, and in the three days after they left the Old Stone Bridge they covered fifty miles.

Each evening they had spoken until almost midnight with the Twisted Folk of wherever they had reached, before sleeping soundly until dawn-light. Martin was enjoying himself in some ways, for George was always friendly, unassuming company and he liked travelling with Hex and Crook. Both names were those under which they had joined the Companions, and neither was yet ready to reveal any other name, although Martin had twice overheard Crook address Hex as Walter. Neither bore the brand of their people really conclusively; Crook, being the survivor of a pair of Siamese twins, carried the scars of separation down chest and abdomen, Hex's skin was patched with many purple blotches, ridged and crinkled like deep burns. "Birthmarks," he explained. "Over most of my body. Not surprising if you'd ever seen the shape of my mother's womb."

Their third evening passed as had the previous two, only the setting changing, this time being a clearing in the trees; previously it had been a hut in a tiny settlement, benches in a village square, somewhere to talk to the heads of the local families. George felt as if he were not needed, for though Hex and Crook were friendly enough often the conversation would fall into the local dialect and dark references, leaving him understanding little. There appeared no real boundary to the Glassy Country, or if there was it was wherever the Twisted Folk were in the majority, though even this was the vaguest of demarcations. To George's eye there was no difference whatever between people whom the other three readily categorised. Even then, Hex, whose family actually came from the Glassy Country, found some over whom he could only shrug. "Maybe one of the Daylight People. With some it just comes down to a frame of mind."

But there were Daylight People who were quick to repeat the cautions to Littler. "Not too far in, George," they would say. "Two or three days is plenty. After four it's too many." When George explained their errand as far as he could understand it, they would nod. "Yes, the King's won his wars. There doesn't seem any accounting for it. Maybe he's just lucky." But, as this was the side of the coin they could see already, it was of little help.

Some of the Daylight People who followed the many trades and lives of the forest, particularly the tree-guarding foresters themselves, of the same profession as George, spoke unenthusiastically of the King: "Why should he help you? He has no reason to do so." Better, they said, to seek the help of the Green Man, and when George protested that such a creature existed only in the imagination, and was just an old name, they laughed and replied that the Green Man was older and deeper than the King, far deeper, and would live to forget the King, and the Matrix too, to say nothing of the transient Daroi, and anyway the King of the Glassy Country was just as likely to be a figment of the imagination. "How can we tell?" asked the foresters. "But please go no further into this land. It doesn't suit us."

Hex urged George to take their advice. He liked the forester and had no wish to see him hurt. Perhaps he might be able to tolerate what awaited him in the palaces of the King, but Hex had never heard of any of the Matrix people reaching there, at least not in his lifetime. George, as ever, said little, except one night, looking into the fire, he spoke more than just a few words: "You are kind and caring, all three of you. But you must realise that I came with Hereward to help him whenever I could. He was a good man, living quietly in our village and we took his eye out for no reason, except perhaps that he was different from most of us. On all this journey so far I have only been a hindrance to him. But now, for the first time since we left the woodlands around Hay, I may be some use. Don't tell me it is dangerous and unwise. I know that, but I also know that if I were the King I would think little of the Matrix choosing only your folk to go into danger."

That night, as he lay in his blankets, George's mind churned like a millwheel. Is this real, he thought, this strange land we are in, behind us the great river with its long stone bridge pulling people to it, and my comrades on this journey? Tomorrow shall I wake up in the woods near Hay and smell logs, sawdust, fur and leather, feel the air icy and see the frost bright on the grass and know this was something remembered from a dream? Probably one day it will seem so, he thought, but for the present we must see it through. And because he hoped one day to strike a blow for Hay village and the woods around it he fell gently asleep.

The days passed as the four travelled on. Martin watched everything carefully. If ever he got back to the low valleys south of Ingastowe Cathedral he would have many tales to tell, but the ones they would always ask to be retold, he thought, would be those of that land where the Twisted Folk lived undisturbed with their own King, living in wide open villages, even houses with glass windows set on hills, as if no one had ever come to round them up into the village square or shatter the windows into crackling fragments.

Martin saw that the trees were mostly the same big trees that grew in the forests of Westermain, oak and ash and hornbeam, sometimes with other familiar trees among them, sycamore, lime, wych-elm, maple, even the grand purple copper beeches, yet despite such old friends he was not at ease, and he could tell that George felt the same. Beneath their feet many of the flowers too were the same: in the glades, dog's mercury, monk's hood, white fumitory, and when they walked in valley bottoms there were meadowsweet, brooklime and violets. Some Martin could not name, but it was not these unnamed flowers that made him anxious. Born and bred among wild plants he knew their seasons and uses, when to plant and when to pluck, and he knew that there was nothing that always grew straight, but here it was different. The day before he had noticed what should have been the meadowsweet's small creamy flowers occasionally gummed together in a brown stained ball as if they had tried to open but had lacked the energy. He had seen how from the fleshy stems of the brooklime the leaves were here and there broken off, the leaves themselves empty of colour, and what should have been blue flowers only a dusting of ash-coloured seedheads. Today the differences were clearer, he thought, and, too, they were often at eye level, with the trees' lower branches marred by leaves that were scabrous and noduled, and behind the leaves the unpredictable pattern that is almost not a pattern, of the outward thrust of twigs and branches, was not always there.

Martin had never known of the snowflake's refinement revealed by the microscope's lens, but he knew of the artistry of the spiders' webs and the whole of his world was full of living shapeliness. So why did so many of the twigs hang awkwardly downwards instead of lifting their tips to the sun, some even doubling back, ingrowing, as if they wanted no part of the rain and the air? What meant these galls and excrescences on both branches and leaves? Martin was fond of oak-apples which, too, are galls, but these blemishes and lumps that he saw were different.

Hex only shook his head when questioned: "You get used to them if you live in the Glassy Country." Crook merely frowned.

"How far in did your family live?" Martin asked.

"Not very far," said Hex.

"Further in than we are now?"

"No, nothing like as far."

"So would you be used to this?" Martin had picked up a small bird, one of the finch family. There were the tiny intricacies of overlapping feathers and the delicate fashioning of folded wings, the elegance it shared with all birds, but this finch had never perched neatly swaying on a branch, had never revelled without knowing it in the springy balancing of twigs in an airy green lattice of other twigs, for its claws were rounded scaly lumps and its life had been a struggle, club-footed, along the ground, never able to rest, an invitation to predators.

"Yes," said Hex. "But in here there are more of these distorted things."

"And tomorrow, will there be more still?"

There were. And the next day there were more again. When the fifth evening came the four travellers again held council with the local families. Crook had stripped to the waist and Hex had opened his shirt wide, both displaying their disfigurements clearly thus. The faces and forms round them at their meeting-places were odder now, and there were currents of unfriendliness insinuating themselves into the conversation. Martin found himself more welcome than the others. George was unmistakably from the Daylight People but Martin, long-legged, short-bodied, with his bouncy walk and wide round eyes, reminiscent of a cheerful frog, was inescapably one of theirs in light or shade. Sometimes he was addressed as if the others were not there, their speech growing stranger as the nights passed. 'Martin-Martin', they would call him, in voices that throbbed deep from the chest, or whistled through lips pinched into pursed holes. One woman seemed to have no mouth at all but sucked liquid through a straw into a hole pierced through her cheek, squeaking at Martin through the hole.

"Martin-Martin, who lives in the light," she mewed like a kitten.

"Martin likes being in the land of unright," added another.

"Martin-Martin, are your eyes bright?" asked one whose eyes wore the greasy scale of thick cataracts.

"Look hard, here is the people of despite," slobbered another, whose tongue moved wetly behind a few straggly teeth, and when he saw firelight shine through her jaws Martin realised, horrified, that there was no flesh where the cheeks should have been, as if leprosy had eaten them away.

"Martin-Martin, where is journey's end?" they said. Try as he would he could find no names to call them by. At times they addressed one another with the names of their afflictions. "Blindy, do you wonder where they wend?"

"Well, I think that will depend," said Martin, and the folk around him shrieked and cackled and patted him on the back.

"Martin-Martin, Tyr's friend."

It was a girl behind him and she put her hand on his shoulder. As he glanced back to look into her face she caught his eyes with hers and held them. He knew what she was doing, and knew to look nowhere else.

The women of the Glassy Country wore elaborate clothes, gaudy in red, pink and orange, their dresses flounced, tiered and ruffled over many petticoats, and many favoured fur tippets, embroidered shawls, scarves and bandannas spangled with seedbeads and mother-of-pearl, mantillas and veils. To Martin they all seemed to be heading off to dance at a forest wedding. The men were not dissimilar, though preferring black, often with gold trimmings, beneath long coats buttoned up to the neck. They too often added dandyish touches, a grey pelisse, a velvet hat with a feather plume, lace and aiglets tied at the throat. The girl was watching him for the tell-tale down and back flutter of the eyes in search of the deformity that had to be there, but he knew better. It was there, just on the edge of his vision, a sort of hairy patch the colour of port wine that crept up from under her collar, spreading its stain on her jaw. The twilight and the girl's movements gave it the illusion of life, a parasite emerging from a hiding-place beneath the collar of her gown, then slipping back. Martin would not look, but he took her hand and sang a song for them that he had learned when he was very young:

Never drop your head, never bow your knee,
Though you're twisted your heart can be fair;
It's only our fate, we weren't born to walk straight,
But we're free as the water and air.

Never drop your head, never bow your knee,
We feel pain but we feel no despair;
No need to repent, our minds weren't born bent,
We're born free as the water and air.

His song went before him and wherever they stopped he was asked to sing it. On the edge of the Glassy Country there had been names, but here the folk either had none or would not reveal them, just as Martin had only by accident heard Hex's true name and still did not know Crook's. There was something sad, he thought, that they should use no names. It made them less than they might have been.

He was angry and sad at once. His own body he knew well and was long resigned to it. All his life the differences had put him in danger, but somehow he knew that the world had always been thus, that long before the coming of the Twisted Folk there had been people who had inherited more than their share of danger and hurtfulness and death, along with their mothers or their skins or their gods. He was not angry or sorry for himself. He had seen much of the strange and fascinating world: the quirky life of an actor, the blue ocean under the *Swan*'s keel, the Big Grey River and the Dole River, the dust in the white quarries of High Altai, the elegant spaces of Aunt Nana's home, the glistening bayonets of the Companions, the frightfulness of Lokietok.

Though he might feel cramped in his body alongside the strength and endurance of so many of the Daylight People, he had not been cramped in his life. Indeed it felt expansive to him, for it contained the friendships of Hereward, George Littler, Demetrius and others. He knew without thinking that through one's friends one lives some part of other lives, and that though this may be distressful when those lives are stunted or sad or never seem to awake, there is also a delight in the fortune of friends. Sometimes he trembled at his closeness to men who were so unafraid. He and all his people had had to live pinched by circumstances wider-reaching than they could understand, pressures which kept them on the fringes of their own lives, but Hereward cared nothing for such constraints, and Martin thought of the cousins, Lucas and Lee, of Urbano de Vito, and all his company, who cared as little, knowing that, though men like this were apprehensive of what was dangerous, of the powers of water and metal, of the perils of sickness and sick minds, what did not intimidate or confuse them was the abstraction of authority. They knew it was nothing.

Sadly, the further the four of them journeyed into the land of the King the more moving became the plight of those living there. They wore their many-layered clothes to distract even their own eyes; no word for 'I' or 'my' seemed to exist in their speech, as if they mattered to themselves as little as the dance of mayflies over the stream; a few nicknames and that was all, and their fancy of calling him Martin-Martin was not teasing but scratching the itch of their envy.

He thought of the crooked flight of birds that flapped feathers off their wings with every beat, of blind rabbits with pus oozing from eyes and nostrils, of snakes with two heads, and the buds that would not open, the chlorosis of leaves, the curse that lay on the land. Another settlement and no way to keep the tears from filling his eyes. "The Glassy Country makes me weep."

"Martin-Martin tears are cheap," an armless man said.

"Twisted Folk will always creep." A girl who sounded to Martin strangely like Kit.

"Martin-Martin, we have fallen deep," added another. "The pit too wide to leap, the sides too steep."

"Go away," said the girl. "Take your questions to the King. Ask quickly at the last inn, then go back to Tyr. The King is bad company to keep."

The next two days were worse than whatever had gone before. On the first of those days and the night that followed they saw no one though all four sensed that they were watched for most of the time. The trees had fallen away and they were climbing to where a plateau seemed to level out ahead of them. A broad highway had once been here; though wind-blown drifts of sand and soil partly obscured it and clinging mosses and liverworts mottled the surface, it stretched ahead of them like a wide fissure through the spurs. The viaducts that had once carried it across the gorges that ran down from the plateau had been long since broken, forcing the travellers to climb down into the chasms and up the other side to regain the old road. A low swarthy vegetation grew on either side of the road, what might have been broad-leaved plants like docks, the leaves crinkled and knobbly with reddish growths, while around them coiled brambles with a few paltry leaves and occasional sickly berries. Spiders had entangled many nets of webs among the thorns, sticky rolls that formed thick silken sausage-shapes inside which, like wet sand, were gummed thousands of brown eggs. Of the beautiful geometry of the night-time webs of his own land Martin saw no sign. Here everything seemed to inbreed, to distend into itself, to be squat, bloated, as if the land were ingurgitating every bud and foetus, intumescent in reverse, the snails oozing from their shells, the shabby trees sprouting a few mean leaves in a timid suggestion of green.

That night his shallow sleep was disturbed by noises, croaks, chokings and moans, and in the first light, again hearing noises like those that had made their sleep so broken and restless, he saw an awkward struggle in the bushes where a crow-like bird and an animal like a clumsy rat lay on their sides pecking and clawing ineffectually at one another. Martin, prising the bleeding, draggled bodies apart with his foot, could think of neither but as victims of a predatory land. An obese toad came from under the dock leaves to seize a hindleg of the rat in its mouth and the tugging and shaking began again.

"Come away, Martin," Hex advised him. "Too much is wrong here for us to put right. This is the land of unright, remember."

"It has no graciousness," said George. He had hardly spoken for days, shocked by what was so different from the gentle woodlands of

Hay. "God's grace is in the fleetness of the deer and the floating of the owl." The others nodded, recalling the white of snowdrops and the green of holly, the brown shine of ploughlands and the red of poppies. Above them the sky was a flat grey and occasionally thin rain fell, making the mosses and lichens of the highway easy to slip on, and there was a cold wind, which never seemed to stop, blowing down from the plateau. The land on either side now was bare, eroded shale that more and more frequently turned to expanses of rubble. "What help can we expect here?" wondered Martin.

"Wait," Hex counselled. "The King is near. I can feel it. He is hurting my bones."

Indeed, they seemed to have tired more quickly in the last two days, and were plodding wearily on when two or three miles ahead and a thousand feet above them they saw silhouetted against the skyline a building, tall with high gables, black against the grey clouds. Crook said it had to be the last inn.

An hour later saw them in its courtyard. Looking back over the long way that now lay behind them there was little to see save the desolate plain of that day's journey and far beyond that the sweep of many miles of trees.

Together they approached the inn. It was strongly built, with a slate roof and what in the dusk looked like slabs of slate hung on the walls, though perhaps they were stone shutters, for there were no windows visible. The rain was falling heavily now and Crook pushed open a door that led to a big stone-floored room with boxes, or perhaps settles, pushed back against the walls. It was ill-lit and draughty, though an archway led into another room from which came some warmth and the crackle and smell of a fire.

A man was standing in the arch watching them. "Which room?" he said, peering as he looked from light into dark. Martin thought he must have taken them for someone else. From beyond the arch there was the sound of voices and clinking glasses.

"Well, can we go in there?" Hex gestured past the man.

"Coming or going?"

"Where?"

All four were bemused. "Are you coming from the King or going to him?" asked the man, speaking with an air of sorely tried patience.

"Going to him." Martin was clear enough about that.

"This room then." The man pointed into the echoing space in which they were already standing. "Sleep here. Food tomorrow. What do you want anyway? The madhouses must be empty, the people we get."

They stared at him thinking him like no innkeeper they had ever met. He was bigger than all of them except George, though Hex and Crook were not small, and he spoke with a dry authority. Martin felt sure he had to be one of the Twisted Folk.

"Is there food and drink here?" Crook asked, though there obviously was, for they could all smell toasted bread.

"Yes, but not for you. Here we feast only those who have seen the King. Why, if we welcomed every traveller who came here and went no further, think of the crowds there would be."

His smile made Martin feel uneasy, but the little man persisted. "Have those folk in the other room seen the King?"

"Yes. Or been in his presence. Anyway one of them has. What about you? Who's going to be the one?" A nod towards Hex. "You, if you take my advice."

"Why one? Why not all of us?" George spoke with much the same calm self-control as the innkeeper, who examined him carefully.

His voice was gentler: "You haven't thought this out. Those who ask the King questions are really asking favours, and generally they ask for what amounts to a life or a death. Or lives or deaths. So what do you think he asks in return?" They looked at one another and were aware that the occupants of the other room had fallen silent to listen, but the question did not really invite an answer. "What's your homeland?" asked the man. "You," he glanced at Hex, "are from somewhere on the edge of this country, I can tell by the way you speak. What about you, little man?"

"The valleys south of Ingastowe. In Westermain." Martin hoped the big man would not laugh at him. "Far away," he added. Too far to get back, came the thought.

"Stay away from the King then and get away from here tomorrow if you can. Get clear of this place. It only needs one to ask a favour, so it should be the one from the Glassy Country. He might just survive a meeting with the King. Just! I don't suppose it's any use asking you all to go away now?"

"No," said Crook and Hex together.

"The King will hurt you."

"Our captain has sent us. When he asks we do not wish to say no." Hex spoke and Crook nodded.

"Who is this captain? Is Lamorak back from Regret?"

"Andre-Leander Townsend of the Companions."

"Hmm, I do not know the name, but I have heard a little of these Companions. A small folk but apt in the field. What have Twisted Folk to do with them?"

"We are all Companions together. Same food as Andre-Leander, same dangers as Urbano de Vito, same place round the fire as Franz Schroeder."

"Same grave on Kittiwake Island?" the innkeeper said, staring down at them, and then, seeming to decide, "All right. This is what you do. One goes to the King tomorrow. Don't stay long, keep it to ten minutes, no more. Tonight sleep exactly where I tell you. Don't move about in the night, any of you. Remember that whoever comes to ask a favour pays to ask, he doesn't pay to have it granted. You won't actually see the King himself, at least you won't know if you have or not. This is the land of Unright and you are near the heart of it. No hospitality before you visit the King. No welcome less delay, you understand."

"And afterwards?"

"I doubt you will want to stay."

In the night Martin woke in panic. His fingers scrabbled at the metal sides of the coffin in which he lay, and in a frenzy he pushed open the heavy lid and sat upright. Around him it was as dark as if he were blind. He had not liked it when the innkeeper had shown them that the seats of the settles could be lifted and the space beneath, lined with metal and with a straw mattress to soften it, was where they were to sleep. He heard another lid creak open and a voice said, "Is that you, Martin?"

"Yes." He was glad to be half out of the box. It was his second night in it.

"What's the matter?"

"I was frightened, Walter."

"It's all right, we'll all look after one another."

Martin made himself breathe regularly and deeply, and felt better. He whispered, "Do you mind if I call you Walter?"

"No, I don't mind. Go to sleep."

Martin lay back under the closed lid, and wondered, as he often did, about the strangeness of people. Walter Hex the previous day had been to the King, while the other three had stayed in the bleak room, for most of the time, at the innkeeper's advice, lying in the metal boxes.

Eventually Hex had returned. "Tell us about it, Walter," Crook had said. They had been brought broth, tasting of meat and onions, with brown loaves, and had gone to sit in the warm room, lit with oil-lamps and made comfortable by a big fire. Hex told his story. He had walked for three hours or so, right across the plateau and then down into a shallow valley, with only rock and gravel underfoot all the way, though it had seemed to him that once there were roads built there, even houses. At times he saw smooth patches of what might have been foundations, but it was hard to tell. Then he had seen the King's dwelling. Hex shook his head and fell silent, seeing it again in the mind.

"A great house?" Martin had asked.

"No, big, really big, but not a building, not any shape at all. It was just a place hidden under a cloak of rock and concrete. I think there was something underneath because it had holes, dark holes like caves, I suppose they might once have been windows, and there was a big cave at ground level, like a doorway. I walked all round the place, but it was not much different from any angle, like an ant walking round a pile of earth. I came back to the doorway but it was blocked by rocks a few paces in. I left the sack of bread and the meat and apples there." The innkeeper had asked him to take food for the King.

Crook asked if Hex had seen anyone, and he laid his spoon on his half full bowl, folded his hands and sat quite still with his back pressed to the wall. Then, carefully, leaving nothing out, he told them how inside the entrance he had seen a drum, hanging from a peg driven into the wall. He had taken the drum outside and beaten on it, a deep muffled thumping. All that day he had seen no movement other than the windblown clouds, but then for the first time a hint of presences: vague shapes, grey in the shadowy apertures, as hard to distinguish as green fish in a green pond, visible only as motion, movements high on the slopes as a figure scrambled jerkily between two crags, a chimney-like pillar of stone bulging as a shape half hid behind it. Three more times he had beaten on the drum but, though the sounds brought the flickers of evasive activity, there was no other response. Once he had climbed briefly towards one of the openings but stones came rolling and bouncing down the sloping sides and he desisted.

The innkeeper was waiting with bowls of soup when Hex returned. After they had eaten Hex asked, "Is it always like this?"

"More or less," came the answer.

"Well, I finished up by shouting out our question, and then I put the drum back. I couldn't think what else I could do."

"There was nothing else. You did well. I hope you came straight back."

"I waited for an answer," said Hex, "but there wasn't one. I waited for an hour."

The innkeeper muttered what sounded like 'I told you ten minutes'. The second evening passed and they slept. Martin's claustrophobia woke him and Hex just before midnight, and then they slept fitfully for another hour. Another hour went by, then the innkeeper woke them, knocking on the lids of their metal boxes. "Visitors for you," he said.

XXXVI

Many days later Crook, Hex and Martin plodded into the Companions' encampment about six in the morning. They had tramped through a long night, but there was no rest. Within half an hour they were surrounded by the twenty captains and Townsend himself, who stared hard at his envoys' faces.

The morning was cold in the damp garden of an isolated homestead which had offered Townsend and some of the others a bed the previous night. He had been anxious, uncertain of whether to wait longer, unsure even of the return of the three messengers he had sent. His scouts brought him news of the endless columns of men and herds of beasts that flowed steadily over the Old Stone Bridge; day after day, and still the steady movement northwards went on.

Leafless vine stalks and branches twined up a trellis in front of his face. Among them, the lines of the spiders' webs were silvered with many tiny beads of moisture, clear as geometrical diagrams. A damp mist had shrouded visibility down to about twenty paces and the shrubs in the garden bowed under the weight of water. Somewhere woodpigeons called and once some of them whirred invisibly overhead. The only movement to be seen by the captains, as they stood silently, was thc mist among the branches of the ash trees stirred by a little breeze. They felt uneasy.

"Well, my comrades," Townsend said. "Tell us how it was. All of it."

Crook told them of how it had been in the land of Unright and of Hex's lonely mission to the massive, shabby, concrete mountain, in which they believed the King resided, and of how when there had been no one for Hex to meet he had shouted out their question. "The innkeeper told us a little of the answer. The King must have told him. Or perhaps he already knew. Perhaps everyone there knows all about it."

"Maybe they teach it in their schools." Hex spoke for the first time and Oyvindsen, in whose company he was enlisted, thought how much his voice had changed.

"What part of the answer can you tell us?" Townsend persisted.

None of the three had any wish to recapitulate their time at the inn, time largely spent lying in their metal boxes, while outside the wind endlessly blustered and shouted round the grey building. Once, through a crack in the shutters, they had seen in the darkness a string of lights move by, and the rattle of stones underfoot as some strange convoy passed across the plain of shaley rubble on which the inn stood. There were some things Townsend need never know.

Crook continued: "Only that the King isn't interested in the long ago. That they beat the Matrix once and in the long run they could beat the Daroi. And, anyway, he heard we voted for peace."

Hex laughed. "So we did. Fair's fair." The words hurt his chest and he started coughing, a deep hacking cough that was more like sobbing, and tried to spit out an ill-tasting bile, but most of it dribbled down his chin and on to his jacket.

Townsend paused so long that Franz Schroeder took up the questions: "The point is how did they beat the Matrix? Look, if this King and his folk did do that and have no fear of the Daroi either, as they tell us or want us to believe, where is their strength?"

"He does tell us, or tells you," said Crook. "Why should he care what you believe?"

"Be civil," said Oyvindsen.

"Or what?" said Hex. He retched and spat into his hands, looking down before spreading his fingers wide, as flower-petals spread to the sun. No one could miss the swirls of red in the grey globs. "Meet the King," he said.

"I'm sorry, Walter," said Oyvindsen. "You need help, rest, medicine, not standing here."

"Forget it, captain. I'm not the first and I won't be the last if you go on with this. Not by a million, if there is such a number."

The air was wetter now, tiny droplets falling slowly, lightly, as if the mist were pondering becoming rain. Their clothes began to darken but no one moved. The light bleached the planes of the captains' faces and water hung on their eyelashes. It seemed that the three twisted messengers had brought back an unspoken, unwritten message, or perhaps a lesson, that there was a power sleeping somewhere in the Glassy Country that was better left unwoken. Every captain, every Companion, almost every person living in the whole great expanse of the Matrix knew the power lesson. Sometimes they ignored it or neglected it or found justification for avoiding it but always were as inescapably aware of it as they were aware of the beating of their hearts.

"Time to eat, then get some sleep," Townsend advised his bedraggled envoys. "Give us time to think. And thank you for what you did. No wonder this King is so sure of winning if his people are like you three."

The captains shook their hands and patted their backs. All approved of the logic behind the choice of Crook, Hex and Martin, but none was happy, least of all Townsend himself. "I should have gone alone," he said. "I sent them where I would not go. Also I did not go first into the Daroi encampments. I did not think then I was afraid. You should have told me I was."

"This is a bad time to have such thoughts," said Schroeder, "now that we Companions have perils greater than any we, or those who went before us, have ever faced. Yet what is there to fear? The gods set us here for a little time, then when we have endured it they have other plans for us. You and I will meet again beyond this little world, which even in its smallness we cannot understand, so how can we know what awaits us when we meet among the stars? We were made and, since we were made, then there was a purpose in our making, just as it is in the rain falling to the earth and the trees growing to the sky. Life is purpose in action. Don't be afraid, Andre-Leander. You see further than I, and you must know this."

None of the others had heard Schroeder speak thus, but in its own way his words reflected their own beliefs and certainties. The Matrix people thought of the workings and purpose of creation as gods and God with no differentiation. The many gods were the laws, the one God was the purpose in past conception and future intention, but whether they were set apart or one and the same was sophistry. Self-evidently they existed all around. They were. That was all.

They knew, of course, what Townsend feared. "It will not be long, the dying," said Billy Scarlett who rarely spoke in their councils. "Even for Timmy Halloran it was not long, perhaps less than a minute. Last night he came out and watched the river and the clouds rushing across the moon. I know." Some of the captains were nervous of Scarlett. He would say 'I know' but what he knew was so deeply sunk that it might have been in the seams of old mines with tunnels drowned thousands of feet in water that would never be drained.

"I do not like to think of Timmy Halloran," said Townsend. "Even if it was less than a minute. And the King of the Glassy Country fears nothing." He paused. "If he told the truth."

"It is the truth." De Vito spoke for all of them. "We bought it with the three Twisted Ones, remember."

Oyvindsen frowned. "I do not like to hear them called that. There should be another name. They have brave hearts."

It was raining harder now and they had gradually moved under the shelter of a wide-spreading ash tree. Only in occasional splashes did the rain slip through its leaves.

Someone said casually, "The Daroi will not like this weather," but another was less sure: "Rain will not stop them. They have come far. They too must have brave hearts." Several captains and two of the companies had seen the oncoming Daroi column flayed with fire and missiles at the bridge, but it had only been stopped for a few hours and that because dead men could go no further.

Townsend sighed at the thought: "We cannot do that again. If we stand aside the Daroi will be confident of becoming masters of the Matrix and the Outer Lands. Then all will be different, perhaps better, perhaps not, but different. For the first time in the Matrix's history, I believe, its people will not have chosen its future. The nomads will have chosen for us. Why will this King not tell us what lies behind the legend of the unlucky land?"

His question hung unanswered, though one of the captains tried to console him: "Remember the rectors chose to remain at peace, or not to resist these wandering people." The speaker did not add that therefore the people must wish for this, which, though logical, seemed not quite to ring true.

"You know what that means," replied Townsend. "The organism of the state will not resist but the people may forfeit the state. The Matrix itself is at best only a thin web of authority. If a net decides to catch the water as well as the fish let it first consider the choice of the holes." The captains smiled, amused by the analogy, and Townsend laughed. "I know. I wasn't one of the Children. Never mind. Send the Children to me and see what they think now."

By mid-afternoon the Children had assembled and learned that there had been no proposition or response at all from the Glassy Country. "Is this what you expected, Sammy?" asked one.

"I didn't expect anything," said Sammy. "Of course we expect laws to work, but purposes are different. Same old God and gods."

Townsend almost groaned, seeing a dozen of the Children quivering in their eagerness to tug at the interlacing of physics and metaphysics, or better still to deny their separate existence.

"Come, let us help our general," said Oyvindsen, conscious of being a captain, yet personally turning with regret from the enticing prospect of debating where phenomenon becomes noumenon. "The world of the Matrix has been long in the making. There is much happiness here. Its preservation is not an unworthy end." There was a babble of voices, for to the Children's delight a new opportunity was presenting itself "Stop, stop! No 'good ends justifying bad means' argument. If the gods are false there is no god. I thought we settled that in the academies."

"Yes, but . . ."

"Didn't we say that . . .?"

"In our year we . . ."

Andre-Leander coughed loudly, and they looked smilingly at him.

Those who had known him longest noticed how his fair curly hair was much greyer now, and how, whereas once he had always stood to talk, here he sat, and played with his fingers, picking the nails away. "You're not helping me."

The Children gave themselves a few seconds. Then ideas leaped, split, evaporated from their minds, as spilt milk-drops hop on the red-hot oven top. After some time Sammy took it upon himself to summarise: "Andre-Leander, we have learned more from your deputation than you seem to think. First, the King is confident and secure, and we can only assume that means he and his people can defend their country. They are not large in numbers, certainly far fewer than the Daroi, so they rely on something else. This is unlikely to be weaponry, even using the word loosely. Whatever it may be seems difficult to bring out of their country, and possibly not out of the centre of the Land of Unright. Those nearer the centre appear to be worse in their abnormalities. The King has hurt Walter Hex and perhaps hurts all of the people and the creatures and plants of that land. But though the King tells us nothing that does not mean there is nothing to tell. The legend through the Matrix is that the Glassy Country is unlucky, to be avoided. The condition of almost everything that lives there confirms this, but where is the true history of it? Remember in success one can live with history, only losers need the legend. Probably they do teach it in their schools, as you say Hex said. Hex and Crook are intelligent, probably the little one, Martin, as well. So why do they have nothing to report?"

"I can think of several reasons," said Townsend. "All unlikely."

Another of the Children joined in, none of them being averse to airing a view: "If they were all impossible, the least unlikely would probably be the truth, Andre-Leander. So are our messengers withholding something?" There were some nods, as well as dubious looks.

"So what do I do?"

Oyvindsen said, "Nothing. Three of our best paid a high price, we owe them some trust. And the seed is sown in the King's mind. There are always more radii in a circle."

No one seemed inclined to dispute the analogies, but one said, "What of the big man with the Unman? The twisted ones regard him highly. Some talk of his being the Tyr-figure, sent to make them free. Should we not involve him? At the least if we help him may not the King feel a little kinder towards us?"

"It may be as you say," Townsend answered, "and will cost us nothing, but let us stay true to one another for I fear all our future holds for most of us is much unkindness."

XXXVII

There is no law that says that the life-span of civilisations or regimes or thrones or realms or hegemonies shall be long or short. Doubtless the end is always coming, implicit in the process of growth and ripening, but for it to become clear to the overthrown or dispossessed or superseded may take a day or a generation. Yesterday the struggle seemed never-ending, today in the street we citizens of the capital watch, shocked, the victory parade of our foes. Twenty-five years ago the first newcomers moved in, humble and intriguing, unreal as pictures in a book; today resignedly we empty our houses and move, knowing there is no future for our children here.

Many circumstances favoured the Daroi. The Matrix people's distrust of centralised power worked against them, there being no real tradition of concerted action, with the Outlands always ready to behave as autonomously as they thought wise. Also, particularly to those who had only heard of them, the Daroi seemed to be a travelling race, and as such their only transgression was a sort of trespass. The peace vote had, as often elsewhere in human history, been seen by the Daroi as a puzzling, but inviting, sign of weakness.

Following the vote in the cathedral there were several weeks of inertia at the Matrix's centre, tinged with hope, doubt and a feeling of self-disappointment. Though the Daroi scouts ranged far ahead the epicentre of change lay, naturally, where the leading body of their warriors had reached. The farther out the slighter the earthquake's register; on the far islands and fringe lands of the Matrix the tremors were slight enough for a wife to glance at her husband and say, "What was that?" and forget it again as he shrugged.

Old Man Dorn sat in his tall house on the estuary, looking out the windows at the grey-brown water, not bothering to ask where his skippers sailed the fishing-boats, nor did they tell him of the Daroi, that being only a piece of gossip passed across the sides of boats. For Abbot Huw, Kay and the monks their services patterned the day, as they always had. They prayed for the case of the Matrix, which had always sustained the cause of the unhurried world they knew best. In the village of Venask the new Daroi headman gave flowers to Sylvie Patillo. She was too busy even to throw them away, for the bees at the bottom of the garden had to be retold the story of Demetrius's dying. She had tied black crepe round the hives. Karl-Pieter the woodman moved his family deeper into the forest as he had intended. Far to the north-west the Companions of Merganser were filing up the gangplanks or lining the sides of the ships, laughing and waving to the folk on the dock, though their captain-general frowned and pondered: he did not like the urgency of Townsend's call for help. Babies were born, children played, men and women fell in love, death came by sickness, accident or age, and the birds, animals, trees and plants endured the journey of their own lives.

The funfair journeyed too, finding a meadow, setting up its coloured stalls, swings and roundabouts for three or four days, the organ music washing over the treetops to lure the children to the apricot and scarlet lacquer of its arabesques and scrolling in the dusk that was just enough to disguise the shabbiness. In daylight the funfair was empty and asleep, and the fair people stayed in their wagons or balanced on one foot, an arm resting on an ox's neck, alert and remote as ballet dancers.

"The sights must be wrong," said Alvin Costello, squinting down the barrel.

The stallkeeper smiled. "Have another try," he said. The others looked at the target, a rattling line of small tin ducks, only a few feet away, that had so far eluded Costello. Next to him a small boy's gun discharged a cork which knocked a duck flat.

"Good shot!" Lee congratulated him. "Show Alvin how it's done."

"It's not too hard." The boy was thinking of his mother and choosing a prize of a glass scent bottle.

"Let me try your gun," requested Costello so seriously that the cousins burst into laughter and even Hereward had to smile. The boy retired blushing among other admiring children.

The Companions had not named Costello 'the marksman' for nothing. Even with the clumsy fire-arms and home-made ammunition of his days and ways he had earned the name, and being an engineer at heart in a world that had veered away from engines he was full of admiration for the mechanism of his rifle, understanding the principles in a way that was more usual in crossbow men, and irritated by his comrades' habit of regarding their weapons as useful handles for bayonets.

Lucas had asked a village girl to have a go on the swing-boats with him and there were shrieks and more laughter as he tugged them to precarious heights. Lee licked pensively at an apple coated in candy, having failed to persuade another girl to join him. The cousins may not have been altogether welcome to the young men of the village but the girls clearly found them diverting. Indeed the whole group was an interesting diversion in a shut-off forest village like this one.

Townsend and de Vito had much approved of the idea of helping Tyr-Hereward and thus perhaps impressing the King of the Glassy Country with their good intentions. Hereward had taken some time to recover from the effects of the night foray into the Daroi encampments. Flaps of skin had been torn loose from both below and above his right eyebrow, and that and the blood and shock had effectively blinded him. One of the Companions had sewn the skin and flesh back with tiny neat stitches. Lokietok had carried him back across the bridge. The Daroi set to guard it had shrunk back, shaken and shocked, to let the monster pass through. Each of them had felt his wild faith chilled and the cold clay stretching out its arms to fold him under into a freezing eternity.

When Hereward felt able to go de Vito had chosen three Companions, a group small enough to attract little attention, to accompany him, Martin and Lokietok towards Limber. George Littler emerged from the Glassy Country forests on the day they left and joined them. He said nothing of his journey or of his arrival so much later than the three Twisted Folk, other than that he had needed to rest. "I have not really got over the fever," he said.

None of the seven had been to Limber before so a map was made that marked a route that would steer clear of the Daroi outposts. Hereward liked the Companions' presence: Costello was as quiet as the cousins were noisy, carrying his rifle wherever he went, whereas the cousins seemed not to care that they went unarmed. Lokietok and they tolerated each other's company well.

The cousins teased Martin good-naturedly, giving him a peaked cap on the front of which they had persuaded someone to embroider 'Frog tamer', saying that this was his special talent. He wore it all day long, which delighted them, for they made no secret of their admiration for his journey into the Glassy Country.

The evening was still early enough for there to be many children at the fair. A cluster of them had gathered round a tall, narrow booth made of striped canvas in the shape of a grandfather clock. The cousins were soon drawn to it and before long the others too. "Here I am! Here I am!" came a rasping wooden voice.

"It's Mister Punch!" said Costello who had seen the crooked, beak-nosed man before. Punch beat on the floor of his small stage with his stick. Soon Judy came, and a pig, then a baby, a crocodile and a ghost. Punch defied everyone, not least his audience, who betrayed him at every turn.

"Watch out!" cried the children as Punch crept up to capture the baby.

"Yes, he did!" shouted the children, and "Yes, he did!" shouted Lee as Punch attempted to deny some dangerous antic.

"No, he didn't," called out Lucas distractingly, causing the children to glower at him and his recent lady acquaintance to abandon him for the shelter of a bevy of girls of her own age.

Later in the evening as the meadow filled with people there were log fires to stand around and the fair-men threw on salt so that they burned blue and green. Spicy meatballs and roast chestnuts were for sale where charcoal grill-fires glowed round the fair-site. Under some big plane trees the group found seats – sitting made Lokietok less conspicuous – and ate the spicy food while passing round red wine, drinking cheerfully in turn out of the bottle. The puppet man wandered over and began to talk to Martin, their voices low and mingled in other conversations. "How far to the city now?" Hereward was asking. He was becoming more urgent and impatient with each passing day, Limber sucking him towards it as the driftwood begins to speed up when the whirlpool's spiral tugs it inwards.

"Three days. Maybe sixty, seventy miles." Lucas knew de Vito's map by heart.

"And the Daroi?" wondered George Littler.

"Another three days after that. That's a guess," said Lucas. "Maybe longer, if they want their cattle to catch up."

"No." Lee shook his head. "The young ones and the dogs have got the scent by now. And the quarry isn't even running, Luc."

"Maybe they've made a mistake. Maybe it's a lion."

"A really old one, then. It could have scattered the dogs once. Not now."

A sudden horrified exclamation drew their attention to where Martin sat. "What! Are you sure of that, Pat?"

"Of course," said the puppet-man. "Jacky Dorn is there too, the newest rector of the Matrix."

"I knew that. Andre-Leander told us, though it seems very strange. I am sure he went there to fetch his sister home. But, Kit . . ."

"She will be safer in the big city than in lonely country places like these," the Punch and Judy man assured him. "I get nervous here, even if they make allowances because I'm a showman."

"I know, Pat, I've been one myself," muttered Martin. Not quite a real job, just something to amuse the Daylight People when they had tired themselves with honest labour. He knew the reputation.

"You're safe with this lot around you. But would you come to this fair on your own?"

"No, I wouldn't. But can you get a message to her?" Martin was shaking. "Some time and place. We'll be there." He looked round. "Won't we, Hereward?"

"Three days from now, then, evening, on the Hundredth Step. You can see the Steps from anywhere in the city. I'll send the message through my brother," said Pat Pudding.

"This sister of yours," inquired Lucas, "is she pretty?"

"No," said Martin firmly. "She isn't." A beautiful twisted girl was a dangerous challenge and temptation in one.

Lucas, undeterred said, "I expect she is really," adding to Pat Pudding, "Tell her I shall be coming to Limber myself. That'll cheer her up." There was a ripple of laughter, among it to their surprise a growling chuckle from Lokietok and a blurred notion:

Lucas-man *No-man* *Lokietok-man*

Lucas said calmly, "Thank you, Lokietok. Now it's back to the fair. I shall win a prize at the shooting gallery for Martin's sister Kit. I can't meet her empty handed."

The shooting gallery and all the stalls were doing good business, their tinted lamps drawing clouds of moths out of the woodlands and crowds of local people alike. The air was warm and there was an occasional flickering suggestion of distant heat lightning, just a tongue of light licking the cloud edges. Lucas was aiming one of the cork-guns at the elusive ducks while the others watched and idly talked. The gun gave an amiable pop and the ducks were parading undisturbed when a javelin thudded into the wooden back of the stall where it stuck quivering.

The fair's music had first drawn the young Daroi warriors through the trees, then the splash of colours and the tangy syrup and cinnamon smells, which made their dogs frisk and pull on their leashes. The more the people in the pathways between the stalls drew back at the sight of them the more their swagger grew. There was a shout of delight from the thrower and he came forward and reached out to tug the javelin free, while another swept up an armful of the trinkets that served as prizes.

Alvin Costello had turned almost with the thud of the javelin and in one fluid movement dropped the pop-gun, picked up his rifle and slid a bullet into the breech, so that the nearest Daroi found himself looking into the black eye of the muzzle. "Put them back," said Costello, whose Far Westermain accent was so soft he seemed unable to shout.

The young warriors not in the line of fire jeered gleefully. Their evening was turning out to be more diverting every moment.

Their people were in a way the mirror of the Matrix people: the latter drew back from the intoxicant of power, while the Daroi bristled at the prospect of submitting to any power. On separate continents the same instincts had found different expressions, with the men and women of the Matrix inclined to spaciousness and even solitariness, while for the nomads the beelike loyalties in their mighty tribes gave them a boyish freedom.

In front of the shooting gallery there was a backwash of local villagers and woodland folk, either stepping away to watch better or pushing children to safer spots, then a parting movement as through them came Hereward and the others, save Lokietok, who, unaware of what was happening, still sat on a stump under the trees.

The Daroi youngsters, slim and wiry as travelling races are, looked doubtfully at the massive George Littler and noted how Hereward and the cousins too were bigger and heavier than any one of them. Whether the cousins' smiles were preferable to the grim stares of Littler and Hereward was also doubtful. From the darkness came an interrogation, a snarling question-mark, as Lokietok suddenly missed Hereward's presence.

The dusk seemed suddenly darker round the young Daroi as they moved closer together. Hereward, looking carefully at them, could not think of them as the enemy. The enemy had flung Adelie down on the stones. He was walking surefootedly now in his memory and the beads on the string were big indeed, not likely to be confusingly the equal of the little beads of that evening, such as the stick in Punch's hand and the smooth curve of the rising swingboat, or of the afternoon, with the water cold in their boots as they splashed through a knee-high stream, and the violet stalagmites of wild lupins by the side of the white road, or of the morning, the brown eagle seen coaxing her brood to fly in careful circles round a hilltop and the dew on his face as he woke.

Hereward pushed Costello's rifle barrel downwards and there was a pause, the Daroi letting their hands stay still on their half unhitched throwing lances. He reached across and pulled the javelin out of the planking of the gallery, offering it to the thrower, who nodded as he took it. George Littler plucked a crystal pendant out of the tangle that had been snatched from the stall. "What's your name?" he said, and the young nomad looked up into Littler's face, pale under its black stubble.

"Frick."

"Right, Frick. You hit one duck, you get one prize." He passed over a shiny gewgaw. "Your friend gets a prize when he wins one."

The Daroi knew, being young, that they were invincible and

immortal, and briefly pondered their reactions. None of them knew why he felt his laughing sunlit future dissolving into black dust, but they did see Hereward's gesture to halt and, following his gaze saw the Unman loom, as if the fairmen had erected a shabby obelisk in the gap between two of the stalls. At the new scent the dogs howled shrilly. At once their owners recognised Lokietok from the Drome at High Altai. Now too they recalled George Littler for his size, and they stared hard at Hereward, at first uncertain for then he had been stripped to the waist, but recognition coming.

"You fought the monster at High Altai!" Frick exclaimed. "It was you. I know you now."

His comrades joined in: "The monster came into the camp by the river. It killed Moskander Daro."

"At the wrestling, was that you too?"

Talking rapidly all at once they were hardly ready for Costello: "Who burned Timmy Halloran? Was that you?"

Frick answered haughtily: "No. We are fighters not burners. But it was one death for one. And El Daro died first. Also on the bridge you owed us many deaths. We died first there too." The Daroi thought of the tribe as the holder of tallies and debts, whereas for the Matrix it was the individual, yet the main point was the same and Costello saw it.

"I have no quarrel with you, only with the men who held the rope for my friend. That was unfair. I gave El Daro a quick, clean death."

The Daroi examined him. At first less formidable than those in the group around him, they were wary of his stillness and the way the rifle seemed part of him, even with his maimed hand padded with bandages.

"Still one for one," argued Frick. "Though we of the clan of Zander Bey are more men than the burners."

"So what do you do?" asked Lucas. "Drown people?"

The young Daroi held their heads high and frowned at Lucas. "No," answered one. "Any one of us may challenge. One to one, until no one wishes to continue. The Matrix lord fought well, I recall."

Hereward's attention quickened: "A Matrix lord. Where was this?"

"Back," said the warrior carelessly, gesturing southwards through the trees. For wanderers back was nowhere; it had ceased to be.

"El Daro's day," said Frick, and spat in the dust, to murmurs of agreement.

"It was our custom, not his," explained another. "And he stayed far back from the Matrix lord."

The Daroi were looking inwards, seeing Demetrius hanging from the bell-pull of the shop, in a dirty blue jacket that dripped puddles round his feet. They rolled their eyes and made disapproving noises. Also, El Daro had hesitated, so he was not one of them. The wind and the fire did not hesitate. Or stay out of reach. The Daroi went on to relate the last hour of Demetrius, having seen it all, unlike the Daroi prisoner at the bridge who had known only a little of the story.

After their story both groups watched Pat Pudding make Punch venture out again. Punch seemed in a dark mood. "These shoes, these shoes," he grumbled to himself, and disappeared beneath his stage, though his humped back was visible, bobbing up and down. "Phew, phew," he puffed, emerging to mop his face with a large red handkerchief. "These shoes aren't my shoes. They don't even fit. These shoes are no good." Punch had the shoes in one hand, beating them with his stick. "Where's the frying-pan?" he shouted sulkily. Judy appeared holding the baby but for once Punch was uninterested. He put the shoes in the pan and began to cook them, occasionally flicking them upwards like pancakes.

"Your lovely new shoes!" cried Judy and tugged at Punch's arm, but he only shrieked, "They're no good! They're useless!" and when Judy protested that they were the same sort he always wore, he cried out, "Fry them for supper. Potatoes, cauliflowers. Leeks." Judy was undeterred and picked the shoes out of the pan and took them away, forgetting the baby. Punch looked at it speculatively and picked it up. "Nice piglet, nice pork." He stirred the vegetables in the pan.

"Quick, he's got the baby," shrilled the children, from where, at the front of the watching crowd, they were leaning on their seated mothers' shoulders or sitting crosslegged holding hands with fathers or older sisters, gazing as wide-eyed as were Frick and his friends.

As the fair slowed down the further stalls had lowered their awnings into shutters, while from the nearer ones those fair-men without customers were watching the show. A big orange moon was sliding behind ragged clouds, while lightning gleamed remotely and silently.

Hereward felt at ease: so many things imprinting themselves on his memory but now he had control of them as, like the coppersmith's rubber hammer they beat his metal into shape with thousands of tiny taps. Almost at Limber now, and his anger still tapping out the shape of the future.

"I don't want the baby!" shrieked Punch. "I'll put it in the pan."

"He's putting it in the pan!" yelled Lucas and the children.

"Going to burn it," whispered Costello into Frick's ear.

"I've been walking for ever," Punch complained. "No wonder

my shoes hurt. Ah, here's a nice camel for me to ride on." A ferocious beast with black and gold stripes had appeared, and though the children cried that it was a tiger, he ignored them. "It's a camel. Now I can ride a long way. Riding's for me!" Punch sprang on its back, and Judy came and jumped on too. The tiger roared and tried to snap at him but Punch beat its back and it began to run. He was triumphant. "No more walking, no more shoes. This is the way to travel." Judy said that it might be, but how were they going to stop the tiger. "Like this," said Punch and threw the baby in front of the tiger that bounced on, roaring, as Punch beat it again.

Judy was unimpressed. "That didn't work."

"This might!" Punch pushed her off, but the tiger only ran on. "All roads lead to Limber. We're here." The tiger ran faster. "We must be going to Regret. I think I'll get off now." A ghost, a white skull above a white shift, halted the tiger, arm raised. "Now I can get off!" shouted Punch, but the ghost scrambled up and the tiger ran on.

When Punch demanded the tiger stop, the ghost said, "It only stops for ghosts. Do you want to be a ghost?" Punch thought it must all be a dream and the ghost laughed. "What else is it? But who's dreaming it?"

Together the three figures jolted down off the stage leaving only a black cloth, though for a few moments they could hear from below the tiger roaring and the ghost cackling.

Some big warm raindrops plopped down, making dark craters on the sandy ground, and mothers pulled hoods up on children's heads. Across the fronts of the few stalls still open canvas awnings were flapping down and being tied shut.

The Daroi were reluctant to move on. They would have preferred the Matrix lord, as they thought of Hereward, to be rather less indifferent. The antagonism of Costello was more gratifying than simply being seen as fairgoers, no different from the farmers, foresters, potters and tailors around them. Also the puppets' antics left them uneasy, as with a face, the name forgotten, you feel you should know. When Costello asked where they intended to go they lifted their heads and said, "The city of Limber," but got only the slight response of Lee saying that all roads led there, and Lucas remarking how that left them all with little choice.

"That is true," said Frick. "My people are not afraid to ride on the striped beast's back."

As they parted Costello called out, "We'll meet again, I expect," and then added something the Daroi could not catch though it sounded not unlike 'at the shooting gallery'.

XXXVIII

Two major qualities, one of constitution, one of disposition, marked the Twisted Folk as being set far apart from the Daylight People. The tragic genetic inheritance of Kitfox's folk was a superscription so glaring, and it had over many generations been the cause of so much grief, that the other difference remained not so much dwarfed as unconsidered. The moon often hangs, a chalk-grey medallion against the blue in the bright daytime sky, as clearly present as the big moon of darkness, yet how rarely you look for or even notice it. So it was with the respective peoples of Jacky and Kit: their physicality was the night's unforgettable moon, how they thought and saw themselves more like the daylight's haunting cloudy moon.

The Daylight People never thought of themselves by that name, but occasionally as the people of the Matrix – and this weighed little upon them, as light as air-drifted spiderwebs – sometimes as the people of Westermain, but as the allegiances narrowed the thicker grew the threads, until being the folk of the Big Grey River had strings that could tug at the heart. However, for the Twisted Folk that was both their own name for themselves and everyone's name for them, and they wore it as a file of slaves might once have worn the iron collars that attached them to the slaver's long chain.

The Twisted Folk sensed almost palpably the passing of time. It was not that their lives were shorter, though often enough they were, it was rather that they yearned for some accomplishment to mark their passage on earth. Their condition fretted them and they were disposed to measure time carefully, with tiny intricate watches and exact clocks and histories that were careful of chronology. For the Daylight People the bells that marked the hours were enough, and the sundials and seasons would do just as well. Noah Smith of Hay village, who knew how the church clock worked, was an oddity among them.

Kit and Jacky lay on the grass of the cliff-top either side of a white cloth and what was left of the strawberries and shortcake, pastries and lemonade she had brought for their picnic. He lay on his back, eyes almost closed, and she, her chin cupped in her palms, wondered whether he would ever kiss her. The Daylight People were infuriating, she thought, behaving not only as if they owned the world but as if they owned time as well. She knew how Jacky felt about her and recalled exactly how he had said to Nestor: 'How much chance did you mean to give my woman?' and only the day before the Daroi woman had taunted her with not being able to find a man. Though she was a year younger she thought of him as very young, not so much in experience nor even in his ways but in what was a sort of innocence. To her Jacky seemed to stroll through the world, not noticing its menaces and pitfalls, and to her half-amused impatience it seemed as if the world sympathised with him, rather as if it would be on its best behaviour because that was how he expected it to be.

"If I'd come on this picnic with anyone else it would have been cold or raining or the strawberries would have been unripe," she told herself, "but even the weather doesn't like to disappoint Jacky. The Matrix drags off his sister and then treats her like a princess – they even accept him as a rector of their great realm to sit at their table in the cathedral." She was too honest not to admit that Jacky had agonised over voting for peace with the Daroi, and that he had voted as he had for her sake. In truth his vote had probably reflected accurately the will of those he spoke for, but that had consoled him little.

"Wake yourself up, Jacky," she said, and, leaning over, held a strawberry over his mouth. "Eat some more, you're too thin." When he began to mumble a response she dropped the strawberry neatly into his mouth, which made him choke and cough noisily.

Before she could lean away his arm went round her and pulled her down on his chest. "Say you're sorry," he spluttered.

"No," said Kit automatically.

"You'll have to stay there then, until you do."

He was laughing, his eyes exactly the colour of the sea beyond the grasses of the hilltop, and Kit was trembling, because he was Jacky, brightest of the Daylight People and she, who had teased and tantalised and gibed at him ever since they had met, who had used her right hand to hold the strawberries because her left was so frightful it stayed always under her glove, she was just too different. But she thought to herself how glad she had been to see Jacky when the fat man came to hurt her.

"I might stay a little while," she said. Her hair had fallen either side of his face, as if they were together inside a soft reddish cloud.

"Well, what am I thinking, Kit?"

"You're thinking I'm one of the Twisted Folk." Her answer was truthful, because though she saw clearly into people's minds she knew that some thoughts splash in the mind as openly as whale calves frolic on the waves, while others lie deep in the ooze, hiding even from the thinker.

Her deformity was so prominent in Kit's own thinking that it could distort her mind-reading talent. In truth Jacky had nothing but admiration for the defiance which had brought her out of her distant cramped home to undergo the disdain that came her way as regularly and unavoidably as rainfall, to say nothing of a physical danger, known only to those breeds, like snakes, that make mankind's blood run cold. Those sailors who had brought Jacky and Kit to Limber had certainly felt the old uneasiness, and, knowing the old story of the dark magic woman who bewitched Adam before he found Eve, among themselves had called her Lilith. "Wrong. I was thinking I like the freckles on your nose," said Jacky, for he was young and meant to take her back to the Big Grey River.

Apart from her family's affectionate pecks and hugs no one had ever kissed Kit or held her close. There were strong and attractive men among the Twisted Folk and Kit had always assumed that some day one would ask her brother's permission to woo her – with so many differences, ranging from tiny quirks and blemishes right through to monstrosities, the acts of marriage and procreation were reached by her people only by way of a labyrinth of formalities. But telling herself that she had not forgotten any allegiances and that he was only Jacky, and hardest of all trying not to think of her father, she stayed very still and looked down into his eyes and this time it was too easy to know that he would kiss her, and he did, and after a few seconds, and very nervously, she kissed him back.

As they walked back into the city that evening a thousand thoughts surged in her mind, bubbling and pressing in opposite directions as when in an estuary the sea-tide and river-current dispute each other's sway. Drawn as she was to Jacky, she could not avoid imagining the many obstacles that they would encounter if she chose him as her man. She cherished the thought that he had chosen her, and tried to hold it separate in her head, away from those other thoughts that would smudge it.

"So not one of our girls was good enough," his people would say of him. In their eyes his future would never fulfil its early shining promise, as if there lurked in him some unexpected perversity, not unlike that of one who would weld on his own shackles. Her own folk too, she supposed, would be saddened by her choice. She held his arm tightly, silently vowing she would settle every account with whoever hurt her man.

Back in the house where they lodged they were met by Astolat, who had as always much to say regarding her day, announcing authoritatively that she considered no watery topics to be ever dull, and was investigating water revolving down plug-holes and the colours of rainbows. Her axiom and experiments having been gratifyingly admired, she said casually that Kit had had a visitor who would return later. "I think he was – you know," she added, "sort of all dressed in black and he had a watch on a chain. You know."

"Yes, I know, Astolat," said Kit.

Not paying much attention, and still thinking happily about the picnic, Jacky said, "You seem a bit vague."

"Men," said Kit and Astolat giggled.

The visitor did return later. Or rather, he was not there one moment and then a voice from a corner of the room said, "Martin of Hay's sister?" There was no one in the room but when Kit said, "Who is it?" they heard 'Outside on the stairs' and a shadowy figure on the unlit staircase was looking in.

"It's all right, Jacky." Kit knew by now the movement when he stood, heels lifted and swaying slightly from foot to foot. "I'm Martin's sister. Come in." The man came just inside the door.

"Have you got a name?" he asked.

"Yes. Kitfox of Sheepwash Bend, close by Hay, of Near Westermain. And you?"

"No. Not a real name. From the Glassy Country. Jack, if you like."

"Same as my brother," chirped Astolat, and her eager smile brought the faintest of glimmers to the stranger's sallow face.

"Well, then, Jack Pudding the patterman, since you ask," he said, and his voice spoke from just beside Astolat's ear, making her hop with excitement at the prospect of questions on sonics. "So we don't get mixed up."

"Have you met Martin?" asked Kit.

"No, but he is well, and Tyr-Hereward also." Jacky took a step forward to speak and the message-man took a soft step backwards, putting himself just outside the doorway.

"Don't worry about him," Kit said quickly. Jack Pudding shrugged without speaking. "Can you tell me any more from Martin?"

"If you are still here he will try to be on the Hundredth Step three evenings from now. But he wants you to go home. He thinks you," and he looked at Jacky, "should not have brought her here. You should see she gets home safely."

"I will," said Jacky. He did not like to open a debate on who had brought whom to the city of Limber.

"When I am ready to go, Jacky will take me."

Jack Pudding lifted his eyebrows at this, but when Kit asked him to say more he continued: "My brother says there is an Unman. Always close to Tyr-Hereward. In the Glassy Country we know the story of

Tyr, of course. This may be the true Tyr, perhaps not. We will wait and see. Bad times are coming with these Daroi nomads, but in bad times there are always more chances for change."

There seemed no more information, but Astolat, bursting to ask her own questions, could contain herself no longer: "Would you do your voice again, please?"

Jack Pudding looked at her, thinking that with her froth of blond curls and ribbons, her wide eyes and small plumpish figure she seemed the pattern of all the children who had gazed up wide-eyed at his strange old act, cheerfully familiar in no time with its outrageous and truculent world.

"Ah-ah-ah-ah!" The noise was like quick rattling coughs. It seemed to emerge from the level of the visitor's stomach, then a very fast croaking voice: "Who is it? Who is it? I'm coming up." A sharp face peered from the top of the visitor's cloak, the red, wrinkled face of a little old man, whose long chin and pointed cap curved towards one another like the letter 'C'. "Where's the baby?" snapped the little man. Now, visible from the waist up, they could see his hunched back, and his painted eyes darted round as the head bobbled and jerked.

"Here I am. What do you want?" A different voice this time, high with the clear consonants of Westermain speech, and for a moment Jacky was sure Astolat had spoken.

"No, not you! Run away quick! Where's my stick?" shouted the little man, and "Bat-bat-bat!" went the voice-thrower, and on his shoulder he made the little man beat his stick up and down. Next a different sound, this time coming from the stairway, a wet growl: "Argle, argle, argle."

"Where's the baby?" the little man shrieked out as a bright green head came out from under the other side of Jack Pudding's cloak. It had long jaws with rows of triangular teeth.

"Argle, argle," gurgled the creature.

"It says it's got the baby in a hole in the river-bank," Punch translated.

"It's a crocodile," said Astolat, and the crocodile nodded in agreement. Punch swung his stick but it slid away under the black cloak with Punch following noisily.

"Was that all right?" Jack Pudding asked Astolat.

"No, it wasn't!" said Kit. "Don't ever do that again!"

XXXIX

Cities spring from many different seeds: some are born of one only, where a river shallows to a ford or roads cross on a ridge, then in the first small shelter this provides other seeds germinate as markets open, saints are martyred, masters draw pupils, parliaments argue. War eyes the cities, marks them on its maps.

Limber was much the greatest city of the Matrix, and a great port with a splendid harbour, but it was far from the centre of its empire's landmass. To its south lay a tangle of islands, one being Kittiwake of the Companions, and the city itself looked out across a sea that was blue and calm for months on end, though in winter it could be as foggy and threatening as the far off grey ocean that the Dorn family fished. North-east of Limber lay an empty salt-poisoned land, much of it where a sea-bed no longer fed by rivers was now a brackish marsh and saltflats. Somewhere uncertainly beyond that lay Regret, the Unman city. Which had drawn the other into its orbit was impossible to say, but they existed counterpoised like twin stars, though without the slightest contact, at least since the assault by Lamorak, which, though only a matter of years ago, now seemed some archaic aberration.

To Hereward and his friends, approaching Limber and within only a few hours of reaching it, the city and the sea remained out of sight on the far side of a high ridge. Visible on the ridge top, like fingers of a raised, saluting hand, was a cluster of towers rising above the tree-tops, and a tall granite outcropping which marked the highest point of the Seven Hundred Steps. There was much scattered woodland and many cultivated fields, some carrying grain but also the darker green of cabbages and potatoes, as well as the neatly ruled lines of gardens of celery, leeks and rhubarb. The farmhouses were sturdy, a mixture of stone and white wood, set amidst their fields. A white road snaked up and around the contours of the ridge.

From the sea ships saw Limber as a spectacle of infinite variety. Level after level it rose up the seaward side of the ridge, the domes of St Xavier's cathedral dominating the harbour, its bulk seeming to ride on the harbour wall. The wall itself was a massive construction that allowed the city to climb sheer from the water, though between sea and wall was a frieze of water-gates, piers and jetties, wharves, moles and quays. Upwards climbed the creamy stone and russet tile of spires, colonnades, arcades, crescents, villas and castellations, all dappled and flecked with the green of treetops. Terraces, courts, copings and cornices were awash with the vermilion of thousands of geraniums, bougainvilleas and poinsettias.

From inside the city where, at their rendezvous, Jacky and Kit sat and talked on the rim of a fountain on the Hundredth Step, the honeycomb of edifices and houses provided two different perspectives, the wider one of the great airy expanse down to the many-coloured sea, and the narrower that of the courtyards and doorways, the embrasures, grills, porches and balconies that made the bones of the city. Hereward and the others would meet all this soon, thought Jacky, though as land travellers it would come on them unexpectedly, whereas sailors approaching saw from afar the pageant of Limber.

Jacky knew the music of Limber, the draymen singing, the young girl practising the flute at her window, the fountain playing in its basin, and always the bells, but that afternoon he heard them slightly if at all for he had come frustrated and impatient from the council. Expecting that the rectors would reconsider the steady advance of the Daroi, he had remained silent, listening to a proposition that the refugees be encouraged to return to their Daroi-occupied homelands. Michael Novak had tried to involve him by asking what the people of the Steps wished, but he only muttered: "Arms." When Osric Sheer sharply reminded him that they had voted for peace, Jacky said, "So we did, I forgot," and abstained in the next vote.

As the warm evening drew on the city's many scents and perfumes intensified, ginger and pepper mingling with jasmine and dust, burning pinecones with syrup and candy. Kit and Jacky sniffed at it ascetically and thought of other smells, she of wet, black layers of leaves with aconites pushing through, he of the chill, salt air blowing through buckthorn and over thrift and sea-lavender, scents elusive and cool.

Both saw, but neither recognised, George Littler, as he tramped towards them, wide-shouldered in fringed brown buckskin, his clothes faded and stained the colour of earth and leaves, with people turning to look at him as he gazed around in wonder. Then behind him they saw familiar faces.

"Over here!" Kit's shriek could hardly be missed, and from under the arm of the big man she saw her brother coming forward with his bounding run. Still the same, she thought, just a little white with the dust and wearing an extraordinary hat, and then he was embracing her, inarticulate amid laughter and tears.

"I never thought you would get here," Jacky told Hereward as they shook hands and took stock of one another.

"I knew they would," crowed Kit. "I knew." Her hair was pushed right back and her black glove tucked inside Martin's arm. "What a silly hat!" She pulled it off to look at it.

"My friends gave it to me. Let me introduce them."

Kit saw the men standing behind her brother. A slim black-haired man with a narrow face bowed formally and Martin said, "Alvin Costello of Far Westermain." The other two with their fair cropped hair and freckled faces had to be related, she thought. One was holding a bunch of flowers.

"Lucas." One introduced himself and pointed to the other. "Lee. You must be Kit. We've heard all about you. We got you these." He passed her the flowers and whistled. "Martin, you said she wasn't pretty. I knew she would be."

Kit liked them at once, and had to smile, wondering at herself as she did so, for both had that carefree, cavalier bearing so rare in her own people.

"Nice place, this," said Lee, looking around.

"I'm hungry," remarked Lucas, and, the cousins having thus put things into at least their own perspective, the group made its way back to where Jacky, Kit and Astolat had found a temporary home.

Kit was a fluster of excitement and nerves. Her own attempt to buy the freedom of the Twisted Folk had failed abjectly. Not only had it hurt Jacky but she felt now that it was ill-considered and demeaning. If her people were to become free it should come from some great all-involving deed and not from an isolated bargain with those who gave or withheld liberty for the sake of a vote. She told herself that those who give largesse as a favour often think they have not altogether parted with it. But now her hopes were higher; Tyr-Hereward had reached Limber. Beside him, Jacky and the others seemed younger, easier to understand, as if their thoughts dwelt only on what it was sensible to think about while his strayed into remote areas of the mind. So Kit waited and listened when, after having eaten, the newcomers told stories of what had happened since they had parted on a summer's morning in Hay village.

The events were folded in layers of understatement and laughter, for everyone would rather share a friend's pleasure than pain. Yet where there was pain then the listeners would not wish to be spared but rather to help the teller emerge from the far side of grief's thickets. So there was always in their talk this equilibrium to be found. When George tried to make an adventure story out of walking across the rough floor of the Drome in High Altai pushing each leg into every step like a prisoner in irons, ashamed at his own fears, wanting to lie on the hard sand curled up on his side with his arms over his head rather than help his friend, then they knew there was a terror that had to be sidestepped by George finally saying, "Well, I've had better times." Jacky listened grimly to the news of the deaths of his cousin, Lars Gustafsson, and of Rigger with whom he had sailed often. Then at the story of Nestor everyone grew very quiet and Kit noticed how the men, even the light-hearted cousins, looked away from her, save for occasional glances, and she knew they were ashamed and angry for her sake.

So they came to the matters of Limber and weaving in and out of their account were the Daroi and the changes their coming had brought and was bringing. Alvin Costello's story was the death of Timmy Halloran, and not easily told except as the negative spaces of:

In the night Timmy Halloran
Crossed the river with us,
And we left him there.

Inevitably there came the matter of the imminent arrival of the main body of the Daroi, which could not now be far away. "They were very unsure," said Hereward. "We know. We helped build the new walls round High Altai. Every hour they expected to see the blue flags. Just the names of Limber and the Matrix held them cramped there for months, but only the Companions ever tried to stop them. So, Jacky, how long will you be a rector once they are here?"

"If you ask why Jacky voted for peace," interrupted Kit, "then it was because I asked him. In any case he can only vote as the people of the Steps want him to vote."

"Why did you ask him?" wondered her brother.

"Martin, the rectors, or several of them, said that if he voted for peace then we, all our folk, could live just like everyone else. I know most think we're debased and warped, but we're not. We're not dirty or disgusting or diseased either, though I expect you all think we are, if the truth was known," she ended in a furious rush of words. "Except Jacky," she added, for after all he was why she had sprung up at Hereward's earlier question.

"And me?" said Martin. Kit gave a half-shrug to indicate a small concession. "And Hereward?"

"Of course."

"And George? Alvin? Luc and Leo?"

"Count us out," said Lucas. "Or we want our hat back."

"I wanted to know," interrupted Hereward, "how long Jacky and the other rectors will keep their positions if the Daroi have come to stay." They looked at him and pondered. Here was the impatience again, the driving to stay ahead of time. That's what makes him different, thought George, whose own sense of time was more a sense of the span of lives. Trees grew at their own pace, so did pheasants and crows. There was only so much one could do in a day or a year. He could not see where Hereward's question was leading.

"Who knows?" Jacky shrugged. "Maybe it would be better to leave now. Go back home, I mean."

He glanced at Kit, and Martin, catching the look, felt cold. Just friends, he thought, just be friends, Kit, remember his birthday perhaps, let him stay young and quick in the memory, but no more.

Jacky's tired remark seemed to signal that it was time to sleep, and they found themselves places as comfortable as possible, though for most of them beds were too soft to allow sleep to come easily. Martin was asleep quickly, but his dream-self heard the wind in the leaves, the chime of a clock, the rain on the roof, swimming in his dreams so near the surface of sleep that George Littler knew he could wake the small man by moving a hand softly, without touching, past his face.

So it was easy to wake when Hereward silently left the house. Part anxious, part curious, Martin followed, reluctant to get too close as if danger was in the little garden, and shortly he recognised the feeling as the mental inscription of Lokietok. The creature was unlatching a wrought-iron gate and entering, out of place, thought Martin, amid the ferns and terracotta pots, the small lichened statues and the table where Astolat did her homework and made her models. He heard Hereward whispering and occasionally Lokietok flickered a faint image: "They are here, Lokietok, not far away. You see it wasn't right what they did to Adelie. So what shall we do to them? Just the same, eh, Lokietok, just the same. Once they have a name, once they're not 'they'. You did well to find the garden, Lokietok, very well. Are you looking forward to finding them? They won't like Lokietok and Hereward when we come in the night, will they?" Hereward laughed quietly and the Unman imitated him, the low, throaty chuckle making Martin shiver. Rights and wrongs and talk of the future meant nothing to Lokietok, he felt sure. So to whom was Hereward talking? The Unman part of himself?

The next morning saw Hereward deep in conversation with Astolat, and at the breakfast table his probing questions continued, aimed chiefly at Jacky. Martin, listening, knew he would never let go. "Do you know how many children there are in the Academies?"

Jacky shook his head. "Hundreds probably."

"How many from the Outer Lands?"

"I don't know."

"Astolat says there are many. And some of them compelled to be here, or persuaded, at least."

"I expect she's right. They say there's often been trouble in the past round the Academies – brothers, fathers, friends. Like us, of course."

"Why does Limber do this?" said Hereward, and when Jacky offered no response, continued: "And Astolat? You fought in full battles to stop her coming here." Kit was listening carefully.

"No, there were deaths around Ingastowe all right, though not many to do with Astolat, only those that were up near the estuary. There were others that morning in the fort, but different reasons. No one liked the Matrix's rules and regulations. Little ships, impositions like that. Anyway, we were just making our deaths equal with theirs, one of the river people for one bluecoat. Nobody had to be there, remember. Now I'm here to look after my sister and though she's far from home she's learned a lot, so that seems equal too."

Those of the others who had grown interested in the conversation nodded in agreement. Every land in the Matrix suzerainty had come to accept as naturally as they accepted breathing that the exertion of power must have an equal and opposite reaction. The Twisted People were inclined to mock this principle, its application being clearly denied to them, yet acknowledged it in so far as their own special gifts appeared to be a compensation for and consequence of powerlessness. Martin had once spoken of this to Sammy, the shrewd young Companion, who had suggested that the repression of Martin's folk no longer had any explanation other than to isolate a valuable pool of talent rather than let it disperse into the general population. "The laws of genetics work," said Sammy, "and they don't vary. They're familiar and fair, no favourites, like the outside of God. You have to like gods who aren't slippery."

When Martin said, "That's not much consolation for us," Sammy had smiled and agreed.

The eggs Kit cooked were tasty and the melons sweet. The breeze came in through the windows with a tang of cedar and pepper. The city hummed to itself gently, sounds too homely to notice: wooden wheels, children's voices, chickens clucking, a jingle of keys. Hereward was ready to move. He had never really wondered if the footmarks of cause-effect-cause would not be there to pursue. Sometimes children paddling in a clear stream and tempted to find its source imagine they will find a limpid spring bubbling from some rock cleft and later are disappointed to find themselves wading through wide leaves and fleshy roots, mud sucking their feet. But this quest had always pointed to Limber, not muddying itself, springing surely from the wishes and works of the rectors. The question of why he left in abeyance. If, as Jacky guessed, the Matrix needed to recruit brilliant minds then that was not a difficulty of any sort. He doubted if there could be a 'why' that would delay him for a moment. This was no matter of pursuing the lightning to demand why it struck where it did.

It was still early in the morning when four of them set off towards St Xavier's. Hereward had asked Jacky's assistance, Kit had attached herself to them, knowing this had to be part of the Tyr legend, and Alvin Costello walked a few yards behind them. His eyes flickered searching for any unlikely movement in the street's activities. The grass-stem that sways into the wind instead of with it suddenly focuses the kite's wide gaze. Hereward had queried Costello's presence but acquiesced in it when Lee and Lucas had said, "Andre-Leander would wish it."

XL

Jacky liked St Xavier's cathedral. He liked the moment when the heavy door opened as he pushed and let him see through a dusky curtained arch into a cool expanse full of blue and green light that made the chancel opalescent, as if in some undersea gallery. Beyond the clusters of marble pillars, cut in a creamy stone with swirls of violet, opened out the great airy space beneath the central dome. Here there were seats, many of them, but almost unnoticed in such a vastness. From the high windows the light came down in shafts and beams, dancing on the floor so that the shiny grey and black flagstones responded with unexpected tints of copper and bronze, even glints of mica. A flash of admiration for the ancient architects and builders went through him, and he was pleased that Hereward, who rarely showed his feelings, clearly found the place impressive.

The rectors' big circular table was nowhere to be seen, there being no meeting due for several days, but Jacky thought of it with no pleasure. Those who customarily sat round it did so, it seemed to him, with too confident an assumption of their position, as if 'I who try to speak for you, salute you' was too glibly spoken. Also he felt patronised, very openly by Sheer and his supporters but also by those with whom he felt some sympathy, as if his presence there was some quirky by-play. He had the impression that his predecessor, Kopa, had been similarly regarded.

There were many people in the cathedral though its immensity swallowed them effortlessly. Among the visitors and worshippers and those who sought consolation or guidance the four of them mingled unnoticed, making their way to an opening that led past the cathedral's chapter-house to its library. Jacky doubted that the information Hereward sought would be found there. As he often did he glanced down at Kit to see if she had any ideas, but her attention was elsewhere. She had her old sharp demeanour, quite different from the dreaminess that lately she had lapsed into, even on occasions letting him win arguments. Now she was like the red fox again, putting her feet down so neatly that had there been snow there she would have left paw-marks, making her way towards a man standing alone leaning a shoulder against a pillar. For want of anything better to do they drifted after her and Jacky recognised Alexis Kopa, the previous rector of the Steps. Hereward too came over, while Costello circled them at a distance and watched for someone who was untouched by the mystery of the place.

"Alexis, are we interrupting you?" asked Jacky.

"No, I often come here just to think," replied the other. "But my thoughts are always the same so it's not really an interruption, is it?"

"Would you like to talk about it?"

"No. I think how I've wasted my life. Self-pity. Forget it."

"But," Kit protested, "you were a rector. You would have done lots for the people of the Hundred Steps." She watched Alexis closely with her luminous green fox-eyes.

"I suppose so, but I didn't need to be a rector to do that. Whenever we sat round the big table in here I don't think my opinion counted at all. Or when it did matter the question we were discussing didn't matter. Same thing, really." He smiled at them and nodded his head towards Hereward. An interesting face, he was thinking to himself, the black eye-patch attracting your attention first, of course, then the beaked nose and hollow cheeks framed in longish black hair, features alert with both attention and intention. In Alexis's experience he had come to divide people into two types, those whose energy pressed outwards into the space around them so that you had to respond strongly or be overshadowed, and those who made no such demands, their energy being internally resolving or resolvable. Hereward and, to an extent, Kit, he placed in the first group, Jacky in the second.

"You must have voted in some big decisions," said Hereward casually.

"Yes, I did." Alexis noted the casualness.

"Which do you most think back on?"

"Many. They tend to fade, of course, but the Fence, naturally, since we wanted no more Lamoraks, and the Outlands, the Companions. There were renewals of old edicts, but important ones, about the sea for instance, size of ships, restricted trade and so on. The Twisted Folk – " Alexis made a bow towards Kit.

She was unable to resist predicting Hereward's question. "The Academies? The children from the Outlands?"

"Certainly," replied Alexis, frowning slightly. Knowing of Astolat he had expected Jacky, if anyone, to raise the point. "The Matrix thought it needed to acquire all the creative minds it could. The principle is sound." Alexis did not like the look of the one-eyed man, who had just muttered words to himself that did not sound at all like agreement. "Of course," he went on, "we didn't really need them. There were always plenty who wanted an education."

"So you voted against it?" said Kit.

"Certainly. Whenever it came up. It was always more trouble than it was worth."

"How many times did you vote on it?"

"Three. To scrap it as a policy, that is."

"You proposed scrapping it, every time, didn't you?" Of course he did, she thought. He was so easy to understand. Like Jacky. Time for decisions, time for revisions, the gods' own chosen people.

"Yes. How did you guess?"

"Whose idea was it in the first place to recruit the children?"

Kit was amused by the mild voice. She had found she could feel Hereward's thoughts irregularly as if they existed in an adjacent room with a door that opened and shut for no reason. At present it was open.

"Look," said Alexis. "I'm not a rector now, but I wasn't altogether ashamed of what I did when I was one. As I said it didn't amount to much, but I tried to represent the Steps properly. As far as I know there are no records of how we argued out our decisions. But I always kept an appointment book and I usually wrote down who voted for what, not every time but always when it was close or I thought it was important. Probably the others did too." He smiled sadly, and addressed himself to Hereward: "I don't mind answering for my own decisions. That's why you're here, isn't it?"

"You didn't like the others much, did you?" inquired Kit, already knowing the answer.

"They were always polite enough. But imagine playing chess and your opponent makes moves that haven't any point that you can see. What do you think?"

"Well," said Hereward, who missed his games with Kay, "either they can't play, or else they are lots of moves ahead."

"My fellow rectors can play all right. Now if you come with me you can borrow my notebooks."

Alexis had been a rector for eight years and there were eight books, each small, each with a velvet and enamel cover, gilt edging on the pages and a tiny decorative lock. Hereward and Jacky started reading through them in the early afternoon and only finished as twilight was gathering. They had drawn one another's attention to various entries as many as twenty times. Often Kit and Martin came and looked over their shoulders, while Costello sat patiently at the window and watched the street. George Littler, Lee and Lucas arrived later and listened as excerpts were read to them. Six years ago Alexis had proposed an end to the academies' recruiting system. Of the ten rectors at that time eight still held the position. Jacky and Kit tried to describe them to the others, as Hereward pondered what he was uncovering.

"Osric Sheer," said Kit, "called me a misbegotten little harlot. Earlier he told me the Twisted Folk could be free and equal if Jacky would vote for peace. He wouldn't have kept his word. He is big and strong, the sort who would bully the Children. I do not like him at all."

Hereward smiled at her. "So I gather. Anyway he voted with Alexis." He showed Kit the page; the names were in a long column in order of voting, those in favour underlined. She stared at it.

"It nearly got passed. Five–four, one abstention. And, wait a minute, look, Jacky. Novak voted against repealing it. Does that surprise you?"

"Yes, but look at this other book, Kit. Two years later it all came up again, Alexis proposing to remove the policy again. Now Novak has changed sides and supports Alexis."

"What about Sheer this time?"

"Still the same. Still agreeing with Alexis."

Lucas, whose attention had been caught, suggested that they find the third vote on the proposition. Hereward, finding the appropriate notebook, flipped through the pages.

"Sheer has changed," he announced. "Novak hasn't."

"Try the lady from the Archipelago. I think her name's Serafina." Jacky had liked her decisiveness in the war-peace debate.

"Against Alexis in the first debate," said Hereward.

"For in the second," Jacky read out.

"She's changed her mind. Against now." This from Lucas who had acquired the book from two years earlier.

"Try Colonna, Luke," suggested Jacky. "He's a newcomer to the council but he detests Sheer. He'll vote the opposite to Sheer, I'm certain."

Lucas laughed. "Wrong again. On the same side. Which rector are you looking for, Hereward?"

"I thought it would be someone who voted every time for taking the children, but there were none, so now it's harder to say. Here's someone who voted against Alexis the last two times. Hippolyta of Wild Horse Plains. Is that a woman's name?" What would Tyr-Hereward do now, Martin wondered, thinking of Lokietok's laughter, would he and Lokietok go to visit Hippolyta in the night? "Perhaps she has a little girl."

There was a moment of complete stillness as Martin, George and the cousins stared at Hereward, watching so carefully that they did not even blink, as if their eyes were stiffened with frost. "Don't say that," said Kit. "Her little girl's done nothing, assuming she has one."

"Adelie did nothing. And this Hippolyta's votes turned her into a mindless cripple. That's for sure."

"Let's eat." Lucas had little appetite for where Hereward's argument seemed to be tending, but enjoyed the spicy variety of Limber's eating-places. "Makes a change from eating biltong." Lee and Costello were quick to agree, having often eaten nothing but the dried meat that the Companions chewed on for days on end. When Jacky said sternly that Astolat was to stay and do her homework she scowled, but eyed Alexis's notebooks. Their blue velvet made them tempting, like expensive toys. Still in the locks were the tiny brass keys. "And don't play with those books," he added.

They departed, leaving George behind to look after Astolat, even Jacky being content with George as guardian. Astolat was well satisfied. She had listened avidly to the discussion on the voting sequences and was longing to analyse them for herself. She had found fascinating her recent lessons on probability and hidden patterns, puzzling over the shape of the tide's ripples in the sand and the placement of leaves on branches. The books would be fun and George easy to cajole.

"I'm only just looking at them, George," she said, picking the top one off the pile, reminding him of the fluffy, scuttling partridge chicks that he used to rear, soft, feathery balls, but full of devouring purpose, hurrying about their pen pecking curiously at whatever took their fancy.

As the evening passed he enjoyed watching her. She soon had sheaves of lists, columns and ranks of names, interconnected with a web of lines, groups in circles that intersected other circles that isolated other names in the lens segment. Then she had brought in thirty pebbles, got out her paint-box and put dabs of different colours on them. "Black for Sheer," she murmured. "Cream for Serafina." She had watched the Council in the cathedral and easily remembered each rector. "Grey for the grey-haired man, blue for Michael Novak who lives near the sea." The pebbles were arranged into groups and rearranged repeatedly. She tried to make a probability curve with Alexis at one end, though with no one voting three times against Alexis this idea led her nowhere.

Astolat used her lessons. Knowing that if you asked why a glass was half empty you could ask not only why it was half full but also why it was not either empty or full. George was sent out for more pebbles and questioned until his head spun.

"There has to be a pattern, George, so where is it?"

"Why does there have to be?"

Astolat was tempted to answer 'because' or 'because Sister Francesca says so' but instead replied, "Well, George, they are thinking before they vote. Thinking has a direction, it isn't just random, like rolling dice, and it isn't like a seesaw, which hasn't got a real direction. If I find the pattern it will be an arrow pointing somewhere."

"Like Alexis always voting the same?"

"Yes, George."

"Isn't that a direction, then?"

"I think it's too small a sample, only one rector out of eleven on one topic showing a pattern."

"What about another topic? More, if you need more clues on how they think."

Astolat was full of approval. "We've tried the voters, now let's try the questions." Pebbles were dabbed with blue for sea questions, green for forests, and ochre for the Twisted Folk, as that was the nearest Astolat's paints could get to the colour of Kit's hair. But whichever question she chose the pebbles refused to remain grouped or in sequences that she could seize upon. The rectors seemed not to have long-term or even coherent views at all, never voting unanimously and changing their sides and minds capriciously. Although this only encouraged Astolat, who had no liking for easy solutions and had learned that the more mystifying the flux the more shapely would be the underlying arrangement, it did not prevent George insisting that she go to bed. She departed with admonishments that she would not be able to sleep, and was asleep five minutes later. When the others returned it was to find George trying hard to avoid taking a step which might disturb pages of drawings and trains of pebbles punctuated with brightly coloured feathers and leaves, and trying to decide which knives and spoons were part of Astolat's project and which could simply be washed. The debris was left to wait for the next morning, George having tried to explain its purpose, though Jacky, with his seaman's neat frugality in the use of small spaces, was tempted to sweep it all up.

Long after the others had fallen asleep Jacky and Kit spoke together. He confessed that many concerns were weighing on him, his care for Astolat, and the dangerous unpredictability of Hereward and Lokietok, the hopes of the Twisted Folk and the coming of the Daroi, his own inaction and, though he did not say so directly, his dreams for him and her together.

He tried to explain the difference between his present set of problems and being at sea by night at the helm of one of his father's trawlers. Out there was the wind and the tide and currents each tugging a different way with the backwash off the rocks to consider and the eddies round the promontories, as well as the keel not gripping enough and the gravel ballast shifted, all vectoring in his head.

And that had been easy, he told her, you just let your feet feel the deck sway, your face chill to tell you the wind's shifts, listen to the water under the bow, don't think about one factor because then you neglect the others. "My brother, Andread, told me to be calm and trust my mind to think for me. I asked him, 'If I'm not my mind who am I?'"

"What did he say, Jacky?"

"He said he would tell me when he'd worked it out for himself."

Kit told him that it was easier than he made it seem, that his mind was inside his head but he was both there and elsewhere too, for in his ship there were the planks that touched his feet and the wooden wheel in his hands, and on him the wind's cold breath, and these were all made of the same atoms as his brain and his body, and where did one atom end and another begin? She said that there was no boundary and that all things were part of one another. She reminded him again of the windy nights with the black sea muttering to him that there were sandbanks ahead, still half a mile, said the sea, be ready but don't turn just yet. "You would know what to do, and when to do it out there," she said. "This is no different. Let the moment come."

"What if I go wrong?"

"If you went wrong on your trawler the sea and the wind and the ship would miss you, be sure of that," said Kit. "They tried to tell you, after all. And we are part of them, we gave them their names."

"'How could we leave them, Lord, you know, you are no way to walk alone.' Like the hymn, you mean?" Jacky said tentatively for he was still unsure of Kit's perceptions.

"Exactly right, Jacky. How could we go and walk alone in the sight of the Lord? How could we bear to meet God without the others? We'll all be there, the ox and the ass, the dragonfly and the whale, the peony and the pennyroyal, the water and the wine. And the whole idea of the world, the many gods, they'll need to be there too."

"The many gods?"

"Of course," said Kit. "The god who colours the rainbow, and the one who gives snow coldness, and you and I, we're all in this together."

So, just before they went to sleep the girl from the hollow chamber by the side of the beck tried to tell the young man from the lonely village on the estuary how she loved him. Being both shy and modest and far more conscious than he of their different backgrounds she spoke to him of elevated themes, and he, being diffident conversing of such matters, could not speak his deepest wish and say, 'I will come with you walking in the sight of the Lord.' So she did not put her shyness aside and tell him that she had waited for him for a billion years and more and that if he was to get lost somewhere in the unimaginable future then she would search for ever until she found him.

Though all woke early the next morning Astolat was up before them. She had let the puzzle of the voting lie in her brain all night, even dreaming of the pebbles, until she grew impatient and lit a candle and went into the garden to speak to Hereward, who was sleeping there. In the grey light she placed him among the pebbles and asked many questions, all the while consulting the eight books one after another.

Their conversation woke Jacky who was put through the same catechism, though neither he nor Hereward felt much instructed by it. Astolat was puffed up with enjoyment, but decided to have one more test, so Alvin Costello had his breakfast interrupted. He seemed to her a good choice, as she reasoned, incorrectly, that the cousins might tease her, that George would chiefly be interested in questions on plants and forests, and she did not call on Kit and Martin, assuming, correctly this time, that on Matrix politics they would be prejudiced. As Costello answered her questions she gave several small cries of "Good, Alvin", then fetched a broom, swept all the decorations into a heap, locked the notebooks with a flourish and dusted her hands together, thereby pronouncing the problem manifestly solved.

After a few moments, when no one could bear the waiting any longer, Jacky had to speak: "Would you like some breakfast now?"

"Or would you like to tell us first what you have worked out?" Kit asked, sympathetically.

"I'll do both together," Astolat said majestically, so boiled eggs were brought and salt put in a small pile on her plate and toast alongside it. Lucas volunteered to crack her eggs for her. "I'm not a baby," she said sternly, and between mouthfuls of egg and toast and gulps of milk demonstrated she was one of her Academy's brightest pupils. The story took a while to develop as Astolat felt there were points to prove, such as that she could not have reached any conclusion had George made her go to bed inappropriately early, as her brother had misguidedly suggested. However when she reached her conclusions she had only rapt attention.

"So you see," she pressed on, "there is no pattern in the voting, or at least in almost all of it. But there has to be, because the questions are important, I think, and the rectors always reached a decision, and something always happened as a result. So they have directed the Matrix. I know because they directed for me to be brought here."

"And many other children," Jacky could not help remarking. "Would you like some more milk?" he added, sensing a hitch in the flow of speculation, for Astolat seemed inclined to stop and debate this fact.

"Before I was interrupted, Jacky, I was saying that there must be a direction in the rectors' decisions. They must make sense. Because if they make sense then they make a shape or design. Even if they were random they would make a distribution curve. That's when – "

"We know that bit," said Kit gently.

"Well, there isn't even one of those. Ten votes on the Children, three times, that's thirty votes, and only one rector votes against the idea all the time. According to the curve there should be another rector always for it. That's not much on its own, but it happens all the time. They all change their minds on everything, but not in any sequence that makes a pattern. Not even voting in groups or with friends."

"Are you sure?" Kit was trying to recall who had attended the grey-haired rector's party, apart from Sheer.

"Yes, I'm sure. But there is something interesting. Alexis votes differently. I can always guess the way he'll vote, and so can Jacky and Hereward and Alvin. But they can't do it with anyone else. Nor can I. So, now I've got the pattern, sort of. I knew there had to be one. Sister Francesca said so."

There was a pause, everyone gazing at her. "Well, what is it?" asked her brother, unsure whether any conclusion had been reached.

"The pattern's been removed somehow, or disguised," said Astolat confidently. "Deliberately removed. The votes that Alexis wrote down can't be real, except his own, which are predictable. I suppose they let him think at the time that the others were real, but they weren't. The real pattern was probably nine for, one against, at least whenever Alexis disagreed. No one particularly seems to want decisions taken, yet no one disagrees on a regular basis. But the rectors must know why this is happening, except Alexis, and Jacky just lately. So the pattern is that they're all in it together, but they don't want anyone else to know. That's what I think anyway."

XLI

The cousins looked at the big stone wall. It was solid and ten feet high, but here and there softened with moss and patched with lichens, clumps of ivy clinging to it and butterfly cocoons in the crevices. Where mortar had flaked and crumbled there were finger-holds between the stones. With a glance up and down the roadway that lay on their side of the wall, and seeing no one, Lee climbed on to Lucas's shoulders and pulled himself to the top. The coping was level and wide, easy for him to lie flat and reach down for Lucas's hands and pull him up. Then came Costello, Hereward, Jacky, Kit and lastly, with a struggle, Lokietok was hauled up, all then crouching and looking across fruit trees, glasshouses, a tangle of shrubs and an expanse of lawn. To their left the wall skirted a tall stone house, many-balconied with, dimly outlined against the stars, a parapet on which stood statues and stone urns.

The night was warm and moonless, and the cousins quivered with happy anticipation. Hereward and Jacky felt the same sensations but less intently, being occupied with their purposes, but to the cousins it was simply delightful.

Down from the wall they scrambled, Hereward steering Lokietok clear of crackly undergrowth. Two of the windows went dark; perhaps the occupants were going to sleep for it was almost midnight. Now they were standing in front of the house on the soft turf. Pricks of light bobbed out on the sea, mirrored by a wavering glimmer of fireflies under the nearby trees. Lee and Lucas disappeared to return a few minutes later, having walked silently round the house peering into the unlit lower windows. "It's almost empty," they said. "No furniture, no curtains, and a lot of boxes at the back. Perhaps they're leaving."

"Someone's there," Costello remarked.

"There'll be carts along soon for the boxes. We'll go in now," said Jacky. He laughed quietly, turning to Kit: "Better than our last visit, anyway." They climbed a flight of steps to the front porch. The door opened at Hereward's touch, reminding him of a night in Hay church with eye-fluids dripping down his cheek. He was pleased with the memory, which was still stingingly clear and bursting with power.

"Why didn't we make an appointment?" asked Lucas. "Don't forget to brush your shoes, Lokietok."

They stepped into a high hallway that faced a wide staircase, and paused to listen. From somewhere above came hints of movement and then barely audible voices. They were halfway up the stairs when the voices became loud and clear, quick footsteps echoed towards them along the floor above, and swaying shadows appeared in the light of a carried lamp. The two figures taking the first step down almost collided with Lucas, and saw the others a solid phalanx behind him. It was the grey-haired rector, Jacky recalled his name as Radic, and Osric Sheer.

"What are you doing in my house?" Radic's voice was loud and indignant.

"Just visiting," said Lucas. Hereward came forward past Lucas, coming level with the two rectors, staring in their faces, trying to see if there was anything there that connected them with a young girl kicked senseless a thousand miles away.

When Radic shouted, "Get out of my house!" Hereward punched him in the stomach, the blow throwing him back against the wall where he crouched doubled up and gulping for breath. "You'll answer for this," he gasped, and Hereward dragged him upright and hit him heavily in the mouth so that he fell and lay on the polished wooden floor.

"Come on," said Lucas. "Is this what we're here for?"

"It's what I'm here for." Hereward had not taken his eyes off the rectors. "I don't know about you."

"Let's get into one of these rooms," Costello's soft voice said. "Give them a chance to talk. Isn't that the idea?"

In a sense that was what they had suggested. No one that morning had been quite sure about Astolat's logic. Watching her cheerful, dimpled face, and listening to her squeaky voice had been diversions in themselves, and her having a woolly toy dog on her pillow was no less distracting for her audience. Yet Kit had said, after Astolat had departed for the Academy, that it made perfect sense to her. She reminded them of how the rectors she had bargained with in St Xavier's chapter-house had selves that protected their thoughts, not so much behind shielding shells, as did crabs and woodlice, but concealed by many layers of disguising thought, hidden as cleverly as the larvae that hide in the froth of cuckoo-spit.

The first room off the landing was bare except for a cupboard and a bedstead no one had bothered to remove. "So what do you want to talk about?" said Osric Sheer. He spoke straight to Hereward, almost with contempt.

"We'd like to know which one of you we should beat into a crippled halfwit. One for one. The customary and even-handed justice of the Matrix – and as rectors you will support this."

Sheer shrugged: "I am certain neither of us has ever beaten anyone as you say. Where is the justice, please?"

"I had a friend," said Hereward, "just a little girl, really. She was very clever, so you sent men to bring her to Limber. When she was afraid they hit her head on the stones. Now she doesn't even know her own name."

"I voted against forcing children here."

"Twice, Sheer. Once for."

"How do you know that?"

"Never mind."

Through bruised lips, Radic said thickly, "I never agreed with it."

"Then it's a pity you voted for it. Twice."

"Voting for it doesn't mean I completely agreed with it."

There was a moment's silence and a few frosty smiles. Costello put it into words: "Lots of moves ahead, Astolat, isn't she?"

Jacky shook his head admiringly: "Even if she calls the knights 'unicorn-horses'."

"Well," said Hereward impatiently. "Who is it going to be? I wish it could be everyone who voted, but one for one is justice. Hurry up, or Lokietok can choose."

"Lokietok? Is that what you call it?" Sheer seemed more defiant than Radic. "Poor miserable wretch. Hasn't the creature enough to endure without you dragging it around?"

Cell	*Bars*	*Bowl*
Bucket	*Brush*	*Stick*
Bruise	*Hereward*	*Air*

Lokietok flung images around the room, that were neither quite word nor simulation, as bats are not quite bird or beast. "Choose!" said Hereward. "Whoever it is goes in the next room with me. More than you deserve. Adelie had less chance with two full-grown men, wouldn't you say?"

"Please," said Radic, "not me."

"It had better be me then," said Osric Sheer. He was as big as Hereward. "Come on. You don't bother me."

They walked out together and the others heard the door to the next room open and close. No one spoke, and in the silence they caught new sounds from far outside the house, a formless shouting and a crackle like fireworks. Lee opened a window to hear more clearly and what looked like firelight was flickering down near the harbour, which the window overlooked. Then the noise in the other room began, a rolling, irregular succession of muffled thumps and crashes, hoarse voices, what sounded like wood splintering, and they felt the wooden floor vibrate underfoot. A brief pause and it resumed, this time with falling glass and sobbing grunts. The silence that eventually followed allowed them again to hear the noises from the city and see yellow flames leaping nimbly in distant tree-tops. Lokietok snarled and gibbered, and the images began to transfuse with energy, the room full not so much of sketchy bats as of vultures, colliding with the walls, making men duck away.

The door opened and Hereward came in. There were scratches on his face, blood coming both from his mouth and from between the stitches around his eye, and he held his arms crossed over his stomach as if hugging something invisible. "Lokietok. Please." He gestured to the other room, miming pulling something. The giant did not hesitate, reappearing within moments dragging Sheer casually behind, as easily as if he had been a feather bolster. "Nearly finished. You see Adelie fought hard too and then was kicked senseless. Martin saw it."

"He already is senseless," observed Jacky.

"Yes, but Adelie was brain-damaged too. Anyone in Hay will tell you."

"God almighty, Hereward," Lucas said. "Has it come to this?"

"This is the law of the Matrix that everyone understands. Besides, it was a child. I only want Sheer to pay his dues. Then Radic owes the Dorns for Astolat and maybe for Andread."

Radic took one look at Jacky and would have tried to run but Lokietok was filling the door-frame, arms swinging like an enraged gorilla. "Now, Radic, sit on that bed. Alvin, turn out all the lights," Jacky instructed. "We don't want visitors. Radic, I'm a rector as well as you, so you will answer us, or else explain to Lokietok."

Perhaps Sheer would not have told them, but not since Radic was a small boy had anyone even cuffed him. He was frightened and bewildered after Hereward had knocked him down. He had come to believe he enjoyed pressure and the cut and thrust of spirited, even spiteful, argument, but previously the width of a table and the etiquette of discussion had always protected him. Now the issues and propositions, the themes and theses, were so close he could see in the dim light the gleam of their eyes, feel their breath warm on him, sniff the leathery-dusty smell of them, hear their feet shift and tunics scrape down their bare arms.

"You know me, don't you?" Kit held her glove in her good hand, her paw was on Radic's cheek, and she flexed the claws just as you extend your fingers round an apple. "Of course you do. I'm the misbegotten little harlot you threw out of your party. Now tell us what goes on with you rectors. No shield over the mind, yes, I know about that. It's one of the advantages of being misbegotten. Let us start with the shield. It is new to me. Which of the rectors have it?"

"I don't know."

"Move the shield," said Kit.

"I can't."

Kit edged her claws up just beneath the rector's eye, and let them pierce the skin, tugging down so that Radic's eye widened. "Once again. Without the shield. One more lie, one less eye. How many others have it like you?"

"All but one," said Radic.

"Better," said Kit. "And is that one Jacky now, and Alexis before him?"

"Yes." The questions went on, probing and searching as the others fretted and gazed out of the windows to where the fires were higher now. Kit found herself fumbling as if she were in a vast underground complex of caves, dark in the caverns and serpentine tunnels, not knowing if she could ever find a secret door up to the sun and air. The man's thoughts sprang from sources so unfamiliar to her that she found it difficult to make sensible assumptions, and Radic gradually seemed more at ease. Only the shield questions had really perturbed him, so she renewed that topic, as if idly.

"So just the rectors have the shield, you said. I wonder how you do it."

"I don't know, it's like breathing."

She sensed both that this was true, and how much Radic disliked where this line of questioning might lead. "So you have it and we don't . . ." She was still fishing, still watching his nerves move under his skin, but knowing she had not yet asked the right question. When she did it was simply a rhetorical question: "So who are you?"

Radic was very still and she knew at once he hated the question, and then Sheer, still only semi-conscious, sat up in his pain and shouted, "Don't tell her!"

And that was it. Often in the past Matrix men and women had fumbled towards the question, but in Radic's villa the contingencies and the people had all come together, pulling at the answer as if they had been planets in alignment.

XLII

My dearest father,

Whether my letters or Astolat's reach you I cannot tell. Perhaps not, for we have never heard from you. I have so much to tell you and I do not know the order of its importance, so I will let you work that out.

First of all, Astolat and I are both well. She has not been treated unkindly here, but I shall bring her home soon. I have written of this in my earlier letters but, briefly, she enjoys her schooling and, of course, lives with me. We rent rooms near the centre of this great city.

Secondly, and again I have written before of this, I have become a rector of the Council of the Matrix. One of the rectors resigned and asked me to take his place. Why he chose me and not any one of thousands of others I don't understand, but as you used to tell me, that was what the hooked fish said. I will say more of these rectors later in my letter.

Thirdly, and I have not mentioned this before, I hope to marry when we return. Her name is Kit. She comes from Hay, not so far from our home, about fifty miles I think. Her brother is also here with her. One day, when all this is over, I would like to bring her home to meet you. She is not like our mother but in some ways like Astolat. You will like her.

Now for some very different news. It is so strange that I can hardly believe it myself, but it is true enough. I cannot write about how it all happened as it would take many thousands of words, but some of my friends and I discovered that the other rectors, there are nine apart from me, are not real people at all. They are all Unmen, from Regret, I suppose, or wherever the Unmen live. Not only that but they claim that back through the ages this has always been so; we have always been ruled by Unmen. Writing it like this I can hardly expect you to believe it either, but the Unmen themselves do not deny it – for we have someone from whom they cannot conceal their true selves. They have been put under guard while it is decided what to do with them.

I know what will go through your mind, that it was the wish of the Unmen that our ships should be so small that the waves were able to take Andread. You are right to think so, and it is my duty to remember that they used their powers in this way. I shall not forget.

These Unmen are rightly so called. When they came into the world, who knows? Perhaps when the Twisted Folk came, back in the Broken Years, but they are far different from us. When we ask them why they wish to be our overseers they laugh and say that is the way things are, that there are always rulers and ruled. They say that we men and women of the Matrix, and the Daroi invaders too, have got our noses so close to the ground we can no more be expected to look after ourselves than the simple sheep and rabbits, and even if we remove them other Unmen will take their place. They are insolent.

How strange the world is. I know I shall never learn a millionth part of what there is to learn in it, but I hope one day to make you proud of me. I did not say that the one who can see into minds is my friend Kit. So you see she is a very talented girl indeed. Say hello from me to everyone in the village and the boys on the trawlers. I hope this reaches you so that you will know I am, always,

Your loving and affectionate son,
John Dorn

XLIII

The night that Sheer and Radic were discovered to be Unmen was a wild night across the city of Limber. Though the main body of the Daroi still lay from one to five days' journey south, the leading waves of the nomads were moving fast and carelessly, excited by the prospects ahead, the adventure of the new and the exaltation of the eye, for Limber promised them enticing novelties in awesome abundance. Like the band of Frick and his fellows, those who reached the city first, days ahead of the family groups, were the young and challenging.

A push in the street, a perceived insult from a Limber girl, an apple picked off a barrow – the petty abrasions mounted and the powder keg was awaiting the match. No one recorded who lit it or where. Probably in an atmosphere saturated with crossed purposes, the combustion to violence came more or less simultaneously and independently in ten or twenty places.

As darkness fell fires began to blaze and looting started. The Limber militia were not called out by their marshal but many of them were impatient for this moment, and the Steps provided a natural rallying point, their steep rises, honeycomb terraces, blind walls and secret accesses making them a haven for street-fighters but forbidding to strangers. As the night wore on the militia grew more and more organised and confident and the Daroi casualties began to mount.

About midnight the Limber scouts searching for a rector found Jacky. He was rushed to an assignation with the marshal at the arsenal under the Steps among the old granaries and reservoirs carved into the rock.

The marshal, hoping to reconvene the rectors, and clinging on to legality like a waterlogged buoy which he would prefer to drown with sooner than abandon, heard the news of the Unmen's long domination of the Council with amazement. Though at first he expressed considerable doubt he became convinced, not least when faced by the vituperation of Sheer, snarling, "Of course I'm an Unman, as you call us in your puerile way, you buffoon." When the marshal explained that the militia were dying for lack of effective weapons only for Sheer to reply, "More fools they," he lost his patience. Now he wanted only Jacky's approval, quickly given, and the arsenals were opened and soon his men were volley-firing in the streets. Before daylight the Daroi, bloodied and infuriated, had been driven back on to the western ridges, from where they sent outraged messages winging back to their various clans.

The Marshal of the Southern Matrix, and traditionally the city was regarded as part of the south, Amalrik the Younger, was so called to distinguish him from his father, who had also served as a marshal for a few months, his grave some anonymous ridge beyond the south-eastern frontier. The young Amalrik had hoped for the position, had read of the great days and the old struggles, saddened that he seemed in this interest as old-fashioned as his books. Long before the Matrix had voted for peace he had kept in touch with his young captains and with both Kittiwake and Merganser. Amalrik was forty years old and believed in the Matrix dream with every fibre of his being. He felt his moment had come even before his men found Jacky. The news of the Unmen was strange indeed, and perhaps made his moment more momentous, but he was not one to flinch.

Jacky had not come alone through the tunnels and reservoir pipes. Not only was he accompanied by his comrades of that evening but they brought with them Radic and the battered Sheer, whom Amalrik knew well by sight having seen both at such debates of the Council as he had attended. Once convinced of the alien nature of the two rectors, he sent orders for the arrest of every other rector that could be found. Three more were brought in before day dawned, and the questioning went on without a break, the interrogators using Kit relentlessly to verify the answers. Her face grew papery-pale, her skin tight across the cheek-bones and her eyes dilated, the mental confrontations sapping her energies, feeling as besiegers might if asked to scale a castle wall not once but repeatedly in the same night. Jacky stood beside her, often holding her hand. Name after name emerged and all were men and women who held authority in Limber or beyond. The names of those who lived more than a day's journey away were simply noted, but those within reach were gathered in, among them bishops, teachers, orators, merchant-princes, financiers and holders of great estates.

Morning came and Amalrik's troops braced themselves for the Daroi onslaught. A strange sight was abroad in the city: scores of blue and gold banners flapped and tugged in the wind above each level of the Steps, drawing to them a mass of unexpected volunteers. The war-peace debate in St Xavier's had misled many observers into believing that the demand for peace was a desire for appeasement. In some cases that may have been true, but there were many who wholeheartedly desired peace yet baulked at buying off the Daroi ferocity with their children's freedom. They who cherished that deepest impulse of the Matrix, so deep it was genetic, that they would not suffer any but the least exertion of power upon their lives.

So the marshal's ranks grew full, ranging from the very young who had never worn the blue jackets, to the veterans who had worn them among the strange lands and wild people beyond the southern and eastern frontiers. More came from the countryside around and others on small ships that slipped into the bays of Limber.

Amalrik moved quickly to shore up the city's defences. The Daroi coming from the south and west would have the advantage of the high ground and would fight downhill towards the sea, but if the city could keep its hold on the sea it could not be surrounded. There was no record in Matrix history of any city, and certainly not a great one, under assault, save possibly Lamorak's attack on Regret, the true story of which had never been told. Yet in the far distant past, before the Broken Years, great cities had turned on their attackers and often fought to the death with a consuming fury. If it was its people's last stronghold, and defeat meant the enemy would violate the women and enslave the children, then often a city would die as a pyre that burnt and soaked its name into history with fire and blood.

The Daroi knew nothing of this, and would not have cared had they known, but they needed time to bring up their long columns and Limber had four days' respite to prepare itself. In those four days, as the people learned of the nature of their rectors, the support for Amalrik swelled. A thousand tasks needed to be done, but the citizens spared neither themselves nor the city. In the outer suburbs a defence line of half-demolished houses and barricades of debris was constructed, with a fallback line inside it, then another and then the natural fortification of the spine of densely populated rocky ridge that made up the Steps. Amalrik put together an inner council of advisers, each one being inspected by Kit lest an Unman try to infiltrate, for now reports of the Unmen were spreading wide, and Sheer's remark about the Matrix folk being rabbits was becoming a rallying-cry in itself. In the days ahead 'Come on, the rabbits!' would drive the blue regiments into desperate counter-attacks. Jacky – 'The last rector of Limber' as he was called by Kit and sometimes by Amalrik – was a natural leader, the people of the Steps eager to be near him, but there were other more surprising ones, such as Alexis, whose knowledge of the city was invaluable. Jacky wished to involve Hereward but the latter was in one of his inward moods, spending much of his time with Lokietok. Martin was afraid that the Twisted Folk had been forgotten now the Glassy Country was left behind.

Late on the fourth day the city was unexpectedly reinforced by the Companions who, having hung on the flank of the main Daroi migration for several days, had swung right round Limber with their rapid marching and entered along the northern beaches which the Daroi had not yet sealed off. Nearly two thousand strong, they came like a wish come true to Amalrik, and the people of the city welcomed them with overflowing hospitality. Townsend and Schroeder were equally welcome additions to the council. Andre-Leander, hearing for the first time of the Unmen, frowned. "Has anyone asked them why they are here?" he said.

"Yes, often," he was told, "but either they don't understand the question or say they have always been here and that it would be chaos without them."

"They are strange," said Jacky, "and even Kit often cannot tell what they think. She says that they hide their thoughts from her. She can recognise that and we've learned to deal with it, but they also hide some from themselves."

"Just as well," said Townsend. "Otherwise they would be like Lokietok. Probably the poor creature lacks this shield and cannot dismiss his deepest thoughts. Since they seem to have sent him mad, perhaps it is just as well we can't share them. How many are there here?"

"About forty."

"One's enough."

The next day the Daroi assault on Limber began in earnest.

XLIV

Forty days later any bird bold enough to fly overhead could have easily observed the position of the city's defenders. It was shaped like a thumb extruded stiffly from the hand. The outline of the thumbnail was the walled part of Limber, with St Xavier's cathedral in the centre of the nail. The bone leading back to the palm was the ridge of the Steps climbing back to the transverse cols and crests that overlooked the city from the west. The thumb was smoking along the outline and the area stretching away from its sides was a hazy vista of charred and ruined buildings.

Amalrik had laid down that at all costs the access to the sea was to be kept open, and the little ships of the Matrix had responded gallantly to the call. The Daroi could only watch frustrated as the ships brought men and food and carried away those who did not wish to stay or were asked to go. Amalrik had expected many to leave, for the tumultuous scenes in the cathedral were not many days in the past, yet there were few who chose to depart. Prompted by Jacky, Amalrik sent messengers to the Glassy Country to say that all of the Twisted Folk were to have full and equal rights within the Matrix lands. Kit told Jacky approvingly that he was a proper rector.

A feeling was abroad that its defining hour had come for Limber and the Matrix. The knowledge of the Unmen and of how they had always directed, however inconspicuously, much of the life of the people, and of their removal, had kindled a reaction of 'let's see what we can do without them', an upwelling of energy and opportunity.

Many images contributed but one clear and potent was the sight of one of the sea-gypsies' towering carracks, its masts lifting tall above the sea-walls, its lacquered sides striped black and gold and white, an elegant ship that boldly took its sailors wherever there was water to float its keel. "Our old rectors said we were only fit to sail little drifters and coasters more suitable for rivers and lagoons." The great ship took to their distant homes many of the Children, and the small Outlander ships brought volunteer fighters, one being Jacky's younger brother Magnus, and took others away, including Astolat. She wept when she last saw Jacky, his pale yellow hair making him easy to see on the harbour wall.

Few of the women of Limber would leave though Amalrik gave them every chance. Deep in his heart he was glad, knowing that his men would die rather than break with their women inside the perimeter. But being a marshal of the Matrix he himself fought whenever and wherever there was an assault on the defences, and he died under the flashing Daroi assegais on the twentieth day.

The battle had no variation. At night the Daroi withdrew and the clans reformed and replacements filled their ranks for the next morning's attack. The Limber militia occupied whatever buildings were sufficiently intact to provide shelter, loopholing the walls and barricading the streets and alleys to make as solid a front as they could. When daylight came the Daroi waves battered against that part of the front they had chosen, charging through the gunfire, the arrows and arbalest bolts, into the rooms, onto the roofs, down inside cellars, wherever they could fight hand to hand. Where the struggle was fiercest was a roaring noise like a giant blacksmith's shop, along with towering columns of smoke and dust, so that even the strongest hearts on both sides quailed as they drew nearer to the din. Towards evening no one could tell where the front line lay, so mixed were the antagonists, sharing streets, lanes, houses, floors, even rooms.

Cut off inside the only untaken house in a street Lee died on the twenty-fifth day. For the next seven nights Lucas smeared his face with charcoal and alone in the darkness stalked the Daroi encampments, until Urbano de Vito found out and forebade his forays.

There had been no question as to who should take Amalrik's place. To the people of the Steps Jacky was their own chosen one, carrying as he did the shadowy prestige of being the last rector. He bore a charmed life, and even the Daroi came to know him as the battle raged on; around their night fires one or another would boast that he had fought that day with the young chief of Limber. Jacky had tried to persuade Kit to leave in one of the Westermain ships, but she had laughed and not even bothered to reply. All day long she trembled when he was away, and when he finally fell asleep she drove every caller from the house.

Many of the Companions were placed in the Limber regiments to force them to adapt. The regiments, if they had their way, would fight in the open in line, shoulder to shoulder, keeping their riflemen safe behind a wall of swords, shields and bayonets. It took a terrible toll, not only in the dead and wounded but in the strain on minds. A regiment that fought this way was hardly ready to fight again for days. The Companions taught them other ways, so that the Daroi were denied the furious head-on slashing matches, and were drained by ambushes, booby-traps, falling masonry, and other pitfalls. At night the Companions patrolled the ruined areas, 'the night belongs to us' still being one of their axioms.

Sammy, brightest of the Companions' Children, died on the

twenty-ninth night, and the next day among the bayonets the sandman came for Jack Pudding the Patterman. The Daroi warrior who emptied his pockets was much intrigued by the figure of Punch.

The Companions persisted in attempting to parley, to convey the message that everyone could go fishing together if only the kings and commanders wished it. They intensified their attempts to eliminate the Daroi high chieftain, doing so on the ninth, twentieth and thirty-fifth days. As the Daroi became more conscious of this tactic they screened their overall leader and the tribal leaders with picked bodyguards and instigated their own hunt for the Matrix leadership, inevitably fixing before long on Jacky. Andre-Leander Townsend, nagged by Kit, took the precautions that kept him alive, ensuring that Costello and other marksmen as well as the wild company of Billy Scarlett were always around him. Kit begged Hereward to stay on one side of Jacky and place Lokietok on his other side. Whenever the Limber footmen held their ground or advanced in line they made a fearsome spectacle, though gradually the need grew less for the Daroi were not slow to acquire guns and bows and the blue regiments learned to dig and tunnel in response.

The Daroi dragged their dead out of the wrecked buildings and cremated them at night so that the sea-breeze was the only wind not to blow the smell across the city. The Matrix buried its dead in graveyards until every plot was full and then in gardens, though the fallen Companions were covered in ice and loaded on to the ships bound for Kittiwake Island. The wives and children on Kittiwake saw the ships come in with dread, the cadets with a sense of tremulous expectation, knowing that the higher rose the toll the sooner would Townsend send for them.

The fatigue of the days of close combat and the nights of work meant for most a deadening of thought. As the fortieth day passed few had time or energy to think past the wall or warehouse, trench or terrace, parapet or palazzo they had battled to hold. The Daroi were finding such advances as they made now measured in a few paces, and a counter-attack as often as not seized them back. As attackers and defenders alike began to develop a grudging mutual admiration the fighting was beginning to lose its virulence. Several of the clans were not slow to voice their discontent, particularly if their chieftains were at all unwilling to be first to close with the 'blue jackets'. The current El Daro himself also seemed to them to be not quite deep enough among the glittering bayonets. By the fiftieth day there was little activity and the two front lines were keeping a respectful distance apart.

Hereward was now spending more time with Sheer. In the violence of the events of the past weeks the Unmen had been largely left alone. Neither Jacky, nor Townsend, nor any of their advisers, had time or opportunity to interrogate them, and they stayed in a loose confinement in one of the big Academy buildings. Hereward came at night and his questioning wore Sheer down; though the Unman often lied behind his mind-shield he did not always bother to do so if the questions bored or did not threaten him. He occasionally referred to himself as a rector, though sometimes preferring the title of commissioner, which he implied better described his role. Hereward found the word intriguing, seeing it as a climber facing a cliff will consider various routes but discard them as unpromising or impossible and then choose one which at least has an early ledge or crack that may lead to higher possibilities.

'Whose commission do you hold?' looked an interesting handhold, and 'What was expected of a commissioner?' another. The first did not bear Hereward's weight of interest, Sheer refusing to answer, suggesting that it was too difficult rather than that he would not, but the second had better results.

"It was expected we would act as we saw fit," said Sheer, in one of his more open answers.

"And you saw fit to bring the cleverest children here? To the Academies?"

"Yes."

"Why?"

"Because it was expected of us," said Sheer.

Hereward was unsure whether he was being taunted; probably he was but he had a footing on the cliff-face. There was plenty of time. The Daroi certainly weren't going away.

"We'll have another talk soon," he said.

From the fifty-fifth to the sixtieth day the Daroi flung themselves at the city's defences with a fierce renewal of ardour. Jacky and his council could see no real reason for these fresh attacks, but on the fifty-eighth the Daroi broke through the line of the thumb at about the knuckle and now the defenders were split into two pockets, one centred round St Xavier's, the other along the higher Steps. The boundaries of the pockets were a confusion of cellars, vaults, storerooms, sumps and hollows, places where the bravest shuddered to go.

One of the few who, through the sewers and reservoirs, could navigate with messages between the pockets, Alexis Kopa, died down there on the fifty-ninth night. During the sixtieth day the Companions were shocked as the news came in that Andre-Leander Townsend had fallen in the lower enclave and both Franz Schroeder and Oyvindsen of Thule among the Academies. Up there Urbano de Vito, a few Companions and a handful of militia clung doggedly to the remnants of the pocket, as abrasive as the crinkled barnacles that cling to their rocks. Pry barnacles off and you pry them one at a time.

That night the sound of singing drifted down from the upper Steps. It was the Companions' own song, nearly a hymn, and those lower down knew the news of Townsend's death had reached the cut off position. On a windless night the sound came very clear:

We made a bargain, a compact with God,
If we kept it by sea and by land
And fought for his children, he'd watch over us,
Keep us safe in the palm of his hand.
In his hand, we rest in his hand,
We rest in the palm of God's hand.

One of a company, one among friends,
Together by sea or by land
And when the time comes to go into the dark
We shall go in the palm of his hand.
Since we kept our bargain, our compact with God,
We shall sleep in the palm of his hand.

As midnight came on the sixty-first night the picquets round de Vito's cut-off perimeter reported distant lights out to sea and later much activity in the port below. In the darkness it was not easy to discern details but a ship had berthed at one of the wharves and then came another and an hour later a third, others docking at intervals during the night. In the first faint light of morning the ships could be seen swinging at anchor. Boats scuttled out like water-beetles to the further ones, while gang-planks had been laid from the wharves to the decks of those laid up against the harbour wall.

"Listen to the bugle-calls," said de Vito to the young militiaman standing alongside him on the balcony of what had once been Radic's palatial home.

"What do they mean, Captain?"

"They're not ours." De Vito was smiling.

"Not ours?"

"Not Kittiwake bugles. I know what those ships are doing, though. They're bringing the Companions of Merganser."

*

The militiaman was only eighteen. Already the days of the siege had blurred together in his mind. Some months later he was asked what he remembered of it. All he recalled was a few minutes of one evening. A call for reinforcements and a few of them were moving up towards the fighting, and there were big trees, it must have been parklands, and a tall narrow house with yellow gables. He remembered the colour best of all, and from inside the house there were screams, which made him want to stop and do something if he could, but his sergeant said, "No, later," and they went on. Oddly enough in later years he could never locate the place again, or even work out its whereabouts in the city. Often he wondered if other people's recollections of it all were as slight as his, indeed at times it seemed to him that he had imagined the whole affair.

Coming from the north-west frontier of the Outlands, out near Thule, the captain-general of the Merganser Companions had been weeks at sea with his men. They had traversed two small seas, one big one and even part of an ocean. Companions and crews were salt-stained, crumpled and short-tempered, but Wilkins had been called Silky so long few people thought it not his real name, and wearing his grey frock-coat and white stock he looked enough of a dandy for Crook to wonder, as Silky strolled by, hands clasped behind his back, whether a Glassy Country grandee had come visiting. The Kittiwake Companion, acting as his guide and wondering if all the Merganser people were like this, led him through St Xavier's to the chapter-house, which had come to be Jacky Dorn's assembly point.

"Good to see you, Silky," said Billy Scarlett, the new captain-general of Kittiwake.

"Good morning to you. Good morning, everyone. I'm sorry we took so long. It was a tedious voyage."

"Maybe we'll have some proper big ships soon," said someone.

"Later on, son. Silky doesn't know about all that yet," Scarlett said.

Wilkins said nothing. He was examining the faces, clothes and bearing, calculating the confidence and reserves in the room.

"Jacky Dorn, last of the rectors." Wilkins speculated about whether that meant the boy was in charge. Probably still under twenty-five, hard to say with that half-focused stare, a blade-fighter obviously with all those cuts and scabs on his hands and wrists, another deep one near his mouth. Wait a minute, he does look familiar, where was it? Not that skirmish outside Ingastowe, surely?

"Urbano de Vito, next in line now Franz has gone." Silky had known Schroeder well but this one was new to him, a dangerous man, older than he looks, he thought. Scarlett he also knew of old and was dismayed to see how even brief command of the Companions had gnawed into him.

"Stefan Giorgiou." A militia captain and looks it, one of those who have always believed in the Matrix, stocky and stubble-faced, when was he last out of the line?

"Hereward." One eye gone. All that coiled-up grievance, and he looks at me once and gives one cold nod and now his mind's elsewhere.

"What do you want us to do?" Wilkins asked.

"Break through to the others, up round the Academies, starting about the Two Hundredth Step," said the last rector. "Can you do that?"

The Merganser Companions broke through in the early evening. It had taken them seven hours, even reinforced with Lucas and his militia alongside. Silky Wilkins and his captains had never seen fighting like it. He had led his Companions for five years and scoured the Outlands so that the people of Westermain, Alba, Altmark, Lakeland, Lettland, the Free Coast and a dozen other provinces had lived free of the would-be power-drinkers. On one end of the scale the freebooters and moss-troopers had returned their booty and paid damages so often that they had gone back to farming, and at the other were the magnates and petty warlords who were hanged whenever Silky found them to be killers.

This was different and eventually it was only the Merganser marksmen having plentiful ammunition that cleared a passage back to the pocket. Some of the watching Kittiwake Companions, who had long exhausted their own powder and bullets, were almost tempted to cheer the courage of the Daroi. Down in the catacombs a few isolated Daroi warriors still stood at bay where Lucas's militia with their bayonets had cut them off. One showed no sign whatever of surrendering and the Matrix policy was so stamped on its troops that there was an impasse for some minutes until Lucas arrived to clear the delay. There was an instant flash of mutual recognition.

"You again, Frick!" said Lucas. The young warrior looked as dangerous as a cornered lynx.

"I remember you," he said.

"Remember those ducks?" Lucas glanced round at his men. They looked too tired to be interested. He was tired himself, every joint in his body ached and he was having trouble with fierce headaches that never went away.

"The ducks, yes. Long time ago," said Frick and sighed.

"About ten years wasn't it?" Frick seemed to agree for he nodded at this, watching Lucas carefully. "What a bastard it all is," Lucas muttered. "I wouldn't mind a holiday. Chance to go fishing."

Frick gave a slow shadow of a smile, momentarily far away with young boys his own age and makeshift rods dipping into a sandy river, and whispered something Lucas couldn't catch.

The Matrix troops seemed to have assumed it was safe to go on and the two were left alone. Suddenly Frick sat down in the rubble with his head in his hands and Lucas saw he was crying quietly, sinking into a quicksand of memories that were already closing over him. The minutes ticked by. Lucas recalled Townsend saying about the Daroi: 'We'll beat them, but I expect they'll break our hearts first.' Or was it the other way round? What did we do to make the lynx cry? "Come on, Frick," he said. "There's a beach a few minutes away. I'll go fishing if you'll come too."

"They'll stop us." The whisper was only just audible.

"Let 'em try," said Lucas.

XLV

Not only had the counter-attack of the Merganser Companions retaken the lost Steps, it had come at a time when the Daroi were finding it harder and harder to launch their charges, or rather it was taking the Men longer to prepare for them. There was not a clan left with enough warriors to attack alone and unsupported by others, and to bring three or four clans together with some sort of plan tested the limits of the Daroi's organisation and patience with one another. Like the Matrix people they too strained towards freedom, but being cattle-driving nomads did not yearn for that separateness which was ingrained in the settled folk of Limber and its home provinces, and particularly those of the Outlands. Frick and every Daroi was born with the feeling that keeping the land unrolling beneath their feet and the horizon coming towards them were their guarantees of liberty, and that if they stopped long enough, say for a generation, then the first ties would slip round their legs, even if they were silken shackles as gentle as the affectionate tug of the damp, soft soil. At first they would simply grow too fond of the land, and then would come the laws of property and demesne, enfeoffment and trespass, leasehold and easement, and then the horizon would be for the likes of others, not you, to walk on.

With cows and a clan of a thousand any Daroi could cross the horizon, and if its pull brought the other clans drifting alongside then so be it. Now in the confines of Limber they grew restless, and there was disturbing news filtering through to them of the storm-clouds gathering behind, rumours of trouble and difficulty stalling what should have been the moving waves of people and animals that stretched back as far as High Altai.

Frick had waited for Lucas next morning on the low cliffs two or three miles north of Limber's harbour walls, having walked down from his family's encampment. Lucas rowed himself round to the spot in a small boat. A sandstone cliff made the city invisible from the beach, and Frick, standing on the cliff, saw Lucas below and waved. One scrambled down and the other splashed through the shallows and rather shyly they met. The sand glittered in white and silver-gilt crumbs smoothed by small waves which decorated it with bright stones and tresses of sea-grass.

"Did they try to stop you coming?"

"Who?"

"Well, the Lords of Limber and the captains of the Matrix."

"I didn't ask them. I just didn't want to fight you today."

Frick looked carefully at Lucas and then decided to take the answer literally. He had in the last sixty days been in at least twenty charges, certainly too many to distinguish one from another. Lucas was bound to have faced some of them.

"What about you?" asked Lucas.

"No attacks today," replied Frick. "If there had been would you have come?"

"Probably."

"It's easier for you." Frick had taken off his shoes and was standing ankle-deep in the gentle ripples which the sea shrugged towards them as if it were breathing in its sleep.

"Why's that?"

"My clan look to me now. If I am not there they will say I am afraid, a coward."

"I've never seen anyone less of a coward," said Lucas, recalling Frick in the tunnels, bristling and facing up unshrinkingly to twenty of his infantrymen. "Anyway your clan should look to its chief to lead them, whoever he is."

"I am its chief," Frick said simply. "What there is left of it."

"What about your friends at the fair?"

"Mostly gone. Yours?"

"My cousin Lee is, for one."

"I remember him. And the monster?"

"Lokietok? No, no one's got Lokietok yet. Unmen aren't easy to kill. Not that kind anyway."

"What other kind are there?" asked Frick. He felt more relaxed now and threw his shield and assegai behind him onto the sand.

"We are holding some of the other kind up in the city. They look the same as everyone else. They ran everything here until a few days ago, as far as I can see."

"Ran everything?"

"Yes. For Limber and all of the Matrix lands. At least they made the big decisions."

"So they are the real lords of Limber?"

"Yes," agreed Lucas. "I suppose they are. Or were." Frick contemplated this news for several minutes, long enough for Lucas, thinking he had lost interest, to change the subject: "I haven't got any rods, but I have got a net in the boat."

"We heard the old lords of Limber wanted peace," Frick said. "So these must be new lords we are fighting."

"New enough. Though maybe the old lords were right and we should never have fought with the Daroi people."

Frick frowned. "When I was a little boy, running behind the cattle, or sitting round the fire at night, I listened to older people talking. They spoke of the beasts, of course, and the tales of the clan, and of love and children, but also the saga of the Matrix. Probably we were a thousand miles away so we only had whispers of the Matrix, and every generation before us had passed away and it was still beyond the horizon. I don't think anyone really expected it to be there. Like the rainbow: what if the rainbow really was a great arch that you could climb into another world, wouldn't that be good? It would be dizzy up there but your feet would be firm on the red. That's how we wanted meeting the Matrix to be, and then it was and it wasn't. The land was beautiful with the rainbow's colours and more, forests and valleys, fields and flowers, ice and sunshine, though more like a carpet than an arch. We just walked on it."

Lucas was fascinated by the image, pulling it on and trying it like a pair of gloves. Of course the Daroi would have found beauty in the land, as he had himself, but how strange the thought of their wanting to climb the rainbow, struggling up the challenging steepness of the lowest curves, walking in many-coloured delight on its convexities, crunching their footsteps where feldspar, garnets and rubies mingled like shingle, then feeling the arch begin to slope away under their feet, and the inevitable downward sliding. He wondered whether Frick and his friends had contemplated the idea as far as the descent. "You mean you wanted to struggle for it," he suggested.

"Perhaps, I'm not sure. At least we wanted to earn it, somehow, pay for it with sweat, maybe grief. It was disappointing. I mean you were disappointing."

"I'm sorry you were disappointed," said Lucas.

"I don't mean it like that." Frick shook his head. "Words are hard. The Matrix lord in that village, I told you about him, and the men at the bridge across the big river, and now everyone here in this city. We expected them all to be like these have been."

"So you did want us to fight."

"I think we wanted to measure ourselves against you. We wanted you to be tall so we could be tall too, like those beans you grow with red flowers, they wouldn't be much without the poles, would they? We thought probably your lives, hopes and ideas were more than ours, more noble. Then until we reached Limber you stood aside as if nothing mattered, as if you didn't love this land. We just walked in, hundreds of miles. Apart from once at the big river. We couldn't understand it."

There was a sudden gust of gunfire, like a flurry of hail blown rattling against the glass of a window, and as quickly over. Both men looked over their shoulders but otherwise stayed still, letting the water flow smoothly back and forth past their ankles, softly undermining the sand from beneath their feet. Frick gestured towards the noise: "Somebody's attacking after all."

"So they are," said Lucas. "Yesterday it was us in the tunnels, today we're paddling on the beach. How do you explain that?"

"We wouldn't be standing here, not on equal terms, but for that noise. You'd be polishing my spears for me, or collecting firewood. Or your women would."

"Couldn't you have been picking up sticks for me?"

"Easily," said Frick. "If we had stayed in High Altai and begged to come into the Matrix lands." The hail gave the window another crackling lash.

"Are we going fishing or not?" said Lucas. They pulled the net out of the boat and untangled it on the beach, putting a line of flotation buoys like yellow pumpkins along its edge.

The net was about thirty yards long and when they tugged it out into the water, one at either end, it reached down from their waists to the sandy sea-bed. The sun was hot on their shoulders and the sea flirted and dimpled like an absent-minded coquette. Gradually they extended the net into a long curve and then began to walk it in to the beach until the two of them were out of the water and anchoring it into a horseshoe shape.

"Now we pull it in nice and steady," said Lucas. How many times in the bay below the almond orchards he'd done this, he and his father and Uncle Leo and Lee. The image of his cousin flickered in his mind as he pulled harder on the net to make the thought go away. The net was coming in smoothly, tightening round a shrinking patch of water with grey-green shadows beneath the surface, and swirls that spattered droplets.

Frick, who had not seen the sea before his nineteenth year, was fascinated. Nor did the net disappoint. A few more pulls and it brought ashore, jerking and wriggling in the folds, bright garfish and whiting, blowfish, tiny squids, clumps of weed, sea-urchins' eggs and long-legged creamy-coloured crabs that soon disentangled themselves and danced off sideways. A few of the whiting they took out and shook everything else back into the sea. On the beach there was plenty of driftwood that burnt with green and violet tinges in the flames. The sun shone as the fish grilled on hot stones. Lucas scrambled up the cliff and brought back lemons from a deserted garden, and as they ate they talked idly about little things.

"Do you have a dog, Frick?"

"No. I did have."

"What happened to it?"

"I don't know. Just didn't come back. About ten days ago."

"I've never had a dog," said Lucas. He was sitting with his back to a boulder, looking out to sea, using the knife they were sharing to pick out a few more scraps. "I've never had a wife, or children. Or a house. I can't read very well. I don't have any trade or any land. I don't even have a cousin now. Maybe I'll get some of the things I've never had but he never will. It makes me feel sad."

"I'm the same as you," said Frick. "Except that I can't read at all. But your cousin Lee, he's the same as my friends you met at the fair-day in the forest."

"Just as dead, you mean."

"No. I mean, who made him come here? No one. He would be like you, here because he wanted to be. It was his decision, and the same with my friends. We used to think this land deserved someone better than the faint-hearted Matrix folk. That was then. Now I don't want to be here. Now it's different."

"How?"

"Because now we know you deserve the land, and it deserves you."

"What do we know about you?"

"That's for you to say," said Frick.

"I didn't like it when Timmy Halloran was burnt."

"The burners. I don't much like them. But they were El Daro's own clan, they almost always are, and they didn't like it when your rifle-man shot him in the dark. In the dark it's hard for the heart to find its way home."

"That apart," said Lucas. "I can tell you a Daroi charge takes some stopping."

"Is that right?"

"Let's go for a swim," suggested Lucas.

"I can't swim. I can't read and I can't swim."

"It's easy. I can teach you inside an hour. Come on."

Frick laughed. "If you can I'll get you a nice dog."

"One of those yellow ones?"

"What other ones are there? Come on."

XLVI

Jacky had smiled when Lucas told them that he was going on the beach again the next day. "Take what's left of your company with you, including Urbano. Silky can look after the fighting if there is any tomorrow."

Martin was delighted to go swimming, which he had been wanting to do for months. Hereward came too with Costello, who, after lengthy protests, was allowed to bring his rifle. George did not feel well enough but Lokietok emerged to shamble down the Steps with them. Altogether there were about forty in the group and rather to their surprise about the same number of Daroi were already on the beach.

The two parties clustered separately, each eying the other for a few minutes, unsure of what to do, although Lucas and Frick were quickly engaged in conversation. Before long, however, Lokietok was a fascinating topic of talk among the Daroi, and after they noticed that Frick had brought a puppy for Lucas, who was at once occupied in scratching its ears, a few remarks began to be exchanged. Then a trade developed in coins, bangles, gloves, and ivory charms, and a cautious mingling was under way. The Daroi were mildly scandalised that Lucas proposed to call his new dog Nips and, after various suggestions, settled on Hunts in the Starlight which Lucas accepted cheerfully, saying that it was a name to grow into. The fishing-net was soon out again and several successful sweeps with it enlivened the meeting more. A thick rope was produced and a tug-of-war started. The Daroi, though lighter framed, were spirited competitors and only with a considerable effort were they pulled over the line in a flurry of sand and laughter and skidding feet. When Lucas persuaded Hereward to join him in anchoring the Daroi line the struggle was furiously even, and on the third pull mixed teams were formed and Lokietok was brought in. The Daroi on Lokietok's team were skittish about this as well they might be, tug-of-wars being unfamiliar to them without having dragons pulling on the rope. Frick and Lucas, pulling side by side against Lokietok, were half gasping, half laughing.

"Heave, you cow-herders!" shouted Frick.

"Not so hard, Lokietok!" yelled Lucas. Martin, watching them, thought that anyone who imagined the Daylight People were not crazy should see them now. The sides were so evenly matched that no one noticed the newcomers until they were almost amongst them.

*

The newest high chief of the Daroi looked disdainfully about him. To him most of his own people and many of those from Limber looked like children. He was unsure of the leadership of Frick's clan, nor much concerned, being himself from what every other Daroi clan called the burners, which to him meant only that it was an aberration whenever El Daro came from any other background. Someone drew his attention to Frick, and he walked over and said, "You," and tapped his finger on Frick's chest. The teams on the rope let the pressure slacken and stood upright. The men in the scruffy blue jackets or the faded tan and leaf-green fringed jerkins took only a casual interest but the Daroi, most of them stripped to the waist having taken off their chequered blanket cloaks, looked more like irritated young leopards disturbed at a carcase.

"Have you no shame?" went on El Daro, adding when Frick seemed disinclined to answer: "Our people are dying up there while you play childish games with the men who murder them."

"Is that so?" said Frick. "Well, if you want to help them in the city you go up there and either tell them to stop or do some fighting yourself."

"And leave you to play on the sand with your little clan?"

"We weren't so little before we came to this city."

El Daro had not long been high chieftain. He was aware that after the old chief who had brought them all this way only to die on the river-bank, and then after three more in this accursed place, he was an expeditious fifth choice, and that his authority would go flabby as wet paper unless he could keep demonstrating it. Among the remnants of Frick's clan he saw an opportunity.

"Your bravest warriors are dead. These others must have hung back."

"No one hung back," said Lucas. "We know."

El Daro gestured impatiently as if to sweep crumbs off a table-cloth. Thinking Frick sought to mollify him by silence he flexed his shoulder muscles, feeling the chief's cloak sitting more comfortably, and decided to be magnaminous: "I cannot blame you, even while I pity you." Frick's almond eyes, wide and utterly focused, neither moved nor blinked and El Daro knew enough to recognise the eye of the tiger and to know his own mistake.

"My clan are as brave as the bravest. Take your burners away. They are fit only to drag good men into fires." Frick picked up a handful of sand and flicked it casually into El Daro's face. "Eat that," he said.

Apart from a few knives in belts or strapped to ankles only one of the Limber defenders had a weapon close to hand. Alvin Costello had kept his rifle bundled up out of sight in his greatcoat, and as unobtrusively as possible he stepped towards where it lay on the beach.

Frick's clan had piled their miscellaneous weaponry some forty yards away among the boulders at the foot of the cliff, and both they and the mixture of Matrix militia and Companions were uneasily aware that El Daro's clan was not only well-armed but outnumbered them by about three to one – and had gradually, and now completely, encircled them. El Daro, his eyes still smarting, brushed sand out of his hair and spat it out of his mouth. Turning he shouted, "Take the cowards prisoner! Kill the bluejackets! This is war, not a game. El Daro commands it!"

No one moved. Even the tug-of-war teams stood in their lines. Then somewhere in the outer circle an arm came forward and Urbano de Vito was down on the sand, a lance through his chest. A single crack answered and the lance thrower staggered back out of the ring. Lucas, glancing around fast, saw Costello pull the bolt back and slide another of the Merganser bullets into the breech.

At once the circle of El Daro's warriors pressed in, savagely delighted by the chance to catch the Limber defenders out of their stubbornly held trenches and impenetrable fortifications, and little inclined to take prisoners among Frick's men, whom they had seen for months as subversive upstarts in the hierarchy of the clans. For a few seconds the swirling, stabbing rim of the circle contracted inwards and, though here and there a lance or sabre was snatched away to give the surrounded group a few flickers flashing outwards against the many slashing in, there seemed little prospect other than a massacre. Only in reaching the piled-up Daroi weapons among the rocks lay the slightest hope.

Hereward, Frick, Lucas and others who happened to be on that side of the trapped pocket were intent at once on breaking out, with knives at best and blows and kicks when all else failed. There the circle bulged outwards and the howling Daroi hounds, tearing and biting, leaped in ahead of their masters. Few of El Daro's clan had brought dogs, and of those that were present most had scattered outwards faced by the ravening savagery of the animals of Frick's men. One dog that hadn't retreated sprang upwards into Hereward's face and he tripped in the sand, toppling backwards at Lokietok's feet.

The huge figure had stood almost unmoving in the swaying, shrieking, bloody circle until this moment. For most of the time, since the death of Ragnar, Lokietok had seemed drained of menace, some senescence having overlaid the old rancour and wrath. The flames of a garden bonfire can sink to a hidden glow under a thatch of black ash with only a few tendrils of smoke to warn you not to poke a careless finger into the debris.

Perhaps in the darkness the sequestered demons felt too long demoted. Lokietok roared out a challenge and the men of both sides, particularly those nearest, shrank away appalled, while a shadow seemed to fall across the beach so that men glanced up at the sun. The Unman kicked the dog away from Hereward, the thudding impact of the foot flinging the yelping animal yards away. The Daroi where the line faced Lokietok flinched as their world, face to face with his bleak vision, disintegrated. Now, for them, there would be no feasting after death in Paradise the Blest, safe in the company of the many gods, and the Companions and Limber men alike shrivelled and blinked as Lokietok opened an abyss beneath their feet and an infinite empty space above their heads. Only Martin found in his twisted inheritance enough acceptance of his own insignificance not to be sick and stupefied. Around him he saw men vomit, others drop to their knees.

The Daroi of El Daro drew back as Lokietok stepped forward. Hereward got to his feet, shuddering at the void in his head.

Black	*Black ice*	*Black blood*
Dust	*Dry dust*	*Powder*
Empty	*Still*	*Lost*

"Lokietok!" cried Hereward. It felt as if he called over a great distance. He plunged forward, half-aware of a corridor opening, a gauntlet to run, better than being trapped in the ring. Lucas had dragged Frick to his feet, and both took one look past Lokietok's shoulder. There among the rocks above the high-water mark was an untidy pile of packs, cloaks, water-bottles and, glinting among them, the weapons of Frick's clan. Lokietok was through the circle now, broadcasting despair as a sower unthinkingly flicks the contents of his basket into the furrows.

Black dust	*Dry blood*	*Blowing ice*
Falling	*Without end*	*Nothing*
Everlong	*Not-me*	*Waiting*

The silent protests came thick and fast. Where are the many gods now? Where the fizzing electrons? Where the slow thoughts of the stones? Where the brave tadpoles? Where the bubbling billions of cells and all their bright promise and logic, where the great venture of the metazoans? For those on the beach, as with all forced to contemplate their deaths, there were perhaps no words to crystallise their protests and maybe they were just thinking 'I am' and holding on to that as Lokietok terrifyingly prised their fingers apart with: 'I will not be'.

There was clear space around and before Lokietok and at first slowly, as if awakening from years of sleep with every joint degenerated and every muscle wasted, Frick and Lucas followed Hereward in the steps of the Unman. El Daro's men had drawn back and apart like sandbanks shifted by the Unman's psychic tides.

Dissipation *Oblivion* *Nothing*

Lokietok's images were little changed, though another was added of a dark smothering vortex that was sucking the struggling giant into itself.

The shot hit Lokietok in the back, shattering a shoulder-blade and penetrating a lung. The rifle had come all the way from the Stone Bridge over the Dole River, where it had found a new owner and, though in the frenzied atmosphere a miss would have been more likely, the Daroi rifleman had a wide target. Lokietok went down on all fours and the images slewed and faded. El Daro's men came forward, slowly at first and then running as ancient men ran to pull down a stricken mammoth.

Frick and Hereward were only five paces from the pile of swords, sabres and javelins but the spear-thrusting Daroi were between them and it. Alvin Costello shot the first spear-man in the chest, before the lances and assegais pinned him to the ground. Martin in despair saw Lucas armed only with a knife knock a gun barrel upwards at the last second, and Frick grappled another spear-man wrestling him desperately to the ground. Across the circle the casualties were rising momently and the red sand beneath them was scuffled and wettened into the consistency of wet sugar.

Lokietok came up off his knees, taking a spear in the chest, and stalked irresistibly forward to stand among the heap of weapons. A Daroi sabre bit down where shoulder met neck, but Lokietok took the warrior by one arm and flung him into the yelling throng. Hereward had reached the weapons and grabbed up a short Matrix sword, distinctive among the curved scimitars. Lokietok was tottering, blood pouring from the gashes in his face and the body wounds oozing into his clothes.

Frick screamed, "Yes!" and snatched up a spear. On the further edges of the fighting, nearer the sea, his men and the Companions were being beaten inwards, only their dogs' fury holding a wavering sort of line.

Hereward drove a warrior back from Lokietok and reached a hand across and steadied the giant, surprised that Lokietok's grip was still so strong and amazed that the Unman could stand upright. Then, with utter certainty, he caught in the strange pale eyes for the first time the flash and brilliance of the human spirit.

"Thank you, young Harry." Lokietok spoke calmly and smiled.

There were no images of any kind. For two minutes he battled like a titan among the clan of El Daro as they came from everywhere to drag him down for the last time, beating round him as a gale roars at a great tree. It was their own undoing, for the distraction and respite that it gave was time enough for Frick and Lucas to see all their men armed and drawing confidence from the narrowness of their escape.

El Daro looked down at what had been Lokietok and then across at the ominous sparkling of steel around Frick. He had no choice that he could see so he walked across to them. "Your friend, the monstrous creature, is dead. Do you wish to give in?"

"So you can burn us?" asked Frick. He looked back at the hotch-potch of men that were left, some standing, some leaning on boulders, others stroking and patting their panting dogs, but all listening. "Shall we give in?" There was a ripple of laughter, a shallow ripple that soon expended itself on the beach.

"Then there is nothing more to say," said El Daro, turning away.

"Wait," said Frick. "Think hard. Who ordered the killing today? Remember we were playing little games. You said so yourself."

El Daro shrugged. "I did not wish to see us defeated and shamed by the lords of the city."

Frick turned to Lucas. "Were we defeated?"

"No."

"Shamed?"

"Not at all."

"So," said Frick to El Daro. He was about to say that a better reason was needed but Lucas interrupted.

"Frick, who are these people?"

XLVII

There is no arguing when the dispossessed come to claim their share, particularly if they have been disinherited for hundreds of years. They were coming as crowds move, a few straining forward at the front, the quick and impatient, then the numbers growing thicker and clustered in groups, talking as they came. The sea made one margin for their advance, but looking inland you saw many more of them silhouetted on the cliff-top.

Men and women came together, in almost equal numbers, but wearing no badge or uniform and keeping no formation, the men drollish like beaux on an assignation, many wearing wide plumed hats or silk bandannas, some even in black frock-coats and brocaded waistcoats, the women as flashy as the men, often favouring bonnets drooping with wild flowers, or turbans with cascades, their jackets tasselled and crocheted, but all alike faded and the gold lace tarnished as if the spangles and frills had been pulled out of forgotten boxes in dusty attics.

Few times in history had the dispossessed come thus, and never in the history of the Matrix. No doubt in the long past too, before they had ended emperors and quelled queens, the dispossessed would have seemed tawdry, not an unreasonable perception by the masters and mistresses for the newcomers would have had little concern with the niceties of taste, and as a candle can carry only one flame so only one resolution would have burned in them.

The strangers bore neither insignia nor emblems, wore no uniform nor any mark of rank. Yet they had brought their flags to plant them where they had not been seen for so long that history had forgotten they had ever flown anywhere. El Daro, Frick, Lucas and every man on the beach scanned the flags, looking to find the statements they waved, but found no stars, crosses, lions, flowers or suns woven there, nor any colours, for the flags were black, as if they brought emptiness and waiting.

Hereward watched the advance parties striding past and saw them glance at and swerve round the fallen bodies of men and dogs, reading easily the spoor of the kicked-up reddened sand. Feeling a tug on his elbow he looked down into Martin's face, the excitement glowing there. The little man pointed to the masses that now followed thickly in the wake of the vanguard.

"You know who they are, don't you, Hereward?"

"I think so. What brings them here?"

"We'll ask them." Martin scampered forward and the first group he reached opened up for him. All around him Hereward could hear the remarks and a chatter of amazement and curiosity.

"It's them. Look, you can tell. Look at that one's face."

"And her hands. How many fingers has she got?"

"Glassy Country?"

"Where else? And so many of them!"

"I can't believe it. I can't believe it's happening!"

"Look, some of them are coming over."

Led by Martin several of the newcomers were approaching. Hereward felt their eyes probe him and in the main body walking past many turned to look, and then some turned and spoke over the shoulder so that those behind also glanced across. A woman spoke to him: "Martin tells us you are close to the new rectors of the Matrix." A dozen of the Twisted Folk stood near him. They were a disconcerting mixture. Some carried no mark of their genetic tragedy, though perhaps their clothes concealed much for one wore a dark veil, another an elaborate mask, and there were few hands not wearing gloves. Even with these precautions there were disfigurements plain to see: an apple-sized tumour growing out of a temple, a soft pearly-skinned baby's face with eyes that might have been a hundred years old. As if in the distorting mirrors of amusement galleries there were improbable movements and stances.

"I suppose that's true," Hereward acknowledged.

"And is anyone close to El Daro?" said the woman. She was imposingly tall, with a blue lily tattooed from her right cheek-bone to the jawline, dark glasses hiding her eyes. A man standing some distance away announced loudly that he was El Daro, but the scorn in the fiercely exultant group close to her told a different story.

A sandy-haired man with a scraped face and ripped clothes laughed and said, "I don't think so." She could feel the vitality sparking out of him, and he was trying to catch her eye through her glasses.

"Who are you?" she asked.

"Lucas, madam. Luc to you. Pleased to meet you."

He put out his hand, and, surprising herself, she took it. "Letitia, from the Glassy Country," she said, amused that he was flirting with her in such a situation. "Presumably you are not El Daro, Lucas," she added, aware that he was still holding her hand.

"Certainly not, though I know who ought to be." He reached back and pulled another man alongside him. "Frick's your man."

This, she thought, was someone quite different, young, shy perhaps, but easy to remember, with that face like bronze and long hair dyed red. An innocent, of course, so he'd have the follow-me in him. "Our people wish to speak to yours, Matrix and Daroi alike. Let us go into the city and speak as friends. Meanwhile someone should decide on the Daroi speaker."

"Frick, definitely."

"I did not mean you personally should decide, Lucas."

"No, madam, of course not. Hope to see you again soon."

The small group of Twisted Folk rejoined the main mass that had been moving along steadily, and the Daroi gathered driftwood, built a large fire and put their dead men and dogs on it. The marchers swinging past the fire looked curiously at it as the body fats sizzled and the flames jumped and spat. Lucas drew his men up into line and they stood silent and at attention until the fire began to die down. One of the Companions who had brought his bugle played a series of long, sad calls which, echoing up towards the city, drew many, Daroi as well as Matrix defenders, to the cliff-edge to gaze down at the fire and, with a shudder, smell the roasting smell that the sea-wind took inland.

Lucas sent back a messenger for coffins and the Matrix dead were laid inside and carried back into the city in a sombre procession, many of Frick's clan insisting on helping, Frick himself being one of the carriers for Alvin Costello, while Lucas helped to bear Urbano, who had always been his captain in the Companions. Many volunteered to join Hereward with the laborious weight of Lokietok. Occasionally the giant's coffin had to be lowered and then men came to look down at the Unman. Hereward had combed back the straw-like hair and washed the face. As an afterthought he took Lokietok's ring. Though too big to stay on his own finger he later strung it on a leather cord and wore it round his neck.

"Poor Lokietok," said Martin.

Kit was fretful and fiddled with spoons and forks. She had found a table and enough chairs and invited her guests, but had only heard of dinner-parties, never given or even been to one. Jacky, like most sailors, was likely to eat standing up, she had rarely seen Lucas eat anything apart from chewing on biltong strips, and Martin had a sparrow's appetite.

"It will be a disaster." Kit found it easy to confide in Letitia. "The food will be dreadful, Jacky will drop off to sleep, Martin will pick at the salads, and I expect Frick will want cows' blood and milk. As for Lucas . . ."

"None of this will happen," Letitia consoled her. "Everyone's looking forward to it and thank you for asking me. You've got oysters and omelets which they will all like, and asparagus is my favourite."

"Jacky will want treacle pudding, I expect," said Kit dolefully. "That's what his mother gave him."

They had returned to Jacky's rooms on the Hundredth Step; for two weeks a cautious truce prompted by the Glassy Country folk had settled between the lines. The Daroi had recoiled into ferverous polemics among the clans, made more barbed and vigorous by Frick and his clan refusing to take part, saying they would very soon be inspanning and trekking on, come what may. Lucas, restless without Lee, had told the Companions he was going with Frick. The latest El Daro had disappeared like a spark in the night, and the burners' clan would say nothing but hugged their dishonour to themselves. The rearward parts of the Daroi migration, blooded on the Dole River and only now beginning to reach Limber, were little interested in the shell of a city and too unsettled for more than a few days' sightseeing before ranging on.

"Letitia, we haven't any flowers."

"You've a garden full of them, Kit. The pink hibiscus are lovely. And you don't have to worry, I've seen him look at you."

"I'm worried sick. He has scars all over and dog-bites. I'm sure he's got blood-poisoning."

Jacky sat quietly through the dinner, though few noticed in the light-hearted conversation. Kit had placed him at one end of the table with herself at the other so she could watch over him. On one side she placed Martin to amuse him with Twisted Folk quips and Hereward on the other like an older brother. As survivors of a shipwreck find it difficult to stop being thankful there is a tomorrow for them, so the guests' talk revolved continually round what the near future held, though none wished to raise the matter of George's health, the big man's listlessness and loss of appetite troubling them all.

"Well, Lettie, what do your people intend to do?" asked Lucas.

"Stop calling me Lettie and I might tell you."

"Very well, Letitia."

"We've kept our bargain with the Matrix and so have they, so most of us will stay and help rebuild the city."

Everyone there knew of the covenant with the Matrix. The Twisted Folk, assured earlier by Amalrik and later by Jacky of their full equality among the Daylight People, had put their weight firmly into the scales and the fighting on the Dole had drained the assaults in Limber of reinforcements. With the Old Stone Bridge destroyed and the Glassy Country folk sinking every craft that tried to cross the Dole, few of the Daroi managed to cross from the southern bank during the siege of Limber. It chafed them as a people unaccustomed to having conditions imposed upon them; also they were intrigued by the quality of the Glassy Country's weaponry which, coming from the combination of a people mechanically apt and fuelled by a history of repression, was impressive to a people of spears. Most of all they had lost interest and central direction, thousands of them being of the same mind as Frick.

"We got side-tracked into this battle," he was trying to explain, while putting Kit clearly at rest by enjoying the oysters. "A few start trouble, their clan goes to help them, the violence starts, another clan is drawn in, then others. If only you had shown us you were strong before, not after."

"So, I hear you are travelling on," said Silky Wilkins.

"Some of us anyway. It will be good to be on the move again."

"And where will you go?"

"Where we have never been, general-chief," said Frick and laughed with glee at the enticing prospect. "New mountains, new rivers, new grasslands, not too many thick forests, I hope."

"New animals, new birds, new clouds in the sky," added Lucas.

"And are you going too?" Letitia asked him.

"The world remaking itself every day, Lettie."

"Which direction will you take?" she asked.

"There." Frick pointed to the north-east.

"There?" They looked dubiously at him. "Towards the Fence? But why there?" someone said.

A silence fell as everyone, except perhaps Frick, pondered the question. The Fence was simply a name but it was multilayered with meaning and assumption. It worked much as saying 'the desert' works. Even someone who has never seen a desert knows it carries premonitions, threats, bewitchings and forebodings, being a place where the roads as they approach it dwindle into tracks, the tracks into dotted lines on a piece of paper between one waterhole and the next, if they even exist at all, the land of the simoom, the djebel and the oryx, its very words distancing it from would-be acquaintances, as if the desert wanted no intruders. Even if it lies close to a great city, only a few miles away, why, the desert still exerts this mysterious quality of not being there. And if beyond it lies another image of emptiness such as 'the sea' or 'the wastelands' then whole sweeps of the world take on an unapproachable anonymity.

Perhaps once there had been, or even still in traces existed, a fence of some sort along the Matrix's north-eastern frontier. Somewhere lying in the long grass there might be posts half-eaten by white ants, even, if you looked under the bindweed and bracken, old fence rails or rusted wire someone had once erected. Nevertheless, the Fence was there and nature had made it even more secure for much of that flank of the Matrix rested on vast marshes. Several rivers drained into these wetlands and the beavers had dammed them into intricate waterways, like a pewter-coloured necklace, of lakes and pools. Through secret pathways moved lynx, wolf and brown bear, and everywhere were the waterfowl. To the north of the marshes was a cold, hostile sea-coast of many bays, in which often the icebergs rode as if at anchor or grated onto the stony beaches. The southern end of the Fence petered out into a dead sea, a glittering expanse of salt, often blown by the fierce winds into white dunes. It lay treacherously waiting, full of quicksands under a brittle crystalline crust.

"Yet," said Stefan Giorgiou, "between the marshes and the dry sea is a tongue of grasslands stretching away to the east, flat and with few trees." His enthusiasm making him stammer, he told them of the waving sea of grassland – quaking grass, wild oats, timothy grass, meadow fescues and a thousand others – and of how everywhere was flecked and starred with wild flowers, white campanile and campion, purple scabious and pink yarrow.

"Stefan, are you a botanist?" asked Martin.

"No," said the Matrix captain, and they could see he was blushing. "My mother taught me their names. But I like the plants that grow in the wild."

"It sounds good," said Frick. "Lots of grass for the cattle."

Stefan smiled. "Big, open, windy country, Frick. But somewhere on the other side of it is Regret."

"Is that the way Lamorak went?" inquired Hereward.

"I would think Lamorak stayed up on the northern edge of the grasslands where it runs into the marshes and there are plenty of trees."

"Does anyone ever go there now?"

"I don't think so, Hereward. Why should they? Plenty of room here."

"Ah," said Frick. "A land where perhaps no one has walked but this Lamorak and his men for a thousand years and more. Lucas, let us go there, you and I."

"Neither Lamorak nor anyone else came back, they say." Letitia's voice was quiet. In candle-light she was not so careful with her tinted glasses, so the guests occasionally glimpsed her disturbing red eyes. Martin and Kit thought nothing of what seemed to them a small oddity, but there were others who preferred it when she kept her glasses high on the bridge of her nose.

Hereward pondered her remark, for somehow, by someone, the psaltery had been brought back. He spoke directly to the Matrix captain: "Stefan, why does no one even travel in the north-east? I know land is plentiful here and up there it is lonely and there is no trade, and there is a fence, whatever that means, but somebody must be curious, at least."

"I'm sure they are and it is fine country, the little that I have seen of it. But it is Unman territory. Better that we and they avoid one another."

"Perhaps," said Hereward. "But it doesn't happen. The Fence keeps in the people of the Matrix but it doesn't keep out the Unmen. We have at least fifty of them here in Limber and probably many more if we could recognise them."

"I do not like them," said Jacky. He had barely spoken while the talk swirled round the table, and Kit had hoped he was at ease. Now, suddenly, she was nervous. "Sheer and his like call us rabbits, folk that live from day to day. If it is true that from far back the rectors have always been Unmen then they are right, and truly we are poor creatures. But times are changing and it is good that we should have friends among the men and women of the Daroi and the Glassy Country, for neither people have been accustomed to another folk regulating their lives. As I understand it, the Matrix itself grew out of the desire to stop our lives being at the disposal of others. Nor did we wish this power for ourselves, because we were proud that our ancestors had thrown off the clamp that had been heavy on their shoulders. It is the task of Scarlett and Silky in particular to break the many yokes that they find in the Outlands. But my heart tells me there will be new masters soon unless we are careful. Nature doesn't like vacuums.

Astolat told me that." He smiled briefly but vividly and everyone knew that her cheerful, chubby face had flashed across his imagination. "A moment like this may not come again for a hundred years and more."

He had spoken their thoughts. The Daroi clans, having shrugged off the most recent El Daro, were bubbling with fizzing energy and fresh dreams. News was filtering outwards of how the Twisted Folk marched under their black flags, and in far-off forgotten woods and hidden valleys an anxious new pride was stirring. Outwards from battered Limber went ripples as the Children reached their homes, and more news spread with the men on the returning ships. All revolutions are revolutions of thought and the new ideas came infectious, not only with freedom but with generosity and evangelism, and the feeling that the Matrix had not been defeated but had recreated itself gave its people the confidence to look for reconciliation, though only weeks earlier Kit's dinner-party would have been unthinkable.

"Magnates always come back, Jacky. You are right," said Silky Wilkins. "Unmen, or someone like them."

Jacky sighed. "I am tired. Very tired. I wish to go back and see my father and my sister. I would like to visit Kit and Martin again at their house by the beck." Kit looked at him and shivered, knowing he was not finished and afraid of what he would say next. Was he going to live in his tall house on the Big Grey River and only visit her sometimes? "No more rectoring. I am going to the city of Regret."

"No," Kit said. "Jacky, please." She felt all eyes upon her. Letitia alone had been told something of what she felt for Jacky. Martin may have guessed, but the others who knew her less were surprised by the tone of her voice announcing so incontestably an unsuspected love.

"Someone has to, my heart." He made his words very gentle for her.

"What's driving you, Jacky? Your father? That stiff-necked Westermain blood. Or Lee and Alvin and all the boys in the coffins?" The surmises were coming thick. "Or Frick's friends on the bonfires? Not poor Lokietok, surely? No, I know, it's Andread, isn't it?" The darts sprayed round the target, some missing, others stabbing close. "Don't be the next Lamorak. You know what happened to him and all the fine young men he took with him."

"I only know what everyone knows, that they didn't come back. It makes no difference. All I want is to ask them to leave us alone. I can do that on my own. Sheer can come and tell them I was once a rector of the Matrix too."

"I'll come with you," said Hereward.

"Why do you wish to go?" Letitia was aware of Hereward as a brooding presence, and she was reminded of the keeper of the Last Inn and others she knew in the Glassy Country who looked deep into the future, so different, she thought, from Lucas and Frick who laughed as if tomorrow would never come. Hereward seemed closer to herself, Martin, Kit, and those who grow so immersed in their intentions as almost to forget to live for long days on end, their lives converging on some future experience and conclusion.

"Well, that's personal, but partly the same as Jacky's question. He doesn't know why the Unmen won't leave us alone. Maybe they can see us more clearly than we can see ourselves, since they seem to regard us as helpless rabbits, as Sheer puts it, but I wonder what it is we lack. Is it courage, or intelligence, or generosity, or honesty? I'm sure I don't know, though if they are bright enough to understand then I suppose it's intelligence."

Kit, probing idly at Hereward's thoughts as he spoke, wondered what else he had in mind to ask.

"Or knowledge?" suggested Letitia.

"Come with us," said Frick.

"And climb the Fence," added Lucas.

Even saying it light-heartedly sent a tremor round the table. It seemed perhaps not an apostasy but at least incongruous, as if you were to capsize your boat to see if you could swim.

XLVIII

So they came to the Fence. Of course there was no fence, but everyone knew when it had been crossed. It was like playing the piano, or swimming, or reading; there would have been a time before when you couldn't do these things and a later time when you knew you could. Everyone could say that they had crossed the Fence, without being able to say at which particular moment it had happened.

The land was flat with huge domed skies where towering cloud masses passed endlessly overhead, white continents pushing out ahead of them rolling capes and headlands of distant purple coils that, as the wind brought them closer, unspiralled into vast cotton-white tufts. At evening sunsets set the western sky ablaze behind the travellers, as if far over the horizon Limber was an old lady taking out her shimmering apricot and violet silks saying that if they must leave not to forget there had been a time when she was young and wore such colours.

Stretching far in every direction were the grasses of which Stefan Georgiou had spoken. Walking thigh-deep in the delicacy of dry grasses foaming in every shade of buff, cream, fawn and yellow, it seemed that a million kinds grew interlaced and interspersed, yet each clear and shapely: spikelets of wild barley awns, nodding seedheads of quaking grass, timothy grass's neat beards, delicate airy heads of fescues and windgrasses, yet these only a tiny part of the parade of the grassland's rippling inventiveness.

The fifty or so families that had followed Frick were as contented as their herd in such a place. Along with the Daroi had come about forty other people, tugged along behind Jacky as a comet brings its clinging gases, some from Limber, varying from Stefan Georgiou to the flower-girl from the Hundredth Step who had sold him his first posy, a few of the Kittiwake Companions, and then the black flag of the Glassy Country with a group of its folk including Letitia.

Jacky, Hereward, Martin, Kit and George Littler walked as a group but there were few times when others did not join them. There were two other travellers: one was Osric Sheer who walked silently not even allowing himself the satisfaction of ridiculing the expedition; much less silent was Jacky's younger brother Magnus who had arrived on one of the Dorn ships. Magnus had been living with the far northern Dorns and had heard late of the fighting at Limber but then nothing would have stopped him. He was big and boisterous, enjoying everything so much that Kit wondered if he really was Jacky's brother.

"Father said you needed me," he told Jacky.

"He shouldn't have done," his brother said tersely.

"I loved Andread too." Not an unexpected answer from a Dorn, thought Kit.

The further they left the fence behind them the slower grew their progress, at first imperceptibly, then noticed by a few, but gradually it became clear to all how much shorter was the distance travelled each day. A tendency developed to break camp late and set up early until they were walking east for just a few hours each day. There was no sense of menace ahead, only of the land's reluctance to have them depart. Stay a while, it cajoled them, a day, two days, don't leave too soon, when you have gone on perhaps this will be the land of lost content that you will never see again, except from a far distance.

The Daroi pressed on, clinging together with the loyalty of bees, and the folk from the Glassy Country seemed only to hear faintly the land singing to them – but those born and bred in the Matrix could hardly bear to continue, a number of them turning back and some others saying they would stay and wait for Jacky to return. Everyone began to feel exposed in the wide grasslands; eventually the expedition moved into the trees that grew in the wetter land to their north, though the Daroi herdsmen and animals kept parallel with the main group where there were grassy clearings and easy passage between the trees.

Hereward took to studying the psalter and discussing it with the others, for it was clear that now they were following Lamorak's path. The faded sketch-maps and descriptions jotted in the book years ago were beginning to tally with their surroundings. Hereward predicted that very soon they would reach a wide shallow river, and on the next afternoon they came to it. It was ice-cold, the water clear and, though faintly tinged with a coppery colour, tasted sweet.

It took the rest of the day to cross with the herd and that night they slept with the clamour of a multitude of frogs in their ears. Frick and Lucas came over to spend the evening with Jacky. Both were uneasy and their edginess communicated itself quickly. "I stay awake too long now," said Lucas, when Jacky suggested it was time to sleep. "I just lie there listening."

"To what?" asked Hereward, particularly intrigued in that neither he nor anyone else could conceive of what could disturb Lucas, who had even been at ease sleeping alongside Lokietok.

"Voices in the earth," muttered Lucas.

"No." Frick knew what Lucas meant. "It's the air talking." Jacky, Magnus, Stefan and George were nodding in agreement.

Martin and Kit looked surprised at such unanimity. "You've eaten the wrong mushrooms," laughed Martin but no one smiled.

"The air sings that this is all folly," said Stefan. "Is it the same for you?"

"Yes," several answered together.

"Good. I was thinking I might have the quinine fever."

"I wonder if Lamorak heard the voices," pondered Jacky.

"Lots of his men turned back," Hereward remarked. "That is written down in the book."

Kit asked, "How many days before we reach Regret?" She was deeply perplexed by the talk of voices, and probing the Daylight People's thoughts she sensed that this was no fabrication of the imagination, indeed that the effect was being minimised because these were men who were accustomed to dealing with their fears. Also everyone was saddened by the rapid decline in George's condition as the sickness ate at him. Too often he came into camp long after the main group, with the exception of Hereward and Martin who walked alongside and encouraged him through each painful day. It might be diverting for them to talk of Regret.

"Two days and nights after crossing the river, so the book says," Hereward told them. "Sheer," he called across to where the Unman lay in his blankets listening, "how far is it now to Regret?"

"I don't know," came the reply. "I've never been there."

"Surely you have," said Martin. "It's an Unman city, isn't it? The only one anywhere near Limber."

Sheer shrugged. "I've never been there, didn't you hear? All roads lead to Limber and none to Regret, you know."

"You have to find your own way there," mused Jacky. "Isn't that right?" Kit reached across and squeezed his hand.

"I hope you know what you're doing, Jackyboy," Magnus interrupted. He was three years younger than his brother, bigger and heavier in build but with the Dorn eyes. Unlike his brothers or sister he was placid and easily satisfied, running contentedly in Jacky's shadow. Dogs came at once to him, jostling to be near him, and he knew the names of all the birds and butterflies of Westermain. "Well," he went on, "what are we going to do when we reach Regret?"

"Ask some questions."

"Such as, Jacky?"

"Why these Unmen were running the affairs of the Matrix."

"Good."

"Why our sister was hauled across the Matrix lands to study in Limber. I know we might ask Sheer that but I'm not sure he really knows."

"Good again," said Magnus. There was a pause. "Any more?"

"Well, everyone ought to have a turn. Perhaps two questions each."

Magnus smiled. Such a regulated conversation seemed unlikely. "I've only got one. These Unmen, where are they all?" Kit smiled too, this being her question also.

"What's your question, Frick?" asked Lucas. "And you're not allowed to ask about cows."

The young chieftain frowned. "Nothing really, though I don't like the voices in the air." He brushed his face as if he had walked in the dark into the clinging faint softnesses that spiders spin across doorways or between trees. "Nobody owns the air."

"Is that a question?" Lucas wondered. "Anyway it's probably something the Unmen do."

"Of course it is!" called Sheer from under his blanket as if exasperated by everyone's slowness. "How long is it going to take you to realise this is no place for you?"

Frick said, "It is a good place. The grass is good, the water is clear."

"Well, forget the voices and that is exactly what rabbits would say about the place."

"Let him be," said Jacky. "Only two days, we can be patient that long. Save your questions for the masters of Regret."

But the land did not stop its singing and they walked into a mesh of admonitions, urgent though not menacing, that shimmered ahead and among them as the air dances and quivers over hot rocks or shadeless sand. Even Kit, Martin and the Glassy Country people were beginning to hear the singing.

At their camp on the next night Frick told Jacky that his folk would like to take their herd back to the copper-coloured river and follow it southwards. It was clear that Regret was no destination for them, if the Daroi could be said to have any destination. Of the other two groups the Twisted Folk would come forward, he knew, protected by their strange inheritance, and some of those from Limber who had linked themselves to his quest because of many allegiances and respects, but would be glad to turn back whenever he should choose to abandon the search.

So, in the darkness of midnight, Jacky whispered his plan to his closest allies. Magnus he had known all his life, and valued his generous nature; if the Unmen were as high-handed as Sheer there would be no harm in taking Tyr-Hereward. He was uncertain about the Tyr facet of Hereward's identity, but he was certain enough that Kit and many others believed that without Hereward the pages of the story they were all inside would not be unfolding. Nor is that so strange, he thought to himself, for what would mankind's story be without restless, changeful men and women, just as in the myths there was no rest from the ardent boys even for jarring giants and pillaging dragons.

Martin he asked to stay behind and, when the encampments awoke, to explain their absence should the three not have returned. "How do I do that?" Martin inquired.

"You decide, but restrain Lucas and Frick. It may just be that the Unmen here do own the air and the rocks under the earth."

"It's Kit who'll need restraining," said Martin drily.

The land was as it had been described in the psalter, lightly wooded valleys that wound through sweeps of downlands. It was easy, fast walking in the moonlight, with their moon-shadows clear on the grass. There were wild creatures abroad, patches of darkness that moved and cropped the grass, and for a while an owl hovering shoulder high kept easy pace with them. "An Unman country tawny owl," announced Magnus, seeming inclined to start a discourse on the beauties of the owls of Westermain.

"Magnus, quiet. This valley is starting to narrow, so soon there should be an aqueduct, then it opens out," said Hereward, "and we should see Regret due south of us. Beyond the city is a ravine that also leads south so there will be hills or cliffs on the far side from us. Somewhere near here Lamorak's men hid in the daylight." Now they moved more cautiously and listened carefully. No great city is silent at night, and they knew that even on the far side of the Limber ranges you could hear that city droning and drumming, though it lay invisible miles away and revealed to the eye only by its lights limning the skyline and pale on the underside of the clouds.

Their ears strained for sounds beyond the softnesses of the wind in the grass and leaves. "The book said it had much thatch and wood," said Hereward quietly. "It would have been easier to leave than a stone city such as Limber or High Altai, even Ingastowe. But there must be some trace left of it." Another half mile of walking brought them quite suddenly out of the valley mouth and on to a level expanse like a flood plain, several miles wide. Looking across it they could see clearly the ravine, a dark sombre gash in the long hill-face which was bathed in moonlight.

His thoughts were interrupted by Jacky's voice at his side. "There it is. Just where your book said it would be."

"It's big," said Magnus. "Huge. Though not many wood and thatch houses. It must have changed since Lamorak's time."

"Look at that massive building with three towers," Jacky whispered. "How long must that have taken to build?"

"Not as long as that one over there with the dome like St Xaviers in Limber. They almost look as if they had the same architect. Perhaps the Unmen were once closer to us."

Hereward listened astonished to the brothers. There was no city there, no mighty edifices, no mark of humanity at all, yet they were absorbed in pointing out features of it to him and one another. Even in the moonlight and with only one eye he could make out that the waving grasses stretched unbroken across to the hills at the far side of the narrow plain. The thought occurred to him that the land had somehow conspired to shepherd them to this place. The marshes further to the north and the dead sea to the south, the grasslands that had narrowed to a tongue with the valleys all running into it, meant that anyone travelling east would be headed towards this gap as surely as sand grains in an hourglass have to come to the pinched neck between the two hemispheres. Though he could not understand what was happening, he sensed there was a purpose at work and that it was almost certainly that of the Unmen.

"Jacky, Magnus," he said. "I wish to ask a favour of you. Let us go back to the camp. Do not go into the city. It may be safe, it may not – though that does not concern me or you for we had no care for safety when the Daroi people fought us – but it does concern me that I cannot see this city."

"Hereward, are you ill?" asked Magnus.

"Perhaps," he answered. "I have no way to tell. But remember that these Unmen were for many years difficult to see properly until Kit came and knew them for what they were. I only ask that Kit comes and looks at this city. Perhaps the others too. I could not hear the voices that you and most of us heard, and if this shadow-city comes from the same source let us be careful. Another day will make no difference."

Jacky had never felt that he knew Hereward well, believing that the contemplative part of the latter's nature held him back from fully sharing the present moment, but he respected and liked him for his courage and tenacity. This liking was tinged with sympathy, for Hereward seemed to Jacky to be swept along by forces and furies, chiefly his own, he could never really control. So he turned his back on the city, because now it was there and that was enough for the night, and he had wondered if they would ever reach it. Those unattainable cities either lost in the past or living only in dreams possess a special fascination, being perhaps shadows of the city of God.

Two hours later and half-way back to the camp they met Lucas with Frick and several of his clan, the trackers and their dogs in the dawn light moving fast and easily, following the trail clear in the dew-wet grasses. "I knew you would be all right," said Lucas. "Kit made us come. I told her the last rector of Limber wasn't going to come to any harm on a lovely night like this and up against such as Sheer."

Magnus said, "We found Regret," thinking Lucas was making rather light of developments.

"It's quite a big city," added Jacky, "though not as big as Limber."

"It's easily as big as Limber," protested his brother.

"We'll see it later," Frick said. "It won't run away."

All the day that followed Kit was alternately stormily angry with Jacky or weeping hot tears. When he told her not to make a fuss she spent hours with Letitia, crying and not being much consoled: "The Daylight People are not like us. They do not think far back or far ahead. You were not wise to fall in love with him."

"I know, I know."

"It's the Hereward-Tyr thing, isn't it?" Letitia guessed. "Because if that's all come true and our people are walking in the open at last, then the end of the story is likely to be true also."

"Yes, that's why when I heard he had gone to Regret with Hereward I thought . . ."

"Well, it hasn't happened yet, so stop sniffling. It's just a story so it has to have an ending."

There has to be some sort of end. Sometimes it is an end that comes so imperceptibly that it has no conscious finality, as if you were to go to sleep and not wake, and this end is common enough for mankind and all creatures and creations, yet other ends come either with the inarguable destruction of the avalanche or the predictable certainty of the year's end. Yet overlying every end is that faith that there is no end, that the daffodil will bloom next year, that the water is only ice for a while, and that the one God and the many gods cannot co-exist with or even be cognizant of ends, other than as reference points when what used to be becomes what is. So it was with the anthropoids far back in time when they reached that point when their growing consciousness was so bubbling within them that they knew that they knew and were then human. Yet this was no more a beginning than an end, for the new man was the old creature as surely as the concept of one is augmented rather than extinguished by two. Indeed as one and two are both numerals, so new and old man alike came to be known as hominids.

So the hominids came the next day to a meeting with other hominids as inevitable and as potential with transformation as when some primitive gazed, transfixed, as the cave wall glowed with pictures. Though mingled together there were really two groups, one whose attitude was an instinctive wariness about Regret, these being from the Matrix, some fifteen or so, and a similar number including Kit, Martin, Letitia and the Glassy Country contingent who heard the voices faintly if at all. Of the Daroi only Frick came, the others being but slightly interested, and the thirty-first was Hereward.

Some trees were clustered together in the centre of the grassy expanse Hereward saw in front of him, though what the others saw he could not tell. In the shade of trees that were familiar enough to them all, oak, ash and hornbeam, the Unmen were waiting, sitting or strolling at ease. They seemed in good humour for there were occasional ripples of laughter. The feelings among those approaching were very different, strained by a lengthy dispute over whether the city existed or not, for the Twisted Folk saw nothing of what others stared at in fascination.

"It is a mirage, a trick, Jacky, drawn from the imagination," said Letitia. "Listen to us and Hereward."

"How can it be an illusion for some and not others?" asked Magnus.

"We paid not to see it," Letitia responded curtly. "We've looked at regret itself all our lives." She took off her glasses and her eyes were like hot coals, even redder in the pearly-gray morning mist that had still not cleared after the rain-showers of the night before.

"There, there, Lettie," said Lucas, and when the intimidating red gaze swept round to him he smiled.

Hereward wondered at the change in Lucas. It was as if the laughter and the boyish jests had burnt away in the crucible of Limber, revealing a nature that was formidably composed and calm.

"Do you see this city, Lucas?" Letitia asked.

"Yes. But I prefer to believe you when you say there is only the waving grasses. Though I'll tell my children I saw it."

Lucas began to stride forward and in a few moments the group was face to face with the Unmen. There were six, three male and three female; they could well have been six of the Daylight People and all bore themselves with the same imperturbability as Lucas. To everyone they spoke clearly and courteously, except when they reached Hereward they shook their heads and sighed as if in resignation or a mild exasperation. He said nothing, presuming he would work it out later.

"May I speak?" said Jacky. It was not the same voice Kit had heard him use to Nestor but it was not dissimilar.

"Of course," came the reply, though it was not clear which of the Unmen, or indeed if any of them, actually spoke. Perhaps they nodded agreement.

"Is it true," Jacky was choosing his words very carefully, "that you decreed that there should be no big ships in the Matrix?"

"There are big ships."

"Perhaps, but only if you count the sea-gypsies' ships."

"The question is a fair one," remarked another of the Unmen, though again it was as if, being of the same mind, one spoke for all, rather as the breeze speaks for the wind. "But you will have many questions. That is why you are here, or some of you."

"So," said another, again without the sensation of a different voice addressing them, "we must tell you the full story and let you judge for yourselves. Remember that we only know what we know, and you may hope to learn more than that. After all you may have come to ask why God should tolerate malevolence and cruelty and the rest of the family of demons."

"What would God say to that?" asked Lucas, and Kit flexed her paw in its black glove.

"Probably that God was just about to ask you the same question."

"That's fair," said Lucas and laughed.

"Tell us your full story," interrupted Letitia, "or these Daylight People will debate the day away."

XLIX

In the beginning was the world. It consisted of a vast number of atoms and even subatomic particles. Over many ages this dust of particles assembled into and experimented with a myriad of forms. Eventually came the primates and their especially flourishing branch, mankind. Man is now the pre-eminent species, characterised first and chiefly by the ability to think, particularly to know himself and his environment and control both by thought. To do this mankind had to become conscious of itself, as it were from the outside, and conscious of existing within the two frames of time and space, and of being an individual within a mesh of billions of other individualities. Yet we know that other creatures, too, think and have thought, with minds unrefined and difficult for us to penetrate, so difficult that there is no word for what lies where instinct jumps into and out of thought. Perhaps we may recognise a fraction of the thoughts of dogs or dolphins, but what of the lizards and lampreys? They are sentient and must have some form of mental activity, call it what you will. Let us not forget either the mighty family of plants, and although that is another order of species altogether, plants too have a primitive, diluted, virtually unimaginable kind of consciousness.

Martin shivered as the voice or voices rolled like far-off thunder. Unmistakably the Unmen, too, spoke for a mighty family.

Consciousness is no aberration. It is an immutable phenomenon and a universal law, as much a presence in the structure of the universe as is mass or radiation. Nor was it ever younger than the stuff of the universe, no more than velocity, say, could be younger. Consciousness no more suddenly materialises than does mass, being there however far back we like to trace it, back through the plants to mosses and the cells of mosses, back through the creatures to the first tiny protozoa. This primordial consciousness did not suddenly emerge as a phenomenon when cells were formed. Universal presences have no such temporal limitations. So the molecules which combined to form the cells are not without it either. Of course if we contemplate the thoughts of water or wood, iron or stone, then we have no words, though mankind has always known instinctively of some incomprehensible communication or relationship, marking down megaliths or groves of trees, or certain lakes, as places to meditate upon whatever it could be. Some of you will find this strange, but the ovule becomes the oak tree and the ovum the ox, and you have always found this not strange at all but familiar and natural.

Frick, who spoke the Matrix tongue adequately but with no flourish or eloquence, was surprised how well he understood the Unmen, and he smiled to hear the name of the ox. Near him Martin in his memory ran along green lanes, high-banked with wild roses, over-arched with bee-loud lime trees, happy that if they lived, at least in some way, as he lived, then sometimes they might remember him in their turn. He had always believed it anyway.

We, mankind, are the tip of the arrow of evolution, and because it has been the simultaneous and parallel evolution of life and thought, then the greatest complexity of thought must also lie at the tip. There have been infinite ages and stages in this evolution and many failures and impasses. The great lizards roamed this earth for millions of years in a multitude of forms but they withered away into the stuff of dreams. Perhaps we too shall wither away but that is not for us to linger on. For us it is to live fully and think deeply, widening always the range and complexity of thought. Not so long ago mankind knew nothing of the world that is smaller than the eye can see, nor the other expanse where the stars journey in their wondrous profusion, and even now we are utterly ignorant of the further reaches of either domain. Nor in our recent past were we aware of our place in the gulf of time, of the eternity lying before and behind us. Now that we have partly come to grasp at these great agencies we have no choice but to incorporate them into our thoughts, to think with the depth and scope that such knowledge impels upon us. Indeed, when mankind, in only four or five generations, uncovered these conditions, a great and anxious turbulence muddied the minds of many, and thousands chose to end their own lives, men, women and children alike, lost in waters so clouded they could not tell if they swam up or down and so gave up swimming and drowned. Yet instinct and thought alike could have directed them to the surface.

"Never give up," said Lucas. "Just keep on swimming." He was leaning on a tree trunk, looking as sturdily uncomplicated as the wood itself. Although to Kit, Martin and the Glassy Country folk his stoic response was somehow not quite how they felt, nevertheless others, Frick and Magnus in particular, approved fully.

"What else is there to do," said Frick. It wasn't a question.

"Let the one God and the many gods look after the rest," Magnus added.

We do not disagree because to survive is the working of mankind's instinct, and it has brought our species, and every other species on earth too, across the great gulfs of time to this moment at least. Yet no other species, remember, has learned to reflect upon itself and think thoughts unconcerned with its own physical existence and the continuation of life by reproduction. As soon as mankind acquired the capacity and habit of reflection, itself the precursor to thinking logically or artistically, then a species which had previously existed as more or less an unindividualised mass began to separate into distinct units or personalities. When this happened then there were really living things on earth where before what was alive was life itself. Easier to think of it as the time in the Garden of Eden, when we ate from the tree of self-knowledge.

"And the Lord God said, 'Behold, the man is become one of us to know good and evil.'" Most looked around wondering who had spoken. It was Isobel the flower-girl.

That is true and right. Because that is the direction of evolution, always towards something that is unattainable without knowledge, without a complex and powerful brain. This progression, from as far back as you like to trace it, postulates our recognising good and evil at some point, and, in this way at least, becoming more God-like. The arrow points us onward in our journey towards a greater unity or a closer alignment with God. What this can be is beyond our understanding, but what a quest, what a voyage! The molecules embarked upon it, those billions of years ago. And when their time came how many voyagers – the cells, the anemones, the tortoises, the blue jays, the mice – faithfully sailed and steered the ark of the molecules. Now it is our turn.

"The tree of knowledge." It was Martin who spoke, and they were uncertain where his mind tended. "It grew in the Garden. And there was no way forward towards God unless the fruit was eaten. Was there? So why was it forbidden?"

There was a sense of rueful silvery laughter around them as if the Unmen were unsurprised by the interruption, as a teacher may smile at the bright and wilful pupil who knows a challenge when he or she meets one.

It was not as much forbidden as an either/or proposition. The terms were clear enough. After eating it mankind would be nearer to God but further from innocence. For us to evolve the knowledge and the presence of evil had to be released into the world. It was the price to be paid for the growth in consciousness.

"So does every step forward require some sacrifice?" inquired Jacky.

Every change of state expends energy. Perhaps that energy may be innocence, or it could be time, or many other forms of sacrifice. Perhaps all humans feel at some time that their childhood state was so precious that the acquisition of maturity and experience was not an equal compensation for its loss.

"And if childhood ended and there were no compensations in the after years?"

There was no answer to Jacky's question, as if the Unmen waited for more information.

"Does every step forward require a greater capacity for thought?" asked Letitia.

Require and acquire.

"So the humans who do not take this step are less than human?"

Within their own present they are just as human.

"But," she continued, "to you they are within the past?"

Again the Unmen consented with their lack of response. As a

mother encourages her infant child to walk, they responded more readily to stumbles or false steps. Some of the Unmen were standing, some sat. One rose and stretched, another brushed back her hair from her forehead, a third walked across to drink from a small spring that bubbled among many-coloured pebbles. There was a sense that at least the pause offered no wounds, but the renewal of information might do – after all, they were in the heart of the city of Regret.

Letitia asked, "Has there been another great step forward since the Garden of Eden step?"

"Or a step back?" asked Kit, and she flexed her paw in her glove, and her agitation went shivering through the group from the Glassy Country.

There has been another step forward. What causes such occurrences we cannot be sure, though it may be that the spherical shape of our world means that there can be no escape for psychic pressure any more than there could be an escape for the physical pressure of populations. Our planet is like a kettle, it reaches boiling-point after millions, or at least thousands of years, and quite suddenly the water changes to steam. Perhaps when there were enough people on Earth for every continent to be inhabited then the capacity for reflection burst forth, and then, in another step, when the world was saturated with thought of every sort, then there was no option but to change, as if the water had again become saturated with heat. Inevitably the change was towards the more complex. It always is. Inevitably it involved a greater degree of association or combination; that is always the way forward.

This is a strange universe in which we find ourselves, and among the mysteries perhaps its deepest secret is so contrary, so odd, that it seems less like a scientific principle and more like a cosmic impulse or ambition. It seems that the universe tends simultaneously towards youth and age. That it ages is not difficult to see, for every action, however minute, expends some energy, and on the great scale our sun must eventually exhaust its fires. This is the law that says that everything tends to break down to its simplest parts as the energy runs out which holds its construction together. Yet there is another force or impulse in the heart of things which drives in the opposite direction, a natural growth of organisations and complex unities. We see it easily where the cells yearn towards multicellularity, nor is it difficult to see the progression that has produced the human brain. So far we have no equation to express the relation between the energies of association and dissociation. It must exist and we shall find it. There are other impulses too, that so far we may only observe but are so mysterious that they appear like the fingerprints of God. Wherever we look we find, instead of a descent into formlessness, that there is an order of patterns, symmetries and harmonies, which are held in place by a force thus far beyond our comprehension, yet which we long to be a part of, as the finest music not only pleases with its sounds but intrigues us deeply with the certainty that the composer's design is counterpointed upon another melody which resonates everywhere around us.

The listeners seemed now sunk in dreams. Jacky dreamed the rippling delicacy of sprays of notes that fell like silver droplets when Astolat and her friends had played such music as he had never imagined could be.

This is the direction that mankind has no choice but to take. Our whole ancestry has been one long striving along this road. The atoms assembled into the hierarchy of elements and they grouped into molecules, often one single molecule being an association of thousands of atoms. The molecules groped onwards and from somewhere came the extraordinary scraps of life, the virions, and with the cells what a combination was there, for even the most primitive had drawn together billions of atoms in its formation. Nor did the impulse halt or even slow, for irresistibly the cells clustered in their hundreds of billions to form the tissues of creatures of all kinds. Driven on by this mysterious energy, life is borne along on the torrent of evolution.

The listeners were unaware of listening. There was an impression of words, indeed of more than one voice, yet they apprehended the meaning as if there were no semantic filter diluting the passage of ideas. It was as if they perused the knowledge where it lay stored in the neurons inside the Unmen's minds, as you might contemplate a picture.

The next part of the future, for surely the kettle will boil again, can lie only in a further association of minds and spirits, a development from the one in which we, the Unmen as you call us, exist. The individual cells and whatever creation they have assembled themselves into, similarly exist together, and far from forfeiting any of their separate natures they augment and enrich themselves. There is nothing strange in this. Did not our ancestors instinctively yearn towards and find satisfaction in being parts of groups? What else are the Daroi, and their clans also? What else the Matrix? Limber? Lettland, Alba, Westermain, Thule? What else the Children? The Companions, the sea-gypsies, the believers? And, too, the folk of one village, one church, one monastery, one ship, and of course one family.

Jacky knew it to be true. Not only was he John Dorn of the family of Dorn, as well as the family of Ainsworth, his mother's people, but of the company of the Big Grey River folk, of Westermain, of the Matrix, one of the trawlermen and thus of the cold sea, and he hoped one day to be part of his own family. By virtue of his past and future he was of the great family of man, and more multi-layered and beringed by far than the richest pearl the sea ever gave up.

Hereward thought it to be true. Though he had a few friends and a good many acquaintances, he was usually lonely, and had either forgotten or had never had the comforting presence of parents, grandparents, children, and the far-reaching web that you call family, a web spread not only in the present but into the distant past from where our ancestors can still twitch inside us. Hereward wondered now, as he had before, what it would be like to live in Hay village where everyone had always known everyone else, and where each family was tangled into every other even by links as tenuous as great-great-aunts or cousins by marriage that sometimes you did not know for years you had, where the men and women in the harvest field who had always cut the corn with you were the ones whose children ran races with yours, who sat in the same church pew as their grandparents had, which was the one just behind your own family's place, and, walking down the path from the church door, you saw the same families' names on the gravestones in the waving grass.

How could the people of a planet coming together be any surprise? When our world became dense with individual thought, then the time was ready. In less than one generation our ancestors built machines that linked thoughts across the world. To absorb this function, to make it organic, was an easy step. Then the composite mind had to grow and to purge itself of malignancies. Ironically, mankind had known how to do this for thousands of years. 'A new commandment I give unto you, that ye love one another.' Of course, it was more an old principle than a new commandment, for what is it but the expression of that affinity which everywhere exists whether it draws together atoms or cells or star-stuff or humans. One may conceive of the direction in which this affinity presses under many names: a combination, a union of increasing complexities, a socialisation, and even as evolution itself. What supplies the energy for this affinity is love. Furthermore, since the impulse to association is a universal principle, then love too must have co-existed from the very first moment of the universe, when the principle, foremost among what are often called the many gods, sprang into being and enacted itself.

You may consider there to be a vastness in this love which makes it so distant from the love of husband and wife or mother and child as to be different in kind, but mankind has easily and with delight been immersed in great concerns of mind or matter, in truth drawn irresistibly by the boundlessness of music or of mathematics, yearning towards the stars. Why, those who seem to prefer some little sphere, directing their tenderness to flowers or birds, are not they in love with the vast natural world, even in their affection calling it Mother Nature? It may be far easier to love creatures and shrink from embracing one's own kind, but it is not altogether a paradox. Affinity is driven by love, love is Christ, and to be gathered with Christ, or the one God if you prefer the name, no faith worth considering has not believed this to be the only true end. Nor height, nor depth, nor any other creature shall be able to separate us from the love of God.

"Amen," said Isobel the flower-girl. There was a pause. It was not difficult to sense that the six who were ambassadors or delegates for the Unmen were speaking for some unfathomable disposition of minds and spirits which itself was engaged in a multiplicity of endeavours, of none of which could the listeners begin to conceive the slightest part. Yet a flicker of irony here, a liking for disquisition there, one of the women whenever motherhood was mentioned making the allusion glow and soften, all hinted at various strands of personality in what was being related.

"You are Unmen, far from us," said Jacky. "But I have tried to understand what you have told us, assuming that everyone heard the same as I did."

Kit looked closely at him. She felt over-awed by the mystery of the Unmen, but his voice was level and his tone was that of a courteous equal. Even when he had battled the Daroi as the last rector of Limber he had, it seemed to her, been in part what others wished him to be, as young men often are. Perhaps for most of his life this had been true; certainly she knew with Astolat he was her perfect gentle knight, and she thought it probable that it was his father's anger over Andread's death that had been expressing itself through both Jacky and Magnus. Now he sounded much older.

Everyone heard the same, the Unmen assured him.

Jacky spoke again: "You are no longer men and women as we are. You are newish upon Earth, as you said yourselves. It seems that sometimes you exist as individuals and as a vast combination of minds at other times."

Not at all. There are no separate times.

"Nevertheless you are new, that is clear. You tell us that you are an essential development in mankind's evolution."

In evolution, not mankind's evolution. Whether the development is essential the future will tell us. At present it looks logical and promising.

"So what you are telling us is we are the past, the lime in the bottom of the kettle I suppose you would call us, or rabbits in a big park. It's even got a fence, now I come to think about it."

No. You are quite wrong. No rabbit ever questioned whether it was a fox or not. Even more are you unlike the deposits in the kettle, though they too have a place.

Jacky was silent. The pause went on for some time, though once he caught his brother's eye and Magnus knew he had been told this was not the end of it. Eventually he asked a question that the Unmen had been anticipating, judging by what seemed a collective sigh: "You say you are new on Earth, as evolution goes. How old are you as a people?"

Let us say many years, in our association of minds. That is still very, very young. But as humankind, well, as old as the species is old. There was again the sensation of urgent personalities merging and emerging, and of a sympathetic but wearing patience as if they conversed with the profoundly deaf.

"So you have not been Unmen for long?" remarked Letitia.

Now there was a sternness of reproach in their response: *It is time to stop calling us that.*

"Why? You are very unlike all other peoples." She was nervous when she said it, but had to smile when Lucas said, "Quite right, Lettie."

Because when we developed anew, then shortly afterwards so did you, that is the people who do not exist in union. Certainly we are greatly different from the old people, but you are even more so. You are a little younger than we are, as you had to be. You were formed by mankind.

"We were? The Twisted Folk?"

Yes. And all other folk too, the Matrix people, the Daroi, the tribes that the Daroi passed through.

"So Jacky and Lucas and Frick and the rest are not fully human." Letitia sounded not fully convinced. "And they are fair to look at and whole. So – " and she gestured round at her Glassy Country companions " – where does that leave the red-eyed, the wolf-fingered, and the scale-skinned? And those that never came on the march alongside the rest of us because they had only one brain for two heads, or carried their stomachs outside their bodies like balloons in harnesses? Did you form them too? If Lucas is less than human what are they?"

"Now don't cry, Lettie," said Lucas. He put an arm around her. "I don't like to see you cry."

"Who made Lokietok like he was?" It was Hereward, speaking for the first time. At the words there was a tingling in the air as if the Unmen's hair crackled with static, and skins tightened in concentration with a suffusion of sadness, and perhaps the faintest tincture of guilt.

Himself, since he was convinced that when he came to die the universe would die with him. It is a condition that bestows much power and more despair.

"Jacky, I want to go, please." Close by his side Jacky heard Kit's whisper.

It is time for you to think more deeply on things. Go back now and on the way let you recount your dreams.

The voices withdrew, as did the figures, walking away quietly, and as they went the distance seemed to make them draw close together.

Few slept much that night. Groups formed, split and reformed around the campfires as they were replenished through the dark hours. Jacky was restless and ill at ease, walking from one fire to the next, sometimes pausing to listen to what was being said. Across the valley the Daroi cows lowed and he could hear the flutes' thin music, which meant that everyone there was content. He felt it likely that Frick was untouched by the meeting with the Unmen, and would involve his followers only by telling how he had dreamed of the powers of air, powers that had more to consider than cows and the wind in the grass.

Returning to where his own blankets lay he met Magnus with Letitia. "Jacky, some of us are missing," said his brother.

"Are you sure? Who?"

"Isobel and two of the Glassy Country girls."

"When did you notice?"

"No one has seen them since we left Regret, if that's what the place is called." said Letitia.

Jacky sighed. "So they may never have got back here." He liked Isobel, who was so timid and inconspicuous as to go unnoticed for days on end and had carried her own pack and cooked her own meals without once complaining.

"Did your girls say anything to you?" he asked Letitia.

"Not a word."

"What about Isobel?"

"She did once." Letitia hesitated and took off her glasses to rub them pensively on her cloak, before deciding to continue. "She said she had never mattered to anyone or done anything, but she didn't want to think her life had passed without just one adventure." She put her glasses back and he saw her smile. "She said you would look after her."

Jacky did not hesitate. He knew whom he wanted and, when he called, Hereward, Magnus and Lucas came. He would have taken George, had the big forester not now looked so dreadfully shrunken and ill. They knew the trail well enough to move along it in a steady jogging run that wore away the miles. Above the stars were big and bright, with the Milky Way like a glinting, spangled cape that the night sky had draped across its shoulders. As they ran along the track, still clear in the trodden grasses, Letitia ran sometimes with them, and sometimes pressing ahead, her feet like a leopard's so that in the darkness no twig crackled nor pebble rattled as she passed.

Three quarters of the way to what they still thought of as the city of Regret she announced that there were three women ahead. To the men there was only the darkness, but she laughed. "I can see the paths on the petals that the bees see when they search for pollen."

"Any Unmen?" Hereward inquired.

"No."

As they pressed forward the first faint greyness of dawn came horizontally across the grasslands from the east. Now they could see figures ahead and as the distance grew less and the groups converged they felt a slight unease. In this faraway unknowable land where by night shadows trotted across the plain or snuffled in the coppices, where at daybreak the waking crows hailed one another from dead branches, calling 'crow', and where another empty day came to expose the unwary, the three missing women strolled as if they walked in a garden. Had the sun been up, they may well have twirled parasols.

L

Here was neither the familiar light nor dark. As if in a dream Kit moved in illumination lit from beyond the spectrum, and there was neither up nor down so that she hung floatingly like a moth. A constant hum and rushing was around her, forming the only physicality of her surroundings; as a blind man may know the wind, and as he may touch the wind as much as it touches him, so Kit felt her way among the intensities of movement. She was aware of time passing but not of its speed, and while growing aware of the labyrinth she could not say how long ago she had entered it. Only the moment immersed her, not least because the labyrinth itself seemed fluid, as if it were coherent only in the moments just before and during its own present.

Kit had been in a more conventional maze before, a friendly puzzle of turf paths between yew hedges, where she, Jacky and Astolat had laughed at its twists and backtrackings, but that maze in a Limber garden had leafy green walls to mark where you could not pass, whereas this one had for pathways an activation of atoms, so that it was the reverse of a maze. She carefully avoided the paths, as in the Limber garden a mouse might have scurried through the twists and turns while never leaving the shelter of the hedges.

The labyrinth's conformation was restless and shifting which suited her, for she felt flushed with an unchannelled wrath, partly caused by Jacky who was so perverse and contrary. While to her it seemed simple enough that to be happy they must get back to Westermain, he insisted on confronting the Unmen, wanting to make them acknowledge their responsibility, at least in part, for the blood shed in the siege of Limber, as well as for the size of ships and the abduction of his sister. Yet she moderated her vexation towards him because he was brave and generous, and above all because she loved him. Hereward was Hereward, and exasperating in a different way that she could not articulate, chiefly because he was both himself and also the Tyr-Hereward he did not wish to be, and thus his actions disconcertingly difficult to predict. With Martin she was angry for not trying to stop the expedition to the Fence, while knowing both that he could not have done so and that he was her brother who laughed and joked inside a body that was a tragic jest at his own expense. Yet in the end none of it mattered other than the passion that had recoiled inside herself where she felt it swirling turbulently.

She thought of the shape, that had once been Jacky, lying on the grass, his breathing shallow and getting shallower and his pulse so low that she had spent an hour wondering if it would stop. When she first saw him like this she had shaken him and screamed, "Jacky, where are you?"

The Unmen people had been there again and had frowned at her distress. "It is his wish to know some of what we know," they said, or else their thoughts echoed in her mind. Kit had noticed Isobel among the Unmen and had caught the faintest imprint of her in their response, as if the flower-girl could not bear that the slightest hurt should touch Jacky. With the speed of the fox Kit had singled out this intonation, elusive as if one of the colours should suddenly hint at its unsuspected presence in white light, and she separated Isobel's thought as if excising indigo from beneath white and between violet and blue. Then she was inside Isobel's mind, like opening a magic cave, and in a moment was out again.

In a fury of instruction Martin had been told what to do. Kit was sure that she could return into the coils of thought and that, when she did, her own body would drop into the same catatonia as Jacky's had. So she lay down among some bushes with a blanket over her and told her brother to watch until she awoke. Through the branches she kept Isobel in sight and then reached out, at first dipping with her own talent into Isobel's admiration of Jacky and then immersing herself in it, letting both minds think alike, always imitating, adjusting the coloration carefully so that indigo should not side-step into blue.

All around her was the presentiment and the sense of Isobel, and Kit stayed perfectly still so that not even a tendril of the flower-girl's thought snagged on her presence. Already she was learning fast, and with that sharp nose for danger that comes from being a survivor in a capriciously hostile world. She knew that this dream-world she had entered was not one in which an error could be healed by waking. There was danger here in many forms, the most perilous being that as she had intruded the world may well feel infected by her and at once exude its own antibodies. Yet Kit felt no immediate peril and if she could remain as inconspicuous as a virus then she could adapt to this strange place.

Somewhere in the labyrinth was Jacky, and she meant to find him. So, very gently she let the palpi of her clairvoyance touch with thistle-down lightness on one of the currents. Years ago as a child she had learned to sip sweetness from the nectaries of the white dead-nettles, and now she sucked the flavour of thought, needing no more than a sip to know enough, as nectar tells of honey. Quite suddenly she knew and saw, with such a luminous impact that mentally she had to step back, a universe at once so shapely and unconstricted as to make the moment like that sunburst of reality which would transform a hitherto permanently blind woman's imagination were she between one second and the next to see a many-coloured landscape under a blue and white sky. Isobel and the two Glassy Country girls, she now knew, had become part of that communion for which their selfless spirits fitted them. With a quick throb of sadness she acknowledged that the great future of mankind was not for her, who loved few and fiercely and forgave no injury nor accepted any damage that had ever befallen her or her loved ones.

There flashed in her head a dizzying percept, a thin face, an expression of dissent, the eyes alert but shadowed by the curtains of long hair. Once walking along a dimly lit corridor Kit had been surprised by an unfamiliar face, to find that it was her own reflection in a mirror, and now, although she floundered for a moment, she guessed that it was someone, Isobel presumably, thinking of her and wishing her a happiness with Jacky that would soften her sharpnesses. How Isobel projected this was intriguing, for the Jacky-thought came not as Kit had recognised herself but as symbols: seals, kingfishers, water-rats, blue crocuses and white-flowering chestnuts. At once Kit knew it as a way of saying 'I love you', and became a confusion of waspish possessiveness and self-blame that she should snap at the other girl's admiring affection which wished nothing for herself. 'Whoever loves the blue crocuses,' she thought, 'wants everyone else to love them too.'

On the grass as Martin watched over her the only stir was the wind ruffling her hair, but in the labyrinth she paused to cry a little. In dreams too you can cry.

Though never having been formally taught, Kit had absorbed from her family a vast amount of knowledge of the realms of beasts and birds and plants, and almost as great a collection of stories, beliefs and vendettas. Her mind was eager and open and she grasped, even from the flickering glimpse into the thoughts aswirl around her, that it was Isobel and it was not, being also every Unman or Unwoman that had ever been, though the relation was unclear, for there seemed to be simultaneously a vortex and a crystal-lattice in which the atoms cheerfully hopped in and out of individuality and union, alternating within some greater stability and shapeliness.

In this glimpse of humanity far into a future that was too strange for her to imagine it would be futile to search for real understanding; nevertheless she could not resist taking another peep and another into the serpentine paths, moving gingerly among them, delicately lifting a leaf from the forest floor and another leaf to see if Jacky had passed this way. "Don't hurt him," she warned the labyrinth. That seemed unlikely but her confidence was growing as she realised how nimbly she could manoeuvre, trying occasionally to orient herself towards him. She felt him somewhere close, though near and far were as difficult to express here as was direction. She recalled Astolat on one of her projects saying, "We need some vectors here," and smiled. With every touch on the composite mind something unexpected and fascinating vibrated and now she was touching often and randomly, as when seeing a harp for the first time a child is enticed to pluck at its strings.

Soft-chidden by the violet eyes of unborn babies.

Kit scowled and plucked again quickly.

Scarce-challenging indigo numerals and symbols, known as unquestioningly as by an idiot savant.

Some other time. Again.

Star-charts and a time when far blue worlds glittered beneath for the unborn Unmen.

She paused briefly to watch a world spin.

Sea-choked by green water, the salt acrid in Andread's mouth.

Better, much better, now Jacky could not be far.

Sun-charred in the solar bonfire of the earth's yellow midnight.

What was this?

Spell-charmed by jasmine, flutes, vanilla, orange trees, the cool rain.

So different from the cold fog of Hay in November.

Stiff-clamped in obsidian, encased so tight that she felt her red heart-beat constricted.

Was this the maze's defence? Something trapped whispered a name. Lamorak?

Snow-chilled as the dust in the tombs behind the black railings of Ingastowe Cathedral.

Ingastowe? Why there? Though the nightmare has to be somewhere.

Sweet-chastened by the white certainty of 'I am the resurrection and the life'.

Was it random at all, she wondered, or could the thoughts possibly be seeking her out? Who's the player and who the harp?

Disturbed that the labyrinth might be too aware of her she pondered her next move and found it with the cunning of the virus. In some way which she could not comprehend the Unmen lived simultaneously as an association and as individuals, each form reinforcing and delighting the other. Kit assumed, having seen Jacky unwakable, that her own body would be in the same deep sleep, but knew that Isobel had no such problem, co-existing in perfect ease as the one and the totality so that the join was seamless. Nor perhaps would it have been surprising to topologists that such a totality should have been the creation of a spherical earth rather than of an infinite flat plain of a world that never incurved and concentrated its creatures' psychic energies.

Then she concentrated herself where she had tapped the Andread-thought. Instead of being the tiniest flicker of a presence in the Unmen's thought she now swam in the full river of their creation and knowledge, flowing and volatile, reason and logic beaten into turbulence by intuition, instinct and imagination. Now she knew what Jacky must be knowing, for the Unmen disguised nothing and knew without sequence or duration, for everything touching their heritage and concerns was there. This cognisance was not central or uppermost but without the slightest part of it the rest would have redefined itself or shifted and skewed to some degree, however slight.

Because she was confronted with it all at once Kit transformed the most striking impressions into a picture – she had seen few paintings but she knew her favourites in tapestry and stained glass well enough. There was the Christ-child, like a small sun on his mother's lap, and she had always looked there first, drawn by the nimbus. Through the baby Kit expressed the energy and love that sustained this strange new universe. As the Christ-child lay in his mother's lap Kit understood from her smile all of the world's flowering that had called all creation from the void. Kneeling in front of the mother was a King, she knew it was a King from the intricate golden filigree of the crown and the exotic mulberry-coloured gown: the Unmen's proud quest outside the stars and inside the atoms. Another King, serious faced, clasping his beard, stood further back; in Hay church the little girl Kit had always admired him, thinking his gift, the silver censer, looked so royal a present – as it was, for no other species had ever dreamed of such a one, it being the unmerited favour of the grace of the aspiration towards God. A third King, partly obscured by shadows, was carrying a glass, which her mother, knowing no more than the name, had told her contained myrrh. Now Kit looked at the great landscape of thought spread out before her and knew that as the Unmen strode and strove towards some unknowable future which only their very striving could define for them, so they could not separate themselves from the suspicion of Ragnarok, a confrontation with an evil that ever grew proportionately with them.

In a flash the picture revealed all this and far more, there being no pages to turn, the eye and mind knowing also the husband, one hand on the mother's shoulder, amazed and half-forgotten, looking back to the carpenter's workshop. Thus Kit perceived the Old Ones, thousands of them still on earth where once there had been billions, tough and wilful, yet wistful, loving rarely and awkwardly. Kit was sure now that Hereward was one such, and sadly that they were already more part of the past than the future.

The picture widened and deepened as it had to, for the figures in the forefront were defined and refined by the long-haired shepherds, some holding lambs, pressed against wolfish dogs, and behind again the ox and ass that had shared their stable, and the straw and the beamed roof, the window a hole with wooden slats outside which lay a field where waiting camels grazed. So Kit realised that here were also the yearnings of the animal world in and beyond the stable, and nor were the trees and plants excluded from longing to enter into the glorious liberty of the children of God.

And side by side, laborious, slow,
There come the trees, the grass, the stone,
How could we leave them, Lord, you know,
You are no way to walk alone.

The old hymn's words now reverberated with a purpose so vast that Kit could only tremble. In the distant, dark fields, stretched beyond the window-bars, was the Unmen's promise that they would never desert or abandon their fellow-creatures.

Then in a great wave of sad admiration and realisation came the knowledge of who the casually cruel, capricious, brave, laughing Daylight People really were. A little change to one gene, no more than a fraction of a gene: now remember the past in sequence, not in significance. How much it explained – the casual acceptance of a past that was nowhere highlighted but was simply there, the events in a series, the dead sparrow pushing the dead father one step backwards down the long stairway towards a kindly fading.

So that was how the people of the Matrix had patiently tended the land for more years than they had ever recorded, calmly caring for the air, the water, the forests, the grasslands, relating memories they could not remember, recording myths and taboos which gave every man and woman a chance to wonder, but above all their memory-paths not singling out and preserving the rush of the nerve of power being pressed, because they forgot so steadily and recalled so faintly that they forgot the taste that might have seduced them. How simple and neat it had been, thought Kit, how simultaneously cruel and kind, how nicely containing the seeds of redemption, not quite fair yet not really unfair, with every hallmark of the Unmen.

Another wave of realisation assailed her, revealing that she and all the Twisted Folk were a product of pure chance, that chaotic element that the Unmen knew perfectly well was both ever present, yet increasing with the complexity of their organisation and intervention. With total certainty it came to her that this left the Unmen as truly mankind, that it was they who had once built the pyramids and palaces, sawn down the forests and poisoned the plants, whose works had arisen and also been destroyed and erased with the same intoxication, and, eventually forced to confront their own murderous creativity and recognise that the power nerve could not be unendingly stimulated in the small space of the planet, they had departed on their genetic expedition, ungraspable because it lay always in the future.

Kit had lived almost all of her life in fear of the Daylight People, and she understood well enough why the Twisted Folk were reviled as they were. What she had never known before now was clear as beck water, for she was seeing through Isobel's mind as one might look over the shoulder of a painter as he works. She recognised, the paint still being wet on the canvas, that Isobel had only recently come to terms with what had separated her from the Unmen and what she had acquired.

For a while she had to retreat and compose herself in the void where the thoughts did not run but as soon as she was confident of being indistinguishable from Isobel she went back, this time like stepping round the corner of a house into the rip-stream of the wind, letting it buffet her and bring her dust or rain-specks, pollen or blown leaves, smoke-smells or the steely air off the ice. Then she had what she wanted, the smell of salt, fishscales, hemp, tar and candles, and she sailed along with the thought, the virus loose now, quick and agile, before the antibodies had learned how to grip it. One tiny part of the Unmen's thought was absorbing Jacky, spreading him in an interchange of experience and ideas among an infinity of others, rather as a brief shower, even a few droplets, falling into some remote sea will then belong to all the world's oceans.

Sensing a nexus that held some of the mana of Jacky she burst into it in a fiery display of passion and prickly hauteur, all wilfulness and captiousness, a firework exploding in a high corona in the night, a flare dripping green and red and silver down the black. Suddenly no longer was she sipping at the slightest flavour of a thought but exposed in the full current of a mighty knowledge pressing to a mightier purpose, fuelled and surging with a rapturous love. Now she was inside and part of the picture, smelling the sheep and sweat and unwashed bodies, the wet-grass breath of the ox and ass, the dusty straw-smell, the strange vanilla-smoke smell of incense and, faintly, the fragrant milky baby-smell. The picture's voice was pigeons cooing on the beams, the whisper of ancient tongues, the dogs snuffling, laughter somewhere outside, and a king spoke a few words, deep and gentle, as the lock on the box of his present clicked open under his thumb, and always an undertone of the straw rustling and softly crackling. The baby gave the softest half-yawn, half-sigh. Outside it was beginning to snow.

Now she knew more, far more, experience lashing her every moment, the scene's kinaesthesia engulfing her. The snow dissolving on her black dress sent her stepping further inside the stable; she felt the push of a shoulder on one side and the warm solidity of the ass's flank on the other, and as a king rose stiffly from his knees she could even feel the rheumatism in him.

At the same time the thoughts were becoming aware of Kit. She sensed surprise and fascination, with a penumbra of rejection that hinted of the mind's prime intention, its self-preservation. The antibodies did not exist to combat the Kit-virus, but they would formulate themselves and quickly, and because the mind knew this then Kit knew it too. Inside the picture was far too hostile a place for her, even the harmless air the shepherds breathed was dangerous. Anyway she had learned enough for the present and it was time to let the picture return to its window in Hay church and, with a pang of exclusion, she woke herself into her body.

Martin, seeing her stir and her eyes blink open, sighed with thankfulness. She felt her hand enclosed in his and her paw warm in Letitia's hand. "Is Jacky awake?" she said.

Jacky reached out and touched his world. Its sky was blue and its grass was green. This he perceived with no speculation; before he awoke they may have been any colour at all, but that must wait to resolve itself. Certainly he recalled nothing of yesterday's sky, nor of the grass. He started with what he could touch, rubbing his hands together as if washing them, then felt his wrists and pushed back his sleeves to see his arms. He was pondering the many cuts, all so recent that they were only just knitting together, and was interested to see if the rest of his body was similarly marked – but so many people seemed to want to talk and to expect him to answer that he could not begin to think clearly. After a while they stopped overwhelming him with questions and as the evening drew in he sat among them round the fire and one by one came to sit beside him, talking of what they said had once been and people he once had known.

"Jackyboy," said a solid young man with hair as pale yellow as his own, "we'll get back one day to the Big Grey River and then everything will be all right. Father needs you and Astolat will be missing you. We'll walk across the sea-meadows down to the tide and you can show me the lapwings and oystercatchers. They can't take that away from you."

But Jacky's eyes showed so little expression that his brother made way for Martin, then for Lucas and Letitia, and in the twilight Frick came across from his camp where the Daroi were packing their gear in readiness for the long trek. He came very close and knelt to look into Jacky's face. His torso was bare and oiled like wet bronze and his hair thickened with red clay lay back in a wide coif. He had brought his long narrow shield with the white-rimmed ochre eyes, very like his own, painted on the front. "Remember us, Matrix lord?" he said, and rattled his spear-shaft on the shield, before driving it downwards so that it stuck quivering in the turf by Jacky's ankles. A shadow came swimming up to the surface of Jacky's eyes and his hand went down to where he once kept his gutting knife. Then the fingers loosened and he gazed at Frick in a mild surprise.

Even Sheer came. "I told you, didn't I? Regret isn't a place, never was. It's where the past and future meet, and who wants the future? Maybe slowly, a tiny bit at a time but not hundreds of years in a gulp. That's what you got and you won't get over it. That's why we got out of Regret, same as Colonna and the Novaks and plenty more." Sheer seemed disinclined to go further, choosing to retreat into his usual morose mood, but left everyone reflecting on his words.

It suddenly crossed Lucas's mind that whenever in his dreams he ran along the familiar lanes and paths of his childhood then the dream predicaments did not oppress him, as if the magic of the places was always on his side. Out on the unfamiliar plains of the future his strength would ebb and his friends would die, and he wanted no sight of it. Even the present he liked much less without Lee.

Frick, too, had listened to Sheer. Often when one of the Daroi grew too old to keep up on their long journey he or she would stop at the edge of some river too deep to ford or too fast to swim, and sit on a rock and watch the others cross and go on. What happened then the younger Daroi never asked, but they did know that the future would answer the question for them. Frick didn't want to think about it.

In the cabin on the end of the jetty lived the old man who would sell you a ticket that told you the day of your death. How he made a living no one knew, for no one came to buy. It was one of the grim fairy stories of Westermain and it was vivid in Magnus's mind. He wondered if Jacky had bought the ticket from the Unmen.

"Sheer," said Kit, "you are not telling us enough. This is my Jacky."

"Ask away. You won't like what you hear."

"Let me be the judge of that. First, what is the matter with Jacky?"

"Easy. He wanted to know why. Why did his brother drown, why did the Matrix take his sister, why did he have to fight at Ingastowe, and so on. Not a good idea to ask questions like that, at least in the long run. Of course I could have given him answers that would have satisfied most people. But they always presuppose other questions. For instance, I know that Hereward's girl had her brain damaged. Why? Because she was struck on the head. That's the sort of answer one gets first. But how many other thirteen- or fourteen-year-old children in her village? Maybe ten, something like that, so why her and not them? Answer – because she was the most intelligent, probably for miles around. Right again. Ask why she was born so bright. Or why she wasn't at home that day. Or why her even brighter sister died in childbirth, if she did, and so on. They get harder all the time. Why is Lucas alive and Lee dead? Ever ask why you have an animal's paw?"

"Lots of times," said Kit.

"You bastard," said Letitia.

"Only helping her out. John Dorn must have gone to the people of Regret and asked them to lift a corner of the blanket that stops us seeing the logic of it all. Probably they don't know more than a fraction, but they are the future, or think they are. So what he now knows has overloaded his brain. Nothing strange in that, it's always been a common cause of suicide. He's tough and he won't give up and one fine day he'll wake. Though he'll never be the same again."

"Why didn't they stop him?"

"Another of those 'whys', Kit, I'm afraid." Sheer had never used her name before. She knew she was being taunted. "Though I think I can answer that one," he went on. "That so-called new commandment, that you love one another, that they say energises all their combination or association of minds, well, it means that as far as possible they won't deny his wishes. I expect he was advised to be patient. In his favour is the fact he's one of the Daylight People as you call them, with those strange memory patterns. It's odd he should be here at all. It's usually the Old Ones who come asking awkward questions at Regret, even seeing it as a city to storm. Possibly Hereward came here once. He's got the same amputated mind as your sweetheart's got now."

"What about you?" asked Letitia. "Aren't you one of the Unmen?"

"Of course he is," said Kit.

And so while the pine-cones burned hot and fragrant and the wind came across a thousand miles of open plains and the crescent moon sailed above them, Kit told them some of what she had learned in the vast web of the Unmen's thoughts. She explained how when the evolutionary one-way track towards association had taken much of humanity forward, thriving in a giant trustful fellowship, there had been the refractory, unruly, unbiddable ones who dared not expose themselves to the reciprocity of love. Instinct told them that in the association they could not really understand there would be an end to the secret dark joy of bending others to their will. And being Old Ones, with their nonsequential memories, they could never forget the sweet power-drug and yearned to taste it afresh. "That is why you Old Ones became rectors of the Matrix," said Kit. "Tell me about the war debate in St Xavier's. My guess is that it was a play in which you all had parts, with the end already written. I expect you kept Kopa in the council deliberately, since it was fun having one random vote. When he left, Jacky had to have a part written for him."

"I thought you did that," said Sheer.

"And when was the decision to opt for peace made? Let me guess again. It was when it was clear that most of the Matrix peoples would rather fight. Exactly the same with little ships – most sailors wanted bigger, safer ones. If they had wanted little ones would you have forbidden them instead?"

"Of course. Little ships are unsafe. Look at Andread."

Sheer half regretted this last remark as soon as he made it, particularly when Magnus spoke: "You must enjoy making people do what they don't want."

"That's what power means, Magnus," Letitia told him. "Where's the satisfaction in telling people to do what they intend to do anyway?"

"So why doesn't it make us feel good, our folk and yours?"

Letitia shrugged. "I don't know."

"I know. I saw that in their thoughts too."

They listened, not knowing what to think, as Kit related how first there had been the Old Ones, and of how not many were left behind when most took the next of evolution's steps, and of how a new people had grown up with one tiny genetic change, even this the Unmen being reluctant to engineer. The change in memory had meant that the Daylight People had loved the world and in their care it had healed itself. Though there were times when they felt briefly stirred by some accidental sip of power, when for an hour or a day or a week something in them pulsated when they cut down a huge tree or dammed a river, the world soon pressed and caressed them again in a way that humanity had once known, lost, and never stopped pining for. In their stewardship the skies had grown bluer, the waters sweeter, the air fresher. Preoccupied with the velvet of the peony-flowers, the hovering hawk ruffling its wingtips, and the flavour of gooseberry tart, they no longer exploited the dominion over the world that their exuberant brains and active hands would have allowed them.

"That is why," explained Kit, "we in Westermain find the Daylight People so hard to cope with. They can hurt us one day, yet build a chapel for us to pray in the next." She nodded at Letitia. "Easier for you in the Glassy Country."

"Do you think so?" Letitia was swinging her glasses round and the firelight made her eyes a deep fuchsia. "No one hurts us, I agree, but as for the hurt, the Glassy Country knows how to hurt all right."

"Well, you can live elsewhere now," Lucas reassured her. "By now everyone knows what your folk did for the Matrix. You could come and live in my country. It's a long way away, though."

"Thank you, Lucas, I'm sure it would be very nice. But the Glassy Country might yet make its mark in the story of the world. Of course it marks its people and twists their bodies and sometimes their minds, but we're changing and surviving, and I don't think the Unmen would like to do without us. We heard how they believe their association is evolution stepping forward, because clustering into ever more complex organisations is a universal law. But may this organisation not be in danger of becoming like the pattern of a crystal, all its component parts resembling one another and developing only by adding similar parts?"

There was someone standing listening just beyond the firelight's cone. As people realised, the conversation dwindled and died. The woman who came among them came so easily into their midst that they doubted momentarily that it could really be Isobel the flower-girl who had been too timid even to place her blankets up close to a fire she had not lit but had slept lonely in the shadows. She put one hand on Jacky's forehead and stroked his hair back from his face.

"Don't!" said Kit.

"Only saying goodbye. And goodbye to everyone here, except one. Come, George. Regret is waiting for you now, has been waiting ever since you were born though you knew it as little as I. It is no distance. Walk with me."

George Littler got to his knees and smiled. The sickness had wasted away his strength but he pulled himself upright, and spoke for the first time for two days. "Will there be trees in Regret, Isobel?"

"Every tree that ever was."

"Then it might be for the best. Do I say goodbye now?"

Isobel nodded, and George walked round the circle of his friends and spoke gently with each as if consoling them. They in turn could only speak humbly and simply, and trust he would know their hearts. Then he walked away and they never saw him again.

"I must say goodbye too," said Isobel. "You have learned much, few visitors here have learned more, but you will forget it gradually or write in a book of how you saw it as you wished it to be, as others before have done."

"I saw the city." Magnus sounded very assured.

Hereward thought suddenly of his bubble city, where he had died on the wall, and how Demetrius had said Lamorak and the Old Ones had found a way into the city of Regret years ago.

"I see empty grasslands," said Letitia. "Do you see them, Isobel?"

"Only those who will never go back see what is here. The Matrix folk see the city of their imagination. What you see is nearer but still what you expect to see."

"Is that our mutations working?"

"Yes."

"Which the Unmen inflicted upon us."

"No. Random mutation made the Twisted Folk what they are. You said yourself that the Glassy Country changes and often hurts its people, and there are other places in the world that do the same. Regret made only one change in the many folk that are the Daylight People. I suppose it was inflicted upon them. I suppose a doctor inflicts health on the sick. I can say this because I know now of the past world when it was at the mercy of the Old Ones, who took life away like a long satisfying drink, stamping on insects, poisoning flowers, burning and felling forests, massacring birds and beasts and fish, sending the beautiful, intricate, irreplaceable creatures to join the unicorns and horses in the only place where they could be safe, the true city of regret.

"Rarely did anything at the mercy of the Old Ones find them merciful. It was not possible to change this completely without changing the whole nature of mankind but it was possible to change the perspective of power so that it became part of the background, there but receding into the distance. The change made us into pensioned-off assassins, so absent-minded that the old murderous inclinations were recalled only hazily if at all. And there were compensations: we loved the world and it loved us back. The trees we didn't fell crowded into a shade wherever we walked, the birds the Old Ones almost silenced sang in choirs for us, we came close to entering the magic realm where the animals listen and speak to us."

Magnus looked hard at Isobel, thinking that surely it had always been thus. The butterflies had always come to sit on his bare arms, opening their sumptuous wings in languorous display, for him to tell them their lovely names: red admiral, peacock, painted lady, swallowtail, fritillary.

Martin looked away from Isobel and back into the little coppices and meadows around Hay village that had always enfolded him in a green embrace of lime tree and beech over his head, ferns to his waist, and speedwell, campanile and elecampane about his feet.

When he looked back Isobel was walking away, and Jacky spoke to him: "What's your name?"

"Martin."

"Do you live here?"

"No."

"No, we don't," said a sharp voice from behind Martin's shoulder. "Nor do you. Your name is John Dorn and you live on the Big Grey River in Westermain."

"Is that far away?"

"Yes, Jacky, but I'll see that you get back." Turning to her brother Kit said, "Hold me when I fall." Then she held up her gloved hand so that it was silhouetted against the firelight and called out, "Isobel, wait!" Martin was just in time to catch her before she slithered on to the grass.

LI

The purpose and destiny of the uncountable billions of thoughts which existed within the framework of what was at once a singular mind and a vast multiplicity of minds was no more known to that consciousness than is the precise future of anything else. Being both intrigued by and reconciled to having to endure the effects of the principle of uncertainty was reflected in Regret's own principle that above all it must stay alive while also staying genetically flexible and unshackled. One of the grim features of genetics is how a species refines itself into oblivion, no longer free to respond to its world because it is imprisoned by an earlier response, which has become for it a self-made sarcophagus, adorned with the teeth of the ancient tigers or the armour of the rhinoceros.

The Unmen wanted no such memorial, its symbol a fossilised brain. Decay holds no surprises, so they were pleased to see that the uncertainty that should be inherent in the futures of both the Daylight People and the tetchy, stubborn Old Ones was expressing itself in unexpected outcomes, and the accident of the Twisted Folk was bringing true unpredictability.

Thus the Unmen waited with anticipation in hope that Kit would again flash and flaunt herself inside and yet independent of their consciousness. And she came with the same arrogant aurora, an announcement so confident that the thoughts that immersed her suddenly assumed in her presence a fresh modality, rather as a mesh may unexpectedly display moire patterns. She sensed too a gentle admiration for her agility and dancing poise, but her prickliness and self-will set her as unavoidably apart as a speck of dust is foreign to the eye. Never before had a self-contained consciousness entered the composite mind intact, though some had struggled fiercely to do so. The Unmen were fascinated not only by her presence but by the entry point, having already grasped that Kit's password was the perfect simulation of Isobel. The law of big numbers will one day produce, if it has not already done so, two identical sets of fingerprints, and now Isobel was integrated into the mind there was no way to keep Kit out.

The thought-presence of Kit pulsed with glee, for she had just made another discovery that she had doubted might involve some paradox. She made a sort of showy pirouette full of predatory grace. As before, she was aware of the activity of the Unmen as paths of some force that she could observe from a neutral position, and then when wishing to communicate she would slide into a ganglion of these paths. Inside the ganglion was a moving, shimmering, living picture.

It was a crowd, faces looking upward, but this time with her own image in it, waiting for her, and she wondered momentarily if it was a trap, but she came and merged into her reflection, knowing at once that now the Unmen were directly in contact with her, instead of thinking about her. She felt sure that she could side-step outside the labyrinth of thought and find herself back in the timeless, colourless void among the paths the quanta were tracing. Indeed, so confident was she that she stood on one leg, the other foot cocked back and resting on the toe, poised as a ballet dancer.

Only the picture was uneasy. It was not the stable and Christ-child, but then the stock of correlative pictures you can envisage to visit is limited. Of course she had the little inconsequential pictures that engrave themselves in even the least retentive memories. Peering out of one of the tunnel-house's entrances into a curtain of osiers and bulrushes, with a hem of marigolds, pink speedwell and forget-me-nots, had been the first picture of her little world. Her worst picture, forever renewed by being sewn in the family tapestry, was her father on the barn door, dried blood in his nostrils, goose grass sticky in his hair, but when she tried to understand the greater world she preferred to refer to a few great and symbolic scenes.

She had heard the Companions singing, 'We made a bargain, a compact with God,' and she believed her present image to be a sort of bargain, hopelessly one-sided though it may have been, and it would be proper to state her case quickly and go, leaving the scene for others to visualise and vitalise, as they had done ceaselessly over many ages. Her own situation was uncertain, and the picture in itself simmered with such a psychopathic vehemence that she had to keep whispering in her head that it was her analogue and how else could she express abstractions than in her own terms.

The scene roared with voices, and counterpointed itself with screams, jostling Kit with elbows and shoulders and stifling her inside a rank smell of grease and sweat. The sky was unnaturally dark, the faces awash with mischief, self-disgust, and a dark excitement, the air itself brewing with a blood-lust that spilled over into carnality, and Kit, feeling herself clumsily fondled from behind, spun round with the snarl of an infuriated leopard. The earth shuddered under her feet, and the mob trembled and yelled as the ground spasmed.

Through the heads she caught a glimpse of Isobel, recognising the flower-girl despite her unfamiliar appearance in a long blue-grey cloak with a white hood like a monk's cowl. As well, there were other women, who wept, and one who, looking upwards, stood like marble, her thin hands pressed against her mouth. Seized by impulse Kit pushed and ducked her way through the crowd, giving Isobel a glance like the clang of a cymbal as she passed, and touched the older woman's arm. A wooden post as thick as her waist was embedded in the ground, and there was a pile of stony, reddish, hilltop soil kicked loose around her feet. The face, lolling at its familiar angle, would be above her, she knew.

A few paces away were the other posts. Briefly she wondered how many other people had been drawn to this thought when they had sought for help or consolation. She knew the older woman's name but could not speak it; now, close, she could see the face's skin faded and fragile as tissue paper, the eyes' colour almost drained away. Summoning up her nerve Kit tried to speak, her tongue feeling thick and clumsy in her dry mouth. "When he was little –" she faltered, unsure of how to go on, but fearful of stopping.

The picture shouted its furies and would not wait for her. Some droplets of blood fell past her; she held out the black-gloved paw and some of them fell on it and soaked in. Above, the edge of the moon's disc was crawling across the sun, and in the dusky light the scene seemed almost candle-lit. "He was a good baby and a good little boy," she said, afraid that any question she asked would turn into begging, but she couldn't stop and ignored Isobel shaking her head. "I expect he had nice toys," she ventured.

The woman still looked away though her eyes rose the height of the wooden post, past the dangling feet and the cross-piece, where Kit dared not look; nor did she dare to look at the other two posts, knowing full well they too held shapes stretched wide in the air, poised as high divers poise, momentarily, before plummeting down. "I'm sure you had lots of happy days." At once it sounded inadequate, foolish, but the picture coughed deep and the earth shrugged again, and the woman for the first time responded, nodding. Or maybe it was just a trick of the light.

She could not stay where she was. The hill-top was no place for her, another agony altogether from the long ago, and she not a real component at all, far less a part of it than one vein in one leaf of the nearby olive trees. Yet the passion was not strange to her and she could share in it. After all, how can you think but in images, spreading them like oils on canvas? Even in the barest form of speculation where the intellect proposes to deal in a puritanical reason what can its tools be but symbols? One was one sheep before it was a notch on a shepherd's staff, and though the stained glass scenes of Hay church were cool and decorous they still distilled the sacrifice.

Kit knew that redemption did not come without payment, but she was utterly determined to regain the Jacky she knew. So she cast a final glance across the picture, trying to search out Isobel and transmit her terms. There was a dreadful moment before she could look away when she noticed the long yellow hair of the second of the suspended figures. What if the third should shout defiance in the accent of Westermain as only one of the irretrievable Old Ones could?

Thankfully she slid away into the colourless void where the Unmen did not penetrate. As yet they had shown no sign of their presence other than by the perturbation around her as the vibrations swept hither and thither in their unpredictable circuits, occasionally seeming to develop some main highway as of a prevailing wind, then fluctuating and swelling along new or little-used directions, so that Kit herself danced to avoid them, as small girls, their feet a blur, hop airily over swirling skipping-ropes.

She was confident that the Unmen knew of her offer. It might have been selfish, she thought, but she knew that the woman in the picture also wanted her boy back just as much as she wanted Jacky. She had made two appearances in their cerebral mainstream, so her intentions and ultimatum must be clear. With Jacky back to his old self she would leave the labyrinth amicably. Otherwise she would be more of a virus than a dust-speck. Isobel in particular would have understood straight away, she thought, thus sending the information flowing through the whole organism.

The virus is old, very old, a scrap of coded life in a capsule. It is life living only to replicate itself, and doing so without mercy for it must always enter a cell and transform the essence of that cell into its own. Many times over it turns its prey into itself. The greater organism, whose cells are being colonised, sends antibodies to search out and consume the virus. Whereas the less subtle viruses try to find secret hiding-places the subtlest of the breed can disguise itself as an antibody. This is what Kit had done. At first she had wondered how to transcribe herself on to the fabric of the place she was in and then how to hide. By chance she had chosen the virus's method, which is to alter the genome of the host cell, and by her own cunning chose the defence method of the most cunning of all viruses known to man, and, disguising herself perfectly as Isobel, remained perfectly secure.

LII

Jacky now knew his name was John Dorn, Jacky to most, and Jackyboy to the oldest, of his friends. At least he had been told so and had accepted it placidly. Other information had come too: Magnus Dorn was his brother, Astolat his sister, he had a father in the far off province of Westermain, but his mother and his older brother were dead, and he was a trawler captain by trade. All of this he assumed to be true, though knowing it only as you know others' words. He could not remember clearly what the sea was, and fish had gone from his mind. When Magnus spoke of the siege of Limber it was a story so incomprehensible that he grew bored. In any case a million immediate interests were busying his mind; at night he lay in his blankets and examined the stars, their brightness, their patterns, their long, slow movements, and occasionally he shook his brother awake to demand their names and the story of their names. Sleep came slowly, for there were the grasses to reach out and touch, the moths that came to the dying fire to watch, and the hooting of owls and the squeaking of mice to intrigue him.

The long journey went on and they crossed the Fence, though it meant nothing to him. Twice the migration of the Daroi moved by, following Frick, the new El Daro, as he led them south, avoiding Regret to their east. Now Jacky knew bulls and cows, and the tall long-striding Daroi, happy that up ahead their leader was tugging them along. He liked them, beasts and people alike, and they, liking children, liked him, not least for his ready laughter and simple questions. "How long do cows live?" he asked, and "What makes it rain?"

His questions made Magnus look away helplessly and tough Stefan Giorgiou smashed his fist on a tree-trunk in vexation. Lest he stray and be lost a watch was kept, which suited Jacky well, there being always someone nearby to question. Cheerful in an innocent contentment his features seemed younger, and the old impatient chafing nature disappeared along with the bouts of melancholy and wildness. Everyone knew that he had been in the world of the Unmen, and the experience had left him utterly changed.

Previously he had assumed that his world was governed by cause and effect, by logic and common sense, by codes of graduated responses. In one awe-struck afternoon he had learned that all his beliefs were either not so or at least existed only to provide in an ever-expanding universe a little assurance, as in one's house are gathered comforting clocks, books, armchairs and pictures, these being not explanations but company.

There being no way but forward for humanity those in its vanguard had traversed more of the emptiness that lay ever ahead than those who trod behind. The lacerating truth they passed back to those who yearned to know it, as Jacky had done, was that the only imperative was for life not to fail, lest the universe should have waited and longed in vain to be made conscious and pervaded by the multifuelled energy of that association and affection code-named love. Somewhere in this lay the answer Jacky had asked for, that the imperative of life to surge onwards ever more complex meant that, like the grasshopper multitudes so vast they could ford rivers on bridges of their own corpses, life itself drove forward on a causeway of corpses, not only of all once-living creatures but of most of the ideas and ideals with which, however primitively, they had sought to sustain themselves.

Jacky had always believed in a world that behaved intelligibly, though its reasons were often hidden from him, and found it difficult to rationalise in reverse and say not that the world behaved thus in order to reach some higher state but that whenever it had reached any stage in the progress then much, possibly all, of what had passed before was chance at work finding demonstrably an effective pathway for past-present to crystallise the future.

He was one of a people who had over the long years before his birth and during his short life helped the forests grow deep and rich, the rivers run clear and the seas roll crystal, the rain fall sweet and the very air sparkle and fizz. The means were good, for by and large the plan had been honourably conceived and undertaken. When what seemed ages ago Novak had explained to him how building big ships denuded the forest the argument had impressed him. But to learn that there was no way to know whether actions that were unselfish, imbued with love, or even a certain nobility of spirit, could be said to hold any more or less significance than the chance disposition or adaptation of some gene, that was as frustrating as knowing that there was an answer gestating to be revealed in an inaccessible future. Had there been no answer how simple it would have been, but there lay the future, and the Unmen themselves were not without premonitions for, along with an infinity of other thoughts, the matter of the presence of Kit in their mind-set reminded them that the present had to test every way to the future.

Jacky's overloaded brain adapted as best it could, resembling the thought processes of those saints, artists, or even savants who have forgotten the worldliness which to them is only a distraction. So while he asked if the sun was far away, or why trees grow upwards, part of him, silently, unrealised, was trying to absorb information and possibilities so vast he could never be the same again. So it is in the thoughts of children when for the very first time their minds must accommodate the idea of their own deaths. Never again can they be truly at ease.

Jacky was aware of the woman with the deformed hand. At first she had spoken often to him and spent hours by his side, but she was uneasy company for him. Harder than anyone else she pressed him to recall his past and the impossibility of doing so aggravated him enough for his face to cloud over, and several times he snapped back impatiently that it was a waste of time. Then his voice had enough of the old vigour for faces to turn expectantly as if some long awaited guest were at the door with hand lifted to knock. Once only she had put her arms around him and said, "Do not forget me, my love." He was always conscious of her presence and sometimes when she pushed back her long dark-red hair and watched him with her green eyes he found her attractive, but she could also look forbidding and even ill-disposed when she pulled her black shawl over her head and stared silently for hours into the night-fire. She had few friends, perhaps only one, the little hopping man who anyway seemed to be everyone's friend, although at times she would speak with the big man with one eye, being always, Jacky noticed, very respectful of him.

"How did you lose your eye?" he asked several times, undeterred by shrugs and silence.

"Someone cut it out," was the eventual answer.

"Why?" Jacky was interested.

"They thought I hurt a girl."

"But you didn't?"

"No."

"I'm sorry. It was a bad thing to happen."

"Probably," said the big man, which seemed an improbable conclusion but Jacky had to be content with it.

A day came when they saw Limber again, or saw it in the way men and women do who, revisiting a place, also revisit the past's many overlapping images. Their thoughts would be forever coloured by the thick brown-grey smoke-drifts, the undersides reflecting in coppery red the city burning, the Daroi gongs droning and shields rattling, the smell of dust and the cremation fires, with overhead the storks circling dismayed as the flames devoured their nests, the Companions' ice-packed coffins going up the gang-planks to the ships' holds. Only the last Rector of Limber knew nothing of all this and saw the city afresh, a thousand new-cleared spaces where the hammering of stonemasons and the dust of bricklayers rose as the new buildings brightly rose. From Limber, from its near provinces, and from the ships crowding the harbour, came carpenters, painters, plasterers, metalsmiths and cabinetmakers, to work from dawn into the night, and with them worked the craftsmen of clear and dyed glass, of wrought iron and filigree, of inscribed stone, of polished marble and fine-grained alabaster, artificers, too, in gesso, fresco, and stucco, and makers of lamps and of pavements, designers of verandahs, balconies and balusters, alongside pargeters and mosaicists, fountain-moulders and bellcasters who dreamed the music of water and bells, and hundreds of gardeners vying to plant tiny courtyards with bougainvillea, frangipani and cypress, to shade wide open spaces with cedar trees, to line avenues with plane trees, and to make everywhere else a profusion of roses.

A few of the Daroi, chiefly from among their elderly people, had stayed in and around the city, but the long columns stalled for so long at the Dole River were now snaking past Limber, skirting it to the north-west, putting it into their tales. To give it meaning they were settling on Lokietok, extending the story backwards to the river, and back again to High Altai, already embroidering it into a trial and a sacrifice, adding that the body of Lokietok had not been truly dead in the coffin when it had been borne away to the ship, and some future generation would some day be called on to show the constancy and audacity necessary to fight an unbeatable foe.

Somewhere in their story there was a niche for Jacky, the shining warrior-chief who had fought alongside the monster before escaping from its spell to become one of the white Daroi, already with his cows just beyond the next river. This figure they did not connect with the everyday young man watching the dockmen tug the sardine crates across the decks and on to the wharves.

Jacky looked into an opened barrel and saw the fish, their silver shapes still distinct, though lying as commingled as needles and pins lie crammed in a bottle. When he smiled down the fishermen knew him for one of those who love and respect the fishes. "Are there many out there to catch?" There were, they told him. "And many kinds of fish?" Indeed there were. "Good," said Jacky. "Let us catch only what we must. The other fish must eat too." So far he knew only the fish he had seen on the dock, but the men around him understood him and were pleased to hear him say 'we' and 'us'. Unlike the Daroi they recognised him as the last rector, though surprised he was so humble and unworldly.

A week passed with Hereward, Martin, Kit and Magnus all impatient for news of a ship sailing for Westermain, and then another as the ship was readied for the voyage. They and Jacky stayed with Stefan Giorgiou, who owned one of the few undamaged buildings in the city. He was caring and kind, though perplexed by his guests. Martin was so unfailingly cheerful that it seemed odd he was Kit's brother, for she grew ever more wayward and contentious. Hereward escaped her censures, even receiving faint praise: "Tyr-Hereward has made the Twisted Folk free," she would say. "I don't really know how, but it is done. He is an Old One. He makes things happen. Perhaps without knowing it. It might have happened if he had sat at home in his mill, but somehow change needed him. All Old Ones stir up change. They can't help it." Martin, Magnus and Jacky drew regular dispraise. "My brother is good with earth-things and tricks, that is all," she told them dismissively.

"He is brave," protested Hereward.

"And quite brave, I suppose." Magnus, being hard to dislike, was deprecated differently: "Magnus should lose weight. He should also not be so obsessed with butterflies." When he heard this Magnus, who could have lifted her in the air with one hand, just laughed. "He should be more serious about life," Kit added. And Jacky, whom she adored, exasperated her endlessly. "He should never have gone to Regret," she reproached Hereward. "I blame you for encouraging him. He is so thoughtless." And, "All Dorns are the same," Magnus was instructed. "Astolat will be the same one day. They spend too much time thinking."

Martin could only roll his frog-eyes when he was informed that Kit had foreseen trouble and wretchedness from the moment he had brought Jacky into their home at Sheepwash Bend, but he understood that she was nervous of again confronting the Unmen's power and was preparing by sharpening her claws on anyone close to her. She had told him enough of her trances for him fully to forgive her disposition. As for Jacky, nothing she could say would affect him, for he smiled at every barbed comment, then wished her good morning and asked if she had slept well. She frowned on the many people drawn to him. "Next you'll be healing the sick," she told him.

The last evening before their departure came and time for farewells. To everyone's surprise Osric Sheer came, asking to speak to Hereward. "It's a pleasure talking to you," he said when they had walked along to a quiet spot on one of the harbour quays. "I don't enjoy John Dorn going round being so tolerant and pitying. That's what happens to some people who get too close to the Unmen. Not to us though, oh no!"

"No?"

"No. And I haven't much time for those Twisted Folk who hang around with the Dorns."

"Haven't you?" said Hereward mildly. "Who have you got some time for?"

"Us, of course. You, me, and the rest of us. The Novaks, Colonna, maybe Lokietok, though it wasn't so clear with him. All right, we don't agree on everything, nor would I expect you to, it's not in your nature."

"What do you mean it's not in my nature?"

"You being an Old One. Like me. We're different, we can't help making the future happen. Take the Children, for example. Years ago when the Academies started, then the Children started to regrasp the world."

"I still don't understand you."

Sheer smiled. "Look, this isn't something easily explained in this sort of conversation, but try a simple example, let's say an egg, sitting in an egg-cup. With the sense of sight what would it be? A water-smoothed stone, a paperweight? Try listening to it – nothing, it wouldn't exist. Smell, I'm not sure, something very slight. Touch? Taste? Now if you only had the sense of taste what would an egg be?"

"Not much unless you cracked it," Hereward said.

"Exactly. And with all the other senses too, if they got past the shell there would be more information. But I doubt they could even get close to understanding the true function of the egg, because they've no choice but to try understanding in their own terms. A blind man who can only use touch comes at it down the only tunnel that exists for him."

"So?"

"So every age, or civilisation, develops one tunnel of thought. Look, if people measured their world carefully, dividing the measurements into ever smaller units, so they could analyse it, what tunnel would they get used to?"

"Mathematics. Physics."

"Right. We Old Ones in our age knew our world in inches and seconds, our own lives in four seasons multiplied by the repetition of years, and so on."

"We still do."

"What happens when you don't measure the world," said Sheer, ignoring this interjection, "but watch it grow? Think of it first as the life-cycle, and the dimensions much later. Come on, if you measure a tree, what are you likely to measure?"

"Wood."

"Not if you think of it as seed, sapling, leaf, flower, fruit, all decaying into earth, and shade and home for birds and insects. That's how most of the Matrix folk think. Another tunnel, of course."

"Botanists. Biologists."

"Indeed. Pity the academies missed you. Any other ways to consider this tree of ours?"

"Draw it?"

"Certainly. The whole range from painter to landscape gardener. Good answer but silly question. Such as how many radii has a circle." Hereward shrugged, wondering where the disquisition was going, and Sheer soon continued. "What about the kindly folk of Regret? They grasp the world their way too. I couldn't tell you its name, maybe psychology, though the psyche of a tree eludes me."

"I'm not interested, except where it touches me and the Children, or, more exactly, one child back in Westermain."

"Let me tell you about that. The children came to Limber, the most brilliant and perceptive children on earth, to have a chance to think, not to stultify in forests and hamlets, herding pigs and spinning threads, nor to think in suits of armour like mathematicians or botanists or even artists but to think like children who see the world afresh."

"And all this because – ?"

"Because we are Old Ones, naturally. We bend the world to our will. What else brought you to Limber? Trouble is our name and nature. The Children are the Old Ones' answer to Regret, or what you think of as the Unmen. Why should we fade gracefully into extinction? There are fewer of us than there were but it is nature's way to favour the hardiest survivors. Regret's not the only future while we are still around."

"No need to use force on the Children," Hereward remarked quietly.

"It happened," Sheer went on, "I agree. But only with a few we couldn't afford to lose. Searching minds and Old Ones' blood. Adelie's mother was one of us. Maybe her father. So was Astolat's mother."

"Why not ask their consent?"

"Probably someone did. But that isn't the point. The world of the Matrix was always far too much a place of consent and consonance. It needs injustice to stir it, and no one can deny the opportunities of turmoil. Conflict is the natural state of Old Ones. Bringing some

Children against their wishes stirred conflict, as did allowing the Daroi to reach Limber. Look at the changes in these last few months."

"For the better?"

"Possibly. That's not the point again. So long as change is stimulated it may be for the better."

"Why are you telling me all this?"

"Because Regret didn't want you. They wanted Isobel, or at least she was in harmony with them, and the other two girls and the big woodman. But not you, not Kitfox or John Dorn. So what do you do now? Go back to Westermain and grow turnips?"

"Maybe," Hereward said mildly, adding, "Maybe I might work as a miller," at which Sheer laughed and shook his head.

"They won't let you, I'll tell you that. Anyway everyone else in the village where your mill is has probably forgotten you, but you can never forget. Send me a message. We'll be running Limber again before long and when we are there'll always be a place for you. That's really the point of this conversation."

"Can I help to choose the children for the Academies?"

"Of course."

"And those who don't want to come?"

Sheer had been so lulled by receiving neutral responses that he was on the point of answering. Then, finding Hereward uncomfortably close, he took an involuntary step back. Behind him the dark waves sucked at the stonework of the wharf, and glancing over his shoulder he found himself looking straight down at the restless water. As Hereward took a corresponding step with him, he felt a tremor of fear, not quite panic but more than apprehension, exactly as Adelie had felt on the embankment above the big barley field when the stranger had first taken her thin arms in his big hands. Hereward reached out and grasped Sheer's jacket, bunching it in his fist.

"I'm sorry about your girl," said Sheer, and tried to edge sideways.

"Of course you are." Hereward's sideward shuffle left them in exactly the same position. "Can you swim, Osric?"

Sheer knew it for what it was, the sort of pointless question of the same order as asking Adelie, "Can you run, little girl?" Since the truth is always available, he said, "Not very well," just as the push sent him falling backwards.

That same evening was the time Kit had decided to re-enter the thought-web of Regret. On the next day they were due to board the ship for Westermain. Martin sat with her as she waited for sleep to come. When she was unconscious, her mind resting without even the activity of dreams, it would be easy to slip into the labyrinth once Isobel called her name. Kit was certain that Isobel or someone else would think her and then she would dive into the whole tempting ocean of faith, hope and love in which humanity had always longed to refresh itself for the next endeavour. After all, she was already there and waiting to be resurrected, and Kit had speculated occasionally whether the double presence she had established might not become triple, even multiple, if every time she sidestepped into the no-mind's-land there was another similar but slightly warier personality installed there. The stratagem of the virus is to endlessly replicate itself into safety.

She smiled and Martin knew she was anticipating a contest that she alone seemed to regard as equal. Only with her brother was she confident enough to face questions without resorting to irony, and when he pressed her to be cautious and wait to see what time would bring she told him she had no time: "My babies are waiting to be born," she said, "and if Jacky truly forgets me then they will never be. You remember what Frick said at Regret, 'What else is there to do?'"

Isobel was therefore she thought, and, because she loved Jacky, sooner rather than later she would think of him and then ineluctably of Kit, whose thought-self would then stir and flex its powers. To Kit this was neither strange nor was it familiar, it simply happened. Had she known it her ancestors had called up a not dissimilar miracle by imprinting a codeword into a machine, the only difference being that it was through her quick wits that the Unmen organism unknowingly summoned her.

It was easier every time. One flash of thought, a glimpse of many images passing so quickly that they left only the faintest of impressions – of blueness, cornflowers, lapis lazuli, rosemary, hyacinths in a bowl, wood bluebells, water under ice – and Kit wondered if Isobel was daydreaming her first look into Jacky's eyes as he stopped at her flower-stall on the Steps. Then she was outside the streaming thoughts and undetectable in the colourless no-place she thought of as her own. Already on her last incursion she had proposed her own bargain, although shaken and her own loss utterly dwarfed by the cruel, sad contract that had ended on the stony hill. At least she had been of one mind with the mother, she was sure of that.

Kit wondered what picture she would see when she was steady enough to step into the rush and turbulence of the thought-stream. Though nervous of being swept away, a straw in a torrent, there seemed no point in hesitating so she put her good hand under her long red hair and flicked it back, first left then right, as if she meant to comb and toss sparks behind her, and flounced forward.

Inside the multiplex that she now thought of simply as Regret every one of her senses was fiercely energised, as if it were indeed tumbling water battering her along, striving to see up green-white towards the surface, moss-olive downwards, water's coldness impinging on her open eyes, mouth spitting and tasting at once the water's flavours – stone, root, leaf – and her muscles pulling her through the flood's own muscularity until she found air and balance and swam, in the stream yet looking at it and letting it look at her. So it did, and instead of the unfocused churning and buffeting it placed her primly on the side of another picture, this time drawn purely from her own small past. She knew that it was she who was the source of the pictures but that Regret was in there too, so deeply that it spoke by way of as many advocates as there were subtleties of choice. Kit at first found the picture reflecting less of her own antagonistic mood and presence than seemed to her quite appropriate.

This time it hurt more personally. The field was green, sloping, irregularly shaped, and fat brown cows had turned its lowest corner into a plash of wet hoof-marks. On the high side lay a dark wood and the other way, beyond the cows, the eye was drawn over miles of fields patched with dim green woodlands, until the distance turned everything misty blue. The field itself was too dimpled with hollows to make it profitable to plough and had a scattering of very old oak trees. Here her people had met Hereward, but this time she was much younger. Around her were sitting Martin, her sister Fleur and her parents. They were in one of the hollows, carefully close to the wood's edge, just as some nibbling rabbits nearby were not straying far from their burrows. The girl Kit was lying on her stomach idly kicking her legs and chewing a grass stalk, thinking how much she hated her paw. She had taken her glove off and scrabbled up the grass in a torn patch, using the claw-nails as a sort of protest, both at her deformity and at having to listen to her parents.

"Maybe you would lose something, if you were one of the Daylight People," her father was saying, "something that you would be sad to lose."

"I can't think what," said the girl Kit sulkily. The older Kit who was sharing every sensation even to scrabbling up bits of earth, half sympathised with and half snarled at her ten-year-old self.

"You needn't feel too sorry for yourself. When Jacky falls in love with you he won't even notice your hand." But at the same time, since she had felt it once, she knew how the girl Kit felt.

Her father was speaking again: "Be careful, my love. Sometimes it is better to be patient. You have your own gift, so that, compared with you, everyone, even the Daylight People, is short-sighted."

"It is more than that," interrupted her mother. "She wishes to be free and equal, to walk openly and at ease across the fields and along the village street."

"That too will come. And when it comes shall we have lost something worth keeping? Though perhaps that is always the way of the world."

The younger Kit was not at all persuaded. "And what can we lose worth having?"

It was not easy for her father. He was a simple man but he tried: "I think we shall lose our old friendliness. All Twisted Folk care for one another. Gradually we shall lose our story too, and our songs, our favourite places, like this field."

So this was what she faced. She might have known. The thought-web was letting her know with all the insistence of her girlish memories that her demand was really a choice, with the corollary that all other choices would be extinguished; she could be patient and hope that one day she might again be luminous in his eyes, reinvested with love, or she could hope to convince the Unmen to trade with her for his past. What would come of it there was no knowing, and she wondered how she would have chosen differently in the past could she have foreseen George Littler cough blood or Alvin Costello loaded on the Kittiwake ship or a thousand other hurts.

Regret had not been unkind to Jacky in letting him forget his past hurts and the present sores that his mind chafed at. At least he had not become another Lokietok. She had seen him laugh more often in one day recently than in all the intense times before reaching Regret. Somehow he had learned that there was no need to torment himself with 'Why?' when now all things seemed to figure out the workings of God's heart.

In the nights of the fighting in Limber she had seen him with his nails bitten until they bled, the glass clattering in his hand against the jug as he tried to fill it, his shirt-front stained with food shaken from his fork, and knowing next day would bring the charging Daroi columns to kill him, or to kill the men he asked to stand in front of them, whichever was worse. All this and far more would come back to him; not all of it would be distressing, there would be happiness blended there, but certainly he would be cut off again from the blessed state of very young children who know without needing to understand, as they know their mother's breast, that their world has purpose.

But Kit had not come this far to turn back, and she displayed her wishes for Isobel and the infinitude of others to know, or confirmed them, for she had displayed them before: 'Let him be Jacky again. As hurt as he was. As hurt as I hurt him.'

The girl-Kit was still sulky in the background. Between her parents was a green cloth, with mugs of milk and flapjack scones on it. Her mother spread a scone with butter. "Would you like jam?"

"I don't feel hungry."

Kit thought of another picnic, of dropping strawberries into Jacky's mouth, and of her first kisses, and of all the perfumed fruit of Limber, the guava, mangosteen and granadilla, that the girl-Kit would taste one day. Isobel climbed over a stile in a nearby hedge and walked towards them. The younger Kit glanced up, momentarily interested, though Kit herself could not recall what had caught her eye so long ago, perhaps some bright bird hopping among the leaves, a child's lost kite puffed by the wind across the grass.

"I would choose the same in your place," Isobel said or thought to Kit, and smiled. "Though you understand that he may not, will not, feel exactly the same if you are not the same as you were before he came to us."

"So?" Kit felt sufficiently pleased with herself to smile at Isobel.

"Jacky will gradually recall the random parts of his past that people do recall, though much more than most, having an Old One parent."

"Am I random?"

"Not at all. Not so much time has passed since he came to your house. What he will have forgotten is what he learned in Regret."

"Will he want to go back there and ask his questions again?"

"Yes. He will want to do that, but he will put it aside, and he will pass his life feeling that it should have had more meaning than he could endow it with."

"Then he will be like everyone else," said Kit tartly.

"As much like everyone else as you are."

"What does that mean?"

"It means you must forget too."

"Forget what?"

"This place, and what you have learned about Regret. Particularly what you have done for love."

"Don't lecture me." Kit's green eyes were narrow and coldly hard. The picture stilled itself and dimmed into a moonless night, no night for picnics.

"Otherwise it cannot be the same as it was. Before Regret you loved him. Now you have love with a flavour of pity, so now he is diminished. Think about it. What you should do is let us help you forget all of this, which is easy enough. Is that too much to ask?"

Kit wondered if this was a victory. It felt very unlike one, and she was unsure of the reason, her father's words on correlative gains and losses having not altogether convinced her, then or now. Also she was loath to lose her access to the intriguing thought-world; she had explored only the minutest part of it, and there nagged at the edge of her mind the possibility, outrageous and blasphemous though it seemed, that this might be at least an intimation of the resurrection and the life hereafter which her faith had bethought itself and cherished. "I sometimes felt," she started and hesitated, not wishing Isobel to be amused at her expense, "sometimes, that this place was interested in me." Put like that it sounded unlikely but Isobel neither laughed nor smiled.

"Fascinated," she said, "and very surprised." Somewhere there was silvery laughter and whispers and the pattering of small feet, but no picture came, nor did Isobel seem to notice.

Kit sighed. "Ah, well, there's an end to all that. It will be nice to have him back."

LIII

The ship came up the estuary on the first day of October. There were premonitions of winter in the air: a dusting of sugary frost stiffened the stems of the marram grass that bound the river banks, oystercatchers and turnstones hopped gingerly on a skim of ice fringing the sluices that drained into the Big Grey River. "You must be cold," said Kit to Jacky. "You should have kept Nestor's hat." It was an idle remark, the sort she had made a hundred times hoping he might be prompted to reconnoitre at least some part of the landscape of his past.

"There's our house!" shouted Magnus from the bow and Kit saw him pointing to a tall narrow grey building that stood some distance away from and above the cluster of chimneys poking through the reds and browns of chestnuts and beeches.

"What is this village called?" asked Hereward.

"Ferris's Landing." Jacky spoke absent-mindedly. Thinking how the name seemed unusual, Kit at first thought Magnus had answered. She was utterly unready when he spoke again: "Nestor? Yes, I think he tried to hurt you. I remember the name."

Turning she almost skipped on the dew-wet deck boards and the flash of her smile washed her face clear of the doubt and demur she had been harbouring for weeks. Indeed, now in familiar surroundings, with his father and Astolat, how could everything not return? As the days passed she continued to watch each move he made, anxious not to miss the next step towards himself that he would surely make. She was grateful to Astolat, who buzzed adoringly round her brother, and she was delighted by his readiness to be involved in his sister's many projects as her mind flowered forth sprays of thoughts, complex and deep as the incurving petals of dark red roses.

Though his sister was happy that Jacky was so ready a playmate for her she was also perplexed by the changes in him. So easy to amuse, so patient and calm, he was light-hearted company, but she well recalled him hard-eyed in his rage at her kidnappers, or agonising over the peace vote, or how, before the ship took her from the city, the weight of command had worn him frail. She missed the sharp edges, the dismissiveness of his love; now, she thought, there may be no mountains left for him to climb, and while Magnus and I have to press upwards, for Jacky it is over. And so it should be, she added, there were enough bad times, but something in her was unsure that this placid brother was what she really wanted. And Kit was so unbending and stiff, continually distracted, and even Magnus, whom she had never seen agitated, was short-tempered. When after a week their father had suggested crabbily that Jacky might find some work Magnus spoke to him in a different voice, harsher than Astolat knew he could use, and she was nervous. Old Man Dorn scowled at his youngest son but chose to nod towards Kit and say, "How long is she going to stay? And her freakish brother?"

"As long as they like," said Magnus, the ice layered so thick in his voice a bull could have jumped on it.

"We'll go today." Astolat knew Kit would say that.

"No, you won't," Magnus assured her.

"What's all the fuss for?" wondered Jacky, sitting on the window-ledge pondering the way the clouds were hanging straight smoke-grey curtains down into the river and the distant sea, the season's first snow-squalls.

'Oh, Jacky, forget the wind and sleet,' thought Kit, 'and think about me again.'

But she was determined to leave and Martin was equally ready to go. Magnus came too; he was adamant that two of Kit's folk should not travel alone and that he, Jacky and Hereward should accompany them. The war of the Daroi had touched all of the Matrix provinces in some way for many men had taken ship to the siege of Limber and so far by no means all had come back. However those that returned felt the old rules and regulations of the Matrix were in abeyance now, and Westermain and Alba and Lett and the others were wondering if each would be standing alone in the swirling new times – and if the Companions did not come when they were called, nor the old militia, whose word would be law?

From the Big Grey River to Hay was two and a half days' steady travelling, on the road from first daylight to dusk. The land was quiet and they saw no other travellers along the long straight road, which for many miles was hard earth, worn and trampled down to the chalky rock of the region, dry and dusty in summer though now the autumn dampness was patching it with moss and flat plantains. Closer to Hay the ground would get muddier, Martin knew, and there would be wheel-ruts to twist ankles in, though each village chose a gravel-man to fill the road's cavities as best he could. Where there were arable fields bordering the road the stubble was shaved low and they were empty of life, except when sheep were penned there. The Daylight People had looked after the land for another year, thought Kit.

Late on the second afternoon a cold rain began to fall and, with little shelter to be found in the flat wet fields and not a barn or shed to be seen, they backtracked a mile or so to where a village lay tucked in a fold just off the road. They had glimpsed its roofs as they had passed, lying behind a screen of elms, the trees patched with rooks' nests, to which strings of the birds were returning from their day's foraging.

The inn was empty, warm with a log-fire which tempted them to stand with backs to it letting their damp clothes breathe steam and after a while sit with feet stretched out to the flames, flexing aches out of calves and thighs. As the evening wore on villagers drifted in, and, although the little group had found an inconspicuous bench behind a table, Kit, Magnus and Martin felt uncomfortable at the silent staring they attracted. Hereward simply leaned his head back and reflected every stare, waiting for the villager to drop his gaze or look away. Jacky was happily at ease, quick to smile and converse, and had been drawn to another table where several young men were playing knucklestones, balancing the rough little flints on the backs of their hands between their knuckles then tossing them in the air to catch them, steadily making the combinations of throws more complicated, the hands picking up the stones off the table as a pigeon pecks up grains of corn, then catching the flicked-up stones as they fell clicking neatly on to those already in the palm. To Jacky with his quick hand and eye it was attractive and at first not difficult, but eventually he could not match the complex manoeuvres of the better players.

". . . and so that's what you owe," said a voice in the clatter of laughter and comment.

"Owe? Was it for money? I'm sorry but I don't have any." It seemed to Jacky that suddenly he had fewer friends. Someone nudged his shoulder and he almost lost his balance.

"Come on. Travellers always have money." Someone else pushed him from the other side and his face grew puzzled and a sort of shadow slid across the features. Kit, getting to her feet, saw the shadow come and go and felt the black trapdoor open in his thoughts but close before his cold displeasure could climb out of it.

Kit sighed, then an ivory disc spun in the air and bounced on the table. "Keep the change," said Hereward. "Buy yourself some manners." One of the men picked up the counter and looked at the Matrix star.

"What's this?"

"Good currency." Magnus had not liked hearing his brother apologise; he would have liked two minutes alone with the men who had pushed him.

A voice across the room said, "Rich men from Limber."

Martin, sensing trouble and wishing he was outside, remembered distantly a backgammon game and wondered what it was in the Old Ones that responded to conflict. A netted fish leaping clear, curving down through the air to shoulder joyfully through the water's coolness, responded to its freedom with no more exhilaration. And Old Man Dorn married an Old One so Jacky and Magnus are half-brothers of trouble, he thought, and Hereward a full brother.

"Keep your money, rich man."

"Rich men, Old Ones, lording it over us. Next it'll be the twisters' turn."

"Never our turn."

The voices unnerved Martin, but not Magnus. "Lucky it isn't the Daroi people's turn. They could show you some real games. It took plenty of the Twisted Folk dead at Dole River to stop them."

"Love the twisters, do you?" Laughter, or an imitation of it.

"Far side of Ingastowe they don't love 'em."

More of the same laughter, and Kit and Martin felt eyes turning to look at them. Kit had been careful to keep her hand tucked under her shawl but, although an austere dresser by Glassy Country standards, she wondered if the lacy scarf and spangled shoe-buckles she had not been able to resist would give her away.

More people had pushed into the room and there was the crash of broken glass as a drink was knocked to the floor. The innkeeper and his wife decided simultaneously that this was enough and by pushing and barking opened an avenue for the group to leave. It was still raining thinly but Magnus turned away from the doorway that was spilling loud youths and gestured the others to follow. They did, apart from Jacky, who was turning slowly when the flung stone took him on the side of the head, knocking him down, with the light-streaks yelling so brightly that he clasped his head in his arms as he lay on the ground trying to make sense of the muddy grass wetting his face, its taste pushing clammily into his mouth. The ghosts were wrestling in his head, not silver wraiths but black and red shapes that bulged angrily, filling all the chamber of his mind, and he got up on his feet and even in the rain-streaked lantern-light his friends saw his eyes. Suddenly they looked twenty years older and were narrow and intent.

"Well, Kit," he said. "It's turning nasty. These Regret folk aren't as goodhearted as we thought. Are you all right?" She gasped for words, wanting desperately to know if this was the old Jacky, her Jacky as she thought of him, but the thoughts were too misty, too shapeless, like trying to grasp at the minds of Hereward or Sheer or any of the Old Ones, who, when death came close or the dark mood was on them, stopped thinking in concepts and behaved as if they were the vehicles of some interior agency that was over-riding any acquired personality.

Jacky had taken several steps towards the faces clustered at the door before Magnus overtook him. "Come on, leave them, they aren't worth it," said his brother. "Another time, maybe."

Jacky went on unheeding and when Magnus pinned his arms to his sides he broke free, and only when Hereward joined in could he be halted. Through the rain there were derisive yells, shouts of "Let him come, then," and now several were looking round for more stones.

Hauling Jacky away felt like tugging at a post long embedded in the earth, but when their straining eventually succeeded his whole body quite suddenly fell slack and they guided him gently back to where Martin was holding Kit's hand, dismayed by his sister's choking sobs.

"Why are you crying?" asked Jacky. "It was only some hotheads. They'll feel sorry in the morning." The rain was rinsing the blood through his hair, droplets of it hanging from his ear like little garnet pendants.

A pine plantation, particularly where the trees have room to thicken out, always makes a good spot to spend the night but there were hours of tramping in cold wet clothes before they found one. Nevertheless it was easy to build a hot fire and the pine-needles were a thick soft carpet. Months of travelling had taught them to keep sleeping-bags and blankets dry in packs, and clothes could always be steamed dry without much trouble. It hardly seemed worthwhile sleeping but Jacky was deep asleep in no time and Magnus was drowsy.

Kit was always respectful with Hereward, so much so that Martin occasionally teased her about it. She would reply that always their people had waited for Tyr, and he had done as they expected and changed all their lives. Martin told her that Hereward was one of the Old Ones and it was natural that there were changes in their vicinity, but she shrugged and said that that proved it.

With Hereward clearly not asleep she was encouraged to address him: "Hereward, what do you think will happen to Jacky? He is too trustful and gentle. He worries me."

There was a pause and she wondered if he had even heard her, but then Hereward said that Jacky seemed happier than he used to be, which was not at all what she wanted to hear. "Is he?" she snapped. "Pushed around by little blusterers in some clodhoppers' alehouse for the price of a drink?" There was another pause so she pressed on: "And when stones were thrown in his face you stopped him dealing with them. If that had been Limber . . ."

"If it had been Limber he would have had his infantry round him and Lokietok alongside him." Hereward did not add that in battle he had also watched over Jacky because Kit had never ceased imploring him to do so. "At the inn he had no weapon and there were fifty of them looking for trouble, but that isn't the point."

"So what is the point?"

"The Unmen told us a great deal and I'm not sure I understood it all, but one thought sticks in my head and that is that there exists this force which causes all things to draw together in affinity, the tiniest and the greatest, a force which has always been there and is all we have to keep away the last, long stillness that there would be if the universe wore itself out. One of its names is love, if you can give it a name, and for people like me it seems like some golden land that long ago we left and forgot the directions that would get us back there.

"I suppose I've a few small loves but I know there was no place for me at Regret. There might have been when I was a boy and perhaps once I tried to reach the golden country and the attempt cost me my memory, or maybe I couldn't bear to think of having been there and lost it. My book suggests someone did, and Demetrius thought it might have been me. Isobel got there and George and the other girls, and maybe Jacky still has a chance, but not if he is as dangerous and unappeasable as he once was."

"If he's not who he was then he'll be someone else."

"And you don't want someone else."

"He loved me once. No doubt he loved his family, too, and the grey sea, but I know he loved me. I agree he could be dangerous but only badness needed to be afraid of him."

"You're right," agreed Hereward. "And tomorrow will come whatever we do."

"I'll be pleased to be home again. I know it's not much – "

"It's nice. Nothing wrong with your home. I've been in it, you know. Go to sleep, Kit."

When they awoke patches of pale blue sky were emerging and the rain-clouds had moved east. To their surprise they saw on the horizon the grey silhouette, the size of a hand, of Ingastowe Cathedral. The previous night had brought them further than they thought and Kit and Martin alike began to feel the land responding, not as the empty land of Regret had acted upon them, which had been to catechise them with mystery and awe, but with soft murmurs, familiar as household words: the river lies over the ridge; beyond the green common the woods of Hay start; three miles down the long causeway over the fields that flood every winter and you see the chimneys of

Hay; down through the hazel trees and there's the beck and Mother and Fleur and we've been running along this path towards them every night for the last year . . .

Midmorning saw them in Ingastowe. It was cool and the paths had drifts of wet leaves that muffled their steps. Past the fort and cathedral they came and down one of the steep narrow roads that made them tread gingerly on slippery cobbles. Jacky's feet slipped and scrabbled but he bounced up and laughed, and a man standing on his doorstep had to smile. That night the man knew he had seen the cheerful face before. But, being one of the Daylight Folk, the past was hazy and he recalled little now of the charge up the slope into the blue militia or who had led him in it.

Behind and above them now was the cathedral, its creamy stone geometry floating over a tangle of roofs and tree-tops, higher even than the battlements and keep of the fort, as magnificent as it was different from Saint Xavier's. To Westermain folk the latter had risen in a shimmering fusion of domes and semi-domes, marble bubbles over apses, arches seen beyond arches, windows scalloping the dome rims as if everywhere the architects had striven to echo, in aureolas of marble, limestone, fresco and mosaic, the haloes that encircled Christ, his mother and the saints. Perhaps, thought Kit, Limber is nearer to the ideals of Regret than we are here with our spiky aspirations.

However she was too excited to pursue such speculation for having climbed the track that bordered the green commonland they were now clear of Ingastowe and ahead of them, hidden and waiting, enfolded in the landscape, was Hay. Martin and Kit began to quicken their steps, so much so that Magnus burst into laughter: "I'm looking forward to seeing Hay! It must be a nice place if we have to run to it."

"Sometimes," said Martin. "Most times, I expect, if you aren't one of us. But I have missed it."

"Did you know about our father?"

"Most places have good times and bad times, Kit." Magnus was always at ease with Martin but conversations with Kit made him feel as if he was continually snagging a broken finger-nail on a woollen blanket.

"Down here." Martin turned off where a field lane wound among blackthorn and alders. Now Hereward found himself passing close by the spot where Adelie had been injured resisting Zjelko and his partner.

"No smoke," said Kit.

"No ash-tree!" exclaimed Martin.

The little house would have been damp without a fire burning regularly in its hearth. The family over generations had developed an unobtrusiveness close to invisibility; they had never invited unwelcome attention by letting a plume of smoke rise like a signal but had burnt smokeless woods when possible or diverted what smoke there was by way of a pipe inside the ash-tree, so that sometimes the tree seemed to have caught an unseasonable mist in its upper branches.

After recent rains the beck was running vigorously, tugging at its banks, swirling under the rank rush clumps. Small birds were swinging precariously among the raggy seed-heads. The vicinity of Martin's house had always been an overgrown inconspicuous patch, a neglected awkward angle between the beck and a sheep pasture, where long grass waged a half-hearted engagement with encroaching brambles, and isolated meadow thistles, knapweed and teasels poked up stiff and rusty-looking. Now the patch was churned as if huge animals had wallowed in it. The opening of the terracotta conduit in the beckside bank, into which Hereward and Jacky had once crawled, had been smashed away, its debris a brown stain on the mossy bank, and there were woodchippings and sawdust in wet-yellow splashes round the sawn-off base of the ash tree. Its twiggy upper branches lay discarded on the mud or sticking out of the water.

Round the edges of the roughly dug soil were small domestic articles, stark and out of place: a pair of scissors with orange handles, a framed sampler twisted in half like a broken fan, a wicker basket with red and white ribbon plaited into a handle, a broken milk-jug, a bent weighing-scale. Martin, kneeling, was pulling at what looked like black sacking, trying to loosen it from the sucking mud. Hereward knew it at once as the Sheepwash family tapestry that had covered one whole wall of the family's hollowed-out chamber, a web of the past embroidered on it, names, scenes, symbols, suns, leaves, water in blue-green thread, Kit's hair in red.

Magnus went over to help. When he pulled it came a little and ripped soggily, leaving in his hand a few square feet of muddy cloth. Kit wrenched it from his hands, the fury in her face more than he could look at, so he walked away and stood staring miserably at the ground, trying not to step on the fragments embedded there. His feet moved a lump of earth, revealing another of the forlorn oddments, perhaps an ornament, wood-carved, or a toy of some sort. Thinking anything was better than looking at Kit and Martin, he bent to pick it up. When it would only move an inch or two he squatted and rubbed the mud away. Only when he dislodged the soil from between them and they fell limply separate did he realise that he was cleaning earth off small fingers. Then the shapely little nails and the outline of hand and wrist were plain to see, so that he straightened up with the sort of sobbing gasp that men and women once made when the rack turned and wrenched bone out through muscle.

Even with her back to him Kit felt the shock in Magnus's head. She turned to follow his gaze. Pausing only to take in what she saw, she flung herself down, tearing at the ground. Hereward and Martin knelt beside her, their hair prickling at her high keening moan, a wail rising and falling unbroken as if she had forgotten to breathe. Magnus too began to dig and, with the four of them scrabbling up the clods of earth, the arm led to a shoulder, a breast, a tangle of hair, and then Fleur's draggled face came up out of the mire. Martin ran a finger into the dead girl's mouth to clear it of mud, and Hereward wiped her face with a handkerchief. Kit was wailing constantly and Martin saying his sister's name like a mantra, while Magnus swore quietly, monotonous and threatening obscenities that no one had ever heard him use. The body was small and slippery, naked from the waist down, and when Hereward lifted it up it felt so light it might have been a cloth puppet full of wood shavings.

"Is our mother buried under here too?" Martin asked Kit.

"I hope not," a voice behind them said. "In the name of God."

The voice was unfamiliar, for it had been far away and, it seemed, a long time ago that they had last heard it. The words rang as boot-heels crack on a black road on a winter's night. Jacky had watched them disinter Fleur, and as each limb or feature became clear the years settled on him so that, when they turned to him, his face, always thin, looked narrow and lined. But the blue eyes blazed with anger, and Kit knew at once he was no more, and she doubted ever would be again, the gentle, unassuming young man who had come back with them from Regret.

"Jacky, it's you."

"Of course it is, Kit. Though why I am here and not in the land of Regret I do not know. I have dreamed a strange dream, and awoken to this nightmare. Is this your sister Fleur, as I think it is?"

"Perhaps our mother too," said Martin.

"I think not. Evil must have a limit. Or the world wouldn't make sense." He was back, Kit thought, biting her lip to restrain her bitterness, back and his eyes would light up for her alone – but what had been the currency paid to shock him into his old mercurial, demanding self, his mother's son as she thought of him, as Magnus was his father's child. "Can you carry her?" he was asking Hereward. "Of course you can. She's not heavy. Come on, let us ask the people of Hay to explain themselves. I must pick up a knife somewhere, I seem to have lost mine."

Martin said nothing, and Magnus repeated, "Come on," being delighted to follow again the elder brother he had run after on chubby legs crying 'Wait for me' on countless boyhood escapades. Hereward merely said, "Good," his Old One's blood bubbling hot and heavy, like red soup in a saucepan coming to boil. Kit almost said, "A life for a life," but refrained, thinking there had been an unpleasant symmetry in regaining Jacky and losing Fleur. Symmetries and coincidences have something in common; perhaps it was merely a coincidence.

Fifty yards away was the embankment. They climbed it and walked past the spot where Zjelko had shot at Hereward more than three years ago. There was a house in an apple orchard, the trees leafless but with a few apples still unpicked. A woman pushing a child on a swing saw them, picked up the child and hurried inside. Hereward had been inside the house once before with Hobson the miller, but he recalled it well, and wondered if Artis was still headman. Magnus pushed open the door and there was the dusty living-room with its heavy curtains, just the same, and on the wall the same large fish in a glass case poised among water-weeds, the same old bureau with double glass inkwells for black and red ink but both dry. Hereward wondered briefly if time had stood still here and whether the old headman had even heard of the coming and passing of the Daroi.

Sitting hunched by the fire Artis hardly glanced up as they entered, nor did he rise when they stood in a half-circle round the hearth. Fleur's body lay on the big table in the centre of the room. "My name is John Dorn," said Jacky. "I come from the Big Grey River and I was the last Rector of Limber. These are my friends, Martin and Kitfox, both of Sheepwash Bend, and on the table is their sister."

Artis nodded and closed his book carefully, as Martin spoke: "Why did you let this happen? You told our mother, after our father died, there would never be anything like this again."

Artis sighed. "Nor was there." Martin stared and waited. He was so short and squat that his face was level with that of the seated man, but he held every eye, and eventually Artis had to respond. "When I was headman there were some hard times for your folk, I cannot deny that, but it was never bad as this is bad. Who listens to me now? I have no voice in the affairs of Hay. There is a new young headman. A new man with new ways. Or newish. You would know him, Orr."

"Would I?" Hereward could recall a certain number of the villagers, some quite well, but describing any of them as 'the new young man' seemed unlikely.

"I expect you've not forgotten Zjelko."

"But he's not from Hay!"

"No, but no militia now, no Matrix troops, no rules and regulations from Limber. We're all free now, to do what we want."

"This free, you mean." Jacky took a handful of shirt and lifted Artis out of his chair. "Free to bury little girls, maybe their mothers too. Get on your feet and look." He pushed the older man against the table, and pulled the corpse close. The mud of Sheepwash Bend had mingled with blood in patches like crude poultices. "Closer!" He pushed Artis's head downwards. "Have a look. This Zjelko might have done that on his own, but he didn't dig up and loot a whole house on his own. Perhaps you couldn't have stopped it, but how hard did you try? You should have tried. Before they let her mother go did they make her stay and watch this?"

"Leave him, Jacky," said Martin. "Leave him alone."

Kit watched Jacky turn towards the instruction, and was afraid and uncertain. For the first time came a crawling doubt that she had taken more from him than she had to give.

"What do you want, Martin, exactly?"

"A proper funeral, that's all, Jacky," said the little man, "and not people looking at her like this."

"Is that all you want, Kit?"

"I want what Martin wants."

She could feel the disbelief in Jacky's mind displacing her words, and waited for the objections, but he said, "Oh, really?" so mildly that she was unsure whose mind was being read.

LIV

Hereward went into the mill through the back way, a clutter of black sheds and outhouses with no doors, then through what the miller called the engine-room, a high, narrow white-washed place where, overhead, sagging belts managed to make wheels clack round, everywhere shaking, dust fogging the air and thickening in floury layers on the cobwebs, every surface powdery as moths' wings.

With the sluice channel open and the big wheel turning Hobson would probably be either in the grinding room or shifting sacks, so Hereward went on through the dusty rooms full of the waiting grain bags and up an open stairway to another floor above. Here there was a different noise with the wooden floor vibrating as the grey millstone ground round upon its fixed mate embedded in a wooden case. If he had opened one of the cloudy windows and looked out he would have been able to see the stream beneath, dammed deep to run the waterwheel, the beck gleaming under its tree-lined banks almost back to Sheepwash Bend.

There were two mill-hands at work and he knew both by name, small men but strong who without pausing in their conversations could lift heavy sacks, sacks that Hereward in the time when he had worked here had also hoisted up with them into piles or on to wagons, but always sweating and his shoulders aching with the effort. "You'll get used to it," they would say and smile.

Seeing him one asked, "Come for a job, Orr?" but he shook his head. "Looking for Hobson?" They pointed through an archway. "Nearly time for a drink."

What if he had asked them whether they had raped Fleurfox, or stood by and watched others do it. They were decent men, he liked them, as he had liked almost everyone in Hay. The question wouldn't have made sense.

Eventually he found Hobson in his narrow office with the wide desk that, as always, had rows of bowls on it, each full of grain, barley from the dry limestone fields to the south of Hay, oats from the poorer land nearer to Ingastowe, bowls of wheat and rye. Hereward had seen Hobson hold a handful of grain, smell it, bite down on a few grains, and then name the field which had grown it: Coolan's Cut, Nettlefold North, Cold Ridge, any one of fifty or sixty. Hobson himself had observed his father and his grandfather doing it before him. They shook hands and the miller poured a drink and passed it across before a word was exchanged. When they were sitting he spoke quietly: "Just visiting? Not here to stay, I suppose."

"How's the business?" asked Hereward. "The top floors looked nearly full." There was no rush; after all only one thing was claiming his attention.

"Business is good."

"Life about the same in Hay?"

"More or less."

When Hereward had lodged with Hobson they had enjoyed a game of draughts, one game a night, after supper. An old, slow, subtle game, draughts is all about timing. Hobson knew he was going to have to move one of his central pieces – maybe he should, as generally it was better to move earlier than later when there were no other moves left. So he moved it. "We've got a new headman in the village."

"Headmen don't make much difference. Open a flower show, make sure the roadman's doing his job."

"This one's making a difference." Another of the central draughts. "There's a hunt on most Saturday nights. Sheds catching fire if you object, that sort of thing. No Matrix, you see, no militia, lots of opportunity for fun. Anybody can join in. Nobody gets hurt."

"I'm glad nobody gets hurt."

"Well, no village people, I mean."

"Of course. Just a few Twisted Folk."

"I suppose so."

"Well, if no one got hurt it wouldn't be much of a hunt, would it?"

"No."

"And no militia, as you said. And did anyone think of sending for the Companions?"

"Yes. Nell Cayley said she would. But it's a long way to Merganser for such as us. Anyway it's happened before and it'll all die down soon."

"That makes it all right, does it?" Wherever you move the next piece it gets taken. The miller said nothing, so Hereward went on: "Ever heard of the Daroi?"

"Yes, the Matrix drove them away at the battle of Limber."

"No, they didn't. I was there. The Daroi never took a backward step, unless they wanted to, and another day or maybe two was all we had left in us. It was the Twisted Folk who stopped them at the Dole River. Just as well or there would be a Daroi headman in Hay, and a Daroi miller, and maybe a different sort of hunt. Well, same hunt, different people, if you understand." The miller nodded, it not being hard to understand. "Last question," said Hereward. "Were you at Sheepwash Bend last week? I'm sure you know what I mean."

"Of course not. Did you need to ask that?"

"Good. Because it would be better that a millstone – you know the rest."

"Luke, seventeen," said Hobson, but to himself, for Hereward had gone, striding away along the lane, past where the water-pump stood in the square, the few people he saw either not recognising him or not being interested.

Wishing to know if Nell had really sent for the Companions he turned down what he knew as Baker's Lane. At the end of it was the beck again and on its bank four or five cottages all adjoining, all dipping so low that the Michaelmas daisies in their gardens touched their eaves. He knew which cottage he wanted, having visited it a number of times. Before he could knock there were unsteady footsteps and the door opened.

"Hello, Orr-Hereward." The girl was small and neat with red ribbons in her hair and a narrow face browned by the summer's sun. He felt he should know her. "Don't you recognise me, then?" she said and her disturbing pale eyes inspected him. He thought of long walks, watching clouds, picking apples.

"Adelie. Is it really you? You've changed." It was the best he could do.

"So have you. I'm sorry about your eye. Mama told me what happened."

A woman appeared, and he had no difficulty this time. "Hello, Nell."

"Come on in then," she said. "We need you back in Hay. You've been away too long."

He followed them inside thinking that Nell's house was as full as ever, wind-chimes hanging at the open window, the walls so full of pictures that the frames touched or even overlapped, cupboards and tables laden with porcelain birds and squirrels and hedgehogs. In bowls of water glass fish floated, suspended, seeming so real that they always caught his eye, and two real cats slept on velvet stools. "Sit down, please." She threw some of the embroidered cushions on to the piano to clear a space. Hereward lowered himself carefully, managed to make a small table rock perilously, and caught Adelie smiling at him. "Don't encourage him to wreck my house. Go in the garden and do some weeding!" her mother exclaimed, though as soon as the girl had departed she was peeping in the window and blowing kisses.

He had to ask: "How did she get better? I thought her mind would never recover."

"She will never again walk properly," said Nell. "But Abbot Huw is a great healer. Now I want to hear everything you've done and seen. I hear you managed to reach Regret, even though no roads lead there."

"How could you know that? And did you send for the Companions?"

"Later, later!"

So he tried to tell her as much as he could, though he could do justice to few of the events and even fewer of his thoughts. She asked no questions and wept twice, once when he told her of Lokietok's curious story at the Companions' camp-fire, and again at how the giant died. Much of what had happened he skated over, including his own contributions, so that she smiled and said, "You don't seem to have done much yourself."

"Well, it would all have happened anyway, the important events like the Daroi coming and so on."

"Of course it wouldn't. Something would have happened, but certainly not what did. It needed you. You are one of the Old Ones, change happens around you, it's the way you are. Naturally there are happenings around the Daylight People too, but they tend to be the same ones as happened the day before and all days before, or if there is a change it comes very slowly over generations as it does in the world of birds and animals and plants. Anyway carry on."

So he finished his story and said, "Your turn now."

"All right, though it's hard to know where to begin." Adelie hobbled past the window on some errand of her own. "Have you ever wondered who her father was? Let me tell you about myself when I met him. I was twenty years old and my family was gentle and loving. Indeed love surrounded me in every way for I was, and still am, one of what you insist on calling the Unmen of Regret.

"Does that surprise you? I was small but my hair was like ravens' feathers and I parted it in the middle and held it in tortoiseshell combs and my ear-rings were ivory. My name then was not Nell." Nell seemed to grow as she told it and Hereward could glimpse the black-haired girl from Regret.

"But I was shy and my time chiefly given to learning until the day I saw him. He was so big I could not have encircled his wrist with my hands, thus." She made a circle joining the thumbs and forefingers of each hand. "He had spirit, and dignity too, and he said he had come to defy the Unmen, as he too always called us. There seemed no reason other than that our existence alone made him feel unfree. He said that he could call no man or people his master, and that he was the equal of any of the Unmen kings. Nor could he be reasoned with any more than you reason with the tiger. But he had the tiger's strength and grace and he noticed me standing behind my parents and friends. His name was Lamorak and Adelie is his daughter. You can see it in her eyes and sometimes in her temper. It was eighteen years ago this month that he came for the first time to Regret, when many others followed him for some of the way, and John Paul almost all of the way. He came again about ten years ago, that time with you, of course, and the others. I told Demetrius to go home. The rest of you went into the maze, as I had taught Lamorak to do. But Regret has as many faces as there are people who search it out, not all of them welcoming faces, and few true ones. Tell me again what you and your friends saw this time."

"It was not only saw but heard. There were sounds that seemed voices in the wind and grasses. Then some saw the city, not unlike Limber according to Magnus, though others thought it smaller. The man in my book wrote that it was a smallish place, wood and thatch. Some of the Twisted Folk, at least those who spoke about it, saw no buildings at all. Who spoke the truth?"

"Everyone in a way," said Nell. "Except they were seeing only what they expected to see."

"The same with the people we met?"

"Yes."

"What happened to Lamorak and his men?"

"Remember the first time he came almost all turned back, as I said, and the second time those who came with him were the single-minded Old Ones. My people sympathised with this, we being chiefly of the same blood, and this antagonism has been present as long as there has been Regret. We caused the Old Ones to forget, or to recall a different quest, say, a journey of exploration. There were exceptions – one was Lamorak, who was so strong in will and he had learned much from me, for I was drawn to him and he to me. I do not like to think of what happened to him. With my people – I suppose I shall have to call them the Unmen not to confuse you – it was always the way not to harm any adventurer as far as possible, only to make it easy for them to forget their feud with Regret. Of course Isobel, George Littler and the two girls you mentioned came only with love in their hearts and, being already in a state of grace, met a new world of challenging happiness there. Nor is this new at all. Other thresholds like this have opened up before humanity and always there have been many who held back, like yourself, and some, not so many who, having crossed the threshold, then turn back."

"Like yourself and Sheer and the Novaks."

"Yes, though not for the same reasons. The power urge is not so easy to sublimate. Such as Sheer are not at home in Regret. In the Limber council he found a very desirable place to satisfy his impulses."

"So why did your people allow this to happen? Surely you can counteract the Sheers."

"Not quite so many jumps, please. You are as bad as Lamorak. First, the Matrix folk always complain of others interfering in their lives, such as the regulations on big ships, and rightly so. Surely they want no more interference? In any case Regret never interferes. Secondly, there won't always be Sheers, though it might seem as if there will. After all, Limber has just dealt with several of them and it won't forget that for a while. If and when it does it can learn again, and next time it will learn just that bit quicker."

"What about taking the children? Was Sheer telling the truth there?"

"That was not so easy to understand. Of course, to control other people's children is certain to satisfy the urgency of power, I think, and probably it is more fundamental than to regulate the people themselves. But it seemed more than that, particularly with the trouble it brought the rectors, though remember that most children came willingly, apart from a few, usually from the outlands, with such potential they had to be coerced. Adelie has that talent – with Lamorak's genes she would have made things hop! My opinion is that they hoped, by taking the most brilliant children and educating them to think with every resource and intensity possible, to develop some human future to rival and relegate Regret. That would certainly please Sheer and the others. There is a space held in readiness for creation into which life will expand, though which of its branches will evolve to occupy this future-space and flourish there is impossible to say. Naturally, to us of Regret, though I speak only as an exile, there seems no future more promising or logical than the one we are creating, but then every species carries the same confidence and so it should."

"What about yourself?" asked Hereward.

"Do I wish that I could repent my passion for Lamorak, I expect you mean. Not a day passes that I do not feel blind, deaf and dumb outside the community of spirits I was born into. Yet I never repented for loving my man. I read once of a long-ago queen who mated with a bull, and perhaps that is how some of Regret and even some of my family thought of me, but not how I thought of myself or of him. You must have thought highly of him yourself to have followed him on his second journey to Regret."

"Did you meet him again that time?"

"Yes. Then he had come to conquer or die. It was his Old Ones' blood, he couldn't help it. But he was a man, he didn't ask others to die for him, though others were drawn to his company. I met you. It was snowing, I recall. But you had left your memories in the thought-web. That is how it defends itself. You were restless and one morning you weren't there any more. I never saw my man again nor ever knew where he went, but you were his friend so when I thought I was lowest and loneliest I came to find you. I didn't know how much more lonely and cut off I would feel after I left Regret. Blind, dumb and deaf, as I said, but without fingers to feel, no scents to smell, no hot or cold. But so much worse for poor Lamorak, still with all his strength, wandering through the forests for years with every day and every turning as pointless as the next. Far, far lonelier for him, with no meaning for company. Then that vile arena in High Altai ..."

"I can see there was nowhere for Lamorak to go," said Hereward, "but you could surely have gone back to your own folk."

"I suppose so, if I'd gone on my own. Don't think I don't long to do so every moment. But Adelie is too much her father's daughter, drawing others to her but reserving her own love for a few, strong-willed, haughty, sharp-minded, and not at all ready for Regret."

"Some of her mother's daughter too, then."

"Perhaps. She would never have asked Regret for help. I did, I begged Huw to make her better."

"And he did?"

"Yes. He understands illness of the mind."

"Did you never see anyone else from Lamorak's two journeys?"

"Yes, but only once. By pure chance I saw Demetrius of Venask, here, in Hay, outside the monastery. His father, Constantine, was as bold and reckless as Lamorak, but the son was different. Poor Demetrius, he must have been haunted by turning back. That's why he wouldn't have turned away when the Daroi came to Venask, though he must have had plenty of opportunities. John Paul, Nancy's husband, would be just the same, years of proving he wasn't a coward simply because he couldn't stay with Lamorak when the two of them planned to reach Regret on the first occasion. For most it is better to listen to the sounds of the grasses."

"So it is the Old Ones who usually reach Regret?"

"No, of course not. Many are drawn there each year. It is chiefly among the Old Ones born with their assertive hearts that you find those who cannot forget themselves enough. They long to fight and struggle towards an incomprehensibly difficult Godhead, when their path could not be clearer or simpler. God is love. I hope I can regain the path some day, though it doesn't seem likely. I was glad when you killed that man on the embankment, but to get back on the path to Regret I must learn to love men like that. That's hard."

"Is it possible?"

"Yes, Hereward, it is."

"You've heard about Fleur, the girl from Sheepwash Bend?" When Nell nodded he went on: "Must we all love those who raped her and then probably buried her alive?"

"You know the answer."

"I don't like it, Nell."

"The apes didn't like it when they became conscious of themselves and of time. I'm sure they hated it, but without it they stayed apes."

So agitated had Hereward become that he began plucking at the leather cord round his neck and the ring swung out from under his shirt. As Nell leaned forward and took it in her hand Adelie came in and she too stared at the silver band. "Fetch mine, please," her mother said, holding so tightly to the ring that Hereward lifted the cord over his head and passed it to her. When Adelie returned to put another ring in her mother's hand he saw they were replicas, one being smaller but each with identical engraving. "Your hands were so big." Nell was crying and talking to her past now and Adelie, waving a handkerchief, was looking fretful.

Finally he said, "Do you recognise them?"

"He gave me mine and I gave him his."

"This design – like a figure four?"

"Not a four," sobbed Nell. "An L crossed with an I. Lamorak and Ignellen. I was Ignellen then, not stupid Nell. Poor Lamorak, poor Lokietok! I nearly guessed before. Where is his grave?" She was shaking and, unmistakably, her daughter stared with her father's eyes.

"On Kittiwake Island, with the Companions."

"He would have liked that," Nell choked out through her tears. "Can I keep his ring?" Hereward closed her fingers round it, feeling ill at ease, an eavesdropper listening to long-ago lovers. "Did you guess who Lokietok was, Hereward?"

"Right at the end I suspected, on the beach at Limber. I saw it in his eyes. Letitia said Frick had it, the 'follow-me'." Trying to find something to say as Nell sobbed on he asked, "Are the Companions coming?"

"Yes," the girl replied. "Mother is one of a great company herself. They will come for her. Three days."

"One more question, then I'll go. Who went hunting last Saturday?" They told him the names, some certain, some suspected. "One last question." Adelie managed a sort of combined warning cough and sniff but Nell smiled. "What brought you to Hay?"

"We were lonely, with no friends. Lamorak said you would be a good friend. Don't forget who my people are. They were glad to tell me where the tides and currents had carried you."

"So why not speak of this at the time?"

Adelie was frowning and ostentatiously counting on her fingers.

"Regret doesn't interfere. It just is."

LV

Back at the house of Artis, the man who had sentenced Hereward to lose an eye, they sat around a large table and made their plans.

While Hereward had been visiting the mill and spending time with Ignellen and Adelie the others had also been active. Kit, Martin, Jacky and Magnus had walked miles paying visits, first to the home of Jesse, which lay in a maze of coppices and little intersecting valley-folds so tangled that unless you listened for the sound of the bells of Hay church you could spend hours looking for a way out or, for that matter, a way to get further in, and then to a shabby farmhouse deep in rushes where the fenlands had come back to make it an island.

"We were all sorry about Fleur," said Jesse to Kit. "If this goes on we shall have to move, deeper into the fens. Everyone here has heard about our people at the Dole River and how they are now full and proud citizens of the Matrix, but someone forgot to tell the Daylight Folk in these parts. Anyway is there a Matrix? It seems to mean nothing here."

"There will be one difference." Kit frowned. "These cruel bullies have not met men who fought at Limber. They carried Fleur's body to the old headman's house, so they are in no mood for mercy."

Further on at the old house crouched in the apple orchard, sheltered by wide reed-beds that were full of unexpected brown shining pools, the air around it creaking and whimpering with the flocks of marsh birds, they spoke to the Pascals and others of the Twisted Folk. "You must not let yourselves be chased and chivvied like this," said Magnus, being young and believing all difficulties have answers. In his mind he saw the black flags on the beach outside Limber, and the assurance of Letitia and others like her.

Someone said patiently, "It's not as simple as that." There were so many considerations, some that Magnus might understand, others that he could never be expected properly to know. In the room were a dozen of the Twisted Folk and between them they knew why it was not so simple. We are so few, thought one; the times are not good but they will pass, another; in my grandfather's time it was worse, thought a third; every generation sees fewer of our differences, another. But these were the thoughts they allowed themselves to articulate. Deeper lay others: guilt and penance gave them history and a little meaning, however obscure, persecution brought closeness, and there were the fortuitous talents that emerged from nowhere. Even this room held a mindreader, a mesmerist, a bone-setter and two who spoke to birds and animals, though, sadly, others who felt themselves blemished with no compensation. They sensed also that their predicament of being called on to love and forgive on some great scale was a source of strength, though out of unfairness came strength and tiredness in equal measure.

"In the great world," said Kit, "the people of the Glassy Country have done deeds that have made our folk free, free to live and find happiness as we wish. I know – I have seen it for myself."

The listeners were uneasy. They had known her since she was born and she was young and passionate, and her champions were powerful. She'd had faith in the Tyr-dream and far off, it seemed, their people had helped to make the dream true. Also the quiet one who Martin called the last Rector of the Matrix always stood close to her and nodded when she spoke. Though sometimes, Siward Pascal noticed, he would shake his head as if to clear a mist from in front of his eyes. In a way they would have preferred her to remain far away, engaged in exploits on some distant stage, but not only was she among them but her sister was dead and they all knew the foul circumstances.

Usually the hunt had been just that, a terrifying chase through the woodlands at night for a family chosen at random; humiliation or a beating provided there was no resistance. The Gunnarsens had been too stiff-necked to run and young Theo Gunnarsen spat in the headman's face, said new times were here, and challenged him to choose his weapon. The new headman had laughed and chosen daggers and a few minutes later left Theo Gunnarsen blind. His followers said he had done this before. Also the twisted boy asked for it and should have run. A nearby village had started its own hunt and several others were said to be about to follow the example of Hay. Maybe other provinces were the same.

Martin said nothing. He understood Kit perfectly and sympathised with the others. He thought of his mother; her home gone, she had watched her daughter brutalised. Now, though one of the families gladly cared for her she had only intermittently seemed to recognise her children. When they had told her of the compact the Matrix had made with the Glassy Country she was not interested. "Don't expect things to change much, Martin," she had said in a clear moment, "except for the worse. That is far away. When the Matrix was strong the lands were at peace. There was danger, I know well enough, for I have missed your father every day for fourteen years. But now the militia are gone, they say, and the Companions will probably never come again. Cut down the forest and the winds blow colder and harder."

"We will make a new forest, mother."

"Not in my lifetime, Kit."

The mood had not been dissimilar in the other families they had talked to. It seemed to Martin an irony after the events in the wider world, and he wished that Hex and Crook and Letitia were in Westermain or, almost but not quite, that he could be with them somewhere walking through a far land. Now in the Pascals' farmhouse, the group's last visit, no one seemed ready to speak; all that could be heard was the gabbling of the water-birds and the thrump-thrump of the geese's wings as yet another skein came or went across the fen, and the wind singing and soughing lonely in the reed-beds.

"Let me take care of this headman," said Jacky, eventually. He was impatient with the hesitations.

"He will have fifty helpers, maybe a hundred. This isn't Limber. Remember the inn – and they only had stones."

"What inn?"

Kit looked at him and away, her stomach twisting with the frustration that knotted inside her. It had been so exhilarating to sparkle defiance in the thought-maze of the Unmen, and if her wish had not been so smoothly granted she would welcome the chance to do so again, isolated but expanding to fill the void around her, unconfined as she had never been. Already she could feel the passage of time fraying those memories away. But it was not this that anguished her so much as coming to the knowledge that the Unmen had offered Jacky a glorious chance. She knew enough of his mind to know that when he had changed after his exasperated cry of 'Why' he had not lost his past and its grievances so much as allowed it to be writ small and indistinct in some antechamber of his thoughts. For a while he had become innocent, unhampered, offered a chance to live in love. To Jacky, full of youthful adversary-demanding energy, this tranquillity had given a new perspective that gentled and diverted his mind.

She doubted that this freshness of spirit would ever return. She did know, for his thoughts were familiar to her again, that he loved her and her alone, and, touching gingerly the idea that in this she had now diminished him, she felt the cruel choice that evolution cannot avoid posing – that it is the unfamiliar that holds the promise of growth.

"In truth," he reflected, "I recollect little. But I do remember your sister. When I was sick in your house she brought me nice food to eat, broths and jellies when that was all I could manage. The jellies looked like father's glass paperweight – she had set nasturtium flowers in them. Let them bring fifty or a hundred. The Daroi came in their thousands and they were men like Frick."

"But you had your fighting-men with you." Kit felt around her the furies beginning to close.

"I've got Hereward, Magnus, Martin, you and as many of your folk as wish to help. That'll be plenty. They've got to pay. There were five, ten, fifty, to hold down the little girl who nursed me."

She saw how pale his face was and his unfocused blue eyes gazing elsewhere. If she and Jacky had children, an odd thought fluttered in her head, how would she feel if they too were hard as small diamonds.

"They've got to pay," Magnus repeated, and the Twisted Folk who knew nothing of him thought he looked bigger and more menacing than his brother. "That's right, Martin, isn't it?"

Martin's face was empty. Ever since returning to the ravaging of his family and the harrowing of his home his mind had churned and spilled thoughts like a mill-wheel rolling. Often he thought of George Littler, who had gone to the King of the Glassy Country and done more than any other man or woman to reconcile the fortunes of the whole cat's-cradle of the Matrix, the Daroi, the Daylight People and the Twisted Folk.

It had been after midnight, everything hazy like a dream, hours after Hex had beaten on the King's drum, that the tapping had come on the door of the Lonely Start Inn up on the plateau at the heart of the badlands, and the big man had knocked on the lids of their metal-lined boxes to wake them.

"Visitors – to speak with you," he said.

"The seneschal of the King, maybe," Crook had suggested, half in jest.

"They've come to ask who called for them," said the big man, whom they had given up thinking of as the innkeeper. "I'll turn down the lantern, George, you won't want to see them clearly."

Martin had shaken in horror as the figures entered, and after one glance Hex and Crook would not raise their eyes.

Those elevated to kingship in the Glassy Country were dreadful symbols and yet pragmatic. The people of their land brought them questions and took away the answers. Oracles are not so unheard of, and the kings, being the most malformed of all their people, answered from the heart, perhaps not least because this was the only organ you could assume every generation of the Folk held in common.

"Someone beat the drum."

Martin and the two Companions were astonished at the clarity of the words and the tone, for it was clearly female. The face's reference points – eyes, nose, mouth – depend on their relation to one another, and here features had neither symmetry nor conventional position, mouth above an eye, both ears on the one side, the teeth protruding through flesh. None of the travellers responded, and the remark hung in the air.

Martin was glad of the dim lantern-light; all of his life he had seen people repelled by his own appearance, and he was shocked to find himself flinching now. As his eyes grew accustomed to the light he braved a glance at the King's other emissary. At first he or she seemed not abnormally proportioned but gradually Martin discerned the struts of metal limbs, the dangling reinforced arms and the mesh which held and stiffened head, neck and torso, as insects shelter bonelessly inside their calcified carapaces. Martin had started to weep, silently, and he watched George walk across the room, and with one hand clasp the woman's hand while the other embraced the metal cage. The forester loomed bigger than he had ever seemed.

"We came to ask for help against the Daroi people," George said. "The captain-general thought you could make a legend, some magic, that would send them away and let the Matrix dream survive. But it is not appropriate. I am sorry we have troubled you."

"George!"

"Be quiet, Martin," Hex said gently.

"You've already paid to ask. And Daylight People pay more," said the woman. By facing George she was speaking across to her left where her mouth was, as if uninterested. "What legend did you have in mind?"

"We thought perhaps you could cause the Daroi-people to tremble and look elsewhere for lands to possess. We think that the Matrix once suffered here enough to weave an augury for many generations. They call this an unlucky land."

"Unlucky!"

"I'm sorry. I'm not good with words. Woods, maybe, not words."

"You're good enough. Wait a while. We must think. Go into the other room."

They sat waiting for an hour, speaking occasionally at first but then sitting in silence.

Eventually the innkeeper summoned them. "Here is our proposition," said the woman. "We will talk of payment later. You must draw the Daroi-folk into and through the heart of the Glassy Country. Use your own men at first, fight a long withdrawal. As they advance the Twisted Folk will join you. It is not necessary to defeat them, indeed you must not do so. But they must advance into the lands about this place. Are the Daroi likely to pursue in such a way?"

"Very likely," said Hex. "But what if they pass through and so into the lands of the Matrix?"

"They will not. Dead men do not advance."

"Will all be dead?"

"All who follow you far enough."

"How will they die?" Hex seemed to have become the party's spokesman.

"Of sickness. It will be painful and cruel but the more dreadful the greater the need to remember and embroider it. Their women will have tales and rhymes about it for their babies a thousand years from now. That should be long enough. A long wasting agony of a sickness which poisons all hope and dignity. Apt in a land that is sick."

"And our men withdrawing in front of them? They will have to pass through here."

"Legends are not cheap. Or lessons. But the Daroi will suffer more. There are more of them. That is how the Matrix learned the meaning of unlucky in the long-ago."

It was impossible to tell if the kings were smiling or sad. No one offered any comment and the innkeeper looked around for instruction. "Take time to consider. Or take the proposal back to your friends."

"It is true we are just messengers," put in Crook.

There seemed little else to say, and the group was drifting towards the other room when the big forester turned round and spoke to the two eerie figures. "Thank you for your time and honesty. It may not be much but may God's love comfort and encompass you."

"How is the outside world?" asked the woman-king.

"Wondrous and difficult."

"Do women still have babies?"

"Yes, of course."

"Little voices saying 'Mother' and soft arms round their necks. It is hard not to envy them. So, now you go to take the message of the legend back."

"What message?" said George Littler. There was a long pause as everyone looked at him. Several voices almost responded but did not.

"I see," said the King of the Glassy Country. "And what would you have given our folk in return for the imaginary message?"

"To make everyone free and equal citizens. But the Daroi are a folk too. Would your people be glad of a freedom bought by a million torments? With the little voices saying, 'Mother, make the pain stop, please.' No, let us forget the message and the legend."

"What legend?" said the displaced mouth.

"What message?" said Crook and Hex together.

*

But George was gone into Regret, thought Martin, and there was no one who could stop what was coming.

Jacky was speaking: "I do not know who brought about the death of Fleur or the others. I suppose there must have been others."

Martin asked, "So what do we propose to do?"

Magnus looked surprised and Kit said impatiently, "They do not deserve to live. It is simple."

"Who is they?"

"Those who did the killing, Martin."

"And if one man did it all?"

"Then one man dies. The rest are outlawed. Let them be hunted since they enjoy hunts. What point are you trying to make?"

"Only this," said her brother, more to the Pascals and other Twisted Folk in the room than to his sister. "George said there was always a time for mercy. And that it is for the fortunate to be merciful. Our people are strong because of what happened at Dole River and now, because the Companions will soon be here, and because our time has come. I know what Tyr-Hereward, Jacky and Magnus have in mind, and the Companions' captain will be the same, but it is for us to solve, not them."

"I think you've gone mad. You were too small to carry Fleur's body. If you had done, you would speak differently." Kit in her fury was indifferent whom she hurt. "Next you'll say we have to love this mad dog and his mongrel gang."

"Forgive first, in time try to love. Our Lord forgave on the cross. And loved."

Though Kit railed and stormed and the others tried to dissuade Martin he would have none of it. The Pascal family and their friends were silent for it seemed to them that he spoke like a holy man and that made him brave, and to forgive was braver still, while to love was heroic.

The day was far gone now and they walked back towards Hay in the twilight, mist-veils floating over the fens and meres, frogs croaking and plopping into the water, and once a pike startled them by suddenly churning through the lily-pads of a nearby pool.

Back at Artis's house Kit sought out Hereward. "Tyr-Hereward," she whispered, when they were apart from the others, "please don't let Martin go near those people. Surely he can forgive at a distance. Or forgive them later after Silky Wilkins has hanged them."

"I'll try. It won't be easy."

That night they slept in Artis's house. Kit shared a room with Martin and watched until he was asleep, waking from her uneasy dozing several times half-expecting to find he had slipped away. But he slept soundly later.

Breakfast was enjoyable at Artis's house, though Kit who was finically tidy shook her head at the kitchen where they ate. It was a big room but seemed crowded with Jacky, Hereward and Martin eating large helpings of scrambled eggs and mushrooms, pausing briefly to drink glasses of milk or spread butter on thick slices of bread, among house-keepers and helpers who clattered pots and pans, brought in firewood, heated water and pushed dogs out from underfoot.

Adelie arrived limping and hoisting herself along on her crutches, then dumping them on the floor, where Magnus, entering late and sleepily, tripped over them. "Who left these here?" he groaned. "Is there any breakfast left for me? Can I have my bread fried, please?" Returning from the stove with a vast heaped plate he began to clear a space on the oilcloth-covered table, toppling over a vase of drooping flowers that sent water swirling round the others' plates. Kit followed with a cloth, saying, "Magnus, for goodness' sake!" and so ostentatiously mopping between the crockery while moving a bowl of fried potatoes out of Magnus's reach, that Adelie was overtaken by giggling.

At this point Magnus spotted several empty bowls and said, "Did everyone else have porridge?" in so plaintive a voice that Adelie found herself saying, "I'll make some for you, Magnus."

"No, you won't." Kit propelled her back towards her seat.

"She's a good girl and means well." Magnus gave Adelie a brotherly pat on the shoulder.

"Magnus," said Jacky, "this is Adelie. She uses crutches because she was left nearly dead by Zjelko and one of his friends. They meant to take her away like Astolat."

"Bastards."

"Your language, Magnus." Kit wondered whether she had a lifetime ahead of looking after both Jacky and his brother.

"Sorry, Adelie."

"It's all right, Magnus. I had heard the word before." She found him instantly attractive. Jacky with his thin face and crackling blue stare seemed rather remote, and Hereward she regarded as a kindly uncle. Magnus had the same colouring as Jacky and they were clearly brothers, but he reminded her of a big golden bear-cub devouring honeycomb, which the scrambled eggs did somewhat resemble.

"How old are you, Magnus?" she inquired.

"Thirty-eight."

"I bet you aren't."

"All right. How old do you think I am?"

"Twelve."

"Same age as you? Well, you're wrong, so you lost the bet. Now you've got to make me some porridge."

"I'm not twelve," she protested. "Tell him, Hereward."

Hereward glanced across and smiled almost in disbelief. Those pale grey eyes, Lokietok's eyes, and the black elf-locks tumbling round her face, and he remembered snow on Ignellen's black curls as she came into the cave outside Regret. How would a man feel if he had ten thousand keys and tried them in a lock one after another until with the very last key the lock slid effortlessly open? He had unlocked his memory.

"Hereward," prompted Adelie.

"What was it? Oh, much older than twelve, of course."

LVI

Forming a plan to deal with Zjelko was not easy. He had moved into the Big House in Hay, which was a large place not unlike Nana's house in Venask, standing in its own wide grounds of lawns, a wood, even a small lake, behind ivy-covered stone walls. Hereward recalled it as having been the home of two reclusive old ladies, the Misses Shepherd, who occasionally invited Hobson round to chase out ghosts, and this he would pretend to do by rattling a stick on the banisters and shouting threats, which seemed to do the trick. Another old lady had taken them in when Zjelko had commandeered their house.

How many men were with him was uncertain. Artis thought about twenty, including several disbanded soldiers and various malcontents, both from Hay itself, notably the Jacques brothers, and from surrounding settlements even as far as fifteen miles away. The number itself varied from day to day. As few as six or seven stayed permanently in the house, the others arriving before the Saturdays of the hunts. There were more still, including a few slatternly women hanging to the fringe and known as the 'hunt-followers', an ancient expression the Misses Shepherd had revived for those who could not resist being spectators of the hunting.

Certainly they were well-armed, though only a few carried firearms, and there was reported to be a sentry-roster at the house. Jacky and Hereward were inclined to deal with Zjelko as they had at Radic's villa in Limber by forcing an entry in the night but Kit became almost distraught at the thought. "I went into the Unmen's mind after him," she told Hereward. "Isn't that enough? In any case this is a time for the Twisted Folk. Certainly it is not you on your own who should make their stand."

Most of the morning the group had spent in the kitchen putting a sort of plan together. About eleven Jesse arrived to say that most of the Twisted Folk, both of the wooded valleys round Hay and the fenlands that began about three miles to the south, wished to resist Zjelko themselves rather than leave the confrontation to the Companions.

"In any case," said Jesse, "is it certain that the Companions now exist? It is said that the Matrix has told the provinces to look after themselves, no more militia either. Or more likely the Companions will deal only with magnates or outsiders."

"Magnates start like Zjelko," Jacky said.

Kit looked around. "Where is Martin? Is he in the garden?"

After five minutes searching and Martin nowhere to be found they regathered, with Kit frantic. "The worst case is that he has gone to the

Shepherds' house to try and solve all this by forgiving and forgetting, though I can hardly believe it."

"You couldn't stop him, Kit. He has a big heart. Anyway it may succeed."

"I don't want it to succeed, Jacky. Nor do you."

"No, I don't, I'm afraid. That's why I wasn't fit for Regret." It was the only time she heard him mention his fleeting encounter with the Unmen. "Magnus, go and find Martin. Hereward will be recognised and I stayed here once at Sheepwash Bend, but no one knows you. And be careful."

Kit shook her head. Jacky's logic was sound enough, she thought, apart from telling the golden bear to be careful. She could sense Magnus's pleasure at the prospect of activity, but doubted that he could conceive of such a thing as cautious activity. "Extremely so," she called after him. "We don't want to have anything else to forgive them for."

Now the plan was easier. Not easy but easier, for Magnus had returned. With him he brought news of Martin and of that night's hunt. Some of the information he offered cheerfully, but there were reluctant gaps.

"He looked the right sort, so I just asked him the way in the street."

Lew Jacques was the youngest of three brothers. His face was so flat it seemed always pressed against a sheet of glass. Suggestions hinting at twisted genes in his family had mortified him as a child, and he was an avid identifier of them elsewhere. His black bead in Hereward's trial had never been in doubt. The young fellow Lew met that morning had been looking for Zjelko's house, and hinted he was interested in a bit of fun that night.

"He said I'd chosen a good night. And where was I from?"

Lew thought the fellow looked clumsy and slow, found out that he'd walked from Ingastowe on the off-chance, and told him he was lucky to have met him, Lew. His name was Thorbjorn, and he wondered if Lew had had any twisted women. "Plenty," said Lew, which was a lie.

"He let slip about last Saturday. At Sheepwash Bend."

Lew had liked the way Thorbjorn had laughed at that, and said, "They can't resist a real man, I expect," adding that one of them hadn't resisted anybody, that was sure enough. Thorbjorn had laughed again, saying that he appreciated a sense of humour, and could he buy Lew a drink.

"We had a couple of drinks. And it got worse."

The beefy young man could drink all right, Lew thought. And he was generous. So it was only fair to tell him how the twisted girl had started to scream when they threw the soil in on top of her. Perhaps Thorbjorn had looked a bit pale at the details. Maybe it was the beer.

"'Tonight it's a place called Shawpits. We're setting off about eight o'clock. Great night, friend, you'll enjoy it. Lots of 'em in Shawpits. Another beer? Thanks. We've got one of 'em up in the Big House. Mad as a snake with its tail cut off.'"

"Then he made me lose my temper."

One more or less makes no difference – Lew shared his philosophy with his fellow enthusiast from Ingastowe. Not like the girl who lives down there, now she does look lively even if she is a cripple. A cripple, that would be fun, especially – Lew licked his lips. Thorbjorn was a good listener, he might even suggest a few refinements.

"We took a walk. He had an accident."

Not a bad suggestion a walk, Lew thought. Down Baker's Lane to the beck, might see the cripple, tell her what she had to look forward to, like last Saturday, 'You should have heard her screaming, Thorbjorn.' But why was there a hand on the back of his neck, and here's the wall coming and then the impact of the stone wall meeting his face, flattening it featureless. And what was the voice saying about being lucky? Lucky not to have the earth in his mouth before he was dead? 'Not the wall-stones again, please, Thorbjorn!'

There was a long pause before Kit spoke: "Is that what you call being careful?"

Magnus shrugged, wishing Adelie was elsewhere. "I was careful. He'll survive. One less tonight. I put him in Artis's barn."

"Oh, Magnus!" Adelie wondered where the honey-bear had gone.

"I was upset." Magnus, who was not prone to justifying himself, wished to avoid even the mildest of reproaches from Lamorak-Lokietok's teasing black-haired daughter. "I mean with what he said about Fleur and then saying he would do the same to you."

"Where's this place, Shawpits? Kit, you'll know."

"I know it well, Jacky. I'm only surprised they haven't been hunting there before."

She told them what she knew of Shawpits, that in distant times, centuries past, it had been an open-cast mine, but the green plants had come bravely back, clinging precariously to the slag-heaps' and diggings' harshness, every year leaving a few decaying leaves and stalks for next year's nutrition to feed the ivy and brambles, the droppings of birds, mice and wildcats sustaining roots just a little more, the plants of the wastelands, golden rod, yarrow, coltsfoot, then as the trees came and there was shade, violets and celandines in spring, later foxgloves and rosebay.

Shawpits had become cool, dark and dense. One footpath led through it, a favourite of village boys and girls by day, though less so after dark. Snow always lay longer in Shawpits than anywhere else. From Hollowhills field, where Hereward had once attended the Twisted Folk's meeting, you could look at the dark edge of Shawpits and wonder if the occasional rabbit-track would really lead inside.

Still the plan would not quite come together. It had to allow the Twisted Folk to act for themselves, while not excluding the aching anger of Jacky and his friends. The impulse to act before the possible arrival of the Companions was also strong. "Keep it really simple," Jacky advised. "The more elements it has the more chances it has to go wrong. Fishing is simple, if you keep the boats simple too and respect the sea." He could not help thinking of his drowned brother. "Father should have known that," he added to himself, though Kit read the thought with ease.

There came a knock on the back door and after a few moments Artis led a man into the room. "Someone to speak to you."

The man looked round uneasily. "It was private really, Art," he muttered and then seeing Hereward: "Orr, remember me?"

"Yes. How are you, Shelley? How are the girls?" Hereward had recognised the man at once as an odd-jobs man for the mill. His wife would send his twin daughters to the mill with a midday meal, the small girls carrying it importantly in a large basket under a white cloth.

"They're well, thank you. And I was sorry about your eye. Well, it's thinking about my girls that's brought me here. What happened last Saturday, I mean. And what they're arranging for tonight. I just don't know what to do, and I thought when Art was headman nothing like this happened."

"It did," Kit said. "You didn't get round to noticing it." Her disdain lashed him as a briar pulled aside can whip back its hooked thorns to scour the face of the blackberry picker. Nevertheless, prompted by the old headman's quiet questions he stammered out his story. It had been the appearance of Martin that had focused his gnawing guilt, troubled not so much by what he had done, which was little, but by what he had failed to do, particularly when Martin walked into the Big House to suggest that there could be other happier futures, that neither forgiveness nor generosity were any more or less impossible than they had ever been, if someone would take his hand and vow to start again. All it wanted was the will.

"I wanted to say I was sorry. If someone else had done it first I would have done. There were others who admired him, I'm sure of that. Then Carver Jacques, who's twice his size, knocked him down, and none of us did anything. Not one of us."

"Where is my brother now?"

"In one of the stables or milking-sheds. He'll be all right for a while. Everybody up there's too busy making their masks and costumes."

The listeners wondered if they had misheard the odd-jobs man. Magnus had to ask: "Did you say masks and costumes?"

"Well, mostly masks. It's the chief's idea for tonight. Best outfit gets a prize."

"Two washing-up towels and a bar of soap?"

"Magnus!" Poised to castigate Magnus for his frivolity Kit thought of what he had done earlier that day and closed her mouth.

"I'd sooner not say," Shelley told them. "Except sort of like last Saturday night."

"I wish Lokietok was here. He'd enjoy spoiling their games." The faces turned doubtfully to Hereward; Lokietok's likings might not be everyone's choice. "What are they like, these masks?"

"All sorts – birds, monsters, ghosts, twisters. Sorry, no offence."

"Just what I would expect from him. Decorate it up. Like he made it legal to scoop out my eye. Well, let's go to his party."

Now Hereward had his life back in all its intricate multisensuality. All that afternoon as they constructed the masks he worked in a daze, intent on tugging out his past in streamers and strings, every image lifting with it others that were bedecked with displays of still others. Before long they were spilling out in such profusion that almost all had to be pushed aside to give him a chance to examine a few in detail.

First he picked up his name and polished it. Demetrius mistakenly gave it a flourish, he thought, and maybe Harry Ward as a name doesn't have the clang of Hereward, but it will do nicely. Just so with his wife and son, if only they were still waiting in Thorpe-on-Saye village. If they are there will be no more Lamorak-ventures, no more dreamed city-walls waiting for the siege-towers, he promised. Now he knew how close he had been to them on the journey south from Ferris's Landing. Probably he had been acquainted with people from the stone-thrower's village, only a mile or so away from his own home. Ingastowe Cathedral had always looked somehow wrong seen from Hay, but now he knew why. Its silhouette would have been very different seen all through his childhood from the north.

Instead of a line of events receding first into a quiet dimness and then disappearing now his memory neither recognised nor acknowledged the passing of time. Around him his past burnt in a fiery circle and his frailties and aspirations would never let him out of that circle again. He had always felt that Tyr-Hereward existed only in the hopes of a deprived few but the flares from the past illuminated a timid wishful schoolboy stirring as the princes and earls spoke in words that brooked no dissent. In the light of memory he saw himself seeking out Lamorak and Regret, longing for the great struggle. In this he resembled most men and women since the world began, feeling an emptiness yet knowing neither from where it came nor how to fill it.

His Old One's memory was so deeprooted in the past and so inexplicably selective that he found himself bewildered by the sensation of having been a series of different characters. The boy, the youth, the man, the present Hereward, each gave different perspectives to each individual recollection. Sorting through it all would take a long time but then he had lots of time since now he had a future that had a shape. When the business in Shawpits was out of the way then his future could start.

Artis's wide kitchen table was covered with paste, cardboard, papier-mache, paints, wood and feathers. Adelie, who had been home to eat, returned to plunge joyfully into the jumble. She was full of admiration for Kit's mask which, like her, made no concessions, being the sleek head of the fox she carried in her name, hand, colouring and paw-light footsteps. Kit had taken a chair out on the lawn and sat painting red fur and green eyes. "I can't work in a mess," she told Adelie. Finishing long before the others, she went off to Shawpits to confirm the details of the plan, which she described as full of impulse and improvisation and not much else.

Inside the mess accumulated around Magnus. Jacky and Hereward, with no aspirations to artistry, were well ahead with their masks, which from simple half-comical conceptions had suddenly acquired a warped menace. Whereas Kit's fox looked more like a fox the more she had worked at it, Jacky was transforming his white fish by adding teeth that leaked blood-trails. "It's a kind of pike," he told Adelie with the mild disdain of a sea fisherman for pond and river fish.

"I don't like it," she shivered, "and I don't like Hereward's. What is it anyway?" The mask was pumpkin-shaped and yellow with black eyes that some mispainting had given a squint. Adelie, never short of ideas, added a moustache and glued on a piece of red fabric like a tongue hanging out.

"What's yours, Magnus?"

Magnus ruefully displayed a tangled sculpture of wire and twigs. "It's a butterfly."

"So it is. A meadow fritillary – in its early stages. Would you like me to help you?"

"All right. Time's getting short, though. Better make an egg, like Hereward's."

"We'll make a pig." Adelie knew she would burst out laughing if she caught Magnus's eye.

The night was cool and windy, with the stars gleaming clear and white. The torch flames blowing aslant shed droplets of fire spangling the breeze. Magnus spluttered as smoke blew inside his mask. The drums at the front thumped and there was a rattling of tins and makeshift cymbals, beating out a rough tune. It was hard to say how many people were in the crowd, perhaps sixty, he thought, though the masks made it look more. "Yes, suitably pig-headed," Adelie had said, and he felt confident of his disguise, pressing forward close to the drummers, swinging an axe and bellowing the crude song he had soon picked up: 'Bring on fire, bring on smoke, Burn out the dirty little Twisted Folk.'

The Misses Shepherd standing at a gate watched them pass. "Going ran-tanning?" said one. "Wait till the Companions come!" called the other. Someone threw a stone at the old ladies and there was a laugh as they ducked.

"We are the Companions now!" shouted Magnus, and Kit inside her fox mask gave an exasperated groan. There had already been a longish wait while the Jacques brothers searched for the missing Lew, and if Magnus didn't stop singing so loudly and making grunting noises the leaders, who prefer followers to be paler imitations of themselves, would take an interest in the bobbing noisy pig-mask. She had already caught stray tendrils of thought wondering who this amusing fellow was, though the masks seemed to sieve out any individuality of thought.

Then Shawpits' dark bulk of trees was on them, closing over the footpath like the entrance to a cave. Bats zigzagged skittishly over the crowd as it halted, the late-comers pressing forward in anticipation. The masks bobbed and swung like living gargoyles, the torchlight picking out the animal faces splashed with reds, whites and yellows, raddled-looking dogs' and rats' faces with rouged cheeks, then the clowns and jesters daubed into roues that made Kit shiver as the thought crossed her mind that these gloating satyrs and pasteboard werewolves leering down at her might have been the last sight her sister ever saw. She moved closer to the new headman, noticing as she did so the doltish pumpkin-mask of Hereward, unmistakable with the long red tongue, still just behind him.

From deep inside the wood a voice was calling, a sound like a mother calling to a wayward child. The crowd surged forward, the narrow footpath pulling them in like a funnel. Here the canopy of the trees hid the stars and the dense head-high bramble clumps offered no easy way towards the siren voice still crying, now plain to hear, "Rebecca, where are you? Where's Rebecca?"

"Over here, Rebecca!" yelled someone, and there was a pushing and kicking at the thorny bushes, and laughter as someone slid and fell, cursing, into one of the dips just off the path. Kit knew Shawpits well, not so much its tangled depths but she had visited the cottage that lay on the further side, what she always thought of as the cathedral side. Apart from Lichgate Farm it was the only conventional dwelling that any twisted family occupied, and the ginger-haired Buckles who had all been born there had no unusual features unless one counted their masses of freckles. Red Buckle feared no one and had let it be known that any headman who cared to play knives-in-eyes would find a ready contest in Shawpits.

The crowd surged along the path for three hundred yards or so to where the Buckles' cottage lay behind honeysuckle hedges, the trees above fingering the roof and eaves protectively. The windows had small lozenge panes and behind one a light made diamond-shaped patterns and showed someone reading, the book on a table in front of him. Kit's doubts were swelling; at the very first turn their plan had grown unpredictable.

And unpredictable quickly, thought Jacky, as the first stone splintered into the little panes, bending the leads inwards, and the half-crazed laughter swept about him. He, like Kit, knew the plan well enough, and Buckle must have known it too for Kit had spent part of that afternoon explaining it to the Shawpits families, and this cottage should have been empty. They had planned that confrontation should take place elsewhere, in the two tunnel-dwellings and the tree-house. Through the window Red Buckle could be seen putting a bookmarker in the pages, and then he emerged from the door.

"Everyone at once?" he said. "Or one on one? Not your style though, is it?"

"Clear out, Red!" shouted Carver Jacques, just in front of Jacky who had not once let the mask's black face, white-rimmed eyes and pigtailed hair get far from him. "It's me, Carver. We've got nothing against you. You're not one of the twisters."

"Mother and father were though," Buckle shouted back. "Go home, Carver. Stick to stealing pea-sticks."

There was a sudden flaring of light and a terrified squawking of chickens. "Have a look at your hen-house!" shouted a voice, and Buckle ran across and dragged the door open for the distraught birds to escape. The front row of the mob was yelling in his house before he could turn. When he did the stiletto was half out of his belt but there was no avoiding the fist that knocked him sprawling, nor the second blow as he tried to get up.

"Got to learn to join in the fun!" Magnus shouted over the din, licking his scraped knuckles and accepting the pats on the back with aplomb. The night air was full of raucous shouting, a shattering of pottery and glass being smashed, fabrics tearing and boots kicking open doors and cupboards. Silhouetted figures were rifling boxes and looting sideboards, waving here a flowered curtain, there a garden rake or a box of buttons. "We're getting left out!" bellowed Magnus leading his new admirers into the cottage.

Kit in the moment's respite took the opportunity to drag the dazed Buckle into the ferns. "Please shut up, Red, for once," she whispered into his ear. "Leave it to Hereward, like our plan." She turned at the sound of hysterical laughter and a rush of people came through the door. Several climbed through the broken window as smoke began to fill the rooms. The fire's speed was as shocking as its heat and the height of its flames, the twigs and leaves above soon hissing and sizzling. Everyone watched fascinated and soon to a burst of cheering the roof fell in.

The headman had watched what had happened so far without participating, as if bored, but now reasserted himself. "This way," he said. "Let's burn out some more of 'em!" and his voice left no room for doubt. "And let's find Rebecca."

The laughter was ugly and Kit trembled. Somehow the crowd had to be split if the Twisted Folk were to cope, but they were all starting to trample and hack a path off to the wood's southern side.

To keep a plan simple is an excellent intention and if it remains simple then it may retain its original shape long enough to be accomplished. Unfortunately for planners it is difficult to foresee any but a few elements, and if a plan has among its components a half-drunk mob led by a dozen bullies and brutes, three terrified families and another group of anxious people trying to break attitudes hundreds of years old in one desperate hour, all together in darkness, in a wood so thick as to be in parts impenetrable, in a half-crazed masque or carnival, then it is almost certain to degenerate, first becoming unpredictable and then chaotic. Sitting in Artis's kitchen tugging their ideas into some sort of shape the group had known these probabilities without acknowledging them. They had known that without any plan no concerted action at all would begin – anyway, instinct told them that chaos could reduce the odds they faced.

The one element likely to stay constant was time. The mob would not wish to stay long in the wood, not when they could be celebrating the cleansing of the nasty little sore that had festered there as long as their grandparents had reminded them of their grandparents' stories, and there was no past back beyond that or none that mattered in the memory-fading of the Daylight People. There would have to be time for drinking and sharing out and showing off the new possessions, and that meant no time, surely, for seeking out one after another the three dwellings in the wood, as well as the Buckles' cottage. As one big group it would take far too long, nor would its members be slow to guess that that way the headman and his closest lieutenants would get all the choicest items. They certainly had done at Sheepwash Bend, especially with the girl. But not this time – this time the share-out would be bigger. Maybe next time it would be bigger still.

The plan would crumble, Jacky knew. He had commanded the citizen-regiments of Limber, and their plan was simplicity itself: stand behind the walls and fight; when one goes down another fills his place. Even then it didn't take chance and accident long to undo it all. So it was now. The north side of Shawpits was an obscure tangle even in daylight, partly caused by the villagers' habit of pollarding the hazels from the base so that the trees regrew into a palisade of criss-crossed fans flanking the path. The northern part was wetter and colder, the ancient diggings treacherous beneath the thick ivy. Though just as easy to lose yourself on the southern side, by day it was sunnier and there were even glades of flowers. As Red Buckle's house burnt the mob began to push in among the trees, uncertain where the twisters were but certain they would be found. Magnus's attempts to divert some to the north by yelling encouragement were ignored. "It's easier going this way, big fellow!" shouted someone.

Now the mob was in two groups, quickly getting further apart, one following the brothers Carver and Haakon Jacques, the other headed after the headman and his closest cronies. Out on the fringe of Shawpits Kit had reached her arranged rendezvous with Jesse and all the Twisted Folk he had managed to assemble, some from remote spots twenty miles away, drawn by the name of Tyr-Hereward.

Inside the wood the masked figures smelled the smoke, and heard the noises start. A breeze was pushing the smoke through the trees, thick smoke from fires layered with damp leaves and ivy. The smoke came invisible in the dark, with its uneasy smell, and it was tempting not to stand and cough but to move. The air towards the fringes downwind seemed clearer. With the smoke came a low muttering sound like the far-off running of cattle, the sound of drums beating outside the wood. Where the Twisted Folk had no drums they beat on empty boxes or hollow trees. To the crowd the noise came as Kit had hoped, intimidating in its unexpectedness and making them feel surrounded as if the wood itself had conspired to encage them. Many remembered parents telling them as children not to stray off the path. The drumming paused, then the screams started, high, wavering and agonised, and cries, half-articulated, occasionally a clear shout, "Let's get out of here!" or "This is a mess – I'm going!" Someone was imitating a wounded man moaning for help, an eerie gasping ululation, "Help me, help me, someone help me!" until even Kit's nerves longed for it to stop. Other voices called names out of the darkness, "Peter Archer, are you in there?" and "Peter, Peter Archer, would your father have liked this?" until Archer, who drove the delivery dray for the mill, pulled off his mask, threw it in the bushes and walked away down the path.

Struggling and tripping among tree-stumps and brambles, climbing fallen logs and ducking under low branches, coughing, as uneasy in the unexplained smoke as bees are when the bee-keeper blows smoke in their hive, the two groups began to fray in the rear, the stragglers pausing, half-lost and frustrated. Where the path led out at either end of the wood people began to emerge, one here, two there, then another. Most chose to turn back to Hay, being the quickest way home and avoiding the smouldering remains of the Buckles' cottage. As they stepped out from beneath the trees they saw familiar and strange faces, a mixture of Hay villagers and Twisted Folk who had been assembled there by Artis and Jesse.

Artis had long regretted the sentence that had removed Hereward's eye and his self-disgust had been fuelled by Zjelko's boast of having manipulated the village court. The stragglers were not ill-treated but nor was Artis gentle with them.

"Within three days all of this land from the fens to the Big Grey River will know what Hay village has been up to lately. Before long we shall be a name of contempt among decent people through all of Westermain. The Matrix no longer regulates us here – we are free to act as we will. As our first free action you chose or supported the rape and murder of a child." None of those he addressed had any bravado left and elected either to stay with Artis or go inconspicuously homewards.

Inside the wood the two marauding gangs were pressing onwards, their leaders unaware of their diminishing numbers. The first to stumble on a low doorway was the group containing the Jacques brothers. The other bigger party was swearing and crashing through the trees some distance away.

Carver Jacques kicked the door in with a whoop and looked through a narrow arched opening into a sort of hallway. A doormat and an umbrella leaning in a corner looked harmless enough and he stepped inside. From behind a door at the end of the hallway a voice said, "Go away, please." Jacques gestured to his followers and they came with a rush. Someone dragged at the door and surprisingly it swung smoothly open. Carver Jacques went through it with a laugh followed by another man carrying a large sack over his shoulder; the doormat was already in it.

Jacky, third in line as he intended, pushed the door closed and turned round. Haakon Jacques behind him stared in surprise. "Open the door, you fool," he said impatiently.

"Two at a time," said Jacky.

"What do you mean?"

There was a rush of scuffling, kicking feet and toppling furniture, and then muffled shouting from beyond the door.

"Well, two against two in there. Got to be fair."

Now others were crowding into the narrow passage and there was the sour smell of beer.

"Get out of my way!" Haakon Jacques went to reach for the door-handle and then, seeing the knife coming upwards, took a fast step backwards; he rebounded off the bodies behind him so that the knife missed his chest and came up through his jaw and into his mouth.

There was an uncomprehending pause, a space clearing itself in front of Jacky. He took off his mask. One of Zjelko's men said, "Who are you?"

"I am John Dorn, of the Big Grey River, the last Rector of Limber. If I were you I should go home."

Unexpectedly the door opened behind him and one of the Pascal brothers from the deep fen looked out. "The headman's man is dead. Carver does not wish to be involved any more."

"I see. Then you and your brother are ready for the next two."

"We've got no quarrel with the Pascals," muttered a voice. "They don't live here."

"Of course not. The Bent family lives here, an old man, an old woman, a young man with no hands and two girls. Did you have an appointment?" Siward Pascal was holding a spade, its bright edge dripping wetly. There was noise outside the dwelling and some pushing to and fro at the door, some wishing to enter, others to leave.

"I advise you to go home," Jacky said. "My quarrel is with those who raped and murdered a fifteen-year old girl a week ago. Those who watched or those who thought tonight was their chance, and I suppose that's all of you, well, you've got the rest of your lives to convince your neighbours that it was all a bit of fun, no harm meant."

There was some shuffling and the hallway was less crowded. "I'm choking – my mouth's full of blood." Haakon Jacques' words sent red bubbles spraying out of his mouth.

"Fleur choked on mud while you shovelled it in," said Siward Pascal. "You shouldn't complain."

A shabby pig-mask peered down the passage, quickly taking everything in.

"Come on let's get out of this! He's one of those bastard Companions!" The other masks swung away after Magnus, who shouted as they ran. "The bloody wood's on fire. I'm not staying in it to get burnt to death!" Jacky picked up his own mask and stepped over Jacques with the Pascals following. Within a few moments Magnus was back, returning after a particularly loud imitation of flight. "Going well," he said. "Lots of 'em leaving."

"All right, as far as I can tell," Jacky agreed. "Better than expected."

But elsewhere the plan was in tatters.

The bigger group that had split away behind Zjelko was altogether more dangerous. Around their leader was most of the close-knit clique of his cronies and drinking partners from the fort or Ingastowe's back-streets, malcontents who had spotted easy pickings when in its adversity the Matrix had recalled its troops from the outlands and disbanded the provincial militias. They knew that the communities of Westermain would be disinclined to empower any new authority to oversee their actions. Zjelko had been amused at the thought of moving into Hay, and the promise of his protection in the uncertain times ahead had been tempting enough to see him instated as headman. Always suspicious and jealous of his position, he had been uneasy at the whisper of visitors at Artis's house, and the arrival of Martin. The two events had no apparent connection but clearly the little man knew of his sister's death, and so, Zjelko decided, the talk of repentance and forgiveness would be a typical twister subterfuge.

But any doubts he had could be left in abeyance, it being the day of the hunt, and the prospect of some action had been enticing, particularly if it might involve the insolent Red Buckle.

At the same moment as Carver Jacques made the fatal error of confronting the Pascals, Zjelko, with seven of his closest supporters and twenty villagers, had reached the entrance to the other hidden dwelling. They would never have seen it had not a small figure darted among the coils of ancient ivy, branches thick as arms, that hid a wooden verandah. "Got it," said Zjelko. "Come on, you four with me" – he pointed to four of his bravoes – "then we'll deal with the drummers and screamers, whoever they are. You others stay here." He didn't bother instructing the villagers, who stood waiting, a few with lanterns, some with sticks and others carrying hoes or scythes.

Pushing through the ivy Zjelko was into the entrance so fast and his comrades so eager that Hereward had difficulty reaching the place he wanted, nor in the narrow tunnel could he push past anyone so that now there were five in front of him. Candle-light seeped into the tunnel as Zjelko went through another door, the rest following close. Over their shoulders Hereward could see into the room, which reminded him at once of Martin's home at Sheepwash Bend: tapestry on the walls, woven reeds on the floor, couches pushed back against the walls, a vase of flowers on a small table, and incongruous in the centre the gleam of candle flame sliding up and down the steel blades.

Already the plan was out of control, he knew. He had had no chance to turn and block the tunnel. Everyone in Artis's kitchen and the Twisted Folk in the fen farmhouse had been confident that Hereward would be impassable in a narrow space, as Jacky had proved to be in the house on the other side of the wood. But the mob had not split into three as expected, the formidable Magnus had found himself chasing shadows, and too many of Zjelko's hard-bitten crew had not split up, as they had themselves originally intended, but were crowding into the passageway, some blocking, others pushing, Hereward.

He could hear Zjelko laughing in front of him and then the clash of metal. He knew the two Twisted Folk inside would be wondering whether he was behind one of the goggling masks and when he would help them.

Yet for Hereward, born without knowing it one of the Old Ones, there was more to know. Death to the Daylight Folk was the end of the daylight but to the Old Ones death was and always had been made terrible by the circling of their memories. Lines have no end but the Old Ones shivered and strained at the confines of the circle. Back in the fort, at the Dole River, in the fighting in Limber the prospect of death had not for Hereward been accompanied by loss. Now it was different, and he could not move forward. The way out was to stand still but he couldn't close his eyes and in front of him the deliberations in Artis's kitchen which had filled him with doubt now filled him with dread as they became the present. Perhaps if he waited one minute something good would happen.

But Zjelko was in a hurry and with four of his cronies five to two gave the twisted defenders no hope. One was down clutching his chest and the other's weapon was beaten from his hand. Hereward's tongue moved as thickly as if his mouth were full of soot, but if words formed no one heard them.

"You've been listening to lies about Dole River." Zjelko sounded almost amiable. "You people aren't cut out for this. Where are the women?"

"You'll never see them, you scum!"

"Think so? I'll see more than you. Remember the Gunnarsen boy? So you want to be like him?" He pulled out a knife. "Hold him down." The others closed in.

Hereward sighed. Every part of him wanted to be out of the tunnel, to be left alone with his new treasure of memories, but his voice spoke creakingly and said, "Leave him alone," and he couldn't stop it saying the words. He felt sick but now he belonged in the domain of the earls and the Old Ones' infantrymen plodding forward into the gunfire in the long-ago. Every face came round as one.

"Who said that?" Zjelko stood upright. He didn't like the sound of the voice.

"Just leave him alone." A space was clearing itself around Hereward as if he were somehow contagious.

"Who are you?"

"Never mind that. I don't like blinding."

Another nudge from Zjelko's past but he ignored it. "Oh, don't you!" His voice dripped disdain. "Take that mask off." Possibly there were some in the village who would react like this, but so long as the dissent remained limited to shrews like the woman Nell and the Misses Shepherd it did not bother him. What Zjelko never knew then or later was the illogic that fed the Old Ones, drawn from their irrational memory-paths and connections, and forged in their inextinguishable encounters with the intoxication of power and their obsession with time.

Hereward made a laughing sound like the clatter of the waterbirds' wings. From under his coat came the old rifle and bayonet he had found in Artis's house. In Limber he had never used any other weapon, disliking swords or spears.

Zjelko laughed too: "You're a fine fellow. Put it away before anyone gets hurt, you've made your point. Let's see your face."

"I'll stand no more of your insolence," said Hereward, and though the words seemed to come from outside him they rang with force as if a door had been kicked inwards in splinters. He dragged off the mask and threw it down.

"Well, well, if it isn't Orr! I see what you mean about blinding." Zjelko spoke conversationally. "An outlaw and a killer who was never taken come back. Fancy that!" He came forward in the murky enclosed space, stepping carefully round a small table, his bulk obscuring the candle, bringing wavering shadows as he came.

Another man skirted the table's other side and the two closed in. Hereward suddenly remembered another dimly lit place, the vaults below the fort at Ingastowe and a lantern extinguishing itself – how easy it now was to remember these things – and instead of stepping back he dragged the door shut, took one fast stride forward and threw himself across the table, squashing out the candle flame as he tumbled on to the reed matting on the far side.

He had cannoned into two more of Zjelko's men but now in the total darkness there was some advantage for him and he drove the bayonet point up and around hoping that no one friendly would be in its path. The first upward stab only rebounded off a curtained wall but the second struck solidly and there was a shout of pain. Moving fast he struck again and again and with five possible targets was unlikely to miss often. The room was full of movement, shouts and confusion, and a yell of pain from the far side of the room suggested someone else had lashed out blindly. Hereward bumped into shoulders and backs, collided with the table and tripped over a body, but the bayonet slashed upwards and the butt swung back as he tried to estimate where the door was, knowing that soon it would swing open and let in the unwelcome light of the lanterns outside. He heard a cry for help so the odds were improving, but then what he feared happened. There was a filtering of light and then more spilling in and he saw one of the milling group had pulled the door open. Hereward took it all in at a glance: one down, one crouched over in a corner and a third caught blinking with his back to the bayonet never saw it. Zjelko and another had knives out, and Zjelko holding the young twisted man in a wrestling hold in front of him seemed to have been using him as a shield in the melee. Now the headman whipped the knife over the young man's shoulder and held it across his throat.

"Stand back, Orr. And still!"

Hereward was shaking with fury and there were waves of force scribbled round him, sending the same alarms that Lokietok once flung out.

"I'll do it. Just drop that bayonet!" Zjelko was nearly shouting now.

"Don't drop it!" Hereward could hardly believe he had heard it. "Don't, Tyr," said Billy Peat. "This is our big chance, remember."

It was happening as if in a play, the actors slowing the action to distil the dilemma. Even in the poor light Hereward saw Zjelko's knuckles tighten, the knife begin its penetration and Billy Peat's first convulsion. Then he watched himself coming forward, three fast steps though not quick enough to outpace the knife's incision, but sudden enough to knock Billy sideways and drive the bayonet unstoppably upwards, feeling it scrape as it passed between Zjelko's ribs.

Zjelko grabbed him round the neck and toppled back, pulling Hereward with him. Hereward punched downwards breaking Zjelko's grip and nose with the same blow. The first of the knife blows from Zjelko's last henchman went into Hereward's back and the second into where neck and shoulder join. Billy Peat flung himself at the man, giving Hereward a chance to get to his feet. All his reactions were very slow now. He seemed to be floating, his vision closing to a tunnel and though he felt no pain – even where the metal had gone into his right lung – he certainly could not walk. But he could stand and wait to see what the last man would do – which was to run for the door.

And now, suddenly, it was very quiet so he sat down and leaned his back against the wall.

Zjelko had exerted a rough sort of discipline among his thuggish retinue and while those of them still outside were disappointed not to have gone down the passage this was not the only house in the wood. Their chance would come. They heard some noise from within, beyond the wooden verandah, but that was to be expected. Disappointingly there were no screams, or not yet anyway.

The big loud fellow in the pig-mask joined the waiting crowd, along with a white fish, easier to see than most, and a disturbing looking sack with eye-holes. "Well, what are we waiting for?" shouted the big fellow, pushing to the front.

"Just wait. Like everyone else." The voice sounded disgruntled with the delay but the man never took his eyes off the entrance.

"Oh, dear," said Magnus, and thumped the back of the speaker's head with the blunt end of his axe. There was a moment of astonishment and disbelief not lessened by Magnus shouting, "The pigs strike back!" For those of the villagers whose nerves were fraying and bravado evaporating, waiting in the smoky dark, the thought of a madman loose among them was chilling. Nor had they liked what they had just heard from inside the door, a growling and crashing as if bears fought in a subterranean cave. A number were on their first hunt, drawn by talk of a bit of fun, a few broken windows.

Then the man wearing the fish mask took it off and addressed the village people impatiently: "Go home. In the morning it will all be different. So far you have done little to be ashamed of."

"Except burn my cottage," said Red Buckle, taking off the sack-face. "Go home or we will come and burn yours. That would be just and fair." Most of the villagers began to edge away leaving Zjelko's four retainers to eye the three in front of them. The odds, though roughly equal, did not seem attractive.

"If you four have weapons put them down." Jacky's words dropped into a silence. The masking ivy rustled and moved and the yellow pumpkin mask with the round eyes, black moustache and red tongue that Adelie had added to it came slowly through the greenery, and very slowly, crouching over, one hand cradling his stomach as if holding a small frightened bird, the figure reached a fallen log and sat there. The bayonet looked wet and umber-coloured in the lantern-light.

"Where is Zjelko, Hereward?" said Jacky over his shoulder. There was a silence, then a slow finger pointed back to the entrance. "Dead?" A nod.

There was a stirring among the bushes and two more men emerged to stand alongside Jacky. They looked tough and purposeful. "Now," he said to the four, "your situation is not good. Hereward is hurt, but the Pascal brothers are not. So I will tell you again. Put down your weapons and sit on the grass. Or die. Not a difficult choice."

He barely looked at the crowd of villagers, which in any case was hardly a crowd now. The number was considerably smaller than it had been and those few remaining were rapidly discarding their masks. A few costume-wearers were making themselves inconspicuous. There was a moment of tension and Magnus fingered his axe's edge impatiently, then two of Zjelko's last four turned and ran, pushing through the remnants of the crestfallen watchers and hunt followers, a number of whom ran guiltily with them. The other two hesitated, finding the Pascals too close to them, and threw themselves down. "Let the others go," said Jacky. He turned to look for Hereward but there was no sign of the one-eyed man.

LVII

The boy came alone, walking along the low road into Hay. He was sixteen years old, tall and slender though the wide shoulders hinted at what he might be later. Everything interested him and he stood for some time looking at the monastery buildings, wondering what happened in there. He was in no hurry, and where the beck gurgled alongside the road he stopped to take off his shoes and paddle in the cold, clear water, pleasing himself with the carpeted feel of the mossy stones under his feet.

Many small happenings had drawn him to where he now was. Drinking beer with older boys and young men, he knew in the same way he knew that it was showery weather that the future wanted him, unlike them, to try his strength against it. His friends seemed satisfied enough living in the limits of tonight's play and tomorrow's work, but these, though good and necessary, lay ahead like the gentle buttercupped meadows and orderly fields he could see from his bedroom window. Somewhere else there were cliffs, sheer, glassy, climbing to the sky, of which he thought much, and deep black abysses, of which, so far, he thought hardly at all.

That evening in the inn he had watched them, the way they walked and sat and held their glasses. The woman had seized his attention with her hooded green eyes and occasional startling stare, even, he thought uneasily, choosing to look at him in his group of friends. He would like to have spoken if only to hear her speak, but the muttered remarks around him about twisters and their women held him back. Clearly the little man with her was twisted into the oddest shape, but he had laughed aloud and shown his neighbours amusing tricks with his eye-catching green dice. And the fair-haired youngish man with the scarred hands and arms, and the stitch-marks pricking down his face, he was puzzling to the boy, as if the music in the man's head was for him alone. The big man with one eye was the same, perhaps more disturbing. Somewhere in the books and pictures in his home he would recognise that look, whatever it was. Something like the look of Baldwin in the book of his adventures, he thought.

Later, he had been ashamed when the stone had hit one of the men, and of the thrower boasting of it afterwards. The inn-keeper had mentioned that the party was heading for Hay. The boy had then told his mother he was going walking in the woods for a few days. It was not much of an excuse but she shrugged and said, "All right, just be sensible," since she knew him for what he was. She was surprised it had taken this long.

The sudden encounter in the wood had happened on the second night. The stranger had seemed confident in a snarling way at first but less so as the boy pulled out a bayonet and began to circle silently, closing in through the trees as the firelight diminished. The stranger was always having to pull at the twister tethered on the other end of the rope though who was really tethered seemed less and less certain. The boy told him to cut the rope and reminded him how dark it was getting. Gradually the boy's voice grew more like those other cold voices the stranger had heard the previous night in Shawpits Wood and the stranger untied the rope from the twister's waist and stumbled noisily away.

The boy had sat and talked with the little twisted man until daylight and wished him well. The little man had wanted them to go together to Hay but the boy was reluctant. He did not want to seem to be searching for more thanks, and they had parted.

Later that morning he told himself that it was as good a direction as any. By mid-afternoon he was paddling in Hay beck. With his feet fresh and clean he felt like running but thought it too boyish. There were a few people walking in the same direction and he strode along among them. The street ahead seemed curiously empty and yet interesting. There were flowers everywhere, in tubs, in baskets, in garlands hung over fences and wreaths dangling from door-knockers, and all tied or interwoven or banded with black ribbons. Eventually he found himself in the village square. Now there were more people, standing quietly, looking down at the road itself or hushing the children if their play tended to grow boisterous, and he chose to leave the middle of the road and rather shyly walk close to the walls and hedges. Here the houses were taller and closer together and he could see a church tower behind them.

Then one of the bells began to toll, a deep, solemn, slow sound, and heads turned towards the noise. The people came first, spilling out of the churchyard down a hill into the square to where the boy stood so that in the twilight he saw first the lights of the candles bobbling down towards him, and then the people, the men in plain trousers and jackets, greys and blacks, the women mainly in black, though often with white sleeves puffed out under velveteen waistcoats. A few children slipped out from among the watchers to walk alongside parents, bearing themselves as stiffly and silently as any in the procession.

Then came the cross; the timbers too heavy to be borne upright for long, it was being carried across one shoulder by a brawny young man who had folded a wheat-sack there to ease its weight. When he reached the square he did heave it vertical, and heard someone murmur, "It was never too heavy for George Littler." Alongside the bearer a black-haired girl hopped on crutches and as they passed the boy heard her say, "Is it too heavy, Magnus?" and the young man smiled and blinked the sweat away from his eyes and said, "No, little mouse."

There was music from somewhere, drums, trumpets and trombones pumping out a simple tune that repeated itself. The procession was not marching to it, but somehow taking their time from the beat, walking with dignity. Then the boy saw the pall-bearers and knew it was not a village festival or a saint's day as he had assumed.

The first coffin was so small it must have been a child's, he thought. He caught his breath when he saw the face of the pall-bearer on his side, for he had seen him before, knocked down by a stone in his own village. He was the same man, clearly, but different. The woman bearer on the other side he recalled too, and there was the little twisted man walking with her. The other bearers, the pair who looked like brothers and a red-haired man, he did not know, though it puzzled him for he had never heard of a funeral bringing together Twisted Folk and Daylight People.

"Who's dead?" he asked the woman alongside him.

"Too many," she said, and another, overhearing her, said, "Not enough," thus leaving him still more perplexed.

Then came the second coffin and now the boy knew that he was in the future that all his friends laughed at. It was large and big men carried it. Behind came more of the long procession of mourners from the church and then the boy stood very still. Often he had heard of the Companions and now they came, one company of them only, but he could not take his eyes away from their loping stride, jaunty, almost sinister, their arms swinging across their bodies rather than by their sides, young and lean in the woodland's tawny colours, russets and faded green, some showier with their sleeves fringed from shoulder to cuff, but all wearing flowers. They seemed to strain forward and the boy heard their captain say, "Steady, then," as they went by. Their band brought up the rear and the watchers, when it had passed, streamed on to the road and followed, with the boy drawn along among them.

After a while he found everyone turning up a lane and across a wide field where sheep were grazing. The graveyard appeared unexpectedly beyond a hedge. In the fading light the graves with flowers on them looked as if people dressed in bright colours had lain down to sleep in the grass. A ring of about two hundred people had formed round the two graves and the bearers had laid down the coffins. The boy edged forward and found himself close to the girl with crutches and the big young man. The cross stood straight up, its foot in the grass, and the man held it in both arms as if embracing it, his cheek against the old grey wood. The boy could hear them talking quietly.

"What's the priest's name, Adelie?"

"Father Huw, Magnus, weren't you paying attention in church?"

Back in Thorpe-on-Saye village the boy had attended several funerals; this one was similar, he thought, with the elderly needing no guide along its familiar avenue, the middle-aged still learning not to be uneasy, and the young looking around them like travellers in an antique land. Then the coffins were lowered into the graves with ropes. The small one went first and the boy's scalp prickled at the long wailing cry from near the grave-side. Others joined in and the boy felt insignificant and lonely, outside even the fringe of such lamenting. As the big coffin disappeared the Companions snapped to attention, so he did too and stared straight ahead with them as the bugle sent its sad notes floating one after another across the valley.

"That's how to say goodbye, Adelie. I hope it'll be the same for me one day."

The boy could hear the girl crying, and the twilight was dimmer now. He wondered if it was over but the abbot spoke again:

"The Lord gave and the Lord hath taken away . . ."

"Blessed be the name of the Lord." The boy and the young man spoke the words together, and the man looked round with a smile and reached out a hand.

"Magnus Dorn."

The boy shook the hand and murmured his own name. People were filing past the graves and dropping in flowers. Magnus lowered the cross he was still holding and laid it in the grass. Adelie separated her flowers into three bunches and offered one to the boy. They were autumn flowers, chrysanthemums white and yellow, late roses and Michaelmas daisies.

"Come with us," said Magnus as they joined the waiting lines.

Swallows dipped and swooped using the last light and a pheasant rattled out its throaty call from the next field. The Twisted Folk from the fens carried marsh marigolds, spearworts, white water-lilies and meadowsweet, those from the valleys clutched little blue wood-orchids, and violets and purple heartsease.

Once people had placed their flowers they mingled quietly, neighbours and friends exchanging words, renewing acquaintances, as if a hard rind was being peeled away and the old gentlenesses were back. Perhaps they were even better, for shyly and often self-consciously came little gestures and indications, awkward but well-meant. That Miss Frances Shepherd should say, "Where did you find such lovely violets, Kate?" to one of the old ladies from the lost valley was neither unusual nor stiff, but that Artis's sharp-tongued housekeeper Hilda should pick up a small boy and mop his tears and clean his grazed knee with her handkerchief, ignoring the crinkled purple birthmark that he wore like a skull-cap, that was well worth recounting afterwards. Artis himself revealed to grey Jesse that he had a cottage that no one used if the Buckles had nowhere to go. When Red Buckle later told Jesse that he would sooner live in a pig-sty he was informed that he should change his mind and that but for his hotheadedness Tyr-Hereward might still be alive. Siward Pascal, hearing Noah Smith's regular lament that no one was interested in clocks any more, murmured something about a collection of clocks, not much, of course, but Noah might like to see them.

The boy took two chrysanthemums and dropped one in each grave, where the coffins were now invisible under their multipetalled shawls. On the grave's further side he saw the red-haired woman flick back her black veil and stare at him and the pale thin man with her stared too. Unthinkingly he straightened his shoulders and lifted his chin. He felt nettled when the woman turned away to whisper in the man's ear.

The crippled girl nudged him. "Do you know who they are?"

"Not really," the boy said. "Well, not at all."

Across the grave Kit was frowning. Then she called out, "Magnus," and the big friendly fellow strolled round to her. "That boy. I think it's the same one."

"What boy?"

"The one from the stone-throwers' village. The one that Martin told us about."

"Then we need to thank him," said Magnus. "His name's Harry Ward."

LVIII

The big room had not changed at all since the Christmas morning Hereward had walked into it carrying two pheasants, melting snow dripping off his boots and clinging in glassy beads to his coat, except that it was now a warm evening in October and the table held not two glasses of red wine but supper for a dozen people.

"I hope you're not too tired to eat," said Abbot Huw to Kit. "I expect you didn't get much sleep." It was true and Kit was not the only person there who had not slept the previous night. Most of the visitors to the abbey had spent the long night-hours in Hay church, mostly kneeling on the altar steps, occasionally rising with stiffened joints to sit in the front pews for a while. Just inside the altar rail the coffins lay, one candle on each lid, the wax sliding into odd little sculptures on the sides of the candlesticks.

Only to Adelie was the vigil-watch new. The others had been company before for mothers, fathers, children or friends rather than see them go lonely into the dark. In their thoughts the lids opened and memories spilled out, so that for hours on end Fleur and Hereward walked about the church and turned the old building into some other place, where Fleur played in the beck and called frogs to her for Martin, and told her growing-up dreams to Kit, and brought cool jellies when Jacky's fever frothed in his blood, and the floor of the nave softened into springing grasses for her and the willow and hazel dressed the pulpit in green veils so that she had her baby climbing-place. A few times Hereward met her in their thoughts but more often he was alone plodding stubbornly across the Mesa, or sitting silent in a pew with Lokietok, or fashioning pinecone hedgehogs for Adelie; faintly at the back of the church in the shadows near the big cupboard where the hymnbooks were kept was the young Old One who went to Regret but could find no way in.

"Thank you. I'll be sleeping very well . . ." said Kit and took a glass of wine and a cake with cream on it, ". . . now." She caught Jacky's eye and saw both his stern expression and, without trying, knew his thoughts. She didn't mind. He loved her, and the rest had been fixed and was over. Two nights ago he had been very angry with her. She had not cared then, nor had she cared the next day when she took communion and was supposed to acknowledge and bewail her wickedness. She did not earnestly repent and only acknowledged this by not saying the words when the others did, though she did wonder briefly whether the burden might not later be intolerable. As she had eaten the bread and sipped the thick wine something red-eyed put its tongue out of her mouth and took a sip and then slid back where she could only hope it need never again be awoken.

When they carried Hereward's body out of Shawpits she had been on the edge of the wood. What had actually happened in the dreadful struggle not even Billy Peat had been able to describe. Even days later, with the wounds in his back and throat, his words made little sense, though when someone comforted him he managed to choke out: "I fought along with Tyr when he died. Who else can say that?"

Piecing the events together it had become clear that Zjelko had escaped. "My mistake," said Jacky, who had been in a hurry to reach Martin in the big house. "I saw him come out in Hereward's mask. Keep all our people round the wood and wait until daylight." There had been much to deal with and, when Jacky had left, Kit had walked along the path to the charred beams, blackened walls and smoking ashes that marked where Red Buckle's cottage had been. On the path someone was standing, hands in pockets, and she saw it was Red himself.

"Hullo, Kit. Sorry about Fleur."

"Sorry about your house, Red."

"It's nothing. I'll build another."

"Zjelko is still in the wood, Red. Could you find him for me?"

"I expect so."

"In the dark?"

"Kit, I've lived in this wood all my life. So has my little dog. It's not so big a wood. It would help if you had something of his."

"He took Hereward's mask," said Kit. "Must have left his own behind."

Ten minutes later the dog stood on the edge of a hollow, almost a pit, where thickets of undergrowth looked blackly impenetrable. Kit had gone slowly and delicately down into the hollow, singing gently and listening as a fox listens that can hear one leaf brush on another.

Come now, come now, I'll know if you're there,
Don't be bashful, that's not very fair.

Still she could not see him, but there now could only be one possible spot, a sort of ditch within the hollow, and she could sense something, body warmth perhaps, though there was not a whisper of breathing or a hint of presence. She lifted a frond of ivy as Red Buckle's dog pushed past her, sniffed at the ground and scrambled out of the pit. Following him she was surprised to see Buckle talking quietly to one of the Pascal brothers.

"I don't think much of your dog, Red," she said.

"Zjelko was down there earlier. But it doesn't matter. We know where he is now."

"Are you sure?"

"Forgotten how to read our minds, girl?" said Siward Pascal. "He's a strong man but Hereward must have hurt him badly. He won't go far."

"Please, you two, take me to him."

"Don't fret, Kit. The watchers have just seen him come out of the wood on the Hollowhills Field side."

"I'm not fretting. So he'll hide in the old shelter the pig-boys use down by the newt pond."

"Told you she could still do it."

"Thank you, Red, but where else could he hide on that side of Shawpits? Have they fetched Jacky?"

"No, they say this is Twisted Folk's business, for you and Martin to decide."

"So it is, Siward, so it is. Me, not Martin. Let's not worry Martin. They raped her first, Red, then they buried her alive. You know that. We'll give him the same chance he gave Fleur. A bucket of milk and potatoes, can you get that? Put some pig-meal in."

"Kit!"

"It's fair, Red. You can't tell me it's not fair."

They went towards the wood's edge, walking among bits of cloth, papier-mache, string, feathers, beads, gewgaws, garlands, that were to lie untidily in Shawpits until the autumn rains came to dim and dissolve them.

Kit sang quietly:

Oh, yes, I've found you. Isn't that a worry?
What about my sister? You'll be really sorry.

"Another cake, Kit? They're very good."

"Thank you, Father. This one with cherries looks nice."

The abbot could see her every thought, she realised, and was openly letting her peruse his, showing her the gulf that had opened between her brother and herself, telling her gently that she should say farewell to him because what he had involved himself in was a resolution wider than his family or even his people. She didn't have to wonder what that was, but she did wonder how the abbot could have so obviously been part of Regret and yet not reveal it.

"I suppose you know what I did at Regret," she asked.

"Oh dear, yes."

"I expect you thought it was stupid and selfish."

"Not a bit. It was fascinating. Jacky is lucky to have a defender like you."

"And when he came back had he lost more than I can give him?"

"You underestimate yourself."

"He's in a bad temper with me now," said Kit.

It was two days ago now. He had been in a rage in the grey half-light, his feet leaving dark footprints behind him on the silvery turf of Hollowhills Field, long gaps between the foot shapes because he had come running. "What do you think you're doing?" he had said, and she was frightened but refused to show it.

"Fair's fair," she had said.

He had pulled his knife out then and shoved through the pigs, though where they were milling in the entrance to the pig-boys' shelter he had barely been able to force his way between the jostling hairy backs.

"Put those sticks down, you idiots," he had snarled at the ring of pig-boys, and even in their wildness they had been intimidated and made a wider circle so that the pigs had a chance to shy away. From inside the hut the grunting, snarling, gobbling sounds seemed to fill the valley morning like a meaty-smelling vapour. Through and above the din came a shout that turned into a scream. Then Jacky emerged from the hut, his clothes muddy and the knife red. He came over and looked down at her. She waited, thinking anything she said would make things worse. Inside the pigs chomped and squealed wetly. The oldest pig-boy came over and nervously asked if the pigs should be driven away, but Jacky shrugged and eventually said, "Come on," and he and Kit walked back to Hay together.

The pig-boys found a dry spot on the edge of Shawpits, lit a fire and roasted potatoes in it. It would need time to decide how this should be told in the history of the pigs.

As the evening drew to an end Abbot Huw addressed the men and women assembled there: "Every day sees ends and beginnings all over our world and beyond," he began. "Yet the boundaries between the past and the new times are to be seen clearer today than most of us will see them in our lifetimes. We have said farewell to Fleur and

Hereward, nor are theirs the only deaths. Now, in the absence of those who are gone, those who remain cannot choose but be different, cannot choose but know more. And it is in these moments of change we find our vision widened. Everyone knows that when a woman's mother dies, even if she herself is a mother, she knows more, because she has inherited a different perspective."

Kit watched the abbot. She wondered how many other men and women from Regret could be found in the Matrix lands.

"I spoke in church of the bargain of good and evil. The greater is the one the greater grows the abstraction of the other. Good does not need evil to exist, but it requires the capacity for evil for both to be fully understood. Equally through the lives and actions of Fleur and Hereward the conception of evil is easier to grasp and thus easier to overcome. What has happened over these recent months, particularly for us here in the last few days, is a new beginning: now we know more.

"Yet I wish to speak to you of more than this. It is the nature of good to be creative, to add to the capacity of things, and evil in its envy seeks to disrupt, to degrade and deny, all unions, harmonies and concurrence. So it is that there is an energy and immediacy associated with evil, for the creations of good are the creations and creating of God and grow with a slow, painstaking knitting together. How long does it take to stamp on the butterfly that took a thousand million years to form?"

Not even Magnus stirred among the listeners, though Kit could almost feel the pigs' sharp stamping hooves and their teeth like yellow spades.

"Let me tell you of how the years have shaped us and that way you will see Fleur and Hereward more fully. First you must try to understand more of the One God and the many gods. Of course everyone here is aware of the many gods. They are the laws by which the One God enables us all to exist. Without the nature of solid substances to be hard or soft in various degrees, and for liquids and gases too, all to be simply there and measurable, we could not exist. Matter falls or floats or burns because that is the nature of its own god. Yet these are not so much gods, though I can say their nature is touched with divinity, being rather the seraphim, cherubim and thrones, those orders of angels that throng among us unseen. Then there are higher angels, the principalities and archangels, those mighty and subtle natures that we are beginning to glimpse.

"All are fascinating, but none more so than the archangel of evolution. Here is creation in the purest form we can hope to encounter it, the miracle that every new-born child or moth embodies, and the anger we feel when that creation is threatened before it can bloom fuelled the actions of Jacky and the folk of the Big Grey River, it drove Hereward when Adelie was threatened, and it even engaged the pigs," said the abbot, looking straight at Kit, "in our anger over Fleur. Yes, I felt it too, that anger that runs counter to all I have tried to teach the people whom this monastery serves, but it is there in the characters of our genes. We of Regret have learned long ago to sublimate it. Indeed without doing so there could have been no composite mind, which is a poor way of describing our difference from you, but let that be. Whether or not we were mistaken to sublimate our anger will become apparent with time. To cope in the universe an uncontrollable rage may be an essential quality, and if so the Unmen (I will call us that) will not be the raft that rides the torrent of evolution but will spend some backwater years justifying ourselves as we admire the lilies."

There was a pause as if the abbot needed time to contemplate this possibility, but he went on: "I speak a little of the stream and destiny of mankind but only to allow us to delight in the lives of Hereward and Fleur. The churning water that is evolution does not flow forward in a smooth, predictable rush; the river bed is rocky, the banks are rough-hewn and forever changing, there are powerful currents that swing in the wildest ways. I have heard it said that of all the many gods the god of turbulence is the strangest, and nowhere is there more turbulence than where the Old Ones are. Around them changes happen; it is as simple as that.

"When the Old Ones, such as Hereward, are not the protagonists they seem to be the catalysts, even when pursuing some other course of their own. They have long memories – if they live a hundred years they still remember parts of their childhood as if time meant nothing and, though they forget much, they do not forget in a slow dimming as the Daylight People forget. Especially they recall those moments of inexplicable desire and fierce joy when they bent the world to their wishes. Mountains were climbed because they were unclimbable, though sadly this did not divert them from exerting their wills to change, control and at worst to dominate all that lives. If trees were mighty they were cut down the more avidly, and the more dangerous the animal the more jubilant the hunt. Among their own kind they strove to be masters and leaders and kings, loathing being mastered and ruled."

"But Hereward remembered little or nothing," protested Magnus.

"Regret was formed by the Old Ones and, having made it into the concord which we believe is the future, then Regret became a catchword, just as one may use 'they'. Why didn't 'they' do something about disease, and so on? It was also in the eyes of such as Lamorak a mountainous challenge on their horizons. Against Old Ones, like Lamorak and Hereward, Regret defended itself in the gentlest way it knew, by causing them to forget everything. Is not this how the City of God has always been, kindly in that we are allowed to subdue, even extinguish, those recollections of a past in which one's yearning to be part of it seemed to be attainable?

"Regret drew into its orbit multitudes of the Old Ones, and it seemed that few would wish to be excluded from it. In those early years the Daylight People emerged, often to join Regret, being as human as humanity apart from one tiny genetic change."

"Did the Unmen engineer this genetic change in us?" asked Artis.

"Partially, yes. But there was also a strong disposition even then to live as the Daylight People now do, that is lives that are full and immediate, because they are not spent always searching the past for something irretrievable or asking the future for something unattainable. The change made them perfect guardians of the earth, restoring it in fertility and beauty to a glory that is its proper condition, rather than poisoning and degrading soil, water and air. That toxicity lingers on, strong still in the Glassy Country, fading almost everywhere else, though one sees its presence – "

"In the deformed, the mutants, the Twisted Folk," interrupted Kit, "in the blighted birds and fishes and all of our family? Is that what you were going to say?"

"I would not wish one particle of you different," said Jacky quietly.

"Hmm, well." The smiles and affection around her left Kit for once shy and bereft of words. "I've forgotten what I was going to say. Continue, Father, please."

"That is all there is. Except to ask you to think again of the archangel that sits on the right hand of God. There is no halting the miracles piled upon miracles called evolution. It seems to us, the Unmen, that with our multi-faceted existences we have taken a long step forward, but what of the blue rose of the Daylight People and the black tulip of the Twisted Folk? We only know how much we value them, value also the single brilliant experiment of the Children. Even in my time here I have seen differences – the Daylight People of today are a little more like the Old Ones every year. Perhaps the world is readying itself again for another springing forward. Who can tell what is being gestated? If it is our ally, good! If it is a rival, good also, for they will need to be stronger and fitter. The universe will need all our miracles. It is sad that Fleur had no children. Perhaps Hereward too. May they both rest in the palm of God's hand."

Later that evening those who had been invited to the abbey walked back through Hay. In the main street, just before where Nell and Adelie turned off, was a pump. His head under it, working it with one hand, was the boy, stripped to the waist, his head glistening like a seal's. As they passed he looked up and smiled. "How are you, Martin?" he called across.

"Well, Harry, thank you."

That night Nell slept badly, shivering and unsure of whether she was sleeping or dreaming. In the morning her pillow was wet with tears. "Adelie, get ready," she instructed. "We need to make a journey. I wish to visit the boy's mother."

"What about his father?"

"His father is dead, I think. That is why we are going."

"Can Magnus come, to look after us?"

"Adelie, you hardly know him."

"Mother, how long had you known my father?"

"That was different." Nell tried to think of the differences. "All right, provided he isn't busy."

"He won't be."

LIX

"Those children say they're talking to Auntie Bella again. They ought to be out walking, getting some fresh air." The long journey had made the children's grandfather crotchety.

"I'll speak to them, though they can talk to her just as well when they're walking. And there's no lack of air in this cart." 'Talking-to-Auntie-Bella' had eventually become a family catchword, but Kit, who always used it sardonically, became at her most maternally disapproving when, two or three times, her children had claimed to have really spoken to 'Bella', and that she was nice and had asked after Jacky and Kit.

"Asked after your father more likely."

The children were at once cautious of and unconditionally enthralled by their mother. Their father was much easier to manage and Grandfather Dorn was clay in their fingers. Watching and yearning after their father sailing out with the fishing fleet they extracted from him a promise that they too would soon sail with him. Kit in the first two years of their marriage had sailed with him too, but had been appalled by the green powers and silver-milky agitation of the sea. Her clear and chirpy beck seemed not even the same element as the fathomless heaving whale-ocean. She was immediately inclined to forbid the children's request, and Jacky agreed that a day's sailing on the Big Grey River would be enough, though he thought their talking to Auntie Bella far more unpredictable, particularly as they could do it at the same time as playing with their toy boats and favourite wooden animals.

"Bella will look after them," said Kit. "I suppose." She had to admit that she was happier now that Isobel knew of the children, being at once inordinately proud and nervous where Sven and little Flora were concerned. She had kept her word and never once had she catapulted herself through Isobel's dreamy thoughts into the deep spaces of the mind-lattice of Regret, but what she had not reckoned with was her children absorbing that capability from her as if it had come with her milk, even less that they would play there, it being no more transcendent to them than an intriguingly overgrown garden whose paths only they knew.

Though their mother never ceased not only to watch over but to inspect them, the only blemish she could find was that one of Flora's hands was smaller than the other. When she realised what else they could do she was at first frightened, though finding in her father-in-law an unlikely consolation.

"They're clever children. I think they're clever, anyway. That'll be Laura in them. She was an Old One, you know."

"I suppose they might have some of me in them too."

"They have. You only need to look at Flora."

Kit nearly snapped out, "You mean her hands?" but bit the remark back. Jacky had wanted their daughter to be called Fleur, but the memories were still too corrosive. Even when the baby had sucked at her breast she had sometimes found herself singing,

Come now, come now, don't be hard to find,
Think about me – let me touch your mind.

The cart creaked and the axles complained but she was content to sit alongside the old man and look out from under the canvas hood. Down the roads from the Big Grey River to Hay it had been showery weather and the nights cold, but on the wedding day and afterwards there had been hot sunshine, so that now on the homeward journey plumes of dust wavered behind the cart. Two and a half days it would take, trundling along behind the white bullocks, watching the trees bask in the sun like green cumulus clouds tethered at the roadside, while in their shade the hedges frothed with hedge-parsley, wood avens, purple and yellow vetches, poppies and dog-roses, as if there would never be another winter.

Kit folded her hands across her stomach and smiled her secret smile, happy that somewhere nearby Jacky would be strolling along, probably chatting amiably with Uncle Isak. When he was away at sea she was anxious; although the old man had been pleased when she restarted the fishing records it made her distrust the sea even more, reading of its appetite for men and ships inscribed there. Nor did she approve of the piles of seasoning timber accumulating in the building-yards, and her husband's placating remarks about a 'comfortable' ship.

"Where can you sail this big comfortable ship that's better than home?" she would ask.

How much Jacky could recall of the turbulent times in Limber was hard to tell. She suspected he had quite a lot of his Old One mother's talent of selective retention, and thinking of what she had learned of the addiction of the elixir of power she hoped whatever taste he had inherited for it the sea would be adversary enough for him. Maybe the big ship was a sign of it. Her own more distant memories were like old love-letters fraying round the edges, the characters' black ink a fading grey, a reminder that her people were once part of the Daylight Folk.

Already her father was misty in her mind, and she wondered idly who would remember her when her children and grandchildren were no more, though she hugged the thought of Sven and Flora. Perhaps in the playground of Regret time passed differently from elsewhere. She found this idea unpursuable, but she was contented, thinking only, 'Oh, my children.'

Another night and another half-day and they would be back in Ferris's Landing. Already Ingastowe Cathedral was blue and diminishing on the horizon behind them. The children were watching carefully from the back of the cart, pointing outwards. "That's where he was," said Sven, but hard as they looked there was nothing there except the green curtain of the trees. "Never mind," said their mother.

It had indeed been just here, on the southward journey a week ago, that Jacky had caught up with the cart and smiled up at her. She could even see the ashes of their fire.

"Time to stop," he had said, "while there's enough daylight to make supper. Come on, children, dry sticks, please, or it'll only be grass to eat."

"Not grass," Flora had giggled, and they had set off to search under the roadside trees, where she was diverted by trying to twine flowers in her hair.

"Poppies make your head ache," her brother had told her gravely, and then it had come through a gap in the trees, magical in the twilight, the colour of the dusk, and put its damp nose down and sniffed at Flora and made a soft ruffling sound.

"Sven, the unicorn said 'Hello'."

The creature had turned elegantly, given an equally elegant flourish with its tail, and stepped delicately away as if its poised feet sought out small stepping-stones under the grasses.

The children had come back to their parents so slowly and with faces so rapt that Kit had seized their hands.

"What's happened?"

"We saw a unicorn!"

"We did, really!"

Long into the evening, with the children sleeping, their parents and grandfather had debated what the children had met. But for Kit there was no argument. The horses were back from the fables, back from the past that had poisoned them, still with that special irreplacable grace. Her children would have less of that emptiness that so many generations had felt as one species after another had dwindled and departed. The baby had moved suddenly inside her and she gasped. Then, lest Jacky and his father be alarmed, she had said, "Our baby is glad to hear of the unicorn-horse."

That morning, as the family set off for Ferris's Landing, they had said goodbye to Astolat, who was staying in Ingastowe. Astolat had gathered around her as many of the Children as could be found in that part of Westermain, losing no time in recruiting Adelie, saying that someone with that genetic configuration would be more intractable than any problem she would encounter. Soon the Academy of Ingastowe would be a wildfire of ideas and generating its own Children. When Jacky had asked Astolat for their thoughts on his big ship they had responded gleefully with a dozen models, some so unlike any ship he could recognise that he had needed to send back for explanations. On Astolat's visits to her father Kit could only wonder at her exuberance. "One way for us to reach out and touch the One God is through understanding the many gods. God touches us through the many gods so it has to be reciprocal. It has to work both ways."

"I know what 'reciprocal' means," Kit had said, and Astolat who had heard with awe of her sister-in-law's exploits in Regret was blushingly apologetic. Both were pleased and amused that the peremptory Adelie had been drawn to Magnus and he to her.

Their wedding had taken place in Hay church. Six years earlier when Kit herself had refused to be married in Hay many of the same guests had found their way to the Dorns' tall windy house with its terraced garden clinging to the hillside above the Big Grey River. Martin had come from Hay with Adelie, Nell, Magnus and the boy Harry, travelling north-eastwards with the Pascal brothers, Red Buckle and other of her childhood friends; and then there was the Dorn clan, a variety of uncles, aunts and second cousins, some from distant islands in the ice-latitudes. From Limber had come Stefan Giorgiou, not so thin now but very grey. "Still see Sheer sometimes," he told them. "Must have learned to swim fast the night Hereward threw him in the dock." From the Glassy Country came Crook, who later stayed a month with Martin, and Letitia with Glassy Country gifts, twelve golden cicadas with garnet wings, which Kit's children were later to mistake for bees. "To put behind the pillow, works well," Letitia had whispered. Silky Wilkins came from Merganser and flirted with Kit, and Billy Scarlett the Once-Dead came and perturbed everyone by asking where Hereward was: "He's round here somewhere, can't you tell?" So Kit had to tell him about the boy.

Six years on and another wedding. The Misses Shepherd had offered Adelie and Magnus the use of their big house to entertain their guests. Knowing Nell, Kit had assumed the guests would be everyone for miles around, and so they had been, and it was as well there were spacious gardens as well as plenty of rooms. The boy had been there too, and she had observed him as you might watch and wonder if the bluish-grey cloud just nudging into view over the tree-tops would bulge and deepen purple into the lightning-bearer. He was back now from one of his journeys, and working with Hobson in the mill. In his mind his thoughts had burned clear for her to see – she need not have wondered if dust from the barley-sacks and powder from the flour-sleeves were clouding over the stark bright moment when the bayonet had slid out of his pack. Martin had told her it all and of how the boy had slid a finger along the blade as if to clean it and said, "Come on, then," to the last of Zjelko's brutal followers. For a true Old One those moments would never dim. Nell had also invited his mother and Kit had observed her carefully, thinking that you should walk cautiously near the wife of Hereward and the mother of the boy Harry.

The Misses Shepherds' garden was a delightful place, its lawns wide and smooth, shaded on one side by elm trees where in the early evening rooks arrived noisily like late guests. Old flaky brick walls were pierced by arches that tempted you through to walk on sandy paths among vegetables and herbs growing in patterned beds enclosed by little box-tree borders. Other arches led to orchards or to where raspberries, black, white and red currants and gooseberries grew under nets like soft cages. Kit's children had indignantly released a marauding blackbird that was protesting inside the netting. There were other spots too, and all welcoming – one a bowling-green with a summer-house alongside, another a small wilderness of trees and ferns hiding an unexpected pool where dragonflies flashed their gauzy wings. This reminded Kit suddenly of Shawpits, so that she briefly forgot her matronly composure, particularly when she noticed the pigboys and their charges in the field beyond the spinney.

Adelie had taken Kit by surprise. With her black hair spread wide and threaded with daisies, jasmine and ivy she was striking enough but from her eyes, the palest grey, with only pinprick pupils, Lamorak-Lokietok himself looked out. Sven and Flora were fascinated by her and later in the afternoon Kit had found the three of them sitting in a circle holding hands.

"What are you talking about?"

"Talking to Auntie Bella," laughed Flora.

"Only a game," said Adelie.

There it was again, Kit thought, the raptor that lived inside the Old Ones talking. Perhaps at present Adelie thought it a game but if the game was worth playing it was worth winning. Regret was founded on love but they too were playing hard, for the future, as evolution always plays. It was a brave adventure of a game but everyone was born to play.

"Mummy," said her daughter's voice in her ear. "We've been having an adventure. Have you ever had an adventure?"

"Oh, a long time ago. You'd better tell me about yours, Flora."

"Mummy."

"Yes, Sven."

"The adventure wanted to know when you and Daddy are coming to be in it."

"We're already in it somewhere, children. I expect you'll meet us there some day."

Fox Creek Wines

Government of South Australia

ARTS A

Wakefield Press thanks Fox Creek Wines and Arts South Australia for their support.